# Once Upon a Wedding

### A Fiction From the Heart Second-Chances Anthology

**Jamie Beck • Tracy Brogan • Sonali Dev
K.M. Jackson • Donna Kauffman • Sally Kilpatrick
Falguni Kothari • Priscilla Oliveras
Barbara Samuel • Hope Ramsay • Liz Talley**

Once Upon a Wedding
Copyright © 2019 Write Ideas, LLC

ISBN-13: 978-1-944048-10-5

All Rights Reserved
No part of this book may be reproduced or transmitted in any form by any means, including photocopying, recording, or by information storage and retrieval system, without the written permission of the author, except for the use of brief quotations in a book review.

This book is a work of fiction. Names, characters, places, and incidents are products of the author's imagination or are used fictitiously. The use of locations and products throughout this book is done so for storytelling purposes and should in no way been seen as advertisement. Trademark names are used in an editorial fashion, with no intention of infringement of the respective owner's trademark.

Eleven best-selling and award-winning authors request your presence as they share all-new novellas that will have you humming the wedding march and dreaming of champagne toasts. It's easy to tie the knot with these heartwarming, second chance love stories.

### *I Do, Again by Jamie Beck*
A makeup artist who is forced to become her bridezilla client's eleventh-hour bridesmaid is dumbstruck to discover her ex-husband is a groomsman and he wants a second chance.

### *Weather or Knot by Tracy Brogan*
Two meteorologists with a turbulent romantic history join a team of storm chasers and discover that love, like lightning, sometimes strikes twice.

### *The Runaway Bride by Sonali Dev*
A groom has one night to convince his runaway bride that her fears that he's settling for her are anything but true.

### *Starboard Vow by K.M. Jackson*
A cruise director is taken off course when the country's hottest bachelor – and her secret husband – arrives aboard her ship for a whirlwind cruise.

### *Wedding in Swan Harbor by Donna Kauffman*
A widowed blueberry farmer is reunited with her late husband's best friend when he returns to escort her daughter down the aisle.

### *Snowbound in Vegas by Sally Kilpatrick*
A best man and maid of honor loathe each other…until they're stuck in a cabin meant for a honeymoon.

### *Starstruck: Take Two by Falguni Kothari*
Embroiled in a Bollywood stunt wedding, an A-list manager is torn between doing what is right for her celebrity client or seizing a second chance with the bad boy groom herself.

### *Always Yours by Priscilla Oliveras*
With love in the air at a *familia* wedding, two high school sweethearts separated by their misguided mistakes just might find their second chance for a happily ever after together.

### *Home Sweet Home by Hope Ramsay*
Family secrets tore them apart as teens but a wedding in Sweet Home, Virginia, may give star-crossed lovers a second chance at forgiveness and love.

### *Inseparable by Barbara Samuel*
Thwarted high school sweethearts meet again in the gorgeous Colorado mountains for a wedding…of their children.

### *A Morning Glory Wedding by Liz Talley*
A florist responsible for the break-up of the bride's first marriage gets a chance for forgiveness and a new love with a hunky pastor.

# Author's Note

Dear Reader,

Thank you for picking up our second-chances anthology. We had so much fun planning this project. If Fiction From The Heart is a "new to you" group, let us introduce ourselves. Each of us writes heartwarming, realistic, romantic women's fiction. We hope you'll consider joining our Facebook community (http://bit.ly/FictionFromTheHeartauthors) and getting to know us all better. In addition to hosting giveaways and guest authors in our space, we love to discuss life, love, and books!

This anthology idea came together in a spontaneous burst of excited energy. We love second-chance romances and we love weddings, so we created a series of stories based on those elements. We hope you smile (and maybe cry a little) as each couple finds their happily ever after.

Enjoy!
XO,

*Jamie, Tracy, Sonali, Kwana (writing as K.M.), Donna, Sally, Falguni, Priscilla, Hope, Barbara, and Liz*

# I Do, Again

by Jamie Beck

# Dedication

*This one is for the romantics who read romance to reaffirm their belief in love as the best solution to every problem.*

# Chapter One

## *Ellie*

My curse—the grim fate of unavoidably hurting the people closest to me—has been plaguing me since before I drew my first breath. Some might think that's hyperbole, but my twin—who died *in utero*—would disagree if she could. So would my sweet baby girl, whose heart defect took her away after just two days. Still don't believe me? Ask my dad. He'll tell you, like he's told me and everyone else for as long as I can remember.

In any case, it's why I'll never again find myself preparing to walk down the aisle like the bridezilla client whose makeup I'm applying.

I swipe the bevel eye shadow brush across the palette while pushing through the pang that always accompanies the memory of my divorce. The irony that I spend my days surrounded by women in love who are planning new lives and families isn't lost on me.

"Aren't you done yet?" Sloane whines.

Every time she frowns, she creases the foundation I've flawlessly applied.

My colleague, wedding planner extraordinaire Melissa, had warned me that this bride was a pill. I don't know whether to be grateful for the steady stream of work I get because I can endure difficult brides, or to resent it.

"The way you keep fidgeting, I'd almost guess you want this plum eye shadow to cross above your brows." I lean back while flashing a smile, which puts my makeup palette within inches of the flowing white organza gown hanging to my left.

"Careful!" Her icy blue eyes are so cold, no one could call them pretty, despite their almond shape and naturally long, curled lashes. "That dress probably costs more than your rent."

Two of Sloane's attendants, whom I've mentally nicknamed Tweedledee and Tweedledum, snicker before they each guzzle another flute of champagne. The third, Olivia, whose makeup I did first, went to the restroom at least thirty minutes ago. At this point, I'm guessing drugs or bulimia...or both.

As for the cost comparison, my bare-bones, one-bedroom apartment in Sonoma totals almost two grand per month, so while Sloane's hand-beaded gown probably retails for at least three times that amount, my rent isn't cheap. And paying that rent is exactly why I have learned to tolerate the truly intolerable.

"We're out of chocolates." Tweedledee turns an empty bowl over and makes one of those pouty moues that only looks cute in a rom-com movie.

"Leighton, you don't need more chocolate," Sloane mutters without making eye contact with her friend. And by the way, I use *that* term loosely. From what I've observed this afternoon, these women are, at best, frenemies. They do all look remarkably similar—tall, slender, blonde—while sharing a bitter edge that comes from being perpetually hungry.

When Tweedledum snorts, Leighton bats her leg. "At least my balayage didn't fry my ends like your highlights, Tori."

Frowning, Tori immediately pulls the ends of her hair forward to inspect them.

Within minutes of my arrival two hours ago, I'd felt sorry for the groom. At this point, I'm beginning to think he must be out of his mind to love this snooty woman and put up with her clique. Maybe he's just after her money. Really, that's the only scenario that makes sense given the dearth of genuine joy in this room today. And, not for the first time this afternoon, I think it unfair that someone like her gets to be married, while someone like me had to divorce the man I loved to keep him safe.

"Where the hell is Olivia?" Sloane asks. "And where is Melissa?"

"Melissa went to check on the guests and your groom," I reply.

"She's never around when I need her," Sloane huffs. I bite my tongue, which is twitching to defend Melissa, whose business is booming because she's professional, creative, and solicitous. Sloane's eyes remain closed while I finish applying shadow to the outer corners, then she says, "Leigh, go track down Liv and tell her to get her butt back here. I assume we'll be finished soon" — Sloane opens one eye and looks at me — "and I want to take some candids before the ceremony begins."

I'm not sure if she expects me to do double duty as a photographer, but we'll never get to it if she doesn't sit still.

Leighton pushes herself out of her chair and straightens the gorgeous blush-pink sateen Monique Lhuillier gown before trotting off to do Sloane's bidding.

I pick up an angled lip brush and dab it across the "Rosecliff" lipstick, nick the brush across my wrist — which now hosts a rainbow of colors from the shadows, blushes, and lipsticks I've tested before applying on these ladies — then outline Sloane's lips. She can't talk while I'm creating the fuller-lip look she'd demanded earlier, so I'm taking as much time as possible to paint them.

Tori is sitting nearby, looking bored. Unlike most attendants and brides I've worked with, these two are barely talking to each other. I'd give up pizza, ice cream sandwiches, and my celebrity crush on Justin Hartley for just a single close relationship that didn't end in disaster, so I can't help the bitterness that bubbles in my stomach whenever I see normal people taking their friends for granted.

Leighton returns, looking paler than when she'd left. She's grimacing so dramatically, Tori asks, "What happened to you?"

"Nothing. But Olivia..." She leans back as if preparing for a blow. "I don't think she'll make the wedding."

Sloane's whole body tenses, but she manages to wait until I pull the lip brush away before whirling around on Leighton. "What do you mean she won't make the wedding?"

"She's barfing and sweating, and way whiter than normal. She thinks maybe she caught the stomach bug from her nephew on Thursday." Leighton moves behind the chair and I decide maybe she isn't so dumb after all. At least she's found cover. Tori and I remain totally exposed to the time bomb in the chair in front of me.

Sloane closes her eyes like it's the only way she won't explode. She doesn't even feign concern for her friend, nor ask a single question about her health. Instead, her eyes pop open and she scans me from head to toe. "What size do you wear?"

I'm so taken aback, I blurt an answer before giving it any thought. "A zero, sometimes a two. Depends on the clothes."

As usual, the litany of nicknames I'd been called throughout the years—Beanpole, Broom Handle, Bonejangles—springs to mind as I'm forced to acknowledge my slim figure.

"Perfect!" She claps, and a satisfied grin appears. I swear, that smile on her face is the first genuine one I've seen all afternoon. "You can wear Liv's dress."

"What?" I croak.

Even Tweedles Dee and Dum are blinking in surprise.

"I can't have an uneven bridal party. The pictures will look horrible, and Josh won't have a partner all night long." Sloane stares at me as if I'm an idiot not to understand this logic.

"I'll be Josh's partner," Leighton cuts in.

"No more substitutions. My mother and I have planned everything and I don't need any more surprises or switcheroos!" Sloane spears me with those bright frosty eyes.

"S-surely you have another friend or cousin on the guest list who is more appropriate—"

"Not *your* size!" She rolls her eyes at me as if I'm the moron.

I shake my head. "Sorry, but I'm outta here as soon as I finish your lips."

A glance at my makeup kit leads me to estimate that the quickest I can pack it all up is seven minutes, maybe five if I don't worry about reorganizing it until I get home.

Sloane sits forward now, wearing a placating smile and talking to me as if I'm a child. "Look, obviously I'm desperate. What if I let you keep the gown?"

"I have no need for that." In truth, I do love the bridesmaid gown, with its sweetheart neckline design and sumptuous fabric. I've never owned anything that fine in my life. If I shortened the skirt, it would be perfect for special occasions. Then again, my quiet, mostly solitary life doesn't present me with many special occasions.

"Fine. I'll also throw in an extra two-hundred-dollar tip if you just walk down the aisle, take the pictures, and stay through the bridal party dance. After that, you can take off if you want." She stares at me in a manner that says she fully expects me to capitulate.

"Shouldn't you check on your friend?" I stall, partly out of concern for Olivia, and partly because that two-hundred-buck windfall is hard to pass up. Against my better instincts, I'm actually considering this ridiculous request. I could use the extra cash, and I'd still have some left over even if I used part to surprise the little boy downstairs with that bike his mom can't afford for his fifth birthday.

"And risk getting sick before my honeymoon? No, thanks." She turns in her chair and tells Tori, "Go tell my mom what's happened and have her send my Aunt Agnes to check on Liv and get her dress. Liv's bag is there in the corner, so she can change back into her own clothes and then go sleep in the hotel room."

Tori stands and starts for the door when Sloane calls out, "Don't forget the shoes!"

It irks me that she knows she's won before I've actually decided. "I haven't agreed to stand up for you."

"Three fifty and not a penny more." She crosses her arms beneath her ample cleavage — another possible reason her fiancé might've proposed, I suppose.

"Done." I hear the word before it registers. Looks like I'm no more immune to the power of cold hard cash than the next person. "Now let me finish your lips because right now they look stupid."

As soon as I finish painting her mouth, I turn to the mirror and realize I've got some work to do on myself while she's pouring herself into her wedding dress. Luckily I'd come without any makeup on, so I wipe down my face with some towelettes, apply some primer, and then add a light foundation.

I assume she wants me to minimize my freckles. She'd probably prefer if I were a blond-haired, blue-eyed clone of her posse, but she'll have to accept me, my curly brown hair and hazel eyes, as is. I spy a few spare bobby pins and do up my hair into a cute mop with some fashionable tendrils dangling around my forehead and ears.

This 'do reminds me a bit of my prom, which revives the unwelcome memory of how my high school boyfriend had gotten food poisoning from the oysters at the restaurant I'd insisted we go to before the dance. I call these Ellie-caused misfortunes of lesser proportions *The Curse Lite*.

I'm barely finished with my makeup when Leighton reappears and shoves poor Olivia's gown in my face. "Here, and these are the shoes."

One look at the spike-heeled sandals tells me they're a little too big. I might be slim like Olivia, but she's at least an inch taller, and her feet are probably larger, too. I go behind the dressing screen that Bodega Vineyards provides in the anteroom where bridal parties prepare for the ceremony, and slip into the gown.

The silky fabric glides over my skin, tempting me to find a zillion reasons to wear it in the future, it feels that good. Maybe I can simply dress up each week to watch *This Is Us* with a glass of wine. I barely know Olivia, but the pleasure I'm taking in my new fantasy life makes me feel like a traitor. I slip on her jeweled dress sandals, which are in fact slightly loose but not unmanageable, and tighten the ankle strap. Even when I'm in the heels, the gown's hem is about an inch too long and puddling on the floor.

"Well?" I hear Sloane ask.

I raise the skirt a touch and walk out from behind the screen, surprised to see Sloane's mother and Melissa have rejoined the group, along with Mandi, the adorable little flower girl, Sloane's six-year-old cousin. But I barely have time to acknowledge the familiar ache that squeezes me every time I'm around a child that age because Melissa's exchanging a surreptitious look of pity with me. We're both in a lose-lose situation, but, unlike these wealthy women, Melissa and I aren't in a position to be choosy.

Rebecca Marsten and her daughter study me like they're inspecting the Venus de Milo for defects. Rebecca flips over a bejeweled hand, her expression one of surrender. "I guess we must make do. I'll have the driver take Olivia back to her room with some ginger ale and crackers to help settle her stomach." Then she drops a wad of cash on top of my makeup kit.

"Good. We can't delay much longer or Will might think I'm standing him up. Guess we're out of time for candids now," Sloane huffs. "Let's get this ceremony going. Where's my bouquet?" Sloane is turning in a circle when Tori hands her a gorgeous basketball-size array of pink peonies and white roses.

I feel woozy, but not because of the floral perfume wafting through the air. In all my years of doing bridal makeup, this is—without a doubt—the craziest scenario I've encountered.

Tori tosses a small bouquet at me. "Here you go."

When I catch it, it feels more like a bad omen than a good one. Of course, I'm always on the lookout for bad omens because they seem to dog me wherever I go. The only good news today is that I do not care one whiff for these folks, so they are all safe.

"Liv was bridesmaid number three, which meant she was to be the first in line going down the aisle, so scoot up to the front now." Sloan fiddles with her bouquet to figure out how to hold it comfortably, while her little cousin sways back and forth with her little basket of rose petals. "Your partner's name is Josh, in case you missed that."

"Lucky you," Leighton mutters.

"I'm happy to trade places," I say, having no interest in leading the processional from hell down the aisle. And if the groomsmen are anything like these bridesmaids, Josh will not tickle my fancy, either.

"I said there's no trading," Sloane hisses as her mom adjusts her lengthy veil before kissing her daughter on the cheek and dashing out to take her seat. "Can we please stop trying to mess up my plans?"

"Fine." I lift the skirt again to move in front of Leighton and Tori.

"Don't play with that skirt. It's inelegant. Haven't you ever worn a gown?" Sloane's exasperated tone almost makes me turn around, strip out of the dress, and throw it at her. Then I think about little Owen—who, coincidentally, is the same age as my daughter would've been had she lived—and the bike with training wheels he'll be ecstatic to receive. I also don't want to put Melissa in a worse position with this client. Referrals are the lifeblood of our businesses, and I won't be the cause of harming her reputation.

"It's too long." I drop the hem to demonstrate. "I'll trip if I don't raise it when I walk."

"Maybe I can find some tape," Melissa offers.

"There's no time!" Sloane snaps. "Just take smaller steps so you don't step on the hem. Melissa can find some tape to jury-rig it before the dancing."

Sighing, I give up and simply turn around, figuring I can endure anything for ninety minutes.

Following a deep breath, I shuffle through the iron-and-wood doors and stand beneath the pink and peach tones of the early evening sky. Pachelbel's Canon in D drifts through the air like a gentle cloud. Before I round the corner of the building, I wait to make sure everyone is lined up behind me, ready to go. I glance over my shoulder in time to see Sloane giving me the "get going" signal with her bouquet, so I brace myself for the surprised look that is sure to cross many guests' faces when they see me. Only after I turn the bend do I notice that I forgot to wash the makeup off my arm. *Oops.*

I'm walking like a geisha to avoid catching the hem with my toes, smiling my best fake smile, when the scenery nearly knocks me over. The vineyard, which I've visited before, stretches across rolling hills in a bucolic patchwork quilt of greens, gold, and browns. But it's the flowers that arrest me. Gigantic urns overflowing with ivy, peonies, roses, and hydrangea surround the rows of guests who are facing a pergola so swathed in blooms it looks like it's constructed of them.

The tableau couldn't be more different from my midnight wedding ceremony in the hot-pink-and-white Little Vegas Chapel. Cody and I might not have had the Marstens' money or been encircled by all this natural beauty, but the purity of our young love had bathed that tacky space in an exquisite glow of its own.

I'm remembering this, fighting that twinge in my heart again, when I take my first steps onto the white carpet of the temporary aisle. I look ahead at the unlucky groom and send him a little prayer, 'cause he'll need it. My gaze drifts to the groomsmen, all three standing like penguins beside their friend. One by one, I check them out.

I freeze when my gaze locks with the familiar blue gaze of groomsman number two. *Cody?* His eyes go round as poker chips.

My heart charges ahead like a stampede of cattle, tugging me along until I trip over the hem of the gown. The next thing I know, I'm sprawled flat on my stomach, bouquet tossed aside.

When the crowd gasps, I wave an arm overhead to prove I'm fine, snatch the errant bouquet, and stand with a smile and a shrug. *Well, great.* It's not the first time I've been humiliated in front of Cody, and, judging by the way my day is going, it won't be the last.

My ribs ache from my hammering heart. I struggle to catch my breath and reclaim whatever dignity I had. I won't look back and give Sloane the satisfaction of burning me with a scorching glare, nor can I risk another look at Cody, so I stare at the minister and humbly make my way to the altar despite the sweat rolling down my back.

# Chapter Two

## *Cody*

If I hadn't been utterly paralyzed by shock to see Ellie, I would've rushed to her side to check on her. No matter what else happens in my life, the desire to help her will remain a reflex. Relief—and some other emotions—had whipped through me after she'd popped back up and flashed her cheeky grin.

I'd forgotten how bright that smile could be. After we lost Carrie, Ellie had stopped smiling altogether. Now I can't make sense of how the heck she came to be in this wedding, or what's happened to Olivia. But maybe it's a sign. One I'd welcome if Ellie would. Because no matter how many times I've told myself our divorce had been for the best, I've never been quite convinced. Nor have I met any woman with a heart as big as Ellie's—which is the ultimate irony of our child's devastating ailment.

I'm so deep in my own thoughts, it shocks me when Will and Sloane turn to face the guests as Mr. and Mrs. Gooding for the first time. I literally missed the entire ceremony. That could be a blessing in disguise, though. I'd known today would be hard—weddings always are these days—but having Ellie standing here within reach makes me ache to the bone.

There has to be some crazy story behind her surprise appearance, which is pretty typical of Ellie. It'll be a while before I'll get a chance to peel her away from the crowd and get the skinny. For now, I stare at her, watching her join Josh for the walk down the aisle to the receiving line. When Tori and I follow behind them, I can't drag my gaze from Ellie's back—the sculpted shape of her shoulders and arms, the tight little rump beneath the fitted dress. More breathtaking than the vineyard and floral arrangements, that's for sure.

"What a beautiful service." Tori turns her vapid blue eyes my way. Ever since the double date Will and Sloane forced on me several weeks ago, I've done my best to be polite while keeping her at arm's length. "Will looks absolutely ecstatic."

I shrug, unable to muster much to say when my thoughts remain almost completely consumed by Ellie. I've never warmed to Sloane, but ever since my friend laid eyes on her in law school, he'd yet to see the decay beneath her striking veneer.

"Kind of makes me want to settle down." She's staring at me like I'm made of chocolate. "How about you?"

*Not with someone who's only into me for my career and Pacific Heights address.*

None of these people know about my former marriage—or my daughter—and I'm not about to get into the details with Tori. Law school had been my fresh start after all I'd lost, and some things are simply too painful to discuss.

"Not really." A half-truth. I do think about—or remember—my marriage more often than I like to admit. Being married to Ellie had been the best time of my life. She'd been warm and open and game for anything. Sadly, as much as our whirlwind affair and wedding had taken our families by surprise, our divorce hadn't.

Lots of couples split after a tragedy like we were dealt, and nothing I'd done or said convinced Ellie that we could be happy again someday. So I'd buried my broken heart beneath LSATs, the bar exam, seventy-hour work weeks, and a short string of women who never came close to making me feel the way Ellie had. Seeing her now, after all this time, blasts through those hardened layers of protection like a grenade.

Tori frowns before saying, "I can't wait to be a bride."

That doesn't surprise me. All of Sloane's friends want to be brides, but I doubt any of them will make good wives.

When we get to the receiving line, I find myself standing shoulder-to-shoulder with Ellie. A zing I haven't felt in ages zips through me, straightening my spine.

"Don't ask," she murmurs through a patently false smile as she nods at and shakes hands with the various guests passing by. She still refuses to make eye contact with me.

"It's good to see you," I mutter, because apparently my heart still beats harder for this woman despite how hard *she* fought to push me out of her life.

That gets those round hazel eyes to look at me before she blinks. Her mouth opens and closes without a word, but her cheeks turn crimson.

"Thanks." She stares ahead again, but not before I hear a soft, "You, too."

My body feels like it's floating, which is stupid. I can't help it because, unlike a lot of women I know, Ellie couldn't care less about my profession or my address. She'd fallen for me when I'd been a clueless college senior who'd shown up at Supercuts one day in need of a haircut. My scalp tingles now like it did that day she'd first cut my hair.

The sun blazes overhead, glinting off her honey-colored highlights. It's a picture-perfect day—which is good because Sloane would *not* have accepted anything less—and in the shadow of the makeshift chapel, I can't help but wonder if the universe is sending us a second chance.

I'm wishing the crowd would disappear so I can talk to her, when I hear Sloane bark, "Okay, everyone, meet by the fountain for photographs in five minutes. Ladies, blot your faces."

A quick glimpse of Ellie catches her rolling her eyes. That Sesame Street song "One of These Things" intones through my thoughts as she trails behind Sloane and her friends.

Josh catches up to me, wearing a pleased grin. "I hit the jackpot today with the fresh meat."

"Don't talk about her that way." The words come out so harsh, Josh stops and stares.

"Dude, what's your problem?"

My problem is that if he lays a hand on Ellie, I'll take him out. Of course, I can't tell him the truth and risk that wave of gossip overshadowing my friend's wedding, so I cover. "Isn't anyone wondering what happened to Olivia?"

He shrugs. "Ellie mentioned something about a stomach bug."

"Which doesn't explain why *she* ended up being part of this wedding."

"Who cares why? Even though I told Will not to pair me with Leigh, Olivia would've spent the whole night pushing me on her. Been there, done that. Time to move on. Ellie is a great way to keep Leigh off my back."

When I don't say anything, he jogs ahead to catch up with Will's brother, Bruce, leaving me to stew in my own juices.

It seems like six hours of posing before Sloane is satisfied that she's got what she needs to fill the perfect wedding album. If it wouldn't be out of place, I'd tell her that perfect pictures and rings and furniture do not make a perfect life. Even true love doesn't always guarantee a happy ending, as I know too well. I hope, for Will's sake, there's more to Sloane than I've ever seen, though. He's a solid guy who deserves a good marriage.

During the photography marathon, I notice Josh taking too much pleasure with every chance he gets to settle his hand on Ellie's waist or shoulder or whatever other body part is closest due to the contrived positions the photographer places us in. I'm consoled, however, by that fact that Ellie doesn't look at all interested in him or in playing any of his games.

As soon as we are released to the reception, I follow Ellie and wait for her to emerge from the ladies' room.

She stops short when she sees me. "Cody, please. Don't make this harder on me."

"You've got to tell me how you ended up here." I'm stalling, hoping for an excuse to touch her.

"I could ask you the same question. Are these people really your friends?" The disappointment in her eyes triggers both shame and anger. The women aren't my cup of tea, but Will is a good guy. I probably wouldn't be here at all if Ellie hadn't walked out of my life.

It won't do any good to rehash the past, though. And just looking at her now is making me too happy to be self-righteous. I cross my arms to keep from clasping her hand. "How did you get hooked up with Sloane?"

She sniffs her elegant bouquet, reminding me of how happy

she'd been with the convenience-store carnations she'd carried at our wedding. If I could've afforded it then, I would've bought her a whole damn flower shop. "I had the misfortune of being hired to do everyone's makeup today. Olivia got hit with a violent stomach bug, so Sloane paid me to stand in 'so her photos would be balanced.'" She shakes her head while screwing up her face. "Like having a stranger in your wedding party isn't worse than an empty spot."

I can't help but laugh because this scenario is so perfectly Sloane *and* so perfectly Ellie. "Well, I can't say I'm sorry it turned out this way."

When she looks at me, sorrow floods those golden-brown eyes. "Cody, I'm only obligated to make it through the bridal party dance, then I'm outta here."

"Maybe I can change your mind." I tip my head.

"Or maybe you should remember what happens to people I care about and keep your distance. Heck, I half wonder if the curse is getting stronger and affecting random people in my vicinity, like poor Olivia." Then she smiles and adds, "Maybe I should go stand next to Sloane a while longer."

I'd join her in the snicker if I didn't hate Ellie's dad and his whole "curse" theory with a passion hotter than a California wildfire. Has she had some bad luck in her life? Absolutely. Did my heart shatter when our daughter died? Of course. But Ellie chose to walk away from me after that tragedy instead of clinging to me. That's what I should focus on and why *I* should probably walk away now.

"You never answered *my* question," she says, bringing me back to the present. "How do you know these people?"

"Will, the groom, is my law school buddy. We work together now."

Her lips part with surprise. "Law school?"

It hadn't been something I'd pursued while we were married because I thought the time commitment would've interfered with being a good husband and father, and I'd been content with my job at the bank. I don't regret my new career, but there have been days when I've wondered about Ellie. Wondered if, due to my own grief over our daughter, I'd given up on Ellie too soon. Wondered if she regretted pushing the divorce.

"Wow." She's fidgeting with the ribbons of her bouquet now, obviously at a loss for words. That makes me smile because Ellie isn't often tongue-tied.

"Seems we've both ventured into new careers." I can picture her doing makeup. She'd always been creative and had an eye for color, like the time she painted our tiny apartment azure blue and then threw a bunch of coral-colored pillows and stuff around for contrast. Based on the job she'd done on Sloane and her friends today, she's darn good at her new career. What I can't imagine is why she'd want to spend so much time around couples and weddings after everything we'd lost.

"Well, I'm glad to learn that my sacrifice worked. Look at you now—healthy, smiling, and building such a great career and life for yourself." Her sweet smile makes me catch my breath like always. "You know I always only want you to be happy."

"So you say every time you walk away from me." That comes out a little sharper than I intend.

She frowns, and I can't stand that I made that happen. "That's not fair."

"I don't think fairness has factored into much about our history, do you?" I ask softly.

Her brows raise, then pinch together again.

"Cody!" Josh rounds the corner, then stops, flashes what he probably thinks is a charming smile, and wags his finger. "We'll be making our entrance soon. Tori's looking for you, so how about you go back to your date for the night and leave me a chance to get to know my pretty partner better."

I hear Ellie's subtle little groan.

"Ellie!" The wedding planner comes running over, waving a fat roll of masking tape. "Quick, let's get that hem taped up so you don't fall again at the reception."

Ellie's smile is proof of her relief to have a reason to escape both Josh and me. "Excuse us."

Josh and I watch the two women disappear into the ladies' room. Too soon, Tori spots us and makes a beeline for me. She loops her arm around mine. "Cody, I was wondering where you went."

"You two go over to Sloane before she freaks. I'll wait for Ellie." Josh winks.

All I can do at the moment is concede, but I'm not deterred. Ellie and I have both matured since Carrie's death, and have had time to recover from the worst of our grief. We deserve a second chance. I still see love reflected in Ellie's eyes, and this time I won't let her leave without a fight.

Reluctantly, I walk toward the rest of the group with Tori, but my thoughts are running a million miles per hour, plotting ways to convince Ellie that our love story isn't over.

"You know she's just a makeup artist, right?" Tori says, astutely picking up on the fact that Josh and I would both have rather waited for Ellie than go with her. If she hopes that pointing out Ellie's lack of a college degree will make Ellie undesirable, she will be disappointed. If anything, Tori's attitude only makes *her* undesirable.

"Yeah, I know. In fact, you look very pretty tonight." Just as Tori begins to smile, I add, "She's obviously amazing at her job."

Tori tilts her head, not quite sure if I've just slammed her or not. I'm content to leave her hanging. I don't like to be a total jerk, but I won't stand by while anyone slurs Ellie.

Tori remains undaunted, though. She smiles beatifically. "I guess we should take our place in line."

I let loose a pent-up sigh. If the prospect of another long dinner date with Tori wasn't trying enough, watching my good friend kowtow to his ice princess and her gaggle, while Josh hits on Ellie, will surely test my patience like nothing I can imagine. But I'll get through it if only because, at some point, I'll find a way to steal Ellie away for the heart-to-heart I should've forced years ago.

# Chapter Three

## *Ellie*

"Great timing," I say to the top of Melissa's head while she scurries around near the floor, taping up my dress.

"Really?" She carefully folds a swath of the hemline before applying another short strip of tape to the underside of the skirt. I suppose it's better than poking holes through the gorgeous fabric with a needle and thread...not that we had that option. "I thought you'd be mad that I dragged you away from two good-looking men."

"Two?" I know Cody is gorgeous, but Josh? He's a little too pretty, with his fine bone structure and fair-haired looks. In contrast, Cody has the rugged appeal of a movie-star cowboy — rangy build, tanned skin — with the bluest eyes rimmed with thick black eyelashes. His coffee-colored hair is dense and wavy, even when worn in his new, closer-cropped style. Just picturing him makes me squeeze my thighs together.

"Ah, so you've already homed in on one." Melissa smiles and cuts another strip of tape. "Well, go for it. You deserve a little fun after the afternoon you've had."

I wish I could, but I can't risk it. Too many people get hurt around me, and I could not bear it if anything bad happened to Cody.

"Shh!" I say, although the bathroom is empty except for us. "Honestly, though, how do you manage? I mean, I've only got to deal with these kinds of women once in a while for a few hours. You, on the other hand, have to deal with them and their moms for months at a time."

She raises a shoulder. "Most aren't nearly this bad, as you know."

It's true. Nine out of ten brides remind me of my younger self...all good cheer and hopefulness. I feed off them now, listening to their romantic dreams and memorizing those gooey-eyed looks they get when talking about their intendeds. Whenever I then return home to my empty apartment and the pathetic plants I barely keep alive, I replay all those good vibes in my mind as if they are dear friends.

Then there are days like today, and brides like Sloane, and all the resentment I've stored deep down from years of painful losses pushes up into my lungs. "Maybe not, but the terrible ones really leave a lasting impression."

"Yeah, but I get paid very well. Those good ones keep me loving my job. There's nothing quite like working with a couple who is clearly in love. The kind you know will make it for the long haul. I guess I like having the chance to contribute something memorable to their beautiful story." She stands and sets the tape on the sink. Her lovely sentiment is sinking into my skin like a quality lotion, soothing the char Sloane and her friends have caused. Melissa circles her finger. "Spin."

I feel a tad off-balance, but not because of the spinning. It's the knowledge that Cody and I were that kind of blissed-out couple Melissa adores. We might've only been twenty and twenty-two back then, but anyone who'd met us would've believed we'd last a lifetime despite our mere two-month-long courtship.

But we'd learned the hard way that sometimes even the deepest love isn't enough, especially when one half of the couple is cursed like me. In my case, the most loving thing I could have done was to cut Cody free.

And look at him now—a dashing, young lawyer.

I can't stop my smile from forming, even though I know eventually he'll be sharing that bright new future with some other woman. Please, God, not with the tedious Tori. I honestly can't imagine him having fun with her or any of these people.

In fact, I doubt they even know the real Cody. I bet they haven't seen him make a stone skip eight times, or know that he irons shirts better than anyone's grandmother, or helped him reorganize his collection of Star Wars kites. They probably haven't lain in his arms and wiped damp bangs off his forehead after mind-blowing sex, or lain in those same arms while falling apart from the worst pain any heart could endure.

Then again, maybe he's different now that he's a big-time lawyer. And maybe the groom is a decent guy and friend. I hope so, even though the thought of anything about Cody having changed makes my heart break open anew.

"I think you're all set. The tape should hold long enough. I suspect you'll be taking off at the first available moment?" She elbows me before flaunting a wicked grin.

"Absolutely." Although now a growing part of me wants to stay until the very last dance, if only to memorize as many images of Cody as I can before I have to say goodbye. This night will likely be the last time I ever see him. I'm simultaneously grateful and angry. It would've been easier on me to never have seen him again than it's going to be to try to forget him once more. Suddenly, I'm feeling a lot of empathy for how Cinderella must've felt when forced to flee the ball at midnight. "I'd better head to dinner before Sloane blows a gasket."

"Please do! I can't take any more complaints tonight." Melissa smirks.

I stop at the sink to rinse the makeup off my arm, then glance over my shoulder. "Any word on poor Olivia?"

Melissa shakes her head before muttering a sarcastic, "Olivia who?"

"With friends like that..." I don't even finish the old colloquialism before Melissa laughs.

"You got that right." Melissa grabs the tape from the sink and follows me out the door. "At least I can promise you that the meal will be fantastic."

"And the wine." Bodega wines are way above my pay level, so I plan to enjoy a couple glasses tonight. Being a bit tipsy will make it easier to ignore Sloane's annoyed stares.

"Yes...have an extra glass for me."

I wave, knowing she needs to get back to work. Once again I'm alone in some terrifying, glittery land of rich people who are looking at me like I'm an exotic sea creature. As I approach the bridal party, I see Josh and Cody.

The one thing that I'm confident about now is that Cody hasn't shared our past with anyone. I'm not even offended because I don't talk about it with people, either. What's the point? No one can change the past or erase the pain, and I don't like to incite pity or be a Debbie Downer.

Josh holds out his elbow, so I lightly lay my hand on his forearm. The DJ announces each couple as we enter the tent and I can only assume Melissa supplied him with my full name. We go directly to the head table, where I learn that I'll be sitting between Josh and Cody. A blessing and a curse, like most of my life.

Both men stand to pull out my chair. Josh scowls at Cody, as does Tori.

"Thanks." I sit and stare at the elaborate place setting, slightly intimidated by the number of forks. All the fanfare seems a bit silly to me. After *our* wedding, Cody and I had gone straight to our hotel room and spent the next twenty-four hours celebrating in private. That good memory prompts a little shiver.

It's going to be a long night here beside the man I loved. The one I still love and will always love. I begin to get concerned about what bad luck will befall Cody if I don't rein in my feelings, and suddenly the tent feels oppressive.

On a cloudless night like tonight, the whole galaxy will be on display after the sun sets. My mind wanders, as it's prone to do. If I could move to the moon or Mars, would my curse disappear, and, if so, would Cody come with me? My fantasy is interrupted when the newlyweds are introduced then share their first dance as husband and wife.

I have to admit, from a distance, they look perfectly beautiful together. I note little Mandi restlessly zooming around the reception, probably bored out of her mind. Wait, did she just chug a stray glass of champagne? I don't even know who her parents are. "Josh, do you know the flower girl's family?"

"Yeah, why?"

"I think she just drank some champagne."

Josh laughs. "That's funny."

"No it's not." I scowl.

"Come on. They probably gave her sparkling cider to make her feel big."

"Oh, I didn't think of that." Totally likely. "Still, we should alert them to keep an eye on her."

"Fine. I'll find them after dinner."

"Thanks." I relax. Mandi is now in the back of the tent twirling around and staring at her skirt as it rises into the air. It probably *was* sparkling cider.

Josh slings his arm across the back of my chair, so I lean forward and place my elbows on the table. I'm the only one in the bridal party with such bad manners, but if I sit back, I'm sure his arm will find its way to my shoulders. He's so slick, I worry he'll leave oil stains on my new dress.

"So, Ellie. Tell me about yourself." He leans in to create some kind of intimacy that doesn't interest me one bit.

I stare at him, convinced he has no idea how unimaginative I find his conversational skills. Of course, given the way his gaze keeps wandering to my chest and my mouth, I doubt he puts much value on conversation. "Not much to tell. I'm a makeup artist."

"Do you live in the city?"

By city, I assume he means San Francisco. People like him consider it the only city within two hundred miles of here. "No. I live right here in Sonoma."

"Ooh, sorry. Must get boring, huh?" He swallows a big gulp of wine.

Not at all the word I'd associate with an area where you can enjoy museums, hot springs, wineries, and an unlimited number of festivals. "If you find vineyards and hiking and camping boring, then sure."

"Camping?" He smiles. "Never been, but maybe I'd enjoy pitching a tent with you."

I narrow my eyes, uncertain whether I can credit him with enough wit to have intended the crude pun. *Nah.* My antagonism fades and I reach for my wineglass.

Cody stirs beside me.

He's got his seat pulled so close to mine, the heat from his thigh warms my own. I basically chug my sauvignon blanc and then reach for the wine bottle for a refill. The pretty label reads "reserve," no less. *Fancy, fancy.* I'll savor the next glass.

I hear Tori peppering Cody with questions but can't make out what she's saying over the din of the crowd's conversation.

When the baked clam appetizer is served, I wait to see which utensil Cody uses and then mimic him.

"Do you like to dance?" Josh asks, still not put off by my attempt to be less interesting than a tree stump. There are plenty of attractive women here, so I'm thinking his interest in me is based on my being the girl from the wrong side of the tracks, so to speak. It's clear from the way he keeps flashing his Cartier alligator-strap watch that he thinks his wealth impresses me.

"I do," I say without thinking, then give myself a mental slap. Now I've wasted a perfectly good excuse to turn him down on the dance floor. I should probably slow down on the wine.

"So do I." He dips his nose into his wine glass and then swirls it, and I try very hard not to giggle at the affectation. Honestly, I'd prefer to be sitting on the sandy bank of the Russian River with a Bud Light and Cody than eating caviar and sipping champagne or wine. "I'm a little shocked Sloane went for a DJ instead of a band, but I'm glad. Bands never cover the songs quite right. And Sloane flew this DJ up from LA, so he's got to be hot."

"Mmm." I nod, as if I care. Then Cody's calf rubs up against mine beneath the table and every thought leaves my brain. I clear my throat and, after allowing myself two or three—or five—seconds of pleasure, scoot my leg out of reach.

If my leg could talk, it would echo my heart's sentiment. *I miss him.*

Cody shifts in his seat again, but I won't look at him 'cause if I do, I won't be able to stop. I make myself remember my hamster, Evelyn, and how she got killed because of me. At eight, I'd thought she'd be safe enough in the topless cardboard box in our yard while I ran inside to pee, but I'd been unaware that a mountain lion had been lounging in a tree at the edge of our property. People, animals, plants. Everything close to me suffers.

"Don't you agree?" Josh asks.

## I Do, Again

Apparently he's been droning on while I've been daydreaming. At this point, I figure it's safe to give a vague response, so I shrug and offer a noncommittal "Mm-hmm."

I've got to concentrate if I want to juggle Josh's questions, eat the meal without using the wrong flatware, and stay sober enough to drive home.

The toasts begin and seem to drone on for quite some time. These people sure do love the sound of their own voices, and but none are giving Jim Gaffigan the run for his money that they think they are.

When the groom's father finishes his speech, I think we're finally free from listening to another person speak, but he turns the mic over to his own father.

The older gentleman rises a bit slowly. He's quite dashing in his tux, with his silver hair and alert expression. My keen eye notes all the smile lines around his eyes and mouth, which tell me he's lived his life well, or at least curse-free. He's wearing a wedding ring, but none of the women at his table look anything like I would picture his wife. Most are too young, and one is even older than he.

He clears his throat before he speaks, and I find myself utterly captivated.

"When Will was born, my late wife, Mary, and I were the absolute best, very *worst* sort of proud grandparents. My goodness, how we made people sick of him before they ever met him." He chuckles along with the crowd, then looks warmly upon his grandson, whom I must now admit shares the man's kind face. "I wish Mary could be here tonight to see you and your bride," he pauses, looking heavenward, "but maybe she is. In any case, I think she'd want me to pass along some advice that kept us happily married for forty-eight beautiful years."

I swig more wine, hoping it will loosen the tightness in my throat. My breathing is falling a little shallow in anticipation of what he'll say next. Every hair on my body is raised and I turn a touch to my left because I cannot bear to look at Cody.

Will's grandfather tugs at his bow tie a bit as if he's also having a hard time finding enough oxygen. "I won't waste everyone's time with the standard advice you hear about laughing often, not keeping secrets or telling lies, of forgiving easily and saying nothing rather than saying something hurtful. You know all that. But I have a few other things to mention.

"Always answer the phone for each other. Sounds silly, but the point is, make time for each other even for the small things. And marriage isn't fifty-fifty. It's one hundred-one hundred. Each of you has to give everything you've got to the other. Right now, it's all bubbly and exciting, but there will be hard times, scary times, and sad times as you go through your days. Rarely will you both be strong at the same time, so when you are the strong one, you raise the other up."

My ears are buzzing now as I actively attempt to shove away the image of Carrie's sweet face — those chubby cheeks, petal-pink bow lips, and the swath of Cody's dark hair. Dr. Joshi's sorrowful expression. The tiny white casket.

Will's grandfather is unaware of my struggle as he continues his speech. "Love is a commitment, not a feeling. I know that might sound old-fashioned and funny to you young folks, but it's the biggest truth I know. Every day, wake up and make that commitment to approach each other in love. To work through those tough spots and low points. If you do that, I promise, you'll be standing at *your* grandchild's wedding together, giving him or her this same advice."

The next thing I know, Cody's hand has found mine beneath the table. I go stock-still. His solid grip is both familiar and comforting. My heart is beating so loudly, I'm afraid it'll drown out whatever Will's grandfather will say next.

"And finally," Will's grandfather pauses and holds up his ring finger before wiggling it, "always wear your ring!"

The audience chuckles, but I'm sitting there with hot tears streaming down my cheeks. Tears of sadness and shame for how I'd been unable to live up to that advice.

Will's grandfather lowers his hand. "It's a symbol of that commitment and proof of the vows you took today. It'll remind you — and everyone else — of your unbreakable bond. So be grateful you found each other, be happy, and I wouldn't mind a great-grandbaby to spoil before I meet my maker."

The sob I'd been working so hard to hold inside bursts from my throat. Josh turns to me. "Whoa, boy. A crier!"

I don't even look at him or Cody as I yank my hand free. I shove my chair back and race toward the bathroom. I have no idea how many people noticed my tears, or how Cody must feel at the moment, but the pain in my chest is wracking my body.

I grab a fistful of toilet paper and try to blot my runny mascara, but it's hopeless. I'm practically shaking, certain I can't go back to the reception now. If I return Sloane's money, maybe it won't matter if I duck out before anyone can catch me.

# Chapter Four

## *Cody*

I'm pacing outside the restroom door, about ready to kick it open, when Ellie finally charges back through it like a dog breaking its leash.

"Hey, hey. Slow down, babe." The old endearment rolls off my tongue as naturally as any word in my lexicon. I reach out and grab her hand, which stops her cold. Even with red eyes and a runny nose, she's the prettiest thing I've ever seen. I take the handkerchief from my pocket and offer it to her without letting go of her hand. "Here."

Her chin wobbles, but she blows her nose as loud as a goose and I can't help but smile.

"Don't smile at me. I don't deserve it." She frowns, but I see a hint of a soft smile forming.

"You okay?" I let my thumb stroke the back of her hand and hope she doesn't shrug free this time.

"Of course not. I'm terrible. Just terrible! That was hard to listen to…" Her eyes search the horizon now, clearly avoiding mine.

Five years' worth of conversations we should have had rush to my brain. From our daughter's funeral, to the months of Prozac, to her filing those divorce papers despite my pleas, I'd failed to find a way to bring her back to me.

Throughout all our time apart, I've tried to picture what I'd say if I saw her. Wondered if the reason I could never really get over her was because I hadn't gotten closure. The instant I saw her today, I knew I'll never be over Ellie Carter. And the way she broke down just now convinces me that she's not really over me.

She inhales and blows out a breath, which tells me she's gathering herself together. "So, how's your mom?"

"Fine." Not my most eloquent answer, but my brain isn't quite happy about her segue to small talk, even though I know it's her go-to tactic when she gets overwhelmed with emotion.

"Is your dad still teaching?" she asks, and I see the smile she always sported around my dad. She used to love to listen to him talk about history and would often say that if she'd had a teacher like him, maybe she wouldn't have hated school so much.

I shake my head. "No. He got Parkinson's a few years ago and it's fairly aggressive. He retired early this year."

Her chin wobbles. "I'm so sorry."

And I know she is, because she understands loss better than anyone.

"Well, we all have our stuff, don't we?" That's the truth. Not her stupid curse. She's looking at me now and I wish I could hear the thoughts churning in her mind. Instead, I blurt my own. "If you could go back and do it differently—follow Mr. Gooding's advice—would you?"

I'm holding all the air in the world now in my chest, and it burns. Our gazes lock. Every dream and happiness I've ever had is trapped there in her beautiful eyes. Before Ellie answers me, Sloane comes around the bend with Tori and Leighton.

Their eyebrows all rise in unison as they catch us there, standing close, holding hands.

Sloane's gaze homes in on our hands before snapping to my face. "What's going on?"

Ellie withdraws and my body drains of heat. "Cody came to check on me."

"Why did that toast make you bawl?" Leighton's gaze darts back and forth between Ellie and me.

"None of your business," I answer before Ellie has a chance.

"Excuse me?" Leigh's tone suggests that I butt out.

"She doesn't owe anyone an explanation. The kind thing for any of you to do would be to simply offer support. Speaking of, I've noticed you on your phone several times. How *is* Olivia?" I know full well that Leigh has not been communicating with Olivia, so I hope my point is made.

"Please don't argue. This is Sloane's special day and I don't want to be the cause of any trouble." Ellie looks at Sloane. "The toast made me remember something—someone—dear to me is all. You're very lucky to have Will's grandfather to go to for advice."

Ellie hadn't had anyone like that, at least not that I'd ever met. Her maternal grandparents had been killed in a car accident on their way to her high school graduation, and her father's parents had never been a big part of her life. Her mother was long dead from cancer. Her father—the fool who'd put the whole curse idea in her head way back when and reinforced it anytime something bad happened—had basically withdrawn from her years ago after marrying a woman who got him to move to Maine.

All of her friends that I'd ever met had been as young and inexperienced as we were, and when everything fell apart, my parents and sister were too busy grieving for Carrie and fussing over me to also help Ellie climb out of her deep depression.

"If I need any advice, I'll ask my mom." Sloane shrugs dismissively. "But I'm glad we found you, because we could all use a little touch-up before the bridal dances. And you should certainly fix your face, too."

Sloane gestures for the ladies to follow her, and, like obedient little ducklings, they do.

Ellie draws in a deep breath and shoots me an enigmatic glance. I sense an opening—it's slight, but there.

"I'll see you back at the party." I offer a smile and leave her be.

On my way back to the tent, I'm nearly knocked over by little Mandi, who seems to be overstimulated by the party based on the way she's giggling uncontrollably as she weaves through the crowd. Of course, I can't help but think of my Carrie and then envy her parents.

Shaking that thought off, I'm looking for Will and wishing it had been Tori who'd gotten the stomach bug so I'd be the one dancing with Ellie when the wedding party pairs up. Then inspiration strikes.

I meander through the crowd, smiling and shaking hands, all the while heading in the direction of the DJ.

He's checking his equipment, headphones in place, unexpressive face in concentration mode. The guy might be younger than me, but his reputation precedes him. He's got a thick blue stripe running through his bangs and is dressed all in black.

"Hey, man." I extend my hand. "I'm Cody. This is some setup."

He nods rather than shaking my hand, removing one earphone. "What's up?"

"I have a favor to ask." It irks me that he hasn't given me his name, but I let it go because, in the scheme of things, it doesn't matter.

"Yeah?" He's only half paying attention to me while fiddling with buttons and knobs and God knows what else makes up this elaborate display.

I wait until he gives me his actual attention. "Without getting into too many details, I'm trying to remind someone here of a better time in our life and am hoping that, after all the bridal dances and such, you could play a particular song for me?"

He narrows his eyes. "What song?"

I know he'll probably resist because Ellie's and my wedding song was as unconventional as everything else about our relationship, but I answer, "'500 Miles'—the cover by Sleeping At Last."

I hold my breath. His brows go way up and I note a hint of respect in eyes that are far too cynical for someone so young. "Cool."

Well, I'll take that, although Ellie had been the one to introduce me to that version of the song. "Thanks, man. I really appreciate it."

I turn and leave him to his job, which I suspect will kick into high gear as soon as Sloane returns. Now I just have to make sure I'm near Ellie when those first notes play.

I see Will speaking with his parents and grandfather, so I make my way over to them.

"Hey, buddy," Will says. "Have you met my grandfather, Matthew Gooding?"

"No," I say, extending my hand again. "Great toast, sir."

"Well, one of the benefits of being older than dirt is being able to look back and know how to hold on to what matters in life." Mr. Gooding glances at my bare left hand. "Looks like you haven't found your partner yet, though."

"Still working on it." I smile but hope Will doesn't mistake my meaning and think I'm into Tori.

"Good luck." The old man winks at me. I want to wrap my arms around him and tell him that he might've been a catalyst for my reunion with Ellie, but I refrain and he turns to speak with an older woman by the cake table.

Josh and Bruce find Will and me. It's obvious Josh has been hitting the liquor harder than the rest of us. Sober, he can be an okay guy, if a bit sophomoric. Drunk, he's sloppy, loud, and sometimes even a bit hostile.

"Maybe you outta slow down there," I murmur.

Josh jerks his thumb at me, laughing. "Who brought my mom?"

The guys chuckle, so I shrug. I'm only looking out for Will. It'd be a shame if Josh did something to cause a scene at the wedding. And if I'm being totally honest, the drunker he gets, the more trouble he'll give Ellie. That's an even bigger deal to me.

"Your leg tired yet?" Josh asks Will, who then tips his head in confusion. "You know, from dragging around the ball-and-chain?"

"Ha ha." But Will doesn't even look put out. He looks content, and I have to trust that Sloane has another side she doesn't show the rest of us.

"I'm happy for you." I slap Will on the shoulder. "Marriage is awesome. In fact, I'm jealous. It's nice to come home to a kiss hello and a hug that makes any bad thing that happened that day disappear."

My friends look at me quizzically.

"What?" I ask, licking my teeth and thinking there must be something stuck there.

"How would you know anything about marriage? You haven't even had a serious girlfriend in all the time I've known you." Will's eyes twinkle with good humor.

*Oops.* "My parents have been a great example of how finding the right person can make all the difference in a life." I look over my shoulder, wondering when Ellie might appear. It feels like the women have been gone forever and I'm getting concerned that Sloane and the others are giving Ellie a hard time.

# Chapter Five

## *Ellie*

If these ladies didn't like me earlier, they really don't like me now. Apparently Cody's kindness will cost me...and probably him, too. *The Curse Lite strikes again.* I wish the bridal party dance would hurry up and get over with so I can leave this reception.

Sloane and the others are whispering among themselves while I reopen my makeup case. One look in the mirror horrifies me. How can Cody look at the disaster that is me with such love in his eyes after all this time and so much pain?

Sloane snaps her fingers from her perch, making me realize I didn't even notice that she'd moved to her seat. "Please fix any shine and redo my lips."

The "please" throws me for a second.

"Of course." I look around for something to drape across her chest so none of the powder accidentally drifts onto the beaded fabric of her bodice, and settle on the T-shirt I'd been wearing when I arrived.

She wrinkles her nose like I'm placing a dirty diaper across her cleavage. "Let's be quick, okay?"

*And* there's *our Sloane.* Only someone who's never suffered any real trauma or hardship could lack all empathy and compassion for people like me who are obviously upset. Sometimes I wonder if there is a reason people like me have a target on our backs, while other people—seemingly less deserving ones—get to skate through life like it's a dream in which everything they want comes true.

"You're the boss." I take out some blotting papers and apply them to her forehead, nose, and chin, then brush on a little powder to give her face a freshly finished look.

"I'm sure it's tempting to try to snag a lawyer like Cody, but don't be fooled by his nice act. Trust me, you're out of your league with him," Tori says from her spot behind me.

I swallow back the truth about Cody and me because it isn't my place to out his past here and now. After starting on Sloane's mouth with my lip brush, I reply, "I'm not trying to snag anyone. But if I were, it isn't any of your business."

I don't bother looking at Tori—partly to bug her, and partly so I can concentrate on Sloane's mouth. Meanwhile, Sloane narrows her eyes at me but can't speak while I'm painting her lips.

"Well, just to be clear, Cody and I are a thing," Tori says.

"Good for you." My heart squeezes, but I don't believe her. Maybe they had a date, but he does not care for her. That much is obvious to anyone who knows him.

"That's a stretch, Tor," Leighton chimes in, though she is not coming to my defense so much as taking a swipe at Tori. "You're not any tighter with him than I am with Josh. At least I slept with Josh."

"Giving it all away as usual. No wonder Josh is no longer interested," Tori snaps.

"At least he *was* interested at some point. Cody hasn't even tried to feel you up." Leighton snickers.

*Thank goodness for frenemies!* My whole body relaxes after Leighton confirms my suspicions. I would go kiss her if I weren't afraid of getting frostbite or something.

I finish Sloane's face and step back so she can look in the mirror. "All good?"

She nods. "Fix yourself before you come back to the party. The bridal party dance should be soon, then you're free to go."

Her tone makes it sound like she believes she's delivering some kind of punishment by banishing me, when all I've done since this ceremony began is count down the seconds until I can bolt. *Well, not the whole time.*

The other two don't wait for a retouch, so I take a moment to myself once they all leave.

I can't help but mourn Cody's dad's condition. He'd been as kind as his son, and so full of energy. I wonder if I'm somehow responsible, like his being nice to me back then doomed him to this illness. Losing his mobility must be so hard on him and the family. The only good news—if you can call it that—is that his wife is a nurse who'll know how to care for him and has access to some of the best doctors in Sebastopol.

Throughout the years, I've actively pushed away memories of Cody's family, but I miss those birthday celebrations and family meals. I fondly recall the one vacation we took with them up the Oregon coast. It'd been comforting to be a part of a real family. Mine had always been a bit of a ragtag crew after my mother died just before my tenth birthday, and I'd lost any sense of family when my grandparents died. Except for those few years with Cody, I've pretty much been on my own since my high school graduation celebration turned into a memorial service for my grandparents.

I shake my head and do my best to wipe away the runny mascara and reapply a bit of makeup. I'm in no rush to get back to the party, so I take my time reorganizing my kit and the rest of my stuff so I can make a quick getaway when the time comes.

Eventually I make my way back to the tent, where Sloane mouths, "Finally," and sends Melissa off to cue the DJ.

When Josh sidles up to me, I can smell the whiskey on his breath. "Thought you took off and left me."

"Duty called." From the corner of my eye, I can see Cody trying to make sure I'm okay.

In no time, the DJ announces the bridal party, so we stride onto the dance floor. I stifle a groan when the first notes of one of the all-time cheesiest songs—

"That's What Friends Are For"—ring out. I'm thinking that maybe Sloane's mom picked it, but in any case it reminds me of another Dionne classic—"I'll Never Love This Way Again"— which is more apt for how seeing Cody again has made me feel tonight.

From the corner of my eye, I see little Mandi spinning in a circle, an empty champagne flute in her hand. "Josh, did you talk to Mandi's parents?"

"Oh, no. Forgot."

I glance at the little girl again, now less convinced of the sparkling cider explanation. "Please do it as soon as this dance is over."

Josh nods, but the real reason my concern fades is because I note Tori doing her best to snuggle up against Cody's chest. Any time Cody tries to insert some distance, she clamps down with the arm slung over his shoulder. She's smiling at him, but his gaze keeps drifting to me.

I don't even pretend to look away. I'm tempting fate, and I'll never forgive myself if something bad happens to Cody after the way I've let my heart open up to him tonight.

I'm so lost in my thoughts that Josh's palm is basically on my butt by the time I realize he'd been getting so handsy. Cody scowls at us, so I reposition Josh's groping fingers before a fight breaks out.

"Come on, Ellie, don't be a prude," Josh slurs.

"Don't *you* be a jerk."

He feigns a wound to the chest. "I've been insulted, but I like a sassy mouth."

*Oh, Lord.* "How about you stop talking and focus on dancing so we don't trip. The last thing I need is to fall on my face a second time tonight."

He grunts. "That was kinda spectacular. You should've seen Sloane's face. Heck, that alone was worth the price of admission."

When I shake my head, he asks, "What?"

I don't even know why I think it'll matter, but I tell him what's on my mind, mostly because I want to understand how Cody got hooked up with these idiots. "I don't understand you people."

"What's that mean?" He misses the beat and stumbles a bit, but I'm able to keep us both upright.

"It means that this is your friend's wedding. One of the most important and memorable days of his life — and Sloane's. Yet the way you and her attendants keep snarking at everything and everyone, I'd think you all secretly hate each other. Or maybe you envy each other. Either way, it's not the vibe I usually see at weddings or among friends."

"Trust me, I'm not jealous of anyone, least of all Will." He leans in like he's sharing a secret. "Sloane's been all sweet-as-pie to his face, but I've known her and her two-faced act since college. He's in for a big surprise after the honeymoon."

I'm not shocked, but I still find myself glancing over at the couple. Will looks genuinely happy and in love, and my heart just aches because, when this marriage ends—and I'm pretty convinced it will—I know exactly how he'll feel. Brokenhearted. Unable to breathe. Unwilling to crawl out of bed, not even to eat or shower.

On the other hand, then he'll be wiser about love and free to find someone better suited. That's what I'd expected Cody to do. If he'd taken more time to get to know me before our wedding, he would've seen how disasters follow me around like my shadow, and then he wouldn't have brought me into his life where I did so much damage.

Josh's hand sneaks back down to my butt, so I stomp on his foot.

"Ow!"

I jab a finger at his chest. "Next time it'll be a knee to the groin."

I swear he almost looks excited. I might be in trouble. But then the interminable song comes to an end not a second too soon. Taking advantage of the break, I step back. "Excuse me. I need some water."

Before he can catch hold of me, I duck into the crowd and make my escape. I'll guzzle some water, then leave this place and these people behind. Well, maybe after one last goodbye to Cody…

# Chapter Six

## *Cody*

My blood pressure is spiking. Ellie told me she'd be leaving after the bridal party dance, and Josh's behavior just now wouldn't have convinced her to stay. I spy her at the head table, downing a glass of water.

"What's your deal with that girl, Cody?" Tori asks, clearly perturbed by my preoccupation.

"Why is everyone so surprised that I'd be considerate of someone who got upset? She must feel out of place here."

"She's not in prison. Let her leave if she hates it so much." The petulant tone makes me clench my jaw, which she notices. "What did I do wrong? I mean, I thought we had a nice time at dinner last month, but you never called, and now you're acting like I've got leprosy."

Her voice sounds sincerely troubled, so I sigh. "You didn't do anything wrong. It's just…it's complicated. My heart's not free." That's more than I should say, but it's as close to the truth as I'm going to give her.

Tori's brows pinch. "Sloane and Will told me you were single."

"I am, but there was someone. I don't like to talk about it." I stare at her, hoping she gets the point and stops asking me questions.

Sloane and her dad glide past us during their father-daughter dance. I excuse myself and make my way around the perimeter of the party until I'm standing near enough to Ellie to make sure she doesn't flee before the DJ plays our song.

Small talk with strangers is not easy when I'm keeping one eye on Ellie and the other on the DJ. I note Ellie glancing around as if she's making a decision to go. It feels like a decade before the DJ says, "And now we have a special request, so grab your favorite partner."

I practically leap toward Ellie. I'm perpendicular to her, so I can see her profile. It only takes a few notes for her eyes to widen and her shoulders to pull back as if her body is waking up to all the memories I hope this tune will call back. She cranes her neck like she's searching me out, so I smile. She won't have to wait.

"Can I have this dance?" I extend a hand, which she takes.

I lead her to the dance floor and then take her in my arms. *Finally.* We fit together as perfectly as I remember. She's so slim, yet my hands know the exact location of each curve and where to land for the perfect hold. I want to press her tight to my chest and breathe in the familiar Neutrogena-clean scent of her skin and hair. To feel her heartbeat against my chest, like when we'd fall asleep after making love. In this moment, everything is right in my world. When she trembles, my heart does, too.

"You did this..." Her eyes are watery.

"I did." I'm torn between wanting to look at her and wanting her cheek-to-cheek. "I never go to a wedding where I don't remember ours and think about this song."

She smiles. "It's a good song...or at least this version is."

*Yes!* I pull her closer so that we can speak quietly, and those curls of hers brush against my cheek and neck. "Tell me the truth, Ellie. Are you happy these days?"

"I'm managing." At least she doesn't pretend to be happy.

I ease back so I can see her face. "You haven't changed a bit. It's hard to believe it's been five years."

She bites her lip before replying. "Twice as long as we were together."

We'd met and married within a couple of months, and then got pregnant shortly thereafter. Ten months later we buried Carrie, and a month later, divorce papers landed on my desk at the bank. I've never been able to put those highs and lows into meaningful words.

"And yet tonight my heart is truly happy for the first time since before Carrie died." A gamble, I know, but there'd be no moving forward with that elephant in the room. "Every year I visit her grave on her birthday, hoping I'll bump into you."

"And every year I go the day before so I won't see you and fall apart all over again." Her voice cracks, so I keep quiet for a few seconds.

"I still miss you." The words are out of my mouth before I can retract them, so they hang there above us, like the notes of the song in the background.

She closes her eyes and I see her nostrils flaring like she might cry again. I'm afraid to ask my next question because, if the answer is yes, that means her divorcing me wasn't only about the alleged curse. "Are you seeing anyone these days?"

"You know I'm not." She's emphatic, which makes me feel better.

"How would I know?"

"Because I only left to protect you from more pain. I certainly don't intend to inflict it on others."

"So you plan to go through the next fifty years without having a single close friend or lover?" I can tell my abrupt, irked tone is out of line by the way she stiffens in my arms. I'm about to apologize, when Josh taps my shoulder.

"Mind if I cut in?" he asks.

"In fact, I do," I say and spin Ellie out of his reach.

But Josh has crossed from tipsy to drunk and isn't interested in being ignored.

"She's *my* partner, Cody." He makes a move to grab Ellie's hand, at which point I shove him with my shoulder.

"Back off, man."

"Cody—" Ellie says, but I'm not listening because I know Josh is a hothead and I see what's coming next before it happens.

Josh shoves me, causing me to bump into another couple. I excuse myself but then turn to see Josh trying to force Ellie to dance with him. Everything around us fades to black as my sole focus becomes the way his hands are clutching her waist, at which point I grab his arm and yank.

Josh spins around and tries to shove me again, but I've got a firm grip, so we both stumble across the floor and crash into the table where the wedding cake is situated. The collective gasps of the crowd rise as the cake falls, then Sloane's shrill yelp pierces the air.

Shame cascades over me faster than that cake hit the floor. I've never been so impolite and out of control in my life. Adrenaline is flowing through me like jet fuel.

Josh looks like he's ready to take a swing, but Bruce holds him back. In the midst of the commotion, little Mandi runs toward the fallen cake and then pukes right beside it.

While the guests are all frantic at the sudden turn of events, I whirl around in search of Ellie to discover that she's already bolted. I'm about to chase her down when Will blocks me, looking at Josh and me with utter disgust before he drags us out of the tent.

"What the actual hell, man?" He's looking directly at me. Josh started the fight by refusing to take no for an answer, but I acted like an ass and ruined my good friend's wedding.

At the very least, I owe Will the truth. The whole truth. "Ellie's my ex-wife. We divorced after we lost our baby. I haven't seen her since then, and when Josh kept manhandling her, I lost it. I'm sorry. I know it's no excuse, but that's all I can say for myself at the moment."

"You were married?" Will's anger takes a back seat to shock, and Bruce and Josh both go slack-jawed.

"Yeah."

Will looks back toward the tent, clearly torn between needing to get back to Sloane and being curious about my secret past. "When?"

"I met her just before my college graduation. We eloped to Vegas and were really happy. Deep down, 'this is my person' kind of happy. But she couldn't recover from our daughter's death, so we divorced."

"Whatever," Josh mumbles, shaking his head. I still want to tell him off, but now isn't the time or place.

He waves a hand and stalks off, and Bruce follows him, most likely to keep him from doing anything else so stupid. I figure

Josh'll get punishment enough when he runs into Sloane and her parents, so I keep still.

Will runs one hand over his hair. "I have to get back to Sloane. I'm sorry about your past, but tonight was out of hand. Maybe it's best if you just slip away and get yourself together. I'll smooth things over with Sloane on the honeymoon."

"I'm really sorry, Will. I'd never intentionally hurt or embarrass you."

"I know. But Sloane worked hard to plan the perfect wedding, then Olivia got sick, your ex fell down the aisle, and now this fight and the cake and Mandi..."

"Let me go apologize to Sloane and her parents."

He holds up a hand. "Not now, trust me. You can apologize later."

He doesn't say anything more before he turns away, then he stops and looks over his shoulder. "You still love that girl?"

"With all my heart." Which is beating hard right now.

"Well, good luck, then." He returns to the tent, leaving me alone beneath a black canopy of sky with a million pinpricks of light. If a wish upon a star comes true, does one upon a million stars get special consideration?

I hope Will can forgive me and that our working relationship will remain strong, but I suspect our friendship might never be quite the same. Sloane won't exactly want me around anytime soon, and she obviously didn't take a shine to Ellie. Heck, Sloane probably won't want to see Josh either, but as long as Leighton still has the hots for him, he might get a pass.

With the exception of Will, I can't say I'd miss any of them, but maybe a part of me always knew something wasn't quite deep and true about a friendship in which I was never completely honest about my past.

I jog toward the main building where the ladies had gotten dressed and open a bunch of doors while calling out Ellie's name. Each room is empty, but in one I find the bridesmaid dress hanging beside Olivia's shoes with a note taped to the hanger.

I cross the room to read it and am shocked to see two hundred and fifty dollars taped to its back.

*Sloane,*

*I'm very sorry for all of the ways my presence detracted from your special day. In light of all that has happened, I can't in good conscience keep the dress or most of the money. I did keep a bit, but only because I plan to use it to do something important for a special kid I know.*

*I hope, with time, you'll see that the importance of the wedding ceremony and reception details pale in comparison to the vows, and that you will follow Will's grandfather's excellent advice.*

*Sincerely,*
*Ellie Carter*

I scrub my hands over my face.

When I moved out of my home after our divorce, I said I wanted a new life. Law school took me to the city, gave me new friends, and set my course on a new career path. But the truth is, I've only ever wanted to put back together the life I had with Ellie. Of course, she'll see this cake debacle as another example of how her curse makes me lose people. The last thing I need right now is another hurdle to clear with her.

I have no idea where she lives these days, so I can't storm her place tonight. Maybe the wedding planner knows. As I sneak back toward the tent, it dawns on me that she'll be no happier to see me than Sloane's parents would. I hesitate before choosing not to further disrupt the reception.

It's best if I give Ellie space tonight anyway. Between the Internet and Will's secretary being able to supply me with the contact info for the wedding planner, I'll locate her. In the meantime, I'll formulate a plan of approach so I don't walk away alone again.

# Chapter Seven

## *Ellie*

For the first time in three days, Cody isn't the only thing on my mind. After waiting to make sure Sloane wouldn't come pound down my door demanding the money I'd kept, this morning I drove up to the Walmart in Napa to purchase the Huffy Spider-Man bike I'd overheard Owen begging his mother to buy him for his birthday more than once in the past month.

Open windows—the benefit of an attic apartment lacking air-conditioning.

It's a ridiculous splurge. I certainly could've spent that hundred bucks on some new brushes for my kit, or perhaps something pretty for myself. But even though I have restricted myself to the acquaintance realm with regard to my downstairs neighbors, I know Nadine—Owen's mom—would buy him that bike if she could afford it. Like me, she works hard just to keep the lights on and food in the refrigerator. Her deadbeat ex can't be bothered to pay child support on time or to show up for the kid more than once in a very blue moon.

It stinks that men like that guy get to be dads, while someone like Cody, who would've been a terrific father like his own dad, had his chance cruelly snatched away. Of course, that thought makes me doubly sad, and I'm trying so hard not to stay sad.

The Marsten wedding is a gig I'll regret for months to come. Dancing with Cody, holding his hand, seeing that smile—it's set me so far back I'm practically as raw as I'd been the day I filed divorce papers. I still shudder at the memory of the hurt in Cody's eyes the day he received those.

I give myself a mental shake while I pull into the driveway. After I turn off the engine, I take a minute to write out the birthday card I bought. It's fun to be a sort of Secret Santa, although this is more like a birthday fairy godmother.

After I exit the car, I look around to make sure Owen and Nadine aren't in the yard. I walk around to the hatchback of my old Subaru and open it. My smile is so big, my cheeks hurt. This is the tackiest bike—red and blue, with a big blue web stretched across the front of the handlebars—but Owen is going to lose his little mind from joy.

That thought fills my heart with some much-needed pleasure. It's the closest I'll get to feeling like a mom or aunt or anyone with an important child in her life.

I heave the bike out of the car and roll it across the yard to one of the Adirondack chairs in the grass. The landlord kindly keeps four of them here around a cheap firepit, and I've taken full advantage of both on cool, dry nights.

After looping the bike lock through the chair's arm, I tuck the lock combination inside the birthday card. An imperfect solution, but I'll keep an eye on it from upstairs until Owen claims his prize.

I set the envelope on the seat of the chair—along with a helmet, knee pads, and wrist guards to keep him safe—and turn to go to the outdoor stairs to my apartment, when I bump into Nadine.

She's attractive, if a bit tired-looking, with her dark hair and skin. Chasing after a young boy is no easy feat, though I'd trade places with any mom in a heartbeat if I could.

"Hi!" I wave and try to act cool.

"What are you doing, Ellie?" Nadine asks, craning her neck to stare at the bike behind me.

"Checking out the bike you bought Owen for his birthday." I smile and hope she believes my feigned ignorance, but her single raised brow suggests I'm outta luck.

"I watched you pull that bike from your car through my kitchen window." Her hands come to rest on her hips.

I wrinkle my nose. "I'm sorry if I've overstepped, but Owen's so adorable and I heard him begging you for that bike. I had a little windfall this past weekend and couldn't think of anything I'd rather do. Please don't make me return it. I really need this…" To my horror, my voice breaks apart and tears begin to flow.

Nadine covers her mouth and then she pats my shoulder. "Come on inside and have some tea."

Normally I'd say no, like I have every other time. I don't want to become good friends with her or Owen for fear of the curse, but at the moment, I need company and am in no shape to climb all the way to the third floor.

I nod and follow her, wiping my cheeks dry.

Her home is spare but sunny. Lots of white curtains blowing in the breeze and a comfy gray sectional sofa tucked into the corner of the living room. A pile of brightly colored plastic toys has overtaken the corner opposite the sofa, and that just makes my heart clench and more tears flow.

Nadine leads me to the small oak kitchen table. She quietly microwaves some water and prepares a cup of chamomile tea. When she finishes, she sits down at the table. "I don't mean to pry, but are you okay?"

I sip the hot tea, not knowing how to answer that question. "Probably not as much as I'd like to believe."

"Do you want to talk about it?" She glances at the clock. "I need to pick Owen up in thirty minutes, but I'm all yours until then."

"I don't even know where to begin, and I'm a little afraid you'll think I'm crazy." I bury my head in my hands for a second.

"Aren't we all?" She laughs, putting me at ease. "You know, I figured you didn't much like Owen and me, the way you keep to yourself all the time. It's kind of a shock that you went to all that effort for him…and me."

"Oh, no…I don't dislike you at all. I keep my distance because of the curse." I sip more tea, frowning.

"The curse?" She sits up, clearly curious.

I suppose I can't get out of explaining myself at this point, and before I realize it, I've gone and told the poor woman everything in my life, from my dead twin up through Carrie and this past weekend with Cody.

Nadine sits back. "Well, you certainly have suffered a lot in a short time, but I don't believe in curses. Karma? Maybe. But not curses. And as far as I can tell, karma shouldn't have any need to bring stuff back on you."

"Then maybe I'm paying for sins of a former life." I'd laugh at myself, but it isn't funny. It does feel like I'm being punished for a crime I'm not even aware I committed.

"Ellie…bad luck is just bad luck. You've had more than your fair share, but you aren't causing it. You know what I think? I think this curse business is an excuse—a way to protect *yourself* from more pain."

"No," I insist. I almost tell her that even my dad believes in the curse, but I know that won't persuade her. "I'm tough. Really. I can handle anything. I just don't want to see anyone else get hurt."

Nadine tosses me a skeptical look. "Well, I hope you don't use that as an excuse to keep your distance from Owen and me in the future. I don't know about you, but I can't collect too many friends."

"You shouldn't take risks with Owen's safety." I twine a paper napkin in my fingers. "I almost didn't buy the bike because I worried I might taint it."

"I'm positive he'll get some scrapes and bruises learning to ride it, but that won't be *your* fault." She looks at the clock again. "Listen, I hate to run, because I can see you aren't convinced yet, but we will be talking about this again. I should be back in fifteen minutes with Owen if you want to come down and give him the bike."

"Oh, no. I don't want him to know it came from me. It is supposed to be a surprise…like from a fairy godmother."

"Fairy godmother?" Nadine laughs. "Well, now I have a better understanding of your thoughts about curses. But I don't want my son believing in that stuff, so if you want him to keep the bike, then you have to tell him it's from you."

She grabs her car keys, so I stand and set my teacup in the sink, and toss the napkin in the trash. I don't like my choices, but she has me over a barrel. "Fine. You can tell him it's from me, but I'm going to spy from the upstairs window so you can get all the hugs."

"Suit yourself." Nadine shakes her head and ushers me out the back door. "Ellie, thank you for the generous gift. He'll be over the moon. I owe you a big one."

"You're welcome. And you owe me nothing, especially after having listened to me cry."

She waves and gets in her car. I lug myself up the stairs and enter my apartment. Like hers, it's spare but cute enough. I like bold colors, so my art and furniture look more like Owen's pile of toys than her Zen white-and-gray motif. But none of the cheerful colors make my home truly warm like hers.

Ten minutes later, I'm sitting at the window, waiting for her to return with Owen. The longer they take, the more nervous I become. Has my gift and her compassion somehow dragged the curse back to life? Are she and Owen on the side of the road somewhere?

My heart begins to race, but then I see her silver Kia turn the corner and pull into our driveway. I stick my head out my window just far enough to see and hear, but not so far that I draw any attention.

Nadine gets out of the car and then opens Owen's door. He's already unbuckled his car seat and literally bounds across the grass toward the bike like a spastic kangaroo. "Oh my gosh, oh my gosh. Whoa. Look! Look, Mommy! Whoa, ho, ho!"

My heart fills with light, although a few tears collect because I can't help imagining my Carrie — her dark hair long and curly, her wide eyes filled with light — leaping around the grass after receiving an extravagant surprise. Yet somehow Owen's happy face makes every tear I've shed since the Marsten wedding worthwhile.

I close the window and retreat into my apartment to draw a warm bath. My Cole Porter playlist and a glass of cheap wine will help me relax. I lower myself into the water, closing my eyes, and think about Nadine's comment.

*Is* it me I've been protecting all this time?

# Chapter Eight

## Cody

It's nearly seven thirty when I turn the corner onto the cul-de-sac of neat Craftsman and other style homes where Ellie lives. For seventy-five minutes I've been thinking about what I'll say to her, but now that I'm parking in front of the dusty-rose house she calls home, my mind goes blank.

I kill the engine and take a few breaths before getting out of the car. My dad always says to go all-in in all things because passion is everything, whether for love or work or anything else we choose to do with our time. As such, I've brought pink carnations, and my wedding ring is tucked in my pocket.

When I cross under the cedar arch covered in wisteria, I enter a small yard where four white Adirondack chairs surround a metal firepit. I can picture her out here at night, staring up at the stars. Picture us tossing logs on the fire, listening to Noah Gunderson, and eating popcorn.

I glance at the house and locate the exterior steps that lead to the upstairs apartment. Unit B, just like Melissa said.

*Here goes nothing – or everything.*

I climb the stairs two at a time, but my increased heart rate isn't due to that pace. I'm just eager to see Ellie again. I rap at her door and try to peer through the curtain that hangs in its window.

"Just a sec!" she calls from inside.

I'm practically bouncing on my toes when I see her face peek through the side of the curtain before she drops the fabric like it burnt her fingers. I have to wait a few seconds before she opens the door.

"Cody?" She doesn't blink. "What are you doing here?"

She's in her pajamas, with her wet hair piled up on her head like she just took a bath. She always liked baths, especially when she needed to relax. My best guess is that she's taken several of them since Saturday.

For some reason, I have a bad habit of smiling whenever I'm in an anxious situation. Needless to say, I'm smiling a bit too much now. I thrust the carnations at her.

"I came to see you," I answer. "May I come in?"

"Of course." She finally blinks and takes the flowers. I hear her whisper the word *carnations* before she looks at me. "Thank you for these."

I'm ninety-nine percent sure she gets the significance of the otherwise cheap flower choice. While she fetches a vase and fills it with water, I remain still so I don't spook her.

Then while she's snipping the stems and placing them in water, she asks, "What happened after I left the wedding? Is Will speaking to you?"

There she goes with the small talk again.

"He's on his honeymoon at the moment. I explained everything about us to him when you took off. I think he'll forgive me in time. Not so sure about Sloane."

"I hope it gets sorted out, for your sake." Ellie sets the vase on her table for two—a table that only has one chair.

"I didn't come here for small talk, babe. Seeing you again...and now looking around here—" I gesture at the pathetic little table. "My God, you've really cut yourself off from the world. What a sad fact—for you and the world—because the world is better off when you spread your sunshine around."

Her mouth falls open and a stark flash of gratitude lights those eyes. It's painful to see because it reminds me how alone she is, and of how I'd been too easily run off years ago.

I head into the living room to escape those thoughts, but its rich, bold colors make me long for the past even worse than before. Every articulate, well-thought-out argument I'd prepared vanishes. "Ellie, I still love you. I want you back. I want the life we were supposed to have back. I used to think I could move on eventually, but seeing you this weekend made me realize how I've been fooling myself by pretending I could be happy without you."

Instead of running into my arms, she stops midway between the kitchen and where I'm standing.

"Cody, I'll always love you, but I'm scared. Look at what happened at that wedding! I can hardly believe Sloane let you live after you and Josh smashed into her cake." The concerned look on her face gives way to a little giggle.

Us falling against that cake is a little funny in hindsight, I suppose, but I'm too keyed up at the moment to laugh about anything.

"That was definitely not a high point for anyone, but you didn't cause that. Josh and I did with lousy behavior that had lousier consequences."

Her smile fades and she slumps onto the arm of a floral-print chair. "Neither of which would've happened if I hadn't been there. Seriously, you've got this great new life and job. I don't want to be the reason it all tumbles down just like that cake."

"What kind of awesome life do you think I'm living without you?" I frown at how ridiculous that thought is. Working seventy hours per week, eating frozen dinners, using dating apps that never lead anywhere worth visiting.

She shrugs. "One without heartache."

"Really? So my dad's illness doesn't cause me heartache? Or my sister's ugly divorce, that doesn't make me sad? Or how about the custody case I was working on that we lost, so now a decent father's kids are moving to Europe—think that doesn't keep me up nights?" I let my arms fall to my side, having been a bit more dramatic than I'd intended. "My point...my point is that bad things still happen to me, whether or not you're at my side."

She pulls her knees up to her chest, forehead all wrinkled with doubt. "I'm sorry about those things, but at least you're healthy and safe. You've got a bright future ahead, too."

"A future without you can never be *bright*, Ellie." I cross to her chair and drop to my knees, holding her calves. "I know you're afraid, but you have to get this through your head—nothing that ever happens to me will hurt as much as losing our daughter and you, don't you see that? I miss you like crazy. There's a hole in my heart that I'll never fill if you refuse to give us another chance. The only real curse is your fear. Please, don't let it ruin both our lives."

Some tears leak from her eyes, so I wipe them with my thumbs. My chest is heaving from my speechifying and just being this close to her again. She's trembling, and I know she's torn up trying to choose between what she wants and what she thinks is right.

"I swear I can deal with any loss if I have you."

"But I can't deal with the idea that something could happen to *you*."

"If something is going to happen to me, it's going to happen. You don't control the fate of the world, Ellie Carter. And anyway, if you can live without me while I'm still alive, you can survive if I die—so why torment us both by keeping us apart? Come on…let's put our family back together again. We've both suffered enough, and there's no reason for us to sit alone and watch the rest of the world try to find what we already have together."

Her hands tremulously reach for my face, so I drag her off that chair and into a kiss. She tastes familiar and sweet, like honey and grapes, and my body can barely register all of the sensations coursing through it now.

We roll onto the thick carpet together, tongues and limbs in a hot tangle of desire and joy so sharp it hurts. My heart's beating like a lion on the hunt as my mouth finds her neck and her hands grip my back.

She wraps her legs around my hips and I am lost and desperate to rip away all of our clothes. "My God, I'm never letting you go again."

Through panting breaths, she says, "I hope you don't regret it."

"I won't." I sit back and dig my ring out of my pocket and hand it to her before sticking out my left hand. "You put that back where it belongs, and then we'll make it official as soon as possible."

"You kept it all this time?" she marvels, turning it over in her fingers.

I wiggle my fourth finger. "Didn't you?"

She slips my ring back in place. My heart feels like it's filling all the empty spaces in my chest.

I did it.

I got her back.

"Hang on." She pats my thighs, so I let her up. She disappears into the bedroom, then returns with her tiny diamond engagement ring and plain band of gold, both of which she drops into my palm. "Your turn."

I stare at the rings. God, how young and broke we were back then. I flash to when Will had asked my opinion on the engagement rings he was considering for Sloane. All big diamonds. All set in platinum. "How about if we upgrade yours?"

Her cheeks turn ruby red. "Don't you dare! I don't need to waste money on fancy jewelry, Cody. We both know there's so much more to love and marriage than that. All I ever needed or wanted was your heart."

I smile and slip the rings on her finger. "Well, you've always had that, babe, and you always will."

She stares at her left hand and then stands and reaches for mine. "Let's consummate this new vow."

"Thought you'd never ask." I follow her into the bedroom.

# Epilogue

## *Ellie*

The framed photo from the Marsten wedding that I keep on a bookshelf is the last thing I notice before another cramp makes me pause to catch my breath. I push through it for sixty seconds, then glance at the photo again.

I've no love lost for Sloane or anything else about that day except for how it reunited Cody and me. For that—and that alone—this picture will always be displayed in our home. I am a little sorry for Cody that his and Will's friendship has dwindled, but that resulted more from the fact that Cody left his firm in the city and moved out to Sonoma for a more balanced lifestyle.

Cody comes rushing into the living room with my overnight bag in hand. "How many minutes apart are we?"

*We,* like his belly feels like it's being stuck in a vise. It's cute, though, that he's so in this with me. As for his nerves, I get those, too. We haven't talked much about Carrie lately—sometimes I'm afraid even thinking about her will cause problems with this pregnancy—but I know he worries about how I'll handle things if something goes wrong this time. "About nine minutes. We should head out just to be safe."

I may have thrown caution to the wind when I decided not to let the curse dictate my life, but I still live by the "better safe than sorry" philosophy. And I'd prefer not to give birth on the side of the road.

On our way out the door, Nadine and Owen wish us luck. Owen has been pretty excited by the prospect of babies around the house. I wish he were older so he could babysit, but Nadine and I can trade that chore from time to time.

I roll down my window on the way to the hospital. I've got my seat pushed all the way back so I can fit there as comfortably as possible. My belly is bigger than a balance ball at this point, but the doc has promised me after each round of testing that the twins are perfect and healthy. That's right, twins. A boy and a girl. Cody agreed to name our daughter Lesley after the sister I never met, and we're naming our son Dillon, which means ray of hope.

Right now, Cody looks more panicked than I feel, which says a lot.

"You feeling okay?" he asks without looking at me. His iron grip on the steering wheel could bend the thing, and he's sitting far forward like an old man overly focused on the road.

"At least until the next cramp." I marvel that I'm not the one most terrified, frankly. Having been through birthing once before, I should be dreading this with every fiber of my being. Two babies at once? The pain will be real.

But I can't stop smiling. I think God makes moms sort of forget the realities of childbirth so we're willing to go through it more than once. And lately a little part of me has wondered if maybe Carrie will be a guardian angel over her family, breaking the curse once and for all. That thought always makes my nose tingle a bit and my eyes teary.

I turn my face and blink until those tears clear. "Did you call your parents and sister?"

"They're on their way." He nods, eyes still glued to the road.

I haven't called my dad yet, but I will later. Months ago, Cody warned him to stop referring to "the curse." My dad agreed and has since promised to come meet his grandchildren after they're born.

We arrive at the hospital, and Cody escorts me inside as if I'm made of the finest crystal.

"Why are you so nervous? I'm the one who'll be doing all the work." I tease him while sweat beads across his forehead.

He shrugs, looking right at me. "I want everything to go well."

He doesn't say "this time" but I know he's thinking it. We both are.

"You convinced me that I'm not cursed, and that we can handle anything, so don't go reversing course on me now." I lean in to give him a kiss, but that's not easy when I'm more beach ball than human.

He strokes my head and touches our foreheads together. "You're right. I'm being ridiculous."

Cody bends forward to kiss my stomach and then we check in and get settled in our room.

Several hours, many pushes, and a string of curses later, Lesley and Dillon make their way into the world and our hearts. After natural childbirth, the doctor shot me up with Demerol, so I'm too out of it to risk holding my kids.

Sitting in the chair beside my bed, Cody is holding them both, staring at them with such amazement my heart aches from sheer bliss. He's planting gentle kisses on their downy heads and whispering to them when his family arrives.

Being surrounded by so much love usually makes me afraid that it will all disappear, but today I let it fill my heart because I've finally learned that the toughest battle in my life has been with my own head.

I make a solemn vow on this sacred day that I won't ever again let fear keep me from love.

# Acknowledgments

As always, I have many people to thank for helping me bring this book to all of you, not the least of whom are my family and friends for their continued love, encouragement, and support.

Thanks, also, to my patient editor on this project, Jane Haertel, and to proofreader Jessica Poore, for working so hard on my behalf.

A special thanks to Teuta Nikollaj, a beautiful young makeup artist who spent an hour teaching me the basics of her profession. And also to a fan, Teresa Kennedy, for sharing the story of her memorable turn as a flower girl and the champagne she'd believed was fancy Sprite!

I also couldn't have produced this story without my Fiction From the Heart gals, who've added another dimension of support and encouragement to my life. I'm so grateful!

Finally, to all of you who choose to spend time with my work, thank you, thank you, thank you!

# About Jamie Beck

*Wall Street Journal* best-selling author Jamie Beck's realistic and heartwarming stories have sold more than two million copies. She is a Booksellers' Best Award and National Readers' Choice Award finalist, and critics at Kirkus, Publishers Weekly, and Booklist have respectively called her work "smart," "uplifting," and "entertaining." In addition to writing novels, she enjoys dancing around the kitchen while cooking and hitting the slopes in Vermont and Utah. Above all, she is a grateful wife and mother to a very patient, supportive family.

For more information, please visit www.jamiebeck.com, which includes a fun extras page with Pinterest boards, Spotify playlists, and more. And for monthly updates, fun tips, reading recommendations, and birthday gift opportunities, please subscribe to her newsletter: http://bit.ly/JamieBeckNewsletter

# Weather or Knot

by Tracy Brogan

# Chapter One

There are only a handful of legitimate reasons to be awake at four thirty in the morning, and even fewer reasons to be up, dressed, and standing outside in a torrential rainstorm. At the moment, Allison Winters was beginning to wonder if her reasons were valid enough to warrant her current level of saturation. Surely there were easier, drier, later-in-the-day ways to make a living, but everyone in her line of work had to pay their dues, so on this wet, blustery morning in May, she was paying hers.

As the weekend meteorologist for Channel 7 News in Glenville, Michigan, that often meant standing on the rooftop of the station during what most logical people would refer to as *the middle of the night.* And more often than not, it meant getting up close and personal with moody midwestern weather. Most days she didn't mind the unpredictable outdoors, and when inside the station, she enjoyed the camaraderie shared among her colleagues during those quiet hours when the night owls and the early birds collided. But lately the zero-dark-thirty shifts had started taking a toll. She was tired of eating her lunch at the crack of dawn. Tired of having to skip nights out with friends because she was either working a double shift and covering the evening weather, or because her bedtime came at an hour when most toddlers were still up and ready to party. And she was tired of being the littlest fish in a modest-sized pond. Her two-year contract was up soon, and she was considering a change. Or at the very least, she was considering the possibility of considering a change.

"Cue Allison. In five, four, three, two..."

She swiped rain from her face as instructions from Frank, the segment coordinator (who was nice and dry inside the control room), sounded through her earpiece. She nodded at the cameraman, some new kid whose name escaped her, and swiped again before the shot went live. Not that the swipe did any good. It was too windy to hold an umbrella and she'd stood under waterfalls that produced less moisture than the rain clouds above her head, but so be it. There were people out there who'd be getting up soon for work, and she owed it to her audience, miniscule though it may be at the present hour, to let them know what to expect from the skies today.

"It's a big, sloppy, wet one out today, folks!" she said, plastering on a quasi-cheerful smile. "Get out those umbrellas and raincoats because this extreme precipitation is expected to continue on throughout the day." She delivered the rest of the forecast trying hard not to blink against the pelting droplets, then tossed the segment back to the weekend anchor (who was also warm and dry inside the studio — not that she was bitter).

"Annnnd, Allison, you're clear," Frank announced through the earpiece. "When you get inside, Jessica wants to see you right away."

Allison took one step then halted, the foul weather suddenly second on her mind. "Jessica? As in Jessica Jackson, our news director?"

"Yup."

"Why is she at the station? It's not even five a.m. And it's a Sunday."

But Frank was gone, on to announcing camera shifts to the floor directors and setting up the next segments. The camera kid was already heading inside through a narrow door that led to the stairs. He paused, looking at her expectantly. "You coming? Or are you waiting for the ark?"

She smiled distractedly and followed him in, her shoes squeaking on the linoleum steps as she made her way downstairs and toward the dressing room. If Jessica was there, it had to be important. Allison shivered from a chill that had nothing to do with the rain dripping down the back of her neck, and hoped it was a good kind of important and not a bad kind of important.

In the four months since Jessica Jackson had joined the station as news director, Allison had interacted with her only during the staff meetings. Partly because their work obligations rarely had them crossing paths, and partly because Jessica intimidated the heck out of her. She was stoic and intense in a way that Allison could only hope to emulate, and her focus was always on substance and professionalism. While Allison worked hard to be taken seriously as a scientist and a meteorologist, she had an unshakable fear that Jessica found her frivolous. And she'd never get bumped to a better shift if the news director didn't think she'd earned it.

Allison eyed herself in the mirror of the tiny dressing room, trying to decide if she should change her clothes or freshen her makeup but decided that, at the moment, speed was more important than style. She hung up her raincoat, and simply wrapped a towel around her head before heading down another flight of stairs toward the executive offices.

In spite of the predawn hour, Jessica looked as polished as always, in a close-fitting pantsuit the shade of pink peonies. A surprising choice, perhaps, but she was the type of woman who could wear any shade outfit and still command the room as if she were wearing a military uniform. Her hair was pulled back in a no-nonsense bun high on the crown of her head. Allison instantly regretted the towel and pulled it off as she tapped lightly against the frame of the open door and hoped against hope that her blond hair wasn't sticking up in every direction. She could have at least pulled it back into a ponytail, but it was too late now.

"Good morning, Jessica. Frank said you wanted to see me?" She couldn't keep the question out of her tone. The one that said *Um, do you really?*

Jessica waved her into the room. "Yes, Allison. Come in. Shut the door, please. There's something I want to discuss with you."

*Shut the door? Uh oh, that couldn't be good.*

"Is it good news or bad news?" she blurted out, as if the ten-second warning would give her time to prepare, but Jessica's onyx-eyed gaze was enigmatic.

"Most news is neither good nor bad. It's just news. As in this case."

Spoken like a seasoned news director. *Just the facts, ma'am.*

"Sit down." Jessica motioned to the chair.

She stepped forward and her wet shoes made such an unfortunate farty noise that Allison nearly felt the need to say "excuse me," but certainly Jessica knew it was her shoes, right? Honestly, why was she so nervous? She settled gingerly into the chair, feeling like a seventh grader being called to the principal's office for chewing gum in algebra class.

Without preamble, Jessica said, "I'd like to send you on assignment with a storm-chasing team. You'd leave on Tuesday for Kansas and be gone for a week."

"A storm-chasing team?"

"Yes." She let that linger out there and Allison couldn't help but note that, for a newsperson, Jessica was being very stingy with the details. After a pause, the news director rested her folded arms on the uncluttered desk and continued. "You'll be expected to tape two to four segments per day. Your reports need to be entertaining as well as educational and informative. If the weather is suitably interesting, we may have you do some live reporting. Do you think you can do that?"

"I'm sure I can," she answered brightly. In truth, Allison had no idea if she could, in fact, do that, but she was a jump first, figure it out later kind of person, and she'd be damned if she didn't give this her best shot. Especially since this was exactly the break she'd been waiting for. Segments from the road? With a team of storm chasers? Viewers loved storm chasers. Her street cred would jump by leaps and bounds, not to mention that this was a surefire way to reach a broader audience, and hopefully impress her boss. "May I say I'm honored you have the confidence in my work to send me on this assignment."

Jessica took a calm sip of coffee from her Channel 7 mug. "My assessment of your abilities remains to be seen but the chief meteorologist seems to think you can handle it. It's a week on the road in a cramped vehicle with adrenaline chasers who are probably more interested in footage than science, and the chance of you seeing any truly remarkable weather is questionable. Hannah Freemont will be your videographer. You'll share a room. Still interested?"

"Yes, absolutely." She didn't know Hannah other than to say hello while passing in the hallways at the station, but she guessed they were around the same age, twenty-eight, and had the same work ethic. Surely Hannah would be equally motivated to make this trip worthwhile. They'd be fine.

"All right then." Jessica picked up a manila folder from her desk. "Here's the rest of the information you'll need, and, Allison, I'm sure it goes without saying that I expect focused, high-quality reports that the station can be proud of. We're one spot behind Channel 4 in the Nielsen ratings and it's no secret I was brought on board to surpass them. They just got a traffic helicopter, and if we want to compete with that, we'll have to pull out all the stops. I need you to go find us a tornado."

Allison nodded, accepting the folder. "I promise you'll get the very best from me, Jessica. I won't disappoint you."

"I'm glad to hear that."

Sensing this meeting was over, Allison rose from the chair and walked out of the news director's office and around the corner before doing a silent jig of joy in the hall. Finally, an assignment with some sparkle to it, and a chance to really show Jessica what she was capable of. Catching sight of the oversized clock on the wall, she realized she had just enough time to try to fix her hair before heading back up to the roof for her next segment. Then there were the radio spots to phone in, graphics to make, and a dozen other things to handle before her work day ended. The folder and its information would have to wait, so it wasn't until she'd gotten home, changed into comfy sweats, and microwaved some soup for dinner before she opened it. Two pages in, the spoon clattered against the side of the bowl and chicken broth splashed onto her sleeve as she read the names of who she was about to spend seven days—and evenings—with.

*No, no, no.*

*Just… anybody else.*

*She could storm chase with anybody. Except Dylan Parks.*

# Chapter Two

"Ride-alongs? Seriously? Who the hell approved ride-alongs?" Dylan Parks's scowl was only half serious as he stuffed a couple of clean but wrinkled tee shirts into the well-traveled duffel bag sitting on his bed.

"I did. We need the cash." Chris, his storm-chasing partner and the best driver Dylan had ever worked with, picked up a sock that had fallen to the floor and tossed it at his head.

Dylan caught it and added it to the bag, even though the mate was still somewhere on the floor. Then he nodded. "Cash is handy, but you know how these tagalongs always slow us down. They like to stop and stretch their legs. They want food and bathroom breaks, and if they aren't getting in the way of the shot, then they end up talking too much on the video. There's a huge weather system developing south of Woodward, Oklahoma, and it looks to be a crazy day. We need to get our crew on the road in the next hour."

Chris handed him the leather toiletry bag sitting on the wooden dresser. "Not a problem. All the guys are already here, and our guests should arrive in the next fifteen minutes or so. It's a meteorologist and her shooter so at least they'll know better than to talk over any video."

Dylan looked up from trying to wrangle the toiletry bag in between the tee shirts. He knew *shooter* meant videographer, but it was the other word that caught his attention.

"Her? One of them is a woman?"

Chris grinned. "Even better. They're both women."

Dylan shook his head slowly. "Did you not hear what I just said about bathroom breaks?"

Truthfully, he had no issue with women meteorologists, or women videographers, or women in general. His mother and his sisters had kicked his ass more than once, and he knew better than to suggest that a woman wasn't as capable as a man. Except at one thing. Peeing into a Gatorade bottle when there wasn't time to stop the car. The storms developing in the south were going to be vast, and move fast, and his team had to keep up with them. They'd missed two opportunities last week to get any decent footage thanks to a broken tailpipe that needed repair, and this week was all about catching up.

"She knows the drill, Dylan," Chris said. "I talked to her on the phone yesterday and she sounds cool. Plus, it's good money for nothing more than having them ride in the back seat and do a few segments from the road."

"Road segments? You don't think those will slow us down?"

Chris arched a dark eyebrow. "That's ironic coming from the guy who takes forty-five minutes every day to style his hair. Before going out into a tornado."

Dylan laughed with acceptance and bent to pick up the other sock. "Yeah, yeah, yeah. Okay. We'll make it work. Hey, could you check the batteries for all the cameras? I meant to do that last night."

"Already done. I also restocked the first aid kit, filled up the water bottles, loaded the cooler, put Rain-X on both the Blaster and the Sidewinder, dropped your dog off at the neighbor's house, packed up the drone, and did about ten other things to get us ready. Unlike you, I don't need ten hours of beauty sleep. I've been working since seven this morning so, you're welcome. Now get your shit together so we can get out of here." He turned and strode away, whistling the *Jeopardy!* theme song.

"I'll be ready in ten minutes," Dylan called after him.

"Make it five."

They both knew it would be fifteen.

Chris was the business side of their team, deftly handling all of the day-to-day stuff. Dylan, on the other hand, was the visionary and the risk-taker. They were both meteorologists, but while Chris was all about details and gadgetry, Dylan had earned a reputation for having an uncanny instinct about which storms would turn into tornadic supercells, and which of those supercells would ultimately produce funnels. It was a good balance between the two of them and over the past three years of working together, they'd ironed out any kinks in their system. Except that Chris was always early, and he was always late.

Dylan finished packing and headed outside to the driveway of the house he and Chris rented. The rest of the crew were milling around, tackling various chores. Shaggy-haired Rob, their own videographer, was loading camera equipment into the Sidewinder, an SUV that served as their backup vehicle. Tech wizard Beau was fiddling with wires from the back seat of the Blaster, their primary vehicle, and twenty-two-year-old Nathan, their other driver and an aspiring forecaster, was sitting in a dinged-up lawn chair staring intently at the laptop perched on his long, spindly legs. His ever-present Cubs baseball hat was turned with the brim at the back of his head, adding to his youthful appearance.

Off to the side of the driveway, standing in the grass with their backs to him, were Chris and two women, obviously their guests for the week. The shorter one had deep-red hair woven into two braids. Her khaki shorts were topped with a shapeless blue tee shirt and she held a small video camera close to her shoulder. Then Dylan's gaze traveled to the woman next to her—and stuck. She was a pony-tailed blonde in a dark-purple tank top and black yoga pants that clung tightly in all the right places. She was tall, slender, and had, quite frankly, the best ass he'd seen in a long time. He blinked and adjusted his sunglasses. If the front side of her was half as good as the backside, he'd have to remind his guys—and himself—that ride-along guests were off-limits. Not that he wouldn't welcome a little female companionship, but this was a work day. And he was a professional.

"Up there we have a Vantage Vue portable weather station," Chris said, pointing to the roof of the Blaster. "It's pretty reliable, and, you know... portable. In addition to our own stuff, we work with Channel 17 quite often and they have a Doppler on Wheels mounted in the back of an F-150. Then, just to keep all our bases covered, I always have my Kestrel 3000."

"Kestrel 3000? That sounds like a Quidditch broom," said the redhead.

Chris chuckled and pulled one from his pocket. "It's this thing. A handheld weather station. It tracks wind speeds, temperature, wind chill, heat index, dew point." He handed it to her, and she gave it a two-second glance before handing it back. "What about those pod things that you leave in the path of tornadoes? Do you guys have one of those?"

"Sometimes. We don't have any to deploy this week, though. We do have a drone but so far haven't had much luck launching one. If you get on the right side of the funnel, the drone will get sucked into the vortex, which is what you want, but more often than not the wind shear just smashes it back down to the ground."

Dylan listened to the exchange as he made his way toward them, his footsteps crunching over the gravel driveway. The blonde turned at the sound, and he blinked again, removing his sunglasses, certain that his eyes were playing a not-very-funny trick on him. Because if he didn't know better, he'd say that woman in the distracting yoga pants next to his partner was Allie Winters. But it couldn't be. It definitely couldn't be, because the last time he'd seen her, she'd been returning his engagement ring and twisting his heart up like an F5 tornado.

# Chapter Three

"Hi, Dylan. Um, surprise?" Allison tried to smile but the muscles in her cheeks decided to twitch instead of relax so all she could offer her ex-fiancé was a slightly sheepish curve of her lips. Even that was an effort. So was breathing. If hyperventilating into a paper bag was an option, she would have considered it.

She'd had a few days to prepare for this moment but seeing Dylan in person was still enough to render her both light-headed and heavy-hearted. He looked good. Very good, with sharper angles to his face and more bulk to his shoulders. His dark hair was cut much shorter than he used to wear it, while his eyes were the same bright blue that had lingered in her memories for years. She'd seen photos of him here and there on social media because they had a few of the same old friends, but she'd avoided those as much as she could. She hadn't wanted to know what he was up to. Not because he hadn't been important to her, but because he had.

Dylan halted in place, color suffusing his face, and she recognized how lame her greeting was. She should've warned him, or told Chris to warn him, but truthfully, she was afraid if Dylan knew she was coming, he'd find some way to avoid her. And after the initial shock of seeing his name on that paperwork, she'd realized that *she* very much wanted to see *him.*

"Allie?" His voice rasped, and he quickly coughed to disguise the rattle. "Wow. I... wow." To his credit, he closed the distance and gave her a hug. Sort of. It was the kind of hug you might give an aging relative with fragile bones who always smelled of Chapstick and arthritis cream. The kind that *looked* like a hug but that involved virtually no bodily contact. He took a full step back a millisecond later and she could all but feel the cold front moving in.

"I didn't know you were our ride-along this week," he said, his voice neutral, expressing neither dismay nor joy. Her heart and stomach did a turbulent little cha-cha.

"I didn't know you'd become a storm chaser," she answered. She stole a glance at Chris, wondering if he knew any of the history between her and Dylan, but his mirrored sunglasses betrayed nothing.

"Wait, you guys know each other?" Hannah asked, lifting the camera to film the answer.

Allison nodded, wishing she'd filled her shooter in on the details. They'd had plenty of time to kill during the flight from Michigan to Kansas, but she hadn't wanted to make it a *thing*. So instead, she and Hannah had talked about families and movies and laughed over the fact that they'd both, at some point during their preteen years, kissed a poster of Justin Timberlake. Hannah had admitted to being in a friends-with-benefits situation that was nearing its expiration date, but when she'd asked Allison about her relationship status, she'd simply said, "I'm not dating anyone right now."

That was true. She wasn't. And she hadn't. Not really. She'd had the random two- or three-month sprees with a few guys over the past couple of years, but work was her number one priority, and none of those dates had inspired her to focus on anything different. None of them had ever compared to Dylan either, but that was a fact she'd tried hard to ignore.

"We worked together in Sandusky," Dylan answered, putting his sunglasses back on and turning toward the truck. "I see Chris is giving you ladies the four-one-one on all the electronics. He's the guy for that, so I'll leave you to it. We'll head out soon."

Allison watched him walk away and tried not to think about the last time she'd seen him do that, a tsunami of hot, sticky remorse cascading over her. Guilt over their breakup was like a tattoo she couldn't just scrub away. Although she'd tried.

Chris finished showing them around and introducing them to the other guys, and soon they were on the road, with Allison and Hannah in the back seat, sitting behind Chris and Dylan. Allison wished she could switch sides with her videographer so she didn't have to stare at Dylan's profile all day, although he seemed to have adjusted to the surprise and was taking the high-pressure situation in stride. Not that he had much choice. As the miles passed, the conversation flowed easily enough, but with all topics restricted to weather and storm chasing.

"We communicate with our guys and other teams by cell phone most of the time, but sometimes there's no service out here in the plains, especially when the wind kicks up, so we also keep a set of walkie-talkies charged and ready. Some chasers have ham radios, but we don't bother with that." Dylan was giving them a basic tutorial of what equipment was found inside the truck, and it was plentiful. All the while he kept a laptop open with radar showing the storm system they were trying to catch up to. "We have a police scanner, a weather radio, and some old-school maps, again, in case we lose Wi-Fi. Not that the paper maps do us much good. We stay on paved roads as often as we can, but it seems like more often than not we're flying eighty miles per hour down an unnamed dirt road and hoping we don't get stuck in the mud."

"Why don't you have one of those tank things? Those cars that look like a giant metal beetle," Hannah asked. Her questions so far had been basic, but Allison was glad since it kept the conversation going without much effort from her.

Dylan chuckled. "I assume you mean an intercept vehicle, like on TV? We don't have one because they're as expensive as hell and hard to build. Underneath all that armor is a truck chassis but by the time they're finished, those things weigh about eight tons and get maybe ten miles to the gallon. We like being a little more nimble, but that does mean we can't get as close. It's a trade-off."

Dylan continued on, talking about weather patterns and what they watched for. He explained to Hannah about wall clouds and rotation and hooks on the radar. Most of it was information Allison already knew but listening to his excitement made her smile. It was one of the many things they'd had in common, a geeky love of the weather, and his words triggered a flash flood of memories. Afternoons spent watching cloud formations float by, of challenging each other with forecast speculations, of evenings spent laughing and teasing and encouraging each other. He'd been her biggest fan once. But that was a long time ago, before prevailing winds had sent their lives in two different directions.

Dylan was rambling on like a first-year meteorology student, but he couldn't seem to help it. He had about fifty intense and conflicting emotions creating a blizzard in his brain right now, leaving little room for logical thought and no idea which way to turn. He was a mess and struggling hard not to show it. What the hell was Allie Winters doing in his back seat? And how was it possible she was even more beautiful than he'd remembered? She was like a sexier, more serious version of her past self and that was not good news. Sure, he still had a stash of printed pictures of her somewhere, stuck in a drawer or a shoebox, and even one picture in a frame. A photo of the two of them nestled up on a sofa, with her wearing one of his Ohio State sweatshirts and him looking smug and satisfied because they'd just had sex with each other for the very first time. He knew it was stupid to keep that picture, but he could still remember how he'd felt in that moment. He'd felt like a man with nothing but blue skies ahead. It was the moment he knew he'd marry her someday.

Only he hadn't.

He'd proposed to her, about a year after that photo had been taken, and she'd said yes. That was the best moment of his life. Then two weeks later, she changed her mind. He'd never felt so gutted, not before or since. Looking back, she may have been right about them being too young. Twenty-three seemed like a lifetime ago, but he wished she'd given them a chance. Given *him* a chance. She'd put her career first without even a discussion. It never had made sense, but he'd worked hard to make peace with it. He'd moved on, even getting close to proposing to another woman last year, but something had held him back and he'd ended the relationship instead. Now, with Allie sitting just a few feet behind him, he couldn't help but wonder if she'd been the ghost haunting all his other relationships. Because in the mix of all the emotions battling inside his skull right now, several of them had to do with him still wanting her.

The storms picked up and he tried to focus on that, but none of the impressive clouds he'd had his eye on turned tornadic. That wasn't atypical. There were roughly thirteen hundred funnel clouds per year in the United States, but storm chasers were lucky if they caught more than a few dozen, and more often than not, those funnel clouds came in clusters because storm systems needed all the right elements to come in to play. The science of forecasting improved with each passing season but, just like having your ex-fiancée show up in your driveway, tornadoes were unpredictable.

They stopped by the side of a creek and Allie, donning a black blazer over her tank top, did some short, taped interviews with the rest of the crew. Chris and Beau talked about the tech they relied on while Nathan nervously stared at the ground and mumbled something about why he wanted to be a meteorologist. When Dylan's turn came, Allie gazed right into his eyes and his adrenaline kicked in as if no time had passed between them. His heart had far too good a memory but he shut that down as best as he could to focus on her interview.

"What made you decide to be a storm chaser?" she asked, holding a microphone up to his mouth. He took a breath to calm his pulse. If the question had come from Allie, his old girlfriend, he might have said, "I was restless and bored because the life I'd wanted with you had evaporated." But the question was from Allison the TV meteorologist, so he gave the sales pitch answer instead. "Meteorology and storm-chasing technology has come a long way, but we still don't know why some supercells form tornadoes when others don't. We don't know why some funnel clouds last for a few minutes and others might last for an hour or more. So the more scientific data we can gather, the more we learn about wind speeds inside the funnel, both horizontal and vertical, and the better we'll be able to predict violent weather. And the more lead time we can provide, the better equipped we'll be to keep people safe."

She stared at him for a second longer and he wondered if he was supposed to say something else, but then she thanked him, turned to the shooter, and signed off on the segment.

"Thanks," she said to him again after Hannah walked away and it was just the two of them next to the stream.

"For what?"

"Um, for being a good sport today. I'm sorry about surprising you."

"Well, you've surprised me before. This one was a lot easier to handle." His tone was sharper than he intended, yet all things considered, that was about the nicest way he could put it. But her smile dimmed, eclipsed by the harshness of his words and he instantly regretted them. But why? Why did he feel bad? *He* shouldn't feel bad. He didn't dump her. *She* dumped *him*. With no warning. Still… there wasn't much point in holding on to that anger. It was a lifetime ago, and he was *over* it. He was over *her*.

Right?

Damn it. This was going to be a long week.

# Chapter Four

"So, maybe it's none of my business but are you going to tell me the scoop between you and Loverboy? Because the sexual tension in the car today was suffocating." Hannah sat cross-legged on the rust-and-green plaid bedspread of a budget motel, eating cheese crackers as Allison pulled a floral nightgown from her bag.

All she wanted to do was take a long, hot shower, put on that nightgown, and go to bed. Amazing how exhausting it could be sitting in the back of an SUV all day, but she knew her fatigue wasn't really from that. Dylan had been cordial, even after the interview, but when he'd made the comment about being surprised by her, it was a sucker punch in the gut, a terrible feeling that she just wanted to get rid of. And every damn time he called her Allie, it took her right back to the time when *they* had been an *us*.

She sank down onto the bed next to Hannah.

"We were engaged." The words came out on a long, sad sigh.

Hannah dropped a cracker and her mouth went nearly as round as her eyes. "Engaged? I figured there was some hanky-panky or something but engaged? That's huge. What happened?"

Allison hated stirring up the long-buried feelings, but it was unavoidable now. "We were around twenty-three and both doing internships at the same little station in Sandusky. We lived together for a while. Then he got offered a job in Sarasota."

"Oh! And then he dumped you? Just like a man." Hannah stuffed a half dozen crackers into her mouth and started chomping furiously.

"No, he didn't dump me." Allison shook her head, her chin dropping with the weight of her memories pulling it down. "He proposed, and I was going to go with him. But then I got offered a job in Chicago, and I just couldn't turn it down." She paused again, the words reluctant on her tongue. "Dylan was basically the perfect boyfriend and I loved him so much, but I also worked really hard to get through school. My parents sacrificed so much to help pay for it, and I know if I'd gone with him, my career would've taken a back seat."

"Couldn't he have gone with you to Chicago? There must have been other job opportunities there."

Allie had often wondered that herself, along with a myriad of other what-if type questions. What if she had married him? What if he'd called her after their breakup? What if she'd called him? What if? What if? What if? But none of that mattered now because it was in the past. "I didn't ask him to. And after I broke things off, he just moved away, and we haven't spoken since. Not until this morning."

Hannah handed her a conciliatory cheese cracker. A little square of processed comfort carbs. "Well, a little heads up would've been nice," she said. "I only got a bit of your reunion on tape and it could've been good stuff."

"I don't think that's what Jessica is looking for. In fact, if she'd known there was any history between me and Dylan, she probably wouldn't have let me come, and I need these segments to be amazing. I'm trying to get promoted."

A soft *harrumph* came from Hannah. "Okay, well, just so you know, the stuff we have so far is pretty meh. Hopefully we'll get some better shots this week, though. Chris said the storms on tap for tomorrow should be more intense."

Allison was quickly learning that Hannah was not one to sugarcoat things. "Was I meh, or was it just the circumstances? Because I need to not be meh."

Hannah shrugged and handed her a few more crackers. "You seemed a little tense but given the circumstances, I guess I see why."

A gentle knock rattled their motel room door, and Rob's voice permeated through the wood. "Hey, you guys want some pizza? We're hanging out in our room."

The women exchanged glances.

"These crackers are not doing it for me," Hannah said, rising and pulling Allison up from the bed. "Let's go have pizza. Unless you'd rather just hang out here?"

That was a tough call. A hot shower and a few hours relaxing in a quiet room versus what was sure to be greasy pizza in a tacky hotel room with Dylan and all his crew. The key word being Dylan. Would he even want her there? Her stomach growled, making the decision for her. Dylan would just have to deal.

Two slices, two beers, and two hours later, Allison was feeling full and significantly more relaxed. The crew's friendly banter now included her and Hannah, a pleasant perk to the evening indicating they'd been accepted. Dylan continued to be sociable but professional, which was probably for the best. He'd showered and changed into jeans and a white tee shirt, and as the alcohol mellowed her edgy nerves and lowered her emotional defenses, she momentarily felt an overwhelming urge to press her face against his neck just to see if he still smelled as good as she'd remembered. Realizing where her mind was headed, she switched to drinking water and strategically moved to a chair farther away from him. She needed to focus on doing a kick-ass job this week, and not get distracted by Dylan's good smell.

"Allison, where did you go to school? What's your background?" The question came from Rob, who'd been sitting next to Hannah most of the evening under the guise of discussing photography, but Allison suspected other motives. He was cute in a coltish, sloppy way, and Hannah didn't seem to mind his close proximity. That friend with benefits might be losing his place.

Allison leaned forward from her spot on a lumpy motel room chair. "I got my bachelor's in atmospheric science from Michigan State. I did an internship up in Marquette, and then I spent some time in Sandusky." She'd leave it vague, just as Dylan had. "After that, I took a job in Chicago."

"But aren't you back in Michigan now?" Rob asked.

Dylan was across the room, leaning against a beige laminate dresser and talking to Chris, but she sensed he was tuned in to what she was saying. Especially once she'd mentioned Chicago, the catalyst of their breakup. "I am back in Michigan, yes. Chicago wasn't a great fit for me. It's pretty cutthroat in that size market, and then my mom started having some health problems so when a job in Glenville came up, I took it. I do the weekend weather. It's a pretty good place to be."

"You said an internship in Marquette?" Nathan interjected. "That's way up there, isn't it? Like practically Canada?"

"Practically. But separated by Lake Superior. It's gorgeous there in the summer but brutal in the winter. Way too much snow for me. Reporting during blizzards is my least favorite thing, when you can't see anything and the cold keeps draining your earpiece batteries."

A couple heads around the room nodded in agreement. With various levels of forecasting and broadcasting experience among them, they started comparing disastrous reporting stories, and times when weather had gotten the best of them. Stories of storm-chasing mishaps were revealed, some clearly embellished and oft-repeated, like a game of telephone with each person adding their own spin. Allison found herself laughing right along with them, and more than once, caught Dylan's gaze resting on her, like a snowflake landing on her skin. It was strange to be in the same room, as if none of the sadness had ever happened. As if they were back in Sandusky and sharing one of those sweet nights that ended with whispers and kisses under the covers. That part had always been good for them. All of it had been good for them, except their timing.

"I've got to get to bed," announced Hannah shortly before midnight, putting an end to the impromptu tacky motel greasy-pizza party. They'd be getting on the road early the next day, probably heading back toward Kansas City if the weather systems they were tracking stayed on their current path. Dylan kept his distance as the women said good night to everyone, but then came outside right behind Allison.

"Hey," he said softly, prompting her to turn around. Hannah kept walking. "I'm sorry to hear that about your mom and the health stuff. What happened?"

It was dark, but the yellow lights of the motel gave everything an amber hue, and the sounds of distant traffic could just barely be heard over the wind rustling the tree branches.

"Congestive heart failure," she answered. "Turns out smoking is bad for you."

"I'm sorry," he said again. She thought he might step forward and hug her, properly this time, but he stayed put, just outside his motel room door.

"She's better now. Making lots of lifestyle changes and managing pretty well. Thanks for asking."

"Sure. I always liked your mom."

"She liked you too."

They stared for another moment, and she wanted to say more, but then Nathan came outside, breaking the fragile spell.

"Oh, sorry," he said, eyeing them both before ducking his head and darting toward his own room.

Dylan chuckled, his smile small but sincere. He offered up a short sigh. "Good night, Allie."

"Good night, Dylan."

# Chapter Five

"So, are you going to tell me what happened between you and the hot weather babe?" Chris asked, not bothering to stifle his yawn. He was still in bed the next morning, although Dylan was uncharacteristically up, dressed, and ready to go, pouring water into a tiny coffee pot sitting on the counter next to an ice bucket. He didn't respond to the question.

"Well?" Chris prompted, tossing off the covers.

Dylan shrugged. "Not much to tell. We dated for a while. And then we didn't." *She broke my heart and left me for dead. But I'm over it.*

"Uh-huh. Is that why you turned Buckeye red the minute you saw her? And why you've shaved for the first time in two weeks? I haven't seen your face so baby-ass smooth in I don't know how long."

"Shut up," he said without heat, taking the joke in stride. Chris would understand but Dylan just didn't want to talk about it. "She was... important. But it was years ago. I'm over it." Saying it out loud didn't make it feel any more real. He *was* over her, but having her around was stirring up a lot of memories and a lot of emotions that he'd much rather leave unexamined.

Chris wandered into the bathroom, flipping on the light and standing there in a gray tee shirt and plaid boxers. "Are you sure? Maybe her being here isn't a coincidence. Maybe she tracked you down to see if the old flame was still burning."

Dylan shoved the coffee pot back into its spot. He *really* didn't want to talk about it. "Damn, Chris. I had no idea you were such a helpless romantic."

"I believe the phrase is *hopeless* romantic."

"Yeah. I know." Dylan grinned, determined to change the

topic. "Now get your shit together so we can get on the road."

Half an hour later they were outside in the motel parking lot, and the weather was perfect, if perfect meant ideal conditions for supercell formations. It was hot, humid, and he could practically feel the instability in the atmosphere.

Chris ambled up next to him and sniffed the air. "Smells like tornadoes. Let's get going."

Nathan rushed forward and set his laptop on the hood of the Sidewinder. "Check out this system," he said giddily. "The radar is blowing up."

Dylan peered at it for a scant second and agreed. Yep, today would make up for all that driving around yesterday, and he was ready. More than ready. He wondered if his eagerness to see some impressive weather was amplified by his desire to encounter a funnel cloud or two for Allie. It's what she was here for, after all. Maybe he wanted to impress her a little bit too. Prove to her that he was good at what he did. Because he was, and if that impressed her? He was okay with that. Because wanting to *impress* her had nothing to do with *wanting* her in general. Right?

She and Hannah emerged from their room a few minutes later, travel coffee mugs in hand. He noted that today's stretchy exercise pants had the same emotional effect on him as yesterday's had, which was damned inconvenient. In all honesty, hearing her laughter last night hadn't done him any favors either. Neither had catching a whiff of her perfume as she'd passed by or watching her press a bottle of beer to her lips as she drank. Being around her was messing with him far more than it should. Yes, she was still beautiful, and yes, he was still attracted to her, but he'd taken this ride once before and it ended with an ejector seat straight into misery. No thanks. He'd be polite, and even considerate. He'd help her get her job done, and maybe they could even have some fun doing it because he was a make-the-best-of-it kind of guy, but if she was here chasing anything other than weather, she was too late.

"Let's get this show on the road," he said, opening the car door for her as she reached his side. She smiled up at him, and he reluctantly found himself smiling back.

"How's it looking today?" she asked innocently.

He deliberately glanced at her cleavage. Because, hey, *cleavage*. "It's looking pretty good from here," and he heard her chuckle as she slid into the back seat.

"This is the system we're following," Dylan said, pointing to the radar screen of his computer as the Blaster traveled north on Interstate 183. "Based on these forecast models, I'd put money on supercells developing near Hays, Kansas, by midafternoon. This system is moving at about forty miles per hour and we should be ahead of it soon. That's right where we want to be."

Allison nodded, anticipation rising inside her like a helium balloon. Her tornado forecasting skills were woefully untested, but she agreed with his assessment. Looking out the window she spotted low clouds on the horizon that appeared to be full of moisture and perfect for producing a storm. And hopefully perfect for getting some great footage. This morning in the motel room, she and Hannah had reviewed her segments from yesterday and they weren't awful, but they weren't awesome either. Just average, but average wouldn't impress her news director. And average wouldn't get her promoted to a better time slot.

As it had yesterday, conversation inside the car revolved mostly around weather-related topics such as forecasting technologies and industry politics, but it also took a few verbal detours toward more pressing matters, like which Avenger had the most impressive skills, whether or not craft beer was worth the upcharge, and if rap musicians were the twenty-first-century version of troubadours. That was Hannah's theory, prompting laughter by all as both the men said in unison, "What the fuck is a troubadour?"

When they stopped for gas, Dylan casually followed Allison into the adjacent convenience store and down the candy aisle. They perused for a few seconds before she spotted what she wanted and grabbed two red-and-yellow bags.

He scoffed good-naturedly. "Honest to God, Als, you're the only person I've met in my entire life who actually eats Raisinets."

She smiled. "Well, somebody else must be eating them or they wouldn't keep making them. Maybe you just need to broaden your scope. You know, meet more people?"

"I meet plenty of people. I just happen to know that you're unique."

Her laughter caught in her throat. He'd said it to tease her, of course, but his cheeks flushed immediately, his knowledge of her candy preferences a spontaneous and accidental reminder of their shared past. She felt her own cheeks heating up, and suddenly she wanted to ask him each and every question that had lingered since their breakup. Was there anyone else? Had he been in love again? Did he miss her or hate her or worst yet, had he stopped thinking of her at all? She could hardly expect otherwise. She'd left him. He didn't owe her any of his brain space, but the intimacy of his innocent comment stirred up far more questions than either of them could answer while standing in the lackluster candy section of a dingy roadside convenience store with fluorescent bulbs buzzing above their heads and twangy country music playing in the background.

But later... she'd ask him later. At some point before this week ended, they would need to talk. Really talk.

For now, she simply plucked a Snickers from the shelf and held it out to him. "Still your favorite?"

He eyed it for a moment, as though she were holding a baited mousetrap rather than candy, but then his lips slid into an easy smile. His eyes met with hers, and his fingertips oh-so-casually grazed over her hand as he took the Snickers, sending stupidly delicious tingles zinging every which way inside of her.

"Still my favorite," he said, holding her gaze, and making all those zinging tingles suddenly zero in on the most logical, yet least convenient, spot of her whole body.

While her brain may have had other plans, and her heart had worked hard to get over him, she still had one lonely erogenous zone that had never really forgotten him. Other lovers had been clumsy or rushed or too much of this and not enough of that, but Dylan had been just right. He *knew* her, her rhythms and her needs and her vulnerabilities. He'd known when to be playful and when to be earnest. And he'd trusted her to know all the same things about him, but she'd tossed that all away for a career. A career that often left her standing on the rooftop in the rain. And *always* left her with no one to go home to.

## Chapter Six

"See that rain wall?" Dylan's voice rose with excitement as he pointed out the open window of the Blaster. "Chris, how far away do you think that is?"

Chris leaned forward from his spot in the driver's seat to get a better look off to the west. "I'd guess about a quarter of a mile."

Dylan nodded, leaning his head and shoulders out of the car for a second before popping back in. "Let's pull over for a minute." He turned toward the back seat. "Allie, this looks like a good place to do a segment. We've definitely got some strengthening rotation overhead. Looks like a funnel may be trying to tighten and drop."

"We can get closer," Chris said, but Dylan shook his head.

"No, this is close enough for now. Another couple of minutes and we may have to get back in the car."

Chris stole a glance in Dylan's direction but pulled over to the side of the two-lane road and rolled to a stop. On either side of them, fields stretched out as far as Allison could see. There was a single farmhouse in the distance, a faded red barn next to it, and a smattering of trees here and there while above them hovered darkening, ominous clouds pulsing with energy.

"That is one scary looking sky," Hannah said as they clamored from the car.

"You are not wrong," Allison agreed. As a meteorologist, she'd seen her share of powerful weather, but it was more of the thunderstorm and blizzard variety. This was something else entirely. This system was big and real and roiling right above their heads. Her hands trembled as she scrambled to clip on her microphone pack.

"Dude, why are we so far away?" called out Nathan as he, Rob, and Beau scrambled from the Sidewinder behind them lugging various forms of recording equipment.

"We're giving Allie a chance to do a segment before this supercell unleashes," Dylan called back. "Get whatever footage you can."

She felt a rush of gratitude at Dylan's answer. His job was to get his crew as close to the action as possible but even after everything she'd put him through, he was willing to have his entire team stop here just for her benefit. It was a sacrifice and incredibly thoughtful. Now she owed it to each of them, as well as to herself and Jessica Jackson back at Channel 7, to do a skillful job of reporting. She certainly wouldn't have to fake the adrenaline coursing through her system. She was excited and nervous and scared and thrilled. And a little nauseous at the thought of that system overhead getting even meaner, as if Mother Nature were on a hormonal rampage.

"Can I get you on camera for this?" she asked Dylan as he walked toward the edge of road, eyes on the sky. "Could you describe what you're seeing for the viewers?"

He turned back to her, his fast smile a bright flash under the darkening sky. "Sure. Come stand over here and with any luck we'll capture a funnel dropping during your report. I'll just keep talking until it does!" His enthusiasm was infectious, and she smiled back, setting aside her concern that he might actually be right. Judging from the looks of that sky, a tornado could unleash at any moment to reach down and pluck them from the ground. It was like wanting to see a ghost but not *really* wanting to see a ghost because that would just be too flippin' scary. She wanted to see a tornado, but when faced with the reality, *did she?*

Ignoring her fear, she and Hannah quickly ran over a few details as she threw on her TV meteorologist blazer. She couldn't very well report in just a tank top, and within seconds, the videographer had the camera poised and ready. Dylan stood next to Allison with the fields behind them and the undulating storm system overhead, a wonderful and exciting backdrop.

"This is Allison Winters with the Channel 7 Weather Team. We're fortunate today to have meteorologist and storm-chasing expert Dylan Parks as our guide. As you can see, we've got some severe weather developing. Dylan, can you tell me what's happening in the atmosphere right now?"

"Absolutely, Allison." He turned to the camera like a pro, far more relaxed today than he had been yesterday. "Folks, we've got a robust supercell forming just east of Ridgemont, Kansas, and all signs point to this system being a prolific tornado producer. Right now, we're about four hundred yards from a rapidly rotating rain wall and I can see by the cloud formations that there's a significant rotational updraft. What most people may not realize is that it's not only the circular motion of a funnel cloud that does damage. It's also the vertical winds inside the tornado. It's those suction vortices, sometimes multiple vortices inside one tornado, that cause the most destruction. So far, we don't have a way to measure that vertical wind speed, but we know it's even more intense than the outer bands of the storm."

Allison nodded, and rather than adding her own observations, she prompted him with another question because he was a natural in front of the camera. He'd been fine at reporting back in their Sandusky days, but this new and improved Dylan was polished and sure of himself. His easy charm lit up as he talked about wind speeds and air pressure and stovepipes versus wedges. His style was thoroughly engaging and in the back of her mind, Allie was thinking it was a shame he wasn't on-air all the time. Then again, she might not be the most objective viewer at the moment because, standing so close to him, she was thinking as much about his face as she was his words, but still, he was mesmerizing.

A few more questions and weather-related banter left her pleased and optimistic. The segment was fun but professional, engaging and informative. Thanks to Dylan, Allison was going to deliver just what her news director wanted. She wrapped up just as drizzle started to mist the air.

"How was that?" he asked, his smile turning a little sheepish.

"Amazing. You're really good at this. I sincerely owe you one."

"There's an understatement." His voice was low and a subtly crooked eyebrow indicated he was teasing, but her response was cut short, becoming a distressed yelp as a bolt of lightning arced across the sky. The sound cracked, reverberating in the air around them and she instinctively grabbed ahold of Dylan's arm.

Hannah squeaked loudly at the same time. "Damn, that's bright on camera!"

"Back in the trucks, everybody." Chris called out the instruction, but his guidance was entirely unnecessary since they were all already scrambling like circus clowns trying to jump into a too small car. Nervous scuffling and laughter turned to relief as soon as they were back inside the relative safety of the vehicles, slightly damp from the rain and thoroughly energized by the potentially near-death lightning strike.

"That was a little too close," Chris said, putting the SUV in gear and pulling back onto the road. "I think it singed my nose hair."

"I'll be sure to include that detail in my report to Channel 17," Dylan replied as he put the phone to his ear to call the station. "Hi, this is Dylan Parks in the Blaster. We've got rapid upward motion just west of Dumont. I'm looking at my screen and that hook is coming around pretty fast. Do you see it on the radar?"

The rain increased as he continued talking, and Chris drove them toward what any logical person would be heading away from. Something plunked against the roof. Hannah ducked, clearly not enjoying any part of this. Allison looked over to see her shooter's cheeks pale in the bluish light of the storm. Another plunk sounded, followed by another.

"I think we've got hail," Allison said, and sure enough, the plunking grew more rapid and loud. She peered out the window to see marble-sized hail bouncing on the ground.

"Shouldn't we be slowing down?" Hannah asked, struggling to keep her camera poised in her shaking hands. "It seems like we should be slowing down."

But Chris didn't slow down.

"We're in good shape, Hannah," he answered. "This one is traveling away from us." As he spoke, more lightning flashed.

"There it is," Dylan exclaimed. "A cone coming down. You see it?" He was talking to them while also delivering information over the phone, his voice getting louder as his words tumbled out. Allison tried to make out the formation. They passed a tiny copse of trees next to the road and suddenly, there it was. A fully formed funnel reaching from the sky. It seemed to be moving in slow motion, a graceful, gentle thing, but of course, it wasn't. She knew that and her heart jumped into her throat. She could hear Hannah all but hyperventilating in the seat next to her but couldn't take her eyes off the storm.

The tornado grew, stretching from the clouds until it made contact with the grassy field, and Allison was glad to see that, for now at least, there appeared to be nothing in its path other than farmland. It was an oddly morbid sort of excitement—being so thrilled to watch something so destructive—but the power of it had to be honored. Dylan continued talking to the TV station, Chris kept driving, and Hannah kept the camera pressed to her window capturing as much as she could. Meanwhile, Allison had the luxury of simply watching and observing, hoping to soak in every part of this so she could retell it on air.

They followed the funnel for what seemed like forever, and yet no time at all. They were at the mercy of the sky and she was so fully captivated, it was hard to determine just how long they'd gone on. But then the rain decreased, and just as suddenly as the funnel had appeared, it magically withdrew. She glanced at her phone to see it had been less than fifteen minutes, but an experience that would last her a lifetime.

A minute later the rain stopped completely and both Chris and Nathan pulled over to the side of the road so the crew could catch their collective breaths. While everyone else jumped from the car, thrilled with the chase, Hannah emerged much more slowly, her complexion now decidedly green.

"You going to toss some cookies?" Beau asked her. "It's okay. You wouldn't be the first one."

Hannah's expression went from pathetic to grateful, then she bent at the waist and puked into the tall, wet grass on the side of the road. Allison started to move toward her, but lanky Rob got there first.

"She's okay," he called out, giving the group a thumbs-up with one hand while he patted Hannah's back with the other.

"How about you. Are you okay?" Dylan asked, suddenly next to Allison.

*Okay?*

*Was she okay?*

*She was better than okay. She was ecstatic!*

She beamed up at him, flooded with exhilaration. "I am fantastic! I loved it!" She very nearly threw her arms around him but caught herself in the last second.

He smiled back. "That's my girl. I thought you might like it. And you didn't really get to see much that time because of the rain wall. The good news is this system isn't finished with us yet. After we regroup, I think we can find you another one."

# Chapter Seven

Dylan was on a mission. He was always on a mission when they were chasing, but this was different. Seeing Allie's excitement from that modest funnel cloud made him more determined than ever to encounter something truly impressive. Fortunately for him, nature was providing, and the supercells were producing one after another. The rain had cleared, leaving the air hot and sticky with visibility significantly improved. He spotted indistinguishable pieces of debris swirled up into the air surrounding a massive wedge they'd encountered just moments earlier.

"Let's stop for a second. I think we can jump out for some footage. You up for it, Hannah?" he asked.

"Oh, sure." Her voice betrayed her lack of enthusiasm, but Dylan had to hand it to her. She was tough. After that first bit of hurling she was right back in action. You didn't become a news videographer if you couldn't handle seeing rough stuff, but even the toughest couldn't always handle the motion sickness triggered by hanging out in the back seat of an SUV and watching everything out your window spin in circles.

"That thing is massive," Allie said breathlessly, her eyes round with awe as she came to stand next to him. The rest of the crew gathered around the Blaster with each of them holding up some kind of recording device.

"And loud," she added.

"Sounds like a jet taking off, doesn't it? I'd say it's about five hundred yards away," he all but shouted as he pointed his phone to get some video. "And about a quarter of a mile wide. See how the whole updraft is rotating. That thing is going to cause some real damage."

"There go some power lines!" Nathan's voice crackled with nerves and excitement as flashes of light popped in the distance and dust kicked up from the earth. As they watched for a moment, the group was uncharacteristically quiet. Chris stood a bit behind the rest of them, talking to Channel 17 on his phone.

"We don't have much more time," Dylan said. "That thing is on the move and I don't want to end up too far away from it. Allie, let's just get some video of you with the funnel in the background and you can just add a voice-over later. It's too loud for good sound quality anyway."

He started to step away so she could be alone in the shot, but she reached out a hand to stop him, her face betraying no small amount of concern.

"You want me in the video?" he asked.

She nodded again, and he smiled as she gave a thumbs-up to Hannah, who had stepped back to frame the shot. He could see from the light on the camera that she'd already started recording. As they faced the storm side by side, he leaned close to her ear. "You okay, Als? This one is definitely a monster."

She'd be fine, and her fear was healthy. Only a moron would be this close to such violent weather and not have a healthy dose of anxiety. Her earlier enthusiasm was now tempered with some good old-fashioned common sense.

"I'm good. I just can't believe how gigantic it is. The clouds fill the entire sky and that funnel looks like a skyscraper. I just can't wrap my head around the scope of it." She leaned into him as they stood watching. Dylan tried not to read anything into it, her closeness, her pressing against him, but damn it felt good to have her there, to *feel* her, especially while sharing something that was a major part of his life. His arm went around her waist, as much from old habit as hesitantly rekindled interest. He'd been fighting the attraction since she'd shown up in his driveway and it was getting tedious. All things considered, maybe it was worth exploring that a little. What was life without risk, anyway?

Far too quickly Chris, who was always the voice of reason, said, "Guys, that thing is growing and moving fast. I think we should get back on the road." His partner was right, but Dylan was reluctant to let Allie go. His arm, of its own accord, tightened around her before dropping away, and her shy smile told him she didn't mind the extra squeeze.

Back in the car, they drove on for nearly fifteen miles before the funnel finally dissipated. In spite of its size and intensity, the destruction appeared to be minimal and no one had been injured. For that, Dylan was grateful. It was the dark side of what they did, seeing the aftermath of the wind's fury, especially when people got hurt. Today, scattered power outages, a handful of damaged homes and businesses, and lots of shredded tree branches seemed to be the worst of it, so his crew's general mood was elation tempered with fatigue as they stopped for the night at a roadside motel just north of Townsend.

"Anybody hungry? I'm starving." Beau pulled a metal case full of computer equipment from the back of the Sidewinder to take inside his motel room. "There's a barbeque place across the street."

While murmurs of agreement came from the others, Allie caught Dylan's eye. She leaned toward him. "Do you think maybe we could, you know, have a little time? Just the two of us? It seems like maybe we should… talk."

God, he wished talk was a euphemism for something else. They did need to talk, of course. They had a lot to discuss, and he had a lot of questions, but after today's excitement, what he mostly wanted to do was kiss that spot just above her collarbone in the way that had always made her sigh with pleasure. Would she still? Would she melt into him the way she once did when he pulled her close? Better yet, would she wrap her legs around him if he pressed her down against a mattress? Because that's what he wanted to do. Sure, he wanted to talk, but mostly he wanted to take her to bed and remind her of all the ways they were good together.

His response was far less specific. "Sure. How about we meet back here in half an hour? I could use a shower, then we can grab something to eat."

Her response was equally neutral. "Sounds good. See you in half an hour."

"Do I need to find someplace else to sleep?" Hannah teased as she dropped off her bag in their motel room. "Because I will if you want me to. Just leave a sock on the door."

Allie couldn't stop the blush, or the chuckle that bubbled up in her throat. "No, you do not need to find a different place to sleep. Dylan and I just have a bit of… reminiscing to do. That's all."

"Are you sure? Because he's been leering at you like a man who just got released from prison. Does he know that you're just *reminiscing?*"

"Of course, he does. My gosh, Hannah. This is a business trip, for goodness' sake. Not a booty call."

Hannah pulled off her tee shirt and replaced it with a clean one. "I'm not judging, mind you. To be perfectly honest, I think you should climb all over that. I won't tell anyone. Besides, you guys were engaged once. This one wouldn't even count."

Allison laughed out loud at that. Hannah's suggestion was tempting, and she certainly couldn't say she didn't want to. Watching Dylan work today had been a thrill, but even more than that, it had been fun. It wasn't just seeing the tornadoes, it was observing him in his element. *Dylan* made it fun, and if memory served—and it did—he knew how to make rolling around in the sheets pretty damn fun too. But where would that get them? Other than the obvious perk of having had great sex, of course. But was that a good enough reason? Her emotions were already as tangled up and gnarled as some of the twisted trees they'd seen demolished by the winds, and any kind of physical interaction would only complicate things. Sure, she couldn't deny that every instinct told her to go for it, but truthfully, it was a risk even just going to dinner. There was so much history, and she'd ended things so very ungraciously. There was just no telling where the night would lead them. Crying was a distinct possibility.

"I think it would still count," she said to Hannah, "but I'll keep you posted. If I don't come back to the room, well… don't wait up."

Allison showered as quickly as she could but by the time she was out of the bathroom, Hannah had already left for dinner with the others, and she was a bit relieved. She desperately needed a few minutes of quiet before facing Dylan across a table. Over the past few days they'd been able to chat without ever leaning in toward anything substantial, but when it was just the two of them in a restaurant, there'd be no place to hide.

She put on the one sundress she'd brought with her, stashed among the leggings and tank tops and her single on-air blazer. It wasn't dressy and she hoped it didn't seem like she was trying too hard, but this occasion did call for something at least a hint nicer than what she'd been wearing. She left her hair down, whipped on a little mascara and lip gloss, and grabbed a denim jacket in case it cooled off later. All of that had taken twenty-five minutes, so she sat down on the edge of the bed and waited. She didn't want to be the first one outside, even though it was silly to just sit there. Then she pondered the idea of maybe going straight to his room, skipping dinner altogether, and just having her way with him. He'd probably be a pretty good sport about that. Her cheeks heated up at the thought even as her intellect warned her it was a terrible idea.

Instead, she waited three more minutes, then left the room. Dylan was already outside, leaning against the Blaster and staring at his phone. He looked up at the sound of her shutting her motel room door, and his smile was slow and dangerously sexy. He liked the sundress. She could tell.

"I didn't think you'd be ready yet," she said, feeling stupidly anxious and totally at a loss for clever words. He was wearing jeans with a blue-and-white striped polo shirt. Nothing fancy but it set her heart to skipping.

His broad shoulders gave a little shrug. "I was motivated." He moved away from the SUV and slid his phone into his back pocket. "There's a little pub-type place down on the corner. Want to go there?"

"Sure." *Again, she was so very clever…* Conversation at dinner just might be a study in monosyllabic speech.

The walk to the pub took just a few moments and soon they were seated at a square table with a multitude of initials carved into the surface. Looking around, Allison realized most of the other tables had carvings too. It seemed to be a theme. Other than that, the inside of the pub was uninspired, with cheaply paneled walls and a green velvet-topped pool table over in the back corner where a couple of scruffy men of indeterminate age and social graces were playing a round. Neon signs advertised various brands of beer and liquor, and a dartboard hung on the wall right next to the restroom sign, leaving Allison to wonder how many people walked out of the bathroom and got nailed in the forehead with a dart.

It wasn't very crowded, with only a dozen or so other diners, and at least their table was next to an oversized window, giving them a full view of the tiny town. Not that it was much to look at. It didn't matter though. She'd probably be staring at Dylan most of the evening anyway.

"Hi, folks. Do you know what you want?" A pudgy waitress wearing a black tee shirt that very nearly but not quite covered her belly handed them each a plastic-coated menu. "Don't get the cod. It's today's special but just trust me. I don't recommend it."

Dylan chuckled and smiled up at her. "What do you recommend?"

"I recommend you eat someplace else." She burst out laughing and thwacked her notepad against the edge of the table. Allison and Dylan laughed, too, exchanging equally bemused stares.

"No, but seriously," the waitress continued, sobering up as abruptly as she'd laughed. "Other than the cod, everything is pretty good. I like the shepherd's pie and we sell a lot of lasagna." She bent closer, displaying an impressive length of cleavage, and put a hand to her mouth as if to impart a secret. "It's Stouffer's so it's pretty good."

Allison nodded. "Good to know. Maybe we could have a minute to look over the menu?"

"Sure thing, honey. I'll be back in a minute with some water."

Dylan smiled over at Allison, his expression apologetic. "I'd suggest we look for someplace else, but this may be the nicest place in town, and at least they serve drinks."

"I'm good with it. And I haven't had Stouffer's lasagna in a long time."

# Chapter Eight

This bar was a D-list dive. Normally Dylan wouldn't have even noticed. He and the guys ate at places like this all the time because they typically had the best greasy cheeseburgers, but tonight it would've been nice to find someplace with just a bit more ambience. A bit less grime. He had no idea how the conversation with Allie would go, or what twists and turns it might take, but tonight might very well be the last time they shared a meal together, just the two of them. The last time they'd been to a restaurant, she'd dumped him. At the very least, this night had to go better than that one had.

The waitress returned and jotted down their order. "You folks hear about that twister south of town?" she asked. "It was all over the news. Sure as heck am glad it didn't do much damage here, although my cousin did lose part of his chicken coop. Then again, that thing was half falling down already. A butterfly could have tipped it over."

"We did hear a little something about the twister," Dylan said, handing her his menu. Typically he would've mentioned the storm chasing but this waitress was already on the chatty side. If he told her why they were in town, she'd likely pull up a chair and yakkity-yak with them all night. He didn't want to hear more about her cousin's chicken coop because, regardless of how much trepidation he had about anything Allie might have to say, he wanted to get that conversation going. He wanted it out of the way. If it went south, he'd finish his beer and call it an early night. But, on the off chance that it went well… No, he couldn't even let his mind wander in that direction. Not yet.

"So…," Allie said, after the waitress delivered their drinks, a beer for him and a vodka and cranberry for her. "Um... how *are* you?"

He stared at her for a moment because, for such a simple, basic question, it had a lot of potential layers to it.

"I'm not quite sure how to even answer that," he finally said. "I mean, I'm good. If somebody had asked me last week how I was, I would've said I'm great. I love my job. It's full of opportunities. I have a great crew of guys to chase with. In the off-season I work at the National Weather Service. My bills are paid. I have a dog. So it's all good, for the most part, but right now I'm sitting across from a woman who dumped me after I'd proposed. I haven't spoken to her in almost five years and suddenly she shows up in my driveway, unannounced, and says she's going to spend the week in my car, watching me do my job, and you know what? That has me feeling just a little off-balance. How are *you*?"

Damn. He didn't mean to sound so sarcastic, and he hadn't intended to unload on her that way. He didn't even realize he'd been stuffing all that shit down. Maybe because he hadn't been forced to think about it in a very long time, but with her right there in front of him, it all just kind of spilled out. He saw her eyes get sparkly with moisture. He didn't want her to cry, and he certainly didn't want to be the reason for it, but... maybe she did owe him an explanation. Something more substantial than *we were too young*.

She blinked and pressed her lips together for a second but maintained his gaze.

"What kind of dog?" she asked softly.

His brain tried to register the ridiculousness of the question and against his better judgment, he let out a chuff of laughter. "Seriously?"

"I thought we could start with the easy stuff. What kind of dog?"

He sighed but started to relax again. He could play this game if she wanted to. "A Bernese mountain dog–lab mix. Her name is Judy. I didn't come up with that. She was a rescue."

Allie nodded and took a drink. "Cute. When you work for the weather service, do you stay in Lawrence, or do you live someplace else?"

"Chris and I rent that place in Lawrence, and we have offices in Topeka."

She seemed to think about the next question before asking. "Why did you leave Sarasota?"

That answer was easy. He took a swig of beer. "Because I was miserable there. Too many Floridians. Not enough flamingos."

Her lips twitched with a smile, and he relaxed a bit more. They could do this. They were mature adults who could discuss the past, even though theirs had been turbulent. Even though her breakup style had been that of the scorched earth variety. Even though half the reason he'd been so unhappy in Florida had to do with his broken heart.

"Are you seeing anyone?" she asked.

That question knocked him right back to square one, and his chest tightened. He wasn't seeing anyone, and he hadn't in nearly a year. No one significant, anyway, but that really wasn't any of Allie's business. At least not until she'd earned the answer.

"My turn to ask some questions," he said. "How long did you stay in Chicago?"

She'd gotten more from him so far than she'd expected. It was only fair she did some sharing too. She definitely owed him that. She owed him complete honesty.

"I moved there about a month after you left Sandusky for Sarasota. I stayed almost three years, then I went to Glenville when my mom started getting sick."

"Were you sorry to leave Chicago?"

"Not really. It was expensive to live there. I didn't like the traffic, and the people I worked with kind of sucked. Not all of them, but enough of them to make working there difficult." Maybe she should add that for the first six months she cried pretty much every single day because she missed him so much. She'd cried after six months too. Not every day, but often enough. Some nights she'd slept with his old sweatshirt wadded up like a stuffed animal. Eventually she got tired of her own tears and decided to move forward. But every single time she'd cried, she'd wondered if breaking up with him had been a mistake. And now that question was fresh on her mind again. So much for total honesty. He wasn't necessarily ready to hear that part yet.

"Do you have a dog?" he asked, smiling ever so slightly.

"No. I don't even have any houseplants. I can't be trusted to take care of anything that's alive. I'm too forgetful. I'm not good at taking care of things."

His look turned contemplative as he paused. "You moved home to help take care of your mom. Seems like maybe you're learning how."

That was just like Dylan, to defend *her* to *herself*. Ironically that had been one of her greatest fears about getting married. He always saw her as better than she was, and she couldn't face that moment when he figured out his loyalty had been misplaced. And so, she'd gone and proven it by saying yes, and then saying no. But still, here he was, trying to give her the benefit of the doubt.

"Maybe I am, but if you'd married me five years ago, I would've been a shitty wife."

He turned his face away to stare out the big window of the pub for the space of a heartbeat, then turned back to her. "I guess we'll never know what would've happened. All we know is what did happen."

"And I'm really sorry about what did happen. Do you hate me?"

"Does it seem like I hate you?" His tone was resigned, as if it would have been easier for him if he did.

"No, but you're a very nice person and maybe you're just being extra nice to me, even if I don't deserve it."

He stared at her for a moment as if measuring his words. "Why did you break up with me, Allie? I thought everything was so good with us."

A very justifiable and not unexpected question. "It was good with us. Really good, but at that time, the thought of being married terrified me. My mom gave up everything when she married my dad and he never appreciated it. He still doesn't. She has a PhD in physics, you know, and she ended up being a stay-at-home mom because my father likes to have dinner waiting on the table when he gets home. And honestly, when she found out we were engaged, she wasn't very happy. Not because of you. She adored you, but she was worried that all that work I'd done to become a meteorologist would just take a back seat to your career."

He frowned, lines forming across his forehead. "But I'm nothing like your father. Did you think I expected you to give up everything? Did I ever treat you like less than an equal?"

"No."

No, he hadn't. Not ever. He'd treated her like a partner and a true friend. She'd just been too young and inexperienced to appreciate how rare that was. She'd thought her parents' marriage was the only kind there was. The kind where wives sacrificed everything, and husbands benefited and took you for granted.

She gave a little sigh. "I realize it doesn't sound logical now, Dylan, because we're older and hopefully wiser, but it felt like an insurmountable thing to me then. I don't blame my mom because she thought she was looking out for me, but she didn't understand I could have both a husband and a job. I guess her perspective on marriage tarnished mine, and she was pretty persuasive. Looking back, I think I finally understand that I was afraid if we got married, I wouldn't be able to live up to your expectations of marriage, and I also wouldn't be able to live up to my own expectations as a meteorologist. I was in an unwinnable situation. I know that's no excuse, but it's the only explanation I've got."

His frown gradually turned to reluctant acceptance, but she could see he was struggling with it. "We would've done okay, you know. We could've stayed together. Or had the world's longest engagement. It would've been good."

"Probably." She sighed because she agreed. "But would you have given up your job offer in Florida to follow me to Chicago? Be honest with yourself. Or would you have expected me to go with you instead?"

He shook his head, the frown returning, as if he wanted to understand her but was frustrated nonetheless. "I don't know, Allie. You never gave me the option of making that decision. You just decided for us. It seems like something we could've talked through."

The waitress came and delivered their food with little fanfare. "Two homemade lasagnas, wink wink. Can I get you two another round of drinks?"

"Yes," they said in unison, breaking a bit of the tension.

Allison smiled but felt more weary than amused. "I'm sorry, Dylan. I wish I could go back and handle things differently. I can't tell you how many times I thought about calling you."

He took a swig of beer, eyeing her cautiously. "Why didn't you?"

"I don't have a good answer for that. I guess I just wanted to prove I'd made the right choice and so I threw all my energy into my job. If I couldn't have you, I wanted to at least have that."

"And do you? I mean, are you happy with your job? Was it worth it?"

He was trying to sound conversational, but there was a tone of accusation. She could feel the sense of betrayal behind his words, and no wonder. They'd left so much unsaid the night of their breakup. At the time, she'd thought she was making the right decision but had to admit, in the five years since, she'd never really stopped second-guessing herself. That had to mean something. It also had to mean something that she'd never met another person who seemed to understand her the way he did. No one who made her laugh at stupid weather jokes or coaxed her out of her comfort zone. No one who ever truly made her stop feeling lonely. Maybe that's because she wasn't actually lonely. She was just missing Dylan.

She toyed nervously with the cocktail straw in her drink and considered her answer.

"Those are two very different questions. Yes, I'm happy with my job although not completely. It's not exactly where I thought I'd be at this stage but it's the right place for now because my family needs me. And I've learned a lot over the past few years, a lot of lessons that I'm grateful for, but as far as it being worth it?" Her eyes locked with his, and her heart tumbled. "No. It wasn't worth it. No job was worth giving you up."

Her own admission surprised her and set her pulse racing. She'd never said that out loud. Not to anyone. She hadn't even allowed herself to think it until just this moment, because if leaving Dylan had been a mistake, then she'd just wasted five years of her life chasing a dream that wouldn't ever make her truly happy. Maybe it was time to reorganize her priorities, because suddenly all of the things she'd thought were more important than love started fading into the distance.

Dylan stared back at her, motionless. Outside, the headlights of a passing car sent yellow beams rolling over their table. Voices from the kitchen and the other patrons melded into an indistinct hum, while a billiard ball falling into a pocket caused one player to whoop with victory while his opponent groaned in defeat. The front door opened, and an elderly couple meandered in. And Allison waited.

"Wow," Dylan said softly, calmly, after what seemed an eternity. "Is that why you came on this trip? To tell me that?"

"No. In all honesty, I didn't even know you were a storm chaser when my news director put me on this assignment. Then I saw your name on the paperwork and nearly cancelled. I'm glad I didn't. Even if you decide you don't want anything more to do with me, I'm suddenly very glad to have told you that truth. I just wish I'd figured it out a long time ago."

"Me too." He looked down at his plate, and she could tell he was trying to process all that she'd just said. It was a lot. For her it was a huge burden lifted. The shame and regret she'd carried deep within about how she'd ended things finally started to dissipate. She was being completely honest—with herself—for the first time since he'd walked out of that restaurant five years ago with her engagement ring in his pocket.

But she knew, for Dylan, this *reunion* had been nothing but one surprise after another. He'd had no preparation, no warning, and no time to think about how he felt or what he might want to say. Just as she had with the abrupt ending of their relationship, she'd spontaneously jumped back into his life, and into his car, giving him very few options. It wasn't fair to him, but she'd make amends if he'd let her.

He took another long drink from his bottle of beer then set it firmly on the table. He regarded her cautiously, not smiling but not *not* smiling. The frown was gone, at least. It was a step in the right direction.

"No, I'm not seeing anyone," he said quietly. "Are you?"

Her heart went whump in her chest. This was the opening she'd hoped for. "No. I've only gone on a handful of dates since we broke up. Turns out you're just about impossible to get over."

"So are you." The tension in his shoulders seemed to ease as his face relaxed into a circumspect *almost* smile.

"Well, I guess that's something we have in common then. What would you like to do about it?" She'd made far too many decisions for the two of them. This one was entirely up to Dylan.

His gaze finally warmed as it traveled over her, as if he were remembering old times and imagining new ones. Then there was a smirk. A suggestive smirk that triggered all the right stuff. "Chris is staying with Beau tonight, so I happen to have a room all to myself back at that crappy little motel. I guess the real question is, what would *you* like to do about *that?*"

*Oh my.* And oh, thank God. So many options, but really only one right answer, and one they both clearly wanted. "Well... we could have our waitress put this Stouffer's lasagna into a couple of take-out containers, and we could, maybe, go back to your crappy little motel room so I can show you how much I've missed you for the past five years."

He smiled fully at last, his chuckle mischievous and naughty. "I am not likely to turn down that offer." His hand shot up to signal to the waitress. "Check, please."

# Chapter Nine

"Slow down," Allie said breathlessly, laughing. "I can't walk as fast as you can."

They were halfway back to the motel, and he slowed his pace, but his heart kept pumping as if he were in a sprint to the finish line.

"Sorry. I'm in a hurry." His laughter joined with hers as they rushed to his room. He fumbled with the key card and hoped he could get his bearings before he made a fool of himself pawing at her. Clumsy hands were not a turn-on and he felt the pressure to make this night one for the record books. He knew it would be for him, but he needed it to be that way for her as well.

There were more questions he wanted to ask her, of course. More things he wanted and needed to know, but all of that could wait. For now, he'd focus on enjoying every minute of removing that little flowered dress and leaving it on a heap next to his bed. He'd focus on kissing every inch of her skin just to see if she tasted as good in real life as she always did in his memories. And he'd focus on rediscovering all those little secret spots of her body that had always held such mystery for him. Pacing himself would be essential, but that was a tall order because not only had it been a while since he'd been with *anyone*, it was a lifetime ago since he'd been with Allie.

Two steps into the room, she turned and all but launched herself against him, pulling him in for a kiss that knocked every sense of restraint from his mind. Thank God. She was as eager as he was, and that was not something he'd take for granted. Her arms wove up around his shoulders and he hugged her tightly, reveling in the sensation of her breasts pressing against his chest.

He'd missed those. A lot. He'd missed her breasts and her lips and her skin. He'd missed the curve of her back and the breathy little sounds she made when he was doing things just right. The mere thought of that set his blood on fire. He'd better start thinking about baseball or taxes or cloud formations or something, or else this night would end far too soon.

Allie took a few steps backward, tugging him with her toward the bed while pulling up his shirt. He laughed and pulled it over his head and let it drop to the carpet.

"Damn, woman."

She leaned back an inch and looked up at his face, her eyes bright, her cheeks already flushed with anticipation. "Too fast?"

"Not hardly." He picked her up under her bottom and took the last few steps until they tumbled to the mattress. The headboard gave a loud wooden creak of protest, but they ignored it. If he needed to pay a security deposit for broken furniture, so be it.

Allison had planned on taking things slow, maybe start with a little kissing just to see if the memories held up to reality. To see if it felt *right* between them, but they'd stepped over the threshold of his crappy little motel room and suddenly she couldn't help herself and she'd jumped into his arms. Now they were wrangling on the bed and she was tugging enthusiastically at the waistband of his jeans while he nudged the hem of her sundress up to her waist. His hands were warm as he stroked the length of her thigh, resting his palm against her hip. Her whole body was alive and trembling. She might have felt teary with joy if she hadn't been so impatient with desire, her physical longing equal to the tender cravings in her heart.

He leaned up on his elbows to gaze down at her for so long she finally asked, "What?"

He shook his head. "Nothing, I just want to memorize you like this."

His words were meant to be an endearment, but they sounded too much like a goodbye, so she arched up and kissed him again, stopping all conversation. She needed him now, before she thought of any reasons why this might not be the best idea. She eased her mind with the knowledge that this was Dylan, the same Dylan who had always loved her well in the past. Her Dylan. At least for tonight.

Hours later, as they lay spent and satisfied in the creaky motel bed, he toyed with a strand of her hair, staring at it as if it were something magical. They were side by side, facing one another with the light from the bathroom illuminating the room just enough so they might see one another, but not so bright they couldn't doze off if the mood struck. Or in this case, if that mood *didn't* strike. Again.

The first time had been frantic and lusty, leaving them breathless, laughing with wonder, and tossing off the sheets to cool their heated skin. The second time they'd taken the scenic route and explored each other's bodies, meandering around curves and muscles, loitering over peaks and valleys until Allie thought she'd die from anticipation. Then Dylan sent her senses spiraling into blissful oblivion. Again.

"Is it my imagination or are we even better at this than we were five years ago?" she asked, tucking the motel blanket under her arms.

Dylan's chuckle came from deep in his chest. He looked adorably sleepy as he gave her a lazy smile. "I remember it always being pretty good, but you might be right. We may have set a new standard."

She smiled back. "Pretty remarkable considering the bleak surroundings." She looked around the budget motel, taking in the bumpy stucco walls, cheap artwork, and bland color scheme.

"And the lumpy mattress and the noisy headboard," he added.

"I liked the noisy headboard. I just hope we didn't keep the neighbors awake. Please tell me none of your guys are next door."

"Okay. I won't tell you that."

A mild rush of embarrassment ran through her. "Awesome. I guess I won't worry too much about doing the walk of shame to get back to my own room then. So much for discretion."

"I think that ship sailed as soon as I asked Chris to bunk with Beau. Sorry."

Allie laughed. "Hannah told me she'd find someplace else to

sleep too. I guess this cat is entirely out of the bag. I hope that doesn't make things awkward for the next few days with the crew."

Dylan rolled onto his back and pulled her with him. "I'm sure they can handle it, although you might want to prepare for some teasing. I'm sure I'll take the brunt of it, but these guys are not subtle with their humor."

"Duly noted." She snuggled a little closer. "I should probably go back to my own room, though. Don't you think? I don't want to overstay my welcome." She didn't want to leave. She wanted to stay right where she was, but it seemed polite to at least make the offer. He glanced at her, that little crease of a frown on his forehead.

"I'll walk you to your room if you want to go, but… I was kind of hoping you might stick around until morning."

She smiled. "I thought you'd never ask."

# Chapter Ten

Bright sunlight streamed in through a crack between the curtain panels, and Dylan felt Allie stir beside him. She sighed softly, still asleep, and he marveled at how the night had played out. Better than he could have imagined. He breathed in the scent of her hair and resisted the urge to wake her with a kiss. He'd let her sleep instead, because they hadn't gotten much rest last night. Fortunately, the storm systems they'd be following today were not too far from their current location.

He heard the shower turn on in the room next door and tamped down a chuckle. Nathan and Rob were on the other side of that wall, and he could hear them talking. Not clearly, but well enough to know that whatever noise he and Allie had made during the night was probably not a secret. He was either going to get teased mercilessly or applauded. Or quite possibly both. Neither idea bothered him, although he didn't want them ribbing Allie too much. She could probably handle it, but he wasn't entirely sure yet how he felt about everything, and until he'd made up his mind, he didn't want his guys getting too involved.

Actually, that wasn't entirely accurate. He mostly felt amazing about what went on last night. This morning, he felt taller and stronger and smarter, like her kiss turned him into a superhero, but he knew all of that was basically pride. His ego and his body were thrilled with this latest turn of events. But his memory wasn't as happy. His memory knew what it felt like to lose her. He wasn't ready for that again, but another goodbye was practically inevitable.

The truth was Dylan loved his job. Storm chasing was an adrenaline rush, but more importantly, the information they gathered was useful. They were the front line of forecasting because no radar system, regardless of how advanced it may be, could beat human teams on the ground. Radar couldn't tell when a funnel made contact with the earth, or see the mini vortices surrounding the storm, and he knew it was those smaller funnels within that often determined which structure was going to be demolished, and which would escape damage. He had an instinct for what he was doing, and he didn't want to give it up.

But Allie's life was in Michigan. Her family was there, and though she said her mother was improving, it sounded like they needed her. Her question last night needled at him, because when she asked if he would've given up the job offer in Sarasota to follow her to Chicago, he knew what his answer would have been: No. He wouldn't have given up his opportunity. Not at twenty-three. He would've suggested she get a job in Florida, or that perhaps they could try a long-distance relationship. He wasn't a chauvinist like her father, but five years ago, he may have thought his job was slightly more important than hers. That self-reflection made him uncomfortable and left him feeling selfish. But who was right in that situation? When you had two career-minded individuals living in different places, neither was wrong for wanting the other to relocate. Which left them at an impasse. It put them right back where they were five years ago.

Allison felt the mattress shift as Dylan got up and she opened her eyes in time to see his smooth bare ass as he went into the bathroom and closed the door. She stretched like a cat and smiled into the beam of sunlight, feeling thoroughly satisfied and decadent. She grabbed her phone from the nightstand to discover a text from Hannah:

> *I hope you're proud of yourself, young lady. staying out all night like a harlot. your father and i have been worried sick. just kidding. hope you had a great night. i expect a full report. see you at breakfast.*

Dylan came back out a few minutes later with a towel wrapped around his waist.

"Hey, sleepy. I was just going to jump in the shower. How are you?" He dropped a kiss onto the top of her tousled head.

"That depends," she answered, tugging on the towel. "Can you come back to bed?"

He smiled. "You have no idea how much I want to say yes but we have to get moving. Everybody else is already heading to breakfast, and this morning's forecast has some storms developing east of here. We need to get on the road."

Her disappointment was probably out of proportion to the circumstances, but she had a nagging sensation that last night might have been their only night. At least during this week. And maybe for good. She had no idea what the future would hold, and she wanted to gather up as much time with him as she could.

"Do you think..." She let the question linger because she didn't dare ask.

He sat down on the bed. "Do I think what?"

"Do you think we have a chance?" she whispered, as if saying it too loudly would tempt the fates, and not in their favor.

"Do you want us to have a chance?" He wove his fingers in with hers.

"Do you?"

His sigh came from down deep, and her heart preemptively began to ache.

When he spoke, his voice was slow and thoughtful. "Do you remember how you felt yesterday when you stood and watched that massive tornado?"

She nodded, not sure where this was headed as he continued, still looking down at their entwined hands. "When I see a storm like that, I'm captivated. I know it's powerful enough to annihilate me, but I'm fascinated anyway. I'm always torn by wanting to get closer and closer but knowing how dangerous it is. Sometimes I take risks that I regret later, and other times I remember to be more careful. And sometimes I rush in and it all pays off."

He looked up and into her eyes. "Allie, that's how you make me feel. Still, even after all these years. Everything I feel for you is dangerous and risky and powerful, and I can't lie. I don't want to get hurt again. Not like last time. You nearly destroyed me. I don't know what the payoff would be if we tried again because even if you have all good intentions now, we live in two different cities.

Two different states, even. We each have our own jobs, our own careers, and they don't currently overlap. I don't know what to do about that."

All the warm, happy buzz from last night was replaced with a strong dose of stark, harsh reality. She knew he was right. Their lives didn't intersect. She couldn't expect him to uproot his world to work around hers, and she had her own obligations and plans that kept her in Michigan. Saddest of all, she knew she'd made it hard for him to trust her with his heart. She might still love him, and he might even still love her... but sometimes love just wasn't enough.

Her sigh matched his. Deep and heavy. "I don't know what to do about it either. I guess all I can ask is if maybe we try to make the most of these next couple of days? I don't want to crowd you or make things awkward for the rest of this week, but I want you to know, Dylan, if last night is all we get, I'm still really happy to have had this time with you."

She meant that with all her heart, but even as she said the words, she knew, deep down, that those few hours they'd just shared weren't nearly enough for her. Now that he was back in her life, she wanted to keep him there. She didn't want this week to be about closing an old chapter of her life. She wanted it to be the beginning of an entirely new story. But how?

"I like that idea," he said, nodding slowly. "We'll make the most of this week and then"—he pressed a soft kiss against her bare shoulder—"then we'll talk again before you leave. Let's not put a lot of pressure on figuring things out right now. Especially because you've got me all confused and...I don't know. I can't really think straight when I know you're naked under that sheet."

She laughed, but he silenced her with a kiss that sent her senses spinning. And when he pressed her back against the bed, she laughed again.

"Isn't everybody waiting for us?" she asked, pushing the covers aside to grant him more access to her body.

"They can wait," he murmured against her throat.

She sighed with relief and kissed him back. A few days from now they might have to say goodbye, but for now, this would have to be enough.

# Chapter Eleven

"I don't know about the rest of you," Chris said loudly to the group as Dylan and Allie finally walked into the diner for breakfast. "But I detect a distinct change in the atmosphere around here. A frost warning has been averted."

Hannah nodded, staring pointedly at Allie. "Is it possible that storm clouds have made way for sunny skies?"

"Okay, okay," Dylan said, chuckling. "Everybody get it all out of your systems. All the jokes at once so we can move on, and let's remember we're all professionals here. And adults."

"I am barely an adult," Nathan answered. "And I heard stuff last night that I cannot unhear. I think I deserve some hazard pay for that."

Allie's cheeks turned crimson and she ducked her head, letting her hair fall over her face as she turned toward Dylan. With his arm around her waist he could feel her silent laughter. The ribald comments continued while everyone shuffled around adjusting chairs so Dylan and Allie could join them at the table. Somewhere during the commentary, she was dubbed *Tornado Allie,* while they, as a couple, were christened *Dyllison.* No one, fortunately, questioned their history and better yet, no one questioned their future. It's was just good-natured ribbing and Dylan felt a surge of gratitude because the underlying message from his crew — his friends — was all positive.

As the rest of the week progressed, the group shifted into a subtle new routine. By day, they'd chase storms, stopping for Allie to do her segments, and even managing a couple of live reports including one with a stovepipe funnel cloud touching down in the background right behind her. Meanwhile, Dylan and Chris and their crew captured a fair amount of useful data and aided Channel 17 with some on the spot reporting. Professionally, it was a great stretch of bad weather. The kind they lived for.

At the end of the day, they'd have dinner as a group at some mom-and-pop dive, and then came Dylan's favorite part. The time when he and Allie would head off to their own room and pretend that everything was going to be just fine. Dingy motel rooms with squeaky beds and questionable soundproofing became their temporary oasis from the world outside. During those luscious midnight hours, he showed her all the ways that he still loved her, even though he never said it. And neither did she. They both knew it was unspoken, but also recognized that saying the words out loud would only complicate matters. He tried, and failed, to keep his heart from the equation, knowing she had to go home at the end of the week.

On Saturday the weather turned particularly fierce, spawning no less than two dozen funnel clouds stretching from one end of Tornado Alley to the other. They followed one intense wedge for several miles until downed power lines across the only access road left them trapped in a tiny Oklahoma town that had suffered significant damage just an hour earlier.

"The mayor states an early warning system gave residents time to find shelter and there are currently no reported injuries," Hannah said, reading the news story from her phone as Chris carefully pulled the Blaster into a grocery store parking lot littered with broken tree branches and other debris. Nathan parked next to him with the Sidewinder and soon the crew was gathered outside the vehicles with everyone surveying the surrounding damage. The front awning of a hardware store dangled precariously from the roofline. An uprooted tree had demolished the tiny coffee shop next to it, and several other shops were all but flattened into piles of kindling. This was a part of the job Dylan would never get used to, the human toll in the storm's aftermath. Allie came to stand beside him, her face etched with sadness and disbelief.

"These poor families," she said. "So much destruction. Oh my gosh. Look at that."

He followed her gaze and across the debris-littered street stood what was left of a tiny country church. The entire front wall and much of the roof was now missing. The steeple lay on the ground, but the pale stone altar and the back wall full of windows remained. And standing on the front steps was a cluster of tuxedo-clad men and a minister.

"Holy shit, it's a wedding party," Hannah said, instantly lifting up her camera.

Allison lifted her hand, halting Hannah. "Let's get their permission before doing any filming. I don't want to be insensitive. Hopefully they'd like to talk to us, though." It was a fine line between reporting a story and exploiting a situation, and she wanted to be on the right side of that. The crew followed as she made her way through the rubble with Dylan close to her side.

"Is everyone okay?" he called out as they got closer.

The men turned in unison. They were various ages and sizes, with one man markedly older than the rest. Most of them shared a notable family resemblance.

"We're okay," answered the tallest man. He had dark hair and a neatly trimmed beard. "Y'all with the news?"

"I am," Allison answered. "I'm Allison Winters with Channel 7 News in Glenville, Michigan. We don't want to intrude but if you don't mind sharing, I'd like to hear about your experience."

He nodded and stepped forward. "Sure thing. I'll tell you all about it. I'm supposed to get married in this church today." He pointed over his shoulder with his thumb. "Guess I'm glad it didn't fall down when we were all inside."

"I'm so sorry for your troubles," Allison said. "Would you mind if we talked to you on film?"

His suddenly broad smile seemed out of place, given the circumstances. "Sure thing. Can we go grab my bride? She'd get a real kick out of being on TV and so far it hasn't been the best day."

"Absolutely." Allison nodded at Hannah who instantly started filming. They'd get as much raw footage as possible and tighten things up in editing. "Where is she?"

"Over here." He gestured for them to follow as he and the rest of his dazed and bewildered groomsmen walked behind what was left of the church. The back part of the building seemed to be untouched by damage. He opened a steel door and called inside.

"Mariska! Hey, Sugar Bear. We got news people out here. Want to come be on TV?"

Seconds later a short, round bride in an audaciously frou-frou dress appeared in the doorway. He took her hand and helped her step outside. She was half his height, even with a four-inch monstrosity of a veil on top of her black hair, and in spite of the dismal situation, she too had the biggest, brightest smile. Allison found herself smiling back at this defiantly happy couple.

"TV? Why sure. I'd love to be on TV. Wait until my sister hears about this. That'll teach her to skip my wedding just because of a little tornado warning."

Allison gathered some basic information before suggesting they return to the front steps of the church for filming the actual segment. She wanted the destruction of the building as a backdrop to the story. She wasn't particularly religious, but even she recognized that the symbolism of the pristine altar, standing untouched amid all that destruction, couldn't be missed.

"Just be natural," she said to the couple once they were standing where the doors should have been. "Please start with your names and then tell me anything you'd like to share about today."

As they spoke, the wedding party and several guests gathered around, along with the rest of Dylan's crew and a smattering of other bystanders. There were bridesmaids in sparkly turquoise gowns, the minister wearing a white collar smudged with dirt, and a weeping mother of the bride who kept a lace hanky pressed to her mouth to stifle her sobs. She was visibly, and understandably, distressed but the rest of the attendants were stoic and probably in a bit of shock.

"I'm Remi Martinez," said the groom. "And this is my bride, Mariska Garcia. We were getting pictures taken before the ceremony, and doing them in shifts, on account of Mariska didn't want me to see her before the wedding. Me and the guys were in the chapel when we heard the sirens go off. I could already hear the wind start to howl, and let me tell you, superstitions aside, nothing was going to keep me from getting to my Sugar Bear."

Mariska's sparkly eyes welled with tears as she gazed up at him lovingly and clutched his brawny arm. He got a little misty, too, pulling the silk pocket square from his tuxedo jacket and dabbing at his eyes. "I sure as heck wasn't about to hunker down for a tornado until I knew she was safe, so all us guys high-tailed it to the back where the gals were. I grabbed on to her tight, and we waited out the storm."

By now even more of a crowd had gathered to observe what was happening, with everyone listening intently even while the sound of chain saws hummed in the distance as rescue crews began the arduous task of cleanup.

"He sure did grab on tight," Mariska added. "I could hardly breathe but even when we heard the front of the church falling, I knew everything would be okay. Remi always takes such good care of me and I can't wait to be married. Guess that'll have to wait though." She glanced back at the church, the first hint of sadness passing over her face.

"We were supposed to get married at four o'clock today." Remi nodded, gazing over at his fiancée. He paused for the space of a heartbeat before adding, "And I say let's do it. Sugar Bear, I know this isn't the day you'd planned, but we've got the preacher here. What do you think about making it legal right now? Right here on the steps?"

The bride gasped, but her joy was obvious and instantaneous, and Allison felt her own breath hitch at the sweetly romantic gesture. A murmur of surprise and encouragement rippled through the collection of guests as Mariska cast a glance back toward what was left of the modest little church. Remnants of wedding flowers and silk ribbons were scattered about amid dust and debris, but the afternoon sun shone brightly through the handful of stained-glass windows that remained, creating a kaleidoscope over the mess. If you squinted a little, it looked kind of pretty. Mariska must've thought so too, because she turned back and grinned at Remi as she offered up a taffeta-rustling shrug. "Happily ever after, here we come!" she said.

Allison cast a smile directly at Hannah's camera. This wasn't her typical weather report, but certainly the news director back at Channel 7 was going to love it. A little drama, a little resilience in the face of adversity, a little bit of a love story. It had all the elements of a really great segment, plus it was just plain adorable. Allison caught Dylan's eye and could tell he was thinking the same thing. And from his expression, she suspected that he was also thinking about *them,* and a wedding that should've happened but never did. She should fix that.

"You kids want to get married right now?" the minister asked, and for a second, Allison thought he was talking to her. Her cheeks flushed, and Dylan chuckled.

"We do," the bride and groom said.

"Right now," Mariska added, clearly not interested in taking any chances on another postponement.

There was a bit of jostling and strategic rearranging as the wedding attendants moved to take their places, and Allison took her cue to step aside. She joined Dylan just a few feet away from the bride and groom. Hannah and Rob kept filming as someone played the wedding march from their cell phone, and the bride's mother never stopped crying.

The ceremony was brief, in part because, as the minister explained, "The good Lord saw fit to blow all my notes away, so you'll have to bear with me. We'll make this one a quickie." He mentioned all the standard things about loving and cherishing, and Dylan slid his hand into Allison's giving it a squeeze that went straight to her heart.

"And as we're gathered here today to celebrate the marriage of these two fine people," the preacher added, "always remember this: When life's storms come your way—and they will—grab on tight to the people you love and don't let ever go. Don't ever take a moment of sunshine for granted and believe that above all else a rainbow of hope is always on the horizon."

An hour later, under a white tent hastily re-erected by a collection of strangers, the reception caterers set up a buffet line to feed whomever was nearby: family members, wedding guests, rescue crews. The newlyweds welcomed everyone, and a glowing sense of unity and celebration prevailed. It was magical for all of its simplicity, and the storm-chasing crew filled their plastic solo cups to toast the bride and groom more than once. Allison was feeling mildly tipsy, and overwhelmingly sentimental. It was no wonder, what with all the love in the air. She couldn't help it.

Dylan came over and sat down next to her, handing her a paper plate piled high with pink frosted wedding cake, and held up two plastic forks.

"Feel like sharing?" he asked.

"I do," she said, smiling at her own brazen innuendo.

Dylan chuckled but said nothing.

They ate the cake, watching as Remi and Mariska danced in the grass to the sound of more cell phone–provided music, and Allison sighed thoughtfully. This could have been her and Dylan, if she'd never given him that ring back. Not the tornado part, or the demolished church, of course, but they could have been a happy couple facing the future together, knowing they'd always have each other to depend on during those life-storms the preacher talked about. Maybe it was time for her to do some grabbing on tight.

She turned to Dylan. "You know that stuff the minister said about hope always being on the horizon? And not taking any sunny moments for granted?"

"Yeah." Dylan nodded slowly, not looking her way until she took ahold of his hand. When his eyes met hers, she felt utterly vulnerable but thoroughly optimistic by the warmth in his gaze.

"Well," she said, "I guess I should tell you… I'm pretty sure I'm in love with you again. Honestly, I'm not sure I ever stopped. I don't know what to do about it, but I'm entirely positive I want you in my life. If you'll have me, I promise I'll never break your heart again."

A smile tilted the corners of his mouth ever so slightly, as if he were fighting it. "Are you sure that's not just the wedding vibes talking? Maybe all the matrimony in the atmosphere has you light-headed and confused?"

She sensed the teasing in his tone and smiled. "I'm not confused. Maybe for the first time in a long time I'm absolutely certain of what I want. I love you. Maybe it's like *The Wizard of Oz*, you know? It took a tornado to teach me that all I ever really needed was what I'd had all along. You're all I need, Dylan. There are lots of news stations and lots of jobs. We'll figure something out. If you still want me."

He stared at her for so long she thought, for a disastrous moment, that he might not think she was worth the effort. Maybe he hadn't forgiven her after all, but then he smiled, and all was right with the world again.

He pulled one of her hands to his lips and gave it a kiss. "Allie, after being together during these past couple of days, I'm not sure I could give you up again. Turns out I never stopped loving you either. I tried but… I just love you. Rain or shine."

She reached up and pressed her palm against his cheek. "I love you too. Rain or shine. And if I catch Sugar Bear's bouquet, you might just have to marry me."

# Epilogue

## Six Months Later...

"Hey, isn't that my sweatshirt?" Dylan asked as Allie climbed into bed beside him. "I thought I'd lost that thing years ago."

She smiled. "It is yours. I used to sleep with it in Chicago on nights when I was really missing you." She tried to nudge Judy toward the end of the bed, but the oversized dog wasn't budging. It had been a month since Dylan transferred to the Michigan branch of the weather service and moved in with her, but she and the dog were still working out their jealousy issues and trying to establish who got to sleep the closest to him. So far the dog was winning.

Dylan snapped his fingers and Judy relented, casting a doleful glance at Allie.

"Well, the good news is," he said. "Now that I live here in Glenville, you'll never have to miss me. So you can give it back."

Allie shook her head as she adjusted the pillows behind her. "Sorry, I'm never giving it back. It's mine now but you can wear it sometimes if you want to."

He eyed her for a moment with a frown that was not at all menacing. "I think that promotion of yours has made you awfully sassy." Then his smile turned mischievous. "But maybe we could work out a trade. I have something of yours that I've been meaning to give back."

"Really? What?" She plumped up the pillows behind her again, trying to get comfortable, and pushing against the dog with her foot to no avail.

Dylan twisted to the side and opened the drawer of the

nightstand, fumbling around for a moment. Then he turned back to her, his smile now adoring and sweet. Her heart gave a little skip as he held out a closed fist, and slowly opened it to reveal a tiny black velvet box. He reached out with the other hand and popped it open, and there was her engagement ring. He'd saved it all this time. Allie's breath cut short in her throat, and she blinked in elated disbelief.

"Allie, I love you, rain or shine," he said, his voice husky with emotion. "I was wondering if you might want this back. But I should warn you, I come with it. If you want the ring, you have to marry me. Like, actually marry me this time."

Tears sprang to her eyes, and joy filled her heart. "You know I'll probably be a lousy wife, right? I'm a terrible cook and I can't even take care of a houseplant."

Dylan nodded. "Yep, I know. But you're everything I want. I think you're damn near perfect, and anyway, even if you're a lousy wife, you'll always be the best meteorologist I've ever worked with."

Like a rainbow after the storm, Allie could see nothing but happiness on the horizon. There were a million things she wanted to say to him. A million ways she wanted to express her love, but words couldn't capture all that she felt.

So she said the only thing that mattered.

"In that case… yes. Yes, yes, yes, yes, yes. And, yes."

## *The End*

# Acknowledgments

Even a short story requires a long list of people to thank and my gratitude is boundless for those involved in this project. Thank you to Jordan Carson, Terri DeBoer, Rachel Ruiz, Derek Haas, Matt Kirkwood, and the rest of the wonderfully friendly team at Wood TV 8 in Grand Rapids, Michigan, for letting me pester you with innumerable questions and loiter around your workplace. Who knew there was so much going on at four o'clock in the morning? Thank you to Meteorologists Ellen Bacca and Melissa Marsh for also answering a long list of questions. I appreciate your time and attention to detail. Thank you to all the storm chasers who post videos of their exploits which I watched on a repeating loop while drafting this story. Please note, any errors in this novella with regard to meteorology or weather science are entirely my own.

Thank you to Jessica Poore, my editor-extraordinaire who fine-tuned this story. May this be the first of many projects we work on together. Regardless, we'll always have Seattle and watching Jensen Ackles take off his jean jacket. Le sigh...

Thank you to my wonderful friends at Fiction From the Heart. Without you, this story would never had made it into the hands of readers! I cherish your advice and support, so thanks Jamie Beck, Sonali Dev, K.M. Jackson, Virginia Kantra, Donna Kauffman, Sally Kilpatrick, Falguni Kothari, Priscilla Oliveras, Barbara Samuel O'Neal, Hope Ramsey, and Liz Talley.

Thank you, Jane Pierangeli, for early reads, coffee, conversation, and all the stuff.

And finally, thanks to my beautiful daughters, Webster Girl and Tenacious D. Your love and support bring me endless joy. Without you, none of the rest matters.

# About Tracy Brogan

Tracy Brogan writes fun, funny stories full of laughter and love. She's a three-time finalist of the Romance Writers of America RITA award for excellence in romantic fiction, a two-time recipient of the Amazon Publishing Diamond award, and the winner of three Booksellers Best awards. Her Bell Harbor and Trillium Bay series have been on the Amazon and Wall Street Journal bestsellers lists and have been translated into dozens of languages. A native of Michigan, the state shaped like a mitten, Brogan is prone to pointing to the palm of her hand to indicate where she's from. Her daughters, Webster Girl and Tenacious D are very proud of her. At least that what she says.

To follow Brogan on social media, you can find her here:

**Facebook:**
www.facebook.com/tracybroganwriter

**Facebook Group:**
www.facebook.com/groups/FictionFromTheHeart/

**Twitter:**
www.twitter.com/tracybrogan

**Instagram:**
www.instagram.com/tracybroganbooks/

Or email her at tracybrogan1225@gmail.com

# The Runaway Bride
## by Sonali Dev

*This one's for my Fiction From The Heart sisters.*

*Jamie Beck, Tracy Brogan, K.M Jackson, Virginia Kantra, Donna Kauffman, Sally Kilpatrick, Falguni Kothari, Priscilla Oliveras, Barbara O'Neal, Hope Ramsay, and Liz Talley.*

*Thanks for being my emotional coconut oil
and making this journey so much smoother.*

# Chapter One

All of Nisha Raje's dreams were about to come true, because all Nisha had ever wanted was to marry Neel Graff. The back pages of her middle school notebooks were witness to her dream, filled from top to bottom with her fantasized signatures as "Nisha Raje Graff." And now it was happening. For real. Even the insistent ball of panic that had been pushing against her stomach walls for the past six months—ever since Neel proposed—seemed to have eased up. For the most part.

Nisha tiptoed down the marble stairs of her parents' mansion. Every inch of the five-acre estate in Mountain View, California, that she had grown up on was blanketed in twinkling lights. Every inch of the mansion was swathed in flowers. Garlands of marigolds, farmed specially on the estate for the wedding, threaded together with jasmine flown in from India, hung from every wall. The Rajes were known for taste not restraint. Even so, 'The First Wedding In The Family' excuse had made Nisha's mother lose all her usual sense of subtlety. Or maybe it was the fact that Nisha was marrying her parents' best friends' son, a boy Nisha had been in love with since before she knew what being in love meant.

Her mother, like every other person who loved Nisha, assumed that Nisha was ecstatic.

And she was.

Truly.

It was near midnight but the living room was still noisy. Her mother, her aunt, and a handful of her mother's friends who were staying over the night before the wedding were getting progressively louder over their drinks. The mehendi ceremony had started early that afternoon with henna being applied to hundreds of hands by twelve artists.

The bride of course was assigned her own artist. Nisha had sat in one place from eleven thirty that morning until three. Her butt was still numb but the henna, drawn on her feet all the way up her ankles and on her hands all the way to her elbows in gorgeously intricate patterns, was the prettiest thing she had ever seen. At the sangeet-cocktails after, Neel had cupped her hands in his and searched for his name hidden away in the patterns. The memory of Neel's hands on hers made a warm tremble ripple across her.

That ripple that dragged like feathers across her skin, leaving warmth in its wake, was what Nisha had been clinging to every time doubts rose inside her. Why was she marrying someone who had chosen someone else over her years ago? And the eternal question that would not go away: was he settling for her?

Of course he was.

But they were right for each other. The way her heart sped up every single time she thought of him, that proved it, didn't it?

"Make sure Nisha doesn't find out." One of the auntie's hushed voice stopped Nisha in her tracks. She'd been trying to avoid being seen on her trip to the kitchen. She needed some tea. What she definitely did not need was any more bride-gushing from the aunties. Or unsolicited and unedited anecdotal advice about wedding-night sex. Aunties plus wine was usually a combination her siblings and she lived for. But not right now, when any thought of The Biggest Day Of Her Life was making her stomach cramp.

She padded into the alcove next to the den Ma and the aunties were having their little gathering in.

"Well, isn't Nisha going to find out if the woman shows up at the wedding?" another auntie's voice said.

"That woman will not be coming anywhere near my child's wedding," Mina, Nisha's mother, said with her usual tiger-mom-protecting-her-cubs spirit. "Neel isn't that stupid. And Sunita will put an end to it if Neel has any wild new-agey ideas about inviting his ex to his wedding."

Sunita Auntie, Neel's mother, had been Ma's best friend since

Ma had moved to America after marrying Nisha's father some thirty years ago. Neel and Nisha's fathers and Sunita Auntie had become friends while doing their medical residencies at Stanford. Mina and Sunita had dreamed of their children marrying, possibly from the day they were born, with almost as much hope as Nisha had. Sunita Auntie had been almost as heartbroken as Nisha when Neel had taken one look at Barbara Lovett in high school and fallen hard.

Was Barbara back in town? Had Neel really invited her to the wedding?

Nisha was going to be sick. She pressed a hennaed hand into her bare belly between her tank and flannel pajamas. Her jeweled belly button ring pressed into her palm. Neel's honey-brown eyes had gone all dark with heat the first time he'd seen the ring. Nisha had gotten the piercing when Neel had proposed to Barbara at their college graduation, needing to do something to prove to herself that she wasn't boring-old-Nisha. Always proper. Always doing the right thing.

"I'm going to call Sunita and make sure she nips this nonsense in the bud, if it is even true," Nisha heard Ma say as Ma moved toward the living room where Nisha was eavesdropping.

Nisha backed away so fast she almost tripped over her own feet. Spinning around, she ran down the corridor and up the back stairs to her room. Her heart hammered against her ribs, her mouth felt dry.

The walls of her room seemed to close in on her. She ripped her phone off the charging cord. The last call on her phone was from Neel. He'd called to say good night. It was their last night apart before they became husband and wife, tied together forever. Nisha had always felt tied to him, even when he had wanted to be tied to someone else.

She took a breath, tried to slow her spiraling thoughts down, and called him. He had danced with her all evening. The heat in his eyes had felt so real. How could he do this to her?

"Nish?" His voice was groggy when he answered his phone. "What's the matter, love?"

The British endearment stabbed at Nisha. Evil-Ex Barbara and Neel had gone to Oxford together for grad school. During the years that they were there Nisha had done everything in her power to never think about their cozy grad-student life in an idyllic English town. She had even avoided the Harry Potter movies, knowing that they were filmed where Neel and Barbara were living out Nisha's dreams.

"Nish?"

One part of her wanted to hang up. She didn't have the strength to give him any more leeway and she knew that he would convince her that his actions were entirely logical. It was his lawyer's gift, but also his power over her. Anything he said, she wanted to believe.

No. This was ridiculous. It was just wedding nerves. She had decided to marry him because she knew that he was over Barbara, that he *wanted* to marry Nisha. All Nisha had to do was be a grown-up about this, act like the twenty-six-year-old she was and have a level-headed conversation. It's what Neel always said: *All we have to do is communicate and be honest and we can get through anything.*

"Did you add any new guests to the list that I might have missed?" she asked, trying to keep her voice light but strong.

Silence.

Silence was never good. But with Neel, it was terrifying. Neel was a communicator, not quite the silent type.

"Well... Umm... I haven't added anyone. No."

"Was there someone you were thinking of adding?" *Now, on the night before our wedding?* Suddenly, something struck her, something she had not thought of until this minute. Barbara was in town and if Neel knew that, it meant he'd hidden it from her. He'd lied.

"Have you met her?" She hadn't meant to ask that but the words just came out, and there was no lightness or strength in them.

Another long silence followed. "I hadn't planned on it."

Nisha's ears started to ring. She could not believe what he was saying. She could, in fact, no longer hear what he was saying. The phone slipped from her hands. She shook out her limbs. Her arms were numb. Everything from her shoulder sockets to the tips of her fingers felt like it was buzzing with a million bees. The henna felt wet on her hands, the dry maroon stain running into rivulets.

She could not cry. Would not cry.

She picked up her phone. The screen had shattered. A million little pieces held together in a spider web pattern. Despite the broken screen, she knew the phone worked, because it rang and Neel's face flashed across the splintered glass, also split into a million pieces. She let the call go to voicemail and stared out the French doors.

Lights twinkled everywhere. All the trees around the house were blanketed in lights. Pushing open the French doors, Nisha made her way onto the terrace outside her room. It had been a few years since she had lived in her parents' house, but this would always be her room. After graduating from UCLA she had come back to live here while she got her MBA. The fact that she had moved out when she got a job was something Ma was still grouchy about. If Ma had her way, all her children would live at home the way they did it in India. At least until they were married.

Marriage.

Nisha yanked up her tank top and wiped her eyes. The baby pink came away with black stains. Kohl eyeliner was impossible to get rid of completely no matter how much you scrubbed it off with eye-makeup remover. Much like how she had felt about Neel all her life. No matter what he did—whether he fell in love with another woman and gave up his admission at his dream school to follow her to the college she wanted, or he followed her across the globe to a foreign country—Nisha's heart had always found it hard to scrub away how she felt about him. Who she was around him.

Tomorrow there would be five hundred guests on these grounds for the wedding. Then one thousand more than that would be at the reception in the city. The entire house was edged in lights like a bejeweled princess. Even the pool house was lit up. The sangeet-cocktail ceremony had taken place by the pool. The glass stage and dance floor that had been installed over the pool was backlit with fluorescent light that seamlessly changed colors. Nisha had always dreamed of a glass dance floor over the pool for her wedding. She'd dreamed of walking across it to the altar. And now here it was. Last night everyone had danced and danced on it like celestial beings floating over water.

An image flashed in her mind. Neel's face when he'd first joined her on the dance floor. Terror. She'd ignored it and extended her hand. He'd taken it, the way he always took her hand, as though it were a precious thing he'd found by accident. He'd let out a breath, and then he'd seemed happy again.

Breakfast would be served on the dance floor tomorrow before the wedding ceremony in the west gazebo, before they turned it into the aisle she would walk down. Neel and she had chosen the gazebo as their altar because it had been their favorite place to hide as children. Their place, where she had shown him how to fold origami swans and he had learned how to braid her hair from YouTube videos. Where they had shared everything. Before he had decided he didn't want her.

There in that gazebo she had agreed to marry him six months ago.

Because she had believed him.

And now he had lied to her.

What was she going to do?

The beating of her heart was brutal. She could not possibly have a panic attack. Not the night before her wedding with a hundred houseguests here.

No, she couldn't think about the wedding.

But how could she not?

How could she marry a man who had met his ex behind her back days before their wedding? Not when he knew how she felt about him settling for her. Not after the promises he'd made. If she hadn't craved tulsi tea and gone down to the kitchen to get it, she wouldn't even know. Had he considered letting Barbara come to their wedding? Would he humiliate her like that in front of all her family and friends?

Without knowing why, she went back inside and crossed her room, then back out into the passageway and made her way down the stairs. The aunties were still in the living room laughing away about something. Ma guffawed — the way she only did when she'd imbibed a tad too much wine. Everyone was so happy. For Nisha.

"All right, bottoms up, darlings. We have an early morning. Time to get some beauty sleep," Ma said as they all raised their glasses and downed what was left of their drinks. The party started to disperse.

Nisha couldn't face Ma. She couldn't face any of them. But she had to get away, get out of the house. Avoiding them, she ran back up and made her way out to the balcony again.

Without thinking about it she took off her flip flops, tucked them into the band of her pajamas, and threw her legs over the railing. The cherry tree that had always grown too close to the house but that her mother loved too much to have chopped down had a branch that grew right into her sister's balcony. Nisha made her way along the wide overhang that ran around the house and climbed onto Trisha's balcony. Inside, her sister was passed out across her bed, a distant cousin passed out next to her. The girls had danced all evening and had too much to drink. It was close to midnight. Every room in the house was filled with sleeping guests dreaming about Nisha's long- awaited Big Day tomorrow.

Grabbing the branch, she pulled herself onto it.

# Chapter Two

Nisha scrambled down the tree, her hands finding purchase in the craggy branches. Her siblings and she had done this all the time when they were kids and apparently, it was like riding a bicycle. Neel wasn't the only one who could climb trees when he was desperate. But she couldn't think about that right now. She couldn't think about how madly romantic he could be.

Her bare feet landed on the freshly mulched ground and looked around to make sure no one had seen her. Then she retrieved her flip flops from the elastic band of her pajamas, dusted her feet off, and slipped them on. What on earth was she going to do? Had she really jumped out of a balcony to run away?

Was that even what she wanted to do? All she knew was that she couldn't be in this place, she couldn't lie in front of all those people tomorrow. Never in her life had she done one single thing that wasn't what everyone expected of her. She was her family's pride and joy, the child who had worked hard to not give her parents one moment of pain. Her three siblings all had personalities as big as their parents' own outsize personalities. So rebellion came more easily to them. Even though it was rebellion Raje-style, passive-aggressive and respectful of who they were expected to be. But at least her siblings had made mistakes. Lived.

Nisha had toed the line. Always. But tomorrow, the wedding… she couldn't go through with it only because it was what everyone wanted. Not when Neel had lied to her. Not when he didn't want her. Not when the woman he did want was back in his life.

Avoiding the security cameras, she made her way around the house and across the back patio and to the pool house. The mess the three hundred guests had left behind was gone. Cleaned up by the wedding planner's crew like it had never even happened. In the distance she could see the gazebo, the white-painted wood was dressed up to be a wedding altar, the sides swathed in marble inlaid with precious stones and the dome replaced with an intricately carved finial. The perfectly harmonious Taj Mahal–like beauty of it made her heart give another brutal squeeze.

Everything around her was achingly beautiful. On the inside she felt uglier than she ever had, and she hated herself for it. She wasn't one of those women who ever talked down to herself about her looks. She'd always been comfortable in her skin and it wasn't easy. Not when you had a mother like Mina Raje.

Her mother had been one of India's most renowned beauties. To be her daughter meant that every single person who met you searched your face for the signs of Mina's legendary beauty. Nisha and her sister, Trisha, had lived their whole lives identifying that search in people's eyes, recognizing the cataloging of their deficiencies where they didn't match up to their mother. Their noses a tad too wide, their eyes not quite as large and almond-like. What was this nonsense about almond-shaped eyes anyway? It was a little brown nut with striations. No one wanted eyes like that.

Nisha hadn't cared. She had chosen to see her own beauty, mostly because she knew that Trisha needed to see her do it. Her little sister was brilliant, but navigating emotions and familial expectations defeated her. Nisha would not let anyone tell Trisha that she fell short in any way.

Now here she was falling short at her own wedding.

She walked toward the altar, every moment she had spent in there with Neel blooming inside her and popping like a bubble. She was almost at the marble path that led to it when someone moved in the gazebo. Nisha dropped to her knees, like a thief in her own home, and crawled behind a tree. Yash, her older brother, stood and searched the surroundings. He'd clearly heard her approaching.

What on earth was Yash doing in the gazebo by himself in the middle of the night? Someone giggled and Yash looked down at the sound with an expression Nisha had never seen him wear. An expression she would kill to see on Neel's face. That's when she noticed that his hair was mussed and his shirt was open down the front. Wild joy shone in his eyes.

*Holy shit!* Her unflappable, always perfectly put together brother was with a woman, and he looked destroyed, as though she had stolen him from himself. He threw another look around the night and looked back at whomever he was with, then with the most tender of looks he reached for her.

The moment felt so intensely private, Nisha backed away, turned around and ran across the lawn. Yash had been betrothed to a family friend's daughter for a year, but Nina wasn't here for the wedding. She was off in Mongolia doing research. Then who was Yash with that made him look like that?

What was wrong with the world today? Yash wasn't a cheater.

Then again, she had believed that Neel wasn't a liar, that he was honest to a fault. But he had met with his ex and forgotten to mention it. The sense of being squeezed between plates of glass pressed into her. Every cell of the good girl she'd always taken so much pride in being told her to go back to her room, but her feet refused. They led her to the break in the electric fence that had been left there so wildlife could move freely through the estate. Just like that she was on the winding road that led up the hill to the Anchorage gates.

Living on an estate that had a name might be something she had taken for granted in many ways, but she had never been ungrateful for her gifts. Her family descended from royalty in India. Nisha had spent every summer of her childhood at the Sripore Palace, the ancestral home from which her forefathers had ruled their kingdom in India for hundreds of years before colonization. Their mother had been one of Bollywood's most successful stars, but her parents had relentlessly pounded Nisha and her siblings with knowing how fortunate they were and insisted they find ways of giving back. Her family's good name was their greatest wealth.

Running away from home the day before her wedding was going to embarrass her parents. She could see the scandal clearly. The media was covering the wedding. *People* magazine was doing a cover story on it. A documentarian had been following Neel and her around for weeks now.

The right thing, the sensible thing, to do would be to go back, wake Ma and Dad, and share her fears with them. But she couldn't do it. She couldn't taint her parents' love for Neel. At least not until she'd had a moment to think about it. She looked down at her phone. The broken screen flashed with fifteen missed calls from Neel. She didn't care. There were seven voicemail messages from him, twice as many texts. No one else had tried to reach her, which meant that he hadn't told anyone else. That was so Neel.

On unsteady legs, she made her way down the street lined with thick redwoods and came to the turn where the private road into the estate met the main street that connected them to the rest of civilization. Even this late, there was a steady stream of cars whizzing past her. It was probably not a good idea to walk down the street in the dark without reflectors on. She may be feeling out of character but being hit by a car and ending up dead the night before her wedding was a bit too irresponsible for her.

Good to know she had limits.

Turning around and going back home felt impossible, but she couldn't stand here at the street corner all night either. She scrolled through her contacts. Everyone she knew was in the mansion sleeping soundly, passed out from the day's pre-wedding celebrations and resting up for tomorrow.

Her finger stopped on a name. Chris Parsons. Chris was her ex-boss. Ex because he'd requested a transfer from his position as her boss just so he could ask Nisha out. Nisha had refused a few times. Charming and kind as Chris was, Nisha had only been interested in short meaningless flings in the year after Neel had returned from England with his heart broken after Barbara had chosen England over him. After working with Chris for a year Nisha knew that the sincere, nerdy single father deserved someone who wasn't just looking for a distraction to keep from throwing herself at the man who had broken her heart.

Something moved in the shrubs a little distance away.

"Hello?" Nisha called. Was someone following her? Had someone seen her leaving the house?

No one answered. Maybe it was an animal. Not a comforting thought.

As fast as she could, she called a cab from the service her family had an account with. Her heart raced as she sat on a boulder by the side of the road and waited. She typed a text to Chris, then erased it. Then typed another one and erased it. Chris wasn't invited to the wedding, because — *hello!* — what kind of asshole even thinks of inviting someone who was interested in them to their wedding to *someone else?*

Maybe she should never have gone out with Chris at all. But after Neel returned, Barbara-less and one diamond lighter, Ma and Sunita Auntie had wanted to rekindle their matchmaking as though the intervening years hadn't happened. Nisha had been so livid at their callousness that she had threatened to kill herself if her mother did not back off. When Ma had rolled her eyes at Nisha's drama, Nisha had gone out with Chris.

The idea of her daughter going out with a widowed father had finally made Ma take Nisha's wishes seriously. Ma had backed off from pushing Nisha and Neel together, and Nisha had done the right thing and not strung Chris along when she had no intention of ever being in a committed relationship with anyone.

The cab pulled up to Chris's house in San Francisco, a beautiful, albeit beat-up, Victorian he had inherited from his wife's grandmother. Nisha got out of the car and watched the cab drive away. It was October in the Bay, and she was glad for the near balmy temperature from the Indian summer. She made her way to the steps that led up to the front door. It had been over a year and a half since she'd seen Chris.

Okay maybe she hadn't thought this through. She pulled up the number of the cab service again, but she could not go home right now. She just couldn't.

Even as she was staring at her poor broken screen, the front door opened.

"Nisha?" She had never seen Chris in sweats and a T-shirt. The thought that she really didn't know him at all hit her. Followed by the realization that there wasn't a single avatar that she hadn't seen Neel in. She'd held his hand when his father died when he was eleven and he couldn't cry anywhere but with her. She'd let him climb into her balcony and hide in her room when he got drunk in high school and couldn't go home. And she'd seen him ecstatic about Barbara.

Nisha dragged herself up the steps to Chris's porch, realizing for the first time that she was in her pajamas. She, Nisha Raje, who never went anywhere without makeup and a painstakingly put together outfit was standing at a virtual stranger's door in flannel pajama bottoms and a ribbed tank top with eyeliner stains. A car turned onto the street behind her and Chris put an arm around her. "It's okay. Come inside. It's going to be okay."

## Chapter Three

"I am so sorry to wake you." Nisha was about to burst into tears when she noticed a little girl, some six years old, sitting on the carpeted stairs in a onesie with two fingers pushed into her mouth, her huge eyes studying Nisha.

"You didn't wake us." As soon as the words left his mouth a scream burst from upstairs as a child broke into the most godawful wailing.

"Make yourself at home. I'll be back in a minute," Chris said, his eyes exhausted. With that he took the stairs two at a time and disappeared, leaving Nisha with the child sitting on the steps.

"Hi!" Nisha said, awkwardness engulfing her. "I'm Nisha."

The girl sucked her fingers with renewed gusto.

"What's your name?"

The girl stared at Nisha as though she hadn't even spoken.

Nisha looked around her, trying to act as though her being here in the middle of the night was perfectly normal. "It's a little late for you to be up, isn't it?"

The child rolled her eyes and threw a glance at the top of the stairs where her little sibling—Nisha couldn't for the life of her remember if Chris's younger one was a boy or a girl—was still shrieking.

*How stupid are you?* The girl's look said. *Who can sleep in this noise?*

Nisha was about to smile when something like a knock sounded on the door. She jumped. The girl's huge sleep-filled eyes widened with curiosity, maybe a little excitement. How was she not afraid?

"I'll see who it is," Nisha said unnecessarily, trying to affect calm.

Unlike Chris's daughter, Nisha was freaking out. Not for the first time that night she asked herself, what was she doing?

She peeked through the peephole and who she saw only multiplied her panic ten times over.

Was she seeing things?

It couldn't possibly be Neel.

"Who is it?" she asked like someone in some classic film.

"Nish? It's me. Can you let me in please?" There was something in his voice that she'd never heard before. A thread of panic that matched her own.

Every instinct inside her told her not to open the door — a stupid metaphor for her life!

"What are you doing here?" she asked. Yes, she opened the door because she was an idiot.

"I could ask you the same thing," he said, looking as though she had taken an axe to his heart. Good, that's exactly how she felt.

"How did you know where I was?" Was he tracking her location?

He was about to answer when he noticed Chris's daughter sitting on the stairs.

The speed with which his expression softened made Nisha's heart squeeze.

He threw Nisha a look she could only call disappointed and waved to the child. When she didn't respond, he looked around the foyer, searching for someone. When he found no one, he threw Nisha another incredulous look and went to the girl.

"Hi!" He sat down on the step next to her.

She watched him in silence.

"Who's that?" He stroked the leg of the rabbit sticking out from her death grip. "Won't you choke her if you hold her so tight?"

The little girl blinked at the rabbit in horror and let Neel straighten the thing in her arms. Her hold on the toy gentled visibly.

"She...?"

The girl shook her head.

"He..." The girl nodded. "He looks like he's going to live."

Another fresh wail broke out upstairs startling Neel.

The little girl patted Neel's arm. "It's okay, he screams every night. He just wants Daddy to hold him."

"Every night?" Neel asked, as though they'd been chatting for hours. "How do you sleep?"

The girl shrugged in a way that said 'such is life.'

Neel's smile was sad but sincere. "I'm Neel."

"No way!" She sat up straighter. "He's Neel too!" She pushed the rabbit at him.

"No way!"

It was like Nisha wasn't even there.

The crying continued and Nisha wondered if she should go up and check on Chris, given that these two had no need for her.

"Do you like hot chocolate?" the girl asked, suddenly chatty.

"You know anyone who doesn't?" Neel asked drily.

That got him a smile. "Neel loves hot chocolate." She held up the bunny. "Can we get him some?"

"Sure. Not sure how to make it. But I can look it up." Neel held up his phone, entirely unfazed by the bizarreness of the situation. "But first I think we should make sure your Daddy is okay?"

The child upstairs stopped screaming and Chris appeared at the top of the stairs with a little boy asleep in his arms. Chris started when he saw Neel sitting next to his daughter.

"Chris, this is Neel. Neel, this is Chris," Nisha said, sounding as stupid as she felt.

The two men nodded at each other and looked at Nisha for more information. She had none to give.

Chris came down the stairs, his eyes on his daughter. The little girl had snuggled into Neel. All of five minutes it had taken her.

"Neel is going to make us hot chocolate using his phone," she said and Neel smiled.

"Do you mind going to your room, Punkin?" Chris said in a tone that explained why this child had such a self-possessed air about her. Nisha's parents hadn't started talking to her like she was an adult until she was indeed an adult. And Ma still talked to her like she was a child sometimes.

"After Neel," she held up the rabbit to make sure no one mixed up the two Neels, "gets his hot chocolate."

Chris came down the stairs, the shadows under his eyes making Nisha wonder where he got his patience from. If she ever had children, please God, could she be this patient?

"I'll make you some later." He seemed pretty certain that arguing with her would get him nowhere, but he tried nonetheless.

"No! Neel will!" She pointed at the human Neel.

Neel stood. "I can do it. I don't mind," he said to Chris.

Chris gave the barest of nods.

The two men made their way into the kitchen, one with a child on his hip and the other with a child practically hanging by his pant leg, a child who hadn't known who he was until ten minutes ago. If Nisha had ever believed that she would run away the night before her wedding, this is most certainly not how she would ever have imagined it to go.

Following them into the kitchen, like a piece of furniture they could not see, she pressed herself against a wall. Neel really was reading instructions off his phone for making hot chocolate and it was so unbearably endearing, she pressed a hand into her belly to keep her ovaries from addling her brain.

"Do you have chocolate chips?"

"Semi-sweet or dark?"

These and other questions, just as ridiculous, were tossed about the kitchen between Neel and the girl as Chris and Nisha watched.

Either Neel really needed to concentrate on putting chocolate chips into milk and microwaving them, or he couldn't bear to look at Nisha right now.

He drizzled marshmallows into the cup and handed the smitten little girl her hot chocolate.

"I'm Mishka," she said. "My mummy was from India. Mishka means a gift."

"I didn't know that's what it meant. But that makes perfect sense. It's so nice to meet you, Mishka. My mummy is from India too, and she called me Neel after the blue-throated god, Shiva. Neel means blue in Sanskrit."

"Why was his throat blue?" Mishka asked.

"You need to get to bed, Punkin," Chris said, throwing a look at Nisha and Neel. Poor guy. The little boy on his hip had dozed off on his shoulder, but his lip was still trembling as though he was only taking a break from crying.

"As soon as you put him down, he's going to start shrieking again." Mishka pointed at her brother.

"Does he only cry when you lay him down flat?" Neel asked, pushing his glasses up his nose, his intense thickly lashed eyes focused on the little boy.

Chris looked like he wanted to slap Neel. "Are you a doctor?"

"No, but my mother is an Ear Nose Throat specialist and my father was one too, and I worked at their practice from the age of fourteen. I think you should get him checked for an inner ear infection. He's probably in intense pain when you lay him horizontal."

"That makes perfect sense," Mishka said, echoing her new best friend. "It would be nice to be able to sleep."

All the adults in the room had to laugh at that.

"Can I hear the story of Neel's blue throat before I sleep? Please, Daddy, please!"

Chris shook his head, but she let out another particularly endearing 'please' and he gave in.

In keeping with the surrealness of the night, the two men sat down at the dining table and Mishka climbed into the chair next to Neel. Nisha didn't move from her post by the kitchen door.

Neel still hadn't looked at her and Chris looked justifiably lost in his own home.

"Once upon a time in a land far, far away..." Neel started. "Gods and demons shared the earth. But they were sworn enemies. One day they found out that at the bottom of the ocean lay a magic nectar called Amrut, and that it would make them immortal—which means it would make them strong enough to live forever. The only way that they could get to the nectar at the bottom of the ocean was by churning up the water." For the first time since he had walked into Chris's house, Neel looked at Nisha.

"Neither the gods nor the demons could churn the ocean by themselves. So, they decided to help each other out by working together. They used a mountain as the churner, and used ropes made out of giant snakes to make the mountain spin and turn the water.

"For days, then weeks, then months they churned and churned, pulling at the ropes from either side and waiting for the nectar to rise up from the bottom of the ocean. Instead, one day the ocean turned hot and poisonous and started to boil over, destroying everything around it and burning away their land and homes. They panicked and went to Lord Shiva, the powerful ascetic god, for help. Shiva knew what had happened. When you churn things up in search of something good, the bad stuff—the poison—comes up before the good, and you have to get rid of that first. The only way to get rid of it and stop it from destroying the earth was for someone to drink the poison.

"Neither the gods nor the demons were willing to drink the poison to save their friends and their world and help them get to the Amrut. So Lord Shiva drank it for them. It turned his throat blue but he saved the earth and let everyone get to the nectar they had worked to churn up. And that's why he's called Neel Kanth, the one with the blue throat who drank poison to save the earth."

For a second there was complete silence.

Then Mishka bounced up and down in her seat. "Can you tell it again? Please…"

Neel laughed. "I think your dad needs some sleep. But if we ever meet again, I promise to tell it again."

Mishka hugged Neel and looked at her father. "Daddy, I've decided that when I grow up instead of marrying you, I'm going to marry Neel."

Neel looked at Nisha again. Damn it. Tears stung at her eyes. She hated this man and what he did to her.

When Mishka had gone up to bed, Neel held out his hand to Chris. "I'm so sorry to barge into your home like this. But thank you for letting us in."

"I have no idea why you're here," Chris said. "But Nisha doesn't have to leave if she doesn't want to."

Neel bowed his head. "I just wanted to make sure she was safe."

Nisha wanted to bang their heads together. Two men in a pissing contest to save her. But she was the one who had come to Chris's house, so at least him she couldn't be angry at.

Chris turned to her. "Do you need a place to crash? I have a guest room." If he knew tomorrow was her wedding day, he gave no indication of it.

"Thank you. But I think I've churned up an ocean and it might be time for me to drink the poison."

Neel turned to her, the bottle brown of his eyes blazing. "I'll wait outside for you." And with that he was gone, ever the gentleman giving her space, but with every confidence that she would follow.

"I don't know what's going on here." Chris looked at the door Neel had left through. "But you're too precious to let anyone hurt you."

It wasn't easy to forget that she had hurt him. Maybe that's why she had chosen to come here, because she needed to be reminded that at least for someone she had been precious, the first choice. She saw now that she had done a cruel thing by showing up at his door.

"I shouldn't have barged in like this," she said. "I just needed somewhere to go…" She trailed off. There was no way to explain what she'd been thinking. She had no idea what she was doing. For the first time in her life, she didn't know what she was going to do next.

Avoiding the little guy on his hip, she attempted a hug. His arm had to be hurting, he'd been cradling the sniffling child for a long time. As lightly as she could she stroked the soft fuzz on the toddler's head. "They're beautiful, and so lucky to have you. I… I'm so sorry."

That wasn't nearly enough. She knew that. But it's all she had inside herself to say.

"Will you let me know what the doctor says when you take him in?"

Chris shrugged, and Nisha let herself out.

# Chapter Four

Nisha shut the door gently behind her and heard the click as Chris locked it.

Next to her, Neel leaned back into the brick wall of the porch. He was wearing light-washed jeans and one of those soft white cotton kurtas he slept in. The supple fabric stretched across his broad frame and hugged his lean runner's muscles. He'd taken the time to change his pajama bottoms but not his shirt.

"Are you tracking my location?"

He pushed off the wall. His glasses caught the porch light and obscured his eyes. But the set of his lips told her he wasn't happy with her accusation. Neel was obsessed with justice and being fair. It was one of the many things about him that made it impossible not to love him.

"Are you insinuating that I don't trust you?"

She had to laugh at that. He was here, when he should have no way of knowing where she was, and still she knew without a doubt that he trusted her. Every damn person she knew trusted her.

"I wish. The whole problem is that no matter what you do, what anyone else does, all of you just trust *me* to do the right thing. You trust that I'll be okay with whatever you throw at me, trust that I'll always be there for you. Waiting. Of course you trust me. Because I'm too much of a damn wimp for you to think I'd ever step out of line."

He had trusted her to be here waiting after being with someone else for eight years. Everyone had trusted her to be waiting. And they'd been right.

His face softened and he reached for her, but she stepped back.

The last thing she needed right now was his sympathy, and if she let him touch her she'd never be able to think.

"Is that what this is about? You came to another man's house the night before our wedding to prove that you can 'step out of line'?"

Maybe. "Or maybe I'm here because I had to get away because I was lied to the night before my wedding by the man who can't stop going on and on about *honesty!*"

He looked like she had slapped him. "The reason I didn't tell you that Barbara was in town was that I knew exactly how much it would hurt you." He waved his arms indicating her reaction proved he'd been right and she considered shoving him. "And I didn't want to give you another thing to worry about when you were already so stressed out about the wedding."

This time she did shove him and spun around and started walking. She hadn't been stressed out about the wedding, not even for a minute. Social events, no matter how large, never stressed her out. The wedding planner was fantastic, but Nisha could actually do her job for her in half the time. Organizing things was something she thrived on.

He fell in step next to her.

"Can you at least tell me why what I just said made you angry?"

"Because it proves that you don't know me at all." How damn ironic was that? She had overheard their mothers talking once about how he was just experimenting with Barbara, trying out something unfamiliar because their lives were such a bubble of the familiar.

"I don't know you? You've been my best friend since we were in diapers."

"Yet you lie to me about your ex being in town and want to blame my stress over our wedding for it? I thrive on the gigantic social shindigs of our set. It's like the most obvious thing about me, Neel! If I weren't from the family I'm from, I'd be an event planner myself." That made her sound like an elitist, spineless snob. But it was true, her MBA was her pathetic attempt at proving that she wasn't the stupidest of her siblings, The Stupid Sister.

"I know. It's just…" Yeah, go ahead and figure your way out of that one, counselor. "I didn't lie to you, Nisha. I ran into her by accident. That's the truth. I didn't tell you because I didn't want to hurt you."

She kept walking, and when they came to Page Street, she turned onto it. They were right by Steiner and the Painted Ladies and that thought made her realize that they'd never been on a real date. A date where they wooed each other. Put their best foot forward to see how the other might react. The thought made her inexplicably sad. "How did you find me, Neel?"

He walked past her, turned around and started walking backward so they were face-to-face. "After we spoke, when you wouldn't answer my calls or texts, I drove to the Anchorage to make sure you were okay. I saw you get into the cab and followed you."

He had driven out to see if she was okay?

She could tell from the look on his face that her own face had softened. If she accepted his excuses for lying to her, she'd be an even bigger fool than she'd already been.

When she didn't answer, he turned around and fell in step next to her. For a long while neither of them spoke, they just walked along the updated Victorians that were the soul of San Francisco. By night as by day, the houses stood uniquely individual yet utterly cohesive, their heads held high as though they were proud of that identity.

She wanted to ask him where his car was parked and if anyone knew where he was right now. Practical considerations about parking violations and who might be worried about him.

What was wrong with her?

Her grunt of frustration broke the silence.

He cleared his throat in response. "Am I allowed to ask a question?"

"Evidently, you are free to do anything you damn well please." She kept walking. Without meaning to she turned down Steiner Street.

"Why did you pick Chris's house to go to?"

Was he for real? She turned to him, her hands in fists. "Because our lives are so darned interwoven I had no one else I could go to who wasn't at the wedding or wasn't tied to you. And I couldn't stay home. Because..." Because he had taken her home from her. Because she couldn't comprehend a home without him in it.

If she had hit him, he would have looked less punched in the gut. "Are you telling me that you feel trapped?"

She was. She was trapped by her own feelings for him.

Dear God, how was she in this place? Unable to say anything honest to him. Unable to have him say anything honest to her.

She sped up, but he kept up with her easily. He was letting her set the pace, but staying on her heels, not letting her walk away from him.

"I thought honesty was important to you. I thought it was the one thing we had," she said.

That made him stop in his tracks. "Are we still talking about me not telling you that I ran into Barb?"

Every time he said her name it felt like a knife stabbing Nisha's skin. How had she turned into this woman? The entire time he had been with Barbara, Nisha had shut them out. Gone on with her life. Let him go, because she would not covet another woman's man and she would not blame a woman for a man's betrayal. Even when her siblings and cousins said mean things about his girlfriend—mostly because they thought they were showing solidarity to Nisha when he brought her to family things—Nisha hadn't joined in.

"I don't know. And I don't know why I went to Chris's."

"Do you have feelings for him?"

When had Neel turned into such a hypocritical asshole?

She almost lied and said yes. Just to see some of what she was feeling reflected in his eyes. "You know what? I wish I did. It would make everything so much easier. He's lovely, and his kids are a joy. Even though his daughter has questionable taste in men."

Despite themselves, they both smiled thinking about Chris's spunky Mishka.

"I so badly want to have feelings for him. For anyone." She stared up at the starless sky, the full moon bright despite the competing light of the streetlamps. "But I'm a slab of ice. I'm the vacuum inside a bubble, a ceramic tile. You've turned me into baked dirt!"

He grinned, and she glared at him.

"How can you be happy about this? How can you be so cruel?"

Again, he reached for her and she stepped back.

"I like being the only one who melts you." His eyes got intense with the need to understand. "I admit that's selfish, but how is it cruel?"

She started walking. How thick did you have to be to not see how hypocritical that was?

"What's gotten into you, Nisha? I'm sorry I didn't tell you. But I don't understand why you're this angry. This is not at all like you."

"That's the whole point, don't you see? That's what I've been trying to tell you." She shook her shoulder-length hair out. It had a leave-in treatment in it to make it especially shiny on her wedding day. But right now, in the middle of the night, with the magnificent painted ladies across from her and the love of her life next to her it was dull and lifeless, and weighed down.

She met his confused eyes. "How would you know what's like me and what is not like me?"

He opened his mouth to respond and she put a hand in his face. "If you tell me again about how we were friends in diapers I'm going to scream. It's been a long time since I wore diapers. We're not kids anymore. We haven't been for a long time. And yet, for six months now we've been playacting at being adults. When we're actually adults." She had been playacting at being in love, when she was actually in love. "How did we get so messed up?"

Instead of arguing with her, Neel chewed his lip thoughtfully. All his intense focus turned inward and away from her. His gaze went to the painted ladies. Even in the middle of the gray urban night the matched facades were whimsical and poised. Obviously he agreed with what she had just said.

"You're right. I'm sorry. I was an idiot. We don't know each other at all as grownups."

Her hand pressed against her belly. Her belly button ring pressed into her palm, grounding her. Part of her wanted to take back her words. She wanted to be back in her room, not out here trying to convince him that they were a lie. But a lie was a lie and no matter what, she couldn't live one, not with Neel.

"You're right," he repeated. "We can't get married if we're strangers."

Her throat hurt, a lump gathering there like a ball of thorns. She squeezed her eyes shut to keep the tears at bay. They could never be strangers. But if he didn't have the kind of feelings she needed him to have, then knowing now instead of later was the only thing that might save her.

He looked at his watch. "It's a little before two o'clock. We have six hours before your makeup person for the wedding shows up, right? That gives us at least five hours to change that."

"Excuse me?"

Reaching out, he took her hand. "I'm asking for five hours. To get to know each other. Complete honesty. The us no one else knows. We only tell each other things we've never told anyone." His eyes were clear, sincere and intense, one hundred percent Neel. "If at any point either of us feels like we're done, if we don't like what we hear, I drive you home. We'll figure out how to tell the family together."

He made it sound so easy. "That's it? It's that easy for you to walk away from me?" she said.

He pinched the back of his neck, refusing to call her out for being deliberately obtuse. "No, it's that hard to see you struggle with being with me."

Before she could process that, he tugged her hand and started toward the steps that led into Alamo Square Park. The action was too much of a throwback to when they'd run off to their gazebo as children. Only now there were tingles where their palms pressed together. She was doing it again, letting her timelines get mixed up, and throwing in her hormones certainly didn't help.

They ran up the steps and turned down the path that led into the park.

"Five hours, that all I'm asking for. I'm trying to do the right thing. I thought this was what you wanted."

It was. But she wanted it to be what he wanted too. "I don't want your charity."

He was about to deny it. Because it would kill him to hurt her, she knew that. That was the problem.

"Yes!" she said too loudly, surprising him. Surprising herself. She pulled her hand out of his. "My answer is yes. Let's get to know each other. When do you want to start?" Best to get this over with.

They stopped by a tree, its majestic canopy and broad, gnarly trunk turning the park into a dark fairytale land. The shadows under it were intimidating but he led her into it and she went.

He sat down, crossing his legs and relaxing into the uniquely Indian pose of the Buddha, perfect for both conversation and meditation. Nisha sank down next to him on her knees, not as rooted.

The tree bed was covered in smooth river gravel. Neel started to pick some out and made a small stack. "So, should we lay ground rules?" When she didn't respond, he went on. "We pick truths about ourselves, only things we've never told anyone else. Does that scare you?"

She shrugged, drinking in the focus in his eyes. He was locked into his goal. She just wished it came from wanting her and not wanting to *do the right thing*. "Not if it doesn't scare you."

His smile was filled with relief and a little something else that made her heart race. He picked up one smooth rock without looking away from her. "Every time I go, I pick up a stone from this stack and place it between us. When you go, you do the same. Until our stack of truths is bigger than the other one we don't leave. Sound okay?"

She shrugged again, but her chest was tight.

"You want to start?" He extended his hand to her, palm up with the smooth stone in the center, an offering. A chance to let everything inside her out. A chance to finally know what he had never been able to say to her.

She took the stone from him.

# Chapter Five

It felt infinitely stupid to take the stone from Neel. Even stupider to fold her fingers around it and press it to her chest as though it were a talisman, infinitely precious, as they sat under a tree in Alamo Square Park in the middle of the night about to rip through whatever chance they had.

"You want honesty." Despite her best effort she couldn't keep the tremor out of her voice.

His gaze fell to her fist pressed into her heart and his fingers twitched, but she couldn't handle him touching her right now.

"Here's my first truth…" Why not start big? *I know I wasn't your first choice, but I don't want to feel like second best. I can't live like that.*

The words wouldn't come out and she sprang up, unable to sit there with him face-to-face on the dewy lawn. His jeans were thicker, more resilient. Her pajamas flannel, more easily soaked. Did everything have to feel like a metaphor?

He waited for the words to come, but they wouldn't. He picked up a rock and placed it at her feet. "I used to pee in my mother's rose bushes."

A laugh snorted out of her. She covered it with her fisted hand.

Sure, Sunita Auntie loved her roses. But still, his admission was hardly a deep-dark Truth. Surely this wasn't what he meant when he said they were going to be sharing things they hadn't told anyone else. "Why is that even a secret you've never shared with anyone?"

He made a face that said 'just you wait' and patted the spot in front of him that she had abandoned. "It was the summer of sixth grade. I had just watched *Big Daddy*."

"The Adam Sandler movie?" She sat back down, his first truth stone between them.

He nodded. "I became obsessed with the idea of peeing outdoors. No one had told me it could be done. It totally blew my mind."

"Very touching." But she was smiling.

"That's not the end of it. That was the summer Mom experimented with…" Mortification tinted his cheeks over the neat line of his stubble.

"Oh God. I think I know where this is going." She pressed her hands into her ears. "I don't think I want to hear this."

"Yup. You don't."

"Please tell me this wasn't the Summer of Gulkand."

"Bingo!"

Oh no! His mother made the most delicious gulkand, a sweet rose petal jam. A rose petal jam that involved crushing rose petals with sugar in a glass jar and leaving it out in the sun, and letting the heat from the sun 'cook' it. Which meant there was no real cooking involved, nothing that might kill germs. And Sunita Auntie had made the most delicious ice cream with it.

"Oh my goodness. I can't even tell you how much of your mother's gulkand I've eaten." She punched his arm. "Why didn't you stop us! Neel! I think I'm going to be sick."

The ass was laughing. "At first I didn't know where the gulkand was coming from. By the time I figured it out, it was too late. Everyone was hooked."

She gagged and he rubbed the spot where she had punched him.

"The good news is—"

"No! How can anything about this be good news?" Unbelievably, she was laughing and wanting to throw up at the same time.

"The good news is, I only peed in one corner and my aim wasn't great. And when I realized what she was doing with those roses, I did the math, and based on percentages and probability there is only a ten percent chance that any of the gulkand you ate might have come from roses I… um… watered."

She slammed a hand across her mouth. "Oh no!"

"What?" he asked, watching her with suppressed laughter shining in his melting honey eyes.

"Poor Trisha." Her little sister was one of those nerds who ate like a camel. She forgot to eat when she was studying, which was pretty much all the time, and then when she did get to food, she basically demolished everything in front of her. "Trisha ate a full jar of the stuff at your house once. Oh my God. How am I going to tell her?"

His laughter hiccupped to a stop. "Hey now! We're in Vegas today. None of this leaves us. Ever."

Fair enough. "Did you ever eat any of the gulkand yourself?"

He nodded. "Threw up for two days after I found out. Mom believes to this day that I'm allergic to rose petals. I'm definitely allergic to *her* rose petals."

Still smiling, she put her rock down next to his. "I always wished I was as smart as my siblings."

He stopped laughing and watched her. She had never said those words out loud before.

"I mean Yash and Vansh are the world's most insufferable know-it-alls. But can you imagine growing up with Trisha? No one is smarter than her." Her sister was unarguably a genius. "I remember when mom was working on getting Yash to memorize the periodic table at the kitchen island. And Trisha recited the entire thing while playing with her Legos on the floor. She was four."

She smiled at the memory. She remembered the day like it was yesterday. "I remember the expression on Ma and Dad's faces. They both ran to her, kneeled in front of her, and asked her how she'd just done that. Trisha simply led them to the study and showed them the chart on the wall. She'd looked at it and her brain had photographed it or done whatever it was her brain did."

Neel's smile was knowing, but he waited, aware that there was more.

Nisha swallowed. "I had just finished reading my first chapter book. An abridged version of *Little Women*. I was six. Ma loved that book and I remember being so excited about telling her and Dad that day. But I never did."

"If it's any consolation, Trisha makes me feel stupid too. She helped me with my SAT prep, remember? And she was in fifth grade."

They both laughed.

For all her sister's brilliance, Trisha struggled with people and feelings and other everyday things. "Sometimes when I see her struggling with normal life stuff, I take comfort from it. I know that makes me a terrible person."

He reached out and stroked her arm. "You're a perfect big sister. You've always made it easy for Trisha to navigate the normal life stuff she finds so hard. And you've never made her feel less for it. Trisha worships you and it's not for nothing."

This was true. Nisha would die for Trisha. And kill anyone who hurt her.

Neel picked up another stone and balanced it on the other two. "I'm afraid of water."

"Excuse me?"

"Yeah." He looked off into the distance, as though his mind was suddenly miles away.

"Wait a minute—that doesn't seem correct." But it had been years since he had joined them at the beach. Or the pool. And he'd been a very good swimmer when they were young. "You were on swim team in school. No, wait. It was only until sixth grade." She pressed a hand into her heart. "You stopped getting in the water after your father died."

He blinked in surprise that she had made that connection. "Dad had been on the US Olympic swim team before med school. He taught me how to swim when I was two, I think. We swam in the ocean every day at the beach house when we were there."

In spite of both his parents being doctors, they hadn't caught his father's bile duct cancer until it was stage four and he had passed away within months of being diagnosed. They'd all been in shock at the speed of it. Neel had spent a lot of time at the Anchorage for those first few years because it had taken Sunita Auntie a while to get back on her feet after. Nisha remembered shadowing him constantly.

He looked at her as though he'd never seen her before. "You're right. I haven't been able to go near the water since he died. Mom sold the beach house soon after it happened, and I've been really good at not letting anyone find out."

Yeah, no kidding. Here she was thinking she'd obsessed over every little thing about Neel and she'd missed something so big.

"Neel?"

He looked up from the stones and met her eyes, the grief from years ago fresh again.

"The dance floor at the cocktails last night. It's over the pool. Why didn't you say something?" He'd been there when the wedding planner had shown them the sketches. He'd been there when they'd done the walk-through. It had been obvious how uncomfortable he'd been the day of the walk-through, but Nisha had thought his discomfort was about the wedding and she'd worked hard not to dwell on it.

For a moment Nisha thought he wouldn't respond. There was something he wanted to say, but he was afraid to say it.

*Well, welcome to my life, buddy!*

She picked up the stone he had placed in their truth pile and pressed it into his hand. "I thought we were being honest."

He wrapped his fingers around hers. "You were so excited about the dance floor. It made you so happy. How could I say anything?"

She moved closer to him, scooching across the wet grass. Guilt nudged at her for not having asked him what was wrong when she'd seen the terror on his face yesterday. "The dance floor wasn't what made me happy."

His eyes did that thing they did, darkening with the intensity of his reaction to her response.

His own response seemed to stick in his throat. "Last night, once I was on the floor with you I forgot about the water under us. Honestly, I've been missing it recently."

A smile bloomed in her heart as he put the stone in the truth pile. "Anything else that you hate about the wedding but didn't say?"

A smile nudged at his lips.

"You might as well tell me."

He picked up another stone and tapped it on the ground. "Well, I'm not sure about tiger bread for the wedding breakfast."

She gasped. "Shut. Up. Who are you and what did you do with Neel?" Neel was such a stereotype of someone from the Bay in his eating habits, he was a cliché. "Turn in your Boy from the Bay card, now!"

He touched his heart as though she'd shot him. "I just don't like the idea of eating anything that looks like chapped skin."

"Whoa now!"

He shrugged, but the smile on his face was all him, so comfortable in his skin, so at ease laughing at himself.

She forgot she was staring at him until he pushed a stone into her hand. More of those tingles sparkled up her arm as skin touched skin.

"I've never been to Twin Peaks," she said. It took her a moment to be able to look away from the stone and at his face.

The usually crystal-clear brown of his eyes darkened with understanding. He remembered.

"Not ever?"

"Not even near it. If I have to drive past it, I take the longer route."

Her cousin Ashna—her uncle's daughter who had moved to America when she was in middle school—had grown up with Nisha and her siblings. Ashna had loved to play this game she called Your Dream Thing, where everyone had to come up with their dream something. Like their dream dessert, their dream vacation spot, their dream career. Wherever they started they always ended up on their dream boyfriend or girlfriend, or their dream date. It was just part of being teenagers, this need to bring everything back to their imaginary dating life. Imaginary because dating, at least before college, had not been encouraged in the Raje family. Their parents believed it to be too much of a distraction from school.

They had been playing Ashna's favorite game in the Rajes' attic playroom one evening when Nisha had shared her dream date: holding hands on top of the world. At the top of a mountain from where you could see everything.

The next day Neel had come over, a book tucked under his arm. He'd found it at the library. Twin Peaks, San Francisco's Highest Point. They had pored over the book sitting in their gazebo with their heads together.

"Someday I'll take you there," he had said.

She was fifteen. He was sixteen. She had taken it as a sure sign that he would be asking her to the spring dance.

"How come you never went?" He put a finger on the stone she had put down.

He had to know that there could only be one reason.

But they were making a game out of spelling out things that laid them bare, so she'd paint him a picture if he needed her to. "I had psyched myself out about how special it would be for so long, that it became one of those things. It was never going to live up to how I'd imagined it. Like anything you've wanted to do for so long that starts to feel too momentous to actually do it."

There was an odd expression in his eyes. "I know exactly what you mean." He reached for another stone and placed it with the others in their combined pile. "I was going to ask you to spring dance in ninth grade."

"Why didn't you?"

"Raj Krishnan asked you and you stopped talking to him."

"I stopped talking to him because he tried to kiss me and he started crying when I pushed him away." Another stone went from her pile to the center. She picked it up then put it back. "Actually, he started crying because I punched him."

He pressed a hand into his forehead, obscuring the anger that flashed in his eyes. "Why didn't you tell me?"

"I didn't tell anyone. I felt dirty. I felt like if Ma found out, she'd force me to leave our school and go to a different school or make a big deal about it with the teachers." Nisha's mother's overprotectiveness was legendary, her childhood as a child-star had been anything but normal and she was determined to keep her children sheltered, something she had never had herself. "And I thought if you found out then you'd never ask me out. And all I wanted was for you to ask."

"Why didn't you say something?"

"Say what?"

"Something that helped me know that you wouldn't stop talking to me if I asked."

"How could you think I would—could—ever stop talking to you?"

"I don't know. At that point, asking you just... it just felt too momentous to do. I was too scared."

So, he had moved on and forgotten about it.

And then he had met Barbara. He hadn't been too scared to ask *her* out.

Nisha stared down at the tiny pile of truths they had made. This honesty thing had been fun. But there were things they couldn't get into. Why had she agreed to this? She had so much more to lose here than he did.

"We were kids, Nish. I only realized that it even mattered to you when I introduced you to Barb and she noticed. By then I believed myself in love."

Nisha felt angry embarrassment flush across her face. She could see it now, Barbara telling Neel that Nisha had feelings for him. She almost stood, but something in his eyes stopped her. It wasn't regret exactly, but it was something close to it, and a plea for her to stay. Why couldn't she trust what was in his eyes, even when she did believe it?

Because he *had* chosen someone else over her—something she had believed herself to be over. And because he *had* lied to her about it—something she could never get over.

Picking up a handful of stones, she held them over the pile. "I know I wasn't your first choice, but I can't go through life feeling like second best in this too. I just can't." She let the stones drop, knocking over the careful tower of truth. Then without waiting for his answer, she stood to leave.

# Chapter Six

Nisha's foot was asleep and it was hard not to limp as she turned away from Neel.

She heard him rise behind her.

"Watching you get into that car today was the scariest experience of my life." He was so close that the heat of his body wrapped her up. The tremor in his voice vibrated against her earlobe.

She didn't turn around, she couldn't move. "Of course it was. Not going through with the wedding would destroy our mothers and if I know anything, I know you would never want that."

His sigh was deep and hurt. "We have very strong mothers, Nish, but they would never want us to be with someone we don't want to be with." He slipped his arms around her. "I was terrified because if you left me I wouldn't know how to go on."

He'd been hurt once, he didn't want to be hurt again. Could she do that to him? Put him through that pain again? It would kill his faith in relationships forever. Was it an act of courage that he was letting himself believe in a relationship again? Or was he taking what was safe because it was there?

"Not having you in my life for so long was horrible. I didn't realize how horribly I had missed you until I saw you again."

The breath she was holding whooshed out of her. She was so tired of all the questions she couldn't ask. She leaned back into him. He pulled her closer and rested his chin on her head.

She'd seen them like this in her dreams a million times. Fitted perfectly together. For all her misgivings, not one thing would she change about how she felt in his arms, his racing heart beating against her back, his heated breath fanning her cheek.

Every cell in her body was alive. Desperate attraction and deep peace, that wildest of combinations, sparkled around them.

She let her arms wrap around his. Could they do this? Pick and choose truths that gave each of them what they wanted. What about wanting the same thing? What did they have to do to get there?

Be honest, maybe? Was that what he was trying with the truth stones?

"Do you know why I never saw you for that year after you came back from England?"

He pulled his arms tighter around her, holding her as though he would never let her go. "Of course I know. You told me. I was heartbroken and you couldn't bear to see my pain." He pressed a worshipful kiss into her hair. It wasn't as though he wasn't grateful for how much she loved him. She knew he valued her feelings. It was his feelings that felt like a mirage she was chasing.

"That isn't why," she whispered into the night.

For a year after Neel came back from England, Nisha had avoided him with singular focus. After coming home, he had started working for a law firm in San Francisco. That first year he had attended all the family parties and hung out with the old gang—her siblings and cousins and their parents' friends' children, people they had both grown up with. Everyone followed his lead and went on like nothing happened.

Everyone except Nisha.

Nisha had refused to meet him. Not in any overt sort of way. But if she knew he was going to be somewhere, she simply didn't show up. She moved into sales at her tech company and traveled for work as much as she possibly could. If Neel made inquiries about why she was avoiding him, no one told her. She didn't make it easy for anyone to talk about him around her and he didn't make any effort to seek her out.

Eleven months after he came back, when she didn't show up for the Diwali party at her own parents' home, he left the Anchorage without a word to anyone and drove to her apartment. She was in her pajamas drinking Malbec, eating mint chocolate chip ice cream, and watching reruns of *Full House*. Not her usual

Diwali, but better than coming face-to-face with Neel and seeing the pain of Barbara's betrayal in his eyes.

The buzzer in her apartment building had almost shorted out after he'd refused to give up when she pretended not to be home. He had tried calling her, but she wouldn't answer her phone. Finally he had walked around to her balcony and thrown pebbles at her window. When she still didn't respond, he'd shouted up to her, "I know you're in there, Nish. I'm going to climb up to your balcony. If you don't want me to do it, you have to come out and tell me. I'll go away if you tell me to go away. I swear."

His stupid, politically correct wildness had made her heart spasm so hard it shot a wild mix of pain and electricity all the way up and down her spine.

When she still didn't respond, he had climbed the tree outside her second-floor apartment and jumped, or rather stumbled, onto her balcony, falling on his knees and elbows and scraping them through the silk kurta and churidar he was wearing for Diwali.

When she finally came out to the balcony, she had found him bleeding at his elbows and knees through his ripped clothes.

The first thing he'd done on seeing her was wipe her tears and ask why she was avoiding him. "It's been a year, Nisha. Why won't you see me?"

The truth had come tumbling out. "Because I can't bear to see you in pain."

He had held her face in his hands and kissed her like she was the first breath he'd taken after years of suffocating. To no one's surprise, Neel kissed like he did everything: he put his soul into it.

Even now, standing under a tree with his arms around her, just thinking about that kiss made her want to turn around and kiss him and let herself forget all her doubts.

That day she had done what she couldn't do today, what she hadn't been able to do since. She had wrapped herself around him, with arms and legs and every living cell in her being and taken what she had craved all her life.

That night had been magic and it had led to them being together almost every day for the next six weeks. Six weeks of heaven and hell rolled into one. Six weeks when she'd finally had what she'd dreamed of, but six weeks during which she had held her breath waiting for him to realize she wasn't what he wanted. Just the way he had done before.

Six weeks when she hadn't been able to say one real thing, because she'd felt like she was living someone else's life. He'd proposed after those six weeks, and the six months after had been another whirlwind of real desire spinning together with playacting and living in fear of Barbara's return. Because Nisha had seen his pain after he came back, and she couldn't forget about it.

She pressed back into him and pulled his arms tighter around herself, as though he were her coat against a frost she'd suddenly walked into, her armor against slicing swords that had sprung up around them. The idea that she might lose this made her tremble, this safety of his arms around her, this elemental rightness that she experienced when she was touching him.

But the sense that it was all in her head, all borrowed, just wouldn't leave her.

"You put a handful of rocks in our truth pile. We still have hours. Talk to me, Nish. Please," he said against her cheek, his words falling like caresses on her skin. "Tell me what's hurting you."

"The reason I didn't... I couldn't bear to see you that year after you came back was because... because I saw you just after you came back," she said quietly.

His body changed behind her tightening with surprise and focus. She held on to his arms as tightly as she could.

"That first week when you were still staying with your mom. My family was visiting yours and our families were in Sunita Auntie's backyard. Your housekeeper told me you were in your room, and I ran up to you without thinking about it." She wished every day that she hadn't done that. "Your room door was ajar. You were sitting on your bed."

The pain in her voice was so naked, he tried to turn her in his arms but she held on tight. She couldn't let him see her face right now. "You were just sitting there with tears running down your face, your crying completely soundless, as though you'd lost everything. You didn't even notice me standing there watching you."

"Why didn't you say something?"

Finally, she turned in his arms and looked up at him. "Say what? That I recognized your pain? That I knew exactly how you felt? Because the way you looked that day was exactly the way I had felt when you started seeing her."

His head bowed at that and she felt terrible adding to his burden of guilt. But sharing it lifted some of the load off her own shoulders and she felt like she could stand up straight for the first time since they had found each other on her balcony that night.

The understanding in his eyes was new, different from anything Nisha had seen there in six months.

"I'm sorry." He stroked her face. "It was fresh pain. I don't know exactly how to explain it but it wasn't what you think. It felt like coming home after failing at something. It felt like I had thrown years of my life away. It felt like I had let my parents down—Mom and Dad were high school sweethearts and their marriage was the cornerstone of my childhood. You know that. And I had fallen for someone who never chose me. She always chose what she wanted and if I followed then I followed. But I had to come back home. I could never live anywhere else permanently, never forsake my home and family. By the time I left, the pain wasn't so much about losing her—at that point it felt like I'd never had her—but about the colossal waste of it all, because I had really tried to make it work. It felt like I had lost my innocence and faith in love."

She cupped his cheek. The shape of his face, the lines of his jaw, the texture of his stubble, it all pressed into her palm with such intimate familiarity that her already aching heart squeezed.

"I'm sorry." She stroked his skin with her thumb.

He pressed her hand into his cheek. "Nisha! I don't feel that way anymore. Don't you see? None of this is about her. It's about us. It's about how lucky I feel that I found you."

"Because I always follow where you lead? I'm always there where you left me. Waiting. Always doing what's expected of me like a damn wimp with no spine."

"Is that what this is about? You don't want to marry me because it's what everyone expects you to do?"

She pulled her hand away, spun around and squatted down next to the stones. They had made quite a truth pile. She started to stack it neatly again, the biggest stones at the base, the smaller ones layered over those. "No. I don't want *you* to marry me because it's what everyone expects *you* to do."

He knelt next to her. "The fact that you can always be trusted to do the right thing is what makes you stronger than anyone else I know. Not a wimp. It's exactly why I want to be with you, need to be with you. You're my compass."

All the truths they had told made an incomplete pyramid. Nisha picked up another stone and placed it at the top. "You know how you said you never told me about meeting Barbara because you thought I was stressed out about the wedding? I was never stressed out about the wedding. But I was stressed out about marrying you. I was stressed out about making a mistake because I was sure that if she came back, you'd realize you were making one."

"And me not telling you about seeing her convinced you that you were." He adjusted the stones she had rearranged and added one more. "That day a year and half ago, when you saw me sitting on that bed crying after I came back home, I had just spoken to Barb on the phone. She had called and apologized. She said she'd made a mistake and she was ready to come home to me. But it was too late. I couldn't go back to that, to the emptiness I had felt for the last years of our relationship. And I realized that I didn't want her to give up something for me after all. We just wanted different things in life. When you saw me that day, I had finally let her go and I felt chewed up and spat out. But also relieved and ready to put myself back together again."

She traced the finger he was touching the stones with. "Why did you never tell me?"

"We never talked about her. I was afraid of talking about her with you. Not because of how I felt about her but because I knew how much it hurt you to hear me talk about her. I thought showing you how I felt about *you* was enough. I'm sorry."

"Is that why you've never told me why you want to marry me?

Because you don't think I need the words?" Although she was no longer sure she meant that. Maybe words weren't the only way for someone to tell you they wanted you.

For the longest time he didn't answer. They sat there staring at their finished pyramid of truth, stable enough now that knocking it over would take work.

Suddenly he sprung up to standing, an odd fire in his eyes, and held out a hand to her. "Will you go somewhere with me?"

She stood, somewhat more slowly, more deliberately and took the hand he offered. "Yes."

# Chapter Seven

They retraced their steps back to where Neel had left the car outside Chris's house. Nisha still couldn't believe she had barged in on the poor man like that. It felt like it had been years since she'd done it, not hours.

She clung to Neel's hand, or maybe he clung to hers. They walked in silence, like lovers. They were lovers, weren't they? Nisha had just never taken a moment to think about them that way. If the life blazing in the palm of her hand where she gripped his was any indication, her body knew things her mind was only now starting to grasp.

The car ride felt endless, but it had been barely a few minutes when Neel turned to her. "Will you close your eyes for the rest of the drive?"

"You're not planning to slit my throat and throw me into the bay, are you?" But she closed her eyes.

"You're just going to have to trust me, aren't you?" Without her vision, his voice was like silk on her skin. "I wish I had a blindfold."

"I guess you're just going to have to trust me, aren't you?" she said. "Then again the blindfold sounds promising." Who knew the simple act of closing your eyes could make you so bold?

"Nisha Raje!" he said with mock pearl-clutching indignation. "Is there something you've been hiding from me? Do we need to go back to the truth stones?"

"Well, some things you might have to discover without your truth stones, Neel Graff."

His laugh was warm and intimate and she felt it with her entire body. She leaned back into the plush seat of his mother's Benz. He lived in the city and refused to buy a car.

The car pulled to a stop and Nisha's heart beat with so much anticipation that she had to remind herself to be careful, to manage the hope rising too fast inside her. When he opened her door, took her hand, and helped her out of the car she realized that there was no care to be had with Neel. That ship had sailed far too long ago. She had been a fool to even think she could ever control it. But she deserved the truth, both to tell it and to hear it. Every relationship deserved that.

She hadn't opened her eyes and he never asked her if she had. Not once. She'd asked him to trust her with it, and the fact that she might not keep her word didn't even enter his mind. This she knew for sure.

"Just a few more minutes, babe," he said in that way he had of speaking close to her ear, as though he couldn't get close enough. It made goosebumps dance up and down the back of Nisha's neck.

A swirling breeze caressed her skin and she shivered.

She lost him for a few moments, then felt the drape of a heavy silken coat around her. "Neel, please tell me you didn't just put your wedding sherwani jacket on me."

"I packed my reception clothes into the car last night. It's all we've got. And it looks better on you anyway." He wrapped his arm around her and led her down a path.

It struck her that she could walk like this with him forever. On the heels of that thought came another realization: he hadn't once asked her to go home, or asked if the wedding was on. He'd focused only on what was bothering her, on what had made her do the craziest thing she'd ever done in her life.

Her heartbeat went insane, and just like that she knew exactly what she would see when she opened her eyes. She knew exactly where they were.

They came to a stop and he rubbed her arms, the soft friction of the silk exactly in sync with how her insides were feeling, warm and liquid and wrapped up. "You can open now," he said.

She squeezed her eyes tighter and shook her head. Tearing up with your eyes closed was the strangest sensation. "I can't." She couldn't bear the hope in her heart, it was too much.

## The Runaway Bride

"It's okay, love." He kissed her lips—the gentlest of touches, the most tempting of promises. "Everything is going to be okay. Open your eyes."

The view from Twin Peaks through the haze of tears was an ocean of flickering lights. With a gasp of awe, Nisha turned a full circle, both hands pressed into her heart. Their beloved city blanketed in golden stars wrapped around them for as far as the eye could see. A full, round moon hung over it all like a luminous pearl, like the final dotting of a signature.

"That's Market Street," he said, pointing at the bright red line of a lit up street.

"It's so beautiful. And look at the Bay Bridge!" The scalloped outline of the Bay Bridge sauntered off into the horizon.

They walked along the stone wall admiring the clarity of the night and the beauty of the city with the embrace of the bay and the two bridges radiating like wings from it. Like tourists, they pointed at things they recognized, enjoying their home with the awe of strangers.

"I'm sorry it took me so long to keep my word and bring you here."

She turned to him. "No, Neel! Don't apologize. This is perfect. This is so much better than I ever imagined it could be. I don't know why I thought it wouldn't match up to my expectations." Reaching up she grabbed his beautiful face and kissed him.

He picked her up and fitted her against himself, drinking in her kiss.

"So is this," he said against her lips. "Kissing you, touching you. Being with you. It's even better than I ever imagined."

She hopped up on the wall and he pulled himself up next to her.

The Sutro Tower, in all its awkward sculptural glory, stretched out toward the sky in front of them. "There's almost something comical about the Sutro's stance," she said.

He smiled. "He's just more squat than all the other towers. Don't judge. On cloudy days you can only see the top and it looks like a ship floating on the clouds."

"Like from a plane. When I was young and we flew to India for the summers I always imagined that the clouds were the ocean and our plane was a ship."

"I still do that every time I fly." He tangled his fingers with hers and studied her hand in his.

On her finger was his grandmother's engagement ring.

He traced it, then pulled it to his lips and kissed it. "Mom never offered me her mother's ring when I was with Barb. But the moment you and I started seeing each other, she put it in my hand."

Nisha met his gaze. "Does that scare you? The pressure of our families' expectations?"

He shook his head. "Not anymore. It used to. I also thought it was funny how excited Mom got when I told her I wanted to ask you to marry me. But I understand it now. Mom knows me and she recognized something in me when we got together. Our parents can recognize our happiness, I think."

Nisha made a face, and he raised a brow at her. "You might as well say what you're thinking."

"Okay. This isn't personal, but I'm so glad Sunita Auntie didn't give you Nani's ring to give her. I don't think I could ever forgive her if she didn't return the ring after you broke up." Wearing this ring felt like such a responsibility. Nisha couldn't imagine it in the possession of someone who didn't see its worth. It was a link across generations, something that reinforced that they were part of something larger than themselves, family. But also that family didn't work without them and their bond with each other as individuals.

Neel's mother was still livid that Barbara had not returned the ring Neel gave her. Nisha could not imagine Sunita Auntie's hurt had her mother's ring been taken from the family.

"I have another truth to tell," Neel said quietly.

Nisha waited, an odd kind of calmness wrapped around her.

"My meeting Barb wasn't entirely an accident the way I made it seem."

She said nothing and Neel took a breath. "She came to my office. I had no idea she was going to, she didn't call ahead. She wanted to return the ring I gave her." His gaze was fixed on Nisha.

"And she wanted to make sure you weren't marrying me on the rebound or caving in to family pressure."

His lips twisted in a smile. "You're crazy to think your siblings are smarter than you. I don't know anyone who's smarter than you at reading people. And that requires the kind of intelligence that can't be gained from books."

"What did you do with the ring?"

His smile was wide, almost smug. All Neel. "I asked her to donate it to Yash's campaign fund."

Nisha had to laugh at that and kiss him again. "You won't stop until I'm completely and totally in love with you, will you?"

Nisha had just quit her job to manage her brother's campaign for state senator. Yash would run for the highest office in the land someday. It's what he had been groomed for since the day of his birth. Nisha had always known she'd work on his political career someday and that day was here. Raising funds was Nisha's highest priority right now.

Someone with the last name of Lovett had donated ten thousand dollars this week and Nisha had sent the form letter thanking the person as Neel had known she would do.

Had that been his way of letting Nisha know, without actually bringing Barbara up? "Why didn't you just tell me?"

"I should have. I wasn't lying before when I said I didn't want to upset you. But it wasn't because I have feelings for her. It was because of how I feel about you. When Barbara told me she wasn't moving back to America with me, what I felt then was nothing like what I felt today when I watched you get in that cab."

"How was it different, Neel?" She needed to hear the words. Needed him to say it.

He pressed her hand into his heart. "When she told me she wasn't coming back home with me, I knew we were over. It was this deep knowing that had been coming on that just fell in place, because coming home was all that mattered. I didn't think, even for a minute, that I'd stay. Her surprise at that, her belief that we would always follow her dreams no matter what I wanted, that had felt like being kicked in the gut.

"When you got in that car today, I knew I was going to do

anything, anything to keep you from leaving me. These six months with you, I've been more myself than I've ever been in my life. I haven't been playacting, Nish. You fill me up. You make me the man I want to be, you make me whole. You are me. Tell me what I have to do to be worthy of you, to have you stay. I'll do it. You're my home. Please don't leave me."

The words flooded her heart. It swelled with love and hope. This night had filled in the cracks and plugged the leaks that had made it impossible for her heart to hold these precious feelings. Now she could no longer remember how that felt.

She snuggled into him and he picked her up and pulled her onto his lap. She could never have imagined that his kisses could be more intense, more hungry, more tender, more rough. But they were now. Because the terror that came with them was gone. She was the girl he wanted to be kissing. Knowing it changed everything. With that touching of their lips, she was the girl on her dream date, at the top of the world with the boy she loved.

"I had one more truth too. Something you have to know."

He let out a mock groan and pulled her closer. For the first time Nisha saw his fear too. Now that her own fear had parted the veil she had kept between them, his was clear as the night sky reflected in his eyes. It was all the more precious to see it, because he fought to hide it. He didn't want it to get in the way of her truth.

He would always be this person — someone who wanted her to say what she wanted, be who she wanted without influence, without pressure. It's how he wanted everything in his world to be — honest and true to its natural, naked state.

Well, it was time for the big truth, the one that was at the heart of everything. The reason why she had left her home today. The reason they were sitting on a stone wall with their legs dangling over San Francisco to fulfill a childhood promise.

Words it was stunning that she hadn't said until now.

"I love you, Neel. I've always loved you. I've known it from before I knew how a girl could love a boy, way before I knew how a woman could love a man. My love for you is so much a part of me, I don't know who I am without it. Before you marry me, before we make vows about family and duty and sickness and health, I want you to know that. That you hold the power to destroy me. Because that's how much I love you."

He was shaking when he pressed his forehead into hers. "I know," he whispered. "I've always known. But I was too much of a coward to take that on. You've always terrified me. Because I didn't know if I could live up to what you saw us as. I was terrified of you — am terrified — of what we can do to each other. But I'm even more terrified of not having that. Not having *us* and what we are together. I love you. You hold the power to destroy me too because the one thing I know for sure now is that I was put on this earth to be with you. Please, please let me be your husband."

She turned in his lap and straddled him. Her arms pulling him as close as two people could get. And there on the top of the world she claimed him as her husband in the truest sense of the word.

# Chapter Eight

It was five a.m. when Nisha walked through the gap in the electrical fence and made her way to the gazebo where she would be marrying the man she had wanted to marry for as long as she could remember. Despite a night spent not sleeping, energy coursed through her limbs.

Her phone rang and she pressed it to her ear, smiling so widely her cheeks hurt. "You have to stop calling me, Neel. No more talking until I see you at the altar."

"You sure you don't want to elope? I still have Mom's car and we can make it to Las Vegas in seven hours."

"First, you need to slow down with the driving. Second, I think that car has served us well. We don't need to abuse it even more." She would never be able to look her mother-in-law in the eye after what they had done in the poor woman's car.

"You know I'm buying this car from Mom, and then we're going to keep it safely in our suburban garage until our children are in college, and then we're driving all the way around the world in it."

Perfect as that sounded, she laughed. "I left you five minutes ago, darling husband. You couldn't possibly have gotten drunk in that much time. You sound positively high."

"I'm drunk on you, darling wife." His voice fell to a whisper, pure heat in her ear. "Given how much of you I did drink."

She moaned into the phone. "Neel, please. I'm going to run into people, I cannot be walking around with dilated pupils. And smelling of sex because I'm wet."

It was his turn to moan. "That's it, I'm coming up there to pick you up. Spend the rest of the night with me. The wedding isn't until ten."

"Don't you dare. You need to get some sleep or we're going to sleep through our wedding night."

"Baby, I don't think we're going to have luck sleeping through a night anytime soon."

She laughed. "Is that a promise?"

He laughed and groaned all at once. "Nisha, you're killing me."

"I'll see you at ten."

"Nisha."

"Yes?"

"Thanks for running away."

"Neel."

"What, love?"

"Thanks for finding me."

When Nisha reached the pool, the crew was busy setting up. Garlands of marigold and jasmine hung from the trees surrounding the pool area where chairs covered in embroidered gold silk had been set up for the guests. Between the chairs, a processional glass aisle floated over the pool which was covered in rose petals and floating candles.

Rina, the wedding planner, started when she saw Nisha. "Nisha! Everything okay?"

"For the most part." Nisha waved at her.

"What's wrong?" For all her training to stay calm in the face of bridezillas everywhere, Rina looked nervous.

Nisha put a hand on her shoulder. "Don't worry. Everything looks beautiful. You've done such an amazing job, thank you! But there is one thing I need you to change."

"You made them change the entire wedding setup on the morning of the wedding and you want us to believe you're okay?" Trisha said as Ashna, Trisha, and Nisha made their way up to the top floor of the mansion to see their oldest cousin, Esha.

"I just didn't feel like walking over the pool to the altar, it seemed a little too over the top. I want solid ground. Every bride is allowed at least one tantrum."

Trisha and Ashna exchanged glances. They looked beautiful in their cream and gold lehengas, their hair in updos, jewels dangling from their ears and draped around their necks, glass bangles jangling on their wrists. If they knew she was lying they said nothing. They had been treating Nisha like a princess, bringing her breakfast and chai as she had her hair and makeup done. It was The Biggest Day Of Her Life and her sisters were doing all they could to make it perfect.

Their cousin Esha would not be attending the wedding. She hadn't left the uppermost floor of the Anchorage for over two decades. She was their oldest uncle's daughter and she'd moved in with them after an airplane accident had killed both her parents. Esha, who had been six at the time, had miraculously survived the crash that had killed everyone else on board including her parents. But after the accident she had started to have seizures if she experienced the stimulation of any human contact outside the family.

It was almost time for Neel and his wedding procession to arrive and, in keeping with tradition, the plan was for Nisha to wait with her girl cousins for the barat to arrive. They were going to wait in Esha and their grandmother's suite of rooms because Esha never left her suite when there were strangers on the estate but also because Nisha could never get married without Esha participating in the ceremony in some way. Once the groom's wedding procession arrived, Ashna and Trisha would take Nisha down to the venue and her parents would walk her down the aisle to Neel.

Esha and Aji gasped when they saw Nisha in her red and gold wedding lehenga. The thing weighed twenty-five pounds, silk woven with gold thread and sprinkled with Swarovski crystals. It looked even more beautiful today than when Nisha had picked it out. She felt glorious in it.

"You might be the most beautiful bride I've ever seen," their grandmother said, as Nisha leaned over and touched her feet for blessings. Aji kissed Nisha on the head. "May your marriage be a garden of blooms that flowers forever."

Nisha grinned and Esha cupped her cheek. "It's gone," she declared, looking into Nisha's eyes in her ethereal way.

Esha had the gift of clairvoyance that no one could explain. It had come on after the crash, and the family guarded Esha and her secret fiercely. Nisha often found Esha's declarations hard to understand. But with this one, she knew exactly what Esha meant.

Nisha nodded and let Esha pull her close. "You deserve this joy. Don't be afraid of it."

Nisha sat down on the rattan couch on the sprawling balcony between Esha and Aji as Ashna and Trisha leaned over the railing to keep an eye on the groom's procession that was making its way up the winding road to the Anchorage gates, led by an Indian musical band and dancers.

"How can anyone not be terrified of The Biggest Day Of Your Life?" Ashna said, staring out at the procession. "I can't believe you convinced Neel to get on an elephant. He looks adorable, by the way. Not that you're allowed to see him until you're at the altar."

"I think Ma and Sunita Auntie were the ones who convinced him to get on the elephant," Trisha said. "That elephant is gorgeous too!"

"I think Neel would ride a tiger to marry our Nisha," Esha said, taking everyone by surprise.

The family tended not to make sweeping statements like this, given that everyone was familiar with Neel's wanting to marry someone else less than two years ago.

"I think a tiger is a bit much, but Neel would get on almost any large domesticated animal if I asked him to," Nisha said, not missing the smugness in her own voice.

That took Trisha and Ashna by surprise. They exchanged a look, some sort of realization dawning on their faces, then high fived each other. They smiled just as smugly as Nisha and leaned over the balcony railing to get back to their reporting of the procession's progress.

Their grandmother watched Nisha. The relief on her gently lined face was palpable, even though Nisha had never before noticed that she was worried.

"You're glowing. The Biggest Day Of Your Life suits you," Ashna said.

"I won't mind the whole Biggest Day Of Your Life chaos if I glow like that," Trisha said.

"The Biggest Day of Your Life isn't your wedding day," Esha said in her soothing voice. "The wedding day is just the day when everyone who loves you makes you feel special. The day that's the real Big Day is the day when you decide whom you're going to spend the rest of your life with." Nisha couldn't be sure, but there was a knowing glint in Esha's eyes.

"Well, then Nisha's biggest day was in middle school," Trisha and Ashna said together and burst into giggles.

Nisha didn't correct them, but she smiled at Esha, who seemed to know how very lucky Nisha was that her wedding day was indeed that day for her.

Suddenly Trisha and Ashna bounced on their heels from their sentry post at the railing. "The barat is at the gates. It's time to go down!"

Nisha gave Esha and Aji another hug. They would watch from up here. They had a clear view of the gazebo-turned-wedding altar and the newly laid out aisle that circumvented the pool area and cut across the lawn. Knowing that Neel wouldn't have to walk over the pool made relief spread through her.

She made her way down the stairs of the house she'd grown up in, flanked by her two sisters. Her smile stretched from ear to ear, because not every woman got to have the biggest day of her life on her wedding day.

"What are you thinking right now?" Trisha asked as they reached the porch where their father was waiting for her in his princely regalia and her mother, who always looked like a princess, had tears shining in her eyes.

"I'm thinking I have to give Rina a bonus for moving the wedding aisle from over the pool to solid ground at such short notice."

Trisha looked at her like she was crazy. But when Nisha walked down the aisle to the ceremonial melody of shehnai flutes, Neel looked at her like he would never be the same again.

"Thank you," he mouthed as she walked up the steps of their gazebo, and in an act that would be the scandal of their set for the rest of their lives, he picked her up and kissed her full on the mouth, before the wedding ceremony had even started.

# About Sonali Dev

Award winning author Sonali Dev writes Bollywood-style love stories that let her explore issues faced by women around the world while still indulging her faith in a happily ever after.

Her books have been on NPR, *Washington Post, Library Journal,* and Kirkus Best Books of the year lists, but Sonali is most smug about Shelf Awareness calling her "not only one of the best but also one of the bravest romance novelists working today."

Sonali lives in Chicagoland with her very patient and often amused husband and two teens who demand both patience and humor, and the world's most perfect dog.

Find more at www.sonalidev.com.

*Loved the Rajes?*
Get more of Nisha and Neel and this fabulous family in
Pride, Prejudice, and Other Flavors

# Starboard Vow

### by K.M. Jackson

*To Will*

*Sailing around once with you is never enough.*

# Chapter One

Jules Monroe straightened the seam of her already straight uniform skirt as she squared her shoulders and tried her best to focus ahead with her usual open and friendly smile. It was the big day. Game time! She was on.

As the chief social director on board the cruise ship *Elegance*, Jules was a master at making people feel comfortable and welcome. She'd done it all her life growing up. The middle child in a turbulent household, Jules was a born peacekeeper, and she had a knack for defusing difficult situations and putting folks at ease. So much so that the first chance she got she ended up making a career out of it, when she left college and by a weird happenstance ended up a fill-in for a friend who needed help with what seemed on the surface like easy summer money.

Turns out it wasn't. The first summer Jules spent as a third stewardess and general assistant for a private luxury yachting company but still, it was during that hard summer she'd found both a career she'd come to adore and a man she'd come to love.

To some, she was the maker of fun, to others the designer of dreams, but Jules' favorite moniker of late was 'The Princess of Party Times.' Too bad today though, she felt like anything but. More like the 'Countess of Crocks' or the 'Baroness of Bullshit.' Yeah any of those would suit her much better right now, she thought, as she was lined up with her fellow chief crewmembers, all dressed perfectly in the pristine officer whites, smiles bright, not a hair out of place, as each stood side by side waiting for their special VIP passengers to arrive. Jules continued to smile as her jaw started to ache from the strain of it, and she feared her perfect façade would crumble at any moment if *he* didn't arrive soon and put her out of her misery.

Jules swallowed down on the lump in her throat and once again sent up a prayer to God, the universe, just anything or anyone who would listen with a divine ear that she could get through the next few days without completely losing her job, her dignity or shit in general. Moving from those big thoughts she went macro and momentarily fretted over the state of her clinical strength deodorant as trickles of sweat formed between her shoulder blades, the late afternoon Miami sun bearing down on them with a vengeance. She squirmed slightly and her friend, and right-hand woman, Dina, snorted from beside her and gave her a quick nudge. Jules looked over and was slightly comforted by Dina's cheeky grin and saucy wink.

"Don't worry about it," Dina whispered. "You've got this. You are a strong, professional woman. You've made it through the last year without him, so you'll clearly be able to survive the next four days in his presence. Hell, by Monday I'm pretty sure Mr. Big Superstar will be brought down a runner or two, at least that is if I have anything to do with it." Dina gave another hard snort getting a dangerous glint in her eye that sent all sorts of warning bells off in Jules' head.

"Maybe it's you who should calm down," Jules whispered out of the side of her mouth. "You know I love you to pieces, but I don't need you making this awkward situation any worse by going all destructo on me. Things will be tense enough, not to mention weird. And what I really need to get through this is calm. So please, just let's keep it cool. It's the only way I'll get what I need out of this cruise."

"Need? Oh, you mean sex," Dina whispered in a way that said she might as well have been using a megaphone.

Jules gave her a side elbow. "Ugh!" she hissed. "You know that is not on the agenda. The order of this cruise is cool, collected and by the end of it all," Jules swallowed once again before she said the next word, "divorced."

"Yeah, yeah, yeah, I hear you," Dina replied. "You know it will be a lot more convincing if every time you said the D word you didn't swallow as if just the thought of divorcing your absentee mega star husband would break you in two." Dina sighed and gave Jules a quick but too deep glance. "Though I still think that one for the road for old times' sake is not the worst idea. You know, see if that pony still has pep."

Jules blinked. How was she friends with this woman?

"What is this I hear about old times' sake and ponies?" It was Brenden Fox, her friend and chief steward and of course, he would walk up just when Dina was saying something saucy. Though the odds of Dina saying something saucy at any moment were usually relatively high.

"Nothing," Jules responded quickly.

Brenden raised a teasing brow her way and she took in his soft hazel eyes, suddenly shining brightly, and watched the edge of his lips quirk up transforming his normally sweet innocent look into something entirely opposite.

She gave him a quick eye roll. She could not deal with both him and Dina today. The two of them on tag team would be too much. Still, Brenden did have a way of making her smile. He was disarming with his classic, good looks, broad shoulders, strong jaw line, copper tanned skin and sandy blonde hair, cut the military style way that made him look a bit like an extra from an old 80's heartthrob come to life.

"Nothing," Jules said, focusing on the work at hand. "It was just Dina going on like she does. You know her, always trying to get someone hooked up. It's not like we're working on the Love Boat here."

Brenden gave Jules a pointed stare, his expression suddenly more serious and turning slightly smoldering. "Well, I can't say that I fault her there. Nothing wrong with love. You say it as if the L word is a bad thing." He stared at her a beat longer before wiggling his brows.

Jules gave him a light tap on the shoulder. "You really are incorrigible. As if you know a thing about love," she said, her mind going to the fact that she'd had more than a few chances with him as he'd made it clear early on that he was available and interested in her, but she never entertained him, and he never pushed. Not that he had to. Jules knew she was nothing more than a friend to Brenden. Any offers were purely of the hookup kind, and a man like Brenden could and did hookup as frequently and with as much variety as he liked.

"Hey, I know plenty about love," Brenden protested. "Just ask anyone who's been with me. I'm one of the most loving guys there is out here. I'm so loving I could write a book on the subject."

"I'm not sure if what you would write would actually count as a love story, Brenden. More like a lust story," Jules countered.

"Love, lust? As long as each person comes out feeling good in the end, I don't see much difference between the two." He grinned, his smile once again going toward the sexy side that had passengers swooning and lining up four deep for any drinks he was pouring for the night, or whatever else he happened to be serving up.

Meanwhile, it was taking all Jules had just to keep up with the conversation because truly, she was only half listening. Her not whispered quietly enough conversation with Dina had gone into dangerous territory and sent her mind even further into a tailspin. She took a deep breath and smoothed back her already well-smoothed and contained dark curls. She needed to get her head on straight. Time to get it together since *he*, aka Aaron Manning, would be coming on board in just a few moments.

That's right, *the* Aaron Manning. This year's hottest, well, just about everything if you let the entertainment trades and social media tell it. He'd made Hollywood breakout star list, *Fan Stan* magazine's most heroic hero list and just this past month, *Entertainment Now's* sexiest bachelor list. Jules held back tightly on a frown. That one, she had to admit grated on her.

She and Aaron being technically married and all.

Though, to his credit—and was she really giving credit here?—but still, to his credit, he'd barely made the list, coming in at number 25 out of 25. But yeah, the fact remained, even if no one knew it, he was her freaking husband. So what that it wasn't public knowledge, and that they had not been seen together in going on a year now, or had it made a year? Jules felt her thighs go taut. Yep, it was definitely a year.

At least for her it was a year in any and all ways. She knew it in her heart, mind, and body. As for Aaron, she didn't know what he knew. All she could surmise was from what she'd gleaned from the internet and gossip sheets. And though he didn't seem like he dated around, he had been photographed repeatedly with one woman, his leading lady from their Starboard franchise, Poppy Roberts.

Aaron and Poppy. The current couple on everyone's lips. Are they, or aren't they? What the hell tabloids? He was her husband. Though he didn't wear a ring, it shouldn't take more than a cursory search to find out that Mr. Hotshot, whether he did or didn't wear a ring, was legally a full on married and attached man. At least for the moment he was. After this cruise, she hoped not so much.

For now, he was her husband and if any of the aforementioned news outlets had researched past their noses, they could have fairly easily found that out. Jules let out a breath, fighting against the anger simmering just below the surface of her chest. What right had she to be mad at some anonymous news outlet? Wasn't this what she wanted? Wasn't it what she'd signed on for when she left Aaron last year? She should be happy about all the headlines. If she wasn't, then it was all for nothing. The headlines let her know that her objective had been achieved. Now all she had to do was stand in the truth of the fact that she was right all along.

Just then a small parade of dark town cars and two sprinter vans with darkly tinted windows pulled to the curb at the end of the dock. Captain Giardano let out a small cough which was more than enough of a signal for the crew to once again assume the positions and prepare properly for their VIP guests.

Jules locked her knees tight against the overwhelming impulse to run. Not that she knew which direction she'd go anyway? Forward or back. The fact that she was struggling with that thought scared her the most. Where would she go and who would she run to, she thought as the door of the first van opened and way too quickly, she got her first glimpse of her husband, Aaron, in over a year.

"Whoa," Dina said, from by her side, "are you sure about this? That man looks so good that even my non-committal ass would ask for his hand. Woman, what are you doing?"

Without thinking Jules let out a low moan as she took in Aaron's tall, dark and way too handsome figure. Dang it! In the past year he'd somehow gotten more sexy, alluring, and downright more mouthwatering than ever before. Jules swallowed. Shit was she drooling? She hoped she wasn't drooling. She let out a long breath before answering Dina. "You said it. My overtime celibate ass is right now wondering the exact same thing."

## Chapter Two

Once again, Aaron Manning vowed to himself that he'd win Jules back. Forget her stupid divorce papers and to hell with nights sleeping alone. He wasn't leaving this ship without his wife by his side.

Yeah, that's what he told himself. Too bad his quickly beating heart and shaky knees didn't quite get the memo, he thought as he prepared to exit the van and make his way to the cruise ship *Elegance* and be face to face with Jules for the first time in way too long.

But why should he be nervous? He asked himself for the hundredth time in his head. If anyone should be nervous it should be her. She was the one who left with hardly more than a word. She was the one who served the papers first, also with hardly more than a word. Aaron reached for the door handle and paused. But he was the one that let her go. And he was the one that didn't chase her back. Instead, heading in the opposite direction over and over going from film shoot to film shoot in pursuit of his career ambitions.

"You just gonna sit there or we going to get out? It's your call," his manager Morris said from by his side.

Aaron looked down. He was no longer holding the door handle but instead looking at a wide-open space where the driver had stopped, come around, and opened the door. Shit. When did that happen?

Aaron shook his head. "Yeah, of course I'm getting out. Let's go."

Morris let out a sigh. "Listen, I know you're nervous. So am I. But I have a feeling everything will work out fine. Jules is a level-headed woman. I'm sure she'll see reason."

Aaron turned and looked at Morris. He really should and wanted to be mad at Morris for his part in all of this, but he couldn't. No, he had to take responsibility for the fact that Jules left. Putting it on someone else was the cowardly way to go. "I'm not sure this is a case for level headedness. We're way beyond that. Though any positive love thoughts you can send my way will be appreciated."

Morris nodded, though he still looked nervous. Aaron knew he was worried about the repercussions of both Aaron getting back with Jules and those of what would happen if he didn't. Both would probably affect his bottom line. Aaron gave him a reassuring smile. "Come on, man. Have some faith in me. I've got this," he said and stepped out of the van and onto the dock.

Aaron tried to walk confidently and think of the objectives of the cruise. As far as gigs went, this was a glorified vacation and a paid for one at that. The fact that his wife was *The Elegance's* chief social director only fell in line with his philosophy of combining work and pleasure. So, win/win there. Work because the cruise was put forth by the studio as a chance to continue to promote his movie *Starboard* and an opportunity to sit with the principals and hash out agenda items for *Starboard 2*, the sequel.

Aaron frowned to himself as he thought of the grueling hours of filming and re-takes and how if he had Jules to return to or by his side during those long days and nights, how much more tolerable they would have been. He missed her so much over the past year. More so when he'd return home from shooting, alone; the silence of his apartment only reminding him of their last night together. Jules burned him up. Making love to him as she did that last time as if she knew it would truly be their last time. He guessed she did. He was the one that found out too late that she'd overheard the conversation between him and Morris about the studio thinking it would be best if he'd kept the fact that he was married to Jules as hush as possible. That it would be better for their plans and his career if he'd appeared as a single man about town.

The worst was that a part of him got the logic, and he was stupid enough to admit that to Jules. But they had positioned him as a renegade bad boy with a secret heart of gold. Supposedly both unattainable and completely obtainable at the same time. The fact that he was selling himself as every woman's or man's fantasy, well he could see how having a wife might stall things a bit. Especially with the 16–25-year olds who were just discovering him. Hell, it might even screw with over 44 demos that he hoped to obtain as fans too. But none of that mattered to him. At least not really and that's what he'd told Jules. What he'd tried to make clear. He guessed he was nowhere near clear enough though.

The next day, when he'd come home from the gym, all that remained of Jules was a Dear Aaron letter telling him to pursue his acting career whole-heartedly without any encumbrances. She being the unnamed but eluded to encumbrance. She'd told him that she was taking an offered job with a new cruise line and would be gone for four months. That he should put his all into his work and not mention the fact that they were married, to anyone. He guessed as some form of placation she'd added that she'd contact him once she returned, but when the time came and he thought, no hoped, that she'd be back, all that he got instead of his wife was a set of official divorce papers to warm his bed and his heart.

Aaron didn't sign and he wasn't warmed.

If he had signed the papers, it would have pretty much nullified their marriage with absolutely no demands or restitution requirements on either of their parts. Signing would make it as if their marriage had never happened, as if their love had never happened. All without giving him any chance to say his peace.

But what would he say to her? The papers felt so final. It was as if she had already given up on him, and it scared him like nothing ever had before. So, Aaron ignored them. Crap move but it was all he could do to both hold onto Jules and get through the grueling schedule set on him by the studio.

Yeah, he'd made small gestures to try and get in touch with her. A few calls and some texts. But they went without a response. No longer.

Now he was here, and he was saying what he had to say to her. Face to face. That way there would be no ignoring, dodging, or beating around the bush for either of them.

Aaron glanced up at the big, white ship with a powerful sleek design, and pulled his shades out to cover his eyes, feeling the need to put some sort of physical barrier between himself, the outside world, and his emotions.

"You ok, man?" came Morris' voice from by his side. "Like I said, don't worry. Jules is probably still not tripping. It's been over a year. Surely she's not still upset about what happened."

Aaron felt an anger he tried to long bury bubble up anew with Morris' words. Of course, Jules was still angry. Hell, he was too. Sure, it wasn't all Morris' fault. It probably wasn't his fault at all, but the fact remained, it was the overheard conversation with him that had sparked Jules leaving. And worse yet, Morris knew beforehand that Jules was leaving Aaron and didn't alert Aaron. Instead, his manager let him go to his final call back with the Starboard director and studio execs, and he missed Jules' departure and his last chance at keeping her by his side.

His gaze slid Morris' way. "I wouldn't bank on that. Jules is not one for forgetting or lightly letting things go."

Morris cleared his throat nervously. "Well, if anyone can convince her than it's you."

Aaron shrugged and strode forward. "We'll see about that won't we."

## Chapter Three

There was no time to back out now, even though everything in Jules was telling her to run. Yep, it all was fine and good when Aaron was just a memory that she was sending divorce papers off to via international post, but now he was striding toward her in the flesh and bone and looking somehow more attractive even than when she'd last seen him.

His shoulders had gotten broader, though Jules told herself that was possibly a trick of the sunlight glinting off the bow of the ship. His hair was longer than she'd expected it to be. Inky black with a slight wave, it was cropped in the back from what she could tell from where she was but slightly past his ears on the sides and in the front, long. It went to the point of covering the top of his dark aviator style sunglasses that thankfully protected her from what was no doubt the devastation of his dark eyes.

The sunglasses, with his shoulders, his dark denim jeans and a black tee shirt covered with a leather motorcycle jacket, not to mention his confident long-legged stride, had him looking like every bit the box office draw that he reportedly was.

It was then that Jules noticed the rest of the crew as they exited the other vehicles. Oh boy, it looked like they were being invaded by a sea of Hollywood coolness as the pack made their way toward them in muted colors of blacks, tans, and greys, toting backpacks and duffels that were over stuffed but seemed to have seen their fair share of travel. Immediately, from the bored, almost unimpressed looks on their faces, Jules knew this would not be an easy bunch to satisfy and that, on top of dealing with Aaron's presence, she'd have the added pressure of entertaining this lot. She almost sighed. There was the Starboard crew, their fans, and some special VIP press who were handpicked to cover the Starboard peeps during their "downtime." The whole thing had to give off an air of being carefree and natural while still being choreographed and staged to within a hairsbreadth.

No matter, she was up for the challenge. When she'd taken the *Elegance* position, she signed on for this kind of excitement and if her husband, well, soon to be ex-husband, wasn't a part of this particular sailing she'd be downright giddy over the challenge. Jules smiled. She could do this. She *would* do this, because she had to, she thought, trying to not let her smile falter. Because before she was Mrs. Aaron Manning, she was just Jules Monroe, assistant cruise director. After this journey, she'd still be Jules Monroe, and she hoped she'd still have the title of chief social director to go with her name.

It was with that thought that Jules heard Aaron's name. It came high and musically pitched from a voice no one could escape if they were anywhere near any form of media. "Macaroon," Poppy Roberts yelled as she ran up on him from behind. "Wait up!"

Jules watched as a slim, petite woman with reddish, blond hair sprinted on impossibly high heels and linked arms with Jules' husband.

She mentally kicked herself for having the thought. Her husband. Crap. She had to stop thinking that way. If she was going to have any success with convincing Aaron to sign the divorce papers, she had to get the thought of him as her husband out of her mind. So really, Poppy was doing her a favor by giving her this memorable image at the very start of their voyage. Though he didn't come right out and say it, maybe the rumors were true, and Aaron was actually up for this divorce. Could it be he figured the time to move on was now, as well?

Jules' frown deepened and she felt a hardness come to the set of her mouth as she stared at the duo and the way Poppy latched on to Aaron while looking up at him adoringly. She flashed Aaron a bright smile, the same one that earned her numerous marketing endorsements, and she scrunched up her pert little nose at him with a laugh.

Jules bit back on a growl and right on time because when she blinked, Aimes Webber, the movie's director, stood before her.

## Starboard Vow

"Hello," she said, blinking once again, to clear the image of Aaron and Poppy away and focus instead on the unassuming man in the wrinkled khakis, vest and Zeppelin T-shirt.

"I'm Jules Monroe. The ship's social director. Please let me know if there is anything I can do to make your stay with us more enjoyable, Mr. Webber." Jules would have known the famous director even if he wasn't wearing his signature vest. He was pretty much a celebrity in his own right but still, there was no dismissing the all-seeing look in the man's direct dark gaze. Something told Jules that there was little that got past him.

He looked at Jules seriously at first before his stern features morphed into a wide smile. "Jules Monroe? Like from the sitcom? And you're the ship's social director? Like a cruise director. How clever," he chuckled out with a twinkle coming to his eye. She'd never thought of her name as clever by any means, not with the job she had. But at the least it was an ice breaker, though most times it was the butt of countless jokes.

Aimes turned to Brenden, "So, are you Gopher?" he asked, giving the name joke more time than it deserved.

"No, sir," her co-worker said. "I'm Brenden, the chief stew. Thankfully I'm not quite as bumbling as Gopher, though honestly, I always fancied myself more of an Isaac type." He tilted his head and gave Aimes a sheepish look. "But maybe I'm just being a tad too lofty in my thinking."

Aimes Webber grinned at this and continued his way down the crew line, finally stopping in front of the captain.

"Oh, I always loved Isaac. Thank goodness for reruns," came that high voice again and Jules wanted to kick herself for momentarily taking her eyes off Aaron. If that was Poppy, then Aaron was probably not far off.

"Nope. Julie Monroe was always my favorite," came Aaron's voice from way too close. "She always knew exactly how to satisfy the passenger's needs."

Jules looked up and there he was. Looking down at her from a spot where she could, with the barest of steps, lean forward, uplift her chin and practically kiss him. It was tempting, so very tempting, even though his expression was deadly serious despite his playful words, which were meant to come off as a light-hearted joke, but Jules knew were anything but. No, the set of Aaron's jaw and the look he gave her told her there was not a hint of playful in him. This man was all about his business right now.

"Somehow, I think you're both too young to fully appreciate a show like 'The Love Boat,'" Aimes Webber chimed in from where he stood.

Aaron smiled down at Jules, his full lips spreading, way more easily than they ought to with that predatory look in his eye, showing his even white teeth, and her heart damn near stopped. Getting smiled at by him, in that sweet, sexy but slightly dangerous way was like getting bitten in just the right spot.

"Maybe," he replied to Aimes while still staring way too intently at Jules, "but thank goodness for reruns. Sometimes things are better the second or even third time around."

And with that he was gone. Down the line with the rest of the crew ending in front of the captain.

Jules felt the most embarrassing pool of saliva forming in her mouth along with a rush of air letting her know she was starring with her mouth open like one of his groupie fans.

"You gonna close that mouth anytime soon?" Dina teased.

"I thought it was closed," Jules replied looked down where Aaron was smiling at the captain as if he didn't just turn her world on its axis.

"Nope. Open and wide."

Jules slammed her mouth shut and looked at her friend. "Well it's closed now."

Dina laughed and gave her a nudge. "You handled that perfectly. Smooth as silk."

"Yeah sure," she said. "If by silk you mean the exact opposite. Then fine."

Jules shook her head and fought to get her composure. She swallowed and plastered her usual smile back into place to prepare for the next incoming passenger. But wait, what was the captain saying? "Please get settled and don't hesitate to ask any of the staff for anything you may need, no accommodation is too small. We're here to serve you. Look forward to hosting you all at my special captain's dinner tonight."

Out of her peripheral she felt when Aaron's gaze landed on her and their gaze clicked. He grinned this time, not quite his star melting smile but in no way any less dangerous. She nodded at him. Trying her best to give back as good as she got. This was no time for weakness or emotions.

But crap. The Captain's dinner. As the social director she had to make an appearance and with this group of VIPs she knew there would be no excuse too big to get her out of it.

# Chapter Four

Aaron made his way to his cabin led by a steward and followed by Morris. On the way he did the usual nodding and smiling at the ship's staff that lined the narrow hallways. He purposely kept his demeanor friendly but slightly closed off, ignoring the overly sexual glances he got from some of the female and male staffers.

When they made it to his cabin, his housekeeper, a cute brunette, feigned surprise and offered him a quick apology over not being quite done with readying his room, though at brief glance around showed nothing out of place in the spacious cabin.

"Thank you, Maribel, that will be all," the steward said pointedly to the housekeeper, who showed little signs of exiting the room. She looked from him to Aaron to Morris, cleared her throat and smiled back at Aaron again.

"Of course," she said, still not moving. "It's very nice to meet you sir. I'm a huge fan."

Aaron smiled at her but kept his expression neutral. He knew that look. She was a fan and a harmless one, but he had to walk that fine line between distancing himself and being insulting. Plus, he also needed to realize there was no need to take his current mood out on Maribel. She was just being nice. "Thank you. Maribel. That's kind of you to say." At the use of her name the housekeeper's grin widened.

"Please, if there's anything that you need, anything at all, don't hesitate to call me. All you have to do is press the button here," she drawled out. Taking her time to animatedly point out the clearly marked service button by the cabin door. "Or text me via the ship's app at 4473 and I'll be happy to assist you," she finally said, her breath light and flirty.

Morris pulled a face over the way Maribel said assist. Maybe she wasn't as harmless as she seemed.

Thankfully the steward cleared his throat again and motioned toward Aaron. "The rest of your bags should be here momentarily, Mr. Manning. Mr. Swift if you'd follow me, I'll show you to your room. It's right across the hall." He turned to Maribel. "I take it Mr. Swift's room is ready? If you'd just come with me for a last check."

Maribel seemed to get the hint, blinking out of the trance she was momentarily in. Or maybe it was she realized taking a chance on Aaron wasn't worth risking her job. He could assure her it was not.

Aaron was relieved when the door clicked, and he was finally alone in the cabin. He let out a long breath and looked out past the large double bed, the sitting area, the huge balcony doors and onto the view of the Miami sound beyond. What was he doing and how in the world was he going to be able to keep his shit together when he was barely able to hold onto his cool after just one brief encounter with Jules?

His Jules. At first glance she didn't seem anything like his Jules at all. Honestly, it had scared him for a moment. Like ice water shot fast through his veins. Though she looked very much the same, he could tell she was somehow changed. Her once bright and welcoming eyes now seem more subdued, still friendly but the shining innocence that was once there was now gone. And it wasn't just that, her full cheeks and the round softness of her body, though no less alluring, had taken a subtle muscular curvature that spoke to intense workouts, something she would've never given time to in the past. Then there were her lips. Aaron practically grimaced thinking of them and the way she had smiled at him, making his mind go to all sorts of past days and long to feel them sweet and pliable beneath his once again.

He ran a frustrated hand through his hair letting out a groan. "As if there was any chance for sweet kisses with the look she'd given me," he mumbled to himself.

Aaron started to doubt this whole idea of coming aboard and trying to win her back as he went to his duffle and pulled out the small jewelry box he had stashed there. Flipping open the black velvet box he looked down at the perfect square cut diamond surrounded by smaller baguettes. He'd noticed immediately how Jules hands were still unadorned. She still wore no rings on her left finger or any finger.

Their own wedding, a hasty one, held just off the shore of Antigua on the one day in which they were docked, and they were able to get their special license. She was ringless then too as they made their vows on the sand officiated by the captain of the *Cordania,* the ancient private cruise yacht they used to both work on. The moon and the old ship as their romantic backdrop. But Jules swore then and there under that bright moon and the shining stars that he was all she needed to last her lifetime, not some ring.

Seeing her now, he wondered if he'd ever truly been enough. Hell, at the very least she should have had a ring to remind her of the love they shared during the past year in which they were apart.

Peeking out of his now open bag, almost mocking him, was a manila envelope and her latest attempt at divorce. In her letter, though brief as it was, she once again made herself the martyr. Saying this was for him. So that he could keep going with his life unencumbered. Aaron snorted just thinking of her ridiculous words. Without her he hadn't had a peaceful unencumbered moment. Why she didn't realize that he didn't know?

But just then for some reason, the image came to his mind of that steward, the annoyingly good looking one, in the too tight uniform who stood next to her just a little too close and got the only genuine smile he'd happened to glimpse from her as she'd made her introductions. The hairs on the back of Aaron's neck prickled in a most uncomfortable way as insecurity and jealousy veered up unexpectedly. What if she was already attached? What if it was her who really wanted the clear break and to get on with life? They had been apart for a long time and she had been the one to leave him, to serve him with papers. The prickly hairs stood even higher and he told himself to get it together.

Of course, they weren't seeing each other. What would she do with a guy like that? All shoulders, teeth, smiles and .... Wait. Aaron laughed to himself nervously as he caught his own reflection in the wall mirror. Shit. That dude was just her type.

Hell, he was every woman's type and he worked with Jules, here. On board this floating aphrodisiac.

Aaron circled around quickly, taking in the cabin fully for the first time. The inviting double bed turned down perfectly, the balcony with its exquisite view and jacuzzi tub, the ice bucket with champagne chilling. It was a total fantasy sex suite! Suddenly Aaron couldn't breathe from the overwhelming thoughts of Jules. He had to get out.

He was about to make a run for it when a knock sounded on the door. He closed the velvet box, and quickly shoved it back into his duffle bag. He didn't know why he was rushing to hide it. It was probably just the rest of his luggage, still he didn't need the prying eyes or wagging tongues of the ship's crew letting his secrets out of the bag, especially not before he'd squared things with Jules.

Opening the door though, instead of it being just his luggage, he was greeted with both his luggage and Morris hopping behind the rolling case. Morris had already changed out of his jeans, tee and blazer and was looking like an extra in the set of a Lampoon's Vacation movie, wearing plaid swim trunks, a cobalt blue tee and a clashing Hawaiian print button down as a topper.

Aaron didn't hide his grimace, though his tone was light when he spoke. "Way to take a theme to the next level M."

"It looks good, right?" Morris replied, glancing at his phone as he side-stepped the luggage and the attendant and entered the room. Aaron shook his head, tipped the attendant and retrieved his case.

"I want to take full advantage of the vacation part of this working vacation while we're on board."

Aaron waved a hand in front of his face, which was still practically buried in his phone. "Yeah, I can see you're fully ready to unplug." He shook his head.

Morris looked up and shook his head before going back to his phone. "As if I ever could with a client like you. Despite my cool ass gear, as your manager I still have to stay on my game while I'm here. You know that this is a pivotal time for you career wise." Morris said, pointing his phone Aaron's way. "And trying to stay on top of things from the middle of the ocean doesn't seem like it's going to be the easiest task. Wireless alone is going to cost me a fortune if I don't want roaming charges. It's like once you're on board you can practically disappear from the real world."

Aaron thought of Jules and her non-communication of the past year. "You're telling me," he said to himself. But to Morris he added, "You'll be ok, I'm sure."

Morris shrugged then gave a nod. "Thanks to you, you're right. Still, I'd better check to see if there is anything that can be done about the connection speeds. This is not the most optimum time to be out to sea, so to speak. I need to keep track of your numbers. We have to make sure to keep riding the wave of *Starboard* and keep your numbers high. The audience can quickly forget and move onto the next latest and greatest between parts one and two of a film."

"Yeah, but I still have Yoskawa's indie film coming out in between the two. It should all be fine."

Morris nodded, but Aaron could feel his hesitance. Morris had strong thoughts about Aaron stepping out in a more serious indie role so early in his career, but it was more. Aaron could sense some of their past problems with communications coming to the surface and haunting his features. The fact that they were where they were right now, on this ship and for the first time both in such close proximity to Jules suddenly seemed to weigh on them. But then Morris smiled. "You're right of course. And you're great in it. I know your fans will follow you no matter what projects you make or what direction you take."

Even though he said it lightly, the heavy weight of his words filled the air in the cabin giving it palatable thickness. Aaron didn't want to go there. In all honestly, he didn't want to go there ever again. He was on the ship to mend the fences and right the wrongs of the past. With Jules, with Morris and, once and for all, set his life on the right path. He couldn't let the feelings of his fans, Morris, or anyone deter him from his current mission.

"Let me put on some shorts," he said, "and I'll join you. I'd like to see more of what this ship has to offer."

Jules busied herself for the next few hours meeting and greeting guests as they arrived and making sure her staff was in place, right where they needed to be. Though it sounded like an easy task, on a ship this size it was anything but. Luckily, she had quite a few years in the business and felt comfortable with the ins and outs of things. The only stickler on this particular cruise was the fact that it had turned into a mini-fan cruise for *Starboard* and in effect turned into a mini Aaron Manning fan cruise.

Though she was initially only slightly anxious over the idea of the cast coming aboard the ship, she wasn't overly concerned because the two lead stars had not been set to sail with them. Obviously that all changed. Jules guessed she couldn't fault the cruise executives or the PR folks for working hard to secure them. In this day and age, a company had to do whatever it took to stay relevant. Once word was strategically leaked that Aaron Manning and Poppy Roberts were confirmed to be on the cruise, last minute sales spiked immediately and the remaining available cabins on the ship were immediately sold out. But still, with all the surprise media and fan attention it made her ultimate goal to speak with Aaron and get him to sign the divorce papers just that much more difficult.

Not that she wanted so much to see him right now, she thought, as she made her way from the Royal Lounge to the upper decks to make sure the new props were in place for the beach bingo games later on the spa deck.

The lounge was quiet, all except the bar set up guys and a few quickly passing through passengers. Most folks were more excited about getting a rail side spot to check out the official departure from Miami. Jules heard the captain's voice come through over the PA system signaling the start of the departure countdown. No matter how many times she set sail, this part always filled her with a sense of excitement married to an overwhelming feeling of melancholy. The idea of charting off for new horizons while saying goodbye to a bit of your past did that to her, she thought as she stepped out onto the sky walkway and took in the view of the pier and its buildings beyond.

Jules turned to her right to get a glimpse of the setting sun, its fiery hues softening to a watercolor wash of blues and pinks. She was about to put up her hand to shield her eyes from light reflected off the gleaming rail but before she could, her gaze was blocked by a larger hand shadowing her view.

"It's beautiful, but you wouldn't want to hurt yourself by looking directly at it."

Shit. She'd successfully stayed clear of Aaron all this time and now here he was. Right in her face. Directly in her line of sight.

"What are you doing here, Aaron?" she asked.

"Why would I not be here? Obviously, this is where it's the best view," he said smiling down at her.

Jules fought not to roll her eyes. Just take his words for what they are, she told herself. Maybe he's not talking about you.

She gave him a steady once over. He had changed from his earlier outfit and was now wearing a sleeveless tee and gym shorts. She tried hard to keep her expression placid, but still her eyes stumbled, the casual look doing nothing to nullify his obvious charm. Jules forced her gaze back to his face and away from the broad width of his shoulders as he spoke again.

"Seriously," Aaron started, "though this trip was proposed to me as an optional journey, the way the word came down from the studio heads made me realize it was in no way truly optional."

Jules shifted her eyes away from him turning to look out over the railing. So, there it was. He was saying the words that she knew to be true. Once again Aaron was taking his dictation from the studio and once again it was studio and his career that were putting her life in a tailspin. But maybe this was for the best. He wasn't here for her and this trip wasn't about her.

But surely that meant he'd sign on the dotted line. She looked back at him, her anger threatening to boil over the top, but she smiled to hold herself in check. "It's good to see you haven't changed in that respect. Still following exactly what the studio heads tell you." She caught the narrowing of his eyes. How his jaw got just a little bit tighter. It shouldn't have satisfied her, this small thing, but it did.

"So, we're starting off like this huh?" he said, his voice thickening with anger. "I don't hear from you going on a year and then when I finally get a communication from you it comes in the form of official court rendered documents." He lowered his voice.

"I thought we were better than that, Jules. I thought you were better than that."

At his words, anger mixed with guilt started to bubble up within Jules. He thought she was better? Who was he to judge her? He was the one admitting to only being on the ship because his bosses told him he had to be. It was on the tip of Jules' lips to tell him off when out of the corner of her eye she saw Morris, coming toward him along with two other women. She looked past them to see a group of four young women in their twenties also coming their way. Their eyes were trained on Aaron with clear intent.

Jules fought back a groan upon seeing the hungry look in the women's eyes. She hated the immediate feelings of fear and dread that came over her upon seeing those looks. She gazed up at Aaron again. "Well as you can see, I'm not better than that. As a matter of fact, I'm just exactly what you see before you. Still, I'm glad you got my papers. I hope to have them returned to me with your signature well before this cruise ends, that way you won't have to deal with wondering what kind of woman I was or am ever again."

She turned to walk away, but Aaron reached out a hand, his gentle touch on her forearm feeling like a clamp. When she looked back into his eyes and then past him seeing the two parties bearing down on them from behind, she quickly stepped back out of his grasp, along the way tripping over the edge of a deck chair. Before she could even get close to hitting the ground his arms were at her back and he was looking down on her. His expression dark and sensuous, sending an immediate squiggle of unwanted deliciousness throughout her body.

He smiled at her. "Look at you, even when you're trying your best to get away from me, the universe still has you ending up right back in my arms."

Jules pushed at Aaron's chest and righted herself. Hoping she could hold onto some semblance of dignity as she came up from the awkward position. She cleared her throat just when Morris and crew reached them, their faces marred with curious expressions. Morris gave Jules an awkward smile, then nodded. "It's good to see you again, Jules, it's been a long time."

Jules nodded and attempted to smile back though it was hard

to be convincing. Morris was one of the only other people who knew of their status and she could see the awkward shift in his eyes as he looked from her to Aaron to the other two women.

*Good to see her?* Though Morris said the words Jules highly doubted their authenticity. He'd made it clear what he thought of her and Aaron's relationship last year when he'd stated the studio's position about Aaron appearing unmarried to his fans. She remembered the talk she'd had with him the next day when Aaron was out, and she was readying to leave as he explained how far Aaron was potentially on track to go. Morris wasn't a bad guy, but he was who he was. She couldn't fault him for doing his job. He'd kept his promises when it came to Aaron and his career. Aaron was where he was today, the top of Hollywood's *It List* partially due to the diligence of his pull-no-punches manager who took the hard line and would openly state the harsh facts about putting career before marriage. Jules knew that Aaron never could, so she had to take the steps that he couldn't in order to see his dreams fully realized.

She tried to think up something else to say to Morris that didn't give away their awkward connection to the gathered women and came up short. Thankfully, they were saved when the ship's main horn started to blow, long slow and loudly in numerous successions of three. The fan girls were torn between taking in the show that was Aaron Manning or the spectacle of departing out into the open ocean. They, along with the other two women, opted for the ocean and went to the railing for the seamless departure. Jules took the moment to make herself scarce, fighting against her heartbeat and hoping that her legs would be strong enough to keep her steady. She cleared her throat, "Good to see you, too, Morris. Um, well, I need to get going. Busy time."

"Oh yeah, sure," Morris said. "But I'll definitely be seeing you around, right?"

She nodded, needing so much to get out of that space in that moment. Being away from Aaron for so long and now to have seen him twice in one day and felt his arms around her was almost too much. "Yeah, you'll definitely be seeing me around. A ship this size is like a small city, and though it may seem big and overcrowded, you keep running into the same people over and over again."

"That's what I'm banking on," she heard Aaron say slightly under his breath but in no way hidden from her hearing.

This time Jules didn't hold back on the hard side eye she sent Aaron's way "But just remember," she said, "this here is my little city. But as long as you play by my rules, there will be no problems." Jules turned on her heels and headed off. Eager to get out and away from the man she married and into a space where she could be comfortable and breathe again.

"Hopefully we'll be seeing you at the Captain's dinner," Morris yelled from behind her back.

Jules stopped short. *Dammit the Captain's dinner.* She gave a brief turn and a nod towards Morris. She couldn't help but catch the mischievous smirk at the corner of Aaron's lips letting her know that, despite her words about her city, he still felt he had the upper hand.

# Chapter Five

"I have to keep the upper hand," Aaron mumbled to himself as he made his way into the Captain's dining room. Almost immediately though, he knew thinking that was nothing more than a pipe dream as he walked in and laid his eyes on Jules, looking devastatingly sexy in a little white dress as she stood behind a chair next to the captain.

Their eyes locked and for the briefest of moments he thought he may have caught an unfiltered second of joy flit across her features. In that moment, he wanted nothing more than to run around the table and wrap his arms around her, pulling her body into his embrace to see what it would be like to feel her heart beat against his once again. But just as quickly as that look flashed, it was gone. Not so much faded but in a blink disappeared, her eyes talking on a cool and impassive gaze as she nodded and gave him nothing more than a bland upturn of her lips.

Aaron frowned. He knew that smile and hated it. Hated the fact that it was directed towards him and not one of the other passengers. That smile was her working smile, warm enough, friendly enough, nice enough and sweet enough to make the guests aboard feel like they had a place in her heart; that she actually cared about them, but he knew the truth. He knew her from the inside and out and knew that was just her, "I'm just doing this to get through the day smile." How did he know? Because he'd seen the true look of joy in her eyes when she was really connecting with a person, and this was not it.

Aaron took a step forward, all his intentions going toward Jules, when the captain's voice pulled him up short. "Mr. Manning, thank you for joining us and for being so prompt. I do appreciate that in a passenger."

Aaron looked around the large roundtable set for twelve and for the first time noticed that, yes, he was the only one from his party there. Dammit. In his eagerness did he completely blow any semblance of cool by showing up too early for the dinner? Trying to cover, he smiled smoothly at the captain. "Please, call me Aaron. I hope I'm not so early as to inconvenience you."

He looked at Jules. She was gorgeous in her sleeveless body skimming dress. "Though being early is not a bad thing. It ensures that I get the best seat at the table." He walked over to her and stood by the chair next to where she stood. "This one looks perfect. What do you think, Jules?"

Jules gave him a hardened gaze as she looked around at the table. "Well, if you hadn't noticed, Mr. Manning, there are place cards to indicate where you should sit."

"Aaron," he corrected quickly and glanced around the table. "I'd think we're way past things like last names. But if you insist. I'd be happy to oblige."

"No," she said quickly, getting his intent. "Aaron. There is no need for formalities."

He looked down and noticed her name. Jules Monroe, written in elegant calligraphy, perched on a card in front of the place setting where she stood. He backtracked a few seats, looking for his own place card. He eventually found it. Four to the left of her. It was well placed in a specific spot for her to have her meal and almost pretend as if he wasn't there. Aaron was sure this wasn't by accident, but by design. He wasn't next to her and not even across from her where he could occasionally catch a glimpse her way. He stopped in front of the place assigned to him, then looked at her challengingly as he picked up his card and brought it over to the chair next to hers. He picked up the card for Aimes Webber and went to switch it with his own. Jules covered his hand, stilling him.

She frowned. "The seating was set up this way for a reason, Aaron. I hope you understand you can't just go rearranging things in order to get what you want."

He nodded, catching the double meaning in her words, and gave her a smile. "Well, I like to mix things up a bit. And trust me, by me switching these cards you are definitely getting the better part of the deal. Aimes is notorious for not keeping his hands on his own plate."

Captain Mike laughed uncomfortably at that, bringing both their attentions his way and reminding them that they weren't alone in the dining room having this little disagreement. "I see you're a funny one, Aaron," the captain said. "Of course, you should sit wherever you like. Call it the privilege of being the first to arrive. Don't you agree, Jules?"

Jules gave Aaron a skewering look before turning back to the captain with a smile. "Yes, you're right, sir. I don't know why I'm such a stickler for these types of things. Please sit wherever you like, Mr. Manning."

"Aaron," he said as he put Aimes' card in the place where his used to be. "And thank you, I think I will. Besides it will give us a chance to catch up."

"Perfect!" the captain exclaimed. "Old friends should get a chance to catch up. Jules why didn't you tell me that you and Aaron Manning were so close?"

Aaron immediately caught the tightness in Jules' jaw along with the look of panic as her eyes widened. She cleared her throat and quickly blinked, making a recovery, speaking up before Aaron could. "Not so much, old friends," she said smoothly, "and, no, it's not like I'd call us close, Captain."

Aaron once again felt heat rising. "Now come on, Jules. You wound me. I'd surely call us close. Maybe even more than close."

Confusion came across the captain's face at the same time as a voice trilled through the air. "I thought you'd wait, and we'd come down to dinner together," Poppy yelled from the entryway as she entered the dining room. Right behind her were the other cast and crew. Right behind them, Aimes Webber entered along with the producer Elena Diaz and bringing up the rear was Morris. Seeing everyone come in together Aaron thought he may have missed a call to meet with the crew in his haste to get to Jules, but he let it go. So what if he did? He wasn't missing out on any precious moments with Jules for anything or anyone.

But Poppy being Poppy, boldly walked up and linked arms with his, giving him the sideways squeeze. He looked at Jules and noticed the tightening of her already not quite smile. She hit him with a sharp look, then turned toward Poppy, the more professional smile back in place. "Thank you all for joining us," Jules started. "Once again, I'm Jules, the ship's social director. I hope to make your stay on board as exciting and fun as possible."

Aaron spoke up. "We're in great hands with Jules. She's a real pro. Always putting her guests' needs first."

Poppy frowned and looked at Aaron. "Wait a minute, you two know each other?"

Oh hell. They were about to be busted. Aaron really was taking things too far. Not just with Poppy but his whole crew was now looking on at their mini drama. Jules quickly stepped around Aaron and spoke up. She had to do something before he blew everything out of the water, so to speak. "We do," she said. Trying her best to keep the turbulent emotions she felt out of her voice. "In a way. Aaron and I knew each other back from his BS days."

Poppy giggled, and Aaron coughed before speaking up. "BS? Jules, really?"

Jules grinned wider and gave Poppy a wink. "BS. Before Stardom of course. Who would have guessed when he was closing down the lounge on our old ship and packing our small theater that Aaron would blow up like he did?" She looked at him, as memories of his dreams and undeniable talent came back to her mind. "But I guess we all had an inkling. Aaron had that spark even back then," her voice came out lower and shakier than she intended, and she blinked, trying her best to come back to her professional self. She turned to the captain. "Sir, now that everyone is here, we should all sit, shouldn't we?"

Jules didn't want to sit but since sprinting from the room wasn't an option, sitting it would have to be. Besides she'd told herself she wasn't running anymore. She had been going from job to job and ship to ship in her race against truly facing Aaron and the end of their marriage. She took her seat, fighting against the mixed feelings she was suddenly having and prayed she could get through the next hour with her dignity and her nerves intact.

Dinner was served, the passengers given choices of fish or a pasta dish prepared by the chef to accommodate all dietary options. Jules was relieved when Aaron didn't go all-in acting laser focused on her, but still she couldn't help but feel his strong presence radiating from her side during the meal. The warmth of him just those few inches away made its way to her bare arms and heated her down to her core when it should be sending prickles of irritation. *Dammit, it felt good to have him next to her.* Jules stopped mid chew, uncertain where that thought had come from. She swallowed hard and then coughed trying to push down the suddenly unpalatable fish, but really it was the thought of liking the feeling of Aaron by her side.

Aaron turned her way, "Are you alright?" His eyes were full of concern, and for a moment he didn't look like the mega star he was, but she caught a glimpse of the man she used to love. The one that she thought she'd share her forever with.

Jules grabbed her water glass and chugged. "I'm fine. Don't worry about me. There's no need."

"There is every need," he said, his voice full of enough force to silence the ongoing conversations around them.

Jules stilled. What was she going to do with him? She couldn't have him bringing all this attention down on the two of them. Jules smiled and snorted out a laugh trying to both cover up her choke while at the same time his ridiculous misstep.

"Just pay attention to your food," she hissed under her breath while giving him a playful, but she hoped hard enough to get the message across, slap on the arm.

He smiled at her with devilish eyes. "Why should I when it's so much more fun laying attention to you."

Jules bit back a groan. The man was incorrigible, and she suddenly didn't have the energy to play his games. There was still a long night ahead for her, so she turned away from Aaron to face the man on her other side. Too bad, focusing attention on Ivan Erickson on her right turned out to not quite be the best of ideas either. The striking blonde with his sharp features and equally as sharp senses greeted her with a soft smile that went totally against the tough guy image he'd portrayed on screen and in the public eye. "Don't let our fearless leader bother you, Jules. He loves to tease but he's essentially harmless," Ivan said, nodding his head Aaron's way.

Jules almost rolled her eyes but remembered she was

technically still on the clock, and though she was with a group of A-list actors, she had to pull out all her not quite award-winning acting chops too. She smiled instead. "Oh, I know he is. I'm just giving him the business. We're old fri—" she caught herself again. "Acquaintances. We go back. He gets that I'm only teasing, too."

"Do I," came Aaron's voice from over her shoulder.

"Really?" Jules said her head swiftly turning back to Aaron. "Can't you just focus on that side of the table?" She almost pointed her finger his way but stopped herself as she caught sight of a glaring Poppy.

"What is going on over there?" Poppy pipped up. "What are you three going on about on that side of the table? Teasing? Yes, Aaron is a huge tease. The biggest."

Jules blinked. *And just how the hell would Poppy know?*

There was another uncomfortable moment of silence then a chuckle. "Poppy you really missed out not trying the pasta. The shrimp are delicious," came the voice of Elena Costa, one of the producers from Poppy's side.

Poppy paused, looked at the woman and let out a breath. "You know I can't touch carbs Elena." She turned back Jules' way, not ready to let the earlier moment go. "Yes, that's our Aaron, a total tease."

Jules took a few gulps of her water then stilled, daintily putting her glass back down. She looked at Poppy. The thought of Aaron teasing the starlet made her blood heat. But why was this woman so intent on getting to her? Did she know more about her and Aaron than she let on? Was Poppy really something to Aaron and had he let the actress know about their past? Jules pondered for a moment then wondered why a woman like Poppy Roberts would be concerned about her and why in her current state she'd even care.

"That he is," Jules replied, not willing to let Poppy, Aaron, or anyone see her true emotions. "Though I guess you would know, having worked so closely together on your film."

She saw Poppy's eyes get a distinct glimmer of self-satisfaction at the same time she felt a wave of tension radiate off Aaron.

"Don't I, and too well," Poppy said, a blush coming to her

already peach hued cheeks. Jules felt heat rise up her neck. But wait, why should she care who Aaron was teasing when they haven't been in each other's presence in the past year? They were getting divorced anyway.

"It's really not anything like that. You know how I like to joke around…with everyone." The end of his reply was more directed at Poppy than it was her. "But it's no big deal," Aaron said sheepishly.

"Of course, it's not," Jules said before turning back Ivan's way. She wouldn't give Aaron anymore of her energy.

"Tell me," she started toward Ivan. "Are you excited about the next movie and where your character is going?" Thankfully this was the right question for the surprisingly sweet hulk and Ivan started to wax on about his character and how he was looking for more development in his villainous role. Jules nodded appropriately and tried hard to keep up but couldn't help being distracted by the last encounter with Poppy and thoughts of how Aaron could have possibly gotten on with teasing the other woman.

Thankfully, she was saved from further small talk when her phone vibrated, signaling it was time to be off and make sure all was in the rights for the rest of the evening's activities. She's never been happier for a night shift in the lounge in her life. Stealing a quick look at her phone she sent a text to the lounge that she'd be down to check prep soon before nodding to the captain to signal her departure.

"Thank you all for coming tonight, but I must excuse myself. The work of fun is never done," she said with a smile that was failing by the moment.

"So, it would seem. Text from your boyfriend," she heard Aaron mutter from by her side.

"No, my teasing buddy," she countered back before thinking.

Aaron quirked a brow, and Jules gave her own challenging one in response before turning back to the dinner party. "Please be sure to check out the itineraries that have been left for you in your cabins if you care to enjoy any of the ship's public activities. And please check your private emailed itinerary for your group activities. Though you have a few public appearances, I'm sure there will be plenty of opportunities for you all to enjoy your time while onboard."

"Here's hoping," came her soon to be ex-husband's reply, but thankfully she'd already given him her back and wouldn't satisfy his immaturity by turning around once again.

# Chapter Six

Well that went about as expected, Aaron thought as the vision of Jules hightailing it out of the dining room came once again to his mind's eye. Over the past two hours, Aaron couldn't get dinner with Jules out of his mind.

He had to admit though, Jules was a smooth one and she'd gotten smoother over the time they'd been apart. Though he didn't expect her to immediately fall for his charms and into his arms, he also didn't expect so much outright disdain from her. If anything, he was the aggrieved party here. She was the one who'd run out on him. Literally skipped seas! Taking up contract after contract and cruising right out of his life.

And now he was right here, practically in front of her, and he didn't get even a hint of an apology? No, all he got was more dodging and sidestepping. Still, he was acting like a bit of an ass, he'd give her that. But shit if she didn't bring out the immature teenager in him. There was no playing it cool on his behalf when it came to her. It was like any bit of chill he had was left on the dock in Miami as soon as he was back in her presence.

It was all about to come to an end, tonight. Jules would hear him out once and for all.

With all his self-pep talking, Aaron paused as he heard the sound of smooth thumping salsa music coming from the ship's Beach Lounge mixed in with the loud yelps and ruckus hollers of the fun-having cruisers. Maybe coming here to look for Jules wasn't the best idea. He should have just called her, left her yet another message. But then again, he'd come off as stalker-ish if he left her anymore messages, not that showing up literally on her job didn't take things way to the limit. Oh hell, he was really doubting himself now.

He was just about to turn and head back to his room for the night when the DJ's voice stopped him short.

"And up next we have sexy dance demo from Jules and Brenden! Always a cruise favorite, these two will be sure to heat up the room and get this party really going!"

Wait, what? His Jules? Who was she heating it up with? Before he could stop himself, Aaron was swinging open the double doors of the club, his eyes frantically searching for his wife.

"Isn't that Aaron Manning?" He heard one woman squeal over the loud music.

"Oh my gosh, yes!" came another voice.

"I heard he was on board, but I expected him and the rest of the stars to stay to themselves for most of the cruise. I can't believe he's here!"

Shit. He should have thought this one out a bit more. Miles warned him about just wandering around on the ship wherever he wanted without any backup or plan. But he wasn't all that used to this new thing called fame and didn't think he ever would be. Anyway, right now all he wanted was his wife. He looked left to right, trying to see past the swirling colored lights and multitude of faces. He nodded and smiled as he walked further into the room, his mind and heart fixated on getting to Jules.

Finally, he saw her, though obviously she'd not seen him because she was intent on her demo, or maybe it was the man she was doing the demo with because Jules, his Jules, currently had her attention completely focused on the tall blond with the too wide shoulders and too broad smile to see anything else. They were spotlighted in the middle of the dance floor, her right hand comfortable in his as she looked at him with dark smoldering eyes and smiled at him through deeply rouged lips. She was giving him a smile that was warm, open and way too friendly to not be sincere and, in that moment, Aaron wanted to break the two of them apart more than anything else in the world. The perfect smile, broad-shouldered jerk gave Jules an equally as smoldering look back as he gyrated his hips and twirled her in and out towards his body, letting his hand skim across the bare patch of skin exposed on her lower back due to her tight cropped tee shirt.

Aaron hated the way the short flirty satin skirt she wore flared out with each turn and swished against the guy's thighs. Entranced, Aaron didn't turn away and continued to watch. His gaze going to her legs, gorgeous and setting him on fire with each of her quick steps. Each flick of her foot only stoking his anger.

Suddenly he felt like a toddler who had his most favorite toy taken away. Only Jules wasn't a toy. She was his everything. Someone he couldn't live without and didn't want to try to live without any longer. Finally, the music stopped, and Aaron let out a breath. The DJ spoke up. "Alright, that was incredible. Now, who will have a go of their own. Grab your partners and join in for your lesson. Are there any takers for a lesson from either Brenden or Jules?"

Once again, Aaron acted without thinking. His body being propelled forward. He could see the other cruisers, some openly pausing in their own merriment to stare at him curiously. But he only had eyes for Jules, and finally, she looked his way. Upon seeing Aaron her eyes went wide and her deep red lips formed the shape of an O. Their gazes locked as she turned from an eager older man with a hungry grin who was trying to get her attention.

"I think I'm in need of a refresher," Aaron said, as the rest of the room faded away.

"What the hell are you doing? Don't make a scene, Aaron," Jules hissed. She could not believe this man. He should be in his cabin or at the most with the rest of the VIPs of his crew in the VIP area. Not here. She looked around and saw no one from his camp. Only curious fans and lots of cell phones.

"Everyone is staring," she said, trying to get his head on straight. She looked to Brenden, but he was already elbow deep in another VIP passenger named Drucenda. She'd been on other cruises with them and was one of their status elites. There was no way Brenden was not giving Drucenda her lesson, though the woman was an excellent salsa dancer in her own right. Brenden shrugged and smiled as if to both apologize as well as give her an I told you so. Still, Jules was about to turn away from Aaron and take the older man Orson up on his offer when a hand snaked around Aaron's shoulder. "I can give you a lesson."

Freaking Poppy? How had she magically appeared. Jules had

just scanned the room. Maybe she had a tracker on Aaron. Jules stared at Poppy a moment and her familial hands on Aaron's shoulder. Jules stepped forward. "Thanks, but I've got this."

Aaron grinned stepping out of Poppy's grasp. Annoyed with his satisfied grin, Jules couldn't help her own bit of satisfaction when she caught Poppy's scowl as Aaron moved away from the woman and walked further toward her.

"Hey there, Pop. I thought you promised me a dance?" Morris said from by Poppy's side.

"Did I," Jules heard Poppy say looking over at Aaron. "Oh, yeah, I did." She took Morris' hand and pretended to shimmy something that wasn't quite a Salsa, but Jules gave her a C for trying.

It was then that Aaron moved in closer and smoothly slipped his arm around her waist, taking Jules' mind off the silly little floorshow entirely.

Shudder, swoon, melt. Crap his hand felt good. Wait. Concentrate woman. He only just put his arm around your waist. It wasn't that big a deal. Just keep it professional and you'll be alright. Besides, she looked around, they were in the middle of the Beach Lounge's dance floor with just about every eye on them. She had to keep her distance and stay professional.

The music changed to something with a slightly slower tempo, supposedly to let the more novice dancers keep up, but all it did for her was accentuate the sensuousness of the nature of the music. Aaron's fingers splayed and the heat of them radiated throughout her back as he pulled her closer to him. Unwillingly, she let out a long and low breath as the present slipped away and she was suddenly transported to the past. To a moment where all was warm and wonderful, and she felt nothing but happiness and hope in the arms of the man she loved. It was everything. Her breasts against his hard chest, the quick beating of her heart making steady time with his as he dipped a hip low and her body immediately moved to his rhythm.

They were dancing again. Moving, swaying, going with the rhythm of the music while also following the beat of something else entirely. Something they always shared when they got within a certain distance of each other and mysteriously synced together.

It was as if their bodies became one and each movement, beat, and breath was a direct reaction to the other. For the moment, Jules let herself go with it. Lost herself to the overwhelming feelings of being in his arms again. She missed that feeling and when he looked her in the eye, and they clicked, it was as if she was shot with a love dart right square in the center of her chest.

Just then the music changed tempo again and thankfully the spell was broken before she could be fully and completely drawn in by Aaron and his charms. Jules blinked and it was no longer just the two of them but them and the hordes of questioning eyes taking in their sensual dance and her, dammit, way too emotional responses. Aaron swung her out then pulled her in close once again. She held up a hand to his chest, blocking him but not the feel of his rapidly beating heart, the large hand on her thigh as her traitorous leg still came up on its own and wrapped around his behind. *Shit. Body come on! Get with it and catch up to the brain!*

"We need to talk," his voice was husky and deep against her ear.

From the feel of him under her thigh it didn't seem like talking was on his mind.

"Yes, but now is not the time," she said.

His eyes got deadly serious. "Then make the time and soon. I won't hold out. If you don't set it, then I will, and I don't think you'll be happy about my time or place of choosing."

Jules sucked in a breath as Aaron pulled her in again with a wicked grin, then he gave his bottom lip a lick that sent her insides to liquid along with just about every other woman in the near vicinity as she heard a corporate sigh wave throughout the room. Jules blinked back into conscious. It was time to get this straight. To get him straight. "Like I said, now is not the time. I'll find you later. Don't mess this up for me. I didn't get in your way. So please afford me the same courtesy."

Putting on her smile once again, Jules let out a breath and pushed away from him. It was too easy though because he'd already let her go and she'd almost stumbled back on weak legs. She made her way to the small stage and the MC, taking the mic from his hands. "Great job everyone. Let's keep this party going and don't forget the drinks are flowing. DJ, bring that quick beat back and get this floor shaking!"

A cheer went through the room and she looked towards the bar noticing that Brenden had gone over and was now flipping bottles in the air while standing and gyrating. Thank goodness for his sweet soul. He probably sensed the tenseness she was feeling and even if he didn't, she was grateful for the distraction from where she and Aaron had made such a show on the dance floor. She looked back to where Aaron had been standing, expecting for some reason to see him still there, but he was gone. Her eyes instantly went to the doorway but all she saw there was the quickly retreating figure of Poppy, her strawberry blond hair flying behind her. No doubt she was chasing behind wherever Aaron went off to. The thought left Jules with nothing but a sinking feeling.

# Chapter Seven

Aaron couldn't get the shower cold enough, so he gave up trying. There was no cooling off from that dance with Jules anyway. As the water streamed over his body, he gave up on torturing himself and turned the tap to hot, letting the water temperature match that of the blood pulsing through his body, and proceeded to soap up. He let out a sigh and put his head back against the shower wall. He was exhausted. Not so much physically, though this had been a long day, but mentally. No, emotionally, since though geographically he was currently in the same location as Jules, he didn't feel any closer to her.

Check that, he thought, as the image of her flashed in his mind. The dilation of her pupils, the pulsing of her lips and slight beads of perspiration that he saw dapple her skin at the end of their dance—there was no faking that. She may say she was totally over him, but her body's response to him said something different. Something instinctual, almost primal. She couldn't hide that. And he couldn't hide or deny what her reaction did to him.

It was probably for the best that they were interrupted by the crowd and her getting skittish. He almost, without any talk, let it all go and took her right then and there on the dance floor with all eyes on the two of them. Wanting to taste those sweet lips like nothing he'd ever wanted to taste before in his life. At this he didn't care who knew how he felt, but knew he had to tread carefully, or everything could blow up in his face. A move like that and she could good and well be done with him forever, plus his career could be over. Or close to it. Sure, he could maybe get past the studio but the press, the internet? They could be quite unforgiving.

But what did his career matter? Yes, he was well on the way to something big, but with each small victory he'd gotten, it felt incredibly hollow when he couldn't share his joy with Jules. The fact that she'd cut herself off from him completely burned him beyond belief. It was so unfair and one sided. Sure, a part of him, the logical part, got her reasoning but his heart could never quite catch up. The fact that she used him and his career as her excuse for their break just didn't sit right.

Aaron dunked his head under the spray, trying to wash the dark thoughts he was having from his mind as he rinsed shampoo out of his hair. Dark thoughts mixed with pent up sexual frustration didn't bode well, and he'd frankly had his fill of both over the past year. Turning off the shower in frustration, he dried off, wrapping a towel around his waist as he stepped back into his suite. He grabbed a beer in further pursuit of cooling down and once again reached for the divorce papers she'd sent as he pushed aside the box with her ring in it. He growled. She was hell-bent on him signing and now. Why was that?

Could it have something to do with the handsy stew with the fast hips. Aaron didn't want to really consider it but for some reason he couldn't get past how good and how right the two of them looked out on the dance floor. They seemed happy, comfortable and in sync. For the first time since he'd seen Jules on this trip she wasn't visibly tied up in knots and her lips weren't drawn in a taut line. With that dude she was relaxed and Aaron's selfish ass, while he knew a part of him should be happy or at least relieved for her, well, truth be told, he hated it.

"Why can't she be that relaxed with me?"

Just then there was a knock on his door, and he gave another frustrated huff as he put the papers back in the envelop and threw them on the counter. It was after midnight. He hoped like hell it wasn't Maribel. The maid had been to his room twice in the short time he'd been back. He was certain he'd put the do not disturb light on outside, but for all he knew it could be Morris. The guy never quit.

Aaron looked down at his towel and paused, but if it was Poppy, he was going to give her a piece of his mind once and for all.

Padding to the door, Aaron looked out the small peephole, jumping back in surprise when he saw Jules' angry expression on the other side.

He looked down at himself in the towel once again and grinned before opening the door wide.

Jules' brows shot straight up upon seeing Aaron standing in front of her dressed in only an *Elegance* issued towel. What the heck? Did she just walk in on something? She knew she was taking a huge risk coming to Aaron's cabin at this time of night, but she wouldn't be able to rest if she let things stand another moment with the way they were. After his display in the Beach Lounge, she had to put a stop to things. But, it wasn't without a small amount of fear that she'd knocked on his cabin door. Afraid that he wouldn't be alone after seeing how Poppy had run out of the lounge behind him. And there he was, opening his door in only a towel, looking like sex on tap.

Jules shifted her eyes left to right, then closed her gaping mouth, trying hard to control her whirling thoughts. "I'm, um, sorry. This was a mistake. I shouldn't have disturbed you. I can, um, come back when you're not so busy or text me and we'll meet to…" she let her gaze go over Aaron's shoulder, toward the bed. Not able to get a clear look her eyes went back to him. Towel, chest, face. "…morrow. We could meet somewhere discreet for coffee when you're free and talk. Well, catch up," she stuttered, trying to cover in the case of listening ears.

She turned, her rapidly beating heart loud in her ears, when Aaron's voice penetrated her mortification. "No, we're having this out now."

His hand was on her wrist then and he was pulling her back around.

She looked behind him again. Then shook her head. "Aren't you busy?"

He let out a frustrated sigh and looked at her deadpan. "Busy doing what Jules? Tell me what you expected to walk in on here tonight?"

Just then Jules heard the click of one of the crews work doors opening down the hall. Shit. She didn't want to get caught outside of Aaron's room at this time of night. Though she could come up with any number of excuses to be here, it would still take a day to let the question die down. She pushed at his naked chest, backing him up, and walked into the cabin.

The fact that she felt relief at finding him alone made her feel incredibly foolish. She'd told herself months ago that it didn't matter what Aaron did. She'd walked away. But still, upon finding the cabin empty, the only signs of habitation coming from him did give her an undeserved sense of satisfaction.

"So. You didn't answer my question," Aaron said, coming past her, his voice smooth and sexy as he looked her in the eye. His eyes were beautiful. Despite being laced with anger and questions they were dark, sharp, and smoldering. Her gaze shifted, looking for someplace else to rest and get a break but everywhere she looked it was all him. His hair, damp and clinging to his forehead and the nape of his neck where droplets of water clung then trailed down. He was all shoulders, chest, abs and oh lord, that towel. She stepped back.

"You want to put on something so we can talk?"

Aaron laughed. "What? You can't talk with me like this? It's not like you haven't seen me in less. Besides, I would think being on this floating paradise you see men in lots less than this all the time."

She rolled her eyes. "It's not the same!"

"Oh, really what's different? Is it the towel? Maybe? Am I wearing too little? Would it make you happier, more comfortable or stoke your fantasy if I were say wearing a tight white officer's uniform?"

Jules frowned. What was he talking about? But then it hit her. Brenden. He was jealous. This was the second time Aaron had brought him up. So, he actually thought that though she was still married to him she'd be sleeping with another man? And another guy on the cruise. It was almost too much. "Are you kidding me with this? What makes you think I'd be into Brenden or anyone for that matter. We are still technically married."

Aaron let out a growl and rubbed his hand through his hair. "Technically? That's all you see me as Jules, a technicality? Damn, woman when you left, I thought it was harsh, but I didn't know you could be cruel."

"Well, what do you see me as? It's been a year, Aaron, and you and Poppy look pretty close. Let the tabloids tell it, you and she are practically engaged."

He stared back at her. Jules noticing for the first-time real hurt in his eyes. Her heart seemed to fracture with the image.

"So what? This is how you've squared it all in your mind," he said going and picking up the manila envelope. "You went and got in your head that I've moved on and was bedding someone else, while still married to you, while I was still hopeful to get back together with you, dammit still waiting for you. I can't believe you thought so little of me."

Jules couldn't have felt lower. She hated the way Aaron was looking at her. She'd left so she'd never have to see that particular haze of resentment in his eyes and here she'd gone and put herself in the direct path.

"I'm sorry," she said, her voice steadier than her actual feelings. She never wanted to cause him pain. She loved him more than anyone in her life. She only wanted to see him happy. This is what this past year had been about, hadn't it?

He threw the envelope on the bed. "Sorry? For what exactly? Making assumptions about me, my fidelity or walking away from us without even giving me a chance to be the man I said I was."

Jules looked down at the envelope on the bed, then back up at Aaron. Once again, her mind went to war with her heart and her body. This wouldn't do. She had to stay strong for herself, but mostly for Aaron. "I'm sorry for a lot of things, Aaron. But for walking away I'm not. It was the best thing for both of us. Look at how your career has gone. You are on your way to the top. I know you wouldn't have gotten there with me hanging onto you."

In a flash, Aaron strode across the estate room toward her. "What are you talking about? So what if you were by my side. At least we would have been together."

He was close, so very close, his emotions practically pulsating from his body onto hers. She needed to keep her cool, but it was almost impossible with him so near.

She looked up at him. "Yes, we would have been together, but it wouldn't have been the same. Every other interview you did would have been about your movie, yes, your great acting and then the question would come up about if you're single or married. The fact that you were married would have closed the doors for so many fans."

"So what, it would have kept the door open for us though," he said, his voice full of desperation and longing. "I wanted you with me. Near me. Loving me. I needed you, Jules."

Jules closed her eyes a moment and took a breath. Was what he said true? Did he really want her with him through those interviews, shoots, and all the days that had passed? She knew she wanted to be with him, but still there was the fear.

"I needed your love, baby."

Jules opened her eyes and looked at him. He was everything to her and he was there. Finally, there in front of her. She thought of all her lonely days and even lonelier nights. How lost she'd felt. How much sorrow and shame she felt for how she'd ended it. She'd needed him too.

The revelation of it hit her hard in the heart, and at the same time in places she'd essentially kept closed off for the past year. Only opening to Aaron in her fantasies in her most private times and thoughts. She reached up and slowly slid her hand around his neck. Tipping up and leaning forward she let her lips meet her husband's once again for the first time in so very long.

The rush was incredible. Like all her past fantasies came to life in 4D. He invaded every one of her senses at once as his lips softened and pulsed under hers and his hand came around her waist to pull her in close to his body. Instantly, Jules felt his hardness on her upper belly and heat pooled between her legs. Easy, she was always so damned easy when it came to him. With that thought, doubts started to crowd her mind as his hand went down and cupped her behind softly while he coaxed her lips apart with his tongue.

"Don't do that, Jules," he said, his voice a low whisper into her mouth. "I know the moment you start thinking. Don't think right now. Just feel. It's been way too long, and this is heaven."

"Heaven," she breathed out. He was right. It was heaven and why was she denying herself this bliss? Jules let her lips open to receive Aaron's tongue at the same time she ran her hand across his chest. He felt perfect. He let out a small moan as their kissing dominance switched and she sucked lightly on his tongue. Enjoying the throb of life within her mouth. The feel of them as one. Their breaths and bodies melded as they sunk to the bed.

Jules wrapped her legs around Aaron's waist as he pulled back and looked her in the eye. His stare was long as if he was trying to really see her, to both see her and memorize her at the same time. He was looking deep. Deeper than he'd ever looked at her before. She stared back at him. He was still her Aaron, the same but still she could see how he'd changed over the past year. It wasn't just the slight physical change in his body, he'd changed mentally. The old Aaron never looked at her this hard, he didn't study her in this way. Their relationship, though close to perfect, she could now admit had been more about him, even when he was loving her. That man was easy, this man was not and it worried Jules that she couldn't read this Aaron's thoughts the same way she once did.

He leaned down and kissed her on the pulsating point of her throat. Instinctively she arched her back, her breasts pushing up at him.

"So, are we doing this?" he asked, gazing into her eyes.

She nodded. "I don't see how I can stop."

He smiled and Jules was both excited and chilled at the same time. No, there was no way she was stopping. He was here and she wasn't missing out on this opportunity to be with her husband at least for one more night.

# Chapter Eight

Aaron woke with a smile. Jules was still there. Warm and perfect by his side. Last night had been more than he could even dream of. They made love three times, and he was exhausted but also exhilarated. Not that he could brag over much. The moment he was inside of her the first time last night, he'd come so fast it was almost embarrassing. Of course, in true Jules form, she didn't let it pass.

They were breathing hard and she was ready, so ready, naked and under him, happy and complete from her own satiation under his hands and mouth and there he was as ready to go as he'd ever been in his life. He was so excited when he finally sank deep into her, he couldn't hold back and let go within moments. Gah! Seconds maybe. Some action star he was. They were each silenced and panting hard when suddenly Jules burst out laughing.

"What's so funny. This is embarrassing and you're laughing. You really have changed."

"No," she said. Leaning up and kissing him. "I guess you really did mean what you said about not being with anyone else. I, well, enjoyed the compliment of your quick release."

He groaned, quickly followed by a laugh, looking her in the eye. It felt so good to be with someone he could trust this much. "Fine, Mrs. Smarty pants. Game on. Be prepared for a long night. I may have been quick that time, but I've got a strong rebound. You will rue those words," he said, leaning down and taking her nipple into his mouth.

She giggled and wiggled under him. "Oh, game on for sure. I look forward to seeing how well you score tonight, Mr. Manning."

Aaron couldn't stop smiling thinking about it. And having her with him now, having her in his arms, made him feel complete.

"What time is it?" Jules said, suddenly bolting up and jolting Aaron out of his musings.

"What?" he asked, confused by her jumping up and at the same time nervous because she was way too quickly moving out of the space of his arms. Aaron pulled her back in and down towards him, relieved to have her body next to his once again.

"Where are you running off to?" he asked. "It's only 6:30. Way too early for you to be getting up. Besides we barely got any sleep last night at all."

Jules groaned and brought her hand up to cover her eyes. "Don't remind me. What did we do? What did I do?"

Aaron couldn't keep the confusion from his voice. "Honey, I know it's been a long time for the both of us, but I'm sure you don't need to have me explain to you in detail what we did. Now if you'd like a repeat of it to further your education, I'll be happy to oblige," he joked.

Jules pushed at him and went to get up. Immediately noticing her nakedness, she grabbed at the sheet covering them and used it to cover her own body. Aaron cocked his head at her when she looked down and noticed that her sheet swipe left him naked and at full attention. He raised a brow "Like I said, would you like me to explain further?"

"Ugh. You are infuriating," she replied, as she threw the sheet back on him and reached down to the floor, grabbing for her discarded panties and bra from the night before and quickly putting them on. Jules turned back Aaron's way as she pulled her shirt down over her head and let out a frustrated sigh. "Aaron, I don't have time for this right now, and honestly I really did just come here last night to talk." She smiled and, in that smile, he could see the memory of what they did the night before fluttering across her mind. There was no regret in that smile, only sweet pleasure, and he felt his body twitch with the longing to bring that pleasure back to her once again.

"Okay, fine then," Aaron started. "Let's just say we talked in our own special way. You and I were always great communicators, Jules."

Jules looked at him, her expression going blank. "You know as well as I do that what's going on between us will take more than a fantastic night between the sheets."

Aaron swallowed and closed his eyes against her cold words. Finally, he looked back at her, wanting to say so much but not able to truly control his thoughts as they tangled together. "A night between the sheets? So that's all last night was?" he asked. "I thought we were on our way back to building something special. Enough of this being apart Jules. It's time for us to come out into the light once and for all."

Aaron tossed the sheets aside and went to get up and head to his duffle. He was about to reach inside for the box when Jules put her hand on his and stopped him.

He turned around and took in the desperate and scared look in her eyes. She shook her head. "No, last night was more than just a toss in the sheets and you know it. Last night was the goodbye we should have had but didn't and that was my fault. I'm so sorry I robbed you of that. I should have given you a proper goodbye and in person instead of leaving like I did. But we're over. We have to be over. More than anything, Aaron, I want to see you happy, and I want to see you succeed. And for you to do that, I can't be in your life." Tears pricked her lashes, and Aaron's hands shook with the need to wipe them away. Catch them before they fell.

"I know how this business is," she continued. "I know what the studio said, and they were right. You ask Morris and he'd agree. This is for the best." She paused for a moment, and he could see the wheels turning in her head. She swallowed. "Who knows if it was later in your career, maybe three or four years down the line, and you were a little more established, things could be different, but I won't have you hold on and wait for me. It's just not fair. I want you to live truly, freely, and happily; do everything it takes to realize your dream. I won't be the one holding you up from that."

Aaron was stunned speechless. She couldn't be more wrong, but he didn't know what it would take to get through to her. He watched as she put on her skirt and slipped on her shoes. She bent to pick up the discarded envelope from the night before from where it had ended up wedged between the loveseat and the nightstand.

"Please sign," she said. "Do this for you. Don't let anything hold you back anymore."

And with that, she went to his door, opened it carefully, looked out he supposed to make sure the coast was clear and then she was gone.

## Chapter Nine

Jules was in full panic mode and it annoyed her more than anything else. She didn't do panicking. She was the queen of cool and prided herself on that fact. But there she was after one night with Aaron and she didn't know herself or her mind anymore. Thankfully, she successfully snuck out of his room and back into her own, though there'd been a few hairy moments in the hallway when she'd almost gotten caught by a couple of folks from the cleaning crew on her way down to her cabin.

She was lucky enough to have made it up in the ranks and have a cabin to herself. At least there would be no need for explaining. She didn't know what excuse she'd give a roommate if she had to. Fraternizing between crew was generally frowned upon but a regular occurrence in their line of work where the tours were so long. So once hookups happened it was big news. It was even bigger news though if said hookup happened with a passenger. That was pretty much a no go.

But Aaron wasn't just a passenger. He was technically her husband, even if no one knew it. And try as she might, she couldn't hang what they did last night in the hookup category.

After a quick wash up, Jules changed to get in a run on the treadmill in the staff gym. She wasn't on call until later that evening but had to get rid of some of her anxiety somehow. She found the gym empty except for Angelo who was pretty much a workout fiend. She greeted him and got a nod back, between his bench presses when a text came through on her phone.

Crap, she should have known he'd not give up so easily. Annoyed, she marched towards the VIP guest gym.

"What is it Aaron? Why did you call for me?" she asked her

arms crossed over her chest, eyes squarely on his and not on his chest straining his tank top or his thighs giving his workout shorts a workout of their own.

He looked her up and down. "You going for a run this morning?" he asked. "I had a feeling you would be. You usually do that when you have some things you want to work out in your mind. Why don't you run with me? I have some things I want to work out too?"

Jules frowned. "Staff don't usually exercise with guests. At least non-trainers don't. Now if you'd like a trainer, I'd be happy to call one for you."

He gave her a bland smile. "You know I would not. I'd like you to run with me. I'm not asking for anything more. You can at least give me that." His look grew more challenging. "Besides, I'm a VIP don't you all pride yourselves on doing just about anything for your VIP's. I'd think this would be nothing."

They stared at each other for a few moments, but Jules already knew that Aaron had won. He was right, they would do anything for their VIP's or at least close to it. If she said no she'd probably come off as petty and she didn't want to give him that type of power. Why let him know he was getting to her that much. She needed to be cool and just get through this.

"Fine, I'll run with you."

"Great!" He grinned wide and reached out to grab her by the hand and pulled her towards the outside sky deck. When Jules pulled back, he turned to her. "It's a beautiful day. Why not take in some air while we run?"

"Why can't we just run on the treadmills here. It's quiet and there's nobody around. You can still get your workout and I'll be right here, too."

He tilted his head and gave her a challenging glare. "Have you always been this timid?" The fact that he asked the question both infuriated and embarrassed Jules.

"What do you mean timid? I'm not afraid of anything?" she protested.

He shook his head. His eyes softening. "Really, because from where I stand it looks like you're afraid of everything or at least everything when it comes to being seen with me."

His words hit her hard, but Jules couldn't let him know that. "Okay. We'll run outside. This ship is big, and a few laps around will be a good workout. Most people are probably still asleep anyway, getting over the parties last night," she mumbled to herself.

Aaron nodded and headed out. "Come on I'll race you. Let's see if you still have some of your old speed, Mrs. Manning."

Jules felt heat rise in her cheeks at the use of her married name. She couldn't tell if it was anger or joy, since she hadn't heard that name in so long. Still the rush of pleasure was undeniable, and instead of arguing she followed Aaron out onto the sky deck.

As they ran Jules took in how finely-honed Aaron's muscles had become. How truly, devastatingly handsome he was. He was so much more then he appeared on the screen or the internet blogs, or in the tabloids. This man was magnificent and, for a short time, he'd been hers.

Was she a fool to have let him go without even a fight? Maybe she was, but she couldn't help but be happy for him. He was indeed talented, and he was doing what he was meant to do. That was incredible. Jules let go and, in that moment, took in the cool breeze kicking up from the ocean as the *Elegance* made its way, cutting swiftly through the choppy seas. There was no land on either side of them, only blue water and wind against their bodies as the two of them ran, their movements and breaths keeping time with each other.

They made it two whole laps around the ship without talking, or teasing or bickering and thankfully, without seeing any passengers; for that time, Jules was happy. It almost felt like old times. On their third lap Jules felt curious eyes trained her way as the ship started coming to life and morning passengers came out to take in the splendor of the day at sea. That too, felt too close to old times, the early days when Aaron's star was early on the rise and he was just starting to get recognized. She was always getting harsh looks, questioning glares that made her feel like a third wheel in their relationship for two.

Jules' gait faltered when she caught the questioning eyes of a couple of twenty somethings looking at her and Aaron. She faltered even more when one of the deck crew members winked at her as she passed while he was putting out chairs for sunbathers. And, oh no, was that a paparazzi lens trained their way?

Aaron stopped and looked back at her. For the first time she noticed how far she'd fallen behind him.

"Hey, what are you doing way back there? We've got two more laps to go, Jules. Come on, this is a workout not a walk out," he yelled playfully.

She nodded and gave him a thumbs up. She wouldn't show her fear, not now when she only had to get through these next days. That's all she had to do and then this would all be over. There would be no more judging eyes and no more speculation. Aaron ran in place waiting for her giving her a shrug and a big smile. In that moment, it was as if the sun became even brighter and she got a new burst of energy. She ran fast and went past him, poking him in his side. "Now who needs to catch up?" she teased and stuck out her tongue.

"Oh, you'll pay for that," he said, running to catch up to her.

No doubt I will, Jules thought to herself, no doubt I will.

## Chapter Ten

Jules should have known the feeling of joy she had wouldn't last. She successfully finished her run with Aaron and thankfully extricated herself from him without any further talk of reconciliation, though none of divorce either, but she was happy enough to leave it as it was with just their run. She made her way back to her cabin for another quick shower and change before heading to the staff dining hall. She'd barely finished, when her phone buzzed again. She half expected it to be Aaron but saw it was Dina with an SOS, telling her to meet her at her cabin right away.

"What the hell is going on," Dina started in. "Are you and that star hubby of yours back together? Why do I have to call out to you for this kind of info. Shouldn't I be the first, well, at least the second to know?"

Jules pulled up short, before letting out a huff. "No, we are not back together. What makes you think that?"

"Well, you were up bright and early running together. And frowns aside, your skin is positively glowing."

Jules sighed. She couldn't deny either, but, damn, news traveled fast. "Doesn't this crew have anything better to do than gossip?"

Dina shook her head. "You know we don't. Now spill. What is the dirt? Did you or did you not finally end your drought last night?"

Jules gave her friend a hard stare, but Dina saw right through it and squealed. "Yay! I'm so happy for you. It was way overdue. I was about to send you to medical if you didn't jump that good-looking man. I'm so happy for you." Her face went serious then.

"But I am going to miss you. It will be boring here without you. But promise me you'll invite me once in a while to your fabulous Hollywood parties, will you?"

"Would you slow your roll," Jules said. "Who says I'm leaving? It's not like Aaron and I are back together. My plan is still on track."

Dina looked confused. "Your plan. Honey, that plan was crap. This plan is so much better. Take your man and go be happy. Live your life."

Jules shook her head. "It's not that easy."

"Why the hell not?" Dina admonished. "You and your plans and need for control, thinking everything must be mapped out to a T. Sure, nothing is that easy, but it doesn't have to be as hard as you're making it. Where is it written that you must live your life for everyone else? And why are you making him live his that way, too?"

"I'm, I'm not."

"If you say so. Listen I know I'm over stepping, but I'm all in now. Why is it you slept with him last night when you have had plenty of offers in this past year from plenty of good-looking eligible men for sex and more? And how about him. From the looks of things with him and that Poppy, I'd say it's pretty much one-sided if that. Seems like a lot of show for me. Why was it less than eight hours in that man's presence and you couldn't keep away from him?"

Jules was stumped. Why, was a darned good question. She'd told herself it was a goodbye, but what was it really? If she was honest, she wanted it. Not it...Aaron. She needed him and needed him desperately in every conceivable way. But how could she be with him when she was such a hindrance to his life? The realization of it all hit her square in the heart at the same time that her stomach let out a loud growl. Saved by the bell! Jules shook her head.

"I don't want to deal with this right now, Dina. The fact that I slept with Aaron last night was a form of closure for me, and I'm glad I did it. But now I'm ready to move on. Come on, let's eat. As you can tell, I worked up an appetite last night."

# Chapter Eleven

It was just a run, Aaron told himself, trying hard to not get excited about his time with Jules that morning. But still he couldn't help it. The little bit of time he had with her was more precious to him than anything he could imagine, but along with that, the thought of having to disembark without her by his side as his wife was almost more than he could bear. He didn't know how he could possibly go on without her. On the outside it looked like he'd made it just fine, but in reality, he was anything but. Back in his room after showering, he rubbed a weary hand across his forehead as he waited for the call time for meeting with the crew to prepare for the fan meeting they would have on board. There was also a private meeting scheduled with the director about *Starboard 2* and he and Poppy's romantic arc. Though he knew the movie and his personal life were separate, it was time to make it clear with the director and the rest of the studio heads that the line must no longer be blurred.

Poppy was a good actor and they worked well together on screen. Aaron also liked the direction of the new script, but he'd no longer be a pawn to advance another person's career. This was ending now. He and Jules' happiness was worth so much more to him, even if it meant this would be his last moments in the spotlight.

Aaron sent a quick text to Morris letting him know that he was on his way, then headed off for the meeting.

The day progressed better than Jules expected. Thanks to Dina she had been able to squash the rumor mill amongst the rest of the staff about what could possibly be going on between her and

Aaron. Everyone knew that she was a stickler for her job and would do whatever it took to keep the guests happy or at least that was the way Dina had spun it. In the end, the star run turned out to not be such a big deal.

She spent the rest of the day everywhere at once, losing herself in her job, though thoughts of Aaron were never far from the forefront of her mind. Especially when she thought of the following night's masquerade party. It would be a big hit with the guests and staff alike, she was sure, but she couldn't help being nervous about the Starboard crew's role in it all. There would be a special meet and greet opportunity for their super fans on the Starlight deck with cocktails. She hoped it all went well and everyone was on their best behavior. When thinking of this event, she didn't know if she was more nervous about the fans or the crew.

She'd successfully avoided seeing Aaron for the better part of the day and found herself in the VIP pool area later that afternoon, her eyes roaming for who, she didn't want to admit. When her gaze finally landed on Poppy, looking gorgeous and sexy seated next to Elena Costa, Jules knew she'd made a wrong move.

She was about to slip back out when Poppy's gaze snagged her, making escape unavoidable, so she made her way over.

"How are you two doing today?" Jules asked. "I was just stopping by to check on everyone to see if there was anything special you needed. Also, to ensure you're all set up for the masquerade event. If there is anything you need costume wise, we have plenty of supplies in our prop department." Jules fought to keep her smile bright.

Poppy gave her a slow up and down with no response. Jules immediately wondered if the woman had a clue about where she'd spent her night. She was about to speak, but Elena chimed in first. "We're good. Looking forward to it. Thanks so much. You're doing a great job, being as thorough as you are. I have to commend you."

Jules shook her head. "It's nothing. I enjoy my job and making people happy."

"Yes," Poppy finally said. Not a hint of America's sweetheart in her voice. "I'm sure you do. But don't worry about us. We're good. We'll put on a great show for you when the time comes."

What the hell bee got in her bonnet? Elena put her hand on top of Poppy's and smiled up at Jules. "Really, we're great. Thanks for checking. We'll see you later then? You all will be having games, karaoke or bingo or something, right?"

Jules knew a dismissal when she heard it, so nodded. "Of course. You can just check the daily schedule." She walked away, stopping by the bar to let the bartender, Alexis, know to keep them happy, which of course she was already handling.

Heading out of the pool area, Jules was glad to get away but ran smack into Morris before reaching the stairs to the next deck. She couldn't help the sigh that escaped her lips before her mind could catch it.

"Good to see we're still on sighing terms, Jules," Morris said jokingly.

Jules shook her head. "Some things never change, Morris."

He nodded. "True that. Though some things, surprisingly do." He looked around. "Listen, can you please spare me a couple of minutes?"

Jules wanted to tell him no, but her curiosity got the best of her. What could Morris have to say to her after their last conversation when he essentially told her she was no good for her husband and his career? She nodded to the clusters of observation seats near where they stood. "Come on. But just a few."

Morris looked nervous but relieved as he gestured for her to lead the way.

Jules sat and Morris followed. He opened his mouth to speak but no words came out. Jules could have made it easy for him, but she didn't want to, so she just stared. Long enough to let it get a touch uncomfortable.

Finally, Morris spoke, his words coming out on a nervous laugh. "Aaron was right, you have changed."

Jules pulled back in shock. "What? That's what you sat me down to say? Um, thanks, now I'm leaving."

Morris reached out a hand and gestured for her to please stay. "No, wait. It's good. It's a compliment."

She tilted her head. "Funny, it doesn't feel like it."

"No, it is. I don't know if you were always like this, but I don't think so. I see a determination in you that I didn't see before. I kind of like it."

Jules was getting more than annoyed. She couldn't care less what Morris saw in her. "Morris, this conversation is ridiculous, and I don't know why we're having it. Let's just agree to live in each other's spaces for the next two days and, don't worry, I'll be out of your hair and a distant memory in no time soon enough forgotten."

Morris looked at her hard, his eyes softening. "Is that what you really think? As if you could ever just be a distant memory or forgotten. Don't you know how you've haunted me for the past year, Jules?"

Jules blinked. What?! Was this a joke? "What the hell are you talking about?"

"Listen, Jules, I'm sorry. Okay. It's not easy for me to admit when I'm wrong, but I was so wrong when it came to you and Aaron, and I'm truly sorry."

Wait. Jules took a breath as she tried to absorb the fact that Morris was admitting to her that he was wrong. It shouldn't matter to her, but she had to admit there was some satisfaction in hearing the words. Still they were hollow. "You don't have anything to be sorry about, Morris. It wasn't like you were wrong. I told you that."

"But I was. Very wrong. I overstepped, and I didn't put my client first. I was too young and eager for money. I'm damned lucky Aaron didn't dump me."

Jules thought about that. It's probably because Aaron never knew about the fact that Morris knew that she was leaving. He looked at her. "I'm going to stop you there. He knows."

She couldn't hide her shock.

"Yes, he knows that I was aware when you were leaving. But you don't know that he tried to get to you. He wanted to stop you from leaving, but I didn't tell him when you were going. You left the time of your sailing, and I scheduled his final audition to conflict. By the time Aaron made it to the dock, you were already gone. I was a total textbook ass, and I chose my client's career over his ultimate happiness when they should have been one in the same."

Jules was stunned, and for the moment she just sat in silence. She couldn't believe all that had gone on without her or Aaron's knowledge, but as she thought it over, she looked at Morris and wondered if she would have done anything different for Aaron. It didn't change the fact that she still had written the letter. Still had left. All that had changed was his audition time and the fact that he had been running to try and catch her, but she was gone.

Jules sighed as she thought once again of Aaron's now blockbuster status. She glanced back into the pool area and saw Poppy as she got up from her lounge chair and slipped into a pair of flip flips, tossing her hair over her shoulder and looking every bit the star she was.

Jules looked back at Morris. "Like I said, you have nothing to apologize for. We're cool. It's all water under the bridge."

# Chapter Twelve

The fans were lined up for the masquerade party and the air was palpable with excitement.

Jules adjusted the ribbon of her gold lace mask and let out a breath. She felt pretty in the ship's shite and gold one shoulder issued formal dress. The drape of hers hugged her curves perfectly and made her feel like a goddess even if she was technically on work duty. The Goddess of the Night. Jules scrunched up her face. Wait, that didn't sound quite right, put that way. No matter, she looked great and she was there to make everyone's dreams come true.

But what about her dreams? Jules sighed and looked up at the night sky. It was a perfect evening for being under the stars. The sky was inky black, and the moon was high and bright. The sea was calm and, though Jules knew they were traveling toward Antigua at a fast clip, the *Elegance* cut through the water so smoothly, it was as if they were standing still.

Jules turned to give the space another check. High round candlelit tables dotted the deck but left plenty of room for mingling and dancing. The guests filing in looked terrific in their costumes, like something out of a Venetian fantasy. A small dais had been set on the back railing for the *Starboard* meet and greet, but the Starboard cast would be arriving individually in costume to mingle with the guests. The theme of the party was "guess the star" and it gave the guests an opportunity to potentially speak with the cast of *Starboard* in a more intimate and casual setting.

The wait staff were outfitted in various Venetian harlequin style costumes and snaked in and out of the guests with an assortment of delectables. Everyone seemed to be having a wonderful time, but Jules couldn't help but stay on edge. She mingled and smiled at guests as she quickly spotted Ciro Santos in a pirate's costume that did little to hide his swashbuckling nature. Ivan Erikson made a dashing Musketeer, looking cute with his dark mustache and goatee. His impressive height gave him away. Poppy, on the other hand, was barely concealed, going full Antoinette with hair teased into a high birdcage, feathers, and flowers. Her dress must have been brought on board in its own steamer trunk, it was so wide. Yes, she wore a mask, but the way she spoke in that high distinct voice, you could tell she wasn't even trying to hide her identity. But why should she? The woman was having fun, at least by the looks of things, as a bevy of fans male and female vied for her attention.

Still, Jules looked for Aaron.

Just as she was passing a pillar, a waiter stopped in front of her with crab cakes. "Care for a taste?" he asked soft and low. "I hear they're delicious."

Jules looked past the court jester costume and the harlequin mask to the eyes she knew too well. Aaron quirked up a lip.

"You know I can't eat on duty," she said.

He grinned. "Good thing I can," he leaned down and captured her lips in his own. Once again, Jules' world stopped. Everything went dark and then bright as color flooded all her senses with sparks of light. "Aaron," she breathed out when he finally pulled away.

"God, I love hearing you say my name woman."

All she could do was nod. Just then she heard a click that sounded eerily like a camera shutter, and Jules jumped and looked around nervously. She moved away from him. "What are you trying to do? Don't you care if you get caught?"

He shook his head. "No, I don't. Now, if you care if you do that's another story. But I'm no longer living a lie."

Jules snorted. "Says the man in the full costume, stealing a kiss." She licked her lips, practically still tasting him before turning to walk away. "Can you get it together, please. It's time to be on. There's a Q&A coming up and I'm sure you've got eager fans waiting for you."

Jules stared out at the assembled guests as they looked up at the Starboard dais with eager anticipation. So far, the crew had successfully answered the usual fun questions. How did it feel like to shoot on location? Did they film their own action scenes? What sort of adventures would there be for the next movie, which Aimes Webber successfully sidestepped well? But suddenly the air changed when a question came out from one man who didn't seem much like a fan at all. Jules sucked in a breath when she caught sight of the long-angled lens holder from their run.

"Aaron, you've essentially hit it big with *Starboard* and have been breaking hearts since you hit the screen."

"I wouldn't say that," Aaron chimed in, "though I could not be more grateful for the opportunity to be a part of the Starboard cast."

The man nodded. "Like I said, breaking hearts but for the most part you've been cagey about your love life. All fans have to go on are the reported close friendship between you and Poppy."

Aaron frowned. "Was there a question there?"

Poppy chimed in from Aaron's side suggestively. "We're very good friends."

Aaron blinked and smiled at her. "That we are," he said. "I'm lucky enough to have lots of good friends," he said and the women in the crowd giggled. "But," he continued. "I have long had a love in my life, and she likes to keep our private life private."

Jules sucked in a breath.

The questioning man smiled. "A love or a wife?"

A collective gasp went through the crowd, and Jules would have passed out if she wasn't in such shock.

Aaron looked at her, smiled, then turned back to the man deadpan. "Love or wife? Is there a difference because to me they are one in the same?"

The man nodded and tilted his head. His gaze went from Aaron to Jules and from Jules to Aaron, and suddenly all eyes were now on her. Jules couldn't breath and she felt like she was going to faint, but before she hit the floor Aaron's arms were around her and he was lifting her toward his chest. "Don't worry, darling. The initial shock only stings for a moment and the best part is after this I'll kiss all the hurt away."

# Chapter Thirteen

It was another perfect day in paradise when they pulled into Antigua. Jules prepared carefully for the day, making sure her staff were in place and all the other passengers were well in hand and ready to go ashore for their different excursions. There would be shopping and sightseeing, diving and snorkeling, lazing and lounging. The tranquil island paradise was about to swell in population by a huge percentage and Jules had a lot to prepare. She also knew she was totally deflecting and playing an avoidance game, trying to block out the events from the night before.

But there was no blocking; the news was everywhere. Her phone was blowing up constantly, Dina was just about out of her mind, and though Jules was able to get away from the crowds and Aaron after he'd whisked her away last night, in the end there would be no getting away. She'd finally have to face it all. The world knew she was Mrs. Aaron Manning. However, if she stayed that way was another thing entirely.

She made sure her makeup and uniform were perfect as she got on the tinder boat to meet the Starboard crew for their special excursion of a beachside BBQ off one of the private islands. Jules wanted to give the assignment to someone else, but when she woke, she told herself she could see this through. It was the last day and, come tomorrow, it would all be over. They would leave and she could get back to her life. Surely Aaron would wake and see the folly of this all. Heck, Morris was probably talking sense into him right that moment.

She had her smile firmly in place when the Starboard crew arrived. She was prepared for lots of looks and some questions but was surprised when all she got was the usual questions and complaints about their destination, what there would be to do on the island and what type of food would be served. Wait, did she dream what had happened the night before? Jules frowned. But it all seemed so real. She looked around as the departure time came and no Aaron or Morris showed. She glanced at her phone; no messages from him.

Her heart sank. Well, she guessed she didn't dream it and maybe she had gotten her wish. Aaron must have decided this morning that it was all too much. She was sure she could expect her signed papers when she returned.

Jules put on her work smile and hit the PA. "Are we ready to have a great day?" she asked the assembled crowd.

"Yeah sure." Came the bland reply from Poppy which strangely mildly cheered her. Yep life would surely go on.

When they pulled onto the private island, Jules thought they may have hit the wrong shore. This was supposed to be set up for a BBQ. There should be a volley ball net, a BBQ pit, and where were the lounge chairs? What had gone wrong? She turned to her chief officer. "I think we should maybe be on the other side of the island. We're about to crash some poor person's wedding."

He smiled at her. "Yeah, I think we just might."

Then Jules saw him. Aaron, looking breathtaking in a black tux under a sheer archway. He was staring out at the boat, and even from the distance she could see the nervousness in his eyes. Poppy came up to her, "Are you going to keep that man waiting? Because I sure wouldn't," she said.

Jules blinked back tears and suddenly wanted to hug the brash starlet.

She couldn't get to Aaron fast enough, kicking sand as she went. "What is all of this?" she asked when she reached him.

He shrugged. "I figure if I'm going down, it's not without a fight, Mrs. Manning." Aaron opened a box, showing her the most beautiful ring she'd ever seen in her whole life. Platinum and diamonds that sparkled as bright as the night sky. "It's been too long that that finger has been bare."

She shook her head, "I told you before I didn't need a ring."

"And I told you all I ever needed was you."

They kissed, long and slow, and this time it was everlasting. When they pulled back, the rest of the Starboard crew stood around them, and Jules noticed that Dina was there and Brenden too.

Dina held up a dress bag and waved it her way. "How about we have us a wedding? You know I always wanted to be a guest at a fancy Hollywood type party," her friend joked.

Jules nodded through her tears. "How about we do that. I've always wanted to go to a fancy Hollywood type party myself."

Jules couldn't resist wrapping her arms around Aaron once again and feeling his lips on hers. She couldn't wait to say her vows to him once more. She'd vow to kiss him good morning, while from him all she wanted was to be sent off to sleep at night with an 'I love you,' assuring her a sound sleep and sweet dreams here ever after.

## **The End**

# Acknowledgments

First and always thanks to God for all my blessings and inspiration.

Thank you to Amy for your help and incredible eye.

Thank you to the amazing sisterhood that is Fiction From The Heart. You women are a true inspiration. Jamie, Tracy, Sonali, Donna, Sally, Falguni, Pricilla, Barbara, Hope and Liz, what an honor it is to be in this anthology with each and every one of you and what a joy it is to have discovered our friendship.

And finally, a special thanks to you, our dear readers and members of Fiction From The Heart. You make what we do a true pleasure!

With love,
KMJ

# About K.M. Jackson

A mother of twins, K.M. currently lives in a suburb of New York with her husband, family and a precocious terrier named Jack that keeps them all on their toes. When not writing she can be found on:
Twitter @kwanawrites
on Facebook at www.facebook.com/KmJacksonAuthor/ and
on her website at www.kmjackson.com.
Please sign up for K.M. Jackson's newsletter here:
http://eepurl.com/cFvzKD

# A Wedding in Swan Harbor

by Donna Kauffman

*Dedicated to those who are contemplating reaching
for that second chance.*

*A new start, a fresh beginning.
In life, in love, in whatever you need it to be.*

*I took that leap, and the result is blissful.
I am wishing the same for you!*

# Chapter One

"That's the one! We're definitely saying yes to this dress."

Lily Dawson looked from the bridal shop mirror, down to the admittedly very pretty plum-colored dress she wore, then to her daughter. The corner of her mouth lifted in a dubious smile. "I don't think the mother of the bride is supposed to show cleavage."

"You look amazing." Faith nudged her mom with her elbow. "Come on, live a little! Your only child is getting married, embarking on one of life's great adventures. Take the plunge with me. Do something a little risky." She wiggled her eyebrows. "A little risqué. I'm taking the biggest leap of my life. Surely you can show a little boob."

Hazel eyes met matching hazel eyes in the mirror. Lily did a little shoulder shimmy, setting the aforementioned cleavage to jiggling. Faith snickered, and they were both lost in a fit of giggles.

"If we're putting this up for a vote, I'd like to enter a yes, please," came a very deep voice from behind them.

Lily's gaze lifted to meet a pair of oh-so-familiar green eyes in the mirror at the exact moment Faith turned around and squealed in glee. Lily's daughter launched herself into the arms of her father's oldest and dearest friend. Lily instinctively covered her exposed cleavage with her hand, pressing her palm against her suddenly racing heart.

"Uncle Sam, you came!" Faith hugged him tightly, then let go and grinned up at him. "I knew you would."

Sam chuckled. "I get an SOS from my favorite girl? Of course I did."

"SOS?" Lily asked. Forgetting about her exposed cleavage, she turned to her daughter. "Is something wrong? What happened?"

"No, it's not like that," Faith assured her. She linked her arm through Sam's. "I just—I was going to tell you, but we got all caught up in dress shopping for me, then for you, and planning everything..." She trailed off, glancing up to Sam for help.

Lily looked from her daughter to Sam Fletcher, her late husband's best friend, a man she hadn't seen since he'd made a surprise appearance at Faith's sweet-sixteen birthday party. That had been eight years ago. He'd spent all of his adult life quite far away from his Maine hometown, working in the most dangerous places on earth, doing things he couldn't talk about. So, it hadn't been surprising that he'd been overseas and out of reach when Dan had so suddenly been taken from them four years ago.

He'd called the second he'd been able to, mere hours after she'd buried her husband. She couldn't even remember much of what they'd said. She'd been too numb at the time. She hadn't spoken to him since. Not because he hadn't tried, or because she was hurt or angry. She was neither. It had mattered to her only that he stayed in Faith's life, and he had. That was the most important thing. The only important thing.

Now, though... now he was right there, right in front of her, unavoidable. And she was forced to admit she wasn't thinking about her daughter or her late husband when she looked at Sam Fletcher.

His expression was open, easy, and reassuring, but he glanced to Faith, making it clear that his unexpected appearance was her story to tell.

Lily looked back to her daughter. "Whatever it is, I'm sure it's okay."

Faith nodded, took a short, steadying breath. "It's just... I should have told you sooner. Everyone knows Max and I aren't exactly traditional." She laughed. "I mean, we're getting married in a barn on our blueberry farm, right? No groomsmen, no bridesmaids. Max's dad is his best man, and you're my matron of honor." She smiled. "The whole town is basically our wedding party anyway. We love our small-ceremony, whole-town-reception plan, but..." She trailed off again, and her gaze went to Sam, not exactly pleading, but clearly asking for a little assist.

Sam slid his arm from hers and laid it around Faith's narrow shoulders, the more-than-foot-plus disparity in their height mitigated a little by the fact that Faith had stepped back up on the riser next to her mom. "Your little rebel here might be a teensy bit more like her traditional parents than you'd think," Sam said, his voice a deep rumble filled with sincere affection as he glanced down at his goddaughter. He looked back to Lily. "Her wedding party might be a bit different, but she didn't want to walk down the aisle by herself."

Lily's gaze flew to Faith's. "Oh, honey—"

Faith stepped away from Sam's reassuring hold and took her mother's hands in her own. "Mom, it's okay. Truly. It's not a sad thing. I thought doing all of this so differently, it wouldn't matter. I mean, of course it matters that Dad isn't here, but... you understand, right? I thought it wouldn't be this sad, glaring hole if I set things up a little differently. If I didn't do the big walk down the aisle, if we just kind of gathered together, like we planned. Only... I kept thinking that I want that moment, you know? Where I step out into the aisle, and Max sees me for the first time in my dress? I thought about asking you to escort me, but I want you by my side at the altar. I want to walk toward you as much I want to walk toward Max. I'm so proud to be your daughter. I know that doesn't make any sense, but—"

"It makes sense," Lily said, her voice a little rough from the emotion she knew was swimming in her eyes.

Faith squeezed Lily's hands. "I want you there. So..." She glanced up at Sam. "I asked Uncle Sam if he'd walk me down the aisle." Her gaze went back to her mother's. "I think Dad would really like that. With both Pops and Grandpa gone now, I just..." She trailed off.

Lily immediately pulled her daughter into her arms. "It's a wonderful idea," she said, and meant it. She pressed a kiss against Faith's hair as she held her tight, then let her go. "It's a lovely, sweet thing to want, honey." She looked up at Sam, felt her pulse kick up another notch, and looked immediately back to her daughter. She'd deal with her own issues with Sam Fletcher in her own way, on her own time. This was Faith's special time. "I'm all for it." She took a moment, then looked up at Sam and smiled. "Thank you," she said, never more sincere. "For coming all this way, for being there for Faith. I know it's not always easy for you to pick up and go, and we both—"

"Actually—" he began, but Faith spoke at the same time.

"Oh no! Mom, I just realized we've got the cake tasting in ten minutes," she said. "You better go get changed."

Lily glanced in the mirror, immediately remembered her exposed cleavage, and was proud of herself for managing a bright, reassuring smile, and for keeping her hands by her sides and not covering herself. She might not appreciate having to admit it, but possibly her twenty-four-year-old daughter had a point. Lily could try to be... a little more spontaneous. *But could I please be spontaneous somewhere else? Anywhere else? Wearing anything else?* She met Sam's green eyes in the mirror and felt the warmth steal across her face. Then spread.

"I'm really glad you were able to come," she told him, relaxing when she noted that he comfortably held her gaze and that his eyes never left hers for even one moment. *Of course they didn't. Like your forty-five-year-old-mother-of-one cleavage is so enticing.* Lily liked to think she'd matured a bit from the geeky farm girl she'd been, newly thirteen and hormones all a-flutter, when she'd first laid eyes on Sam Fletcher. *And yet, apparently she hadn't.*

"It's my pleasure and honor," he told her, shooting Faith a fast grin. "I'm looking forward to meeting your groom. Making sure he's worthy." He held up a hand when Faith started to say something. "I owe that much to your dad."

"Dan knew Max," Lily said somewhat abruptly, knowing she sounded a little defensive, protective maybe, despite not meaning to. Lily knew Dan would, in fact, be very happy to know Sam was looking out for his little girl's best interests. Maybe it was the inference that Lily hadn't already properly vetted and approved Max herself, or that her approval wasn't enough. Which was equally silly, since clearly Sam had been teasing. "We all love him, and his family," Lily said, shifting her gaze to Faith, her smile coming naturally then, even as she silently wished she could magically transport herself to the dressing room and away from this quickly spiraling conversation.

Back in their school days, long before she'd started dating Dan, she always seemed to find herself either suddenly and hopelessly tongue-tied or blurting things that never came out the right way when Sam Fletcher was around. That apparently hadn't changed either.

"If cake is waiting, I won't hold you two up," Sam said with a smile, graciously letting the subject drop. He turned and looked around.

"How did you know where we were?" Faith asked.

"I didn't," Sam said. "That was a happy surprise." A man with a measuring tape came bustling toward them, and Sam gave him a nod. "Looks like I'll be needing a tux," he said. "And I didn't happen to have one on me when you called," he added, winking at Faith.

Lily tried very hard not to imagine the six-foot-three, all-grown-up Sam Fletcher in a tux, and failed. Quite spectacularly. She swallowed against a suddenly parched throat. "We shouldn't hold you up, then, either." Lily managed a brief smile, then took Faith's hand and headed straight to the dressing room. She didn't even care if she looked like she was escaping. She was. One good thing about being that forty-two-year-old mother of one, and a widow, was that she'd gotten over worrying about what people thought of her. All that mattered was Faith, her farm, and taking care of the people who helped her run the place.

Used to her mom's no-nonsense approach to dealing with things that made her uncomfortable, Faith just laughed and waved over her shoulder at Sam as she trotted to keep up with her mother. "The cake will still be there when we get there," she told her mother, a little breathless, her cheeks still pink with delight over seeing Sam, or from all of the wedding planning, actually.

Lily quickly changed back into her jeans and hoodie and breathed a bit more easily. Definitely more her speed.

Faith stuck her hand inside the dressing room. "Hand it over," she said, wiggling her fingers.

"I can hang it back up," Lily said, tucking her feet into her work boots. She hadn't had time to change into something more presentable before racing to town to meet up with her daughter. It had been one of those days when one crisis got solved and two more popped up. She honestly hadn't expected to find anything to try on anyway and assumed she'd scope things out, then come back later by herself to find something she felt comfortable wearing. She should have known her daughter's enthusiasm wouldn't allow for window-shopping.

"We're not hanging it back up. We're buying it. I mean, did you see the way Sam looked at you?"

Lily yanked the curtain open with a bit more force than was necessary. "Faith Marie!"

"Mom!" Faith parroted back, pasting a mock look of shock on her face, then breaking into a peal of delighted laughter. "If you could see your face right now. And don't even try telling me you two weren't trying hard to pretend you weren't checking each other out. How long has it been since you've seen him?" She waved her hand like she was fanning her face.

Lily knew her mouth was still hanging open and had to snap it shut again, just so she could set her daughter straight. "Sam Fletcher was your father's best friend and like an uncle to you. Your dad, Sam, and I have known each other since we were kids. The very last thing I would ever do is think—"

"Oh, you were thinking," Faith said, her knowing smile making it clear she was perfectly okay with that. "Dad told me you knew Sam before he did. Grandpa said he worked at his hardware store when you were in high school."

"Middle school," Lily told her. "He was fourteen. And I didn't know him. I mean, everyone knows everyone in Swan Harbor, but we weren't friends. He only worked for Grandpa that one summer. I think it was his first job. I spent my summers working on our farm and babysitting for our neighbors to earn extra money. Our paths really didn't cross." She could hear the nervous babble, but she couldn't seem to stop. "And we definitely didn't run in the same circles in school. I was a science and art geek who spent her spare time drawing or playing in the dirt growing things, and Sam was the quintessential golden-boy jock who dated cheerleaders and prom queens." She laughed. "In fact, he was the one who introduced—"

"You and Dad," Faith finished, looking more intrigued by Lily's blurted explanation, not less. "I know. He and Dad were friends, and Dad had a crush on you but was too nervous to say anything, so Sam approached you and told you Dad wanted to take you to the movies and that you'd be missing out on the best thing that ever happened to you if you didn't say yes." Faith smiled and batted her eyelashes. "So, you asked Dad out, and the rest is legend."

Lily did smile at that, and her heart squeezed, but in a good way. "I did, and it was. I loved your dad with every part of my heart. In that respect, Sam was absolutely right. Dan Dawson was the best thing that ever happened to me." She pulled Faith in for a hug. "And he made it possible for the other best thing to happen to me." She kissed the top of her daughter's head. "You."

Faith hugged her mom back, then straightened. "We're still getting this dress. And don't think you distracted me from my original point. You and Sam might have been worlds apart back in the day, but that was back in the day. Things are different now. You can't pretend that oglefest out there didn't happen. I'm surprised the mirrors didn't steam over."

Lily's mouth dropped open, then closed again just as quickly. "I'm going to pretend this conversation never happened. At least this part anyway."

Faith's teasing smile shifted to one of love and earnestness. "Mom, no one would ever doubt, for one second, that you and Dad weren't the best partnership, the best team, the best parents, ever. I wish, every single day, he was still here. But he isn't. That is our reality now. And he wouldn't want you to be alone. Not forever. And honestly, Mom, who better to forge a new path forward with than someone Dad trusted the most?"

"We need cake," Lily said quite abruptly, simply unable to even consider what her daughter was saying, in any context. She took Faith's hand. "Lots and lots of cake." She hung the dress on the restock rack and was perfectly willing to drag her daughter from the store if necessary.

Faith snagged the hanger as they went past. "I'll just come back and buy it, so you might as well save me the trouble." She waved to Sam, who was now on the riser, being measured for a tux, as they passed.

"Fine, fine, let's just—" Lily stopped talking at that point, not trusting herself to say anything further. Nor did she trust herself to so much as glance in Sam's direction, certain the entire inappropriate discussion she'd just had with her seriously misguided daughter would somehow show over her head in a flashing, neon-lit conversation bubble. Instead, she focused on getting them both to the front of the small bridal shop. Swan Harbor's only bridal shop. Lily knew that every single person in town would know exactly what dress she bought before the sale had been completed. Just as she knew they were likely already gossiping that Sam Fletcher was back in town over coffee and blueberry pie across the street at Dixie's place. Lily supposed she could console herself that at least the blueberries had come from her farm.

Ten minutes later, she and Faith were two blocks over, seated at one of the little bistro tables at Brooke's Bakes, breathing in the rich scents of delicious buttery cake. Like Dixie's, and the bridal boutique, Brooke's was the only shop of its kind in town. Lily and Faith could have driven into Bangor and taken advantage of the much broader array of options in the city, but it was important to Faith to be loyal to the shops and businesses where she'd grown up, on the farm started by her great-great-grandfather. Lily was proud of her daughter for that, amongst many other things.

"So, you're not upset?" Faith asked. "About Sam, I mean?" She lifted a hand. "Not about what I said in the dressing room—I stand by that—but that I asked him to walk me down the aisle? I should have told you right away, and I wanted to, but... I guess I didn't want to hurt your feelings, or make you think I was disrespecting Dad."

"Oh, sweetie," Lily said, releasing some of the tension she'd been carrying since Faith's little recitation in the dressing room. "You could never disrespect your father, it's not in you. I think you're paying him tribute by asking Sam."

"Good," Faith said, relieved. "Because that's how I saw it." She paused, then said, "I know he hasn't been home in ages. And that you two haven't talked much in the past few years. I know we both understood why he wasn't at the funeral, so I assumed things were okay between the two of you, but maybe I should have asked if everything really is okay."

"Everything is fine," Lily said and knew Faith wasn't totally buying that simple statement. Lily debated glossing it over, but her daughter wasn't a child any longer, so she decided to share at least part of it. "I think, back then, it was hard — and this isn't remotely fair or even rational, okay? I know that, I knew it then, and didn't blame Sam. I knew it was my problem. But I think initially it was hard because there Sam was, traipsing all over the world, putting himself in harm's way, no family back home worrying about his survival—"

"And it's Dad who ends up dying instead of him," Faith finished softly. She laid her hand over her mother's and squeezed. "Mom, you were grief-stricken, we all were. No one would blame you for that. I mean, you don't still feel—"

"No, no, of course not. I was very grateful that he continued to keep in touch with you. He's your godfather, and he's always taken that role seriously, and I truly respect that about him. Always have. Especially with your dad gone." She turned her hand over and laced her fingers with Faith's. "With Gramps and Pops gone, too, I thought it was really good that you had him in your life, that he was there for you. I know how much you mean to him, and vice versa. I've always been thankful for that. But he was your dad's close friend, and yes, we all grew up in Swan Harbor, but honestly, Sam and I never really spent much time together, as kids or adults."

"But he always spent time with us when he was home."

"He spent time with you, and he and your dad would go off and spend time together. I wasn't really part of that, and that was fine," she hurried to add. "I loved that they'd kept their friendship strong for so many years and over such a distance. Your dad treasured that, and I treasured it for him. But Sam and I... we both cared deeply for your dad, for you, but that's pretty much all we had in common. It's not like Sam and I ever sat down and talked. I was on the periphery, which felt normal. So, I don't know what I would have said to him, once your dad was gone. Since he remained connected to you, I felt like he had what he needed, in terms of still feeling close to your dad. And you had what you needed." She lifted her shoulder. "That's all that mattered."

Faith nodded, taking it in, giving it honest thought. "Thank you, Mom. For telling me all of that. It does make sense. And it means a lot."

Lily nodded, thinking how lucky she was that she and her daughter had always been able to be direct with each other, that talking things out came naturally to them. To that end, when she noticed Faith was still toying with her napkin, she came right out and asked, "Is there something else? Are you nervous about the big day? How is Max handling all the planning chaos?"

Faith seemed to realize she'd twirled her napkin into a tight spiral and gave a rueful smile, putting it back on the table. "I'm excited, nervous, too, I guess, but not about marrying Max. I just want the day to get here so we can throw this big party and get on with the adventure, you know?"

Faith's eyes were shining with real happiness. She was just so certain of herself, of this next step. Lily knew that and had to remind herself she'd been two years younger than her daughter was now when she'd married Daniel Dawson. They'd still been in college when they'd eloped. They'd been so very certain, too. And they'd been incredibly fortunate to discover that they'd been right. Lily had meant what she'd told Sam. She loved Max, loved his family. They were a generations-old Swan Harbor family, too. Also like Lily and Daniel, Faith and Max had more or less grown up together, too. They'd been a couple even longer than Dan and Lily had been, sending little notes back and forth to each other as early as sixth grade. Best friends, thick as thieves, they'd been finishing each other's sentences before they'd even reached puberty.

Lily felt a pang in her heart, a little stab of loneliness, of missing her other half. Daniel had been all of that for Lily, though it had taken the pair all the way to high school before they'd started dating.

"How did Dad and Sam become such close friends in the first place?" Faith asked. "I don't think I ever asked either of them that, or if I did, I don't remember the answer. I mean, they couldn't be more different."

Lily laughed. "Truer words. Actually, Sam was responsible for that, too. Your dad was kinda nerdy, like your mom." Lily's smile was a fond one. "I was into science. Your dad was a math whiz. He was a bit... socially awkward at times, definitely reserved." Her smile spread to a grin. "Whereas I didn't care so much what people thought and didn't have a problem speaking my mind."

Faith laughed. "*No*," she said, pretending to be shocked. She propped her elbows on the table and her chin on her hands. "Tell me more."

"You know how it is, there are always those kinds of kids who make fun of kids like your dad and me. I blew it off, because why would I want them as friends anyway? I didn't get them, and they surely didn't get me. I think your dad tuned it out for the most part, too. I was just more obviously dismissive of it. Sam happened to see a bunch of kids picking on your dad one day early in their freshman year in high school. And he stepped in, took care of it."

Faith's eyes widened. "He did? Like... how? Beat them all up?"

"No, nothing like that. Sam got most of his height early on, and he was pretty much the most popular guy in school and everywhere else. He didn't have to do much more than step in for the others to take off."

"And Dad? What did he say about Sam doing that?"

Lily laughed again. "See, this is the part of your dad that you and I know, but people who didn't know him, like those other kids back then, not so much. Your dad had this quiet, dry sense of humor that was so wickedly sharp and utterly unexpected. I loved that about him. In fact, that was a large part of what made me fall in love with him, his ability to make me laugh at the most unexpected moments. When the other kids sulked off, their fun ruined, Sam turned to your dad to see if he was okay. Instead saying thank you, Dan just looked at him and deadpanned, 'I was just about to deliver a withering setdown, but I guess your way works, too.'"

Faith's eyes went wide. "'Withering setdown'?" She hooted. "That is so Dad. What did Sam do?"

"What we all always did—he laughed. He was so caught off guard by it, he basically decided he liked Dan right then, and that was that. They were going to be friends. In Sam's mind, they were from that moment on. To Sam's credit, he never stepped in again. He truly befriended Dan, sat with him at lunch, they hung out together." She laughed. "Your dad's social circle was definitely different for having Sam as a pal. But in return, your dad was the one who helped Sam keep his grades up enough so he stayed on this or that sports team when they were in high school."

Faith nodded. "Sam told me that without Dad he'd have never made it into college."

"Their bond was as tight as it was true. I'm glad it continued after Sam left Swan Harbor." Lily smiled. "And I'm glad we chose him as your godfather." She leaned back in her chair, her smile turning wry. "I have to say, I didn't think he'd make as great a one as he has, what with his lifestyle, his work. I should have known, given how his relationship started with your dad, that he'd always stand by you, just like he stood by Dan."

Lily didn't miss the considering look in her daughter's eyes, but before she could say anything, Faith said, "I'm so happy he could rearrange things to get back a little earlier than he'd planned so he could be here in time for the rehearsal and all the other parts leading up to the big day."

Lily frowned. "What do you mean, earlier than planned?"

"Ooh, cake!" Faith said in response, sitting up straighter and picking up the Brooke's Bakes signature pink linen napkin and shaking it over her lap.

Brooke reached their table a moment later, carrying a tray loaded with slices of every possible kind of cake in existence. "I can feel my jeans getting snug just looking at those," she laughingly told Brooke.

"Oh, Brooke, this is amazing." Faith's eyes were round as she looked from the display to the baker. "I will never be able to pick one."

"Maybe we should wait for Max to get here before starting," Lily said.

Faith laughed at that. "Have you met him? He still eats like he's a college linebacker. He has never met anything with frosting he doesn't love. He will be no help whatsoever."

"Except for keeping us from inhaling all of this ourselves," Lily said, looking at the array of plates and wanting every slice.

"True," Faith said, and they both laughed.

"You all take your time," Brooke told them, beaming proudly at their reaction. "There is a card under each plate with the name of the cake and frosting on it. I'm happy to do any frosting on any cake." She handed Faith a small sheet of paper. "This is the full list, the pricing, and some notes on the bottom about which frosting is best for certain kinds of decorating. I have a whole binder filled with photos of decorations and cakes I've done in the past for you to look through as well."

"Thank you so much," Faith said, taking the price sheet, which Lily promptly took from her hand.

"I've got this part," Lily told Brooke.

"Mom—"

"I know you and Max want to handle this yourself, but I want to help."

"You're letting us take over the farm for our wedding and reception—"

"And I'm taking care of the cake." She smiled up at Brooke. "Whatever she wants is fine with me."

Brooke nodded, then looked to Faith. "It's not often I get to make the wedding cake for two of our own. I'm so excited to be doing this for you. If you don't see what you want, or have questions on any of it, you've only to ask."

"You're the best," Faith said, eyes shining. She looked at Lily. "And thanks, Mom. You really don't—"

"I really do," Lily said, then picked up her fork and wiggled her eyebrows. "The only thing left to do is figure out where to start."

Forty-five minutes later, they were both leaning back in their chairs, dizzy from the sugar rush. "I can't take another bite. I also can't decide. I'm sorry," Lily said. She sighed, her eyes closing. "They are all *so* good. I'll have to jog around the fields for the next week to make up for this." She opened her eyes and met her daughter's gaze. "And it will be so worth it."

Faith let her fork drop to the last sampler plate, then looked at the tray. "What just happened? We only had to taste them."

They both laughed, then groaned a little as they looked at the cake carnage littering the table. They had made notes. Faith and Lily had both written notes all over the chart Brooke had given them. "I don't even think I can read my own writing," Lily said.

Faith nodded, squinting at something she'd scribbled on one of the cake cards. "It's like we were in a carb frenzy."

"What happened here?"

Lily's gaze jerked up and met Sam's smiling eyes. First with the exposed cleavage, now in a cake coma... Couldn't he ever, just once, catch her in a good moment? *What happened to not caring what people think?*

"Wedding cake deliberations," Faith told him. "I'm sorry, you missed it." She lifted a plate that had a dab of frosting on the edge. "We lost all control."

"I remember Brooke's cakes. I can't say I blame you." He swiped a dollop of cream cheese frosting with his fingertip and popped it in his mouth. He closed his eyes and nodded.

Lily told herself not to watch, then didn't even try to listen. Her throat went dry all over again as she watched him in his cake-frosting bliss.

From the corner of her eye, she caught Faith looking at her, then at Sam, then back at her, a very satisfied smile on her face. Too satisfied. Lily's eyebrows narrowed.

Faith simply smiled sweetly and popped her frosting-covered fingertip between her lips.

Lily was going to have to have a little talk with her daughter, it seemed. She glanced up to Sam. *Is he in on this?* He seemed oblivious to the undercurrents. Of course, he wasn't. Lily Marie Foster Dawson was the last woman on earth Sam Fletcher would be interested in.

*And he's the last man on earth you can be interested in,* she reminded herself. Not that she was interested. Sure, what red-blooded woman wouldn't swoon a little? He'd been a good-looking kid, and he was a strikingly gorgeous grown man. *And then some,* her little voice helpfully offered.

Still, if she was ever tempted to take her daughter's advice and open herself up to so much as considering the idea of dating— God, just the word *dating* made her want to crawl back into her rambling old farmhouse and never come out—and even if Sam Fletcher ever saw her as anything but the geeky girl from school he'd quite successfully matched up with his nerdy best friend, the very last person she could consider fair game was Sam Fletcher. Ever.

"Did the tux-fitting go okay?" Faith asked.

"I didn't know there were so many body parts a person could have measured," Sam said with a chuckle, "so I certainly hope so."

*Oh my God, Lily Dawson, get your mind out of the gutter.* She immediately pretended to study her cake notes and did not—repeat *not*—think for one more second about the parts of Sam Fletcher that she might like to measure.

Feeling like she was quickly losing control—of herself, of the situation, of life in general—Lily pushed her chair back somewhat abruptly and stood. "I'll go talk with Brooke, tell her we need some time to decide," she said, then unashamedly and unapologetically escaped. Again.

Like that was going to fix anything. Sam Fletcher was back. And in Swan Harbor, there were only so many places a person could hide.

## Chapter Two

Sam Fletcher drove his old pickup down the long dirt and gravel lane toward the Dawson farmhouse, the suspension squeaking and groaning as the tires bounced over the ruts. He'd lost count of how many times he'd driven down this particular stretch of road, to this exact destination. First by bicycle, then eventually behind the wheel of this very truck.

The Dawsons had been a second family to him. Hell, a first family more often than not. He'd had two safe havens back then — school and Dawson Farm. Three, if you counted the playing fields outside school. He'd never known his mother, who'd passed giving birth to him. An event his father had held him accountable for the rest of his life. As if Sam had had some control over that tragic event.

Sam's Grandma Ruby had been a much-needed buffer for the duration of his childhood, moving in full time after the death of her daughter, to take care of her only grandchild. Sam had loved her so unconditionally, thinking about her still made his heart tighten up. She'd passed just after his twelfth birthday, and he'd missed her every single day since. Most of them spent anywhere but at home. Many of them spent right here.

He pulled up in front of the white clapboard house with the green tin roof. The original structure, built by the first Dawsons to settle in Swan Harbor, was long gone, but the current farmhouse stood on the exact same spot. Originally small and square, a two-story saltbox with a deep front porch, topped by two dormer windows and a stacked stone chimney, it was now a rambling series of add-ons and upgrades that somehow managed to make the place look all the more charming with age. Deep flower beds framed the porch that now wrapped around the side. The big oak tree in the front yard, with its squat, immense trunk, still guarded the homestead, giving shelter with its massive umbrella of leafy branches.

A tire swing hung from a lower branch, as it always had. The only bare spot in the thick green lawn was the round circle of packed dirt just below it. The tire sported a fresh coat of white paint, but somewhere along the line, likely once Faith had left for college, Lily had transformed the swing into a hanging planter-bird feeder combo of sorts. Purple and white petunias trailed out of either side, and a wood tray sat snug inside the tire, filled with birdseed.

Lily might have become a Dawson by marriage, but she shared their happy, good-natured view of the world, their love of whimsy, and it showed everywhere he looked. The old, refurbished bicycle parked by the mailbox, the mesh basket on the front porch also filled to overflowing with a cascade of colorful, blooming flowers. The menagerie of birdhouses attached to various fenceposts and tree trunks, each one a clever, colorful design. His smile grew as he noted the little Airstream model perched on top of the corner hitching post, with a little black capped chickadee sitting proudly on top, staking his claim to the shiny little abode.

Sam walked up the white gravel path, shaking his head as he saw that Lily had positioned a knee-high rubber barn boot at the edge of each step leading up to the porch. She'd painted each one a bright color and turned them into planters as well. Green-and-white-leaved ivy spilled over the tops of each one, trailing along the rail and steps. He knew she'd opted for farming full time over pursuing her passion for art, but she'd managed to find a way to bring it into her world, nonetheless.

The Dawsons couldn't have asked for a better caretaker to inherit their century-old farm and homestead. If a newcomer to Swan Harbor were to pull into the spot where he'd parked and look around the place, he or she would see only joy and a home lovingly maintained. No hint of the sadness and tragic circumstances that had struck this family even harder than his own. He admired Lily Dawson for a lot of things, but maybe that above all. This wasn't a front, a happy face painted over a sad reality. This was Dawson Farm. It lived on with an in-your-face cheerfulness that was impossible to resist, and he couldn't imagine a better tribute to all who had come before.

Faith came bursting through the screened front door and raced down the porch steps to meet him just as he reached the bottom step, a broad smile on her happy, pretty face. She might be twenty-four going on forty, but in that moment, he saw only the little girl, with wild red pigtails and a ridiculously adorable splash of freckles across her nose, begging him to push her faster, and higher, in that tire swing. How was it possible Dan's little peapod was getting married? He remembered coming up with that nickname upon seeing the grainy ultrasound photo Dan had sent to Sam's middle-of-the-ocean outpost on the aircraft carrier he'd been assigned to while working a naval intelligence case. Dan often called Sam a hero for his efforts in reducing threats to US sovereignty, but Sam remembered telling Dan that he was the far braver one, tackling parenthood, and he'd meant it. Sam would take braving the high seas and flying into inhospitable territory every day of the week. Twenty-four years later, he was pretty sure he'd taken the easier route.

"Thank you so much for coming out to help," Faith said, breathless and looking lovelier than ever with a happy flush in her fair cheeks.

Her hair was darker now, more an auburn brown, and the freckles had long since faded, leaving a strikingly beautiful woman in their wake. She had her mother's coloring and her father's lean frame. She was the best of both of her parents in more ways than that, and Sam hoped she knew how fortunate that made her.

"I know you must have a ton to do with all you've got to organize now that you're back in Swan Harbor for good."

"I'll have plenty of time for all of that," he told her, and that much was true. He was still coming to terms with many of the individual elements of his decision to return to Swan Harbor, but looking into Faith's smiling, happy face, he knew he'd made the right choice. He needed to cut himself a little slack on adjusting to it all. The wedding as a distraction, it turned out, was just what the doctor ordered. "Until you say your I-do's, I'm all yours."

She hugged him again, then took his arm and turned him away from the house, her enthusiasm palpable, her energy making him feel that much older. "We've moved the equipment out of the big barn," she told him. "Henry — our new field manager, I think I told you — he's raking the dirt floors to smooth them out and remove any debris. Meaning it's a big dust bowl in there at the moment. Once that's settled, we can start laying the temporary flooring." At his raised eyebrows, she laughed. "They're sort of like big square puzzle pieces, kind of like shipping pallets, only solid on one side, that lock together and form a temporary hardwood floor. I know it sounds crazy, but apparently getting married in the great outdoors has become trendy, so there are companies now whose entire purpose is to make all kinds of things that help to —"

"Bring the indoors to the outdoors?"

She laughed. "Pretty much. We're not doing the whole barn interior. Just enough to make a decent-sized dance floor. The rest will have a heavy roll of this kind of Astroturf-looking carpet. Heavy enough that it won't bunch up and trip folks but will also keep the hems of everyone's dresses from turning brown and won't ruin their heels."

He shook his head and chuckled. "Sounds like you've got it all worked out."

"I know it sounds fancy, but it's not really. With having the wedding here and friends helping with catering and photos and making our own table decorations, it's actually pretty simplified and down to earth. Our supply manager, Jake, plays in a band, and they're providing the music." She shrugged. "Honestly, we didn't have all that much left to do but get the tables and chairs. So, Max and I had a little leeway in making it look a little polished."

"It sounds great," he told her, meaning it. "Can't think of a better way to get launched than surrounded by the people who've loved you your whole life."

Her eyes immediately teared up, and his smile fell as he thought he'd screwed up and made her think of Dan, but then she was hugging the air out of him once again and saying, "I'm so happy you're here. Now everything is perfect." She leaned back and dashed the dampness from the corners of her eyes.

Eyes so much like her mother's. Sam tried not to think about that, especially now. Dan's wife was seeing her only child walk down the aisle. From all appearances, every aspect of the event was happily anticipated, with everyone cheering on the happy couple. You couldn't ask for more than that. But Sam knew Lily had to be feeling at least a few pangs with Dan not there to see Faith on her big day and Lily's empty nest maybe feeling that much emptier. Faith hadn't lived at home since college, but Sam knew she was out here all the time. He suspected that as Lily's daughter set up her new little cottage in town with Max, her trips to the farm would become fewer. In a town as small as Swan Harbor, they'd see each other often enough, but both mother and daughter were moving on to new stages in their lives, nonetheless.

Despite all the things Faith had been telling him, about trying to get her mother to look beyond just running Dawson Farm and get out there and get a life… he was pretty certain Faith hadn't meant that Lily needed to be looking in Sam Fletcher's direction. To be honest, Sam was surprised he was thinking about looking in hers. He'd never thought of Lily that way. Well, once upon a time, he'd found himself intrigued by the daughter of his first boss. She was smart, almost intimidatingly so to a guy who struggled to keep his grades up, but it was her confidence, her directness, that he'd admired most. She hadn't put up with fools, and she hadn't seemed to care one whit that she wasn't running with the popular crowd. He'd liked that about her, too.

Same reason he'd taken a true shine to Dan. The moment Dan had mentioned he was interested in Lily, though, that had ended Sam's growing fascination. Dan was perfect for Lily, and Lily for Dan. Sam would have been a terrible choice for her, and given where his life had led him, it was good all around that things had gone as they had.

He smiled. Not that Lily Foster had ever made him think, for so much as one second, that she'd have given him the time of day, even if he had made his interest known. *Smart girl, indeed.*

Now life had turned everything upside down. Dan was gone. Sam was back. With no plans to fly off again this time. He wanted stability, to feel grounded. He wanted to be home. His thoughts wandered to that moment earlier in the week when he'd gone in to get fitted for his tux and had his head completely turned around by none other than Lily Foster. That dress had been something. But it had been more than that. At least for him. Her head bent next to her daughter's and their delighted peals of laughter were what had caught his attention in the first place. Seeing her had all but stopped him in his tracks. And he was old enough now, with enough life experience under his belt, to know he hadn't been the only one so surprisingly affected. At least it had sure looked that way to him. Then and in the bakery later.

If she had been any other woman, he might have pushed things just a little, to determine the lay of the land, to see what was what. But Lily Foster was also Lily Dawson, and widow or not... Dan had been his friend, his ally, his safe port in the wild, out-of-control storm that had been Sam's home life as a child. Looking at Lily and thinking of her in any way other than friend, wife of Dan, mother of Faith, felt like a betrayal. *And yet, you were thinking, all the same.*

He looked over his shoulder at the rambling farmhouse, and his heart filled right up. Dawson Farm would always feel like home to him, that would never change. Just knowing it was here and that he'd see it from time to time... that was enough. He'd look out for Faith, and for Lily. He'd keep that promise to Dan. Not that either woman seemed to need looking out for, but he'd be there for them if and when they needed anything.

Nothing less, but nothing more either.

He turned his attention forward, internally and externally, and followed Faith to the big barn. He let her excited chatter wash over him. Just being here soothed him like nothing else ever did, ever could.

"Oh, Faith, there you are. Good. Max and I need you to—" Lily abruptly stopped as she realized her daughter was not alone. "Sam," she said, neither welcoming nor rude. Mostly surprised, gauging from her expression. And not necessarily happily so. He couldn't tell.

"We need all the strong hands we can get," Faith said by way of explanation. "He offered to help, and I wasn't about to turn down free labor." She looked up at Sam, gave him a wink, then looked back to her mom, gave a little head jerk in Sam's direction, and smiled. "I'll go talk to Max." And she was gone, leaving Lily and Sam standing there, staring at each other.

Leaving Sam to wonder what that wink at him and nod to her mother had meant, because... it couldn't have been encouragement. Could it? She hadn't just left him alone with Lily because she was hoping the two of them would...? *Stop looking for excuses to make it okay. It's not okay.*

The silence between them was awkward when it shouldn't have been, and he hated that, even though he understood it. Or at least he thought he did. He needed to fix that. He owed Dan that, and Lily, too. "I've wanted a chance to talk to you," he finally began. "For a really long time. Too long. To explain—"

She didn't let him finish. "It's okay, Sam." She met his gaze directly then, and he saw sincerity, but there was a kind of distance there, too. He supposed he'd earned that but couldn't help thinking about how she'd looked at him in the dress shop when she'd first seen him again. That reaction, that moment of awareness, had been an honest one, too.

"If it's about not being here for the funeral, Faith and I both understood why. Truly. I know she's said as much to you, and it's sincere. If anything, I'm sorry I didn't think to try and change things so you could be there. Delay the funeral, something. I was really just so overwhelmed, and I wasn't thinking clearly. There was so much—" She blinked a few times, then glanced down, then back up, her gaze clear once more. "I'm sorry you weren't there, but for your sake, not for mine. I know that was hard for you, not to have that chance to say goodbye, and I'm truly sorry."

Her heartfelt apology undid him. He had promised his closet friend he'd always watch out for his family were anything to happen. Of course, they'd always laughed at that, the assumption being that if anyone was going to meet his maker earlier than expected, it would be flyboy-Navy-fighter-pilot-turned-naval-intelligence-officer Sam Fletcher. Not quiet, unassuming, accountant Dan Dawson.

"I should have been here," he said quietly. "For you both."

"I know you would have been if it were possible." She lifted her hand, like she was going to place it on his arm, but then let it fall back by her side. "It was a terrible time for everyone. You included. I understood, and more importantly, Dan would have understood." She pressed on when he would have refuted that. "You know he would have, Sam." When Sam merely gave a quick nod, she went on. "We got through. I'm sorry we weren't there for you, that you had to handle it on your own, while doing... all the things you were doing. Are doing. We are grateful for that, for your service—"

"Don't—"

"It's the truth." She surprised him then by suddenly smiling and letting out a short laugh. "My goodness, Dan dined out on stories about you. He loved being the guy with the inside track on what the amazing Sam Fletcher was doing to keep America safe. You're our hometown hero."

Sam rolled his eyes at that but smiled with her. "If it got him a few free meals from his clients, then I'm happy to have helped."

Lily nodded, still smiling in reminiscence. She looked back up at him, and he thought she seemed... settled now. Looking into her eyes, he saw acceptance, peace. Her words confirmed that. "It's been four years, Sam. Yes, we miss him every day, but we long ago decided to honor him by remembering all the good, thinking about him with joy. He'd want to be with us in shared happiness, you know? It's the Dawson way. And it's a good way to be."

"You're right," Sam said, and meant it. "That's a really good way to look at it. That's exactly what he would want." His smile grew. "It's like you knew him or something."

She laughed at that. "We both did, you and I, in our own ways."

She smiled up into Sam's eyes, and he was struck again by what a beautiful woman she'd become.

"I want this time to be joyful," she told him. "And I want us—you and me—to be okay."

"We're good, Lily. Truly. I'm happy to be here. For Faith, for you, and for myself."

"She's so excited to have you be part of this." Lily paused, but her gaze held his. "I'm glad you're here, too, Sam. I am."

They stood there a moment longer, their gazes still connected.

"Faith sounds happy," he told her. "She and Max seem like pretty smart kids who have really put thought into the decisions they've made."

"Have you met Max, then?" Lily asked, surprised.

He nodded. "I ran into them in town yesterday." He smiled. "He's a hard guy not to like."

The corner of her mouth pulled up in that wry grin she had. "So, he's passed the godfather test, has he?"

Sam waved his hand as if still undecided, then laughed when Lily gave him a knuckle to the arm. "Yes, I think she's chosen well. I mean, come on, a grade-school teacher and high school football coach?"

Lily beamed. "It's true. Could they be any more adorable? They've signed a lease on a little cottage in town, with the prospect of buying it one day." She laughed. "I'm a little proud of her. I guess that shows."

"You should be. She's turned out to be a wonderful young woman," Sam said. "To the surprise of absolutely no one. Seeing as she won the parent lottery and all."

Lily ducked her chin briefly. Her cheeks had flushed with a hint of pink when she met his gaze again. "We got lucky with her," was all she said. "I sometimes think she's the wise one and we're the ones fumbling around, praying we get it right."

"You got it right," Sam said. He motioned to the farmland surrounding them. "Looks like you're still getting things right here, too."

Lily glanced around, the satisfaction he saw on her face all the answer he needed. "Things are going well here, too, yes." She looked back to him. "We're all doing okay."

He nodded. "I was thinking that as I drove in. The place looks even better now than it did before, which is saying something. Pops Dawson would be mighty proud of you," he said, referring to Dan's father, who'd run the farm prior to Lily taking over, as his father had before him and his grandfather before that.

Lily looked pleased by his comment but said, "I can't take too much credit. Pops had this place running like a top when he was in charge. All I have to do is keep up what he started."

Sam grinned. "You were the daughter he never had."

Lily laughed outright at that. "You mean I was the son he never had."

Sam laughed with her. "True. No one was more relieved than Pops when Dan announced he was going to be an accountant, not a blueberry farmer."

Lily nodded, still chuckling. "A farmer he was not." She looked around, and Sam could see all the love and devotion she had for the land, for this place, shining clearly from her eyes. "For all that he loved this place and the Dawson heritage, Pops never held that against him."

"With you already part of the picture, he knew he was leaving it in the right hands."

She nodded. "It used to be that my only real regret was I couldn't find a way to hold on to my family's little farm, but when my mom passed, my dad didn't really have it in him. He was running the hardware store full time, and I was too young to take it on." She smiled. "The folks who have the property now are raising alpacas."

Sam's eyes widened. "Okay."

"Actually, it is. They've improved on our old house, and the place looks really good. Sarah and Wendy both buy blueberries from me, so I get updates, and they've had me out to see the place. Wendy is the farmer, really. Sarah is a weaver, and they spin and dye their own wool. They clearly love the place. Honestly, it's like it all worked out the way it was supposed to." She took in a deep breath and looked around the farm again. "I fell in love with this place the moment I saw it. Dan used to tease me that I only asked him to that dance way back when because I was angling to see his farm."

"He got the girl and she got the farm, and they lived happily—" He broke off, and his smile faltered, but she smiled at him.

"We did do that," she assured him. "For the ever after we had. Every single day. I was thrilled to get to work with Pops, for him to show me everything, teach me everything."

"He could be a stubborn cuss," Sam said, relieved she'd handled his slip so kindly. "Thought he knew every last thing about every last thing."

Lily laughed. "Well, most of the time, he did. But he also cherished what his wife brought to Dawson farm, all the color and the life, her little whimsical touches, just like Pops' mom brought to the place, each in their own way."

"I was thinking that you've found a way to put your passion for art to work," Sam told her. "I like the boot planters," he added when she gave him a questioning look.

"Ah. That wasn't me. Well, not all me. Faith saw a picture in a magazine with boots nailed to a fence and turned into planters. So, the two of us decided to see what we could do with that. A mother-daughter project." She let out a short laugh. "If I was the son the Dawsons never had, Faith was definitely the daughter they never had. She has a real eye for design. She's already started sketching ideas for their little cottage. I can't wait to see what she does with it."

"An artist like her mom, then."

"Maybe back in the day I was, but I'm a happy farmer these days. I leave the sketching to Faith." She tilted her head slightly. "How did you know I was into art?"

"Your dad had some of your pen-and-ink drawings up on the wall in the hardware store. You had a really good eye. I mean, I was just a kid who knew nothing about anything, but I thought they were pretty great."

"Right, I forgot about those." She shook her head and gave him a wry grin. "Amateur hour to be sure. Faith has ten times my talent. I thought maybe she'd go on to art school, or get into graphic design, but she knew early on her calling was teaching. In middle school, she helped tutor other kids in English, and she knew right then. Her conviction never wavered either." Lily shrugged. "My dad wanted me to pursue art, but I knew my passion was digging my hands in the dirt, watching things grow. Dad was happy for me, just as I'm happy for Faith. We're all doing what we were meant to do. She's a great teacher. Her kids adore her."

"You guys coming?" Faith called out, and they both turned to see her in the doorway to the barn.

Max poked his head out, saw them, and grinned, waved. He was a good foot taller than Faith, with broad shoulders and a head of dark, shaggy curls. Sam knew from Faith that he'd kept his curly locks despite pressure from the athletic department to present a more clean-cut look. His young student athletes seemed to idolize him much the same way Lily said Faith's students looked up to her. Sam suspected the kids identified with Max's youthful exuberance. He would have when he was their age.

"The dust has settled," Faith shouted. "We're ready to go."

She started to say something else, but Max took Faith's hand, turned her in a little spin, and pulled her, laughing, back inside the barn.

"Looks like we need to give that pair a dance floor," Sam said.

"I don't think it matters, really," Lily said with a laugh. "I'm pretty sure they're dancing on air."

"Oh, to be young and in love," Sam said, happening to catch Lily's gaze as she glanced from the now-empty barn door back to him.

"It's a special time," she agreed.

Sam would have thought that comment would have her reminiscing about the days when she and Dan had been planning their wedding, which had also taken place on this very farm. But her gaze seemed outwardly focused. In fact, it seemed to have caught, and lingered, on his.

Once again, the moment spun out. And like before, where it should have felt awkward, or at the very least wrong, it didn't. Maybe it was the glow of the impending wedding, coloring everything with its hopeful, joyous hue, or maybe it was the woman standing in front of him, smiling up at him. Probably it was a little of both that had him putting words to his thoughts before he could think better of it. "You're right. Love is always a special time, no matter when it happens."

Her eyebrows lifted, just slightly, but her pupils shot wide at the same time. Surprise and awareness.

He didn't know what had possessed him to say that to her, or what he'd even meant by it, but her reaction, that latter part, wasn't helping to clear his head one bit.

"We'd, uh... we'd better get inside," she said, her voice a little throaty, which did all kinds of things to him he definitely didn't need to be thinking about, much less feeling, in that moment, or any other.

"Right," he said, knowing he should clarify what he'd meant, or... or something. Only he had no idea what that something would be.

She turned away before he could decide to do anything, so he simply followed Lily to the barn, hoping he hadn't ruined the seemingly easy and natural détente they'd just reached. None of which kept him from watching her as they headed up the path. She wore old jeans, mud-covered barn boots, and a gray hoodie with Faith and Max's college name and emblem stamped in navy blue on the front. Nothing about any of that was geared to turn a man's head, and yet, his gaze wasn't on the new fencing that had been put up since he'd been there last, or the color coming into the blueberry fields, as it did every June.

No, his gaze remained on the subtle swing of Lily's hips as she strode up the last incline toward the barn doors. Her stride wasn't meant to entice. She was simply covering ground in the same no-nonsense, direct way she did everything else. And that was what had his attention. Not the old jeans, or the way they fit... but the woman who wore them. She had his attention. Like she had one summer, a very long time ago, when they'd been barely more than kids. Like she did, quite suddenly, once again.

Sam couldn't stop picturing the happy, contented look on her face as she'd smiled up at him, laughing about Pops, about her luck in ending up on Dawson Farm. The only thought he should be having was how Dan had been the luckiest guy on earth to have had those eyes smiling up into his every day of his life.

Not wondering what life would be like if she'd keep looking into his own eyes the exact same way.

# Chapter Three

Lily let herself in through the mudroom door off the back porch, taking her barn boots off before heading into the kitchen. She went straight to the stove and put a kettle on. Summer had arrived, that brief, lovely season of sunshine and warmth in Down East Maine, but the nights could still be quite chilly. After a long day of lugging, pushing, hauling, and stomping to get that flooring into place, all she wanted was a cup of hot tea, a long, steam-filled shower, then warm food. Any warm food would do. Soup, maybe, she thought, as she sank thankfully onto a stool that fronted the large marble-topped island positioned in the middle of the oversize kitchen. She thought about starting a fire in the big stone fireplace that took up most of the wall on the opposite side of the room, but that would mean getting up. Something she didn't plan on doing until the kettle whistled. Maybe not even then.

The back door swung open, making Lily jump, as Faith and Max came bustling in on a burst of happy conversation and laughter. She'd just started to lower the hand that had flown to her chest at the sudden intrusion, only to keep it there when she saw Sam follow them in. Lily immediately sat up straight but managed to catch herself before she smoothed her hair. Which would have been useless given she'd started the day with a hastily assembled ponytail, and that had been nine or ten hours ago. No amount of smoothing would repair the irreparable. It was silly anyway, on several counts. One, Sam didn't care about her hair, sloppy or otherwise, and two, he'd been out there right along with the rest of them, doing more than his fair share of hauling, shoving, dragging, and stomping. He'd seen her hair. Along with the rest of her.

She closed her eyes briefly and gave herself a mental shake. *What does it matter anyway? I thought we went over this.* She'd been relieved that she and Sam had had a few minutes to talk before they'd gone into the big barn. For all she'd more or less avoided him over the years since Dan's death, thinking she had nothing to say, she'd realized immediately how silly that had been. Sam was easy to talk to, and once they'd gotten their apologies out of the way, she'd really enjoyed chatting and laughing with him. She might not really know him all that well, in any direct, one-on-one way, but he was family to Faith, and to Dan, and by close association over so many years, apparently to her, too. At least it had felt that way. Mostly.

She tried hard not to think about those few moments when it seemed like things were less family and more... personal. And not in a bad way. She'd been trying hard—and failing—to not think about what he'd said there at the end of their talk. Obviously, he'd been speaking in general terms, but boy, the way his gaze had penetrated hers... she'd felt like she was coming down with hot flashes a few years early.

Clearly, she had misread that entirely. Wishful thinking. Except she wasn't wishing for any such thing. *Yearning, maybe.* She closed her eyes and willed herself to shake off... whatever the heck it was she was doing and feeling. About Sam Fletcher, of all people. *Just stop it.*

Maybe once the wedding was over, she'd take her daughter's advice and think about signing up on one of those dating sites. When Faith had first offered to help her do that, she'd given the very thought a hard pass. The hardest of passes. She knew they were popular and had become a commonly accepted practice, but she simply couldn't even imagine herself doing it. She was too old-fashioned. Faith had pointed out that Lily could use a dating site just to talk with single members of the opposite sex, sort of wade in and get comfortable with the idea of dating. She didn't have to actually meet any of them. Lily had initially rejected that idea as well.

Only now she was giving it a second thought. Maybe if she was talking with other people her own age, men who'd found themselves single for whatever reason, as she had, she wouldn't be having such a huge, unexpected, and entirely inappropriate reaction to Sam. That's probably all it was. She had a backlog of hormones long overdue for some attention, and they'd simply responded to the first eligible target.

*Good,* she decided. *Good.* She had a plan, she'd execute it, and that would be that. She'd distract herself for a little while, the wedding would happen, she'd see the happy couple off. Then Sam would head back out to parts unknown, she'd return once more to her blissful, solo, steady, and in-charge-of-her-own-life routine. Contentment was all she should be feeling right now. That and a little fatigue from a long day. She had it all under control.

Then, at Faith's bidding, Sam walked over and set about starting a fire in the fireplace. And Lily watched, helpless to look away as he crouched down, thigh muscles flexing below that lean waist and those broad shoulders she'd noticed far too many times throughout the day. He bent forward and quickly, expertly arranged the logs and the kindling, and she was forced to admit that she wasn't even close to having things all organized and under her control.

Instead of contentment, she felt utter self-awareness, like her skin was suddenly intensely sensitive, where every little shift in the air put her body on full alert, all tensed up. Not from stress, but in that anticipatory way it got when all the other senses went on high alert, ready for some new stimulus. In a good way. A really, really good way.

*Only this isn't good. Not good,* she told her traitorous body. *Yes, he's somehow ten times sexier now than he ever was before. Yes, I'd have to be dead not to notice that. And, apparently, I'm not dead. Yay, me. Good to know. Now can we please, for the love of all that is holy, move on already?*

Then Sam drew a long match along the stone built into the hearth for just that purpose, and that prickle of awareness flared as the match caught flame, into a moment of such intense need she had to press her thighs together and look away to keep the soft moan at the back of her throat from slipping out.

"Mom?"

Startled, Lily turned to find Faith standing right behind her, an expectant look on her face. She hoped the dim lighting hid the heat flooding her cheeks. Flooding her... everything. "Sorry, I was—what did you say?" She carefully did not look back to see what Sam was doing. Or more to the point, now that the fire was lit, where he was looking... or whom he might be looking at.

"I just got a text from Brooke," Faith said, appearing mercifully oblivious to the undercurrents in the room. Or at least the ones emanating from her ridiculous, pent-up mother.

"Is there a problem?" Lily asked right as the kettle started to whistle. She jumped, perhaps a little more than was warranted, at the sudden shrill sound, eliciting a frown of concern from Faith, but ignored that as she all but leaped off the stool, relieved she had something to do with her hands, and her brain. Anything to keep her from looking at Sam, thinking about Sam... everything about Sam.

"No, the exact opposite." Faith beamed. "She's so sweet, she's setting up a private little tasting for me and Max after she closes tonight. I sent her my top four choices—"

"You picked cake?" Lily asked, surprised. "When?"

Faith laughed. "I basically narrowed it down to four flavors that I thought would please the most people. No decisions on frosting yet."

"But it's your cake. You should pick what you love most—"

"Mom, was there any flavor we didn't like?"

Lily laughed, too. "Good point. And now Max gets to be involved, too, which is great. Let me know what you two end up choosing." Lily would text Brooke the moment Faith and Max were gone and make sure the two soon-to-be newlyweds got whatever they wanted.

"We will." Faith leaned in and kissed her mom's cheek.

Lily gave Faith a quick, one-armed hug. "You coming back out here tonight? Are we still working on the seating arrangements tomorrow? I've got a buyer from Machias coming in around nine, but then I have a few hours before I have to head back out. Henry can cover things while we sort that out."

Faith shook her head. "Actually, I was going to ask if we could put that off until tomorrow evening, after dinner. Since tomorrow is Saturday and we're both off, Sandy asked if we could come meet her by the lighthouse out on the point. She wanted to take a few more casual engagement photos if the weather holds."

"I heard no rain till next week. The storm they predicted went out to sea."

"Next week?" Faith said, suddenly looking anxious.

"Wednesday morning, gone by Thursday. Windy Friday, which will dry everything out. Then sunny and gorgeous for the big day on Saturday." Lily smiled reassuringly. "Just like I ordered."

Faith made a show of crossing her fingers. "Good. Sandy said the light would be better in the morning, so we're meeting early. I thought I'd stay in town tonight, so we'll be right there close by. I don't know how long it will take, or if we'll do other locations tomorrow. But I'll keep in touch and see what we can work out."

Lily knew that meant they'd stay in Faith's tiny apartment that night and smiled. The two had gotten the keys to their cottage a week ago, and Lily knew it might seem silly to some since the pair all but lived together anyway, but she thought it was sweet that they'd agreed that neither of them would spend the night in the new cottage until they were husband and wife. Lily had already told Faith that someone better take a picture of Max carrying her over the threshold and thought maybe she should text Sandy about that right after she texted Brooke about the cake.

"We'll get everything done," Faith assured her. "And why is the bride reassuring the mom?" she asked with a laugh. "Shouldn't it be the other way around?"

"I can't help it," Lily told her daughter. "I like having you around." With the wedding taking place at the farm, Faith had been spending a great deal of time back at home, and Lily had gotten used to having life and laughter in the house again. She'd miss it double this time, she knew. "If you were a more miserable kid, it would be so much easier."

"Darn me for being so decent and kind." She gave her a quick, tight hug. "I blame you."

Lily hugged her back, then turned to hug her future son-in-law, who stepped in to say goodbye as well.

"Thank you, Mama Lily," he told her with a fast hug. "We'll

send you some pictures if we get any good ones tomorrow. Sandy said she'd send us some proofs right away."

"They will all be good," she told him. "And thank you. I'd love to see them."

The two made their way out through the mudroom door, and Lily turned back to the stove and kettle and busied herself making a cup of tea and sending a text to Brooke. She smiled and went ahead and sent one to Sandy, too, about the idea for a threshold photo, just in case it could somehow be worked out.

"I don't suppose you have some instant coffee hidden in one of these cupboards."

Lily jumped, again. How had she gone from being hyperaware of the man to forgetting he was still there? She'd like to blame it on wedding brain, what with running the farm and juggling so many details about the impending nuptials and all, but truth be told, she'd been managing all that just fine. She was a champion list maker. She was well aware that her sudden bout of scattered thoughts and jumpy behavior coincided with the moment Sam Fletcher had stepped back into her life.

And voted yes on her cleavage.

"Sure, yes, of course," she said, trying to cover her gaffe with a bright smile before turning to open another cupboard. "I can brew a pot, though. You don't need to drink instant."

"You know what, on second thought, don't go to all that bother. I should probably head on out. We've all put in a full day, and I'm sure you still have work to do this evening. I know the farm doesn't stop running just because there's a wedding in the works."

Lily nodded, smiled, and actually relaxed a little. It was nice being with someone who understood how her life worked. Sam had witnessed it firsthand, being on the farm as much as he had while growing up, and he'd put in his fair share of time in the fields over those years as well. Thinking on that made her smile grow.

"What?" he asked, noting her amusement.

"I was just thinking it's funny how I've lived in this house for most of my adult life, but it has been as much a home to you in your lifetime as it is to me. You all but lived here for a good number of years when you were a kid."

"Are you trying to tell me if I want coffee, I can fix it myself?"

His grin was a quick flash of white teeth, matched with a crinkling at the corners of his eyes that did things to her pulse she really didn't want to think about, much less admit to. How was it possible he just kept getting better looking? Gray hair was threaded in at his temples now, for goodness sake, and even that just added to his sex appeal.

She smiled at his teasing question and ignored the urge to fan herself. "No, but by all means, please do. My casa really is kinda your casa, too." She nodded toward the cupboard over the counter. "Some of the things in the cupboards have changed over the years, but as you probably recall, Frannie was the queen of organization. Things are pretty much where they've always been. I didn't see much need to fix what wasn't broken."

Sam smiled fondly at the mention of Dan's mother. "Working on a farm where things break on their own all too frequently, that makes sense to me."

She grinned. "My thoughts exactly."

He walked around the counter, and she scooted around to the other side and perched on her stool. He was lethal enough to her equilibrium from across the room. She needed to regroup before she dealt with having him within arm's reach.

Hand on the cupboard door, he glanced back at her. "You sure you wouldn't rather—" He nodded toward the hallway that led to the study at the front of the house that had been used as the farm office since before Pops' time.

Her suddenly raging libido made taking him up on his offer to let her get to work the sensible course of action. But that would be rude and inhospitable. Two things the Dawsons would never stand for, and she didn't intend to change anything about that either. She shook her head. "I'm going to sit here, sip some tea, take a few moments of downtime before tackling a mountain of paperwork, and enjoy this very nice fire you were kind enough to start. There's no reason you can't join me."

"A hearty invitation if I ever heard one," he teased. He lifted a hand to stall her reply. "I appreciate the offer, thank you. And I'm happy to brew my own cup. Do you still make Frannie's old blend? If so, I'm not even going to apologize for being an impolite freeloader. I've suffered through some godawful coffee for far more years than I care to count. A cup of Frannie's coffee would be one of the best welcome-homes I could ask for."

Lily smiled over the rim of her cup. "Like I said, if it's not broken."

She laughed when he closed his eyes as if in prayer. "Frannie Dawson. An angel on earth and in heaven."

Lily nodded to the pantry. "The cannister is in there, second shelf from the top. I've been trying to wean myself over to tea, so out of sight is out of mind," she said.

Sam had stepped into the pantry and ducked his head back out. "How's that going?" he asked, sounding dubious.

She stared down into her teacup. "I had to experiment with different flavors, but I like it well enough. It's definitely better for me at the end of a long day."

Sam set up the coffeepot, and Lily inhaled the rich scent of the beans as they began to brew, somewhat surprised at the ease with which she was holding up her end of the conversation. Especially given the riot of sensations he'd so effortlessly fired up inside of her. She hadn't blurted out a single awkward thing. *Yet.* "On cold winter mornings and weekends, I still treat myself to a cup."

Sam looked at his watch. "Well, it's not winter, but it will be Saturday in a handful of hours."

He'd already taken off his jacket and boots in the mudroom, and yet even in sock feet, he still seemed to take up all the space in what was, by any measure, a large, airy kitchen. Something about that pale green, long-sleeved T-shirt that was just the right amount of strained over his broad shoulders, worn untucked over jeans that were also just the right amount of worn and snug... She jerked her gaze back to her cup of tea before he turned around and caught her ogling him.

He'd always been that way, she thought. Larger than life in attitude, charm, and physical size. That much hadn't changed.

In other ways, though, he was proving to be a little bit of a surprise. When he spoke, the confidence was still there, but it was assured now, rather than cocky, earned from life experience and understated because of it, rather than being put out there because he was trying to impress. He still exuded a kind of raw energy, but it was... steadier now. Under control. He knew what he was capable of but no longer felt the need to make sure everyone else knew it.

She supposed that side of him had always been there, it just wasn't the part he'd projected to the world. She knew there were certain other aspects of his personality Sam had kept tucked away, especially when he'd been younger. The vulnerable, less-than-fully-confident side Dan had assured her was there, which Lily knew had come from Sam's home life.

He wasn't all flash-and-dazzle now, with his brash charm and impossible-not-to-respond-to grin. That part of him still surfaced in flashes, to be sure, but with all of that more or less banked, the wisdom gained and maturity reached shone through, allowing her to truly see him for all the things he was.

On the one hand, it was that very change in him that had allowed her to relax as she had, chat with him like he was the old family friend that he indeed was.

On the other hand, she suspected she'd be replaying a lot of little details of this time spent together, over and over, when she was lying in her bed later. Alone. Maybe then she'd find a way to sort out and manage this other energy between them. All glowing embers one minute, to a sudden shower of sparks the next, then back to simmering below the surface. At least that's how it felt to her.

She shoved that thought aside and purposefully thought about Dan, about how much he'd like knowing Sam was here and that she was keeping him company on his return home.

And that was when she knew she was really in trouble. Because rather than thoughts of her late husband putting any ideas she might have about becoming more than just a good friend to Sam Fletcher back where they belonged... she heard her daughter's voice echoing through her mind.

*Who better to forge a new path forward with than someone Dad trusted the most?*

Even more alarming, Lily honestly couldn't disagree with

Faith. She knew Dan would agree with her, too.

Feeling like her life had suddenly become a train rapidly going off the rails, Lily glanced up just in time to see Sam nod toward the pot and wiggle his eyebrows. "Care to savor just a small cup?"

No. No, of course she didn't. Shouldn't. *No savoring anything. Not out-of-bounds coffee. And definitely not out-of-bounds family friends.*

Which didn't explain at all why when she opened her mouth, what came out was, "Yes, I think I would."

And that was the honest truth. Yes, she would. Yes to the coffee, yes to Sam, yes to whatever the heck was happening to her every time she looked at him. Yes.

*Yes. Yes. Yes.*

All of it was true, no matter how hard she tried to make herself believe otherwise.

And just like that, she shut off all the alarm bells, the whispered words of advice, the endless worries, and just... all of it. Lily Foster Dawson shut it all down. Then she carefully set her teacup down, too, with a definitive little click.

She looked at Sam and, for possibly the first time in her entire life, made the very conscious decision to throw caution straight to the wind and do exactly what she wanted to do. "Pour me one, too, please." She folded her arms on the marble-topped island and thought nothing had ever felt so freeing as the dry smile she shot his way. "As they say, it's coffee o'clock somewhere."

# Chapter Four

"You bought Terry Jamison's airfield?" Lily sat her coffee mug on the island top. "How did I not know that? We've spent, what, the past four straight nights talking?"

It was Tuesday evening, and Sam and Lily were both enjoying their second cup. He'd left after that first cup last Friday. They'd spent that evening talking about the wedding, about Faith and Max, the soon-to-be newlyweds' plans for the future. It had been relaxed and easy, given it was a topic they shared an interest in. He suspected they could have easily continued on to other subjects and talked until the fire burned to embers, but he hadn't wanted to overstay his welcome. He'd thought at the time, given she had work to do, that maybe he already had. So, he'd headed out with a wave, and she'd waved him good-bye, calling out a last thank-you for his help in the barn.

Then somehow, he'd ended up back on her doorstep the following afternoon, ostensibly to see if there was anything else he could do to help set things up. He'd spent the next four hours building the stage setup for the DJ and rolling out the green turf carpeting, so they'd be ready when the tables were delivered for the reception. Lily had invited the whole crew in for a beer afterward, but they'd all been putting in time after their own long workday, and for one reason or another, each one had peeled off and headed to their own homes and families. Leaving Sam to decide if he should stay or go.

Lily had asked in him... so he'd stayed. They'd enjoyed another pot of Frannie's coffee instead of the beer she'd offered the others. Talk of the wedding prep left to be done had turned—when he'd asked about one of the neighbors—to her catching him up on all the goings-on in Swan Harbor over the next hour. He might have lingered on the steps leading down the front porch to his truck that evening a little longer than was necessary. He liked how she looked, standing in the open doorway, the glow of the house behind her, the light of the rising moon playing shadows across her face.

He'd been so tempted to walk back up those steps, close the distance between them so she'd tip her face up to his. He'd palmed his keys instead and made himself climb into his truck before he could change his mind. He'd noticed in his rearview mirror, though, that she'd remained standing there until the main house finally dropped out of sight.

Sunday, Faith and Max had come out for dinner, and Faith had invited him as well. Afterward, Faith and Lily had spent hours over the kitchen table organizing the seating arrangements for the reception, so Max and Sam had gone down and shot some pool. Sam had been happy to have the time with Max, to get to know him better. He'd headed out when the kids had, but he hadn't missed the quick look of disappointment on Lily's face when he'd slipped on his jacket when they'd grabbed theirs. He hadn't minded that look either, had even thought about hanging his jacket right back up again. But things were good between them. Life felt good. Really good. And he didn't want to do anything to change that, then or now.

Yesterday afternoon, he'd been back to help set up tables as the regular workday on the farm was winding down. A dip in the temperatures as the predicted storm had drawn closer had had him deciding to stop in at the main house on his way out and get a fire going, so the kitchen would be warm and cozy for Lily after a late meeting with one of her distributors. She'd been coming in just as he'd been heading out. She'd been surprised and touched by his thoughtfulness. He'd been relieved she hadn't felt he'd intruded by taking it upon himself to set the fire. She hadn't at all. Instead, she'd asked him in for a coffee so he could enjoy the fruits of his fire-building labor.

He should have said no. Should have continued to let things follow their own path while not putting too fine a point on just where he was hoping that path would lead.

Which was a flat-out lie. He was coming to admitting exactly where he wanted it to lead. But he also knew he wasn't willing to ruin what friendship they had—the old one, or the new one they were building—by pushing for something she didn't want. If this was all there was to be, then he'd be happy for it. Better to have this than have nothing. Though he was growing more and more convinced he wasn't the only one thinking about what else there could be between them.

Still, they had time. Time to get used to the idea, time to make sure it was what they both wanted, time for everyone else to come to terms with the idea that there might be something brewing between the late Dan Dawson's wife and his best friend. No need to push.

But he had said yes to that coffee. Just a cup. She'd talked about distribution issues and other day-to-day aggravations that had been taking too much of her time, when what she wanted to do was just enjoy the anticipation of the wedding and focus on dotting all the i's and crossing those final t's. She'd apologized for dominating the conversation with her venting, and he'd told her, sincerely, that he hadn't minded a bit. He'd offer her an ear, and a shoulder, anytime.

Now it was Tuesday. He'd helped with reception tables. They'd gotten them all set up a day earlier than planned because of the storm due to hit later that night and last all the next day. Sam had offered to take her out to dinner afterward, give her a little break, the closest he'd come to asking her for a date. She'd countered by offering to cook him dinner, given all the help he'd been to them. They were both pretty beat, and neither one of them needed to be slaving over a hot stove, so they'd compromised with pizza delivery and a cold beer.

That had been hours ago now. The dishes had long since been cleared and washed, the leftovers stored, and beer bottles put in the recycling bin. He should have been on his way, following his rule about heading out once things began to wind down. About not pushing. Only she'd been the one to dangle the offer of a weekday cup of Frannie's coffee. And he was only so strong.

One cup had led to a second, proving his rule had been a good idea. Only, sitting on the stool next to her, the fire burning low behind them... he was having a hard time remembering why any of this was a bad idea.

"All this time we've spent talking, and I can't believe I didn't know that," she said with a laugh. "I didn't even know Terry was thinking about selling. I need to get off the farm more."

"You've had a lot on a plate that is always pretty full."

"Yes, but at the very least you'd think I'd have wondered what it was you were doing all day every day when you weren't here providing free labor. Or at least asked."

He lifted his mug. "I'll take being paid with Frannie's coffee every day of the week."

She laughed. "Good thing, since that's pretty much all I've managed to do to reimburse you."

"And Sunday dinner and pizza."

She rolled her eyes. "Hardly enough to count for even base wages."

Sam could have told her she'd repaid him ten times over, more than that, with conversation and shared laughter.

She rested her elbows on the table then, cradling the mug as she looked at him with unabashed curiosity. "So, why an airstrip?"

"Airpark," Sam said with a laugh. "As Terry would be quick to correct you. And because it seemed like the right thing to do."

She stared down into her mug for a moment, so he couldn't read her expression. "So," she said at length, "does that mean you're staying? To run it?" She glanced up, met his gaze. Hers was unreadable. "Or will you hire someone to manage it?"

He'd made it sound like not mentioning it had merely been a thoughtless slip, but he hadn't brought it up on purpose. He and Terry hadn't finalized the deal, and Terry didn't want word getting out until things were fully settled. Frankly, Sam was surprised it hadn't gotten out anyway. Secrets were hard to keep in a town this small.

That wasn't why he hadn't told Lily. She'd have kept his confidence. He hadn't because of the expression he saw on her face just now. Or, more to the point, the lack of expression. She'd likely — and reasonably — assumed he would be heading back out to parts unknown once the wedding was over. Sam suspected that was why she'd been so relaxed around him, simply being herself. Not that she was a guarded person, but they were grown adults, and things had gotten beyond the point where they could deny that, if the situation had been any different, they'd have likely made a move toward exploring their very clear attraction to each other. Instead of settling for family dinners and a little conversation over a nightly cup of coffee.

Only now she knew. And she looked a lot guarded. Which was exactly what he hadn't wanted.

"I'm staying," he said, holding her gaze, trying to read what was going on behind those gold-green eyes. He smiled, trying to lessen the tension that had sprung up between them. "I guess you could say I retired. I've left my former line of work, at any rate. I do have to travel back to Washington at some point to tie up a few loose ends." He was supposed to have flown back over the weekend to finalize turning his condo over to a realtor to handle selling it for him and arrange to have his stuff trucked north. He'd put it off to stay and help with wedding setup. Or so he told himself. Then he'd put it off again and stopped lying to himself about why. As long as Lily Dawson was inviting him in for coffee, he was going to be in Swan Harbor so he could say yes. "I left a bit sooner than intended," he added, one corner of his mouth kicking up a little higher. "Someone needed my arm for a little stroll."

Lily's expression warmed instantly. He liked how thinking about her daughter and the impending wedding made her entire face light up.

"I had no idea you were juggling that much," she said. "And you've been helping out so much more around here than you could have possibly planned on. You must have a million things that need doing. I owe you a lot more than pizza." Her expression wasn't guarded now. Her gratitude shone quite sincerely from her eyes. "I know I've thanked you and thanked you, but you've really gone above and beyond. Just being here for Faith on her special day was gift enough."

He turned his head to look at her more directly. "I'll always be there for her, Lily. For both of you."

She held his gaze for what felt like the longest time. "We're here for you, too. You know that, right?"

"I do," he said and thought at once how simple this should all be, could all be, and how complex and complicated it was, all at the same time.

She looked down at her coffee mug, ending the moment, then shifted on her stool so she

faced the island table. "Will you be flying? Giving lessons?" She glanced at him, her curiosity sincere and not simply polite.

But the mood had shifted, and he respected that she was going to need a little time to process this change in how she had thought things were going to play out between them. She'd assumed his role in her life would be nothing more than periodic pit stops, as it had always been before.

She smiled and added, "I'm sorry, I have no idea what running a regional airstrip requires."

"Airpark," they both said at the same time, in the same droll tone, and shared a laugh. The moment, the humor, helped to nudge things back in the direction of where they'd been.

"It's nothing like what you're used to flying," she said.

He shook his head. "No, and I'd be lying if I said I'm not going to miss certain parts of my former world. Flying would be at the top of that list, which is why I'm doing this. At least the only danger I'll face here is whether or not Maisy Farnell's cows have gotten loose and are roaming the runway again."

Lily spluttered a laugh. "That is true."

He chuckled with her, and a little more of the tension eased between them. They both sipped their coffee, and the silence played out for a moment or two, not uncomfortably, which was a relief. One of the things Sam liked most about the time he'd been spending with Lily, both in the house over coffee and working side by side with her out in the barn, was that it had been effortless. Their communication came easily, naturally, which in itself shouldn't be a surprise, but the truth was, they hadn't really ever sat and talked that much. And never one-on-one.

Lily was an open and direct person, but in the past, she'd generally left Dan and Sam to do all the talking during his visits. He knew it was because his visits had been infrequent, that she'd simply been giving the two men time together to catch up. She'd tease them about needing "man cave time" and leave them to it, whether it was playing pool on the generations-old slate table downstairs or having a beer and firing up the barbecue out back, maybe taking a drive around town and chatting up some of the locals while Sam was in town.

She'd always welcomed Sam warmly and been sincerely happy each time the two old friends were reunited. But somehow, even with so many years having gone by, though Sam had gotten close to his goddaughter—largely because Faith had pursued a relationship with him and had made use of the modern technology at her disposal to keep in touch—he'd never really bridged that gap with Lily. Not that he'd seen it as such. But that had been the end result.

Now, when they reminisced about things like school and town events over the years, the memories they shared weren't because of their connection to Dan, but because they'd both grown up in Swan Harbor. And though he'd meant what he said about being there for her and Faith, the reason he was lingering over a second cup of coffee had nothing to do with making sure he remained connected to his late friend's family.

Maybe it was because he'd spent the past few days driving around his hometown for the first time in quite a few years, bombarded by all kinds of memories and emotions, and not just those related to Dan but to Sam's whole life in Swan Harbor. Whatever the reason, the truth of it was, the second he'd entered the bridal shop and spied Lily standing on that riser in that amazing dress, head bent with her daughter, laughing like she might have when she'd been closer to Faith's age... he hadn't seen her as Lily Dawson, wife of his late friend, mother to his goddaughter. He'd been looking at Lily Foster, daughter of his first boss, the only girl in school who hadn't seemed to give a rat's ass about impressing him. Lily Foster, who just happened to also be Lily Foster Dawson, all grown up.

And single.

Wandering into that territory this late at night, fueled by too much caffeine and not enough sleep, was probably not the best idea. Especially given the bomb he'd just dropped on her. "I should probably be taking off," he began, setting his mug on the marble surface.

Just as she said, "Speaking of things I should have mentioned sooner, I was sorry to hear about your father's passing."

He stilled for a moment, and it was his turn to be caught a little off guard. A lot off guard. Wherever that had come from, it only proved just how far apart their trains of thought truly were. He settled his weight back on the stool, just for a moment, admittedly curious to find out why she'd chosen that moment to mention his father, of all things. "No need to apologize," was all he said.

"Sorry, that probably wasn't the right way to bring that up," she said. "I was just thinking about you moving back here and thought maybe it would be easier now because..." She let that trail off, and he saw the color rise in her cheeks from embarrassment, but she pushed on. "I know you and he weren't close, but it can't ever be easy, losing a parent. And I... just wanted to extend my condolences." She looked down then. "I wasn't thinking. I'm sorry. I shouldn't have said anything."

The one thing he would have to get used to, living in his hometown once again, was that everyone in Swan Harbor knew about his past, his childhood, and his less-than-ideal home life growing up. It wasn't something he ever shared with anyone in his day-to-day life now, nor had it been for as long as he could remember. So, he wasn't used to talking about it. Not that it was the kind of thing one ever got used to discussing.

It turned out, though, that he didn't so much mind hearing it from Lily. In fact, she, of all people, could truly sympathize. She'd suffered more loss than pretty much anyone he knew, the particulars of which he knew more about than most. Just as she also knew his situation, understood his loss more intimately, given their connection, than anyone else in Swan Harbor would.

"You never need to apologize for kindness," he said. "It was... challenging, but not in the way it was for you." He knew she'd been young when her mother had gotten sick and passed away, just as he knew her father had passed a few years after Faith had been born, also from a long illness. "Thank you," he added. "For sending flowers. I would have called to say that, but... I did mention it to Faith."

She glanced up and waited until his gaze met hers. "They were for you," she said kindly, but with an even edge to her voice. And that was all she had to say. She knew what he'd suffered at his old man's hand. She paused, as if deciding whether to continue, but then went on. "I have to admit, we were all pretty shocked when he up and sold your old house and took off for Florida back when he did. Barely said a word to anyone about it. If he hadn't used Hank as his realtor, we might not have known until after he was gone."

"Would have been just as well," Sam said, no warmth in the accompanying dry smile, but without real rancor either. Watching his father slowly waste away from a long-term illness, one that had caused the old man to leave the cold of the North for the heat of the South, and bitch about it every single day of what he had left of his life, had sapped most of the harbored and deeply seated anger out of Sam. Most of it. The rest he'd made peace with many years earlier, when he'd chosen to live life on his own terms. Meaning mostly as far away from Swan Harbor as he could get. The only reason he'd come back at all had been for the Dawsons, and eventually Faith, and Lily, too.

"I can understand leaving your former line of work, taking a new direction with your life. I guess I'm kind of surprised you'd pick Swan Harbor to settle down in." She smiled, picked up her mug again, and cradled it between her palms. "You've seen a good part of the world. What, you couldn't find someplace with milder weather that had an airstrip in need of managing?"

And just like that, with nothing more than a dry smile and a wry comment, things smoothed right out again. Something settled inside of him, and he thought that was what being with Lily was like. She turned him on, yes, but the attraction he felt was so much more than that. It was this. This kind of moment, of kinship. Whatever happened, wherever things went between them, they'd have this. They'd keep this. He'd make sure of it.

"I like it here," he said. It was the plain, if not so simple, truth. "I know there was a fair bit of bad, but that's all in the distant past. There was a whole lot of good, too. And I miss it." His lips curved more deeply. "After spending extended time in some pretty inhospitable places, Maine winters will seem like Palm Beach."

"Well, I wouldn't go that far," she said with a laugh. "Maybe you've forgotten just how bitterly cold it can get. And how much snow you'll have to clear off that runway."

He chuckled. "Also true. If I could just get Maisy's cows to figure out how to run the snowblowers and front-end loaders, I'll have it made."

Lily nodded. "Cheap labor, too. I hear they work for peanuts. Or is that carrots?" She pretended to ponder that. "Apples, maybe? I'll be happy to donate some blueberries, if that helps."

"I can work with that." Their gazes caught, held, as did their smiles, then lingered for a moment, then another. He liked that she didn't look away. He liked even more the hint of pink that bloomed in her cheeks when he let his smile slide into a full-on Sam Fletcher grin. *Definitely not wise.* He pushed his stool back. "I know you still have never-ending paperwork to do. I'd offer to help, but ask any of my superiors about my report-writing skills, and they'd be happy to tell you just how little help I'd be." He stood. "I'll let you get to it."

She slid off her stool, too. "I'm glad you stayed," she said, and sounded like she meant it. "For pizza. And for coffee."

He nodded even as he took a small step back, putting a little more space between them. He wanted to tell her how much he'd enjoyed all the nights they'd sat and chatted over coffee in front of a crackling fire. In this place he loved, that still felt like the best part of home. He was pretty sure he'd never get tired of it. Or her. But that was where things got complicated. And he wasn't ready to go there. Not tonight, at any rate. *One step at a time.* "Yeah," he said, then cleared the bit of roughness from his voice. "Yes, I'm glad I did, too."

"I think Dan would be pleased," she said, her expression open, honest, her words sincere, but she seemed to be searching his gaze at the same time. For what, he wasn't sure. "That we're keeping the Dawson-Fletcher connection alive and well."

And just like that, the complication was thrust, front and center, right smack in between them. Not that there would ever be a way around that fact. Sam didn't know what a possible path forward with Lily Dawson would, or even could, look like. However, he suspected if Dan knew the kind of thoughts Sam was trying really,

really hard not to have about his wife in that moment, his old friend might not be all that pleased with the kind of connection Sam was wanting to keep alive and well.

"Always," he told her, meaning that. "No matter what."

She was gazing up into his eyes much the way she had that first day, when they'd been on their way to the barn. There wasn't a single suggestive note in her tone or demeanor. And for a split second, he thought she might step forward, put her hand on his arm, tip up on her sock-footed toes, and kiss him on the cheek. In gratitude, of course. Gratitude he definitely knew he hadn't earned. Not in that moment anyway, not with what he was thinking.

He cleared his throat again, then glanced at the fire. Anywhere other than into those pretty hazel eyes. "I can bank the fire if you—"

She glanced at it, as if surprised by the offer. It was barely more than embers now. "I think it will burn down just fine. Thanks, though."

"Well, I'll just grab my coat and boots and be out of your hair." A crack of thunder rattled the windows just then, making them both jump.

"That doesn't sound good," she said, looking toward the big bay window that faced the expansive backyard and the woods and farm beyond. She looked back to him. "I guess we've been sitting here talking longer than I thought. It wasn't supposed to get bad until later." She glanced at the clock. "I guess later is now." She looked back up at him. "I know you said you were fine staying in town when Faith offered the guest cottage here the other night at dinner, but they're calling for some pretty nasty wind and flash flooding. Maybe you should bunk out there tonight."

He was searching for the right words, some tactful way that didn't insult the offer, or clue her in to his real reason for not wanting to be lying in a bed less than fifty yards from where she would be lying in hers, when she let out a rueful laugh. "I should warn you, though, it does not look like it did when you used to stay out there."

Admittedly curious, and thankful for the reprieve, he said, "Oh? How is that?"

"After Dan died, Faith and I kind of turned it into... What do they call them these days? A she shed? Only in our case, we kind of made it into a whole she cottage. Faith paints out there, and I do some stitching and other things." She grinned. "Okay, okay, we mostly watch really bad eighties movies, dance to music that we'd never listen to in public, and eat too much junk food. All of which we could do right here in the house, seeing as I'm the only one living here, but somehow doing all of it out there makes it seem more, I don't know, rebellious."

"Rebels with a boom box," he said, laughing with her. "I like it."

"Yeah, well, you say that now. We might have... overdecorated. Faith picked out things she'd always wanted as a kid but never asked for. I might have gone a bit beyond adding the recommended touch of color. Silly, but harmless fun." She looked around the kitchen. "I think we both just needed to create an environment that was exclusively ours, put our own stamp on it, if that makes sense. I love this house, and I really didn't want to change a single thing in it."

"It must have been hard," he said, his tone sobering. "So many memories here."

Lily nodded but said, "Even at the worst of our grief, it didn't feel oppressive. It was the exact opposite for me. It was comforting, like being held in the arms of all the Dawsons who came before. I felt... safe, I guess. Like it would be okay because the Dawsons had always triumphed, and I would, too. Or at least that's how I chose to look at it, to feel. Celebrate rather than mourn, though I did plenty of that, too. That probably sounds morbid, or creepy, but—"

"Finding comfort during the hardest time in your life in a way that also happens to honor the best of what this family has always been about? I can't think of a more loving and healthy way to process your grief."

Her eyes widened a bit at his heartfelt testimony. "Thank you," she said. "I never thought of it that way." She smiled. "I will from now on, though."

It was a marvel how she'd come through it all, not just the loss of her husband, but all who had passed on before. Yet, she was positive and upbeat, as was her daughter. Getting to that point wouldn't have been easy, though. As she took another look around the room, a satisfied smile on her face, he was glad that his words had brought her an extra measure of comfort.

"All that said," she went on, "it was admittedly kind of nice to go a little wild out there, carve out a spot that the Dawson women could call their own."

Sam was more than a little charmed by her cottage confession. "Well, the Dawson men have had the man cave downstairs for generations now, so it seems more than fair." He walked over to the mudroom and slid on his boots. "As much as I appreciate the offer, though, I think I'll head back to town. No need to go to the bother of getting things set up out there. Sounds like the rain is already coming down."

"All the more reason—"

"That old truck has made it through far worse. There's only the one really low creek crossing, and it can't have been raining long enough to be over the banks just yet."

"You're giving the famous Dawson hospitality a bad name," she teased. "But okay."

He chuckled. "Then I'd just have Annie mad at me for checking out of her B&B early," he told her and took an inward sigh of relief when she laughed with him. They'd settled the issue with no hurt feelings. Just standing there a few feet apart, looking at her with her eyes shining, lips curved in that wry way they often did, it was harder than it should have been to keep himself from closing the distance, ducking his head down, and kissing her good night.

"Thank you again," she said. "For all the help over the past few days."

"Anything else I can do?"

She shook her head and walked with him down the hall toward the front door. His truck was parked out front. "We've got some decorating to do in the barn over the next few days, which we saved to do then since the rain won't matter for that part. We've got to set all the tables, decorate the chairs. But I'll have plenty of hands on deck for that, given the storm. I expect we'll get most of that done tomorrow. The rest doesn't really happen until it's showtime." She smiled up at him when they paused at the front door. "So, you're a free man until it's time for rehearsal on Friday. You'll be able to stay for the rehearsal dinner, won't you? Jonny is coming out and putting on his famous Down by the Sea buffet. Lobster roll, haddock, shrimp."

"I think my eyes just rolled back in my head in bliss," Sam said. "I haven't really had time to indulge in my hometown favorites since I've been back. Sounds like I'll be able to take care of that in one swoop." He put his hand on the doorknob. "You can count me in. I'm happy to contribute something, too. Maybe dessert?"

She looked offended. "We'll be having Frannie's blueberry pie, thank you very much. And her blueberry-lemon crumble. Faith and I will be slaving over a hot stove all day Friday putting those together." Her expression warmed with affection. "I think I'm looking forward to that part more than the dinner itself." Her eyes got a little misty. "Before she goes off and starts baking in her own kitchen." She laughed self-consciously and dabbed at the corners of her eyes. "I never cry, but I'm starting to think I'm going to be a total mess at the wedding."

His reaction was instinctive, without actual thought to the possible consequences. As one would with a friend, which she most certainly was — in truth now, not just by association — he put his arm around her shoulders and pulled her in for an affectionate hug. "Oh now, Mom, she'll only be twenty minutes away. I'm sure there will be all sorts of family baking still going on in that kitchen. I seem to recall holiday cookie-baking being an epic event at Dawson Farm."

The minute their bodies came into full contact, Lily stilled. Then Sam stilled, too, as he realized what he'd done. After an evening spent keeping his desire for her in check — hell, five straight days and nights of keeping himself in check — he'd gone and blown it without even thinking. He perfunctorily finished the light squeeze, then had every intention of letting her go and heading straight to his truck. He'd steer clear of Dawson Farm the rest of the week, till he was needed for rehearsal. Maybe catch up on the dozens of things he'd let slide because he couldn't seem to stay away.

Only, she looked up just then, and her gaze caught this. Her eyes were big, surprised, but also... aware. There wasn't a doubt in his mind about that. Because he was aware, too. Aware of just how she felt, firm and strong in some places... warm and incredibly soft in others. She had a physically demanding job, so the strong part wasn't a surprise. It was the soft parts that hit him like a sucker punch, messing with his equilibrium, making him pause that infinitesimal moment too long.

"Sam," she said, hardly more than a whisper, confusion in her eyes now, too. And desire. Right there. Right now.

"I'm... I'm sorry," he said, unable to look away, much less step away, but knowing he should. "I didn't mean anything by it—" And maybe he hadn't. Not in the moment. But it was a very conscious decision not to let her go now.

And, heart thundering inside his chest, he was also very conscious of the realization that she wasn't stepping away either.

# Chapter Five

Lily had absolutely no idea what might have happened next, and maybe that was for the best.

*Because you don't know want to know? Or because you do?*

She had no time to reflect on that either. At the exact moment she'd watched Sam's eyes grow dark and felt her own body respond with a staggering flood of need, a white flash of lightning slashed down from the night sky, so close it lit up every window in the house, making them both flinch hard. Sam had instantly turned them away from the front door and pulled her deep into the shelter of his much larger body, as if instinctively anticipating a full-on assault. Before either of them could react to their bodies being so utterly and intimately pressed together, there followed a deafening crack of thunder that quite literally shook the house.

There was no doubt the lightning strike had to have hit something in the backyard. Once they got their bearings back after the reverberations died down, they both turned and took off back down the hall to the kitchen. Sam had her hand in his and led the way, careful to keep her behind him.

The moment they entered the kitchen, Lily moved beside him. Through the big bay window at the back of the kitchen, they saw a shower of glittering gold and red sparks filling the air, followed by a loud whooshing sound, as if an enormous gust of wind had been forced through a tunnel, followed immediately by a bright orange glow that seemed to explode and fill the backyard.

"Fire!" Lily shouted and would have taken off toward the door to the back porch, only Sam clamped a wide palm around her upper arm and spun her right back around and into his arms, where he held her gently but firmly in place until he was sure she could focus and listen to what he was saying.

"Call the fire department," he told. "Get them on their way here. I'll go see what's been hit."

She started to argue. It was her farm, after all, her responsibility.

"I have some training with this, okay? With fire and explosions anyway." He caught her gaze, held it, until she nodded. "We've got this. It's going to be all right."

She nodded again, then took a deep, shuddering breath. She wasn't going to be any help if she went off half-cocked. "Okay. Thank you," she said, letting the breath go and trying to get on top of the adrenaline rush that felt like it was doing the Indy 500 through her bloodstream. "I'll make the call. I'm okay. Go." But she pulled him back around when he turned to leave. "Be careful," she told him. "Don't let anything happen to you."

He'd been nodding, but he paused, just for a split second, and she knew he understood she wasn't just saying what anyone would say in that moment. She was issuing the request, very specifically, to him.

"I'm not going anywhere," he promised her, then without hesitation, he leaned down and pressed a brief but solid kiss to her temple. "Next time, I'll just say yes to the cottage and spending the night," he said as he straightened and turned, shooting a quick glance heavenward. "No need for the Dawsons to go throwing lightning bolts down on us as a reminder not to ignore Dawson hospitality." Then he flashed that full-on, sexy-as-hell Sam Fletcher grin, added a wink, and was out the door.

Lily shook her head, as if trying to make sense of all that was happening, from the hard jolt of the lightning strike, to the feel of his lips pressed against her skin, coupled with that wink and grin. It was too much to process all at once, so she tackled the only part she could.

She grabbed her cellphone off the kitchen counter, her fingers shaky.

*I didn't mean anything by it.*

His words echoed through her mind even as she punched in 911 on the keypad. Maybe he hadn't, maybe that kiss had been reassurance from one friend to another, too. But she'd felt his body pressed against hers, seen that look in his eyes up close... and all of it had sure felt like it meant something.

She went back to the bay window while quickly giving the dispatcher her address and explaining what happened. She gasped, and her shoulders went slack when she saw the trunk of the big oak tree in the backyard. It wasn't as thick and squat as the one out front, but the tree was equally old, equally cherished... and was now split right down the middle. Half of the tree branches hung drunkenly over the potting shed and equipment shed that lined the north side of the backyard, though mercifully they remained upright enough for the roof of either building to not have been crushed or damaged.

Despite it being long past nightfall, Lilly could see that clearly, because the other half of the tree was on fire, illuminating every detail of the backyard.

The flames raced along the branches that hung downward toward the yard, obscuring her line of vision. She couldn't see the cottage behind it, but she thought it was far enough back to be out of the way. Most of the bent and damaged limbs were lying across the circular gravel drive and small parking lot that took up the space immediately behind the house. Had the tree been split in the other direction, the roofs of the cottage house and the main house, both substantially higher than the outbuildings, would likely have been torched as well.

She hung up with the dispatcher, already hearing sirens in the distance, and was out the back door and down the porch steps an instant later, running for the hose.

Sam emerged from somewhere right behind her, a black silhouette framed by the orange and yellow glow behind him. "Don't aim that at the fire, it could—"

"I'm going to aim it at our roof, douse it, get it as wet as possible," she said, raising her voice to be heard over the roar of the fire. "Can you get back to the cottage to soak that roof? In case the sparks carry? There's a path on the other side of the fence, away from the tree, behind the sheds, that leads around to a path leading over—what am I saying? You know where it is." She turned and bent down to yank on the faucet, turn on the water, when Sam put his hand on her arm.

"Lily," he said, but she jerked her arm away.

"We can't let the sparks hit the house," she told him, had to all but yell at him over the noise of the tree burning. She never knew fire could be so loud.

Sam took her arm again, only this time he turned her and pointed upward before she could jerk free.

She looked up… and felt the rain stinging her cheeks, then silently ducked her chin and shook her head. It was raining. Hard. No need to soak anything. "Sorry. All I could see was this beautiful old home that's been in the Dawson family for generations going up in flames." She turned and hung up the hose, then scraped her hair back from her wet cheeks and forehead, feeling abruptly helpless now that she was no longer on a rescue mission.

She turned and looked at the tree, having to prop one hand on her forehead to block the rain and provide a shield from the bright glare of the fire. But she couldn't look away. She reminded herself to be thankful that the buildings had dodged a big bullet, but her heart was squeezing painfully all the same as she watched the majestic old oak burn. There was no changing it, no going back, and nothing she could do to fix it.

The scream of the sirens grew closer as smoke started to billow up, along with the flames.

Lily pulled the front of her sweatshirt up and over her mouth and nose and held it there with her hand, but her eyes watered all the same, and not just because of the smoke, until she finally squeezed them shut. She felt Sam's arm slide around her shoulders as he gently pulled her in and tucked her against his side, allowing his much taller, bigger body to shield her from the brunt of the storm and smoke.

"The rain isn't enough to put it out, but it will keep it from getting worse," he said, leaning down so his mouth was close enough for her to hear him without having to raise his voice. "Why don't you go inside? I'll meet the truck and emergency personnel—"

She was already shaking her head. "No, it's my farm, my

responsibility." She looked up at him, squinting against the raindrops clinging to her lashes. "Thank you, though. For all of it."

"I didn't do much more than assess and make sure nothing else had caught on fire."

"I hate feeling helpless." She looked to the tree, then back to him. "Maybe it just felt better to be helpless together," she said, trying for a faint smile, missing it by a good mark as tears continued to gather at the corners of her eyes, mixing with the rain tracking down her cheeks.

The first truck rolled down the lane, and they both turned and jogged through the muddy puddles around to the front yard. Sam's long-legged pace would have put him there well ahead of her, but he'd taken her hand, measured his stride, and kept her with him. She liked that his instinct was to be a partner and not simply a commander. A protective one, perhaps, but he didn't run roughshod. He treated her as an equal. She found she liked all of those things. Even the protective part, given it came packaged with all the rest.

Sam made arm motions for the emergency vehicles to take the drive around to the back, inasmuch as they could. When three more vehicles pulled in behind the two fire trucks, Lily knew, given how wet and muddy the ground had been to begin with, that there would be deep tire ruts, and the yard would likely be all torn up by the time this was over. She couldn't think about that now. She was just thankful they were there and would stop the tree from burning completely to ash, as well as keep it from falling and harming anything else. *Grateful, just be grateful.* And she was. Sam gave her hand a squeeze, then they parted to help direct the various crews so they could do what needed to be done.

It was close to two in the morning before the trucks pulled out again. The fire was out, but what was left of the tree still sent up thick plumes of smoke. She'd been warned it would be doing so for a few days, even though the rain was likely to continue until morning. She'd also been given strict orders to steer clear of it and the immediate property behind it until the fire marshal came out to check it over.

Lily had already been on the phone with Faith, assuring her everything was okay before she heard the news some other way. Faith and Max had insisted they wanted to come out anyway, offer moral support, and just be there as part of the family. It wasn't until Lily told Faith that Sam was there with her that Faith agreed to wait until the next day. Lily made the two of them promise to go on to work in the morning like normal. Then they'd meet up afterward if Faith wanted to come out. It was just the tree. Everything else would be all right.

Lily didn't want to think about what the place was going to look like once the sun came up. She hadn't mentioned that part to the soon-to-be bride either. It wasn't until Lily finally, wearily, climbed the steps to the back porch and re-entered the kitchen that she gave any thought to just how drenched and muddy and smoke-grimy she was. She took off her shoes, which were trashed now. When she'd first raced out the door, she hadn't been thinking about appropriate footwear. By the time she had, it had been too late.

Sam had climbed the steps behind her but stopped on the back porch after she stepped into the kitchen.

"I'm soaked," he said when she looked at him expectantly. "I don't want to make a mess."

She spread her arms wide and glanced down at herself, a wry smile on her face, exhausted, and beyond caring at this point. "What's a little more mud and muck? Come on in."

He took his muddy boots off on the back porch, then stepped carefully inside and went straight to the mudroom in a few long strides where he slid out of his sodden jacket. He hung it up in front of the specially installed space heaters the Dawsons had always used to dry outer gear in the winter months.

"Coffee?" she asked, and they both laughed, maybe a little harder than was warranted, but it felt good. Cathartic, after hours of tense observation and helpless anxiety. Now that he'd peeled off his jacket, Lily realized everything he wore underneath wasn't just damp but plastered to his chest and arms. Outlining every muscle, every flat plane.

And just like that, she was right back to where she'd been

before the lightning strike had quite abruptly ended... whatever it was that had been happening down the hallway by the front door. She was too exhausted now to put up much of a defense against it either.

"I, uh—" She looked away, gestured down the hall. "Max has a few things stashed upstairs that I'm sure will fit you. Let me go grab—"

"I could just head back to the cottage—"

"Fire chief said we can't go anywhere near the tree," she said. "Or behind it until the marshal gets out here. He's afraid some of the burnt limbs could come down in the storm."

"I'll head back to Annie's, then," Sam said. "Let you get some rest."

"It's the middle of the night. Past that, even, by the time you'd get back to town. No need to wake her up, coming in that late. Besides, you'll trash your truck if you climb into it like that."

He grinned at that, and even as tired as she was, her pulse shot straight up. "You've seen my truck, right?"

She let out a tired laugh, tried to ignore the prickling awareness of him in that sodden shirt and the aching need he seemed to so effortlessly rouse inside her with nothing more than a flash of that grin. She should let him head out, let them both regroup. Apart. But that felt too selfish, given all he'd done that night. All he'd been doing for her, and for Faith, for days on end now. Surely they were too exhausted to do, or even want to do, anything other than crawl into separate beds and pass out.

"Still," she said, "you're here. It'll be morning before too long. Take the guest room upstairs, next to Faith's old room. Max's stuff is in the dresser in there, and there are probably some things stuffed in the closet, too. You can use the hallway bathroom, take a good hot shower, and we'll tackle tomorrow tomorrow." She smiled. And tried like hell not to imagine him in that shower. Peeled out of those wet, oh-so-clingy clothes. Failed. She had to clear her throat to get more words out. Not looking at him any longer would help, too, but that was apparently too much to ask of herself.

She needed to go to bed, too. Alone. *Going to bed not alone would probably help with all that pent-up stuff a lot better,* her little voice helpfully supplied. That she ignored. "Well, 'later this morning' I guess is more accurate now."

"If you're sure," he said, looking perfectly willing to drag on that wet coat and his muddy boots and head back out into the storm.

She was already starting to feel the chill from her sopping-wet clothing seep past the surface of her skin to somewhere near bone-deep. He could only be feeling the same. "I'm sure." She found another smile. "I'd hate to think what the ghosts of Dawsons past would toss down at us if you didn't accept my hospitality offer after their last little display."

He winced even as he smiled. "True that. Well, I appreciate it," he told her and left his jacket hanging in front of the heaters.

"If you want to turn on the boot dryers in there and bring in your boots—"

He shook his head. "They'll be fine." He sat on the big wooden chair perched in the corner of the mudroom and pulled off his wet socks.

"Max should have some socks up there, too," she offered. "And, uh, whatever else you need."

He shot her a quick glance, his eyebrow cocking up along with the corner of his mouth, but whatever he might have been about to say, he clearly thought more wisely of it.

Had it been any other night, or any other... anything, she might have made a boxers-briefs-or-commando joke. But making suggestive banter, no matter how jokingly intended, didn't seem like a wise move.

"Could I bother you for a towel?" he asked, then smiled. "Like of the beach variety? No point in me dripping all the way through your house and up the stairs."

*Dear Lord, now he was going to strip? Right there in her mudroom?* She closed her eyes briefly against that mental image, then wondered why she continued to even bother. "Uh, sure. Cupboard above the dryer." She motioned, then glanced away as he turned to reach for it. She stared down at the puddle forming at her feet on the tiled kitchen floor. "Speaking of dripping, I might as well drip myself right on up the stairs and out of these wet clothes."

Even as the words left her mouth, his gaze had been swinging back to hers. But now it seemed to pin her there, to the spot. He'd already been smiling, and that didn't change, but it was the way his gaze homed in and focused. All on her. She knew, even from across the room, that those green eyes had probably gone all emerald dark again. Just as they had right before lightning had struck.

She jerked her gaze away and braced a hand on the counter so she could peel off her own soggy socks. The rest was going to have to wait.

"Why don't you go ahead and hop in the shower first?" he told her. "When I hear it shut off, I'll wait a few, then take mine."

Seriously, she couldn't take much more of this visual bombardment. She'd never sleep again. She'd never been the shower-together sort, but she couldn't help but wonder what that would be like. With Sam.

She turned toward him, soggy socks in hand, just as he reached for the hem of the double layers of T-shirts he wore and did an immediate about-face, tossing them in the general direction of the door to the back porch. She'd deal with... everything tomorrow.

She'd turned toward the arched door that led to the main hall and the staircase that led to the second floor when he said, "Lily."

Just her name. Quietly, without a hint of suggestion, teasing, or... anything. In fact, he sounded quite serious.

She didn't even bother bracing herself. If he was half naked, no amount of bracing was going to help. She glanced back. *Still clothed,* she noted. And wasn't reassured in the least when her immediate reaction was disappointment rather than relief.

"Thank you," he said. "For... letting me in."

Her breath stilled inside her chest, because she knew he wasn't referring to her opening the door of her guest room to him for the night. He was thanking her for letting him into her life. Not as the wife of his best friend, but just as herself. As the woman she was right now. "I... feel the same," she said, meaning it. He'd brought parts of her back to life that she hadn't been sure she'd wanted to have resurrected, maybe ever. He'd made her feel things. New things. Different things. He'd made her curious, made her want to reach for things she hadn't allowed herself to even consider, and reminded her how that kind of constant anticipation could be both heady and terrifying.

"I've been wanting to come back to Swan Harbor for some time now," he went on. "But in all honesty, I wasn't sure how it would really be. How it would feel." His smile was slow, sincere rather than flashy. "This has been a very good welcome-home. Far better than I could have allowed myself to hope for."

Despite all the intensity flying around the room, she felt herself relax. This was all rather terrifying, sure, some — most — of the things he was making her feel. Whether it was his sincerity, his maturity, his... everything... she couldn't say. All she knew was that the thrill was rapidly starting to outweigh the fear. Partly because her first reaction on hearing he was staying... had been joy. She'd been happy that their long talks over coffee didn't have to come to an end. Maybe ever.

Mostly, though, it was because this was Sam Fletcher, a man who had always had her entire family's best interests at heart. Like her apparently far-wiser daughter had said that first day, if Lily was ever going to trust herself to move forward and reclaim this part of her life... who better to take that step with than someone she knew and could fully trust? Someone who that very same wise daughter loved and respected so much she'd chosen him to escort her down the aisle on the happiest day of her life?

Lily's smile was slow, as was his, and she felt the pull between them intensify when she let hers slide wide. "Paying for hours and days of free labor with pizza and coffee, then following it up by your home-away-from-home almost burning to the ground, all in the midst of a raging rainstorm," she replied, then to her utter surprise at such an important, crucial moment — at least in her mind, because she was tossing her hat directly into the ring now and directly at his feet — rather than blurt out something awkward, or run for the stairs, she wiggled her eyebrows — *wiggled her eyebrows* — and said, "Yep, I really know how to show a guy a good time."

# Chapter Six

Sam was standing in the backyard the next morning, watching the still-smoldering tree, when Lily emerged from the house. Her hair was wet, fresh from the shower, combed back from her face, but worn down around her shoulders instead of in her standard messy ponytail. The sun had returned, the early morning beams catching on her dark auburn hair, making it look like sparks flickered along the damp strands. She wore khaki field pants that hung on her frame, a loose, pale aqua T-shirt that clung to her slight curves just enough to make him notice, and a large, unzipped gray sweatshirt that hung halfway down her thighs. There was nothing remotely sexy about the outfit.

And yet he found himself pressing his curled fingers deeper into the pockets of his pants—well, Max's pants—partly to disguise the effect she and her baggy, shapeless outfit had on him, partly to keep from reaching for her, which seemed like the most natural thing in the world to want to do in that moment. Like joining him in the backyard after a morning shower was how they started every morning. Together.

Somehow, he'd managed not to walk straight to her last night, scoop her up in his arms, and carry her straight up to bed. But despite the fact that they'd each slept alone last night, he hadn't missed the change in her when she'd teased him before heading up the stairs. Like she'd come to some kind of decision. One that might scare the bejesus out of him and thrill him right down to his marrow all at the same time. He wondered if a good night's sleep had changed any of that for her.

Because it had changed things for him. Though there hadn't been much sleeping involved.

"If the offer of the cottage is still open, I found a path around to the back that won't have the fire marshal writing me up," he said by way of greeting. "I thought with the tree situation, and the wedding in a few days, I could be more readily available to help if I stayed here." As she drew closer, he saw her face was as freshly scrubbed as her hair, her skin a bit pale, and there were shadows under her eyes. The aftereffects of the long night before, no doubt. He wanted to press his lips to the soft pulse he saw beating at her temple, then gather her in close and maybe talk her into going back to bed. To sleep, get some rest. Then... who knew after that?

He knew what he'd want after that, just as he knew his face looked more the worse for wear than hers did, because he'd lain in bed thinking about that want until the sun started creeping up over the horizon.

"I got my muddy things out of the house." He smiled. "I might have taken a sandwich bag of Frannie's special grind, too. If you're okay with putting me up in the cottage, I'll move the rest of my things over from Annie's later." She hadn't said anything as yet, so he met her gaze, held it. "I haven't said anything to Annie. So, if you'd rather keep things as they are—"

"The offer stands," she said, her voice steady, open, if maybe a shade softer than usual. Her gaze shifted back to the tree, and he could see the hurt there, like looking at it caused her actual pain. He suspected it did. She was a farmer who'd spent her whole life nurturing life from nothing more than tiny seeds, tending to them, watching them grow. Seeing this big, beautiful tree she'd looked at, lived with, walking beneath its outstretched boughs every day for the better part of her life, now disfigured, half scorched, and bereft of all its majesty would indeed likely cause her physical pain.

Lily Dawson was smart, direct, self-assured. She'd been dealt a lot in her life, but it was her nature to stand up to it, not bow down. Find her way forward, for herself, her daughter, her farm. She wasn't given to overtly feminine trappings or flirtatious banter, though she'd quite shockingly surprised him on that score the night before. Twice. First with her talk of going all girlie rebellion on the cottage, then again later with her parting remark. Must have shocked her, too, because she'd beaten a hasty if soggy retreat right after the words left her mouth, before he could reply.

Watching her now, however, he realized she wasn't quite as rock solid as she put on. Yes, he'd seen her be loving and affectionate with Faith and worried, at times, for her only child, too. But that kind of softness was different. She was fully and utterly maternal and very open about it, and it was a good look on her. But this... the vulnerability he saw now, was a side he hadn't seen. *Because you were half a world away when she was hurt the last time.*

Not that losing a tree, no matter how magnificent or integral it might have been to her life, was in any realm of comparison to the heavy, far more personal losses she'd sustained. But it was as close as he'd come to witnessing loss, in any form, in her, so it felt significant to him. Seeing her ragged edges, ones she wasn't trying to hide from him, drew him in all the more and left him feeling helpless.

He shifted his attention to the grounds, the yard, the gravel lot, the muddy driveway, which all looked exactly as one would expect, given the heavy equipment that had rolled through there in the middle of a rainstorm. "I talked to Hank this morning," he said, keeping his voice a little quieter now, but still direct, forward-moving. He suspected she'd revert to much the same in short order. Maybe it would help if he started. He didn't know, but it was all he had. "I figured, as a realtor, he might have a few contacts. People who can spruce up a place to get it showroom-ready for the big day. He gave me the name of some folks who could come out and level out the ruts. He said he's got a guy in Machias who might be able to lay sod before the weekend. If that was something you wanted to do."

She kept looking at the tree and, other than nod, didn't say anything right away. Maybe she wasn't a morning person. He'd never been around her first thing in the morning. Generally, when he'd come up to the house when visiting Dan, she'd long since been up and gone, out in the fields, or somewhere on the farm, doing whatever it was a farmer did to keep an operation the size of Dawson Farms running smoothly. So, he'd always assumed that that had made her a morning person.

He glanced back at her and fought an odd urge to smile. *Or maybe not.*

"Thank you," she said a moment later, the words filled with sincere gratitude. He saw her take in a slow, deep breath, then let it out the same way.

She nodded, maybe at the tree, or maybe at some thought or internal decision she'd just come to, or maybe in response to him. He didn't know. He wanted to know. Wanted to know everything about her. And he stood there a moment longer, thinking how amazing it was, after all these years, how little he still did.

"She's going to have to come down, isn't she?" Lily said, looking at the ground now, out at the fields, back to the house. Anywhere but at the tree. Or at him. He suspected she was trying to get her emotions under control. He'd give her all the space she needed for that.

"Looks that way," he said. "I'm sorry, Lily. It must feel like losing a stately guardian."

She looked directly at him, surprised, then nodded. "That's exactly what it feels like. I couldn't find the right words." She did look back to the tree then, and her shoulders sagged. "Thank you. Having the right words helps."

He turned and stood beside her, looking at the tree.

"It looks so much worse. In the light of day," she said, her voice quiet, just a breath above a whisper. "So horribly sad." From the corner of his eye, he saw the sheen steal across the surface of her eyes, saw the tiniest tremble of her bottom lip. She didn't try to hide it, but he suspected the frown that followed was her way of trying to at least stifle it.

He'd have to be made of stone not to react. And while he'd spent a good part of his adult life pretending to be made of stone, in situations ranging from the merely harrowing to the downright terrifying, that one tiny quiver utterly undid him. "Come here," he said, loosening the arms she'd wrapped around her middle, then turning her gently into his own. He shuffled her close, cupped the back of her head, then sighed when, rather than pull away, she pressed her forehead to his chest. She rested her hands lightly on his hips as she let the breath she'd been holding come out. It was shaky, and there might have been a sniffle there, the beginning of a soft sob.

"It's okay," he told her. "Holding it in just keeps it all backed up."

"It's a tree," she said, her voice thick with unshed tears. "It's just a tree."

"It's your tree," he corrected. "It's a Dawson tree."

She nodded against his shirt, and her breath caught, then shuddered as she still tried to hold her emotions in check. "How do you get that?" she said hoarsely. With a watery laugh, she added, "Of course you get that."

He pulled her closer, sliding his arms around her, and after a brief hesitation, she slid hers fully around his waist and pressed her cheek to the front of shirt, her face turned outward.

He bent his head, pressed his cheek to her hair, so his lips were close to her ear. "I'll take her down for you. Okay?" he said, the words a deep rumble. "You don't have to be here. I'll do it right. Have the wood milled, not cut into firewood."

She glanced up, met his gaze, looking startled, horrified by the very idea of her lovely old oak being reduced to firewood.

"Not that she'd mind keeping you warm, but I'm thinking it would be more meaningful to build something with her. So, she'll keep standing for many years to come."

Lily's eyes widened, then she nodded, sniffled again as a tear finally formed and escaped from the corner of her eye, tracking down her cheek. It took every last bit of control he had not to bend his head and kiss that tear away. He wasn't used to feeling so protective. Not like this, at any rate.

"That is… perfect," she said, then surprised him by letting out a soft laugh, even as another tear broke free. "Who are you, Sam Fletcher?"

He smiled at that. "What, I'm not allowed to have a sensitive side?"

"I knew that about you," she said, surprising him again. "Or you and Dan would have never forged a friendship in the first place. I guess it was the intuitive part that caught me off guard." Her lips curved in a kind smile, even as that tear continued the rest of its way down her cheek. "Maybe it shouldn't have."

Sam had gone a little still at the mention of her husband, his friend. Maybe because he was thinking and feeling a whole barrage of confusing and clarifying things... and assumed a mention of Dan would jerk him right out of it.

It hadn't.

Maybe she wasn't feeling any of the same things he was, despite her flirty parting comment the night before, despite standing deep in his arms right now. Maybe he'd misinterpreted that bold smile of hers last night. And maybe this was just a friendly hug. Well, it *was* a friendly hug, but...

Her smile faded slightly, and a concerned look crossed her face. "What is it?" she asked, and he realized the direction of his thoughts had caused him to frown.

"Nothing," he said and quickly smoothed his expression, offered a small smile, then reached up and brushed away the tear that now clung to the corner of her mouth. His fingertip lingered there, not intentionally, but her gaze jerked fully to his at the touch. Any doubts he'd harbored that she wasn't as affected by being in his arms as he was by holding her so close were instantly erased.

Neither of them said a word as their gazes continued to hold. Unable to stop himself, even knowing he might be making the biggest mistake of his life, he slowly drew that fingertip along her lower lip. It quivered again, but this time for an entirely different reason.

"Sam," she whispered, her eyes searching his as if she looked to him for answers, or for permission, or for whatever it was they needed in order to take another step, then maybe another. He could feel a fine tremor race over her skin, and she trembled, just slightly, in his arms. Or maybe he was the one feeling a little shaky.

"Lily," he began, having no earthly clue what he was about to say, whatever intuitiveness he might have had fleeing just when he needed it most. "I—" He paused, his gaze dropping from those big, wide eyes to her mouth, which parted on a little gasp, almost undoing him completely right there. His gaze went right back to hers. "You matter to me," he said. "And not just because of Dan." He intentionally put that there, between them, where Dan would always be in one way or the other, in hopes that it would become a place they would be comfortable with. Open with. "This isn't... I'm not—"

"Right," she said, misinterpreting him, her expression shuttering immediately. "You're not wanting this. I—we shouldn't—"

He tipped her face back up so her gaze met his once more. "I don't think I've ever wanted anything more in my entire life," he said. Blurted, actually. Lily Dawson style. Actually, Lily Foster style.

Her shocked look at what he'd said, or maybe the way he'd said it, sparked a reaction he hadn't seen coming. She laughed. "Oh, thank God," she said, looking both delighted and relieved. "I thought maybe I'd just fabricated it all in my head, seeing what I wanted to see."

"Wait—" He lifted her face back to his when she ducked her chin and wiped her eyes. "What?"

She smiled up at him, her eyes still glassy, her face still too pale, and all of her was just so damned beautiful to him.

"I feel like—have been feeling like—I'm just meeting you for the first time," she said. "And at the same time, there's such an easy comfort with you, all the time, like I've known you my entire life. Because that is true, too. I have. And it so confuses me. Because I never thought you'd—" She broke off, shook her head, then let out another short laugh. "Sam Fletcher. And Lily Foster." She looked back up to him. "I mean, really? Who would have seen that coming?"

"Me," he said without hesitation. "From the moment I saw that pen-and-ink drawing in your dad's hardware store the summer I turned fourteen." Her expression shifted from shocked to stunned as he went on. "Followed quickly by you coming in on my first day on the job, all five-foot-nothing of you back then, and informing me in no uncertain terms that your father was not going to tolerate me standing around and staring at stuff. I told you I'd already stocked everything he'd told me to stock and asked if those initials on the drawing belonged to you. You said yes, which blew my adolescent mind, then shoved a broom in my hands and told me, 'When in doubt, sweep.'"

"The first of many blurted idiocies when I was around you,"

she said with a laugh, her cheeks charmingly growing pink with embarrassment. "You had the tendency to sort of suck the air out of the room when you came in. In the very best of ways, so my adolescent-girl hormones thought. At least that's what I blamed for feeling so lightheaded when you were around."

Now it was his turn to look a little stunned.

"Oh, come on. You, of all guys, knew the effect you had on the opposite sex."

"Maybe, but not you."

"Ouch?" she said on a laugh.

"No, I didn't mean I didn't see you as a member of the opposite sex. It was just that you weren't like any of them. You didn't seem to care one whit about me or what I thought. Of you, or anything else." He smiled. "It was both annoying and intriguing as all hell. You fascinated me from that moment onward."

She shook her head, smiling, but clearly believing he was embellishing his little story. "If all that's true, why didn't you say something? You were hardly shy."

"I would have if you'd have come by the store ever again that summer. At least while I was there."

"And make an idiot of myself in front of you again? With repeat matinee performances every Tuesday and Thursday afternoon?" She laughed. "Even then, I had a better sense of self-preservation than that."

He wiggled his eyebrows. "You remember after all this time that I worked my very first after-school job on Tuesdays and Thursdays?"

She merely lifted a shoulder and owned it. "Maybe. But again, if you'd been oh-so-very intrigued, as you say, we went to the same school. You could have made your curiosity about me pretty clear if you'd wanted to," she said, a teasing smile on her face. "I know you wouldn't have cared if the cool kids saw you talking to the science and art geek, because that didn't stop you from rescuing Dan from those idiots who harassed him half to death, much less becoming his good friend afterward."

"Actually, it was because I rescued Dan that I never pursued my fascination with you. Okay, that's only partly true. You intimidated me."

She laughed outright. "I find that impossible to believe. You could have had any girl in school panting after you with hardly more than a wink."

"They weren't you. And it's one thing to encourage the obvious, and maybe some guys would have taken your ambivalence as a challenge. Me... well, maybe some of that cocky swagger was there to cover up what insecurities I did have." He shook his head. "You seemed like someone who would see straight through that. I don't think I'd have risked that. Not back then."

"Sam," she said, such soft empathy in that one whispered word, then fell silent again.

"In the long run, none of that mattered anyway," he went on. "Once I learned Dan had the biggest crush on you, and saw how perfect the two of you would be together — if I could ever get him to take his head out of his ass long enough to ask you out — I was out of that picture for good. And more than a little relieved. No risk for me, and the reward of seeing my best friend deliriously happy? Win-win."

She might not have wanted to believe it, but he suspected she knew the truth when she heard it. And he'd meant every word.

"Besides," he said, a slow smile curving his lips, "I was right."

She nodded, her smile sweet, and a little sad. "You were. I know I've thanked you before, for telling me about Dan and his crush on me." Her tone turned wry as she added, "When you failed to help him with that head-and-ass issue." Her smile grew, and her eyes were shiny again, but in a good way. "So, I could ask him out and take care of that for you."

"It worked, didn't it?" Sam laughed and pulled her close, their hug this time a tribute to the friendship between all three of them, and though the sadness was there, too, it was a good memory, one he wanted them both to always cherish. Sam knew that if anything was to come of this, Dan would always be with them. And in honoring that, he'd also never come between them.

Sam wanted to tell her that, so she'd know where he stood, but when she leaned back, smiled up into his eyes, he saw that she was already there.

She shook her head, still smiling, and held on to his gaze.

"What?" he asked.

"I don't know what we're doing," she said. "Or if we should be doing."

He loosened his hold but didn't let her go. "We're not doing anything," he said. "Yet. Lily, just because we both want, doesn't mean we have to jump."

"I don't know what I'm ready for, Sam," she said, as baldly honest as she'd ever been. "How could I, right? Maybe it will be weird. Maybe I won't be able to handle it. Maybe you won't."

"All of that is absolutely true."

"If anyone had told me you'd stroll back into town and we'd end up spending every waking minute together, and now I'm standing here, blubbering all over you and acting the fool over a tree, I'd have laughed them out of town."

"Nothing about you is foolish."

She raised one eyebrow and gave him a considering look. "You've been inside, right?" she said, nodding to a point behind him. "You've now seen the she cottage."

"That's not foolish," he said with a laugh. "More… overtly whimsical."

"Nice save," she said with a nudge to his ribs.

"Taking the Dawson love of joy and humor to the next level."

She laughed at that. "Oh, it's next-level all right. Faith and I might have gone a little overboard with the grief therapy."

"I don't know. I kind of like the unicorn shower curtain," he said. "It's too soon for tasteless jokes," he deadpanned. "So, I'll just leave it at that."

A bark of laughter burst out of her, and she buried her face in his jacket and kept snickering. "So… so bad."

"Well, that depends on what you thought I meant," he said with mock pride. "Maybe I was identifying with the joy of racing through a meadow of glittery flowers and butterflies."

She gave him a little thwack with her palm. "I know exactly what you were identifying with," she said, her ensuing giggle ruining the imperious delivery entirely. "Or think you were anyway."

"Did you just smack my backside?"

"Maybe," she said, then snickered again. Then he did. "I'll never be able to look that unicorn in the eye again," she said, and they were both lost, laughing until they had to wipe the dampness from the corners of their eyes.

When their gazes met, it almost took his breath away all over again. She smiled up into his eyes, then reached up and traced her fingers over his cheek, down his jaw, and that gentle touch, that first real touch from her, rocked him in ways that had absolutely nothing to do with hormones and needs. She was looking up at him exactly the way she had that day when they'd first walked out to the barn. Only this time, all that joy and affection—and, yes, desire—was for him. And he knew he'd happily spend the rest of his days doing whatever it took so she never stopped.

"I do want, Sam. I want to find out where this might go, where we might go, together," she said. "Neither of us can know what we're ready for. But I think if we matter enough to each other, and Faith matters to both of us, and we honor Dan's memory—as we have been—then if it turns out that this isn't right for either one of us, we'd do what was best for each other. Right?"

"Yes," he said, the word hardly more than a rasp. She had the damnedest ability to take his breath away. "Absolutely." He cupped her cheek. "I don't want you to hurt. Ever again."

If it was possible, her eyes grew even more luminous. "Life offers no guarantees. We know that better than most. Just like we know that sitting on the sidelines doesn't guarantee we'll be risk-free. The way I see it, I have someone standing right in front of me who makes me feel so many wonderful things I didn't think I'd ever feel again, who brings new joy to my world, fills me with the best kind of anticipation, with hope. If that's not worth taking a risk for, taking a chance on, what is?"

He covered her hand, still pressed to his cheek, then lifted it and wove his fingers through hers. "I want that chance, Lily." He lifted their hands and turned them so he could press a kiss to her fingers. "Fair warning," he said, smiling up at her, his lips still brushing her skin. "I plan to make the most of it."

She smiled. "I plan to let you."

He closed his eyes for a brief moment as both wonder and not a little fear filled him. Fear of the unknown. Fear of not being enough. Then something else she'd said struck him, and he lifted his head and tucked their joined hands between them. "About Faith," he said. "I'm happy to talk with her, assure her our hearts are in the right place, a very good place. I'll respect her feelings on this, make sure she's okay with—"

"Are you kidding?" Lily broke in, a grin stealing across her face. "I'm pretty sure that will be the one thing we don't have to worry about. In fact, I'm not entirely sure she didn't ask you to walk her down the aisle, in some part, because she was hoping for this very thing."

Sam knew he looked every bit as shocked as he felt. "Faith? Was playing matchmaker? With us?" He was well and truly speechless.

"That first day," Lily said, "at the bridal shop... well, let's just say that maybe she saw the inevitable before we bought a real clue."

He chuckled and shook his head. "I don't know how I feel about that," he said in utter honesty.

"I'll be honest with you. I told her in no uncertain terms to just pack that idea up and put it away," Lily said with a laugh. "Probably because it was too much to even consider, given I was already having an almost impossible time handling my reaction to seeing you again. I mean, you were Dan's best friend, godfather to my only child, and there I was, getting all hot and bothered because you were voting yes on my cleavage."

"Yes on your...?" He was confused for a moment, then realized what she meant and grinned. "Well, in my defense, that dress did do wonderful things for said cleavage. And you seemed torn. So, I thought I'd offer some assistance in the decision-making." He laughed when she swatted him again. "But Faith as matchmaker...I'm still wrapping my head around that. I mean, to me, she'll always be that pigtail kid on the swing out front. And this Saturday, she's just playing dress-up for her pretend wedding. You know? How did she become such a smart young woman?"

Lily beamed at the compliment. "She's had good people in her life. Loving people," Lily said. "You included. She just wants that for everybody else." She laughed. "Having bride brain just exacerbates that."

"Who's calling someone a bride brain?" a voice called out from just behind them.

# Chapter Seven

Lily all but leaped from Sam's embrace, then spun to face her daughter. "Faith!" The word came out on a rather high-pitched squeak, after which she pasted a ridiculously over-the-top smile on her face. Like she could erase what her daughter had just seen by distracting her or pretending it hadn't happened.

"Mom!" Faith mimicked with a laugh.

"What are you doing here?" Lily asked, quickly crossing the yard to meet her. As if putting fast distance between herself and Sam could erase what Faith had clearly seen. "Why aren't you teaching?"

"Storm knocked down a bunch of trees, which took down the power lines and knocked out a transformer. No power, school is closed." She ran up and hugged Lily tight before she could do or say anything else. "I'm so glad you're both okay."

"I told you everything was fine," Lily said, still in Faith's tight embrace.

"Am I wrong in thinking I was just seeing what I think I was just seeing?" Faith whispered excitedly in her mother's ear. She leaned back, but held on to her mom's arms. "Because, honestly, I didn't think you'd let yourself go for it." She lifted one hand above her shoulder, palm out. "Up high."

Lily's laugh was partly delighted and mostly mortified, but she gave her daughter's hand a quick swat with her own. "Very funny."

Faith leaned in again, lifting a strand of Lily's damp hair. "Long night, late morning. So... does he... you know, live up to the packaging?" She wiggled her eyebrows.

Lily's mouth dropped open, then snapped shut. "Okay, new

rule. We may both be adults, and you know I have always had an open-door policy, encouraging you to come to me with anything. No topic is off-limits. That remains true." She held up her hand to stop Faith from replying. "However, the reverse does not apply."

"Is it wrong for a daughter to want to share in her mother's much-deserved happiness?" Faith asked, devilish delight dancing in her eyes.

"Sharing is fine. Oversharing, not so much."

"Where is the line in the sand?" Faith wanted to know, clearly not remotely deterred.

"Um, well, as long as we don't stray into any territory that involves wiggling of eyebrows as a means to convey one's point? We're good."

"Got it." Faith's expression immediately shifted to one of utmost seriousness. She leaned in close and asked in a hushed whisper, "So, purely for academic purposes, as a measure, one might say, of your satisfaction with where things stand so far, on a scale of one to ten, then, would you say he's, like, an eight or a nine or...?" She leaned back and held her chin between her fingers, a most professorial expression on her face... which was ruined entirely by the way the corner of her mouth kept twitching.

It took everything Lily had not to laugh outright.

"I'm not wiggling my eyebrows," Faith pointed out, her face a study in exaggerated seriousness.

Lily knew her daughter was far more outrageous than she was, and Faith certainly hadn't gotten that from her father either. The difference was that Lily knew experience often trumped audacity. *Two can play this game.* She leaned in, the epitome of let's-share-our-deepest-secrets, and whispered, "Well, we haven't actually done anything yet, but I was reading this website that had some pretty wild suggestions on various positions—"

Faith leaped back like she'd been stung by a bee. "Wow, okay! Well, that's fabulous, Mom. I'm—hoping that goes well for you."

Lily's smile was unrepentantly one of superior smugness, and a quick glance over her shoulder told her that while Sam might not have heard the specifics, he'd drawn the right conclusion. If that devilishly sexy smile on his face was anything to go by. He just nodded in her direction... then wiggled his eyebrows as he gave her a quick thumbs-up.

*Oh my God.* Lily's mouth dropped open, and a hot flush flooded her face. So okay, he had heard every word. Of course he had. She whirled back to Faith, expecting her daughter to be sporting the smug smile now, but Faith had finally looked past her mother and Sam and spied the tree for the first time.

"Oh no! I was so focused on you two." She turned to Lily and threw her arms around her. "I'm so sorry, Mom. I'm so glad you're okay and the house is okay. But..." She trailed off and looked back at the tree, and Lily could see her daughter's heart in her eyes as well. "It's like losing a member of the family." She looked at her mom. "It will have to come down, won't it?"

Lily nodded. "The split goes all the way to the ground inside the base of the trunk." She told Faith about Sam's idea of milling the wood and building something from it that would continue to honor the tree. "I don't know what we'll build, but something that will be around for a long time."

Sam walked over to them then, and Faith put one arm around his waist, the other around her mother's shoulders, as they all looked at the tree.

"How about a gazebo or pergola?" Faith suggested. "Right where the tree is now. I mean, even with half of it gone now, there should still be enough wood for something like that. Then we can still sit under her, and have picnics like we did when I was little. As will future generations."

"Oh," Lily said on a swift intake of breath. "That would be perfect."

"You raised a pretty smart kid," Sam said, leaning down and kissing the top of Faith's head. "I think that is exactly the right thing."

Faith looked up at Sam, then at her mom. "I think this is exactly the right thing, too."

They didn't have to ask what she meant.

"Well, honey, it's —" Lily began.

Just as Sam said, "We don't know what it might be or not be, but having your blessing while we find out means everything."

He was smiling, but his words were as seriously spoken as she'd ever heard him.

Faith slid her arm from her mom's shoulders and turned to hug him fully. Her phone buzzed as she let him go, and she slid it out of her jacket pocket. "Text from Max," she said, her face lighting up. "He's off today, too." She looked at Lily. "We're going to go spend some time doing something that has absolutely nothing to do with wedding planning. I know it sounds terrible, but we need a date night." Another text came in, and she looked, well, like a woman about to get married. "Max just invited me on a picnic. That's so sweet. I knew I picked a winner."

Faith gave her mom a noisy kiss on the cheek, then tipped up on her toes and pulled Sam down so she could buss his cheek, too. "You kids behave," she said, then took off across the small lot toward her car. "Don't do anything I wouldn't do," she called back, then turned and jogged backward a few steps. "Insert eyebrow wiggle here." Her laughter trailed behind her as she climbed into her car.

"Well," Lily said as she waved and watched Faith's car disappear down the long drive. "I stand by my bride-brain assessment. She didn't even notice that the yard looks like we had a monster truck rally here last night."

"I'm sorry we won't have enough time to take the tree down properly before the wedding, but hopefully Hank will come through on the lawn part at least. So folks can park and get over to the barn without too much trouble," Sam said as Lily turned back toward him. "One less thing to worry about."

Lily nodded. "Thank you for looking into that." She smiled. "Yet another thing I owe you more coffee and late-night pizza for."

He stepped closer and took one hand in his. "I'll take you up on that," he said, then gently turned her fully toward him. "Maybe we'll do something really crazy and go out to eat."

Lily's smile spread to a grin. "You mean, like on a date?"

"Is that still a thing for people our age?" He urged her closer and took her other hand in his as well. "Full confession," he said. "I have no idea how this is supposed to work. Or what the proper protocol is."

She laughed. "Don't look to me for guidance."

"Dinner seems to be a nice place to start." He moved closer, and she tipped her head back to look up into his eyes.

"Haven't we already started?" she asked, a breathless note in her voice.

"It sure feels that way to me," he said, his own voice dropping deeper.

"Good," she said. "Then I'd love to go out to dinner with you, Sam Fletcher. You know the whole town will be talking. Are you ready for that?"

He chuckled, that low rumble that sent shivers of anticipation right down through her. "Oh, I'm pretty sure they're already talking. We're standing in the middle of your backyard, in front of God and a whole lot of Dawson Farm employees. Unless they think you and I are standing this close because you've got something in your eye… I think that ship has sailed."

"Well, then, let's make sure they're not getting the wrong impression," she said, delighted when his eyebrows lifted in surprise as she tipped up on her toes and brought their lips a breath apart. "I don't know what I'm doing either," she whispered. "But I think this is the part where you kiss the girl."

His eyes went instantly dark, like emerald fire, which thrilled her down to her toes. "Something tells me we're going to figure this out just fine." He brushed his lips across hers in a teasing glance. "I especially think I'm going to like this part."

A soft moan escaped through her lips. "Sam," she breathed, not caring that she sounded needy and maybe a little demanding. Now that it was happening, now that they were taking this step—this giant leap—she wanted to go ahead and jump already. Her impatience surprised even her.

"We can give the rest of the world a show later," he said, his lips touching hers as he spoke. "Right now, for this first time, I just want it to be us." He shocked her by bending down and scooping her up in his arms, a sensation she could honestly say she'd never once experienced in her adult life. "I hope you don't mind."

She looped her arms around his neck. "And here I thought I'd already been swept off my feet," she said, a bit dizzy with all the things she was feeling.

"House, or she cottage?" he asked. "For that kiss... and maybe a morning cup of coffee."

"House," she said. "It's a part of both of us. And I'd like us to start as we mean to go on." She saw such raw emotion fill his eyes, hers filled right up, too.

He carried her to the house, and she pressed a private smile against his shoulder as he carried her over the threshold.

*Who knew she'd be the first one to do that this week?*

The moment they stepped into the kitchen, he let her feet slip to the floor but held her close, arms wrapped around her. If she'd thought anything about this moment happening between them, Lily supposed she'd thought, given Sam's flashy grins and heated looks, it would be like those scenes in movies where the two leads finally lose control and start tearing off clothes as they kiss and fumble their way to the nearest bed.

She should have known nothing would go as expected with Sam.

He slid one hand under her hair, cupping the nape of her neck, looking into her eyes the whole time, so much filling his own it was hard for her to know what all he was feeling.

"Hello, Lily Foster Dawson," he murmured. "I'm Sam Fletcher."

"Hi, Sam Fletcher," she said softly.

"And I've wanted to do this for what now feels like my entire life." He lowered his mouth then and finally took hers.

She sighed and leaned into him, her entire being responding to the feel of his lips on hers. They were warm and firm and so very different from anything she'd felt before. So very Sam. She loved all parts of that. New beginnings. For her daughter and now for herself.

He took his time kissing her, slowly, endlessly, learning every contour, taking in every breath and sigh, before finally parting her lips and taking her more fully.

The moan started somewhere deep inside of her as she willingly responded to his deep, slow, sensual slide with every part of herself. Her arms tightened around his neck as she decided this wasn't going to be just about taking, it was about giving, too. She kissed him back and was rewarded with a very gratifying groan from him in response.

He finally lifted his mouth from hers but kept her pulled up against him, up on her tiptoes, as he rested his forehead on hers and took a slow, shaky breath. "So," he said, sounding not a little stunned. "That went well."

She smiled, and any doubts that might have lingered about taking this step with this man vanished once and for all. She felt confident and vulnerable all at the same time and knew she could be both with him, freely and openly, and he would be right there for all of it. Just as she knew, heard in those very words, both of those things in him. And knew she'd be there for him, for all of that, too, and so very much more.

"I don't know," she said consideringly. "It's been a while for me. I think I need more practice." She slid her hand around the back of his neck and shifted her lips close to his once more. "Possibly a lot of practice."

"Is that so?" he said, and she knew she'd never tire of hearing that gravelly note in his voice. "It felt pretty damn perfect to me." He surprised a squeal out of her as he lifted her and set her on top of the center island, then stepped between her legs, his arms still around her. "Maybe we just needed to be on a more even playing field," he said and let a full-on Sam Fletcher grin curve those lips she was dying to taste again.

"Hmm, maybe," she said, possibly squirming a little as he teased her with a kiss to her jaw, then to that soft spot just below her ear. She let her head drop to the side as he kissed his way along the side of her neck, gasping as he reached tha curve into her shoulder.

"Better?" he murmured against her skin as he pulled her legs around his waist and scooted her forward until they were flush up against each other.

"Best," she managed, pressing her thighs against his hips against the ache that had bloomed, hard and fast and deep inside of her. He moved against her as he lifted the hair from her neck and softly bit her earlobe, and she thought she might come apart right there, fully clothed, in her kitchen. "So, very, very best."

"Oh, there's always room for improvement," he said and found her mouth again.

"I don't see how," she gasped helplessly. "But I'm game to find out."

He shifted, looked into her eyes, and his were filled with so much joy. "I can promise you that we are going to make the very best use of every minute, hour, and day we have together."

"I want that," she told him. "All of that. And you. Every one of those days." Her eyes twinkled. "I'm kind of looking forward to the nights, too."

His gaze grew dark, and she could feel his immediate response to that. Every inch of it. "If we're making our own rules, then why wait until nightfall?"

"First you corrupt me with weekday coffee, now this?" she teased. "Whatever have I gotten myself into?"

He lifted her off the work island and wrapped her up tight against him, then headed for the hallway to the front stairs. "Hold on to me, Lily Dawson," he told her. "We ain't seen nothing yet."

And he was right. So very, very right.

# Epilogue

Breathless, Lily rolled to her back, then laughed when her head slipped off the side of the bed. At least she thought it was the side of the bed. "I thought the kids were supposed to be the ones honeymooning," she managed, still trying to regain her breath. She spied her dress, the "cleavage dress" as she'd forever think of it, lying discarded in a heap on the floor right where it had landed. Two days ago. "I'm supposed to be running the farm."

Sam kissed his way along her hip and across her abdomen. "You gave everyone off for the week," he reminded her.

"I did, didn't I?" she said. "No more champagne receptions for me," she added with a sigh, then a bubbly laugh followed. Because, honestly, it was the best decision she'd ever made.

He grinned against her skin. "You were very happy and sweet." He lifted his head as she shifted so hers was back on the mattress again. "So very happy."

She sighed, but she couldn't keep the goofy smile from taking over. "I might have been a little tipsy. But they were just so beautiful, and those vows they wrote? I mean, there wasn't a dry eye. Who knew Max was a poet? It was so romantic, and then you looked at me that way you do. And I was just so… in the moment. I couldn't help myself."

"You wanted everyone to be happy."

She nodded, then squealed in delight when he lifted up and slid her fully back onto the bed and right beneath him. "I do want everyone to be happy," she said, wrapping her arms around him. "As happy as they are." She lifted her gaze to his. "As happy as I am."

He settled his weight between her legs and looked down into her drowsy, contented, beautiful face. "Mission accomplished," he told her, then lowered his mouth once more to hers.

# About Donna Kauffman

**Donna Kauffman** is the *USA Today* and *Wall Street* Journal bestselling author of over 70 novels, translated and sold in more than 26 countries around the world. The recipient of multiple RT Book Awards, she is also a National Readers Choice Award and PRISM Award winner and a RITA finalist. Born into the maelstrom of Washington, D.C., politics, she now lives in the Blue Ridge Mountains of Virginia, where she is surrounded by a completely different kind of wildlife. A contributing blogger for USAToday.com, she is also a DIYer, a baker, a gardener and a volunteer transporter for the Wildlife Center of Virginia and Rockfish Sanctuary. Please visit her online at www.DonnaKauffman.com.

# Snowbound in Vegas

### by Sally Kilpatrick

*To*
*Jamie and Tracy and Sonali and*
*Kwana and Virginia and Donna and*
*Falguni and Pris and Barbara and*
*Hope and Liz*

*If it weren't for you, this story wouldn't have happened.*

*And to Wendy Cope who brought the coffee — literally — essential oils, a silly hat, and most importantly, unwavering belief in me when I needed it most.*

# Chapter One

Either Geo Russo was drunk or his best friend's wedding was about to be officiated by Dolly Parton. He stepped back into the groom's room to question the groom.

"Dylan, are you really going to be married by the Queen of Country?"

The groom, taller and blonder than Geo, clapped a hand on his friend's shoulder. "Fiona *loves* Dolly, and what Fiona wants, Fiona gets."

"You are smitten," muttered Geo.

"And you are cynical and destined to die alone if you don't get off your glum ass and find a nice girl," Dylan said as he straightened his tie.

Geo looked around the tiny groom's room at the Mountain Bliss Wedding Chapel and told himself to take deep breaths. Every surface in the place—as in most places in Gatlinburg, Tennessee—was wood: paneling, flooring, furniture. All of that wood reminded him of growing up in a dingy trailer, even if the wood there had been, for the most part, fake paneling.

Mind you, he had nothing against trailers. His grandmother had a double wide that was nicer that most of his friends' houses, but his father had no desire to maintain the home or keep it clean. He'd been too busy working on get-rich-quick schemes rather than doing an honest day's work, and Geo had been awfully busy staying out of his way.

Come to think of it, his so-called cynicism had started in that very trailer.

"Well, I'm never letting you set me up again," he said.

"Aw, come on, Gee, that date was a hundred years ago, and

you're still pissed off about it?"

"Damn straight. That woman is a menace."

Dylan sobered. "She's grown up a lot."

"Haven't we all?"

Geo had grown up a lot, too, but Truvy Fuller had been like nails on a chalkboard. He couldn't stand her. She couldn't stand him. Back in college they had forged an uneasy truce only because she was Fiona's closest friend, and he was Dylan's. He knew that Fiona and Dylan still had this crazy notion of fixing up their respective best friends together, but love did *not* work like that.

Heck, in his experience, love just didn't work.

At all.

And he had the divorce to prove it.

"Seriously, man," Dylan said. "Truvy would be *perfect* for you, and I've seen the way you look at each other."

"She's an attractive woman, I'll give you that, but there's more to relationships than sex."

Dylan grinned. "Oh, I don't know about that. The things Fiona can do—"

"I'm going to stop you right there. Don't be an ass who kisses and tells. I see Fiona like a sister, and I would like to keep it that way."

"Such a prude. Must be all of those years in that crazy church."

Geo sighed deeply. He'd never told Dylan about his hatred of wooden interiors, and he wished he hadn't told him about the church he grew up in, an independent affair that solidified his father's belief that men should be the absolute rulers of their households. It also fueled his quests for money with its sermons on the prosperity gospel. As a boy, Geo had soaked up his father's righteous indignation at being left by his mother. As an adult, Geo had learned that his father wasn't telling the whole truth and nothing but.

Of course, that didn't stop him, even now, from wondering why his mother hadn't taken him with her. If she couldn't stand his father's inability to hold down a real job, then why had she left Geo behind? And why hadn't she put her foot down when his father insisted that they name their son after the car in which he had been conceived: a Geo Storm.

He still hadn't even figured out the logistics of having sex in a Geo Storm much less why any self-respecting mother would allow her son to be given such a name.

Whatever.

His nemesis, Truvy Fuller, poked her head around the door. "Guys, it's time."

*Ten minutes earlier, in the bridal suite*

"I don't get what you have against Geo," Fiona Macland said as she tried to balance the cheap veil on her head. It had been a last-minute addition, and Truvy didn't understand why her best friend felt the need for a veil in the first place. One, she was no longer a virgin. Two, she wore a smart beige suit rather than a wedding gown. Three, the veil had already proven itself a pain in the ass, and she informed Fiona of just that.

"Dylan said he'd always dreamed of being able to remove a veil from his bride's face before he kissed her, and he's going to get what he wants."

Confident that Fiona couldn't see her, Truvy rolled her eyes. Dylan was full of big ideas and grand gestures. Better Fiona than her because she couldn't live with a man that spontaneous.

No, she needed order and quiet. Life had thrown her enough curveballs already; she didn't need a groom who made crazy last minute requests.

"Fiona, are you sure about this? It was awfully sudden."

"Sudden? We've known each other for years. Besides, sometimes you just know. It was either get married now or wait until both Dylan and I had been at our new jobs long enough to get some vacation. Our leases were both up. It was fate, kismet if you will."

"If you say so," Truvy said as she adjusted the veil with an army of bobby pins. If it were really fate, then Dylan and Fiona wouldn't have broken their first engagement a year after they both graduated from college and one month before the wedding. Truvy was afraid that the ten-year anniversary of their college reunion had Fiona worried that she would never marry and thus she'd settled for what she knew.

Of course, when she'd told Fiona this, her friend had pointed out that she'd had time to date other men, and she preferred Dylan's quirks to any of theirs.

Fiona sighed. "I swear you and Geo are perfect for one another."

Truvy almost choked on one of the bobby pins she held between her lips, turning to spit the last three across the room. "Fiona Macland, that was the *worst* date I have ever been on, including the time I went out with Gregory Calhoun."

Fiona laughed so hard, it ended in a snort. Somehow, she still made it charming.

Gregory Calhoun had been a linebacker at their high school, and Fiona had bet Truvy twenty dollars that she couldn't survive an entire date with him. Truvy had let the giant down gently when he asked for a second date—and then collected her twenty dollars from Fiona.

"He's actually a nice guy. You saw he married Candace, and you know she doesn't suffer fools."

"What can I say? I was young and stupid and hung up on appearances," Fiona said as she applied another layer of pink lip gloss.

Fiona might no longer be hung up on appearances, but her mother was going to have a cow—no, an entire herd of cattle—when she found out her daughter had gotten married in a Gatlinburg chapel. Come to think of it, the first wedding had probably been canceled because Fiona and Dylan had fought constantly over how the wedding would go. He wanted something simple; Fiona would agree to almost anything to get her mother off her back. Meanwhile, Fiona's father was still mad about all of the deposit money that had been wasted, and he still didn't like Dylan Alexander.

Probably easier to elope and then break the news to them.

Truvy shrugged. Not her circus and most certainly not her monkeys, and boy was she glad of it. The Maclands had a mansion down by the Tennessee River that had more rooms than she could imagine, but with all of that space there wasn't much affection.

Truvy still remembered overhearing Fiona's mother telling her, "If you're not going to put on lipstick, then don't come home at all. You look like a homicide victim without lipstick."

So, it was no wonder that Fiona used to deal so much in appearances; it was what she'd been taught.

Truvy, on the other hand, had grown up across town in a modest frame house that was alive with noise and emotion. First, her father's drunken bellows had kept everyone cowed; then her stepfather's kind patience and sense of humor had cleansed the home through joy and laughter. When she settled down—if she settled down—she wanted to create a home like that one: simple, not pretentious, but full of laughter.

She certainly wasn't going to waste her time with anyone who might turn into her father, and no matter what Fiona said, Geo I-Show-Up-For-First-Dates-Wasted Russo was not in any way perfect for her.

"Hmmm," Fiona said as she pressed her lips in the mirror and looked at one side of her face and then the other. "I've never understood how you could find so much to love in Gregory Calhoun but so much to hate in Geo."

"I don't *hate* Geo."

Fiona arched an eyebrow.

"I *dislike* Geo. He was insufferable that night, and we decided—quite maturely, I might add—that we would have to agree to disagree and learn to tolerate each other for yours and Dylan's sake."

"How magnetic of you."

"I think you mean magnanimous."

"See? You're insufferable, too." Fiona poked a finger lightly into her oldest friend's chest, but she grinned as she said it.

There was a time when Truvy would've gotten her hackles up, but she laughed instead. "You're probably right, but I'm afraid Geo Russo and I will *never* see eye to eye."

"Never say never."

"Fiona."

The bride batted her eyelashes. "What?"

"You promised."

"I did. I promised never to interfere in your love life ever again."

Outside the door in the hall, the grandfather clock started to chime. Truvy looked at Fiona. "I believe that's our cue."

Fiona smiled radiantly. "Then go get the boys, and let's get me hitched."

# Chapter Two

Geo took several deep breaths. The sanctuary of the church was also done in suffocating wood, only there was more of it once you added the pews. To make matters worse, he didn't care for churches anymore, so it was taking some real will power to stand beside Dylan. He allowed himself to rock back and forth on the balls of his feet while they waited for the ladies.

Truvy came first, of course, wearing some kind of dress that wrapped around her. The dark green complemented her red hair and green eyes. That wrappy style also amplified her cleavage. He couldn't stare at that, though, so he looked at the walls, but they were wood, so he immediately looked back at Truvy, focusing on her eyes.

She smirked at him as she passed to her side of the altar. She'd no doubt noticed him staring.

The tiny organ in the corner broke out into the bridal march, and both he and Dylan looked to the double doors that flung open dramatically to present Fiona Macland, heiress to the Buttercup Flour fortune.

Geo had half-expected Fiona to wear an outrageous designer gown because she could've afforded it, but she'd decided on a simple suit of all things. The veil on her head looked ridiculous, but Dylan was grinning like a jackass eating saw briers, so it really didn't matter.

Their officiant, a Dolly Parton impersonator who was a shade too tall and a shade less endowed than her namesake, ran through the marriage quickly. Heck, they no doubt had another wedding coming through in an hour or so. It felt as though Geo had blinked, and they'd come to the part where it was time to kiss the bride.

Dylan lifted the veil, and Fiona looked up at him with such love. Bride and groom paused to take in the moment, then reached for each other, Fiona on her tip toes and Dylan bending over until their lips met.

And then their tongues met.

"C'mon, y'all, save something for the honeymoon," the officiant said in an almost perfect imitation of Dolly.

Bride and groom separated sheepishly but clasped hands as they walked down the aisle to "Islands in the Stream." They paused long enough for a photographer to take a picture.

Geo looked over to Truvy, who was wiping away tears.

He resisted the urge to roll his eyes. Instead he offered her his arm and they followed their friends down the aisle. The photographer again jumped out and took a picture.

Geo was sure both he and Truvy would have wide-eyed expressions because taking a picture of them hadn't been a part of the deal.

"Sorry," said the photographer. "You just look so cute together that I had to do it. Want to smile this time?"

Geo looked at Truvy, who shrugged her shoulders and then turned on her megawatt smile, even if Geo knew a close observer would know that it didn't reach all the way to her eyes. He took a deep breath and then did the same.

One more flash and they were free.

"Merle's? You want to have your wedding reception in a place called Merle's?" Truvy asked.

Fiona grinned. "We're just going for a few drinks and a first dance in front of the jukebox. You and Geo will soon be free to go your separate ways."

"I still can't believe that you're honeymooning here, of all places," Truvy said with a shiver as she shut her car door and headed in the direction of the log cabin-type building that served as a honky-tonk a bit off the beaten path. "I would've definitely gone tropical."

Fiona shrugged. "Plenty of romance to be found in a cabin, too."

"If you say so." She held the door open for the bride, and they wound their way through high tops and bar stools until they came to the table where Geo and Dylan sat.

Fiona took a seat by her new husband. This meant, of course, that Truvy would have to sit next to Geo. He smiled at her hesitation. "I don't bite. Promise."

No, but one could never be too sure. She took a deep breath and took a seat beside him. Shame that he was such a raging jerk because he was classically handsome with dark hair and brown eyes, totally her type. He also smelled really good, and that was knowledge that she could've done without.

"So here's the plan," Dylan said. "We're going to toast the marriage. Fiona and I are going to have our first dance in front of the jukebox. Then we're going to go turn in our paperwork before the office closes, and you two are going to go up to the cabin and make sure everything is cool up there."

Truvy nodded. She knew all this. She didn't know why she and Geo had to go check on the cabin together. Seemed to her like Geo could handle that all by himself since he was such a smart lawyer and all that. Fiona had insisted, though, that Truvy purchase some sensitive items that she didn't want Geo to know about.

A waitress brought four beers, and Truvy stifled the urge to order something else. She would drink a little bit to be polite, but she much preferred wine. Beer made her belch, and she didn't want to belch in front of Geo. He had enough disdain for her as it was.

Well, that and she might have been a teensy bit too stringently against alcohol when they first met. Okay, she was a total prig, and she knew exactly why he didn't like her. Warmth flooded into her cheeks, and she looked around nervously to see if anyone had noticed.

No one was even looking at her. Good.

"To Fiona and Dylan, may the course of true love, in your case, run smooth!" Geo said.

They all four said, "Hear, hear!" and drank, then Truvy chanced a glance at Geo. Had he just paraphrased Shakespeare?

That was new.

Fiona cleared her throat, reminding Truvy that she had a few duties left. "To Fiona and Dylan. May you find every happiness, and may your marriage last at least one year for every pair of shoes Fiona owns."

Fiona swatted at her friend playfully, but they all chorused, "Hear! Hear!" and took a drink.

Truvy shook her head. "I still can't believe you got married like this. Your mother is going to be furious."

Fiona shrugged. "She wanted me to marry Giles Fordham. What does she know about marriage?"

Dylan sobered and he put his arm around Fiona, pulling her closer. "We can still pretend—for your mother—that this didn't happen. There's no reason why we can't have the big wedding for her and always remember this wedding as ours."

Fiona pulled a face. "I'm tired of doing things for my mother. If she wants a big wedding, then she can have a vow renewal with my father."

*Unlikely.*

Truvy couldn't help the uncharitable thought. If Mrs. Macland was bad, then Mr. Macland was worse. He only talked to Fiona about how her job was going.

"Let's talk about more pleasant things," Fiona said. "I think it's time that Dylan and I have our first dance as a married couple so we can get the honeymoon started."

Dylan pulled her even closer long enough to kiss her on the cheek. "I like the way you think. Maybe I should marry you."

"You already did," she said with a ridiculous grin.

"That's right, I did. I am one lucky bastard."

"You don't know the half of it," Fiona said with a sly smile as she slipped from her stool and strolled over to the jukebox to pick out their selection.

"My teeth are hurting from all of this sweetness," Geo said.

"Someday, you too will be in love," Dylan said.

Just as Fiona sat down, Jason Mraz crooned the first strains of "Lucky," and Fiona slid back down from her stool with a squeal dragging Dylan with her so they could dance to "their song." Truvy did her due diligence and took several pictures of the bride and groom, being sure to include the confused looks of the bar patrons who had been taken aback by the intrusion of a sweet pop duet in the midst of their country music.

Finally, she put down her camera with a sigh to hum along with the lyrics and watch the newlyweds sway to the song. What she'd give to fall in love with a best friend, to find someone who looked at her the way Dylan looked at Fiona.

She could almost feel Geo's stare. A glance showed that he was studying her—but thoughtfully rather than creepily. He looked away, the hint of a blush tinging his cheeks. Before she could figure out what to say to him, Fiona and Dylan had returned.

"Did you get the pictures?" asked Fiona.

"Of course," Truvy said.

"Great! Can you go take care of... that thing for me then?"

Truvy wanted to roll her eyes, but she wouldn't do it. It wasn't Fiona's fault that she had trouble saying the word condom; that dubious distinction went to Fiona's overbearing mother. Since the marriage would be enough to send the woman over the edge, Fiona had wanted plenty of condoms so she wouldn't have to announce a pregnancy at the same time.

"Man, you got this?" Dylan asked Geo.

Geo nodded, and Truvy bit back a smile at how restrained Dylan was being. Geo looked to her. "Shall we?"

"Let's go," Truvy opened her wallet to pay for her drinks.

"Hey, we've got this one," Dylan said. "It's our super fancy reception after all!"

"Well, thank you," she said before turning to Geo. "If we hurry, then we'll be done in time for me to binge some Netflix."

"Oooh, hot date on the town tonight," said Fiona.

Truvy came around the table to hug her and then Dylan. "Well, this friend of mine was getting married so I had to tell all the boys beating down my door that I had plans tonight. They were inconsolable, I'll have you know."

"I guess that's fair," Fiona said with a grin as Geo hugged them both, too.

Truvy waited until they'd left Merle's before she turned to Geo. "Why are we doing this together again?"

"Because our friends asked us to. Dylan has a surprise for Fiona. Fiona wants you to do something for Dylan. They're both a little nutty, so I don't know. We'll handle it and get out of each other's way," Geo said as he ran a hand through his hair and stopped at the passenger side of Truvy's ever-practical Toyota Corolla. They'd come back for his Lexus later.

"Okay, then," Truvy said as she took a seat behind the wheel. "You've got the directions, so let's do this."

## Chapter Three

Darkness fell quickly as Truvy drove up a gravel road to the honeymoon cabin. Geo couldn't help but notice that this particular cabin seemed more isolated than others. Often the rental cabins clung together on the side of the mountain, but they'd left the last set of matching cabins about a half-mile back.

The road wound sinuously up the side of the mountain, and Truvy had to slow down even more because it had narrowed to one lane. Geo drummed his fingers on his thigh.

"In a hurry?" Truvy asked, her eyes never leaving the road.

"I'm ready to be home."

"Me, too. How much farther?"

He looked down at his phone. "A half a mile, I think? I don't have any service up here."

"You would think we'd get better reception on top of a mountain."

"You'd think."

Geo glanced out the side window. "There it is!"

Truvy backed up a little until she found the narrow gravel path. "There's secluded and then there's secluded. Is this a honeymoon cabin or a horror movie intro?"

"Yes."

"Very funny."

Her words might have been caustic, but her lips did turn up into a smile, and Geo had to admit they were nice, full lips. He also had to admit that he liked making her smile.

The house appeared before them suddenly, a rustic cabin perched on the side of the mountain with a tiny turnaround area in front. Geo would've simply parked, but Truvy took her time turning the car around. "I want my getaway to be unobstructed."

"*Our* getaway, and I know that's right."

"A light on the porch would've helped. Are we sure this is the right place?"

Geo turned on his phone flashlight and searched for the sign beside the door.

*Las Vegas.*

"Who the heck names their cabin *Las Vegas?*"

Truvy shrugged. "Dude. What happens in Vegas stays in Vegas? It's still better than *Pedro's Pleasure Palace,* which we passed a while back."

"Yeah. That did sound a bit like a brothel," Geo said, shining his light so Truvy could see her way up the steps.

She fumbled for the key and entered the door. Someone had already turned on the heat, thank goodness, because it was ridiculously cold for early October. The weather forecast even called for a ton of snow, but Fiona and Dylan weren't that concerned because they planned to be holed up for a week and had thus stocked the place with groceries.

Geo closed the door behind them. "You know where you're supposed to go?"

"Yep." She patted her purse as though it contained something important.

"Well, let's get this over with."

She went for the stairs, and he went for the fridge where he found the plastic container of rose petals. Then he tossed the petals in a path past the air hockey table and the seating area in front of a gas log fireplace, to a small bedroom on the main level of the cabin. He took deep breaths. Wood. Everywhere, the cabin was wooden. He threw rose petals all around and then on the bed, finishing one container and starting on the second. This time the rose petals were white instead of red and he retraced his steps, walking through the seating area to the stairs, and flung petals up the stairs until he reached the open loft where Truvy sat on the bed reading a letter.

"Hey! Don't read that!"

She looked up at him, confusion bunching her eyebrows. "But

it's to us."

His stomach lurched.

*They didn't.*

He and Truvy stared at each other for only a minute before she dropped the letter and he tossed the petal container. Down the steps they ran, but outside a car's engine came to life. Geo flung open the front door just in time to see the tail lights of Truvy's Corolla disappear around the corner.

To make it worse? It had begun to snow. Fat flakes came down fast just as the weatherman had predicted.

"What did the letter say?" he asked as he closed the door.

"You might want to read it yourself," Truvy said softly.

She sat down on the couch, shivering from the cold that had come in through the door. Geo took the steps like a condemned man. Once at the top, he noticed that the heart-shaped jacuzzi tub had been lined with candles. A lighter sat nearby, beckoning someone to light them. Some of the white rose petals had settled against the red tub.

He and Truvy had created the perfect honeymoon situation. For themselves.

He sat down on the bed and picked up the letter.

*Dear Geo and Truvy:*

*Welcome to your home for the next week! I know, I know — we weren't supposed to meddle in your affairs, but we're in love. We can't help ourselves. Also? Did you really think that we were going to honeymoon here in the cold? Brrr. Nope. We're on our way to Hawaii.*

*But don't worry. Uncle Vince has Truvy's car, and he'll check on you if the storm gets worse than expected. He'll bring the car back in a week. In the meantime, just relax and work out your differences.*

*And, hey, Truvy brought the condoms should you really patch up those differences.*

*We stocked the fridge with food and wine. There are games and books in the closet downstairs. Just be careful, Geo — Truvy is a bit competitive.*

*No television, no telephone, no cell service — just a week to get away and get to know each other.*

*Don't hate us too much. Our future children will need their Aunt Truvy and Uncle Geo. Hey, Fiona might have a bun in the oven already!*

*Love,*

*Dylan and Fiona*

*P.S. We called both of your workplaces and told them you needed vacations. They agreed — especially you, Geo, since Dylan is your boss.*

"I'm going to kill him."

"You're too pretty for prison," Truvy called up.

He'd forgotten that the loft was open. With a heavy sigh, he plodded down the stairs to find Truvy in the kitchen with a bottle of wine and a corkscrew.

"What are you doing?"

"Making the best of a bad situation?"

"We gotta get out of here."

She cocked her head to one side. "How exactly?"

"We'll walk."

She looked at him as if he'd lost his mind. "We're going to walk down a steep mountain in the dark and snow in a dress and heels or, in your case, a suit and dress shoes? We both left our heavy coats in the car, even."

"I'll walk."

"It's my turn to remind *you* that *I* don't bite. Frost does."

He paced between the air hockey table and the downstairs bedroom door. "There has to be a way. Surely this Uncle Vince lives nearby. How the heck did they get your car keys anyway?"

Truvy smiled ruefully then turned to pour herself a glass of red wine. "My spare set disappeared about a week ago. I have a pretty good idea who took them. Want a glass?"

"No," Geo said absently. "Wait a minute. You drink now?"

She arched an eyebrow. "On occasion. And this is definitely one of those occasions."

He shook his head. That awful first date so many moons ago, he'd gone into it a bit tipsy having already been into the beer at the frat house. He couldn't even really remember all of the things he'd said to her because, for some crazy reason, he'd ordered another one when they got to the restaurant.

Oh, yeah. He'd ordered another beer because she'd been so obnoxious about it. He couldn't help but laugh.

"What?"

"You were so angry with me about a couple of beers."

Her eyes didn't meet his. "I was a bit of a prudish know-it-all in college."

"A bit?"

"Hey! You did show up drunk for a date."

He held up one finger. "Tipsy. I was tipsy."

Her eyes met him with a force that almost knocked him down.

"Fine. I shouldn't have pregamed before our date. I had my reasons."

"Well, maybe I had my reasons for being a teetotaler."

"We all had reasons," he muttered as he took a seat on the couch.

She nodded as she took a sip. "It's a nice cabernet. You might want to try it later."

"You're saying things like 'nice cabernet.' The world is upside down."

She chuckled. "That it may be. You go your way, and I'll go mine. There are two bedrooms, so we can handle this."

Geo watched her walk to the glass door on the other side of the living room. She turned on the porch light to watch the snow. He wondered how in the hell they were going to get out of here because he had cases to research and clients to meet no matter what Dylan said. She had to have something she was supposed to do.

What the heck did she do?

Nope. He wasn't going to ask. He was going to prowl the cabin until he came up with a solution. She might be okay with doing what Dylan and Fiona had planned, but he wasn't. It was the damn principle of the thing.

# Chapter Four

Truvy took deep breaths and small sips as she watched the snow come down harder and faster than she'd ever seen it before. She would *not* give Geo the satisfaction of knowing he made her nervous. She also wasn't about to tell him that she had nowhere to be, so the situation didn't bother her as much as it should. If Dylan and Fiona wanted to give her a weeklong vacation, then she would take it. She would drink their wine and soak in their hot tub and think on what it was she would do next since she didn't have a job.

Not anymore.

Shame they hadn't left a television so she could catch up on her shows. Maybe they had bought some ice cream so she could at least be pathetic in that way.

Behind her, Geo was tramping around and muttering like a caged panther.

"Is it really that bad to be trapped with me?"

She didn't mean to say the words so sharply, but that's how they came out. Why were they such oil and water? For years she'd thought they'd maybe gotten off on the wrong foot, but, no, here they were again, rubbing each other the wrong way once again.

Geo stopped his pacing. "No. It just feels… claustrophobic."

That made her turn around. "Claustrophobic?"

"Yeah. I don't like being surrounded by so much wood. It reminds me of bad times."

"What kind of bad times?"

He didn't say anything, and she sighed. "I'm sorry. I didn't mean to pry."

"It's not that. I didn't know where to start," he said.

"Start anywhere you like. If you want to."

"My mom took off when I was five. In the summers, my dad didn't have anyone to watch me, so he locked me in one of the bedrooms of the trailer where we lived, only he took almost everything out of the room so I couldn't hurt myself."

She sucked in a breath. "Geo."

"It was this tiny, boring, empty room with wooden walls, only a bucket to use as a toilet and a couple of peanut butter sandwiches. It felt like forever waiting for him to come home."

She wanted to hug him. Correction: she wanted to go back in time and let little Geo out of that room and take him to the park or at least to a licensed daycare. "That's awful."

"Well, it's done," he said, although his chest rose and fell a little too quickly for her tastes.

"Why don't you sit down for a minute and close your eyes."

"That'll make it worse."

"Maybe. Or maybe you won't be able to see the wood so you can imagine any other place you'd like."

To her surprise, he took a seat and closed his eyes. She had the oddest urge to put her wine glass down and then massage his temples until the frown lines disappeared from his forehead and his lips relaxed. No matter what was inside Geo, she had to admit he had a handsome profile, one that would look even better in firelight.

She walked to the fireplace and set her glass down on the coffee table.

"What are you doing?" he asked without opening his eyes.

"Starting a fire."

"That sounds good."

She turned her attention back to the task at hand, glad that her former job as a property manager of cabins just like this one had taught her the correct order of turning knobs and switches to properly light the fire.

A line of gas-induced flames lit along the bottom of the faux logs, and Truvy put the screen back in place. A quick glance at Geo confirmed her suspicions: he was even more handsome in the dance of shadow and flame.

"You know, you were right about closing my eyes," he said.

She took a seat at the other end of the couch, leaving an entire cushion between them. She'd be willing to bet that she was right about massaging his temples, too, but she couldn't make herself get up and touch him. "You'd be surprised how often I'm right."

"Oh, would I?"

He chuckled, and the sound rumbled through her. Nope. She was not attracted to Geo Russo. Just because they were stranded in a cabin together, she would not prove Fiona and Dylan right. Just because she hadn't so much as been kissed in over a year, she wouldn't fall for their shenanigans.

"Feeling better?" she asked as she took another sip of wine. She couldn't help but notice that he'd opened his eyes and seemed more relaxed.

"Yeah. There certainly wasn't a fire in that old room, so that's something new to concentrate on."

"I didn't know all that about you."

"I've never told anyone before."

"Oh." Her voice trailed off. Telling secrets was something one only did with friends. Maybe someday she and Geo could move beyond detached cordiality.

"I bet your life was all roses," he said erasing all of that good will.

She almost spewed her wine. "Well, things improved greatly when my mother married my stepfather. Let's leave it at that."

They sat and listened to the whoosh of the gas, watching the flames dance. "Where was your mom?" she asked.

"Your guess is as good as mine." His voice sounded so sleepy that she might have thought he was drunk, but he hadn't finished his beer back at Merle's, so she knew this could be nothing but the warmth of the fire.

"That's awful," she whispered.

His eyes snapped open. "Oh, for crying out loud. Don't pity me. I got out of there and made something of myself."

"I know that," she said. "It's just—"

"It's just nothing. I don't even know why I told you about it."

They sat in silence, his eyes glued to the fire. Finally, she said,

"Would it help if I told you something about myself then?"

"I think it would."

Men. So surly when they thought they'd given up a weakness, as if she were an opposing army looking for a place to strike.

But then again, now that she'd uttered the words, she didn't want to share any of her weaknesses, either, so maybe it was a human response rather than a masculine one.

"I got fired on Friday."

"What? Why?"

She shrugged. "My boss asked me a question, and I told him the truth."

"And what truth was that?"

"That I wouldn't fudge the numbers for his taxes."

"What was your job?"

"Property manager."

"But I thought you were going to be a lawyer, too?"

"So did I," she said as she took a longer pull of her wine, almost emptying the glass. "So did I."

"What happened?"

"My stepdad got cancer. I had to drop out of school for a while."

"Is he—"

"He's in remission now." And thank the Lord for that. She wouldn't regret the time she spent helping her mother because that meant more time with her stepfather.

He shifted on the couch facing the fire, and, for a minute, she thought he was gesturing for her to come sit down next to him. For a minute, she wanted to.

"I bet that was tough, taking care of your stepdad."

She smiled at the thought of Marty. He'd cracked jokes about being Lex Luthor when he lost all of his hair. He'd insisted on tipping her whenever she went to get him a milkshake because that was the only thing he wanted to eat.

He'd told her that he and her mom had everything under control and that she should go back to school. Maybe they did, but Truvy had seen how haggard her mother was at the end of the day. She would wilt the minute she was out of her husband's sight. For that reason, Truvy stayed behind.

"Did you like being a property manager?" Geo asked.

She snorted. "Not really. But it paid the bills."

"Why don't you go back to law school now?"

She laughed. "On that note, I think I'll have a little more wine. Sure you don't want some? Might take the edge off seeing the wooden walls?"

She cringed as she said it. She shouldn't have reminded him.

"Know what, I think I will have a little wine," he said. "If you'll tell me what's so funny about your going to law school."

"You know, I think I saw some cheese and some of those fancy meats when I was checking the fridge to see if a white wine had been chilled. How about a charcuterie for supper?"

"I think that'd be great, but I also think you're changing the subject."

"Geo, I'd have to retake the LSAT at this point, and I've been out of classes so long. I've probably forgotten everything I once knew."

"Bullshit."

"With such detailed and intricate arguments, I can see why you're so successful in court."

"Come on, Truvy. Don't sell yourself short. I'll help you prep."

She paused, the wine bottle midair. "You'll help me? You don't even like me."

He didn't say anything, and her heart fell a little.

*Don't be silly, Truvy. You don't like Geo Russo, so why should he have to like you?*

But she was beginning to like Geo very much indeed.

"Like has nothing to do with it," he said. "A friend of mine does some LSAT tutoring, and she owes me one. You won't have to look at me if you don't want to."

She poured the red wine in his glass, pausing to appreciate the sound of its slosh. Then she added just a hair more to hers. "I'll think about it."

"Good, you can—"

"I said I'll think about it," she said as she put the wine glasses down and searched the fridge. Sure enough, she found a selection of cheeses and meats. She washed her hands, wondering who this girl making a charcuterie could possibly be.

Then again, she was preparing the little feast for a man who'd washed down a cheeseburger with a Bud Light on their one and only date. She made quick work of slicing up some cheese and taking out slices of prosciutto and other meats. Taking the crackers out of the box would make the whole experience a little too cozy, so she tucked the box under her arm.

"That looks fancy," Geo said as she slid the plate on the coffee table.

"Don't get used to it. You're cooking next time."

He had no answer to that, so she went back for both glasses and brought them to the couch. She hesitated, but the couch had plenty of space, was closer to the food, and she wanted to look at the fire head on. That was it. It certainly wasn't that she wanted to sit a little closer to Geo.

They both sipped their wine and munched on cheese and crackers while watching the fire.

"If you don't want to be a property manager and you don't want to be a lawyer, then what do you want to do? You can do anything you want now."

She hadn't thought about it like that. She'd been more focused on what kind of job she could get so she could pay her rent and not have to move back in with her parents.

But it wouldn't be bad to move in with Mom and Marty if she had a plan. "I don't know."

"Hey, maybe it will come to you while we're snowed in."

"Maybe," she murmured, allowing the fire to mesmerize her as she sank into the bliss of a good Manchego and being just a little tipsy.

"Ever think about our first date?" asked Geo.

"First date? It was a two for one special: first and last all rolled up into one."

He winced. "Come on, it wasn't that bad."

She snorted.

"Okay, you should've shaved your pits."

"I would throw this wine on you if it weren't too fine for such things."

"But now I'm curious. Do you shave under your arms now or are you still a militant feminist?"

"Wouldn't you like to know? You still staunchly defending man's right as the head of the household and not reading women authors because you 'just don't get them'?"

"I didn't say that."

"Yeah, you did."

"Did not!"

"Oh, you think on it."

And that is just what they both did.

# Chapter Five

### *14 Years Ago, Spring of Freshman Year*

"You're drunk."

"Hi, I'm Geo. Nice to meet you," he said with more than a tinge of sarcasm. He would've been able to pick out Truvy easily from Dylan's description—except for the part where his friend had neglected to mention that she breathed fire.

"Truvy," she said as she extended her hand. "And you're still drunk. I can smell the cheap beer on you."

"I am not drunk," Geo said even though he could hear a hint of a slur to his voice. "I just had a couple of beers with the boys before I left."

"Uh-huh."

Great. Just what he needed: a judgy female. "I thought Dylan said you were chill."

She arched an eyebrow.

Oops. He hadn't meant to say that out loud.

"Good thing we aren't *driving* anywhere."

"I'm fine to drive," Geo said, waving away her concern.

"And just how many beers were 'a couple'?"

"Three, okay." And he hadn't wanted to drink them, but his fraternity big brother had decided that afternoon was the perfect time for a little light hazing despite Geo's protests that he had a date that night. He should've canceled the date, but he wasn't one to cancel things, and canceling wouldn't have looked good, either. "This guy in my fraternity—"

"Oh, great. You're one of those," she said, rolling her eyes.

"One of what?"

"A frat boy. Fiona did *not* tell me that she was setting me up with some richy rich frat boy."

Geo almost told her that he wasn't rich by any stretch of the imagination, but the whole point of joining the fraternity had been to make the sorts of connections that would help ensure that he never went to bed hungry again, so he held his tongue. She didn't need to know that.

"Well, Dylan didn't tell me that you were so judgmental."

"Judgmental?"

"Yeah. You don't know anything about me."

"I know that you showed up for our date drunk."

"I am not drunk!"

His voice echoed off the dormitories. He did sound a little drunk. "Maybe we should just call this off right now."

"I'd say that, but Fiona's just going to keep pestering me until we have this date, so we might as well go and get it over with. Besides, I haven't been to the Copper Cellar in a while, and I love their spinach artichoke dip."

Geo grimaced. He couldn't help himself. So they were going to have a meal as well as an appetizer. He'd pay because that's what gentlemen did, but that also meant a little less in his grocery budget for the next week.

"What's wrong with that?"

"I don't like artichokes. Or spinach."

She shrugged. "Whatever. Are we going to do this or not?"

He offered his arm, and she took it for a few minutes until there was enough traffic on the sidewalk that they had to walk single file. Geo gestured for her to walk ahead of him, and it was one of the best decisions that he could've made. Truvy Fuller might be prickly, but she had an enticing posterior.

He had to hand it to Dylan, the woman was a knockout. Even the shapeless long dress she wore couldn't hide her curves, and he'd always had a weakness for redheads anyway. Too bad she was such a shrew. He'd been led to believe that she was fun.

But competitive.

Dylan had warned him not to play any kind of card games or

mini golf or bowling or anything of that nature on their first date. He'd said the woman could get fired up over any kind of competition.

Geo could believe that.

The foot traffic slowed down as they approached Cumberland Avenue, the area that Tennessee students called "The Strip." Before long, they were crossing the street and entering the fanciest restaurant in the immediate area, The Copper Cellar.

Geo quickly stepped in front of Truvy so he could open the door for her. She murmured a grudging thanks and brushed past him to the hostess booth. The hostess, a girl he recognized from his western civ class, showed them to their table immediately. Such was the advantage of being a party of two.

Geo tried to get there in time to pull out Truvy's chair for her, but the hostess blocked him, and he supposed the Copper Cellar wasn't quite *that* fancy.

He wouldn't really know.

Growing up, he thought McDonald's was as good as it got.

A waiter came and took their drink orders, then they studied their menus in silence. Even though his wallet was afraid to ask, Geo said, "What else would you like besides the spinach dip thing?"

"Just that," she said as she put her menu down.

"That's all?"

She nodded. "Most of this menu has meat, and I'm not really in the mood for a salad this evening."

Geo's mouth dropped. "You don't eat meat?"

"No, is there a problem with that?"

"No, no problem." After having grown up in a house where his dinner was sometimes a can of Beanie Weenies — but without half of the Weenies because his father took them as his God-given right because he was the head of the household — Geo couldn't understand ever voluntarily giving up meat.

He turned back to his menu and started to do the math. *Ten dollars for the burger and eight for the dip then ten percent sales tax, so that's basically twenty dollars, but also account for the tip. Oh, and she ordered an iced tea, and who knows how much that costs since they don't* have the price on the menu and —

"Are you okay?"

"What? I'm fine."

"You were grimacing."

"That's my thoughtful face," he said. Mental note: he would have to learn to do mental math without scowling. Of course, if he had more money, then spending it wouldn't be such a problem. He was practically sweating, and they were going to come out under thirty with tip. He could cover that.

"Do you need another beer?" she asked, acid dripping from her tongue.

Her words tweaked his pride. "Actually, I think I do. Would you like anything?"

"No, thank you. I'll stick with tea."

"Teetotaler?"

"I am, actually, and you would be, too, if you'd ever had to live with my bio father. They say alcoholism runs in families, you know."

Oh, he knew. He was probably playing with fire himself, but he'd be damned if he'd let this woman get the best of him and try to tell him what to do. How Dylan could've thought for one moment that the two of them would hit it off, he'd never know.

How Fiona could've thought for one second that this Geo character would be perfect for her, Truvy would never know.

First, he'd been five minutes late. Then he'd come up reeking of beer, and she didn't need that again. The day her bellowing, belittling alcoholic father had moved out of their house had been the best day of her life. She'd promised her mother that she would never drink too much herself nor marry anyone who did.

But if Geo wanted to drink himself to death, then so be it. He wasn't going to be her problem after tonight. She'd even help him get his precious beer. She raised her arm to flag down the waitress.

"What the — ?"

Her cheeks flushed pink. "Is there a problem?"

"You didn't..."

"I didn't what?" Oh, she was going to make him say it.

"You didn't shave under your arms," he said incredulously.

"And why should I?" she asked, even as she crossed her arms over her chest. Not shaving was a small way to fight the patriarchy, but she couldn't quite get used to it. Years of being programmed to make herself beautiful for the eyes of men wouldn't be undone in a couple of months.

He held up his hands in surrender. "No reason. It surprised me a little, but it's no skin off my nose."

The waitress appeared at that moment, and he hesitated for just a second, but then he ordered his beer, and they each ordered their food. She'd expected a frat boy like him to be an expensive steak and potatoes kind of man, but he chose the cheapest burger on the menu.

"That grease is going to kill you," she said, regretting the words even as they came out of her mouth. Why was she antagonizing him? She wasn't going to be his keeper after tonight. If he wanted to clog up his arteries, it wasn't her problem.

He lifted his beer in a mock salute. "We all gotta go sometime."

She closed her eyes for a mere second and took a deep breath. "You know, we're going to be in here for at least another thirty minutes, so we might as well attempt pleasant conversation. What's your major?"

"At the moment? Psychology. I'm thinking about going to law school."

Of course he was. No doubt he was interested in those branches of the law where he could make lots and lots of money — probably at the expense of poor people.

"What about you?"

"Women's studies."

He choked on his beer. "Ah. I get the underarms thing now."

"Do you?"

"Sure. That's why you didn't like me holding the door open for you, isn't it?"

She shrugged. "It was kind of you, but not necessary."

"Good to know you're not militant."

"What's that supposed to mean?"

"You know, a feminazi."

"I object to that term on about a hundred different levels. All I want is for women to have *equal* rights, and that's why I'm going to attend law school, too."

"Well, my apologies. Seems I can't say anything without irritating you. Wonder why that is?"

"You showed up drunk. You're a part of an organization that props up the patriarchy and—"

"The patriarchy?"

"You don't think men are still in charge of everything? That women don't have to claw and scratch their way to positions of authority and—"

"Well, sure. But man is the head of the household."

She did a slow blink, mainly to keep her rage at bay. "What did you say?"

"I said, man is the head of the household."

She leaned back, draping one arm over the chair beside her so he'd have to look at her hairy pits. "That's what Paul says. Not Jesus. It's an excuse by the church to—"

"Enough. Let's change the subject."

"All right," she said as a server slid the cheesy spinach and artichoke dip in front of her. Such fatty dip along with all of those carbs in the tortilla chips would be her undoing if she didn't watch it, but she supposed she could splurge for one night. "What have you been reading lately?"

"You mean for class?"

"No. For fun."

"Oh, I don't have much time for that," he said just as his burger arrived.

*Why, Fiona, why? Why would you send me on a date with a man who doesn't read? It's like you don't know me at all.*

"Well, what was the last thing you read that you enjoyed?"

He waited until he was done chewing then wiped at the hamburger grease that had rolled down his hand. "Well, I got some John Grisham books for Christmas. Those were good. Read some Clancy back in high school. Stephen King, I guess."

Not a single woman writer. Typical.

"Nothing by a woman?"

His eyes bugged out.

Why had she said that? She was supposed to be making small talk so they could eat and leave. She would insist on paying half, and they would never have to see each other again—

"I guess stories by women don't really interest me."

She scoffed. "But all of us women have to keep reading the same classics by a bunch of dead white men. Okay."

"You are so angry," he said.

"Well, you would be, too, if you were looking forward to being paid seventy some odd cents to every man's dollar."

"Oh, for crying out loud," he said, his voice even more slurred. "I'm not personally responsible for the wage gap. I'm just trying to get an education and make a living."

"You prop up the systems that keep misogyny and racism in place."

"That's it. Let's just not talk. We'll eat. I'll pay. We'll tell Dylan and Fiona that they're batshit crazy and then move on with our lives."

"Fine."

"Fine."

They ate in silence then looked anywhere but each other as they waited for the bill. Truvy couldn't help but glance at him when she was sure he didn't notice. Shame that he was another rich frat boy partier because he was her physical type: tall, dark, and handsome.

Well, okay. He was only an inch or two taller than she was, but he did have unruly dark hair that begged a woman to run her fingers through it and dark brown eyes that held sadness and secrets.

*Too much poetry for you, Truvy. You are not going to make this guy into some kind of Byronic hero. Byron had all sorts of STDs by the time he was twenty-one. You remember that.*

If there was one thing she was going to remember, it was to *not* be a doormat to any man. The way her mother had waited on her father hand and foot and then given up her painting because he thought it was "frivolous"? No, thank you. She was looking for another guy like her stepdad, Marty. She wanted a man who wasn't afraid to wash the dishes or change a diaper, someone who would encourage her rather than hold her back.

Despite her first impression, Geo didn't seem like a bully.

And he had lovely lips. She wondered if he knew how to use them for something other than irritating her.

*Stop. It. Syphyllis. Remember the syphillis!*

To be fair, it was Byron who had the disease, not Geo.

*He is a jerk who cared so little for you that he showed up for your first date drunk. Remember that.*

He had successfully flagged down the waitress, so she quickly looked away before he could figure out that she'd been studying him. Clearing her throat, she added, "I can pay my part."

"That won't be necessary," he said as he reached for his wallet.

"I know it's not necessary, but I'd like to contribute since I obviously was *not* what you were looking for."

He paused midway through taking cash out of his wallet and studied her so thoroughly that she thought she might blush. "I wouldn't say that, but I'll be paying since *I* was obviously not what *you* were expecting."

"Geo."

"I'm paying," he said, his eyes flashing with anger even though his voice was calm. "Tonight, the patriarchy pays. Literally."

Her blood boiled, but she let him pay. He lay down two twenties, drumming his fingers on the little tray that held them. She realized he was waiting for the waitress to make sure no one else picked up the cash, especially not the bus boy in the corner with the narrowed eyes.

If her math served her correctly, he'd left almost a ten dollar tip on a thirty dollar meal—and it wasn't to impress her, of that she was certain.

So he wasn't like other men she'd been out with, the cheapskates who left only however many ones they could find in their wallet.

"That's a nice tip you're leaving."

His head swiveled. "Have a problem with that?"

"No, not at all." She supposed she deserved that since she'd needled him about being rich.

He sighed, seeming to realize that his tone had been brusque. "I used to work as a waiter. It's not an easy job."

"I've been a waitress," she said. "I can second that."

He smiled for the first time, and it almost took her breath away. "Finally. Something we can both agree on."

In silence, he walked her home even when she protested that she knew her way and that the campus was well lit.

"I said I'd take you on a date, and part of a date is making sure that you make it safely home," he'd said.

They stopped outside her dorm, and she was afraid that he might try to kiss her. Instead he held out his hand. "Best of luck to you, Truvy Fuller."

She took his hand. It was rougher and warmer than she'd expected, and she wondered for a split second if she'd misjudged him. "Same to you, Geo Russo."

Then with a nod of his head, he turned and left.

Nah. He was a spoiled rich kid who could, on occasion, show some manners.

That was all.

# Chapter Six

Geo still had his eyes closed, so Truvy could study him. Ridiculously long eyelashes, the hint of a five o'clock shadow. Suddenly, he turned his brown eyes on her full force. "I think I said those things."

She took a sip of her wine. "Yeah, but I was insufferable. You shouldn't have shown up for a date drunk, but you couldn't have known about my past."

She'd been very much on her guard back then, forever waiting for the other shoe to drop.

Man, she was so tired of waiting for the other shoe to drop. What would it be like to trust a guy? To think he might be a Marty instead of a Dad?

"Is that why you were so bent out of shape?"

"Sure. Bent out of shape. Let's call it that."

He chuckled.

"What's so funny?"

"I didn't intend to show up drunk. My fraternity big brother decided that it would be fun to have me chug some beers in front of the other boys. I told him that I was going on a date, but that only made him want to humiliate me more. Man, I hated that guy."

Oh. So it wasn't like he made a habit of drinking three beers before every date. "Then why did you stick with the fraternity?"

"Remember my tale of woe? Of going to bed hungry? I was determined that I would do whatever it took to make enough money that I would never live in an ancient trailer again. Seemed to me that joining a fraternity and making connections would be some insurance. Unfortunately, I didn't get my first pick because, shall we say, my lineage was not great."

And that would explain why he went along with the hazing. He didn't have a lot of other options. A flush of shame washed over her. That also explained why he'd ordered the cheapest thing on the menu.

"It wasn't all bad. Once that jerk graduated, then I got to be the big brother. I didn't pull stunts like that on pledges."

She could see that. He was the kind of man who wanted to do better, not a coward who imposed punishments on others simply because he'd had to endure them.

"Well, I'm sorry I gave you such a hard time about it."

"You didn't know. And you were right. It wasn't cool. Of course, I thought standing you up would've been bad, too."

"True."

They sat in silence.

"Oh my gosh, that's why you were making that face while you looked at the menu!" she said.

"What?"

"You were doing the mental math to make sure I didn't spend more money than you had."

He looked away, and she thought his cheeks might be pink, but she couldn't tell in the firelight. "Yeah."

"Well, I'm glad I didn't order an entree then."

He snorted. "If you'd known, you would've ordered the most expensive steak. Even though you didn't eat meat."

"Geo! I'm not that mean."

"No, but I did order another beer just because you were needling me. Don't worry. I was hung over the next day."

She grimaced. "Well, I'm sorry you got the full force of my women's studies class. I don't hold you personally responsible for the gender pay gap, by the way."

"Oh, good. I don't know if I could bear that."

She threw a small pillow at him. "You are such a smartass!"

"And you're not?"

"Fine."

After a few minutes, he finished his wine and set the glass on the coffee table. "There's one thing I've got to know, though."

"What's that?"

"Are you still not shaving your pits?"

"What is wrong with you?" she asked, wishing she had another pillow to throw.

"I'm just curious."

"Well, I'm not telling."

"Fine. Tell me something else then."

"I do eat meat now."

"Really? You didn't just now."

She put her wine glass down beside his. "Well, I had an awful bout with anemia a few years back, and I now occasionally eat some meats. Grass fed, organic, of course."

"Of course."

"Don't mock me!"

He turned those dark eyes on her again, and she sucked in a breath. "I wasn't mocking. I was thinking that there are two grass fed organic New York Strip steaks in that fridge."

"And?"

"They expire tomorrow."

"And?"

"Maybe we should cook those steaks along with some potatoes and redo our first date so it's not a disaster."

Her stomach felt a little queasy. "Are you asking me on a date?"

He gestured toward the window and the snow coming down. "We don't have anything better to do."

Whatever twinge of excitement she had felt dropped right to her toes. She'd do well to remember that Geo didn't like her and she didn't like him. They were learning to be mature adults about the whole thing and to make the best of a bad situation. Nothing more.

"I mean, I would like to cook for you and show you that I don't usually show up for dates when I'm three beers in."

"There's another cab that would go well with the steaks," she said, "And I wouldn't mind your being tipsy—as long as you share."

"So, it's a date."

"Sure," she murmured. "It's a date."

"Tomorrow we each forage for breakfast and lunch until supper at six. In the meantime, we can stay out of each other's way. Maybe read or soak in the hot tub or something. I guess I could use a vacation even if I hadn't planned on one."

"Yeah," she said, swallowing hard as she realized she didn't have a bathing suit. If she were going to soak in the hot tub, then he would have to look the other way.

He yawned. "It's after eleven, and I am beat. Which bed do you want? Red petals downstairs or white petals upstairs?"

She laughed. "I think I'll take white petals upstairs."

"Cool."

He stood and walked toward the back, and she sighed. It seemed such a waste for all of those rose petals not to be slept upon. She could almost feel their velvety texture on her skin, their fragrance rising all around her. Then Geo would lean down and kiss her and—

*Girl, the first thing you need to do when you leave this cabin is to get laid. If you are thinking about having sex with Geo Russo, then you have officially hit rock bottom.*

But he wasn't any of those things that she thought he was.

Maybe *he* should be her candidate for scratching that certain itch.

*Sure, if only you were his type, which you most assuredly are not.*

"Whatever," she mumbled to herself before crawling over to the fireplace to turn off the fire.

She was tired and cranky. The best thing to do would be to march upstairs and get a good night's sleep.

Geo lay on his back, his hands clasped over his stomach. One thought had been plaguing him for the past hour or so: *if I were to get her naked, then I would know about her underarms.*

Right. Her underarms. It wasn't that he wanted to see how much of her cleavage was real and how much due to a push up bra. It wasn't that he wanted to know what those full lips tasted like. Nor was it that he hadn't had sex in a very long time.

Curse both Dylan and Fiona for setting this up. If he weren't stuck in the cabin with her, then he'd never be having these thoughts. They would've both gone on with their lives being politely cordial with each other, and he wouldn't be wondering so very hard—and the operative word was hard—about what Truvy Fuller looked like naked.

# Chapter Seven

Truvy glanced over at the clock radio on the nightstand. Only three more minutes had elapsed since the last time she looked at it: two twenty-two AM.

Ugh.

Why couldn't she sleep?

*Because the whole room smells like rose petals, and you're having ridiculous thoughts about Geo Russo of all people.*

Fine.

Whatever.

She was going to have to do something to get to sleep.

Now would be the perfect time to test the hot tub. Geo had to be asleep at this hour, and then she wouldn't have to worry about him seeing her without the bathing suit she didn't have.

Or she could be a rational human being and just soak in the jacuzzi bathtub.

No, the water in the pipes would wake him up. Weren't the hot tubs in places like this always full and ready to go?

Only one way to find out.

And once she'd had a nice, long soak in warm water, then she'd have to fall asleep.

*✿*

Geo awoke to a distant banging.

He leapt out of bed first and then took in his surroundings.

Oh, yeah. The cabin. Dylan and Fiona's treachery.

*Truvy!*

He raced out the door, skidding to a halt in the living room before he realized the banging was coming from the porch off the living room. And the light was on.

Surely, no one had climbed up the porch that hung over a mountainside, but, if they had, they were about to regret it.

"Geo, open up!"

After the pounding, he heard a splash. A grin spread so tightly across his cheeks that they ached.

*Oh, Truvy.*

He approached the sliding glass door that led outside and managed to pull it open with some muscle. Sure enough, Truvy sat in the hot tub, her face flushed with warmth. Tendrils of her red hair stuck to her face even though she'd tossed the mass of it on top of her head. He almost couldn't see her for the steam rising above the hot tub.

"Well, well, what have we here?" he asked as he eyed the towel that was on the corner of the hot tub out of Truvy's grasp.

"I, uh, couldn't sleep so I decided to sit in the hot tub for a while, but then I couldn't get the door to open when I got ready to go back inside."

"Interesting."

"If you could please, just prop something in the door, and I'll be inside in a minute."

"I don't know," he said as he stroked his chin in faux contemplation. "That hot tub looks awfully inviting even if the snow is still coming down out there. I might need to join you."

"No!"

"Why not?"

"Because I don't have a bathing suit."

He chuckled. "We're all adults here."

She swallowed hard, and he wondered if that was because she didn't want him to see her or—and this is what he hoped—she was getting curious about seeing him. Only one way to find out: he wrenched his shirt over his head.

"What are you doing?"

"Joining you."

"But I'm ready to get out."

"Then get out."

"I. Am. Naked."

"But are you nekkid? That's the real question."

"Geo, this is why people don't like you."

He shucked his pants. "You'd be surprised at the number of people who seem to like me."

She huffed in frustration, and he hooked his thumbs into his boxer briefs.

"Don't you dare," she said.

"Oh, I'm daring. What happens in the cabin stays in the cabin."

She looked away as he shed his briefs and sank into the water. "I didn't agree to that."

"Doesn't matter if you agreed to it. You want to tell Dylan and Fiona that we went skinny dipping in the hot tub?"

"No."

He leaned back, his arms hooked over the edges of the tub and groaned in pleasure. "This does feel really good."

"Great. Keep your eyes shut, so I can get out."

He sighed but did as she requested. "If I must."

She stepped out of the tub with a splash of water. He could imagine her wrapping herself in the towel. Then she grunted as she pulled on the door. "Did you lock this?"

"No," he said without opening his eyes. "It's just tricky. Needs to be realigned."

She pounded the door with a frustrated sound. "Could you please open the door for me?"

"Sure," he said, standing.

"Wait!" she said, pinching the bridge of her nose just as he was about to step out of the water. "I can wait until you're done soaking."

He sank back into his seat, settling into the rumble of the jets and the warmth of the water.

She shivered over on the porch.

"You either need to get back into this tub or let me open that door for you," he said. "I don't want you to catch a cold."

"I'll get back in the tub, then you can leave something to hold the door open when you get out of the tub."

He grinned. "However you want to work it."

"Now close your eyes again."

He did as she asked, and she slid back into the hot tub.

"This is the best idea you've ever had, Truvy Fuller."

*This is the worst idea I've ever had.*

So much for going to sleep easily after her soak. For one thing, she'd expended a lot of effort and a fair amount of panic trying to open the door. Secondly, she'd caught enough of Geo's physique that her heart raced, much to her chagrin. She'd always suspected him of being soft, but his frame was wiry, almost like a swimmer's body.

It had taken a supreme effort to look away when he'd stripped his boxer briefs. Supreme effort.

Even worse? Or better? But probably worse? Those boxer briefs had been straining.

*That's probably a normal male reaction to any naked woman in the hot tub.*

Maybe so, but it was also a normal female reaction to be flattered at the sign of a handsome man's attraction.

She splashed the water with her hand and made another sound of frustration.

His head snapped forward, and he trained those brown eyes on her. "What?"

"Nothing."

"Oh, it's something."

"It. Is. Nothing," she said through gritted teeth.

"Nothing always means something."

"Except when it means... nothing."

"If you say so..."

"You are insufferable."

He threw his head back and laughed. "So I've been told. You're awfully fun to get a rise out of."

"So *I've* been told," she grumbled.

Suddenly, he sat up straight and floated in her direction. "There is one thing that has been bothering me."

"Really," she said, crossing her arms then hastily looking down to make sure she hadn't inadvertently pushed her nipples to the surface.

She had.

She sank into the water, wanting to die of mortification.

*Maybe he didn't see it.*

One look into his dilated pupils, and she knew he'd seen it. She took in a jagged breath. "Why don't you tell me about this thing that's been bothering you? Then we can get out of this tub before we turn into prunes."

"It's been bothering me that we didn't have a postdate kiss."

She snorted. "You would've tasted of beer."

He held up one finger, and she told herself not to ogle his muscular arms. "Ah, but tonight, I would taste of Crest. I am officially minty fresh."

She sank lower before she crossed her arms this time. "And?"

"And, I would like to kiss you, Truvy Fuller."

She sucked in a breath, her heart suddenly hammering against her rib cage. She couldn't figure out if it was telling her to make a run for it or to lean forward for her kiss. She bit her lip, then immediately stopped since her last boyfriend had said that was a tell that she was turned on.

The corners of Geo's mouth turned up into a smile.

Too late to hide it now, but she could obfuscate. "If I kiss you, will you then let me go back into the cabin?"

He floated back to his spot across the tub. "Oh, I'll let you go back into the cabin right now, if you want me to. I know I was teasing earlier, but extortion is illegal. If I'm going to kiss you, then I want you to *want* to kiss me."

And that was the problem, wasn't it? She wanted to kiss him. She couldn't hold his past actions against him because she didn't want to own her past slights, either.

"What happens in the cabin stays in the cabin?" she asked.

"It *is* the Las Vegas cabin," he said as he crossed his heart.

"Then, I would like to kiss you."

He floated back to her side of the tub and planted his hands on the bench on either side of her. The jets stopped running, and they were left with the warm water, and the feel—if not the sound—of snow landing on the porch railing, the trees, the roof, the ground.

They leaned toward each other, lips meeting gently, almost chastely. He backed away, studying her curiously before they leaned forward at the same time, lips meeting and retreating until she drew her arms around his neck, and he crushed her body into his as their lips tangled and they both gasped for air.

Finally, he broke the hold and eased back to his side of the tub. They looked at each other, both panting. "Damn."

She said nothing, mainly because she'd lost the capacity to form words.

"I think we should probably get out of the tub," he said.

"Uh huh."

*Great, Truvy. So articulate.*

"You first," she said. Averting her eyes took a Herculean effort.

She felt the water slap against her as he left the tub with a splash. Then she heard him wrench open the door with a grunt. From inside the cabin, he called, "It's safe to come out now."

She laughed in spite of herself. No way was the cabin safe.

Not now.

Even so, she stood with a sigh and gathered her towel around her before placing the top back on the hot tub. She stepped inside, shivering. She'd turned the fire off, of course, and she regretted not having an excuse to stay downstairs and warm herself.

Behind her, Geo closed the door and locked it. "So I guess this is good night?"

Disappointment filled her, but she forced her lips to swing upward. "This is good night."

He leaned toward her and she sucked in a breath of anticipation, hoping that he would kiss her again, but then he leaned backwards, running his hand through his hair.

"Sweet dreams, Truvy Fuller," he said before walking down the hall to his bedroom.

"Good night, Geo," she whispered, even though she knew he wouldn't hear her. Then she climbed the steps slowly up to her bedroom where, she had a feeling, she still wouldn't be able to sleep.

# Chapter Eight

They'd stuck to the plan, each going his or her own way the next morning. Truvy had read an Agatha Christie book and stolen glances at Geo, wondering why he hadn't taken their kiss further. Geo had read a Liane Moriarty book, and she had to smile thinking about how he'd once said he didn't read women authors.

She also wondered if he'd stolen glances at her.

She hoped so.

When she realized she'd read the same page three times, she got up and searched the game and linen closet, finding a pack of cards and setting up a game of solitaire.

*Fitting, Truvy. Always playing by yourself.*

"Getting up a strip poker game?" Geo asked without looking up.

"No," she said with a snort. Immediately after the words left her lips, she regretted them. Geo wore only a plain white undershirt and his dress pants. If her memories of last night were any indication, playing strip poker could be enlightening.

*Truvy. One kiss should not have you this shook.*

She turned her attention to the game of solitaire and told her eyes not to look Geo's way again.

Geo's eyes had looked over the same page three times already, but he was having a hard time concentrating. There Truvy sat with her face scrunched up in concentration as she carefully moved playing cards one over the other.

She sat in her bridesmaid's dress, but she was so absorbed in her cards that she'd forgotten and leaned forward with her legs spread. He couldn't see anything, but that wasn't the point.

*Why did you have to mention strip poker?*

Wishful thinking. It had to have been wishful thinking because when she bit her lip like that, it only made him want to kiss her again.

*Geo, get back to the lies in the book. Which are big? Which are little? These are the things you need to figure out.*

Yeah, but the book wasn't anywhere near as interesting as Truvy.

The growling of his stomach more so than a glance at his watch told him that it was time for lunch. "Want a sandwich?"

She looked at him with arched eyebrow. "You cooking lunch as well as supper?"

"I'm slapping meat on bread. If you call that cooking, then sure."

"How about cheese and bread only and you've got a deal."

If she wanted cheese and bread, then he would give her cheese and bread.

Only he was going to toast it first.

Less than fifteen minutes later, his hard work was rewarded with a moan of pleasure. "Geo, what did you do to this grilled cheese?"

He stared at her, the memory of her groan etched into his gray matter.

"Geo?"

"Huh?"

"I asked you what you did to make this grilled cheese so good."

"Oh, I added a little Manchego and American to the cheddar. And butter. Lots of butter."

"It's the best grilled cheese I've ever eaten," she said.

He swallowed hard. He would like to attain a loftier goal than best grilled cheese based on her reaction.

*No. Stop it.*

He couldn't possibly. It was the principle of the thing: he didn't want to give Dylan and Fiona the satisfaction of thinking that their matchmaking had worked.

Well, that and he was a gentleman, dammit.

And she was still Truvy Fuller, so, at the end of the day, they would still be incompatible.

"Why aren't you eating your sandwich?"

"What? Oh. Lost in thought I suppose," he said.

"What are you thinking about?"

*You. Naked.*

"Uh, the book I was reading. Just trying to figure out what the mystery is and all that."

She stopped chewing and studied the book he'd left in the chair beside him. "You like *Big Little Lies*, then?"

"I'm all about it. Who knew so much was going on in the suburbs?"

After a pause, she laughed.

At first he bristled, thinking that she was laughing at him. Then his shoulders relaxed as he realized she was laughing that anyone could think that the inner lives of suburban women—mothers, if you will—weren't twisty, dark, and mysterious.

"I'm just glad to see you reading for fun. Hopefully you do that even when you're not stuck in a cabin."

"One of the perks of being out of school," he said. "I get to read more of what *I* want to read. What about your book?"

"Oh, there's still a homicidal maniac on the loose, but I'm confident that Hercule Poirot will find him or her in the end."

They ate in companionable silence for a while. Truvy studied the last bite of her grilled cheese and then sighed in sad contentment before popping the last bite in her mouth. Her appreciation of something so small made him want to give her something much larger.

*Geo. Stop.*

It was about more than the kiss, though, and more than being cooped up with a beautiful redhead. He genuinely *liked* her.

And that was a good reason not to mess with the tenuous friendship they'd started. He'd cook her dinner and atone for his part of their bad date, but that was it. He might not mind the suffocating nature of wood paneling anymore—as long as he didn't think about it too much—but that didn't change the fact that he'd already proven himself to be a horrible husband.

Loath as he was to admit it, she deserved better than that.

# Chapter Nine

It felt surreal to be getting ready for a date while sharing a shower with a man and knowing you would have to put on the same clothes you'd already been wearing. In a stroke of what she'd thought was genius, she'd even washed her panties in the sink.

Unfortunately, they were not dry.

It would appear that she was going to be going on this date commando.

She went upstairs to drape her still wet underwear on the side of the tub. Those sensible cotton briefs would keep Geo downstairs. They weren't exactly the pair of underwear that she wanted to introduce a man to.

*There's a bed downstairs, too.*

Yes, a bed that she wasn't going to visit because once this weekend was over, she'd go back to being her, and he'd go back to being him. Best to remember that there was something magical about a cabin surrounded with snow. They had no social media or television to distract them. No doubt that's why she was stuck on the ideas of beds and getting Geo into one.

That and his surprisingly tender kiss.

She tugged on her dress wishing she could've put on something more flattering, maybe even some makeup. How ironic that when they'd first met, she'd intentionally been avoiding such trappings. Now that she'd evolved to understand that feminism meant doing what you wanted to do, she didn't have her makeup or hair styling implements.

She'd have to go into this faux date without any of those tools she used to bolster her confidence.

"Hey, Truvy, are you ready?"

"I'll be right down."

When she reached the bottom of the stairs, Geo had reassembled his best man suit, his hair still a bit damp from the shower. He hadn't shaved — there was no razor to be had, and she would know because she'd actually looked — and that simply reminded her that he *had* shaved for their first date so long ago.

He extended his hand, "Hi, I'm Geo Russo."

Ah, so they were going to do this from the top. She took his hand and tried to ignore the tingle of attraction. "Truvy Fuller."

He offered his arm and escorted her the ten steps to the little table then pulled out a chair for her.

"Thank you."

*Still chivalrous.*

"My pleasure," he said.

She looked down at a plate with steak, baked potato and sautéed broccolini. She cut into the steak, seeing that it was well done but not burnt just as she'd requested.

"If I don't eat all of this, please don't be offended. I just can't eat this much meat."

"I won't be offended in the least," he said as he took a bite of his own steak, which still had plenty of pink to it. "Cabernet?"

"Please."

"So, what's your major?" she asked as she took a sip. Another nice wine.

"Psychology," he said. "What about you?"

"English."

He frowned, "I thought your major was women's studies."

"I changed it the next semester. I still have a women's studies minor, though."

"Oh, what does that entail?"

She cocked her head to the side studying his expression, thinking over the tone of his voice while trying to figure out if he was mocking her. She didn't think so.

"Reading literature by women who were overlooked, women's health, women's history."

"What have you learned — other than the wage gap, which is a travesty."

Her heart melted. Not only had he remembered what she'd said so long ago about the wage gap, but he'd just used the word "travesty."

"Did you know that most medical studies are done on men so doctors often prescribe the wrong medication dosages for women? Some women were crashing on the way to work in the morning because they'd been given doses of Ambien that were too high, for example."

He paused midbite. "Really?"

"True story."

The conversation lulled after Truvy had so nonchalantly told him of an injustice against women he'd never considered. Even worse, he had a feeling that was the mildest example she could've thrown out to him. He braced himself for something more, something designed to make him feel guilty.

"What are you going to do with that psychology major?" she asked instead.

"Oh, I'm going to law school."

"Me, too," she said, her eyes lighting up. But then the light dimmed as she remembered they were now in a future where she'd never made it to law school.

"What are you going to do with that law degree?"

"I'd really like to help women in some way. What area of law did you go into? I mean, are you going into?"

He chuckled. "I work in family law. I also take on some juvenile offenders as my pro bono work."

She nodded, and he knew she was thinking of what he'd told her earlier about his childhood.

But she didn't say anything.

Damned if he wasn't seeing why Dylan thought Truvy might be the perfect girl for him.

Truvy fought off a sigh. She could see why Fiona thought Geo was the perfect guy for her. Polite, handsome, interested in helping others—but there was one very important question to ask:

"Do you like to read?"

He grinned because he knew she knew the answer to that. "I do."

"What do you like to read?" she said as she pushed her plate to the side and took a sip of her wine. She'd managed only six bites of steak but all of her broccolini and some potato.

Somehow she had the feeling Geo would be eating the rest of her steak along with some scrambled eggs the next morning.

"I read a little bit of everything," he said with a twinkle in his eye. "Especially mystery."

"That so?"

"You know, I once had a date with this woman who made me think about what I was reading so I've been consciously looking for books that aren't just by old dead white guys."

Intersectional. Be still her heart.

She held his gaze a little too long and finally looked away. She had seen his eyes full of sadness and mystery, but they twinkled with laughter and... lust? He wasn't like Byron at all. Or maybe he was what people *thought* Byron was.

Damned if he still didn't have that unruly hair that made a woman want to run her fingers through it.

There in the small cabin, sitting in the light of candles she'd brought from upstairs with the play of light and shadow bouncing off the walls, she'd just had a perfect date. The snow outside muffled all sound. She heard neither animal nor car, the solitude as delicious as the meal had been.

This wasn't Las Vegas; it was heaven.

"You're awfully thoughtful over there," he finally said.

"I'm content, possibly the most content I've ever been in my entire life."

His smile faded, and she wondered if she'd scared him off.

"That could be the nicest thing anyone has ever said about hanging out with me for two days."

*I think I could live in this moment forever.*

She bit back the words because they were ridiculous. Of course, she wanted to live in this moment forever. She didn't want to go out into the real world where she'd have to start looking for a job.

But she was an adult, and she had to go back to that world. In five days.

"I'll do the dishes," she said abruptly.

"I'll get them in the morning," he said, looking at her speculatively.

"It'll take me maybe twenty minutes," she said, more to keep her hands and mind busy than anything else.

He grinned. "Less if I help."

"Ah, but the matriarchy is taking care of the dishes tonight since the patriarchy did the cooking."

He twirled his wine glass by the stem. "Only if you're sure."

Her heart squeezed in on itself. This weekend in general and Geo Russo in particular were about to spoil her for all future men. "I'm sure."

She made short work of the dishes and even the broiling pan, and Geo came over to dry the dishes anyway. Finally, she dried off her hands and noticed that he'd placed his phone on the table. He pulled her into his arms as Jason Mraz started singing about being lucky, and that made her think of Dylan and Fiona.

"Oh, we're going dancing too?"

"Of course."

They swayed cheek to cheek so his voice rumbled through her, and her heart hammered against her rib cage. "Am I doing better this time?"

"What?"

"That awful first date we need to forget."

"Oh, already forgotten," she said.

"Well, thank goodness for that."

"Where'd you get the music?" she asked as the song switched.

"Fiona downloaded her First Dance Playlist on my phone," he said. "And to think, at the time I was irritated by all of the space it was taking up."

"To think," Truvy echoed, settling into his arms as they danced.

"Now I need to see you to your door," Geo said seriously just as Eric Clapton's guitar left behind the last chords of "You Look Wonderful Tonight."

"Oh, of course," she said. "Do I at least get a goodnight kiss?"

"We'll see."

He offered his arm with mock formality. When they reached the foot of the stairs, he took both of her hands. "Truvy Fuller, I'd like to see you again sometime."

Her heart beat double time. Did he mean it, or was it all part of the game?

"I'd like that," she said.

"How about tomorrow then?"

Ah. He was still talking about their week in Vegas, where everything would stay in Vegas. She forced her smile not to falter. "That would be lovely."

He brought her hands up to his lips and kissed each of those. "Well, then good night."

He turned to walk away, but she grabbed his arm. He looked at her expectantly, and she hesitated. There was that pair of underwear to think about, certainly *not* the impression she wanted to set.

*Truvy, you didn't even shave under your arms for the first date. What does it matter?*

"Would you... well, would you like to come upstairs? Maybe for some tea or coffee?"

Of course, he knew she didn't have tea or coffee upstairs, but why was he leaving her hanging?

"Maybe tomorrow," he said, his voice tight, as if the words cost him.

"Tomorrow," she echoed, leaning forward to kiss his cheek.

Then his arms wrapped around her, and he pulled her close for another kiss that started chaste and quickly became anything but.

"Sure you don't want that coffee?" she asked when they both came up for air.

He groaned. "I am *trying* to be a gentleman and do this right."

"Maybe I don't want a gentleman."

"Ah, but you *deserve* a gentleman," he said, pulling her hands up to his lips for one last kiss before disappearing around the corner to his bedroom.

# Chapter Ten

The next day, after a night of tossing and turning, Geo met her in the kitchen as if nothing extraordinary had happened. She'd replayed the scene a hundred times over in her mind and couldn't decide if she thought he was being virtuous for wanting their mulligan date to go as it would have back in college or if she was offended he'd turned her down.

For heaven's sake, she'd been willing to let him see her least attractive pair of underwear. That should count for something.

After a disastrous round of Trivial Pursuit in which she might've let her temper get the best of her when he got a final question of who wrote *Jane Eyre* while she got a question about freaking Thomas Pynchon, they'd settled in with their respective books. Restless, she'd gone to wash her bridesmaid's dress and now wore nothing but a robe over bra and panties.

The next time Fiona stranded her in a cabin, she *had* to at least leave some pajamas and a couple changes of underwear.

*As if she would ever trust Fiona again.*

Geo had jacked up the heat in deference to her and now only wore a T-shirt and boxers. He put down his book and picked up the pack of cards to play a game of solitaire. Which reminded her of his crack about strip poker.

And he was only wearing two items of clothing to her three.

Why was she letting him decide whether or not they would get some coffee?

And by coffee she did *not* mean coffee, although he had brewed a pot earlier that morning before she got up, which was yet another point in his favor.

There were a lot of bad things about College Truvy, but she'd certainly never been too shy to ask for what she wanted. Sure, there'd been that one guy who'd come in and trampled her self-esteem. Then there was the embarrassment of not making it to law school and even getting fired from her property manager job.

But College Truvy had had some things right even if she'd been too high-handed about them, so maybe it was time for New Truvy to go for what she wanted.

"Ever played strip air hockey?"

Geo almost choked on the water he'd been drinking. "No."

"Me, neither, but I'd like to learn."

"Far be it from me to keep you from it, but now I've seen that competitive streak that Dylan and Fiona warned me about."

"Sure, but whoever loses this game still wins, yes?"

In what parallel universe had Geo found himself?

He was trying so hard to be a gentleman even though he'd wanted to throw Truvy over his shoulder and take her off to bed ever since their kiss in the hot tub night before last. He sure as hell hadn't slept a wink. Nor had he really absorbed a bit of the book he'd been reading, even though he normally gobbled up a Moriarty book like candy.

"All right," he said as he put down the deck of cards. "Let's do this."

He took his spot at the end of the air hockey table and sized up his opponent. Flushed face, very kissable lips, mischievous eyes—he liked what he saw.

"Let's add some stakes to this game," she said.

"You mean other than getting naked?"

"Nekkid. I believe night before last you were hoping for nekkid."

He swallowed hard. "That I was. What's your plan?"

"Winner of each point also gets to ask a question."

He nodded his assent. Fine by him. He had a few questions for the lady.

She turned on the table and sent the plastic puck his way. He evaded her best attempts to score on him as well as he could, but he hadn't played air hockey in years.

Obviously, she had.

The puck clattered through her goal, and she looked up at him in surprise. It was beginner's luck, but he wasn't about to tell her that.

"Your game, Truvy," he said with a shrug, trying to keep his lips from quirking up into a smile.

She shrugged out of the robe she'd been wearing to reveal a lacy bra that barely held in her cleavage.

Good call. He was definitely distracted. "What happened to feminist Truvy to make her switch to English? You haven't talked about smashing the patriarchy once."

She sighed as she fished out the puck. "Life."

"Oh, there was more to it than that."

"Well, I got into a relationship with a guy not long after our date, a bit of a controlling jackass, really. Then I went home to take care of my stepdad. Figured I needed to turn in my feminism card if I couldn't manage to avoid controlling men or even continue my education," she said as she lay the puck on the table and pinned it in place with her pusher.

Geo studied her, irrationally looking for wounds. Of course, her wounds were probably kept inside. That made him want to kill the guy even more. "How does that make you any less of a woman? You got rid of the jerk and took care of your stepfather."

She looked down at the floor. "I don't know. I feel like a failure, but I can't seem to make myself want to date or go back to school. I think I'm afraid I'll botch it up again."

She'd offered herself last night, and he'd said no. That couldn't have helped with her fears of dating again.

"You are not a failure," he said.

*You're perfect.*

Where had that thought come from?

He wanted to go around the table and take her into his arms, but he somehow knew she wouldn't appreciate the gesture any more than he'd appreciated her pity when he'd confessed about how his father had treated him as a kid. So, he changed the subject. "Who was the jackass?"

"Does it matter?"

"No. I just might want to put a hit out on him."

She smiled. "In that case, it was Clark Regis."

"Oh. He *is* a jackass," Geo said, already plotting petty revenge against the guy who'd gone to law school with him. "But you are the badass who came up with strip air hockey, so please carry on."

To say his play was distracted by the bounce of Truvy's breasts would be an understatement. She immediately sank her puck on his side. He drew his shirt over his head and frowned. He hadn't thought this out very well because he was only wearing boxers now. He didn't even have socks because he'd stepped in a puddle of water earlier and taken them off. Of course, Truvy didn't have on much more than he did.

"Fiona told me you were divorced. What happened?"

He scowled. "Fiona talks too much."

"Geo."

"The short version? She left me for another man, a richer man."

"Come on, Geo. You made me tell you about Clark."

"I didn't *make* you. This game was your idea."

She arched an eyebrow at him.

"Fine. I think I got married because I thought it was the thing to do at that time in my life. Then I worked too much and ignored her probably because I secretly figured she would abandon me anyway — at least that's what my therapist said — and then it became a self-fulfilling prophecy."

At least Truvy had the good grace to look embarrassed at having made him admit all of that. "I'm sorry."

"Don't be. I'm not. At least, *now* I'm not."

The puck whizzed his way, and the two went back and forth before Truvy scored again. She jumped up and down in celebration as he hooked his thumbs in the waistband of his boxers, glad the table hid exactly how attractive he found her. "How about you ask me the question and then I'll shed the boxers?"

"Why did you turn me down last night?"

Turn her down? Is that what she thought? That he was rejecting her for some crazy reason? "I am *trying* to be a gentleman."

She nodded at that, and he couldn't read her expression.

But then she bit her lip.

*Focus, Geo, focus.*

He slipped off the boxers, but then stood as close to the table as he could before slapping the puck back on the table, wielding his pusher like a man on a mission because he had a very important question to ask. Getting Truvy to take off another item of clothing would just be a bonus.

She was so distracted by his nudity, it took only a few volleys before he sank his puck in her goal.

She straightened and took a shaky breath before reaching behind her back to unclasp the bra. She let the straps fall down her arms so slowly, and a lump formed in his throat as he waited, waited, and then saw the world's most perfect breasts as the slip of lace hit the floor. Then she put her hands on her hips in a challenging expression that had him wanting to end the game right then and there.

"Truvy?"

"Mmhmm?"

"Did you want me to take you up on your offer last night?"

She blushed. "Yes, I did."

"Are you sure?"

"Absolutely."

"How do you feel about men who toss women over their shoulders and take them to bed to kiss every square inch of their bodies?"

She paused. "If such a man is going to go to all the trouble of carrying me to a bed—and I'm assuming, say, a bed upstairs where there's a box of perfectly good condoms nearby—then I would hope he wouldn't stop at kissing. That's my official stance."

"Good to know." He put down his pusher and walked to the other end of the table then tossed Truvy over his shoulder as he'd wanted to do the night before.

And the night before that, really.

"What happens in the cabin stays in the cabin?" he asked as he mounted the steps.

"It *is* Las Vegas."

"Well, Truvy, I've got some good news and some bad news,"

he said as he lay her down on the bed.
　　She rose up on her elbows. "What?"
　　He leaned over to kiss her. "Supper tonight is going to be late."
　　"Oh?"
　　"But I promise you're not going to mind."

# Chapter Eleven

The next two days they laughed and fixed meals for each other. They rarely wore clothing. Wednesday afternoon came around, and Truvy found herself naked in the hot tub once more, only this time she sat beside Geo.

They'd also remembered to prop open the door with the Trivial Pursuit box because that game wasn't going to be opened again any time soon.

"We only have two days left," she mused.

"How?"

She cuddled under his arm, amused that he'd lost track of time, too. "Saturday night was the wedding. Sunday, our first date. Monday we played air hockey—"

"Strip air hockey, the greatest invention of all time, you mean."

"Then there was yesterday," she said as she remembered sex in his bedroom, companionably reading together on the couch, sex in the Jacuzzi tub, sandwiches for lunch, sex on the table—

She sensed a theme.

"And today," he added.

There'd already been sex today, and if his shifting indicated anything, there would be more sex in her future. She studied his profile, his serious expression even as the water roiled in the tub around them. She would give a whole heckuva lot more than a penny for his thoughts.

Was he ruing the last two days like she was, or was he ready to go back and leave this week behind? With some men, she would think he'd had sex with her only because she was available, but she didn't think that was Geo.

She didn't *think* so.

No matter what, she would soak up every minute of the next two days, every last moment of Geo—just in case. She wanted to ask him what this week meant to him, but she was afraid to break the spell.

That could wait for their last day.

She closed her eyes against the memory of that delicious moment when he threw her over his shoulder. He'd asked if what happened in the cabin would stay in the cabin. Like a fool, she'd said yes.

Why had she said yes?

He turned and nuzzled against her ear. "Getting ready for some afternoon tea?"

She gave a snort giggle then clapped her hand over her mouth in embarrassment, but when she dared meet his eyes, he looked at her as if she were the most enchanting creature he'd ever seen, snorts or no.

"Is afternoon tea anything like postdate coffee?"

"Oh, yes, he said. "Tea, coffee, thee—it's all very similar."

"In that case," she said, standing up and enjoying the sensation of cool air hitting her overly warm body. Even better, his breath hitched, and those dark eyes found a way to dilate a little more. "Let's go upstairs, shall we?"

She'd hardly made it through the door before his lips were on hers. They kissed and touched all the way up the stairs. For a split second Truvy thought he meant to have sex with her there on the steps, but, of course, the condoms were upstairs.

All too soon, she lay underneath him, squirming, somehow still wanting him even as he paused to look down at her, a lock of dark hair hanging over his forehead.

"What are you doing?" she whispered.

"Remembering every detail of this moment," he said.

She sucked in a breath, drinking him in, too. By now he had the beginnings of an honest to goodness beard, and she knew her face was red from beard burn. She ran her hands down his arms, feeling each muscle flex. Then over his broad chest, her fingers scratching through the hair until he took in a sharp breath. Down his body her hands trailed.

Suddenly, he was in her and around her, his fingers and lips working magic at a deliciously slow pace as if this were their last time. Her hands made their way up his back, her fingernails digging lightly into flesh as she thought, *Any time could be the last time.*

The very thought sent her over the edge even as tears leaked down the side of her face.

He followed quickly, panting, and then reaching underneath her to crush her to him as though he'd been thinking the same thing.

*Two more days.*

*They still had two more days.*

## Chapter Twelve

*Two more days.*
*No, one.*

Geo rubbed a hand over his now very stubbly beard, blinking in the harsh sunlight flooding through the skylight. He looked over to where Truvy lay tangled in the sheets. She sighed in her sleep, and the sheer contentment made him want to give her that kind of joy every day for the rest of their lives.

*Geo, get it out of your head, man. This is the Las Vegas Cabin, and she's going to drop you like a hot potato the minute she reaches civilization.*

But not for another day. His mind raced through what was left in the refrigerator, what books they could read, if there was any place yet where they hadn't had sex —

Except... Did he hear knocking at the door?

He leapt from the bed, grabbing a robe, and hurried downstairs. He flung open the door to see an older man in a snowsuit. He held out car keys, and Geo could see Truvy's Corolla back in the spot where she'd originally left it.

His heart sank.

"Fiona said to tell you that she had a change of heart and doesn't want you two to tear each other limb from limb," the older man said as he placed the keys in Geo's hand. "She hopes you aren't too mad at her."

"We're not mad," Geo managed.

The man jerked a thumb at the mountain road behind him where there were now ruts. "Road's not great, but it's passable now if you take it nice and slow. Once you get down into Gatlinburg proper, the roads are plenty clear."

"Good to know. Thank you."

The older gentleman stepped off the porch, but turned to add, "And don't worry about clean up. My wife will get all that. Fiona already asked us to."

"Thank you," Geo said.

Fiona's uncle saluted and turned to walk up the hill in the snow. Apparently, there was at least one more house on top of the mountain.

Geo closed the door against the cold, shivering a little bit. Maybe he could convince Truvy that it was still dangerous, that they should stay longer. Maybe—

*Maybe you're just prolonging the inevitable.*

He turned around and, sure enough, Truvy stood halfway down the stairs, her expression blank. "Let me guess: we have the car back and the roads are doable?"

So much for convincing her to stay.

Well, if she was going to run away, then now was the time before he got completely invested.

He ran a hand through his hair. "Yeah."

"Then I guess we'd better go?"

"Yeah," he echoed. "I guess we'd better."

Upstairs, Truvy shimmied into her dress and looked for her shoes.

She would not cry. She would not give Geo Russo the satisfaction of knowing he'd gotten under her skin this much. If he could go back to his regularly scheduled life after all of their delicious sex, then she sure as shooting could, too.

She stepped hard into her shoe, almost breaking the heel off.

*Calm down, Truvy. You can't be mad, either.*

She paused and took deep breaths, pushing the heels of her hands against her eyes as a reminder that she could not yet cry. Swallowing the lump in her throat, she picked up her other heel and slid it on. Once dressed, she looked around the loft for anything else she might've left and started picking up condom wrappers.

"Fiona's uncle said his wife would clean up," Geo called upstairs.

"Yeah, well, I'm pretty sure she doesn't want to pick up

condom wrappers or empty this particular trash can."

Truvy tucked the box of condoms under her arm and brought the smaller can downstairs to dump into the larger trash. Geo brought the trash from his bedroom and the bathroom and then tied up the bag.

Truvy took her coat and purse from one of the kitchen table chairs. "I guess this is it," she said, willing her eyes to tell his that she didn't want this to be it.

"I guess it is," he whispered.

They said nothing as she oh-so-slowly maneuvered the Corolla down the mountain and back to Merle's where Geo's Lexus sat under a coating of snow. They sat in her car contemplating this.

"Want me to wait until you're sure you can clear off the windshield and get it started?"

"No, I wouldn't want to hold you up," he said. "I know you have a hot date with Netflix that I interrupted."

Oh, God. She wanted to barf. She wanted to cry. Instead, she said, "Netflix gets a little jealous sometimes, but he can wait."

Lame to begin with, the joke fell flat. Geo gave her one chuckle anyway before leaning over to kiss her cheek. "You are one amazing woman, Truvy Fuller. I'm glad I learned that."

She turned to capture his lips with hers even if briefly. "And you're a good man, Geo Russo. I'm glad I found that out."

He opened his mouth as if he were going to add something else, but then shook his head like he was ridding his mind of the thought.

They stared at each other, Truvy willing him to say that one week wasn't enough.

He didn't.

Only after he got out of the car and started brushing snow off his windshield did she think, *Maybe he was waiting for me to say something.*

Well. She wasn't about to float out the idea only to have him slap it back down. She could stand on her own, thank you very much.

Besides, what happened in Vegas was supposed to say in Vegas. Hadn't they both said that at least a hundred times?

# Chapter Thirteen

Geo had sworn to himself that he would never again be in the position of having a woman run away from him, but here he was sitting in a parking lot letting a woman leave. His heart felt as though it wanted to claw its way out of his chest and follow Truvy's taillights.

He couldn't blame it.

Of course, he also couldn't afford to follow his heart. No, he needed to think more with his head. His brain had told him that his first wife wasn't the right woman for him from the beginning, but he hadn't listened because his heart had wanted so desperately to be loved and other parts of him had wanted so desperately to get laid.

*Okay, brain, I need you to remind me of all of the reasons I can't be in love with Truvy Fuller because right now I want to follow her.*

Well, she was a judgmental woman who couldn't handle a little bit of drinking or meat eating or a man having a decent job, and —

And all of those were misconceptions that he'd carried around with him for the past fourteen years, years that he'd wasted without her.

And he'd be damned if he'd squander another second.

He flung open the driver's side door and threw himself into the seat. He tried to jam his key into the ignition but missed the first time because his hands shook so much from the cold.

Or maybe it was nerves.

Would Truvy have still been so receptive to his charms if she'd had any other options? I mean, she was the one who originally pointed out that they were in Vegas.

Yeah, but he was the one who *said* that whatever they did

would stay in the cabin.

*Geo, you jackass. You only repeated it a hundred times.*

Well, maybe not a hundred.

This time, the key found its mark. He had to turn it twice because the car didn't want to start up in the cold weather. Once he got the motor running, he called Dylan.

"Yeah, I know you're on your honeymoon. I don't care. I need to know where Truvy lives."

Truvy tossed her purse and coat on the chair just inside the door. She crossed the room to the sofa and plopped down to turn on her television. A smarter woman would be polishing her resume, but she just wanted to sit down and cry.

Now that she was home alone, she allowed all of her hot tears to flow freely. She was too sad to sob, and she hadn't known that such a thing was even possible.

What had she been thinking?

Men could be so charming when they wanted sex. She knew that. She'd fallen for it anyway. Hell, she'd instigated it with her strip air hockey, as if that should be a thing.

Someone banged on her door, and she sighed. She didn't have the money to buy anything. Jesus Christ was already her personal savior. It was too early for Girl Scout Cookies. Whoever it was would just have to go away. Besides, it was too cold to open the door.

"Truvy, I know you're in there. I see your car."

Geo? But it couldn't be him.

She crossed the room anyway and glanced through the peephole. He stood on the other side of the door, rubbing his hands against his scruff as though wishing he could shave it away.

"Truvy. Please?"

She opened the door, still bewildered. Had she forgotten something?

"Geo? What are you doing here?"

"We, uh. We didn't set up a time for our second date."

Geo's hands curled into fists at his sides. She'd been crying. He had made her cry.

He might cry himself if she didn't answer him soon.

"No, we didn't," she said softly, sagging against the door, still bewildered.

"Can I come in?" he asked.

She looked behind her and blushed, but nodded and stepped aside for him to enter. The minute the door shut behind him, he moved forward to pull her into his arms.

She took a step backward.

"Oh," he said.

"Oh, what?"

He stared at her, and she stared back at him. She was going to make him say it. She was going to make him put himself on the line, and he had sworn that he would never again put himself at a woman's mercy.

Of course, that was before he met Truvy.

Might as well put all of his cards out on the table.

"I think I've—"

"You think what?" she asked, as she leaned forward, her lips slightly parted. They were swollen from all of his kissing, and he wanted to make that a habit.

"I think I might be falling in love with you."

She closed her eyes, and his heart quit beating.

*Way to put it all out there and hedge your bets all at the same time, Geo.*

"I'm not talking about the sex, which is amazing. I'm talking about you."

Her eyes snapped open then narrowed. "You're not just saying that to get into my pants, are you?"

He sucked in a breath, offended until he saw the hurt in her eyes. Of course, that jackass Regis had once hurt her the way Violet had hurt him. Hurting each other seemed to be what humans did best.

Well, second best.

"We're not in Vegas anymore," he said. "I wish we could go back, but I'm also glad we got kicked out."

"Why?"

"Because it was that much sooner that I realized…" He wasn't going to make the mistake of saying the "L" word again. He couldn't say it again unless he knew she felt the same way.

Slowly, torturously, she crossed the tiny living room of her apartment. Stopping in front of him, she took a deep breath. "I think I might be falling in love with you, too."

He wrapped his arms around her, just holding her against his body for a few seconds to remember the warmth of the cabin. He buried his nose in her hair then held her out at arm's length. "Does this mean I get that second date?"

One corner of her mouth curled up into a half-smile, and her eyes twinkled. "Sure. How about in the meantime we Netflix and chill?"

"I thought you'd never ask."

# Chapter Fourteen

## *One year later*

Once again in the Mountain Bliss Chapel, Truvy and Fiona stood in front of the full-length mirror in the bride's room. This time, however, Truvy wore white. She fiddled with her tiara while Fiona huffed and paced.

"And here I thought you'd be happy for me," Truvy said.

"I am happy for you. It's just—"

"It's just that you and Dylan are arguing over stupid stuff and you don't like to be reminded of your vows?"

"Damn, Truvy. Way to cut a girl to her core!"

"Look, you got me into this."

Fiona's shoulders sagged and she smiled with tears glistening unshed in her eyes. "Yeah. And it's the best thing I ever did."

"I'll say. Now are you going to go up to the cabin and take care of things for me like I asked you?"

"Yes, Dylan and I will go spread the rose petals and put the box of condoms by the bed and bring the steaks and wine and all of that so everything will be just like the weekend when you and Geo finally fell in love like we told you to do in the first place."

"So humble," Truvy said with one eyebrow arched.

Fiona smiled ruefully where once she might have grinned. "Don't mind me. I'm sorry I'm being so irritable on your big day. Things are a little tense with Dylan right now."

Truvy hugged Fiona tightly. "They say the first year is the hardest."

"You better watch out," Fiona said with a sad smile.

The clock outside chimed the hour, and Truvy said. "*Your* turn to go get the boys."

Geo paced the little room. "And you're sure she won't change her mind?"

"Truvy?" asked Dylan. "Heck, no. Truvy always knows what she wants. Unlike Fiona."

Geo pointed a finger at his best man. "I know there's trouble in paradise, but I don't want to hear about it today. Tomorrow you can man up and apologize for whatever you did."

Dylan clasped a hand over his heart and scowled in outrage. "Why do you think it was something I did?"

"Because I know you. And sometimes those grand gestures of yours go awry."

"Whatever."

"And you're going to go fix everything up at the cabin just like I said, right?"

Dylan waved away Geo's words. "Yeah, yeah. Fiona and I will drive up there and make sure everything is exactly like it was last year. Blah. Blah. Blah."

Fiona appeared in the doorway, and Geo couldn't help but notice that Dylan looked at her with hungry eyes. "It's time, boys."

This time, Dylan rocked back and forth on the balls of his feet, obviously ready to get out of the chapel. Geo smiled but kept his eyes trained on the doorway.

Truvy Fuller appeared in a floor-length wedding gown with a tiara and long, white debutante gloves. He had to grin because she'd gone all out. She grinned back at him and made a subtle nod to his right and his left, a questioning look in her eyes.

He nodded, and she sighed in relief just as she reached the dais and took his hand.

Then Geo Russo and Truvy Fuller got married with the power vested in a faux Dolly Parton. This time, however, the little chapel was full to standing room only with friends and family.

Dylan stomped his wet boots on the rug as he and Fiona

entered the cabin with the stupid name: Las Vegas.

"Take off your boots!" Fiona yelled. "If you track mud in my uncle's cabin, he'll have my hide."

Dylan muttered under his breath but stepped out of his boots and set them beside Fiona's high-heeled ankle boot contraptions, pair five-thousand and forty-six of her shoes, best he could tell.

"Get the rose petals!" she called from upstairs where she was doing whatever it was she was supposed to be doing.

"I know what I'm supposed to do!" he bellowed.

She appeared at the top of the bedroom loft and looked down on him. "Then do it. I'd like to get home before eight."

Yeah, yeah. Her shows.

These days she was so tired that she often fell asleep on the couch. She was so cranky and not at all like the woman he'd married. She'd burst into tears at the drop of a hat.

Maybe tonight—

The unmistakable roar of his Ford truck had him running to the door and trying to slam his feet back into his boots. By the time he stumbled out onto the porch, his truck was gone. "Son. Of. A. Bitch."

"Uh, Dylan?"

"What?" Now he was irritable, and he didn't like that about himself. Of course, he also needed to get laid. That would help his disposition a lot.

"You might want to read this," Fiona said as she climbed down the last stair with a letter and a small pink box.

*Dear Fiona and Dylan,*

*I guess we owe you some thanks now that we are together. Since the two of you seem to be doubting the wisdom of your own marriage, we decided you might need a week in Vegas to patch things up.*

*We cleared it with your employers who both agreed they would prefer a week without you if that meant both of you came back in a better mood. Do us all a favor and straighten yourselves out. Please.*

*We heartily suggest red wine and strip air hockey. But not the Trivial Pursuit.*

*Love,*
*Truvy and Geo*
*P.S. We're going to Hawaii, bitches!!!!*

It had taken forever to get to Honolulu, but Truvy had decided it was well worth it as she lazed on a white sand beach in the world's most perfect weather, watching a sunset that defied description. "Now *this* is a honeymoon."

"You mean you didn't want to go back to Vegas?" Geo asked facetiously as he put down the Tess Gerritsen book she'd recommended.

She laughed. "Nah. Las Vegas is for people who need to work out some... things."

"I need to work out some things," Geo said with a waggle of his brows.

"Oh, do you now?" she asked.

"Oh, but I do," he said as he got to his feet and started collecting all of their belongings.

"Maybe I have some things you could work out."

"I see. And what are the chances that when we get back to the hotel room you'll wear the leis from yesterday's luau and nothing else?"

"Pretty high," she said, batting her eyelashes.

Geo paused in their walking to look skyward. "I love this place."

"More than you love Vegas?"

"Oh, Vegas will always hold a special place in my heart," he said as he held open the gate that led to their hotel. "But I don't think it matters where I am as long as I'm with you."

"Geo," she said, melting for him all over again.

"As Dolly says, I will always love you."

"Don't you dare sing it."

But he sang it anyway, and she loved him all the more for it.

## Acknowledgments

Special shout out to all of my Fiction from the Heart authors: they keep me on my toes and make me a better writer. I'm proud they let me tag along.

Thanks to Peter Senftleben for his editing expertise—always a pleasure to work with him—and to Sarah Younger for being my agent extraordinaire.

Thanks to Jamie Beck and Susan Sands, who both read early versions of this story; to Sonali Dev, who read a later one; and to my mother, Jane Rowlett, who, as always, has come through with a red pen, a quick wit, and lots of love. Any mistakes are mine and mine alone.

Thank *you*, dear reader. I wouldn't be able to do what I do without you.

As always thank you to my parents (all four of them), my kiddos, and Ryan. I love you and appreciate you and promise that I will one day learn how to meet a deadline without having a zombielike demeanor and relying on alternating pizza places for supper.

## About Sally Kilpatrick

Straight from the buckle of the Bible Belt, Sally Kilpatrick writes southern fiction full of small-town shenanigans. She is a Golden Heart® finalist, a Book Buyer's Best finalist, and a National Readers' Choice Awards triple finalist. Her fourth novel, *Bless Her Heart* won the 2018 Georgia Author of the Year Award and the Maggie Award of Excellence. Her fifth novel, *Oh My Stars,* explores what happens when a community finds a baby in the manger of the local Drive Thru Nativity. Sally lives with her husband and two children in Marietta, Georgia, a suburb of Atlanta. Visit her author website at sallykilpatrick.com or follow her on Twitter as @SuperWriterMom.

**Web site:** www.sallykilpatrick.com
**Twitter:** @superwritermom
**Facebook:** www.facebook.com/SuperWriterMom/

Dear Christine,

# Starstruck: Take Two

## by Falguni Kothari

*Happy Reading!* ♥

Love,
Falguni ♥

*For Truffles*

# *Scene One:*

## *Wedding Crasher*

A throng of paparazzi blocked Tania Coehlo's grand arrival to Suryaganj Fort, a privately owned manor in the Jaisalmer district of Rajasthan, where her client, Ariana Kapoor, was filming her big-screen debut.

It was barely five in the morning, yet the gossip-hungry vultures had jumped up from their makeshift camp the second they spotted her ride—a shiny blue Bentley coupe—and fresh bait.

*Flash. Flash. Click, click, click.*

"*Arre wah*, it's the manager, Ms. Tania."

"Ma'am! Have you seen the rushes of *Padmini*?"

*Flash. Click.*

"Are you here for the wrap-up party, or is it something else?"

"Can you get me into the party as your plus-one, ma'am?"

Tania wasn't sure whether to be honored or horrified that paparazzi had started recognizing her.

As the cameras flashed in her face and the questions got nosier, she fished her sunglasses out of her Fendi tote and slid them on, feeling silly as she did so since it was still dark outside. She regretted asking the chauffeur to take the car's top down on her drive in from the airport. But she'd wanted to bask in the freshness of the desert-scape and marvel at the glorious canopy of stars above—a sight never to be seen in smog-riddled Mumbai.

Not one of her smartest decisions.

Neither was coming to Jaisalmer for the wrap-up party, considering the day.

But it would have looked strange if she'd refused to come and celebrate such a momentous event of Ariana's career. She'd already stayed away from the production for much too long. And, even though her job as a celebrity manager was more behind the scenes, her absence had been noted on several occasions in the last eleven months.

"Ma'am, are the rumors true? Is Veeriana headed for a breakup?"

Tania's belly hollowed at the question as the Bentley lurched forward.

*Stop it. Stop obsessing over him. And the fact that it's Christmas Eve.*

Veeriana was the celebrity couple name given to the stars of *Padmini* by their fans who shipped Veer Rana and Ariana Kapoor's relationship both on- and offscreen.

What would happen if the fans ever found out the truth?

"If Veer Rana and Ariana break their engagement, what happens to the *Padmini* franchise? Will they still work together in the next two movies, ma'am?"

Good question. But moot point because Veeriana was not breaking up anytime soon, and it would be smart to focus on that.

Somehow, the chauffeur managed to steer the car through the inquisitive horde, and soon, they were driving down a meandering, private road with nothing obstructing their progress, except random rocks along the way and a cute little caravan of camels.

Five minutes later, the car pulled up in front of an imposing yellow stone structure that was lit up from rampart to ground and turret to turret as if it were Diwali. The wedding scenes had been filmed this week, Tania recalled.

Suryaganj Fort was situated on the outskirts of the Thar Desert, about an hour's drive west of Jaisalmer city, and had a muddled history with the real Queen Padmini—the reason Javed Ali, the director of the *Padmini* franchise, had wanted it for a location shoot. Now, she knew what the fuss was about. The fort was stunning. Timeless. A glittering echo of an age long gone.

Tania got out of the car with a jaw-breaking yawn and a shiver she couldn't quite control despite the sweatshirt she'd pulled on over her comfy travel jeans for the plane. It was cooler here than in Mumbai. She'd have to improvise with her wardrobe for tonight. Or use her bare shoulders as an excuse to leave the party early.

Settling her tote on her shoulder, Tania walked into the manor's charmingly cluttered foyer, which was brimming with film crew and equipment instead of royal guards and grand furniture. Props and strange apparatus were being trotted in from the wide open terrace doors across the hall while other thingamajigs were being carried out. There seemed to be a scene change taking place out on the terrace or in the courtyard beyond, even at this ungodly hour.

There was no such thing as a nine-to-five workday in the movie business. Filming was done according to scheduling and budget, and sometimes, the crew had to work round the clock to finish within those parameters.

Pulling an all-nighter would explain why no one had stopped her from entering the premises or asked her for her ID. Careless of them. For all they knew, she could be a paparazzo who'd just waltzed in.

Maybe it was just too damn early for prudence.

Tania hailed one sleepy-eyed crew member. "I'm looking for Ariana."

The young man jerked his chin at the courtyard.

"Thanks. Also," she called out when he made to go, "can you point me toward a restroom? And is there any way I can get a double shot of espresso now?"

With a heavy sigh, the man led her to a bathroom and then went off to fulfill her beverage request—or so she assumed since he hadn't said a word to her.

She shouldn't be having another shot of caffeine tonight; her nerves were all over the place. But she was addicted to the stuff.

She'd been subsisting on coffee and croissants for the past thirty-six hours while running around Mumbai, attending to the needs of her A-list clients. As a one-woman celebrity management agency, there just weren't enough hours in a day for her to tackle her roster of eight actresses with blossoming careers without stretching herself thin. She took care of all of her clients' business needs, like managing their schedules, reading scripts, giving advice on projects or endorsements, going over new contracts or renegotiating old ones, publicity, and branding—everything.

Most nights, she fell into bed long after midnight and would bolt upright before her six a.m. alarm went off. She'd trained her mind and body to function well on a minimum amount of sleep, like an emergency room doctor. Injecting coffee into her veins helped, too.

Tonight—or this morning since it was after midnight—she'd barely entered her home and kicked off her black high-heeled pumps when she was blitzed by phone calls from Ariana, demanding that she fly to Jaisalmer for the wrap-up shoot and afterparty. Tania had argued that she was officially on vacation from that afternoon onward until the New Year.

"Then, you have no excuse," Ariana had countered. "Get your butt over here for the celebration. I'm sending the car and the jet, darling. Get moving!"

Tania hadn't been able to counterargue fast enough, and so here she was. On Christmas Eve no less.

Her nerves hadn't stopped jingling since the phone call.

She flushed the toilet and began to wash her hands. The bathroom was as grand as the foyer, minus the clutter, with inlaid marble floors, shiny lacquered doors, and gilded lavatory fixtures that seemed new but weren't. She splashed her face with cold water and dried it on a monogrammed towel.

The vanity mirror wasn't kind to her. The dark circles under her eyes made her look like a horror movie extra.

"You can handle him for one day," she told her reflection. "Even today."

Veer Rana was her client's fake fiancé and costar. That was all. So what if she'd had a brief fling with him last year? It was over, and they had both moved on. She had refortified her heart during these eleven months. She would not be charmed by him again or act starstruck.

With a decisive nod, Tania extracted her kohl pencil, compact, and lip gloss from her tote that carried everything but the kitchen sink and went to work on her face. She was not freshening up to impress him—definitely not. Her job required her to be presentable at all times. And it didn't hurt to look nice while swimming with swans. Not that applying powder and gloss to her face would transform her into a swan. The point was to not look like a zombie, that's all.

Once she took care of her face, she twisted her hair into a French knot with a couple of flicks of her wrist. Her phone buzzed with an incoming message from Ariana while she pinned it all in place.

*Are you here?*

*Yes,* Tania replied, texting with one hand. *Where are you?*

*Awesome! Come to the courtyard. Still shooting.*

Tania replied with a thumb's up emoji and went back to the foyer. It was a wonder she was still on her feet and not hobbling like an old lady. Thank God she'd worn sensible sneakers for the flight and not her usual heeled pumps, though she carried those in the tote for tonight.

She was bone-tired and slightly hungover from Pihu Khanna's birthday celebration—another diva of a client and TV star who'd turned twenty-eight for the seventh year in a row. Heading home from the party, Tania had prayed there would be no more drama until she got her beauty sleep. But, as luck would have it, Ariana had decided to become a diva tonight.

Managing the careers of spoiled, entitled actresses definitely wasn't for the faint of heart, and Tania Coehlo was anything but. She'd cut her teeth on Bollywood divas and bad boys. Her mother, Sonia Coehlo, had only been a dancing extra on movie sets, and she'd still had the airs of a diva, both at work and at home.

It was only after being diagnosed with early onset Alzheimer's at the age of forty-five that Sonia had mellowed down into a little kitten without claws. Still, these past three years had been rough on both of them with the full household burden and medical bills falling solely on Tania's shoulders.

Tania's father wasn't in the picture. Either Sonia didn't know who he was herself or she didn't want Tania to know. The latter more likely. Apart from being an extra on movie sets, her mother had been a starstruck groupie, hooking up with any actor willing to spend wads of money on her.

As such, Tania had been born and raised within the movie industry. This was her world. It was all she knew. And, when it had come time for her to choose a career at the ripe old age of seventeen—college had never been an option—she'd decided that managing the careers of superstars might be a smarter and steadier way to make a living than trying to become one herself, as Sonia had wished. With her average height, curvy body, and bedroom eyes that were a gift from her mother, Tania was more femme fatale than sweet and wholesome female lead material. Not to mention, she couldn't act to save herself. Plus, she hated being stared at.

It had been twelve years since she started her business. She had zero regrets.

What was there to regret? A celebrity manager often enjoyed most of the perks of stardom minus the stress and lack of privacy. Minus the lovely money, too. But who needed all that money when her generous clients allowed her free use of their Beemers and Bentleys? When their private jets flew her from Mumbai to Jaisalmer for a party? When she was invited to their beach homes for the holidays or on their yachts —

Tania cut off the thought. *Do not go there. Do not think about his damn boat or him.*

She forced her mind to go blank. Was this what was happening to her mother's brain but involuntarily?

Before other crazy thoughts popped into her head and since the crew member and her espresso were nowhere to be seen, Tania decided to find Ariana. But, the second she walked onto the terrace and swept her eyes across the courtyard that was bedecked as a big, fat royal wedding, she knew it was too late to keep Veer Rana out of her head.

Dozens upon dozens of people were rushing about — some working behind the scenes, some in front of it, most of them shouting or dancing or moving massive pieces of equipment here or there — and yet all Tania saw was Veer.

He sat on a golden throne in the middle of a raised, lotus-shaped altar that had been constructed in the middle of the courtyard. Resplendent in his wedding finery, he looked every inch like a Rajput king, complete with a thick moustache that curled at the ends. Her chest contracted, ached as she tried and failed not to gawk at the vision he made.

She hadn't seen him for eleven months, and suddenly, it was too much. She couldn't catch her breath. *He* was too much.

Then, from somewhere above her head, Javed Ali's voice boomed, "I want music!" and the giant speakers placed all around the movie set burst into Sanskrit wedding mantras.

*Da-dum, da-dum, da-dum… swaahaa! Da-dum, da-dum, da-dum… swaahaa!*

The cameraman's assistant snapped the clapper, shouting into his own mike, "Ratan Sen close-up. Wedding *phera* scene. *Annnnd,* ACTION!"

On cue, Veer—no, Ratan Sen rose from his throne and gallantly helped his red-veiled princess bride to her feet. He didn't let go of her hand as he led her around the fire, once, before coming to stand in front of their respective thrones once more. In an authentic Hindu wedding ceremony, the couple would go around the fire seven times, each *phera* signifying a marriage vow.

The bride—Ariana as Padmini—stood with her back to Tania, at an angle, which gave Tania an unhindered view of Ratan Sen's face. Like a besotted groom, he smiled down at his bride, marveling at his good fortune. Then, slowly, his moustache kicked up on one side and the smile changed flavor. The hearts dancing in his kohl-lined eyes made room for lust to rise—a look that promised his bride an unforgettable wedding night.

Tania knew that look. As if he couldn't wait to strip her naked and have his way with her. As if the very heat in his eyes would burn away the barriers of their clothes. How many times had he looked at her like that during their monthlong affair? A hundred … thousand … million?

Jealousy turned her insides to ash despite the fact that Veer was only acting. Despite knowing that Veeriana was nothing more than a publicity stunt orchestrated by the producers of *Padmini*. Neither actor was interested in the other in real life.

Tania wanted to tear her eyes away from the scene, from Veer, but it was impossible.

Holy sepulchre, but he was a gorgeous specimen of humanity. Tall, athletically built with a loose-limbed grace that spoke of confidence and health. On his head was a red-and-gold turban with a jeweled broach pinned to his temple, but she knew that underneath was a mop of dense, unruly hair that he kept cropped short. Each of his features had been carefully crafted by their Maker and arranged on his face in such a way that made him look both handsome and beautiful at the same time. Angelic and sinful.

She loved his mouth the best. The wide, wicked slash of his lips that had teased her as well as tormented. That'd spoken words she was so tempted to believe. Words that had the power to destroy her if false. And, when he'd smiled at her like he was smiling at his bride ... *oh God.*

Tania wanted to scratch Ariana's eyes out, which made her the reigning queen of stupid because she had no claim on the man. She never had. He belonged to Ariana and *Padmini* for the next two years. She should not forget that.

And, because she was once again distracted by Veer Rana and the things he made her feel, Tania didn't notice the twenty-five-foot-long jimmy jib swinging toward her.

The next thing she knew, she'd been whacked on her head, and down the terrace she tumbled like Jill, rolling bumpity-bump until she came to a spread-eagled halt at the bottom of the steps.

With her ears ringing like church bells, all Tania could do was blink at the star-studded sky in shock, the monstrously long and large camera crane cutting it in half. A gaggle of human heads popped into her line of vision—most of them wearing wedding costumes and worried expressions. All of them babbling at her and each other.

The crowd parted like the Red Sea and the red-and-gold turban drew closer. The moustache buzzed at her. Why was it buzzing? She wondered what it would feel like against her skin.

He dropped to his knees beside her and gently placed his hand on her forehead. Still buzzing.

His touch was meant to soothe, but it had the opposite effect on her. It was all she could do to not grab the garland of flowers around his neck, yank him down on top of her, and kiss him into oblivion.

*This* was why she had to stay far away from the likes of Veer Rana. Like her mother, she simply could not be sensible around beautiful men.

# Scene Two:

## *Clueless*

His emotions exploding like land mines, Veer followed Tania and Dr. Mehra down the east wing hallway and into the Peacock Room — named and designed with India's national bird in mind — which had been converted into an emergency clinic for the duration of the filming.

Thank God they had a doctor on staff while on location. Production had to, for insurance purposes. Prop crews had a propensity to nail their thumbs to props. Stuntmen constantly broke bones. Entire sets could come crashing down around everyone's ears. Movie sets were hazardous places — as proven.

Dr. Mehra directed Tania to sit on a peacock-inspired divan, so he could continue the examination he'd started in the courtyard. The stubborn woman had refused to be carried inside, insisting she was fine even though her beautiful eyes were round as saucers and still dazed from her fall.

Veer turned to shut the door to keep away the busybodies trailing behind them. Not Ariana. He let her in. She looked as shell-shocked as he felt as she swept in behind them, the heavy skirts of her bridal costume hitched up for ease of movement. She carried Tania's handbag in one hand. *Good girl.*

"Doc?" he prodded after Dr. Mehra had freed Tania's hair from the twisty hairdo and parted it to see the back of her head.

"No cut. No bleeding. That's good. No swelling or bump on the skull yet. Hopefully, it stays that way. The area might feel a little tender for a few days, mind you. Except for some minor scrapes and bruises from the fall, you seem fine, young lady. You were lucky. Let's get you an ice pack and some painkillers and send you on your way."

The fact that Dr. Mehra wasn't a quack didn't alleviate Veer's panic one whit.

"Shouldn't we take her to a hospital for a CT scan? What if she has a concussion?"

The jimmy jib had whacked her pretty hard, and when she'd rolled down the steps, he'd swear his heart had stopped.

Dr. Mehra beamed a penlight into her eyes. "I don't think there's any need. I mean, we could have her X-rayed. However …"

"You can stop talking about me as if I were in a coma," Tania snapped, finally sounding like herself. But Veer was only slightly relieved. "I feel fine."

He was about to call her out on her bravado when Dr. Mehra beat him to it.

"That's good to hear, child. We can table the X-rays for now. But I strongly recommend painkillers because you will start to hurt. The bruise on your elbow will need monitoring. A cold compress should keep the swelling down. On your head, too. Can someone bring in some ice packs and towels, please?" Dr. Mehra shot over his shoulder at Veer or Ariana or both without turning around. The old coot never missed an opportunity to yank their celebrity egos back to solid ground by making them do menial jobs.

"Don't bother them. I'll go to the kitchen and take care of it myself," Tania said and started to get up. God, she was stubborn.

"Sit. Manan will fetch the ice packs," Veer said, resisting the urge to reach out and push her back on the divan. He pulled out his cell phone from the inside pocket of his sherwani jacket and called his valet.

"You guys are making a fuss over nothing," Tania grumbled. But, she sat down again.

"You scared us, honey. Sure you're okay?" Ariana handed her the tote and her phone. Then, she gave Tania a long hug.

Veer wanted to wrap his arms around her, too. Run his hands all over her body to see if she was really okay. But he knew she wouldn't stand for it. Not in front of an audience.

"I'm fine. Really. Go. Finish filming your scene." she tried to shoo them off.

"Are you sure? I do have one more scene ..." Ariana looked around the room, clearly in two minds.

"I'm done for the morning, Ari. I'll stay with Tania and make sure she's taken care of," Veer said, slipping his phone back into his pocket.

"Nobody needs to stay," Tania protested, glaring at him, then quickly looked away. "I can take care of myself."

"No doubt. But I'm staying," he said. Whether she liked it or not—and, of course, she didn't.

She went stiff as a plank of wood at his unequivocal declaration. He was coming to realize that she was going to treat him like a stranger or an unwelcome acquaintance, at best.

Ariana dithered for a few minutes, but eventually, Tania convinced her to go. She didn't get that far with him.

She ignored him while Dr. Mehra cleaned her wounds with Dettol. The skin to the right of her chin was scraped, as were the heels of her palms. It had to sting like a bitch, but she bore it bravely. Veer kept his mouth zipped through it and his hands to himself, even when she flinched. He didn't want to say or do anything he'd regret.

God, she infuriated him, confused him. She'd freaking ghosted him for eleven months. How she'd managed to keep their paths from crossing when he was pretty much joined at the hip to her number one client, he had no clue. If he hadn't been the target of her boycott, he would have admired the level of organizational juggling it required.

But all of that could wait. Right now, her health was paramount.

He'd never been more shocked or terrified as he'd been when the jimmy jib knocked her off the terrace. Watching the whole thing happen, he'd leaped from the stage and rushed to get to her as fast as his stupid *mojdis* could carry him—which they hadn't, not very far, and somewhere along the way, he'd chucked them off.

He was still barefoot, and the marble floor was chilled beneath his feet. He should ask Manan to bring a pair of shoes after he brought the ice packs. It was pure luck that he didn't have a nail or sliver of wood jabbed into his sole since most of Suryaganj seemed to be littered with such debris. He also needed a shower. He was sweaty from being under the harsh lights of the set, and the embroidered sherwani and dhoti he was wearing were making his skin itch.

He took off his turban and rubbed his hands over his scalp, groaning in relief. Even his hair hurt. He needed to scrub the gunk off his face, too, before his skin broke out like a pubescent boy's. But he would not leave Tania's side.

Every Neanderthal instinct he possessed wanted to whisk her away—somewhere far and remote—where he could take care of her hard head and protect her luscious little body by stuffing it inside bubble wrap, so she'd never get hurt again. Yet the urge to shout at her for disappearing on him was bubbling inside of him.

Maybe he should go shower if only to cool off.

No, he couldn't leave her side because, beneath all of the blood-boiling emotions he was currently feeling, there was also joy. A sense of utter peace had settled inside him the second he saw her on the terrace.

She was finally within touchable, huggable distance. A little cross, a little panicked—he knew he made her nervous—but she was right in front of him. Right where she belonged—where they both belonged.

Now, if she'd only relax her rules a little, it was where she'd remain.

# *Scene Three:*

## *Breakfast at Suryaganj*

An hour later, the sun had popped into the sky, raising not only the temperatures in the area, but also the tempers of the sleep-deprived residents of Suryaganj. And Veer had still not gotten to shower.

His valet, Manan, had brought him a change of clothes and loafers after he delivered the ice and towels to the infirmary.

"You really don't need to babysit me. Please, run along. Do whatever it is you do between scene takes."

The ice pack might have helped Tania's hard head from swelling but not her pissy mood.

"I am doing what I want. I'm having breakfast. You have a problem with that?" He raised an eyebrow and continued to demolish his three-egg omelet.

Three times a day, buffets were set up on the terrace to serve the two-hundred-plus production unit. Though the kitchen was open twenty-four/seven for those who couldn't make it to the buffet line.

As one of the main actors on set, Veer didn't need to eat with the crew. He could order his meals to his room or eat in the formal dining room with the other actors and executive personnel, but he preferred to eat with the men. It built a sense of camaraderie and trust, his father had told him long ago. It also kept movie stars humble to be part of the norm rather than the exception. No wonder Dr. Mehra and his father, former Bollywood megastar Tarun Rana, got along so well. They thought alike.

That morning though, Veer had asked the ever-ready kitchen staff to serve Tania and him breakfast in the dining room. He didn't want her to stand in the buffet lines or get elbowed on her bumps and bruises by the boisterous crew.

"Stop staring," she murmured, halfway through their first shared meal in eleven months. Her voice was naturally low-pitched and husky, but when she'd just woken up or not gone to bed at all, it was liquid sex.

Hearing it conjured all sorts of delicious images in Veer's mind.

"No staring. No talking. No texts or calls or e-mails. Any other restrictions?"

When she pretended to not hear him, Veer felt an unholy urge to shake her. What would she do if he kissed her in front of the crew? Or if he spread her out on the table and feasted on her?

He took a large swallow of his protein smoothie instead of acting on any of those scenarios.

"I was under the impression that we'd decided to stop seeing each other romantically until the movies were released. Not platonically," he said, making a gargantuan effort to sound offhand when he wanted to roar. Or whine.

She glanced at the open doors of the dining room. "This is not the place to talk about this."

He didn't care for them to become a scandal either, not when he wasn't free to do anything about it. "I agree. But you've left me no choice."

He was about to start begging her to reconsider their agreement when Ariana strolled into the room in a pink sarong-style maxi dress and a plate of fruit in her hand. Shaan Rana, Veer's older brother and executive producer of the franchise, stormed in right behind her.

"Don't be a brat." Shaan scowled at Ariana. Then, at Veer. Then, he did a double take at Tania. "What the hell happened to your chin? Did you bang it or something?"

The chin in question was missing a couple of layers of skin—like her elbow—and was shiny from an aloe vera application. It also confirmed that his *bhai* didn't know everything that went on at his movie set.

"A runaway jimmy jib hit her. She's suing for damages," Veer said, straight-faced.

"A freak accident. And I'm not ... suing, that is," Tania said, shooting him an annoyed look.

"Which is it?" Shaan's scowl deepened. Talk of money always set him off, especially when he had to give it away.

His brother had been a nervous wreck since they started production back in February, and while Veer empathized with the stress of his job, he also could not help poking fun at Shaan.

"Forget it," Veer said before Shaan had an aneurysm or Tania emasculated him.

His surly brother settled his hands over the belt holding up his cargo shorts. "It's good that you're here, Tania. You can take your client to task and off my hands. She was caught smooching her hairstylist in broad daylight, and now, the media thinks Veeriana is in trouble."

"Jesus, Shaan. What the hell?" Veer stared at his brother, then cut a look at his costar as she sat down next to him with a long-suffering sigh.

But Tania had frozen and was looking at Ariana in horror. "You did what?"

"I didn't do anything" — Ariana waved her fork in the air — "in broad daylight."

Veer sniggered while Shaan's scowl turned sour.

"Of course you encourage her to misbehave."

"Not true." Veer winked at Ariana even as he denied it. He didn't actively encourage Ari to misbehave, but he didn't discourage her either. You lived only once, right?

"You'd like nothing better than for this whole production to blow up in our faces, so you can go back to being a recluse. You never wanted to be a part of it. Admit it," Shaan huffed out.

It was true. Not the bit about him wanting the movie to fail, but about him being a reluctant hero and a homebody.

Once upon a time, all Veer had ever wanted to be was a Bollywood hero, like his father. Luck and family connections had made his dream come true much too soon. He'd been India's teen sensation with a super-hit TV series tacked to his name by the time he was thirteen. But the fame and early success had gone to his head, and he'd succumbed to its glamour and toxicity. By the time he was twenty, he'd been in rehab twice and nearly been arrested once. That was when his parents—both brilliant movie stars, too, and still very much in demand at the box office, even in their forties—had decided to hang up their megastar crowns and buy an organic vegetable farm not far from Mumbai, so they could nurse their youngest back to health. That had been five years ago.

When Shaan had come to him with the *Padmini* script, Veer's first instinct had been to refuse it. But he'd changed his mind for Ari's sake. He didn't want her to be blindsided by the industry or the fame like he'd been.

Ariana Kapoor was one of his oldest and closest friends. Born only a year apart, they had so much in common that they were practically twins. Their parents had been colleagues and close friends, too. Ari's father had been one hell of an actor and director in his heyday. But he'd died of heart failure the year Ari turned eighteen. She'd been preparing to make her film debut that year, but Roy Kapoor had made her promise to finish her education first. Smart man. Ari had honored her father's wish and gone to London to get her degree. As opposed to Veer, who'd only argued and fought with his parents back then.

He'd grown up eventually. And this past year had taught him even more about himself. He knew now that he wanted to be a part of the Indian film industry, which was, for better or worse, in his blood. Though not in front of the camera this time, but behind it. Watching and learning from Javed Ali about directing and visualization had revealed a new purpose and passion in Veer. He had used *Padmini*'s sets to learn everything he could from a master, one who'd happily taken him under his wing.

"Also not true," Veer replied belatedly, sending Ariana an apologetic smile. Reluctant hero or not, she knew he was honored to be her first costar. "Simmer down, *bhai*. Do you want tea? A glass of cold coffee?"

Shaan shrugged off his attempt at bonhomie and began questioning the mental faculties of everyone in the room. Ari was used to his brother and continued to chew on her watermelon through his tirade. If she was pissed or hurt by Shaan's words, she hid it well behind a bored face.

Ariana was a natural-born star. There was no doubt that she

was gifted. He'd been watching her for months now, and he knew just how effortlessly she got into the skin of her character. *Padmini* was a female-centric film, and Ari couldn't have picked a better debut to showcase her talent.

Thankfully, she seemed to have it together off camera, too. Her manager's influence? It wasn't because of Ari's mother, for sure. Nina Kapoor's life revolved around luxury spas and being detoxed and Botoxed most days.

And therein lay the problem. Both Tania and he were fond of Ariana—Shaan was, too—and each of them, in their own way, had sworn to launch her as a star, even while protecting her.

Veer glanced at Tania again. He was being careful not to stare at her for long or directly or flirt with her at all. He understood why she wanted to hide their past involvement, as it was no one's business but theirs. But he couldn't understand why they needed to ignore each other. He was respecting her wishes, though he didn't like it at all. Why was he letting her call all the shots?

She sat with her back straight, looking none the worse for wear from her fall. Her ubiquitous extra-large handbag that carried the secrets of the universe within it was in a chair next to her. The bag had been Potterized by an Undetectable Extension Charm; he'd swear on it. She'd taken out a tube of aloe vera gel from it to put on her wounds and bandages and makeup remover towelettes for him. Her hair was back in the twisty knot, and her tidy little hands were cupped around her coffee mug as she channeled a serenity Buddha while Shaan spewed his usual parochial crap around the room.

Again, he felt an urge to dishevel her.

Every few seconds, she flicked a glance at her phone screen as it flashed with notifications or at him in irritation when she caught him looking at her—like she was doing now.

Veer felt his mouth tug upward, but he schooled his features into grimness. He was supposed to be worried about Ariana being outed. According to Shaan, the media had smelled a rat because of something Ariana had said or done and were now speculating about the veracity of Veeriana.

The whole idea behind a relationship nickname was ludicrous, in Veer's opinion. It didn't stop him from making one up for him and Tania. *Veerania? Tanveer?*

Shaan paused long enough to take a deep breath and then continued the lecture. "I don't even want to imagine what will happen if they sniff out the truth. Do you know what's at stake here, ladies and gentleman? If this gets out, Ariana can kiss getting crowned as Bollywood's next reigning queen good-bye."

Ari arched a pointed eyebrow at Shaan. "I know what's at stake. I'm not an imbecile."

Shaan snorted. "Are you sure about that? Because you're not acting like you do or that you even care. Your life is no longer judgement-free, Ari. Everything you do is going to be analyzed and discussed—repeatedly. Even things you don't do or say will become media fodder. You are a public figure. You've always been one since you were in Nina Aunty's stomach. But it's more now, and once *Padmini* releases, it's only going to get worse. Fans expect certain things, and one of those things is for the object of their fandom to be exactly what he or she portrays to be on-screen. Hero or heroine. So, don't start screaming about double standards."

"She knows that, Shaan. You can stop repeating yourself," Tania inserted evenly.

If Veer didn't hold her in high esteem already, the way Tania refused to be cowered by the formidable Shaan Rana would have nailed it. Forget cowered, she'd subtly rapped his brother on his hand as if he were a naughty kid.

Not that Shaan was deterred by the rebukes from either woman.

"I'm glad to hear that," he went on with a righteous nod. "So, you all agree that we have to squash the rumors. There is NO trouble in paradise for Veeriana. And no more cheekiness from you, Ari. And keep away from that hairstylist!" His brother was many things, but sensitive he was not.

"Shaan, for God's sake," Veer began, but Ariana was already on her feet, martyrdom wrapped around her like the sarong.

"I thought controversies worked in our favor. Aren't movie stars supposed to be gossip fodder? Shouldn't we be titillating our audience on- and offscreen? That's all I'm doing, Shaan. And, while doing so, if I can open people's eyes about love being above gender, class, race, and color, more power to me, right?"

"Save your Miss Universe agenda for the annual pageant, sweetheart."

How was it possible that Shaan was completely clueless about the world or about the fact that Ariana was simply yanking his chain? Tania's heavy sigh told Veer that she knew exactly what her client was doing.

Ari stuck her nose up in the air. And, since she was wearing crazy-high platforms, she made it a point to look down her queenly nose at Shaan, who stood several inches lower. "I refuse to pretend to be someone I'm not, even for the coveted Filmfare award. Besides, who gives a shit who I'm locking lips with in private when I'm being debauched by this sex god on-screen?" She pointed at Veer.

A question for the ages.

However, Veer felt his cheeks grow hot at being called a sex god. But he couldn't stop himself from trying to gauge Tania's reaction to the term. Of course she was ignoring him.

"The world cares, you idiot. And, if you still can't see sense ... then maybe this will help. That hairstylist is fired. You hear me? Her career in this industry is finished. And, lead actress or not, if you don't do as I say, you will be next." By the time he finished shouting, Shaan was red in the face.

"You heartless toad!" Ari cried, and flounced out of the room.

It was a dramatic exit fit for an intermission scene—and clearly bogus. Shaan didn't have the authority to fire Ari's hairstylist, as she'd brought her own team on set. Everyone in the room knew it.

However, as Ariana had opened the door ...

"She is right, Shaan. Why should she pretend? Why should any of us pretend?" He aimed that zinger at Tania, as he was beginning to get pissed off, too. "Jesus, what age are we living in?"

Tania didn't look pleased by his outburst. Too bad. He was tired of her silent treatment. Damn tired of her pretending that last Christmas had been nothing more than a figment of his imagination, alone.

"We're living in the age of pretense, Mr. Rana. In a time when perfect selfies are taken only from one's good side and where filters hide every flaw one possesses. We're all living a lie; didn't you know that? People only see what they wish to see, and they only show what they want to show."

Damn, she was cynical. And, by addressing him formally, she was trying to create an even bigger chasm between them. If that wasn't a smackdown meant to put him in his place, he didn't know what was.

She ignored him again and began to pacify Shaan on her client's behalf. "Ariana understands. She was only teasing you, Shaan. She's just young and … free-spirited; you know that."

Tania was only five years older than Ari, four years older than him, and about Shaan's age. Yet she made herself sound ancient.

But Shaan wasn't pacified. "There hasn't been enough PDA footage of Veeriana, considering you both are together all day, every day. No wonder the media is ready to believe the worst. You guys don't do anything romantic together."

Veer scrubbed his hands over his face, the bristles of his moustache rough against his palms. He needed to trim it again. The newness of it still surprised him. He'd chosen to grow one instead of having makeup stick one on him every day. "Fine. I'll slow dance with her at the wrap-up party."

"That's not going to cut it. They need to believe you are IN LOVE — in all caps. You will hype up the romance, starting now, or the movie will bomb even before we release the official trailer next month."

"I get it, *bhai*," Veer bit out even as he mentally conspired to lure Tania back into his life and his bed. There had to be a way for him to have his cake and eat it, too.

Naturally, his lady love was on a parallel train track, heading in the opposite direction.

She steepled her fingers together and tapped them against her *fuck me* lips thoughtfully. "We could spread an elopement rumor of our own," she began. "Let's leak a couple of photos from the wedding shoot. Make it seem like wedding bells are imminent. Veeriana could also be seen scoping out a temple, hand in hand, while making goo-goo eyes at each other. Let's *give* the media something to speculate about."

Veer snapped out a, "Hell no!" and stood up, glowering down at Tania.

But Shaan was already chortling and rubbing his hands together. "That's brilliant, Tania. No wonder they call you the piranha of publicity. Let's finesse the plan further."

Veer had had more than enough. "I'm going to shower," he said and stalked out of the room.

# Scene Four:

## She's Just Not That into You

This was not how Veer had envisioned his reunion with Tania. He'd thought they'd exchange shy smiles, eager glances, and secret kisses. And their eleven-month hiatus would finally come to a sizzling end on a burst of electric attraction.

He wanted to know why she was giving him attitude when it was she who'd broken up with him. And what was this bullshit about not being friends? Or not even being civil toward each other? Why was she pushing him away?

It was time to get some answers, and for that, he needed to enlist a cohort.

He pulled out his phone and called Ariana as he took the stairs that led up to his suite two at a time. "Hey, sweetheart. I'm sorry Shaan was a jackass. Again. You okay?"

"I can handle your brother. Are YOU okay?" came Ari's reply.

*Am I?*

Then, it struck Veer what Ari had asked. Sensed. He cleared his throat and said, "I wasn't the one under fire, pal."

"Stop pretending, pal. Not you, too. Why didn't you tell me you were interested in my sexy-ass manager? Was this why you hassled me about hassling her to come today and oh-so kindly handled all her travel arrangements? It usually isn't my style or yours to force someone to do something they don't want to, and I was wondering why you were so insistent. Now, I know."

Veer blew out a breath. How could he deny it when it was true?

"She's giving you a tough time because of me, isn't she? Because she thinks it will be a conflict of interest if she's managing my career and at the same time dating my costar ... who happens to be my fake fiancé?"

And Shaan thought Ariana was clueless.

"Ari ..." Veer began, but she cut him off.

"You're a fool, my friend. She, too, if she's demurring because of me. Dumbos number one, both of you."

Veer slowed his strides while walking down a pillared corridor with arched views of the miles of surrounding desert. Last night, he'd been absolutely sure that he needed to fulfill his commitments to the production and Ariana before going after Tania Coehlo.

This morning was another matter.

He picked up his pace again. "You're right. I have been a fool. But I plan to rectify that and win her back ... if you'll help me."

"Back? What do you mean, *back*? When did you have her before?" Ariana screeched through the phone.

Veer laughed full-on, suddenly feeling loads lighter. As if a huge weight had been lifted off his chest. "I'll tell you some other time. For now, this is what I need you to do ..." He explained his plan.

"That's ... possibly illegal. Are you sure she'll be okay with that?" Ari asked.

No, he wasn't. But he had kissed her without her permission before, and she hadn't slapped his face or had him arrested back then. Also, he'd run out of options.

"I'm sure. And try to keep out of sight until tonight, please. Jenny, too."

Jenny was Ariana's hairstylist and the cause of his brother's paranoia.

"Sir, yes, sir. And good luck, sweetie. I totally ship the two of you."

Veer slipped the phone back into the pocket of his jeans, his grin fading.

He needed all the luck he could get. Because, if Tania really wasn't interested in renewing their relationship, he was going to have to let her go.

*Fuck.*

# *Scene Five:*

## When Tania Meets Truffles

Following the directions the crew had given her regarding Ariana's whereabouts, Tania brisk-walked down a narrow, sandy path, past an organic vegetable garden, and toward a cluster of white tents that had been set up at about a ten-minute walking distance from the courtyard.

She'd been trying to locate Ariana since breakfast. She wanted to have a serious talking-to with the starlet about the state of things. Yes, she'd defended her client in front of Shaan and Veer, and yes, she didn't believe Ariana would do something to jeopardize her career, but it never hurt to remind clients what their goals were from time to time. Or what it meant to achieve those goals.

She hoped—prayed Ariana wouldn't do anything foolish just to get back at Shaan Rana. Never mind that the man was the very definition of a male chauvinist pig and richly deserved payback. Not at the cost of Ariana's career.

Veer was nothing like his brother. Not in looks or personality. The comparison came to her mind, unbidden, and of course, as soon as she thought about him, he appeared before her like a magic trick.

Tania rounded the corner of a white tent and came to an abrupt halt when she spotted him sparring in the angry heat of the desert sun. His upper body was deliciously bare, the muscles of his torso flashing with power as he clashed swords with another half-naked man.

She tightened her fists around the handles of her tote, watching as if hypnotized, as he slashed and parried, twisted and lunged, the folds of his silk dhoti billowing with every move.

Ariana was right. He was a sex god. But, more than that, Veer had everything a woman could want in a man—looks, manners, interest.

He wanted her. Even now.

*Did I really say no to him? Am I mad?*

Right. He was still publicly engaged to her client. Still too pretty, too rich, too young, and too much for her.

As she stared, he pivoted full circle, coming to a stop in a backward lunge with a grunt, his beautifully sculpted arms raised above his head. The dhoti slipped an inch, hooking over the sharp points of his hip bones.

Tania bit back a groan, nearly swallowing her tongue. *Do not visualize him naked. Leave. Now!*

She slunk back, preparing to turn on her heel and run down the path when, suddenly, Veer whipped his head toward her, and their eyes met. Held. Clashed like blades of steel.

If she left now, she'd look like a coward. So, she marched forward instead.

"Where is she?" Tania demanded, finally recalling why she was there.

*Holy moly, the moustache looked good on him.*

One eyebrow quirked up. "Oh, we're speaking now?"

She supposed she deserved that.

He straightened up from the lunge to his full six-feet-plus height, lowering his sword arm in a slow, elegant arc. Pearls of sweat rolled down his temples, his neck, wetting the whorls of hair on his heaving chest. He hadn't shaved his chest in a while either. Eleven months ago, he'd manscaped on a weekly basis.

She definitely preferred him with the moustache and chest hair … which wasn't too much, mainly around his pecs, and then it tapered off—

Oh, for the love of God, she had to stop ogling him. It was beneath her.

"I was told Ariana would be here. Clearly, she isn't. Do you know where she is?" she tried again, politely this time.

"No clue." Veer shrugged, prowling off to a coffee table set in front of one of the tents.

Several bottles of water and a stack of towels had been placed on it. He picked up a bottle and drank deep, his throat muscles jumping. Then, with an utterly wicked look in his eyes, he tipped the bottle and emptied the rest of the water on his head, wetting his hair, his shoulders, and his washboard abs.

"Need to cool off. It's hot, yeah?"

Now, he was just showing off.

Tania rolled her eyes, and she was about to put him in his place when a cacophony of happy, excited yaps stole her thunder. A white ball of fur came hurtling around a tent, heading straight for Veer. But, when the puppy saw her, it changed direction and charged at her.

"Truffles?" Tania exclaimed in shock as the puppy reached her and started doing a mad welcome dance on his hind legs. She dropped to her knees, tote and all, gathering the pooch in her arms.

For the next several minutes, her whole face was licked over and over, and she was scolded and greeted quite thoroughly. She reciprocated with kisses and belly rubs and back and leg massages—just as the sweet pooch liked it.

"Oh, how you've grown. Who's a handsome boy? Who's the bestest dog in the whole world?"

She couldn't believe this was the same scrawny puppy that Veer and she had found trying to cross the street near the Gateway of India. They had left the idyll of Veer's boat one afternoon to have lunch at the Taj Hotel and stock up on groceries until the New Year when they spotted the puppy. He'd been a hairbreadth away from being trampled by the sea of humanity and automobiles on Mumbai's roads. They'd plucked him up and taken him to a vet, who'd run tests on him and administered the necessary medication. Then, they'd brought him back to the boat as a foster until the vet found someone to adopt him.

Tania had bonded with Truffles in the three weeks they had spent together. When she'd returned to reality, she'd been as heart-shattered about leaving Truffles as she was about leaving Veer. But neither the dog nor the man were hers to keep, were they?

With her head half-buried in silky-white dog hair, she slid her gaze toward Veer, who'd come to a crouch beside her. His nearness, the musk and heat coming off him, was ... going straight to her head.

He'd kept Truffles. *Why?* He wasn't a pet person, he'd told her so himself. It couldn't be because of her, could it? Because she'd always wanted a dog, but circumstances hadn't allowed her to ever get one?

"You kept him," she said huskily and was appalled to note that her eyes were stinging.

Veer snorted. "I think T-Man here kept me."

God, she'd missed Truffles. Her man's best friend. And, yes, damn it, she missed Veer, too.

"Hey, are you ... crying?" He tipped her chin up gently, then cupped her cheek.

His eyes were dark pools of wickedness still, and full of promises she was too scared to believe; it would be so easy to get lost in him. His mouth parted as if to say something, and her eyes fell on his lips, which were always slightly pink, as if he'd applied lipstick or forgotten to remove his makeup after shooting. It should have made him look effeminate, but she'd never seen a more masculine guy in her life. The moustache made his bottom lip seem fuller than the top.

"Just sand in my eyes." She caught herself as she swayed toward him. And, before she did something stupid like kiss him, she began to scold the puppy's bad-boy owner. "You're not supposed to let him wander around without a leash. Don't you know anything? This property has no walls. He'll run off; that's what dogs do. He could get lost in the desert or get hurt. He could get spooked or bitten by a snake or a wild animal. Or get trampled by camels." She was babbling. *Dear God!*

"Don't worry; he's safe and happy. Someone from my personal staff or the film crew is always with him. See? There's my valet, holding the leash." Veer leaned closer, cupping both her cheeks. "The truth is, he misses you. I miss you," he admitted in an echo of her own thoughts.

Hearts and heat flared in his eyes. He was going to kiss her. The attraction between them was as solid and powerful as ever. Last Christmas, all it had taken for him to seduce her was a two-minute elevator ride down from Ariana's apartment. She'd fallen for him hard in less than a week. He'd claimed he felt the same.

One month later, he'd still gotten engaged to his "best girl" — as the media put it — and Tania had had to watch him put a ring on another woman's finger and smile through the ordeal. The four carat solitaire that still winked on Ariana's ring finger didn't look all that fake to her.

Tania thrust the puppy at Veer, who was only too happy to leap into his master's arms and start licking the water and salt from his chest. Just like she wanted to do.

"I can't do this." She scrambled to her feet. "I shouldn't have come."

She wouldn't make a fool of herself again. She could not be charmed by him again.

So, she did what she should've done last year in that elevator. She picked up her tote and ran.

She didn't even stop when Veer shouted after her, "We have to talk, Tania. You can't keep running away."

# Scene Six:

## *Runaway Bride*

To hell with her rules and playing it safe.

Veer surged to his feet and darted after his woman, their dog in his arms. Barefoot, he didn't get very far.

"Shit. *Fuck!*" Unable to stop his momentum, he hopped from foot to foot as pieces of cacti, sharp-edged pebbles, and bramble — the detritus of a desert — tried to poke holes into his feet.

Swearing a blue streak, he hobbled back to the tent where Manan waited, a T-shirt and shoes in his hands and a smug grin on his face.

"Quit being obnoxious." Veer set Truffles on the ground, yanked on his shirt and shoes in record time, and took off again, his dog racing at his heels as if it was a game of chase — which it was. Chase and catch.

He caught up with Tania in the courtyard, just as she was climbing the steps of the terrace where she'd had her accident — Christ, had it only been that morning? The wedding set had yet to be dismantled, and the marigolds and roses that had suffused the air with their divine scent last night had gone stale already. The entire production unit had shifted to the dunes, which were about an hour's drive away, to set up the wrap-up scene and the party after.

Veer grabbed Tania's arm as gently as possible. "Stop running. Please."

She shook him off and backed away from him in panic. Not *creeped out* panic, but the *let me run away before I do something foolish* sort of panic. It was clear he was getting to her, getting through her barriers. Heat crackled between them every time they were together. They'd nearly kissed twice today.

Truffles plopped to his belly by their feet, pink tongue hanging out from the sprint.

"Please, stop running," he repeated, even when she stood there, unmoving and breathing hard. "I'll go down on my knees and beg if you want me to. Please, give me a chance — give us a chance."

"I did. Last Christmas," she whispered, her eyes huge and wary. Afraid.

He was terrified, too. Didn't she see that? Afraid of losing her. Of losing his mind.

"Give us a second chance then. Don't be afraid, Tania. Everything will work out; you'll see. No one needs to know ... not yet. We'll keep our relationship to ourselves. You won't have a conflict of interest," he said and then cursed himself for bringing up her objections and her obligations when she flinched away from him. "Ari already knows," he added desperately, trying to allay her qualms.

She stepped further back from him. "What do you mean?"

Truffles rose, ambled over and nipped Veer's exposed ankle. He'd swear the dog rolled his eyes at him.

A warning prickle crept down his spine, but he couldn't stop now. He had to convince her. "She guessed. She already knows about us and has given her blessing. It's all fine, baby. She doesn't think there's an issue if we're together while you work for her. We can do what we want. And Ari ... well, she already does what she wants."

Even before Tania held up a hand to stop him from prattling on, it occurred to him that he'd jammed a size-eleven foot in his mouth.

"Let me get this straight," she began, her sexy-as-fuck eyes going flinty. "You think you have fixed my problem by telling my client about something that doesn't concern her but clearly bothers me, and because you and my client have decided to become deviants and eschew time-honored work ethics, you think I should relax my scruples, too, and live it up?"

He wasn't going to answer that. It was a trick question. He ran a finger and thumb over his moustache, which was an answer of sorts.

"Go. To. Hell," Tania declared before she spun on her heel and sailed off through the gaping archway leading into the manor. "And don't you dare follow me," she threw over her shoulder.

*What the hell had just happened?* Veer scratched his jaw in confusion. He'd sorted her conflict, hadn't he?

Truffles whined after his mistress, exactly like his master wanted to do. Then, the dog lifted his leg up and did his business right there on the terrace.

"Jesus, buddy. When are you going to be potty-trained, huh?"

"When are you going to be media-trained?" asked Shaan, striding out of the manor as if it were on fire. "What were you and Tania arguing about?"

"Business," Veer muttered, wondering how long his brother had been watching them and how much he'd heard.

"Keep your head in the game, Veer. We don't need the wrong scandal," said Shaan, confirming that he'd heard enough. "So, it was you who co-opted the jet and the Bentley last night to fetch her. Not Ariana. And on the company's expense?"

*What, everyone is a detective now?* Veer's day seemed to have taken a sharp nosedive.

"I put it on my tab. Don't worry, *bhai*. I'm not abusing privileges." Veer picked Truffles up and headed into the manor. He needed to shower. Again.

Find Tania. Again.

Beg her pardon. Again. Even though he had no idea what he was apologizing for.

Shaan fell into step beside him. "You cannot have an affair with her, Veer. It's too complicated."

"Too late." Veer was fed up with trying to hide his feelings. He adored Tania, and he wanted the whole damn world to know it.

Shaan caught his arm and forced him to a stop. Annoyed, Veer rounded on his brother to chew his head off, but one look at Shaan's worried face, and his anger dissipated.

Shaan was the odd duck of the family, the average-looking Rana. He'd been born with a severe cleft palate, and though several plastic surgeries had rectified the anomaly in his childhood, he'd been stuck with a nasal lisp that no amount of speech therapy or surgery had been able to correct.

With nearly five years separating them, there had never been any rivalry between Shaan and him. They loved and respected each other, and Veer knew just how much the success of this project meant to Shaan. His brother had sunk in a large chunk of his own money into the franchise.

"This is not funny, Veer. The media has been camped at the gates for a week now. We've been denying them access to the production for months. They are hungry like wolves for any news … some gossip. For all we know, the paparazzi have zoom lenses pointed at Suryaganj right now. Or drones. That's why I'm livid with Ariana. And, if you're caught even looking at the wrong woman …"

Veer was sick of the same lecture. "Ari is right. Isn't that what you want? Don't you want us to be in the news … in any way? So, let everyone think there's trouble in paradise. Believe me, that's more interesting than pretending we're living in some ridiculous fairy tale."

Shaan was already shaking his head. "No, nope. The lovebird leads of the movie having a romantic tiff and making up is quite different from you having a side piece."

"Watch it, *bhai*." Veer curled his hands into fists. Tania was not a side piece.

"You watch it, little brother. It won't look good for Ariana if you leave her for a nobody. *Her manager* to boot. I thought you wanted to make Ari into a star. Have you changed your mind?"

Veer inhaled sharply. No, he hadn't.

*Damn it.* What Shaan said was true. It wouldn't look good if Tania and he became a couple out of the blue. Not for them and not for Ariana. The world should be crazy about Ari, coveting her, obsessing about her. If he jilted her at the altar … so to speak … she'd look pathetic. As if there were something wrong with her. The double standards in the movie industry were vile and legend.

Tania had been telling them this all along.

"I can't police both Ariana and you, Veer."

Veer heaved a sigh. His brother had always been there for him.

Through his fall from grace. Through rehab. The Ranas always supported each other.

"You don't need to police me. I won't do anything to mess this up. I know what's at stake, *bhai*."

"That's all I wanted to hear." Shaan patted him on the cheek and rubbed Truffles on his head. "And, remember, there will be media present tonight. So, extra PDA with Ariana, okay?"

Veer nodded, swallowing the bile rising in his throat.

*Two more years of pretending and hiding?*

*Fuck.*

# Scene Seven:

## *My Best Friend's Wedding*

Tania should have left Jaisalmer that afternoon. The situation had been sorted and handled to everyone's reasonable satisfaction. Neither diva—Ariana or Veer—was going to do anything inappropriate or unscripted or outrageous. They'd fallen in line like good little future stars and—

God, she should have left for Mumbai that afternoon.

She'd tried to leave right after her disagreement with Veer. She'd even managed to secure transport to the airport when Ariana showed up in the foyer and dragged Tania to her room for a late lunch. They'd nibbled on carrots and leaves and talked shop until everyone was on the same page once more. Then, Ariana had gone for a shower, and Tania had decided to take a power nap, which had turned into a full-brain shutdown because she'd missed her afternoon espresso dose.

When Tania woke up, it had been evening already, and Ariana had been getting ready for the wrap-up shoot. Not in the full warrior-queen regalia, but the clothes she'd arrive in for the shoot in honor of the paparazzi. Everything was a production in the movie business.

Tania had tried to leave again, making weak noises about nonexistent aches and pains from the fall and catching the last flight back to Mumbai, and once again, she'd been cajoled into staying.

"You promised you'd stay for the party!" Ariana had pouted, watching Tania swallow a couple of painkillers.

She'd promised no such thing. And yet, here she still was, in Jaisalmer, in her little black dress with bow-tied spaghetti straps and sneakers on her feet—because open-toed pumps were a menace in sand—watching the sun go down while her ex-lover seduced his on-screen lover in front of two-hundred-odd people.

Tania hadn't known they'd be filming the wedding night scene there—well, the seduction leading to the wedding night. The set was beautiful in its simplicity, less elaborate than the lotus-shaped altar in Suryaganj's courtyard. Tents had been erected along the ridges of several dunes with Ratan Sen's flag fluttering proudly in the mild breeze on top of each one. There were camels and horses and close to a hundred extras dressed up as the royal guard and loyal servants.

The dunes had been murder to navigate, even in a military-style Jeep, and Tania wondered how the crew had managed to get all that equipment—including a couple of jimmy jibs that she was staying far away from—up there.

Tania and Ariana had arrived at the bottom of the dunes in the Bentley. From there, a Jeep had taken them deep into the sandy hills. Up and down like a roller coaster they'd driven, reaching the set an hour before sunset.

Veer had already been there, dashing about in jeans and a T-shirt and a ball cap, commandeering the troupes. He instructed the extras about what he wanted them to do and how and when. He explained his vision to the cameramen, discussing distances and angles and panoramas and close-ups. Of course, Veer consulted with Javed Ali at every turn, but for the most part, he'd been given the director's chair for the scene.

He came to Ariana last and took her through the scene break-up. As Tania was sitting right next to her client on one of those foldable chairs ubiquitous to movie sets, she could hardly avoid Veer's earnest face.

Not that she wanted to this time. He looked incandescent against the setting sun. His long, trim figure vibrated with excess energy as he explained what he wanted Ariana to do and feel in the scene. He gestured with his hands and body, showing her where he wanted them to stand and how. He was such a graceful man. Self-assured of his place, of his worth. He wasn't even looking at Tania or touching her, and yet her skin came alive simply by his proximity.

She was so screwed.

Finally, he rose and strode into a white tent with *Greenroom 2* written on the flap. When he emerged, he had once again transformed into a king and a groom. Though, in the raw and naturalistic setting of the desert dunes, with his red-gold turban and long robes flapping in the breeze, he looked more like an Indianized version of Lawrence of Arabia.

Tania couldn't have looked away if a sandstorm had hit her in the face.

The scene being enacted was of Ratan Sen and his new bride arriving at a desert camp to spend the night. They were traveling from Padmini's ancestral palace, where they'd celebrated their nuptials, to Ratan Sen's kingdom. Their marriage was as yet unconsummated, and so the sexual tension between the newlyweds was supposed to be as thick and sultry as the monsoons in Mumbai.

Veer and Ariana were completely in character from their fourteenth century clothes to their regal bearing. There wasn't a person watching who didn't believe they truly were Ratan Sen and Padmini.

In they rode in a caravan of horses and camels and palanquins in a breathtaking silhouette against a larger than normal orange sun behind them and endless sand beneath them. A secondary team with proxy actors was shooting the caravan scene several dunes away.

On the main set, Ratan Sen dismounted from his horse and helped his bride out of her royal palanquin. But she was burdened by her heavy wedding skirts, and her bridal veil covered her face up to her chin, so she tripped while rising to her feet. Her husband's arms were there to catch her, steady her. The newlyweds hugged for a long moment while a romantic ballad crooned all around them. Because the scene was a song sequence, each step and look and gesture was stretched to dramatic effect.

Then, Veer began to unveil his bride. Inch by inch, he lifted the veil, heightening the anticipation of what was to come. All the while, the sun was slowly sinking into the horizon.

When Padmini's exquisite face was finally revealed, the rapt audience gave a collective sigh. Just like the moviegoers would,

Tania imagined. Full lips quivering in anticipation of a first kiss, kohl-lined eyes unfocused with desire, Padmini was the epitome of love in that moment. Men would want her, would kill for her. Women would want to be her.

Veer stared at Ariana with his black-as-sin eyes. Hearts. Possession. Devotion. The sun and the stars. Everything was right there for the world to see. Slowly, he bent his head and pressed his hairy lips to hers and …

It was like someone had stabbed a poker straight through her heart.

Tania bit down on her lip, so she wouldn't gasp or cry out. She closed her eyes and counted to a hundred. When she opened them again, they were still kissing.

Even after Javed Ali yelled, "Cut!" Veer didn't stop kissing Ariana. In fact, he gathered her closer and brought their bodies flush against each other.

The paparazzi cameras went wild, and the crowd began to cheer from all directions. Some of the media had been invited to take exclusive photos, which they would release on a specific date.

Tania couldn't look away. She knew it was fake. She knew he was doing what his brother had ordered him to do—play the audience. She knew Ariana was mostly gay and that Veer thought of her like a sister. She knew all of that, and still, her soul felt battered. Her insides hollow.

His kisses were hers. Only hers. How dare he kiss someone else?

She was mad to feel possessive about him. What did she think would happen when he signed another movie, and the script required kissing? What if that actress was straight and available? What would happen when she had to watch him make love to different women on-screen? Date other women for publicity or in real life? Always wonder if he was telling her the truth or was it all a show?

Tania recoiled at the thought and took a step back, bumping into someone.

"I'm sorry!" She froze when she realized it was Shaan and that he was studying her intently, his dark eyes so much like Veer's just then. *Oh God, what is he seeing on my face?*

He plucked two champagne flutes from a loaded tray that a waiter was circling through the crowd. He handed her a glass. Tania drained it in several gulps.

"They're beautiful together, aren't they?" Shaan lifted his glass as if toasting the couple—the actors. "Just look at them. Close to flawless from head to toe. *Nice* to boot. Not like us," he said, cutting her a glance. "We are ... not perfect, you and me. Damaged even. How would we look standing next to that kind of perfection?"

*Not good.* They would not look good. Veer and her did not make a good pair.

Tania took a deep, shuddering breath as her eyes began to burn. *Do not cry.* "Can you ask someone to take me to the airport?"

She handed her empty glass to Shaan and looked about for her Fendi tote. It was sitting on a chair in front of Greenroom 2.

She had to leave. Now. She'd have to spend the night at the airport because the next flight out was in the morning.

Shaan had the decency to look ashamed. "Take the Jeep down from the dunes, then the Bentley to the airport. I'll message the chauffeurs. I'm sorry, Tania. Believe me, I know how you feel. I've been in your shoes."

She wanted to strike out like a cobra and sting him with something sharp and poisonous. But, in the end, she walked away with her head high. It wasn't Shaan's fault that she'd been an idiot.

One thing was certain, though, she never wanted to see any of the Ranas ever again.

Her tote in hand, she reached the spot where she and Ariana had been dropped off at the very edge of the set, but instead of a slew of Jeeps, she found a line of festively dressed camels and shepherds. The camels had fake red noses fitted to their snouts and reindeer antlers strapped to their heads because it was Christmas bloody Eve.

"Where are the cars?" Tania looked every which way and saw nothing but Rudolph-nosed camels. Darkness was falling fast now that the sun wasn't in the sky, and panic was settling into her nerves. She needed to get out of there.

"They're parked at a village a few miles away," said Veer's

valet, Manan, who'd been smoking a bidi with the shepherds.

Could she not get a break from Veer or his valet?

"Shaan said one of the cars would pick me up." The stupid tears welled up again. She would not cry over a man.

"I don't think they can, ma'am. It is not safe to drive in the dunes when it's dark. That's why the cars are waiting at the village. You have to ride the camels to the village. It's a fifteen-minute ride."

Tania stared at Manan. "Are you joking?"

The valet's brows came together in the middle of his forehead. "No, ma'am. Why would I do that?"

"But … I don't want to ride a camel! No offense." The animal idling closest to her didn't seem offended by her rejection. In fact, it looked mighty bored. Its eyes were at half-mast and fringed with long, naturally curled lashes. Women would kill for those lashes. The camel continued to chew on something, grinding its big teeth over and over, as she argued with Manan.

"I'm afraid it's the only way to get to the village, ma'am."

"Can't I walk there?" It would be easier and smarter than sitting on a bloody camel.

She'd asked a shepherd, but Manan shook his head. "It is not safe for someone who is not familiar with the area to walk in the dunes. You could roll off one and get lost in the sands of time."

She gave Manan a narrow-eyed glare. He had to be pulling her leg. But, he looked utterly sincere, and three of the shepherds agreed with him.

Resigned to the fact that this might just be the worst day of her life, Tania sighed and said, "Fine. Which one do I ride?" The sooner she left the sooner her life could go back to normal.

At a shepherd's command, the bored camel was brought forth. It rocked forward, then back, then forward again and sank to the ground.

"How does one sit on a camel in a tight dress?" she asked the men. It wouldn't do to flash them while climbing on.

The answer was sideways.

# Scene Eight:
## *There's Something about Tania*

Veer knew the exact moment Tania walked off the set.

Even immersed in filming, his character kissing Ariana's for all he was worth, Veer had known where Tania was the entire time. And, when she ran away, he was ready.

"Good scene," he murmured, taking a step back from Ariana. He kept his eyes on hers, smiled at her like a satisfied lover as a dozen cameras flashed around them.

"Do moustaches shed? I think I have hair in my mouth," she said, matching him look for look.

He felt laughter bubble up. "I think that's a wrap, but let's wait for Javed sir's verdict." He was quite proud and honored that Javed Ali had allowed him to direct these last two scenes without supervision. Veer couldn't wait to see the rushes, but that would have to wait until tomorrow. Tonight, he needed to be with his woman.

"I'm going to disappear for the night. You'll be okay, fending off the paps? And handling Shaan?" He kept his tone low and careless, even while bursting with impatience inside. He wanted to run after Tania, find out what was going on in that beautiful mind of hers.

Ariana beamed at him and the cameras kept flashing. "Oh my God! Yes! Go to her, you foolish man."

He went into his greenroom as soon as Javed Ali called the production a wrap. He changed out of his costume into dark jeans and a festive shirt. He cleaned his face, hoping, praying that Manan had convinced Tania to take the alternate mode of transportation.

He needed to talk to her. He had to have one night with her. And every single night for the rest of their lives, if she'd have him.

He was going to eat his cake and have it, too.

Shaan would have to understand.

Veer got to the pick-up point where Manan reported anxiously, "Everything went off without a hitch."

He slapped his valet on the back and mounted his own camel in front of the shepherd already sitting on it.

Then, his ride rocked up, and off they went behind his woman at a trot.

# Scene Nine:

## *Crazy, Stupid, Love*

Ten minutes into the camel ride, Tania knew something was wrong. She should have reached the village by now or been within viewing distance of it or near a road at least. But she seemed to be traveling deeper into the desert.

"*Arre, bhaiya,* what route are you taking to the village?" she asked in Hindi. *Where is an Uber when you need one?*

The shepherd mumbled something she couldn't catch and pointed into the darkening landscape. He began to run, the camel following his lead, and she began to witlessly bounce in the saddle.

She'd been strapped into her seat, her tote snuggled behind her, so there was no question of falling off. But, with her teeth and brains jarring with every trot, she didn't know if it was a blessing or not.

The feeling of wrongness ballooned inside her stomach. Shaan had clearly been under the impression that there would be Jeeps available to transport her from the dunes. He'd said nothing about red-nosed camels. And, just as she was trying to work out the oddness of it all, her ride went berserk.

Tania screamed as the camel began to full-on gallop. She clamped her hands around the handlebar in front of her. "What's happening? What's bloody happening?"

Something had spooked the camel.

The shepherd was shouting at her, but she couldn't understand him at all, and his voice began drifting further and further away. She craned her neck to look back and couldn't see a thing. Why wasn't the boy running after her, trying to control his beast or rescue her? Had he twisted his leg? Rolled off into the dunes?

*Jesus, Mary and Joseph, I'm going to die in the desert. No one will even find my body under all this sand,* she thought hysterically.

She began praying. "Think of my mother, O Lord. She's losing her mind." And if the camel kept bouncing her about, so would she. "I'll do anything. Rescue me, O Lord. I'll ... give up chocolate. *Er,* maybe not chocolate. I'll give up cheesecake!" Yes. She didn't like the stuff anyway. "Just make this camel stop galloping. And make it go home."

After what seemed like an eternity of bouncing and shrieking and swearing and promising absurd things to the Almighty One, Tania became aware of a dark, amorphous shape creeping up on her.

*What now?* Was she going to be attacked by desert mobsters? Molesters?

"Tania, listen to me."

She screamed. *The mobster knows my name?* She was so dead!

"Please, stop shrieking. You're freaking the camel out, babe. Calm down, sweetheart."

Oh God. Was she hallucinating Veer now?

But it wasn't her imagination. Veer came galloping out of the darkness on his own camel, and soon, their animals were head to head. He was grinning like a buffoon. She just knew he was even if she couldn't see his face.

"You did this! You kidnapped me. How dare you?" she shouted.

"Quiet, woman," came his amused voice from somewhere ahead of her.

There was a shepherd sitting behind him—was it her shepherd?—who began to make clucking and whirring sounds and kept it up until her camel slowed down, going from gallop to trot to walk. And, finally, to a dead stop.

Tania wanted to jump off, wrap her hands around the rat bastard's thick neck, and strangle him. She'd strangle the shepherd next. But she couldn't do any of that since she was still strapped into the harness. "Get me off this animal!"

"Not yet." Veer's calm yet determined voice wafted out of the ether, and despite her best effort to the contrary, the sure, raspy timbre of it soothed her. He began explaining what would happen next. "Chotu here is going to grab the reins of both camels and lead us to our destination, where — "

"Where nothing," she shrieked again. "Take me to the airport now, Veer."

He didn't speak after that. Neither did she.

She was vibrating with panic and ... excitement. God, she was stupid. Her thoughts scrambled for purchase, trying to figure out what he was about. Trying to decide what she should do.

They had to talk. Finish the discussion once and for all. He was right about that.

Her heart rate was nearly back to normal when they reached a campsite of sorts. More like a luxury oasis in the middle of the desert. A large, concentric area was lit up with tiki torches and electric lanterns. In the middle of it was a ginormous white tent with a campfire roaring in front of it with several chairs and side tables arranged around it.

The camels came to a stop next to a tiki torch-lit pathway and rocked to the ground. Veer got off before his camel was fully seated and came to her.

Mute with shock, Tania allowed him to unstrap her from the seat and help her dismount. It wasn't dark anymore because of all the burning lamps, and she could see his face clearly. He was so damn beautiful. It was unfair.

Her knees buckled as she tried to walk in the thick sand, so he simply swept her off her feet and carried her to the campfire. He settled her in a foldable canvas chair. He took her bag from Chotu, who'd followed them, and put it on a chair next to her. Veer thanked Chotu for his help, gave the man a wad of cash, and sent him on his way.

They were completely alone then.

She couldn't believe he'd kidnapped her. Her eyes tracked him as he went into the tent and came out with a thick, silken blanket with paisley block prints on it that he arranged around her shoulders. She hadn't even noticed she was shivering.

Next, he brought out a bottle of chilled Dom Pérignon and two glasses. He popped the champagne by slicing the blade of his Swiss Army knife across the cork—he was so good at that—and poured it into the flutes. He turned to her, his face solemn as an angel's.

"Happy first anniversary, my love," he said softly.

But she refused to take the glass he held out to her. With a sigh, he set it on a side table by her elbow—her bruised elbow—where it bubbled and fizzed just like her emotions.

He drew a chair right in front of her, sat down, and said, "Okay, let's talk first."

Tania lost it then. She shot out of her chair, launched herself at him, and tried to scratch his calmness off. "How dare you do this to me?"

He didn't fend off her attack. Didn't shove her off his lap. Didn't retaliate in any way. The only time he held her off was when she tried to bite his cheek.

Eventually, the panic, the fear, the fury left her, and she broke down in sobs. It had been too much. This whole day had been too much. She couldn't take it anymore, couldn't fight it. More, she didn't want to fight it—her attraction to this man. Sensible or not, she wanted him.

His arms came about her, cocooning her, and he began to croon sweet nothings into her ear, apologizing to her over and over again. The moustache tickled her skin, just like she'd imagined.

Then, they were kissing. Deep, drugging kisses that she'd missed with all her heart and soul, that she wished would never, ever end. Soft, sweet kisses that made her want to weep all over again. Hard, possessive kisses that were meant to claim, to punish, to remind.

To remind her of what they had once had ... and could have again. Of what she had lost and would lose in the bright light of tomorrow.

"I'm sorry I scared you. I didn't expect the camel to run off like that," he said, sucking on her bottom lip.

"You mean, that wasn't part of the grand kidnapping plan?" She tunneled her fingers through the short bristles of his hair and tugged.

His scent—lavender and lemon and forest—was like a drug to her senses. She was already high, already addicted.

"I'm not that crazy." His mouth slanted up wickedly, but he sobered up within seconds. "Do you still wish to leave? I can have you out of here within fifteen minutes."

She should leave. This was going to go nowhere, and her heart was going to break again.

"I don't want to leave," she whispered, sealing her fate, her throat raw from all the screaming.

She pulled Veer's head down and kissed him until she forgot everything, except what it was like to be in his arms.

*Just one more night.*

# Scene Ten:

## *Reality Bites*

Veer had brought Tania to the camp to talk. Fine, he'd shanghaied her there to make love to her, but they had to talk first. They had to find a way to be together despite the dark forces keeping them apart.

He picked up the champagne neither of them had touched and breathed in relief when she accepted her glass this time.

"To us," he said, clinking his glass to hers, and when she responded with, "Merry Christmas, Veer," the vise around his heart loosened a little.

She hadn't acknowledged his toast. No matter. He was a patient man and the night was young.

He took a long sip of the bubbly and kissed her again, disinclined to start a conversation he knew was going to end in an argument.

Tania didn't seem too eager to chat either. She was curled up in his lap, alternately sipping champagne and kissing him. By the time they'd downed two glasses each, they were barefoot and he'd removed the clips from her hair, letting the thick tresses cascade over her bare shoulders and down her back in an artful mess.

He sat back to look at her and catch his breath, his heart hammering inside his chest.

Wild hair framing a face glazed with passion. Lips swollen red from his kisses. *Fuck.* She was a vision.

"Tania," he began, but her fingers pressed against his mouth, silencing him.

"*Shh.* I don't want to talk." She ran her tongue over his lips. "This is what I want."

He went from half-mast to instantly hard, as if his body had only been waiting for her command. He wanted nothing more than to carry her into the tent and make good on her request. But...

"I want to make love to you, too. Quite desperately, babe."

She scooted off his lap and stood up, holding out her hand. "Great. Let's go."

Damn it, he couldn't. From last Christmas to the end of January this year, all they'd done was screw each other's brains out. If they started that again, without talking first, they'd end up right back at square one. He needed to understand what she was afraid of. What he was doing wrong.

He got to his feet and took her hand in his, so she couldn't run. "Why did you run?"

She stiffened immediately. Her half-dazed expression went through several interesting changes before she settled on the one that told him to tread carefully. Since he'd expected her to pull her hand free from his and make a break for it, he considered her reaction as progress.

"And don't tell me it's because of Ariana's career or the sham engagement or anything work-related because I don't believe you. Tell me the truth, Tania. Tell me why you won't be with me when everything in the universe points to the fact that we should."

The flames of the campfire blazed inside her eyes. For a moment, he was sure she was going to tell him to fuck off or make up another excuse. "You want the truth? Fine. I'll tell you the truth."

She tugged her hand free, but didn't move away. She poured herself another glass of champagne and chugged it down. Then, she began to talk, "You know my mother's story, right? She was a dancing extra at the same time your parents were young movie stars. She wasn't a great judge of character and was easily blinded by glamour and shiny things. She made her living by hooking up with actors—single, married, didn't matter. No one took her seriously much less respected her. I don't think she took herself seriously. Even after I came along, she didn't change her situation. Not much. She just accepted that she was going to be an extra, both in movies and in some man's life."

Tania looked as if she was about to start crying. He went to take her in his arms, but she pushed him away. "Do you want to hear the rest or not?"

He nodded. "I want to hear it." Though it was killing him that she was hurting because of it, because of him.

"I won't be an extra in your life, Veer. I won't be my mother. I can't be her. I'm already stuck on you, and I'm afraid that, the more time I spend around you, the more I'm tempted to give in. I can't say no to you. If you ask me to be your mistress or your clandestine lover or your guilty pleasure... whatever label you want to give it... I'm mortally afraid I won't say no. I won't be able to say no. And, if I give in, I'll never forgive myself. And I'll never forgive you for making me."

She raised her chin defiantly. "Now, can we stop talking and go to bed?"

# Scene Eleven:

## *Pretty Woman*

Mindful of her revelation, Veer bent to pick up the blanket and the nearly empty bottle of Dom Pérignon before following Tania into the tent. He snorted out a laugh when he saw her weaving—not walking—ahead of him.

He jogged up to her and caught her around her waist. "Easy there, lightweight. Maybe three glasses of champagne were too much for you."

She'd downed them pretty fast, too. And she was a compact package. No wonder she was tipsy.

"Four. I had one with Shaan," she paused and waved her hand about. Definitely tipsy, though she sounded lucid enough. "When you were smooching your best girl."

Veer shot her a sideways glance, his grin fading. She wasn't smiling either. Her head was tilted up to the sky, but her eyes were closed.

"Tania," he began and stopped. He had no idea what to say to her. If possible, her honesty had made everything even more complicated.

She sighed, opening her eyes. "Veer."

"Have you eaten tonight?" She shrugged. "Come on. We can both use some food," he said.

He ushered her into the tent, which had been prepared for a seduction that wasn't quite going as he'd planned. The floor was carpeted, the space heated. There was a king-size canopy bed in the middle of the tent, covered in layers of colorful silks and throw pillows. A low table and floor pillows made up a dining area; the table was loaded with covered dishes. He'd asked the chef to prepare cold food because he didn't know what time they'd get there. He'd assumed sometime closer to the end of the wrap-up party. Not at the beginning of it.

Tania shook her head, pressing a hand against her belly. "I'll barf if I eat anything. The camel ride jostled my intestines. We can go straight to bed."

Making love was out of the question. He couldn't take advantage of a drunk, camel-sick woman, even without the other stuff confusing him. But she was right about going to bed. She needed to sleep this off.

"Let's get you out of this dress. Turn around, babe," he said, lowering her zipper when she did.

"You know what you are?" she grumbled as he asked her to raise her hands.

"No. What am I?" He began tugging handfuls of satin up. She wasn't wearing a bra, and he tried not to drool over the delectable little body that had been plaguing his dreams for eleven months.

"You're a hemorrhoid." Her voice was muffled through the satin of her dress as it caught around her head.

He couldn't help but laugh at her. "A hemorrhoid?"

She nodded sagely once her head popped out. "You're like an itch that just won't quit. I have to scratch it. And, it feels so good when I do. So amazing. But afterward?" she paused and pouted. "You're nothing but a massive pain in the behind."

"Okay, in you go, baby." Leaving her black cotton panties on, he tucked her into bed.

Tenderness filled his heart when she fell asleep as soon as her head hit the pillow. He stood by the bed, watching her sleep for a long time, his heart aching at the purple shadows under her eyes. She hadn't had those a year ago, and he wondered if he was responsible for them.

Veer stripped off his own clothes and climbed into bed, but instead of sleeping, he went over everything Tania had revealed to him today. And wondered about the things she was still hiding.

# Scene Twelve:
## *The Proposal*

Tania woke up in the dark, bundled in Veer's arms and silken sheets, a portable heater blasting out hot air close to her. She tensed for a moment, wondering how she'd landed up there, then relaxed as her memory returned.

It was strange, but she wasn't as embarrassed that Veer knew the truth as she'd imagined. About what she thought of her mother. About how he affected her. She'd more or less admitted he could hurt her, that he was the chink in her armor. She'd given him that kind of power over her, and yet, instead of freaking out, she felt relieved.

Mother of God, she'd called him a hemorrhoid.

She burrowed into him, drinking in his scent — musky now, but there still was a faint trace of lavender and lemon. She kissed his chest. He'd left her panties on.

Last night — she frowned, was it last night or this morning now? Was it before or after midnight? It felt as if it was after — yes, definitely after. Anyway, last night had bombed. She'd been too tired and tipsy for any hanky-panky. But she felt good now. Rested. Slightly aroused and getting more so with every swish of silk on her skin and every rub against the furnace that was Veer's naked body.

Veer was a light sleeper. He stirred when she teased his moustache, mumbling about not wanting to spar that morning. She smiled into his neck. He thought she was his trainer.

Ariana and Veer would begin filming the second installment of *Padmini* next month, which had graphic battle scenes in it. Hence, the lessons in sword fighting.

"Are you sure you don't want to spar with me?" she whispered, sucking a love bite into his jugular.

He came fully awake then, and he had her flat on her back within seconds, his hands softly gripping her wrists as he settled on top of her.

Heat flared from her belly all over her body, and suddenly, even the silken sheets were too much stimulation for her skin.

It was always like that between them. Instantaneous. Intense. Immense.

He had the face of a fallen angel. So beautiful that it hurt to look at him.

Her doubts came charging back. *Why does he want me? How can this last?*

"You're doubting me again. Doubting yourself," he said, his voice raspy from sleep.

He let go of her wrists and rolled off, and she wanted to howl at him to come back. Why couldn't she make up her mind? Stick to one reaction?

He sat up, scrubbing sleep from his face. She sat up, too, covering her nakedness with the red sheets.

"I can't help it." She felt utterly wretched. "I keep wondering why you want me. We're like night and day in just about everything but this," she flicked a hand between them, "mutual attraction. Which is bound to burn out. And what happens when it does? I'm not sure I'll be able to deal with it. Not rationally. I feel too much for you."

*There. He knows all my fears now. Most of them anyway.*

"I love you." He looked straight at her as he said it, his gaze fierce, his words solid and strong.

Her throat felt thick and her vision blurred. She wanted to believe him. She did.

"I think I've loved you since that first night, Tania. I don't know if I ever believed in love at first sight, but I do now that it's happened to me."

"It was lust, Veer. Not love," she felt compelled to clarify.

Frustration made his lips go flat, but he went on as if she hadn't interrupted. "You drew my eye the second you walked into Ari's flat, battle-ready to take on Shaan for her. He wouldn't have given Ari half as much stake in the franchise without you. You were wearing a pair of siren-red leather pants that molded over your round bottom and legs like a second skin. Fuck yes, I wanted to bend you over the sofa right there. I'm a guy. We were locked in that flat all day, hashing out the contracts first, then for Ari's Christmas Eve bash. I couldn't take my eyes off of you."

Tania gave a shaky laugh, remembering his heated stares. "I know. It felt like you were branding me."

She'd returned the favor, surreptitiously. He'd dazzled her in his electric-blue velvet tuxedo. But, more than his physical beauty, she'd been impressed—surprisingly so—by his quick wit and worldliness. He was a tremendously well-informed man and had opinions on everything, from politics to potato crops. He was patient and sweet with Ariana and her crazy friends, and with his fans who didn't know the meaning of personal space. Even the trolls. That wasn't to say he was an easy man to be around—he wasn't. But, as Shaan had said, Veer was *nice.*

But, the question wasn't about her liking him, it was about him liking her.

"You branded me, too." He smirked, echoing her words. "Oh, you played a good game of pretending I was invisible once the business was done and the party started. Every time I got close enough to talk, you vanished to the other side of the room. I'd never met a woman so determined to ignore me."

She'd been terrified of him. Of his effect on her. Still was. It was self-preservation to ignore him.

"Exactly. You're only interested because it's novel ... for you to chase after someone."

He picked up her hand and pressed hot, sweet kisses on her palm, her wrist. "I'm not trivializing your fears or telling you what to feel or not to feel, but they are unfounded. The thrill of a chase wears off fast, babe." He kissed her, quick and hard. "That night, I lusted after your luscious body, yes, but I was bowled over by you. I watched you work the room. You have a talent for making people laugh, putting them at ease. You love your job and it shows. Your confidence is an aphrodisiac. I began to wonder what that focus, that tenacity would look like in bed." He nuzzled her cheeks, flicking his tongue over her skin, making her squirm. *From his touch or from his praise?*

And, she'd compared him to a hemorrhoid. *Oh, Jesus.*

"You are conscientious and care deeply for your clients' welfare in a way that's beyond mercenary ... that's rare in our world. I know you have tremendous responsibilities and... God, you are so lovely." He wrapped a hand around her nape and devoured her mouth. "I can't get enough of you. The month we spent together, and the eleven months we've been apart... during which I'll admit I've shamelessly stalked you through Ari... have only confirmed what I'd already realized last Christmas. Why do you think I followed you into that elevator? I was already crushing on you."

He dragged her into his lap. His body was hard as rock, his skin warm as the desert sun. Who needed a heater with Veer around?

"We are not going to burn out. Well, sexually perhaps... after many, many lifetimes, I hope. But I promise you that what I feel for you is not frivolous. It burns brighter every day, my love."

"It's only a case of absence making you addlebrained," she said stubbornly. She couldn't believe him. She shouldn't. But, she couldn't help kissing him back. "I challenged you. Denied you. This is nothing but..."

She couldn't say it. She couldn't call him a spoiled, entitled movie star who was only trying to get his way — even though he so clearly was. And yet he wasn't, was he? There was no need for him to run after her like this, beg her for her time, her attention... because that was exactly what he was doing.

Yes, he had power over her; she'd be a fool to deny it. But she also held his heart in her hands. That was what he was trying to show her.

He tipped her chin up, careful of her bruise that no longer ached, until she was looking into eyes so dark and forceful and knowing. "Marry me. We'll figure the rest of it out, but say you'll marry me, so I can prove to you that what we have is real. That what we feel is true. I love you. I will never stop loving you."

A shudder racked her from head to toe. He was giving her everything. She wanted to believe him so badly.

"I can't say no to you, Veer," she cried. He was going too fast. But they'd known each other for a year now. How was that fast? And he'd waited for her all these months, accepted the rules she'd made without throwing a tantrum. And, he'd kept Truffles.

"Then don't say no. Marry me. Say you trust me. I need the words, babe."

*Oh, yes, he knows me.*

"I'll marry you," she breathed out before sucking in large quantities of air. Then, she said something she'd never, ever told another human being. "I trust you, Veer."

*Oh Lord in Heaven, please, please don't let him break that trust.*

He kissed her to seal the deal, and after a joke or two about itchy hemorrhoids, which broke the tightrope tension between them, he made love to her on the big, silky bed at last.

Their second round of "sparring" took place under the star-studded sky—their butts freezing despite the crackling fire and the heat lamps—so Tania could finally claim that she'd been completely and thoroughly starstruck by Veer Rana.

# Scene Thirteen:

## *A Midsummer Night's Dream*

Tania woke up with Veer fever. But, the feeling didn't strike terror in her heart this time, rather, it brought a giddy sort of happiness to it.

They made love again; they were both making up for months lost. She didn't regret breaking up with him or putting Ariana first or herself. She'd needed those months to realize what was important and what she wanted. She wasn't going to run anymore.

Around noon, they got ready and made their way back to Suryaganj Fort. A helicopter was waiting for them when they walked out of the tent, their hands entwined. It dropped them off on the helipad on top of the manor where Manan awaited their arrival.

"Shaan is looking for you. He's in his office, organizing a press conference for this afternoon," Manan informed.

Veer gave a sigh. "I'll go see what my brother wants … and tell him our news." He smiled his wicked smile at her.

Tania didn't want him to go. She didn't want to be apart from him, even for a second. *Ugh. Don't be so clingy.* She was not going to turn into her mother, unable to function without a man.

Veer was as reluctant to leave her. "Do you need Manan to show you to Ari's rooms?"

She shook her head. "I know where they are. I'll catch up on my e-mails, get some work done. What I can't ignore while on vacation." A celebrity manager was never officially off because divas required constant monitoring. "I'll see you at the press conference."

She tried to tug her hand out of his, but he refused to let go until she shoved him back playfully. She forced herself to walk away. But, before she took the stairs down, she looked back just to make sure she hadn't fantasized the whole night. He was right behind her, and when their eyes met, he winked and mouthed, *I love you.*

He really did love her.

"I'll see you in a bit," he said, giving her a discreet peck on her lips, so Manan wouldn't see.

She floated toward Ariana's rooms, every molecule of her being glowing with happiness. But, just as she was about to knock and enter, it struck her that she should be with Veer when he told Shaan, who was bound to go ballistic when he heard the news. How could she let Veer face his brother alone?

"Oh, you are a moron," she muttered to herself and rushed down the stairs.

The foyer was overflowing with film crew, as usual. This time, they were busy building a temporary podium in the courtyard for the press conference. She walked past them, heading toward the office next to the dining room, and increased her pace when she heard the brothers shouting all the way down the hall.

"Don't you know who her mother is?"

Tania stopped short right outside the half-open office door as soon as she heard Shaan.

"What does that have to do with anything?" Veer said—no, he snarled it out.

"Are you sure she's not playing you?"

"Watch it, Shaan."

Tania pressed her back against the wall, so she wouldn't slide to the floor. Her legs had turned into jelly.

"I'm hardly a judge of women, I'll admit, and she's a smart cookie. I just want you to be careful. Fine. *Fine.* None of my business. But you swore you'd support me in my business. You can't back out, Veer."

"I'm not going to. I am doing the bloody movies." He didn't sound happy about it, but he wasn't snarling either.

Her heart sank. Hollowed. What did he mean that he wasn't backing out?

"Good. Including sticking to the publicity plan. Do whatever you want in private, Veer. In public, you are devoted to Ariana." After a brief silence, Shaan snorted and added, "Who knows? Maybe, in a few months, she'll be out of your system, and there will be no issue."

Tania's breaths grew rapid. She waited for several beats for Veer to retaliate, to set his brother straight. Tell Shaan to go straight to the devil and never return. But he said nothing at all, shattering her soul into a million pieces.

She backed away from the ornate doors, shiny with lacquer.

It was just as she'd feared. He'd made a fool out of her.

Tania Coehlo had turned out to be just as stupid as her mother.

# Scene Fourteen:
## *Definitely, Maybe*

For a full minute, Veer exercised superhuman control over his tongue and his fists and his body, forcing it to stand perfectly still or risk pummeling his older brother into an early grave.

"Shaan, you are my brother, and I understand you've been hurt and disappointed and a whole shitload of other things that all of us humans have to suffer because that's just the way it works. But you have gone the fuck too far."

Veer thrust away from the desk he had been leaning on and began to pace. Shaan was a cranky bastard, but he'd never been nasty, not to women. Their mother would have their asses if they acted out like that. Something else was going on here …

"How deep in debt are you?"

Shaan's sheepish face told Veer everything. "Fuck."

"I've sunk the entire pot into this venture. Plus, what I borrowed from various places," Shaan admitted.

Meaning Shaan had borrowed from nefarious individuals.

Veer had known things were a bit tight for his brother financially. But this sounded worse than bad. "And you didn't think to go to our parents or come to me with your problem?"

Belligerence shadowed Shaan's stiff posture. "I fight my own battles, little brother."

"Commendable," Veer said sarcastically. "If you don't end up in a ditch somewhere or behind bars."

It was a clusterfuck. He threw himself into an armchair, closed his eyes, and thought for a minute.

There was no way Tania would agree to keep their engagement quiet. After what she'd told him last night, he'd be an asshole to even ask.

Neither could he leave his brother in the lurch. Or Ariana. It wouldn't be right to jilt her... but maybe she could jilt him?

"*Bhai*, there might be a way out of this for all of us. But, next time, try not to wait until it's a life-or-death situation to ask for help."

Shaan smacked him on his head for his sass but sat down on the chair across from him. "I'm all ears to your brilliant plan." But, when Veer started outlining his get-out-of-jail-free plot, Shaan was aghast. "Fuck off. No way, man. No fucking way."

"Yes way, big bro." Veer overrode all of his brother's objections. "This whole fiasco lies at your feet, after all. We'll announce it at the press conference."

Elated that things were finally falling into place, he went in search of Tania and Ariana. He dashed up the west-wing staircase, his long strides eating up the length of the second-floor corridor.

He knocked on Ariana's door and let himself in when she said, "Come in."

Ariana's suite was a mirror of his, the decor tasteful and classical — fit for the star of *Padmini*. His friend reposed on her bed, a green mask on her face and oil in her hair.

"Where is she?" Veer looked about the semi-dark room that was neater than it should've been, considering the number of clothes lying about.

"Who? Tania?" Ari yawned. "Didn't you manage to find her last night?"

A bad feeling settled on his shoulders like dead weight. She wasn't there.

He pulled out his phone and called her. She didn't pick up. He texted her while dashing out of the room, not bothering to answer Ariana when she called out, asking him what was wrong.

It was clear what was wrong. Tania had run away from him again. *But why?* Even as he asked himself the question, his phone pinged an incoming message from her.

*Next time, make sure to shut your office door while you belittle someone else's family.*

Veer halted as soon as he read her text. She'd heard Shaan but not him. And she'd drawn her own conclusions.

He took a deep breath and let it out.

He could follow her, catch her, explain, beg, plead, make her listen. But two things stopped him from doing any of that. One, there was a press conference to prepare for. And, two, Tania had run away from him one too many times. She either trusted him or not.

And it seemed not.

*Fuck.*

# Scene Fifteen:
## Love Actually

Tania left Suryaganj on a truck packed with eight crew members and filming equipment that wasn't needed since filming was complete. The rushes were in the hands of the editing director now. It was his job to cut and merge the scenes and make all the different shots look amazing and continuous and cohesive in the final reel.

Over the next two days, the entire production team would disperse and head back to whichever city they called home. Luckily for her, a couple of trucks had been about to leave right then.

Tania got a ride to the airport, where she first bought her ticket and then hid in the restroom and had a lovely, pitiful sob-fest. Her flight wasn't until evening, so she had plenty of time to curse her fate.

Her phone kept buzzing inside her tote, but for once, she didn't care what her clients were doing or going through or how she'd get them out of the fix. For once, she allowed herself to focus on her own woes and bawl her eyes out.

She'd known it would come to this. She'd known he was a smooth-talking Bollywood bad boy who always got his way, and still, she'd fallen for him. After watching her mother and hearing about a million other naive women destroy their lives by falling for the wrong men, most of them from the movie business—yes, she was biased—she'd still believed him.

*Stupid. Idiot. Moron.*
*But he sounded so sincere in the desert.*
*Stupid. Idiot. Moron. You heard him and his brother.*

*But I didn't hear the whole conversation. What if—*

*Jesus, Mary, and Joseph! How much more did you want to hear? How much more proof do you need?*

And so it went inside her head until Tania started worrying whether she had early onset dementia. Like mother, like daughter after all.

Eventually, she came out of the restroom stall, her eyes puffy, her nose leaking, her heart a big ball of hurt. The cleaning women and the ladies waiting for their turns gave her strange looks as she dragged her tote to the sink. She washed her face and brushed out her hair without looking in the mirror. Then, she dragged herself out of there and took a seat by the gates.

Three hours later, when she was nearly dehydrated from her periodic crying jags, all the TVs around the terminal began to broadcast the press conference going on at Suryaganj.

Tania tried to plug her ears, but a bunch of young women—girls really—who sat opposite her, started chattering about Veeriana and dissecting the relationship. Tania's pathetic little heart opened its ears and lapped it all up.

"They look amazing together. I can't wait for *Padmini* to come out."

"No, he's too good for her. I've loved Veer Rana since I was nine, and he was thirteen. He was always sexy. But now? *Uff!*"

"Ya, man. I'd ditch my boyfriend and marry him."

*Get in line, bitch,* Tania thought without meaning to. Then, she mentally smacked her forehead, recalling that she did not want to marry him or want anything to do with him. He was a bad man. A real-life villain. She wondered if she should warn the girls about just how bad he was.

Soon, their sharp chatter turned into full-blown screeching.

Tania looked up from her self-huddle and scowled at the girls. Would they ever shut up?

"Oh my God! They eloped! They are married."

*What?* Tania sat up, her eyes honing in on the closest TV screen like a pair of nuclear missiles. He hadn't even waited for—she checked her watch—three hours before announcing alternative marriage plans? *The bastard.*

Wait a minute, Ariana was her client. How dare the Ranas play fast and loose with Ariana's career?

Tania dug out her phone from her tote. *Damn it.* It was dead. She'd forgotten to charge it. She found an outlet and set it up. Then, she marched up to a TV and started reading the news flashes at the bottom of the screen as it covered the press conference live. She could barely hear the NDTV news anchor, who was waiting for the happy couple to come out of the manor.

*Kapoor-Rana elopement* was emblazoned on the screen.

Tania's legs wobbled, and she had to sit down again. Serves her right for not having dinner, then drinking, then making love—having sex—multiple times, and then getting dumped. It was all so healthy for her state of mind.

"Oh my God!" one of the girls screeched again. "Look! There they are!"

Tania slammed her eyes shut. She couldn't look. She couldn't see them. She wasn't a masochist. *You have to look to get over him,* said the devil on her shoulder.

Acid dripped into her belly as she opened her eyes and peeked. Then, she stared. Finally, her jaw dropped.

"It has been confirmed that Ariana Kapoor has married Shaan Rana, executive producer of *Padmini,* which is set to release in two months. Congratulations to the happy couple. Obviously, the rumors about Veeriana breaking up were true. I'm dying to know how it all happened, Ariana. How does one go from being engaged to one brother to marrying another?"

"Well, love can't be directed, can it?" Ariana said, looking very much like a woman in love as she smiled shyly at Shaan, who, wonder of wonders, was looking at his bride with hearts in his eyes.

*Did all the Ranas possess that talent, Tania wondered?*

Ariana was in a red sari, exhibiting all the outward signs of a married woman, from the *sindoor* on her forehead to the dozens of bangles on her hennaed hands. Shaan was in a jodhpuri suit with a groom's turban on his head. They both had orchid and marigold garlands around their necks as if they had just stepped off a wedding altar.

"You can't do anything but listen to your heart," Shaan said, grinning like a fool in love.

The camera panned to the anchor. "Our hearts go out to Veer Rana who was jilted at the altar, so to speak. However, the single ladies will be ecstatic at these new developments."

*What? How? What the hell?* It was as if a stealth missile had sneaked into her head and detonated her brain.

Tania launched herself at her phone. It was barely charged, but she could turn it on. Several hundred notifications popped up. She X'd all of them.

No message from Veer after her pithy text about him gossiping about her family. Not even an emoji.

Her heart literally skipped a beat. She felt it. *Bum, bum, bum ... long pause ... bum, bum, bum.* It was most odd.

She wondered why he hadn't messaged her. She wondered why he hadn't found her yet. Where else would she be but the airport?

The film crew knew she'd been heading there. They'd seen her climb into the truck. Veer would have asked them. Yet he hadn't followed her.

She buried her face in her hands as she worked out why. She hadn't believed him when he said he loved her. Hadn't trusted him.

No, she hadn't believed in herself. Tania Coehlo, A-list celebrity manager and the piranha of publicity, had doubted her own worth.

*Stupid. Idiot. Moron.*

She called him while running through the airport. He picked up on the first ring. "Veer ... I'm an idiot."

"I'm not going to argue." His voice sounded hoarse in her ear, like he was upset. Of course he was upset. She'd betrayed him, too, hadn't she? She hadn't believed him, hadn't trusted him.

"When you come out of the airport, turn right and go around to the back. Away from the public areas," he said.

"What? Why? Are you here?"

"Of course I'm here. Where else would I be, woman?"

Her heart flapped its wings and soared into the sky. "Oh, I

don't know. Shouldn't you be in Shaan's office, gossiping about my mother?"

"Tania ..." A pause. A sigh. "I'm sorry you had to hear that."

"Veer, stop. Let's forget I heard that." She switched the phone to her other ear, dodging people to get to the main exit. She had to stop being so sensitive. "I'm sorry, too."

Sorry for doubting him. Sorry for running away. Sorry for wasting eleven months of their life together.

Outside the airport, Tania walked briskly down the terminal building and spotted him as soon as she rounded the corner.

In jeans and a T-shirt, Tom Fords perched on his nose, he leaned against the Bentley with effortless grace, Truffles in his arms. Lord Almighty, but they were fine specimens of humanity and canine. And they were hers. All hers.

He'd gone to such lengths to be with her, to show her how much she meant to him.

The puppy started squirming as soon as it saw her. Veer dropped Truffles to the ground, and the pooch raced toward her with unconditional joy and love.

She took her cue from the best dog in the world. Tania ran to Veer, laughing as Truffles took a U-turn and started running behind her, barking madly. When Veer opened his arms wide just like a Bollywood hero—no, a sex god—she was already leaping into them.

She knew now that he would always be there to catch her. All she needed to do was have some faith in them both.

"I love you, Veer," she said, hugging him with all her might, the whole of her heart.

He was squeezing the breath out of her in return. "I love you, too. I won't live without you, Tania."

They hugged for an eternity. Or until Truffles began to yowl for attention.

Veer smoothed his hands over her hair, framing her face. "Want to get married today?"

She blinked at him, positive she'd misheard. "What?"

"The crew is waiting for your go-ahead to start decorating Suryaganj for a Christmas wedding. A pundit and a priest from

Jaisalmer have agreed to officiate the ceremony. My parents are waiting for the jet to pick them up and bring them here—to show their support for Shaan and Ariana. I also told them about us, and they are beyond excited to meet you. They offered to bring your mother and her caretaker with them, if you wish. It is okay, isn't it? For your mother to travel?"

Butterflies began to dance in Tania's belly. "Oh my God. You're serious."

"As a hemorrhoid." A teasing smile curved his beautiful lips, but his dark eyes remained sober. However, the hearts were there. They'd always been there. She'd just been too afraid to believe. "We belong together. I don't want you to doubt that."

"I won't. Not ever again," she said, letting the last of her resistance go.

Veer dropped to one knee then, and held Truffles up to her. "So, Tania Coehlo, will you marry me today and make us the happiest males on earth?"

Tania giggled through her tears, accepting his troth. "Yes, I will marry you today, Veer Rana. Most happily."

# Epilogue
## The Holiday

That year, *Padmini* made it big at the box office and won every possible award at every possible award function. Veer Rana and Ariana became the darlings of the Indian film fraternity and, as Tania had predicted, were inundated with script offers.

Ariana was only too ecstatic to be in demand and had already signed on for six more films after her commitment to the Rana production house ended. She and Shaan seemed to be getting along just fine despite the accidental start of their publicity marriage. Tania was still Ariana's manager.

Veer had been serious about working behind the camera and was in discussions with an award-winning cinematographer about an indie film project, which would feature addiction in teenagers.

But, most of all, Veer was serious about making his wife, the love of his life, wholly and wildly happy.

It had been a year since they had a second chance at love at Suryaganj Fort and two years since that fateful Christmas Eve when he seduced her in an elevator. And so, to celebrate all the anniversaries that seemed to be piling up for them, he brought her back to Jaisalmer for yet another Christmas Eve anniversary special. It was the last one they'd spend entirely alone since their baby was due in less than six weeks.

They drove to the sand dunes in the Bentley, Truffles riding shotgun in the front passenger seat with his new pal, Leo. The top was down, just as she liked it, even though there were no stars in the sky yet.

"The stars are there. You just can't see them in daylight," Veer said, tucking her up against his hard, hot body.

"Even if we could see them, these days, I'm too busy being starstruck by my husband."

That rejoinder earned Tania Coehlo Rana a wicked-as-sin smile from her Bollywood bad-boy husband and a kiss that promised her the stars, the moon, and the sun. For all eternity.

# Author's Note

*Starstruck: Take Two* showcases everything I love about storytelling, from the comedy of romance to the smug happily-ever-after to the drama of Bollywood movies to immortalizing the memory of my precious pooch, Truffles, to working on an amazing project with a bunch of women I have come to adore and admire deeply.

So, many, many thanks to Jamie Beck, Tracy Brogan, Sonali Dev, K.M. Jackson, Donna Kauffman, Sally Kilpatrick, Priscilla Oliveras, Barbara Samuel, Hope Ramsay and Liz Talley for not only inviting me to join the Fiction From the Heart Facebook group and being part of the Once Upon a Wedding anthology, but for every message and e-mail and chat we've shared in the past two years that may or may not have anything to do with writing or books. And to Virginia Kantra, who couldn't be part of the anthology, but was there with us every step of the way regardless.

And lastly, to my readers, I hope you enjoy being starstruck by this little story, just like I am.

Lots of love,
*Falguni.*

PS: If you want to read what came before **Take Two**, sign up for my newsletter and start reading, *Starstruck* here: http://bit.ly/FKMailingList

# About Falguni Kothari

**Falguni Kothari** is the author of messy love stories that are "perfect for book groups" and kick-ass tales about gods and demons. Her novels, most recently *The Object of Your Affections*, are all flavored by her South Asian heritage and expat experiences. An award-winning Indian Classical, Latin and Ballroom dancer, she resides in New York with her husband and belts out karaoke in her spare time.

Find out more at: www.falgunikothari.com

# Always Yours

by Priscilla Oliveras

# Dedication

Every book I write involves *familia,* in all its facets—those I've gained by blood, from friendships, and via my imagination.

Writing this novella was an absolute thrill, as it allowed me to spend more time with my beloved Fernández *familia.* These sisters and their relatives ushered me into the life of a published romance author, and I'm so excited to share them with readers like you.

Sincere *gracias* to my Fiction From the Heart sisters…I'm *so* relieved & jazzed to share my first indie endeavor with you amazing women. The support & friendship in our group are true blessings!

To my personal *familia,* I can't say this enough: *¡Los quiero y aprecio mucho, siempre! (I love & appreciate you so much, always!)*

To readers, those who've been with me and those who find me through the pages of this anthology…my hope is that you enjoy escaping to my characters' world, finding new friends who love and dream and struggle and triumph, just as we all do. *Gracias* for spending some time with us.
    Abrazos/Hugs,
    *Priscilla*

# Chapter One

"*Hola*, Lourdes, it's good to see you."

Bent over the open dishwasher in her soon-to-be sister-in-law's childhood home, Lourdes Reyes froze at the softly spoken greeting. Her heart leapt into her throat, fueled by the flash of mixed emotions—desire, regret, unease—Eduardo Santana's husky voice sent sparking through her.

The handful of wet silverware she held slid from her grasp, free-falling, just like her stomach every time she'd nearly crossed paths with Eduardo since he'd moved back to Chicago nearly two years ago. There were only so many shortcuts a girl could take getting around their Humboldt Park neighborhood when she wanted to dodge someone. She knew all of them.

The mix of forks, spoons, and butter knives clattered into the plastic rack, the jangling mimicking the clash of panic that had rung in her ears and sparked her pulse when she'd learned he and his father were living in their neighborhood again. Years ago, she had foolishly trusted Eduardo with the key to her heart. The same key he'd thrown into the Caribbean Sea like a worthless piece of metal after moving with his parents and sister back to Puerto Rico the summer before their senior year of high school.

Lourdes squeezed her eyes shut, cursing her stupidity in thinking she'd be able to avoid speaking to him. Here of all places. At her baby brother Diego's wedding shower, in a house busting with *familia* and friends, all raucously kicking off a week of festivities. The sand had run out of her hourglass.

"You need some help?" Eduardo offered.

The hesitancy in his tone told her he anticipated her *hell no* response. She wasn't the one who had issued his invite today. That was Diego's doing.

"*No gracias,*" she muttered, determined to be a mature adult. Not the teenager who'd thought her world was ending and had started down a path that almost led her there. "I got it."

She took her time straightening the silverware, picking up the few pieces that had bounced out of the square rack and onto the tray.

This is what a *chica* got for volunteering for clean-up duty. Forget screwing up her manicure because she hadn't found gloves under the sink. This job had morphed into a self-preservation project. Focus on how excited she was for her brother and his fiancée, not on the loneliness she couldn't always stop creeping in on her.

A loneliness that thoughts of Eduardo and the what-ifs intensified. *Ay,* the price you pay when you have years of mistakes and hurts to make up for. Even though Diego harped on her to forget about it. Work on the right now and the future, he kept encouraging.

Easy for him to say. He was a week away from beginning a blissful future with his new wife, becoming part of her wonderfully normal *familia.* Something Diego rightfully deserved. While Lourdes…*pues*…love and romance hadn't been in her life plan, not that she'd *had* any type of plan, for far too long.

Her right now was focused on keeping her shit together. No slip ups.

Her future? Finish cosmetology school. Move from receptionist to having her own chair at CeCe's hair salon. Keep volunteering at the youth center and women's clinic, sharing her story in an effort to help someone else make better choices.

None of which would be on Lourdes's horizon if not for her future sister-in-law.

Lilí Fernández was a miracle worker. The soft-hearted, if also hard-headed woman had been a key player in Lourdes getting herself on the right track. Finally. Pride, a tiny if slowly thriving flower, bloomed inside her. Lourdes couldn't have picked a better person for her little brother who deserved only the best. Especially after the hell she'd put him and their mami through, *que descanse en paz.* Lourdes gave a quick sign of the cross as she sent the prayer for her mother to rest in peace up to the heavens. Then she got back to work, rearranging several serving platters in the dishwasher.

*Sí,* her brother was a lucky man. About to marry the love of his life—his sappy words, not hers. More importantly, about to become part of the type of boisterous, loving *familia* they'd never had growing up, despite their mami's best efforts.

A bone-weary sigh pushed through Lourdes's lips as she straightened. Keeping her back to the archway that led to the open dining and living rooms, she snagged the dish towel off the mottled grey and tan granite counter top.

The soft tread of his shoes on the tile floor warned her of Eduardo's move further into the kitchen. She kept her gaze trained out the window above the double sink overlooking the back yard. Some of Lili's nieces and nephews, along with several neighborhood kids, ran around the thick grass in a rowdy game of tag. The hot June sun didn't seem to bother them as they sidestepped around the wooden swing set and playhouse taking up the left corner. Screeches of delight pierced the air, muffled by the window, closed against the summer heat.

Out of the corner of her eye, she caught the red of Eduardo's shirt. Hands deep in his front jeans pockets, he leaned a hip against the counter's edge. The familiar scent of his earthy aftershave teased her, tugging her down a memory lane she'd blocked off with bright yellow caution tape. *Ay Dios,* the countless times over the years when she caught a whiff of that scent. In a store. On a stranger passing close by on the street. In the bottle she'd once bought and tucked away in a drawer, only to leave it behind when her situation went sour and she had to bug out of the hell hole she'd been living in.

Just like now, that rich, wood and spice scent took her back to days gone by. When everything seemed like it might be okay. Even though her papi had deserted their family, and mami struggled to make ends meet.

When Lourdes had been in Eduardo's arms, when they'd talked about a future together, she'd felt invincible. Protected enough to confess the pain of papi's abandonment and her anger at her mom, even though she knew it was unfair.

And then, just like her papi, Eduardo left her, too.

"You can't keep avoiding me, you know. Not forever," Eduardo said, his deep voice hushed for privacy.

Lourdes sucked her teeth in response. Not the most mature answer, but whatever.

Eduardo crossed his arms in front of his chest. His strong biceps strained against the short sleeves of his red polo, the dark color heightening his deep golden tan. For a second, she nearly reached out to touch his forearm. Treat herself to the feel of his warm skin and the tickly sensation of soft hair under her fingertips.

"*No seas tan terca,*" he muttered.

"I'm not being hard headed." Despite her promise to herself not to engage, Lourdes spun around to face him. Annoyed, she swatted the floral dishtowel at his broad chest.

Eduardo easily caught the end of the towel in his fist. He flashed a grin, his teeth white against his bronze skin.

"There she is." Triumph twinkled in his light brown eyes. His right brow arched in a cocky move she remembered. Only, now a thin scar cut a trail about a quarter of an inch from the edge, extending about an inch above his brow bone. The urge to ask how he'd gotten it nearly had the words springing from her lips. But she didn't want him to think she cared.

She couldn't. Not anymore.

"What are you talking about? There *who* is?" Lourdes tugged on the towel. Eduardo held tight. "I'm supposed to be washing and drying dishes. I don't have time for this."

"What? No time to say hello to an old friend?"

Now it was her turn to arch a brow. Only, hers was more of the are-you-freaking-kidding-me variety. *Friends?* Yeah, right.

One corner of Eduardo's mouth curved down in a disappointed slant. "Come on, Lourdes, don't keep shutting me out."

"Look—"

She broke off as Lilí sauntered into the kitchen carrying a tray of dirty glasses. "Thanks so much, both of you, for sticking around to help."

Eduardo let go of the dish towel to take the tray from Lilí. "No problem. I don't have to rush home. Happy to help."

Lilí beamed, her wide smile, like always, encouraging a similar response from those around her. The girl had pretty much been walking on air since Diego proposed to her at the Cubby Bear over the Christmas holiday.

*Dios mío*, Lourdes had snorted her disbelief when he'd admitted his plan to her. Few women would swoon at the idea of a marriage proposal in a sports bar. Then again, Lourdes knew her almost sister-in-law wasn't *most women*. That, along with her commitment to making a difference in their community, is what made Lilí so special. The type of person Lourdes was hell bent on becoming.

Wanting the marriage proposal to be memorable for Lilí—and not in the *what in the hell were you thinking?* kind of way—Lourdes had started to talk Diego out of his idea. But as soon as she'd learned the Cubby Bear was where the happy couple had their first date, after chaperoning a group of kids from the youth center at a Cubs baseball game, she'd had to admit it was a suave idea.

*¿Quien sabía, ha?*

Yeah, who knew. Back when she'd been tucking his scrawny butt in bed when their mami worked the night shift, Lourdes would never have guessed at the romantic streak hiding inside her brother. Apparently, Lilí brought it out in him.

Envy flashed through Lourdes's chest, hot and unwelcome.

"*Pués*, I appreciate you staying." Lilí gave Eduardo a quick thank you tap on the back of his shoulder, then leaned in to wrap her arms around Lourdes in a tight hug.

For the tiniest of moments, Lourdes froze. The smell of Lilí's favorite coconut-lime lotion filled Lourdes' lungs as she sucked in a shocked breath, before quickly returning the embrace. One thing she had to get used to, one thing she *wanted* to get used to, was the easy, natural way Lilí and her two sisters showed their love for each other.

Lourdes and Diego were slowly regaining the closeness they had shared as kids but rebuilding a bridge that had been impassable for many long, troubled years would take time. She'd known that long before she'd started therapy and begun trying coping mechanisms like journaling about her emotions and recognizing triggers.

"I'm so happy you're here," Lilí whispered in her ear.

Lourdes blinked rapidly, trying to dry the sting of tears before they fell. She swallowed past the fist clogging her throat, returning Lilí's tight squeeze with one of her own.

"There's no place I'd rather be," Lourdes said.

And she meant it. Even though Eduardo stood nearby, a vivid reminder of the happily ever after dream she'd once had back when she was a young, foolhardy girl. Polar opposite of the jaded, but no longer beaten down woman she was today.

His gaze caught hers over Lilí's shoulder. Compassion and—was that remorse?—turned the gold flecks in his honey brown eyes a burnished yellow.

Lilí stepped back, bumping into Eduardo behind her. "*Ay, perdóname,*" she apologized.

Eduardo shifted to the side, out of her way, and set the tray of glasses on the counter beside the sink.

"I'm going to finish saying good-bye to the stragglers, okay?" Lilí made her way toward the archway leading to the dining room.

"Sure, we got this covered," Eduardo said.

Lourdes shot him a glare. "I don't—"

"Oh!" Lilí's exclamation and quick swivel to face them again cut off Lourdes's rebuttal that she didn't need his help.

"I almost forgot." Lilí pressed her fingers to her temple, as if recalling one of the million pre-wedding tasks on her To Do list. "Rosa said she wanted to touch base with you about the pictures for the video. She'll be up once she finishes tidying the basement." Lilí rolled her eyes, her lips tugging up in a rueful grin. "You know her, everything's gotta be in the right spot. Even though I told her I had it covered."

Dread settled on Lourdes's shoulders, making her answering smile feel wobbly and uncertain. Exactly how she felt at the thought of digging through the box of family photos stashed under her bed. The same box she'd pulled out, pushed back in, pulled out, then pushed away countless times in the months since she'd been asked for old pictures of Diego and their *familia.*

She and her therapist had talked about it. About Lourdes' fear of the emotions, the regrets, the shame, that would inevitably mushroom inside her. Old demons she'd once chased away with bad decisions that had only led to more regrets.

"Um, okay. I'll be here. Waiting for her. Just..." Lourdes waved a listless hand at the dirty dishes, wishing she could wash away the past as easily, send the ugly memories down the drain with the dirty water.

Silly wishful thinking that got her nowhere. She didn't need a therapist or sponsor to tell her that.

"Great! ¡*Gracias!*" With a good-bye wiggle of her fingers, Lilí hurried off to the family room and the last of the guests who still lingered.

Sagging back against the sink, Lourdes closed her eyes on a heavy sigh.

¡*Coño!*

No, eff that, this was a *double damn* problem.

"Hey, you okay?" Eduardo's hand cupped her elbow, warmth spreading up her arm, into her chest.

Yearning, sharp and hot, tore through her. *Ay,* years ago she would have leaned into his touch, sought his reassurance.

Now, she couldn't afford to rely on him. Their breakup had decimated her, and she'd wound up making one of the biggest mistakes of her life.

If she let him in, and it wound up blowing up in her face, she risked ruining everything all over again. Her two years clean anniversary was around the corner. Hours of cognitive behavior therapy had taught her that she had to own her actions and deal with tough situations in healthy ways.

The box held demons of her own making. Demons *she* needed to slay.

Opening her heart to Eduardo again wasn't an option. It couldn't be. Even if the longing to do so pierced the depths of her deep, dark soul.

## Chapter Two

The flash of pain on Lourdes's expressive face had Eduardo stepping closer, sliding his arm from her elbow, up her bare arm to the middle of her back. The need to comfort and care for her came as naturally as his need to breathe. It always had. Despite his obtuse insistence otherwise.

"Whatever it is, let me help you," he pleaded.

"No." Lourdes shook her head at the same time she slid to her left and rolled her shoulder to shake off his arm.

"*Mira* – "

"No, *you* look," she interrupted. "I can't… I don't know what you… We cleared the air already. I don't think there's anything left to say."

Frustration swooped over him like a wave crashing onto Luquillo beach back on the Island. "I don't want to just be a name on a list you cross off as part of your steps."

Anger flashed in her dark eyes. "That's not your decision to make." She shoved a hand through her curls, pushing the long dark brown tresses away from her face. Her gaze darted to the archway where Diego, Lilí, and a few others stood chatting in the living room. Thankfully out of ear shot. "You lost the right to share your opinion about what I do the day you admitted on the phone that you'd been thinking we should break up. *¿Te acuerdas?*"

He huffed out a breath in disbelief. Of course, he remembered.

The memory of that call was perpetually burned in his mind. No matter how hard he'd tried to erase it. With her at home in Chicago and him at his abuela's house in Puerto Rico after his family's move, he'd thought it was the right thing to do. Set her free, instead of tying her to someone miles apart, with no foreseeable way for them to be together.

The devastation in her voice had been like a live electrical wire reaching across the ocean separating them. Zapping his soul and strangling the breath from his chest.

Remorse bitter on his tongue, Eduardo kept his mouth shut. She had to know he'd never forgotten their last phone call.

"I've wasted so much time blaming others for what's happened," Lourdes said. "Namely, you and my papi. But you didn't make me take that first hit with Patricia when she offered it. Or the next one. And the next. That's on me. I hafta live with all the crappy stuff that followed." Her voice hitched, her full lips pulling into a tight line as she fought to get herself back under control.

"Hey, don't be so hard on yourself." He leaned closer, dipping his head to catch her gaze with his. "We've both made mistakes, Lourdes. Who the hell hasn't?"

She let out a harsh bark of laughter. "*Por favor,* don't patronize me, okay?"

The glare she threw him over her shoulder as she turned back to the sink might have warned someone else off. Not him. Over a year ago she'd surprised him by showing up on his doorstep, intent on apologizing for her past transgressions—Step Nine in her Twelve-Step Program. At first, he'd taken it as a sign that she might be willing to rekindle their old friendship, if not more. Instead, he'd spent the months since then trying to figure out a way to break down the wall she'd firmly planted between them.

"I'm not patronizing," he countered, picking up the towel she'd tossed aside. "I'm being honest. You don't know what I've done or haven't done in the years since my mami's health problems caused us to move back to Puerto Rico."

"You're right, I don't know. Because we went our separate ways. That's the way you wanted it back then, and that's how it should stay." Lourdes shoved the sink plug in the drain, then pushed the faucet head up and to the left. A squirt of yellow grease-fighting dish soap later, and citrusy-scented, bubbly warm water filled the right side of the stainless steel, double sink.

Eduardo watched her stiffly rub the soapy sponge along a glass platter that'd been used to serve the *pernil* once the tasty, falling-off-the-bone pork shoulder had been pulled from the oven. As soon as she set the platter in the drainboard, he picked it up to start drying.

"I know a lot has gone down, in both our lives, over the years," Eduardo said, determined to find a crack in the wall between them. Feeling close to desperate, but afraid to admit that, even to himself. "But we were friends first, before we..."

Lourdes's dark eyes cut to him as his voice trailed off. The challenge swimming in their depths, paired with the smirk curving one edge of her full mouth, reminded him of the sassy attitude she'd worn like a cloak in high school. One that camouflaged the pain of a daughter abandoned by her beloved father. Confused by the spurts of anger for her mom, even though she'd been the one constant in Lourdes and her brother's lives. Eduardo had been too young, too immature to understand how deep those kinds of wounds could reach. Or how his departure, though forced by his parents, might exacerbate them.

"Before we what?" she asked, turning back to attack the roasting pan. "Were lovers? Each other's firsts? You can say it. But it doesn't matter. There's no going back to what was then. Believe me, I know. Now I'm busting my butt, trying to make things right. Taking it day by day. With the goal of having a life, a future, I can be proud of. One that makes Diego proud."

Her shoulders hunched, she scrubbed at the burnt, caked-on drippings. Eduardo's gaze trailed down the length of her body, starved for the sight of her. The deep purple wrap dress she wore cinched tight around her trim waist, accentuating her shapely hips. The stretchy material hugged her round butt, falling a few inches above her knees and leaving the rest of her gorgeously tan legs for him to appreciate. Her black strappy sandals were a foil for her bright pink toenails.

She was an incredibly beautiful woman, his Lourdes.

*Sí*, he still thought of her that way. Always had. Always would. He'd come to accept that after his breakup with Carmen and the harsh truths she'd thrown at him. Namely, that no woman would ever be able to compete with whatever ghost from his past he held on to.

That ghost now stood before him in the flesh and blood. No longer a figment of his imagination. She was a vibrant, resilient, compassionate woman. One who might have lost her way, suffered much, but who was finding her way back. Building a good life for herself. A life he longed to be a part of.

"If there's one fact I know," he assured her, "it's that your brother's already proud of you. Just like I am."

She sniffed as she finished rinsing off the roasting pan.

"I mean it." Eduardo reached for the pan, covering her wet hand with his.

She stiffened but didn't pull away.

"Life hasn't exactly turned out how we envisioned it," he went on, ramming his head against that damn wall. Determined to get through to her. "Back when we were sitting on your living room sofa, Diego doing his homework at the kitchen table while your mami was at work, we had no idea. I *had* to stay in Puerto Rico to help take care of my mom. Especially with Papi taking on two and three jobs to cover her medical bills. After she died, there was my sister to watch over. And then..."

He stared at their shadowy reflection in the metal pan they both still held. Their images distorted, just like their youthful dreams. "Then it was like I couldn't get out. Couldn't leave Papi alone. But when Franchesca got accepted to Northwestern's law school and Papi said he wanted to move back, I knew it was a sign."

"Of what?" Lourdes asked, confusion and doubt creasing her brow.

"I don't know. Possibilities? Hope, maybe?" At least, that's what he'd felt awakening inside him the moment his dad had brought up the idea.

Lourdes stared up at him, her eyes dark pools of sadness.

"I used to curse hope," she admitted.

"And now?"

She eased her hand out from under his and, with a slow shake of her head, turned to grab the lime green scrubbing sponge floating in the soapy water. "Now, I can't mess with hope. I have to *do*. *Work* for those good things I used to hope for. I'm learning how to trust myself again. And others. But it's not easy."

"And I'm not included in those 'others,' is that it?"

She chuffed out a breath, then slanted him an impatient, side-eyed glare.

Before she could respond, the basement door burst open.

Lourdes gasped, spinning around to face whoever emerged from downstairs. Water dripped from her hands and wrists, plopping onto the cream-colored tile.

"*Hola*, Tía Lourdes, here's a few more dirty dishes Tía Rosa asked me to bring you." Lilí's twelve-year-old niece, Maria, crossed the floor toward them. "She said to tell you she'll be up soon. I think she mentioned some pictures she needs? I don't really know."

The young girl, the oldest child of Lilí's big sister Yazmine, shrugged as she set down her dishes, then dashed off to the back yard to join her sibling and cousins.

As nonchalant as Maria had been about Rosa's imminent arrival, Lourdes had the opposite reaction. Eyes wide, her gaze shot from the open basement door to the hallway leading to the foyer where Lilí stood hugging someone good-bye, then back again. Like a cornered perp checking out his options and realizing there was nowhere to run.

This was the second time Rosa's name had caused Lourdes to freak out. Strange, because as far as he knew, Rosa was the peacemaker of the three Fernández sisters.

"What's going on?" Eduardo asked, as soon as the back door clicked shut behind the child. He held out the dish towel to Lourdes so she could dry her wet hands. "This talk with Rosa has you jumpier than the teen I collared for shoplifting at the corner bodega last week."

"I haven't done anything wrong," Lourdes countered, her scowl defensive.

"I didn't mean you had." He put his palms up, facing her, in a calming gesture. "But something's bothering you. If I can help, I'd like to."

"You can't."

"How do you know?"

"I just… I just do." Her last words were punctuated by a huff as she crossed her arms, the gesture inadvertently drawing his attention to the curve of her cleavage peeking out from the crisscrossed material of her wrap dress. His gaze caught on the gold crucifix hanging on a delicate chain low on her chest, much like the necklace her mother had worn years ago.

Lourdes sagged back against the sink, dejection stamping her face. She gnawed at her lower lip, her frown deepening with each tense second that ticked by.

"Come on. Try me," he urged, stepping closer.

Her eyes fluttered closed, and she hung her head.

Eduardo held his breath, praying she'd let him in.

She tilted her head to glance at him under her lashes, her gaze serious, considering.

*Confía en mí.* The words were a chant running through his head. *Trust me. Trust me.* Over and over, as if, somehow, they might tip whatever mental scale she was using in his favor.

"Fiiine," she muttered.

Relief whooshed through him like a gust of salty hurricane wind blowing in off the ocean.

He nearly pumped his fist in celebration. Instead, he schooled his features in his best friendly cop expression and mimicked her stance — arms crossed, leaning back against the counter's edge — next to her. "Lay it on me. I'm all ears."

When she didn't respond, he nudged her shoulder with his.

She nudged back, surprising him.

Without thinking, he leaned into her shoulder again for another nudge, watching her out of the corner of his eye. The tiniest hint of a smile teased her full lips, warming his heart.

The reminder of her playful side sucked him back to memories of their past. Her witty come backs and often inappropriate sense of humor. How'd they'd cuddle on the couch to watch some TV show after she put Diego to sleep when they babysat together. Only, somehow the TV watching devolved into a tickle fight that inevitably ended with her in his arms, the two of them sharing long, deep kisses. Innocent, inexperienced, *real* love.

A love he'd given up. Foolishly, even if his intentions had been noble at the time.

As if she sensed the dire path his thoughts had taken, Lourdes' mood shifted, her smile fading to a tight line of distress. She shifted, clasping her hands tightly in front her.

Unable to resist offering his comfort, Eduardo covered her hands with one of his. When she didn't pull away, he took it as another positive sign.

"Three months ago, Rosa asked me for some old pictures of Diego and our *familia*," Lourdes said, her tone heavy with doom and gloom. "I guess she's putting together like a…a video they plan to run during the wedding reception." She paused, the tap-tap-tapping of her black sandal on the linoleum floor giving away her distress. "No big deal, you'd think. Right?"

Eduardo gave her hands a gentle squeeze, but remained silent, knowing she wasn't really asking him a question.

"Only," Lourdes went on, "what's inside the box of photos tucked under my bed represents all that was good before. But now's been lost, because of me."

"You can't say that."

"I know. I'm not supposed to blame myself for everything that's happened," she interrupted. "That'll only start a spiral that could suck me back into a world I don't want to be a part of anymore. Ever."

"That's good to hear."

She turned to face him. "I don't want to let Diego and Lilí, or any of her sisters, down. I refuse to. But I can't rely on my therapist or sponsor to walk me through a situation I should be able to handle by now. I *need* to do this. I *want* to do this. For them. And for me."

The determined expression stamping her beautiful face may have fooled most people. But the flash of desperation in her dark chocolate eyes relayed the emotional toll this would take on her. It also solidified his certainty.

"Let me do this with you," he pleaded.

Lourdes's mouth open and closed. Her throat moved as she swallowed whatever response she'd started to give. She ran her tongue over her lower lip before biting it with her teeth.

The urge to pull her into his arms and taste her sweet mouth again swelled within him. His hands itched to hold her, touch her. Soothe her.

But her worries, the past she was working so damn hard to overcome and the role he played in it, couldn't be kissed away. Her trust in him had been broken. He had a herculean amount of work to do if he hoped to restore it.

Gently, Eduardo tucked a curly wave of her hair behind her ear. His gaze held hers and he prayed she recognized the sincerity in his words. "Let me do this. No strings attached. Simply one old friend doing his best to be there for you. Like he wasn't before. Can you give me a chance to right my own wrongs? Maybe...maybe we can bury some old demons together. What do you say?"

# Chapter Three

Lourdes paced the cramped space in her kitchen, the soles of her favorite pair of *chanclas* tapping against the worn linoleum flooring. Her gaze darted, once again, to the digital clock on her microwave tucked into the corner where the laminate counter met the wall.

One minute past the last time she'd checked: 7:12.

In three minutes, Eduardo should be here. Like, no kidding, here. Inside her tiny, cramped, one-bedroom apartment. Something she'd never allowed herself to think possible.

Both being with him again *and* having her own place.

Sure, her apartment wasn't much. Less than six hundred feet, really. But that was her name on the lease. The utilities and rent paid every month, on time, with her own hard-earned money from the salon. Strange, how much pleasure and pride she got writing that check to her super. Those first few months she'd actually walked the check to the guy's office a few blocks over, handing it to him personally. Mostly because she was afraid of it getting lost in the mail, though she had to admit it did feel damn good. Unlike some of the other "homework" assignments Sandra had given her as part of their cognitive behavior therapy sessions.

Not like today's task.

Lourdes eyed the beat-up cardboard box sitting in the middle of the black card table that served as her makeshift kitchen table. One of the box's top flaps refused to lie flat, its corner dog-eared and bent. Like a crooked finger calling her over.

Her heart sped up, fear and anxiety making their unwanted presence known. In the past she would have caved under their pressure, sought an escape, usually an unhealthy one, to dull her emotions. Now she relied on different techniques she'd learned through therapy.

She sucked in a deep breath through her nose on a count of three, then slowly released the air through her lip on a count of six. Repeating the routine brought a sense of tranquility and control, of herself and the situation.

Another slow and steady breath, in and out. She could do this.

A sharp knock on the door startled her, shattering the newfound calm. Her stomach clenched with nerves as she ran her hands through her hair, smoothing her curls and cursing the midsummer humidity with its frizz-inducing power. Nervously, she fingered her gold hoop earrings, telling herself it was only to make sure she hadn't lost one. Knowing full well it was a favorite stall tactic. Sandra had drawn Lourdes's attention to it countless times when she delayed answering a tough question.

The knock sounded again. Insistent and strong.

"Coming," she called, hurrying the short distance to the front door.

Pausing to check the peephole, she was treated to the sight of Eduardo, hands on his hips, looking pretty damn good in a pair of dark jeans and a light blue polo, a pair of Ray-Bans shielding his eyes. Even the tiny peephole's wide-angled, condensed image couldn't mar his *papi chulo* status. And cute, teen-aged Eduardo had without a doubt grown into a man who could only be described as a hunk.

Suddenly, a swarm of bees took flight in her belly. Their tiny wings flapped a million miles a minute, creating a buzzing sensation that started in her core, then hummed through her body. *Cálmate,* she ordered, pressing a hand to her belly and willing her nerves to calm the hell down.

She closed her eyes and muttered a brief prayer for sanity and serenity, adding a curse at herself for acting like such a wuss. A flick of her wrist turned the deadbolt, then she slid the safety chain down the squeaky track and swung the door open before she could chicken out.

"*¡Hola!*" she greeted, wincing at her high-pitched voice.

"Hi." Eduardo removed his sunglasses, tiny laugh lines

fanning out from the corners of his eyes as he smiled.

The bees swarming in her belly moments ago took flight again, stingers ready to do their damage. *Coño,* when it came to Eduardo, their target could wind up being her heart. Damn was definitely right.

*Ay,* how many times had she dreamt he'd show up on her doorstep like this, looking all hot and sexy? His dark hair was slicked back from his angular face, the scruff of his five o'clock shadow and the new scar marring his right brow giving him a tough-guy vibe that had certain parts of her body tingling with awareness.

His lanky adolescent figure had filled out over the years. Now the dips and slopes of his biceps stretched his polo's short sleeves. His broad shoulders and chest made a *chica's* hands itch to roam over their expanse, savoring their strength. At well over six feet, this older Eduardo made an imposing, heart-palpitation-inducing figure. And yet, his easy-going smile remained the same.

When they'd been together, he'd been caring and protective with her. Playful, but disciplined with Diego. Respectful of her mami. *Un hombre decente,* mami had called him. Yeah, a decent man who'd ultimately broken her heart.

"You, uh, gonna invite me in?" Eduardo asked in the awkward silence.

"Um, yeah. Sure."

Lourdes pushed the door open wider, stepping aside to avoid him brushing against her as he walked by. Still, there was no avoiding the intoxicating scent of his wood and spice cologne. No way she couldn't admire the snug fit of his jeans as he strode confidently into her small living room.

His gaze scanned over her worn, but comfortable green microfiber sofa and the scarred wooden rocker she'd found at the Goodwill. Diego had sanded and stained it, along with the low entertainment center along the right wall. Eduardo hesitated in front of her modest TV, stooping to get a closer look at the one family picture she had framed beside it. A photo of her and Diego taken by Lilí the day Lourdes had moved into this place.

Sweaty from lugging the sofa and her few pieces of furniture up the flight of stairs, he'd draped his arm around her shoulders and pulled her in for a surprise bear hug. Lourdes had squealed in protest. Lilí had snapped the pic, capturing Lourdes and her brother grinning at each other like fools. Pure joy shone on their faces, a sentiment they hadn't shared in far too long.

She'd framed it as reminder of how great things could be if she wanted them so. Which she absolutely did.

"I still have a hard time not thinking of him as that little kid who begged us to watch scary movies, then wound up cramming in between us on the sofa," Eduardo said, pointing at Diego's image in the photo.

"A lot has changed since then," she answered.

"Yeah, I know."

He stopped in front of the window overlooking Division Street, glancing up and down the block. She figured it was the cop in him. Diego did the same. Scoping out the neighborhood, always keeping watch.

"Thanks for not canceling on me," he said, turning back to face her.

"I wouldn't..."

She let her voice trail off when he tucked his chin to slant her a *yeah right* look as he hooked his sunglasses in his polo's button-down V.

Lourdes hitched her shoulder. "*Pues,* I did think about it."

"Ha, I figured!" A self-deprecating grin accompanied his bark of laughter.

She rolled her eyes and plopped down onto her sofa. "Whatever."

His smile slipped away, leaving an earnest, sympathetic expression blanketing his features. "I know this isn't easy for you. Going through old family pictures. Having me here."

With anyone else, except for maybe her brother and Sandra, she would have shrugged off the words. Pretended it was all good.

With him, this man she'd once shared her deepest secrets with, she found she couldn't lie.

"No, it's not," she admitted. "None of this is."

Uncomfortable baring her thoughts to him, Lourdes crooked her index finger on the crucifix hanging from her necklace. She slid the piece of jewelry that had belonged to her mom back and forth on its gold chain.

Eduardo stepped toward the rocking chair, setting his hands on the high backrest. The waning summer sun streamed through the front window, bathing him in golden white rays and casting his face in shadows. "But I'm betting, going through the pictures could help put some old demons to bed."

She nodded. "Sandra seems to think so."

"Sandra?"

"My therapist. I started seeing her after I checked myself into the treatment center. Even though I finished the outpatient program, I still keep monthly appointments with her. The accountability helps."

"That's good. You mind?" Eduardo motioned to the opposite end of the couch.

"Of course not, have a seat." Lourdes slid to her right, jamming her hip up against the armrest, as if having a full empty cushion between them offered some sort of barrier.

"I meant what I said yesterday." Eduardo scooted around to face her, crooking a knee on the sofa and resting his elbow along the back of the couch. "No ulterior motives here, other than both of us trying to lay the past to rest."

"You keep saying that, but..." Lourdes shook her head, "...but my baggage isn't yours to carry."

"Maybe I want to carry some of it for you. Maybe I—"

"No!" She pushed off the couch, refusing to let him go on. "That can't happen. I have to face the truth. Shoulder the responsibility for ruining my *familia*. For literally worrying and stressing my mami to an early grave."

Shame filled her, clogging her throat with its tight fist. Tears burned her eyes and she raced toward the kitchen.

"Lourdes, wait!"

She ignored Eduardo's plea, unable to face him. Instead, she tugged open her refrigerator, the frigid air cooling her heated cheeks. She swiped at her eyes, angry at the tears. At her inability to keep her emotions under control. She snagged the filtered water jug off the top shelf, pushed the refrigerator door closed and poured herself a glass, quickly chugging half of it.

Sensing him behind her, she poured a second glass, then left it on the counter as she crossed the few steps to the flimsy card table.

This was a mistake. Inviting him here. Thinking maybe she could do the whole two birds, one stone thing. Go through the pictures and let him get whatever he needed to say off his chest. In the privacy of her home rather than in the kitchen of Lilí's sister's house, their *familia* coming and going through the room.

Instead, she felt like the stone was a boulder, strapped to her back, and she was sinking to the bottom of the Chicago River.

"Look, I appreciate you offering to be here, Eduardo. Other than my brother, who I don't wanna worry, especially during his wedding week, you're probably the only person who understands why I don't want to do this. You used to let me cry on your shoulder wondering why Papi left us. Or, when I felt bad 'cuz I took out my anger at him on my mom. After you left, it got way worse between her and me. I did..." Her voice faltered.

She dragged out one of the metal folding chairs, the rubber stub on the end of the legs protesting against the worn linoleum. Plopping into the seat, she rested an elbow on the black vinyl padded table top and rubbed at the center of her forehead where a headache had started a dull throb. Not from withdrawal, *gracias a Dios*. This was stress related.

Eduardo reached for his water from the counter, then joined her at the table, his expression serious. But not condemning. She expected that to come later, once he knew the whole truth.

"Mami should be here," Lourdes made herself continue. "Excited for Diego's wedding. Instead, she went from dealing with my prick of a father, to dealing with me and my...my messes."

"If you think I might understand where you're coming from, how this isn't a cake walk for you, why do you keep shutting me out?"

Of course, he'd get right to the point. Apparently, his propensity to tackle problems head on, not putting up with any bullshit or skirting the issue, hadn't changed. Those skills probably came in handy as a cop.

"You want the truth?" she asked.

"Always."

"Because I've worked hard to avoid situations that can blow up in my face. And you…"

She broke off, not sure how to put into words the firestorm of emotions and thoughts being near him set off inside her. Not without revealing how much she still cared about him. And that, sharing that truth, ha, making herself vulnerable to any man again, sounded about as much fun as jumping into the icy waters of Lake Michigan in January like those crazies she'd seen on the news. *No gracias,* she'd give that type of fun a hard pass.

"I what?" Eduardo pressed.

She traced a line in the condensation fogging her glass. Thinking about Sandra's words the past few sessions.

Lourdes hadn't backed down from the other difficult conversations necessary for her to start rebuilding relationships she'd ruined. Maybe, like Sandra had implied, it was time she took care of this unfinished business with Eduardo.

Problem was, what if by finishing this, by having the "completely clear the air discussion" needed, it severed any tie, even an unhealthy one, with him?

Lourdes brought her thoughts up short. *¿Estaba loca?*

She *had* to be crazy if she was entertaining the idea that an "unhealthy" anything was the right choice.

"Okay, truth," she said, straightening her seat, her tone confident and strong. The opposite of what she felt inside. "Because you scare me."

Mid-drink, Eduardo choked, water spewing back into and over the rim of his glass.

"*Ay!*" Lourdes jumped up, racing to rip a paper towel off the roll next to the sink. When she spun around, he was wiping his mouth with the back of his hand. Wide-eyed he stared at her, shock and dismay swimming in the light brown depths.

No turning back now.

Handing him the paper towel, she folded a leg under her as she sank into her seat. "I'm guessing you want to know why, right?"

# Chapter Four

Stunned at Lourdes's admission, Eduardo couldn't even utter his thanks as he took her proffered paper towel. Her words reverberated in his brain like a heavy gong swinging from one side of his head to bang on the other, then back again. *You scare me. You scare me.*

*¿Que carajo?*

Thankfully he swallowed those words before they slipped out. *What the hell* wasn't exactly a response that would get her to open up with him. He didn't need Basic Interrogation Skills 101 from the academy to figure that out.

Lourdes's gaze flicked up to meet his, then dropped back down to where her nail picked at a tiny rip in the table's vinyl top. The uncertainty in her eyes clashed with the tough girl set of her shoulders and jutting chin. Like she refused to back down, even if she regretted revealing something so personal.

Her mix of strength and vulnerability awed him. She was absolutely amazing. Breathtaking, really. A vision in a pale yellow sundress that heightened the smooth expanse of her tanned skin. What he wouldn't give to peel down one of those thin yellow straps, press a gentle kiss to her collar bone, show her that fear was the absolute last emotion he wanted her to feel in his arms.

"I probably shouldn't have blurted that out," Lourdes grumbled.

Eduardo shifted uncomfortably in his seat, mentally chewing himself out at the same time he adjusted his jeans on the sly. Seriously, what kind of idiot started indulging in sexual thoughts about a woman right after she admitted he freaked her out?

He made himself look away from her. Instead, taking in the

worn, grey Formica counter that extended from the outside wall to the gas stove behind her. A wooden block knife set and matching pilón stood guard between the stove and a black microwave wedged in the corner. If Lourdes had inherited her mother's cooking skills, no doubt she wielded that mortar and pestle to whip up some tasty *mofongo*. The fried plantain and bacon concoction had been one of Lourdes's favorite foods back in the day.

"Anyway, you were pushing for an answer, so…" Lourdes quirked a shoulder in a *there you go* half shrug.

"*Sí*, I did." Frustration had him balling up the wet paper towel between his palms. "I didn't expect that one though. I mean, I have *never* laid a hand on a woman in my life. How could you think otherwise?"

He tossed the paper towel next to his glass, then leaned his forearms against the table. The puny metal legs groaned in protest at his weight. Intent on changing her mind about him, he spoke without thinking. "Look, maybe the same can't be said for some of the other men you've been with, but you have to believe that's not me."

Lourdes sucked in a sharp breath and reared back so fast, the front legs of her chair rose off the checkered linoleum. A pained expression chased across her face. "What did you hear? Who have you been talking to?"

Eduardo closed his eyes, cursing his mistake.

He sank back in his seat. Pissed he'd let it slip that he knew more than she probably thought he did. He had wanted her to tell him herself. To confide in him in her own time because she trusted him with her secrets, like she had before he'd left.

"Answer me," she demanded. "There's so many *bochincheras* in this neighborhood. What have they been saying about me? Let's see if the gossipers got it right."

Anger pinched her lips together. It flashed in her eyes like a dark storm rolling over Lake Michigan.

"It's not like that. If anyone's talking out there—" Eduardo waved a hand toward the kitchen window overlooking the back alley and the building behind hers, "—it better only be about the good you're doing at the youth center and the women's shelter. Screw anyone who says anything else."

The pugnacious angle of her chin softened the tiniest bit, the narrow-eyed glare she pierced him with shifting toward skepticism. Her right hand clasped the gold crucifix on her necklace, her thumb rubbing over the top part of it like a talisman.

"We heard about your mom's funeral from one of my papi's old domino buddies over here," he continued. "Tito mentioned that you'd been in the hospital when your mom had a heart attack. I immediately started reaching out to a few friends, digging on my own. Privately. Eventually I connected with Diego, asked for your number, but by then he didn't know how to get in touch with you."

Eduardo paused, gauging her reaction to his admission. Hoping she'd see it for what it was, snooping into her private business because he cared. Not because he was hounding for gossip.

"So, you know then." She swallowed but didn't break their eye contact. Her head remained at a haughty angle, though her thumb continued doing its best to shine the top of her crucifix, or maybe bring her good luck. "About how I not only got myself hooked on drugs, but also acquired a talent for hooking up with the wrong guys?"

He nodded, his jaw tight. *The wrong guys.* Ha! That was too tame a description if you asked him. Still, Eduardo kept his thoughts to himself; he'd said enough already.

"Guys who thought I looked a lot like a punching bag, especially when they were high."

Eduardo winced at the brutality of her words. White hot anger at the thought of some lowlife hitting Lourdes whooshed inside of him like a swiftly moving fire he needed to bank, or he'd risk losing it right here, in front of her. And she did not need another man in her life who lacked self-control.

Releasing her necklace, Lourdes crossed her arms. She ran her gaze up and down as if sizing him up. Her tough girl act was in Oscar-worthy form now, but he'd heard the slight tremor in her voice. A tremor that sent a seismic wave of anguish for all she'd been through cresting over him.

Hands clasped tightly in his lap, Eduardo focused on cooling his simmering rage before he spoke again. "Here's what I think. No one deserves what those scumbags did. Especially the *sinverguenza* who put you in the hospital."

She scoffed, her full mouth twisting with a sneer. "You're right, he was shameless. But that's not the worst of it."

"He was in the wrong, Lourdes, not you."

Her eyelids fluttered closed for a brief moment. Her chest rose and fell on a deep breath, whether from relief or the weight of guilt and shame she couldn't seem to let go. He couldn't be sure which.

"I say the same thing to women I meet with at the shelter. It's easier when you're giving the advice to someone else though. Sticking around too long in that relationship, the worry and stress it gave my mom, that's one of the mistakes I have the hardest time forgiving myself for. And yet, I have to." A thin line appeared between her brows, the pain she struggled with obvious. "If not, I can't move forward."

"I know it's not easy. You don't know how much I regret not being here for you. The guilt I feel for breaking it off. At the time, I thought doing so was right for you. Even though it meant depriving myself of something precious to me."

Her chin quivered and she rolled her lips together, turning her face away from him.

"I'm so sorry, Lourdes. And, yeah, I get that the words might not mean much. Not now. But I have to say them anyway. I owe you that, and more." Eduardo reached across the table, his palm up, desperate for her to take his hand. Meet him halfway in his bid to make amends.

Instead, she slanted a look at his hand. Doubt creased her brows, a knife to his chest. His fingers closed in an empty fist. His heart sank a little deeper into the dark shadows of loneliness inside him.

"Am I too late?" he asked, his voice gruff with remorse. "Has the pain I've caused gotten me stuck on the 'off-limits' list? That's why you're scared of me?"

"It's not that I'm scared of *you*."

"That's not what—"

"I doubt there's a mean bone in your body," Lourdes interrupted.

Not true. If you asked his ex, she'd curse him for his inability to commit, for "wasting good years of her life" by stringing her along with one excuse or another.

"It's more like…" Shifting in her chair, Lourdes rubbed at the center of her forehead, muttering an "*Ay Dios mío, chica*" under her breath.

Certain she had changed her mind about sorting through the pictures together and wanted him to leave, Eduardo started to pull back, reminding himself he shouldn't push her if she wasn't ready.

No way would he let himself consider that she might never be ready to forgive him completely.

Suddenly Lourdes covered his closed fist with her hand, halting his retreat. Heat from her touch sparked up his arm, like an electric current zapping through him. Warming the deep chill he'd kept on his emotions since the day he'd told her good-bye.

"I'm scared of what you make me feel," she said on a rush.

If not for the rapid bongo beat in his chest, he'd swear his heart stopped. "And what's that?"

Her dark eyes stared back at him, intense, serious. The tiny speck of white against her lower lip as her teeth worried it gave away her unease.

"Hope. Desire. Longing for what Diego and Lilí have together. For someone to look at me, *all* of me, and still believe in me. Still appreciate and honor me. It might have taken a while to get it through my thick skull, but I know I deserve that."

Shame for whatever part he had played in causing her self-doubt burned his throat. Pride for the amazingly strong woman she'd become humbled him. Slowly, his pulse racing, Eduardo uncurled his fist, laying the back of his hand on the table until his palm lay flat against hers.

"*Gracias,*" he murmured.

That tiny line etched between her brows again at her confused frown.

"For trusting me enough to admit that. Instead of shutting me out. You have every right to."

She curled her fingers, their tips brushing against his palm. A soft caress that soothed his aching soul. At the same time, it had his body zinging with desire and lust.

"As much as I want all that, I don't know if I should," she continued, her gaze on their joined hands. "I'm finally in a good place. Letting myself get close to you again, it's not worth the risk. If things went south and I slipped into bad habits to help dull the pain...I might not recover. And Diego—" her words tumbled on top of each other, anxious and laced with fear, "—he might not forgive me. He's got a *familia* to protect now. I want to be part of that *familia*. I can't—"

"Hey, hey, it's all good." Eduardo sandwiched her hand softly in between his, desperate to calm her. She'd finally opened up to him, yet immediately started pulling away. "I said no strings, remember? We're two friends here. If this goes anywhere else, it's on the slow train, not the express. And only if we both decide we're ready. Okay?"

"The slow train?" Uncertainty colored her words.

He nodded and held his breath. Prayed.

After several painful seconds, she curled her fingers around his bottom hand, pressing their palms together.

"I've been on a fast train to nowhere for a long-ass time. Slow motion with you sounds like more my speed." Her full lips curved into a beautiful smile as she finally met his gaze.

Eduardo gave her hand a squeeze.

Saucy *chica* that she was, she responded with a wink.

Eduardo grinned back, relief lightening the pressure in his chest.

Baby steps. That's what it was gonna take here. He'd waited years to get back to her. Years during which he'd tried fooling himself that she was his past. Any step they took forward together now was a blessing.

"So, you ready to dig through this box and see what Rosa might want for the reception?" He tipped his head toward the beaten-up cardboard box.

"*Bueno,* Rosa's counting on me." Lourdes slid the container closer to them. "I don't want to disappoint one of the new *hermanas* Diego keeps telling me I'm gaining when he gets married."

"Sisters, huh? You always wanted a big *familia*."

Her hands on the box flaps, Lourdes paused and glanced over at him. "You remember that?"

He remembered every detail about her. Hadn't been able to forget, no matter how hard he'd tried.

"*Sí*, I do," he answered.

A deep blush crept up her tanned cheeks. Her eyes shone with pleasure before she turned back to the task at hand.

"Okay, ready or not..."

After a deep shuddering breath, she reached in to pull out a handful of photos. She spread the images across the tabletop, colorful flashes of the past. He caught the tremor in her hand as it moved over the old photographs, barely touching them.

There was one of her as a young second grader in a modest white dress, a lacy veil on her head, silky gloves on her little hands as they grasped a rosary and bible after her First Communion. Another of her older, probably middle school-aged, wearing tight jeans and a figure-skimming dark green sweater, a scowl on her face as she clutched her school books.

Lourdes reached for another one, scooting her chair closer toward his as she held it up between them.

The image sucked the breath from him.

It was her at age seventeen, standing with her right arm around her mother's plump waist. A young, gap-toothed Diego stood on her mami's other side. Dressed in their Sunday best, with their neighborhood church looming in the background, they smiled at the camera. At him, as he snapped the pic.

What-ifs and regrets assailed him like tiny pieces of shrapnel, burning into his psyche.

That day, the future lay ahead, bright with possibilities. None of them aware that his mami's health would soon nose-dive. That she'd plead for their return to Puerto Rico, afraid of dying away from her beloved Island.

Pain over lost dreams choked him. His eyes burning, he placed his hand on the center of Lourdes's back. As if to remind himself that she was here with him. They were finally together again. If tentatively feeling their way.

Knowing how much she missed her mother and the depth of Lourdes's guilt, Eduardo fully expected the tears shining in her eyes when she glanced up at him. But the sad smile tugging up the corners of her lush lips had him longing to offer her comfort. As if she read his thoughts, she leaned into his embrace, surprising him when she tucked her head on his shoulder and snaked her left arm around his waist for a hug.

A sense of peace, of rightness, filled him. It seeped into the shadowed, lonely corners of his soul.

Before he could tug her closer like his body clamored for him to do, she leaned back in her chair again. A trail of sizzling heat where her arm had brushed along his waist burned his skin.

His heart in his throat, he watched as this incredible woman he had never stopped loving dropped her gaze to the photo she held. A curtain of her chestnut, wavy hair slipped down to shield her expression from his view. She tucked her hair behind her ear, a tiny gold hoop earring peeking out from her tresses.

"*Ay*, Diego hated that it took so long for his front tooth to grow in that year," she murmured, warmth in her husky voice. "I can still hear him whining to Mami when she told him to smile big. Ha! I can't *wait* to see his face when this flashes up on the screen."

With his palm still pressed against her upper back, he felt a chuckle rumbling up from Lourdes's chest, shimmying her sexy shoulders.

She held the photo out toward him, and their hands touched when he grasped it. Rather than pull away, she slid her hand to completely cover his. He froze, wanting so much more. Waiting to take his cue from her. Without a word, she gave that familiar squeeze. The one that used to mean, *I got you.* Or, *I don't want to let go.* And later, *I love you, too.*

Instinct had him leaning over to press a kiss to her forehead.

Her grip on him tightened. Closing his eyes, he breathed in the spicy floral scent of her perfume. Time stopped. The sounds from the city street outside disappeared. All that mattered was this woman. The fact that she was in his arms again. A dream…a need he'd held on to for years.

Eventually Lourdes pulled away, turning to inspect the photos again.

"I'll, just, uh, add this to the 'yes' pile, okay?" he asked, his voice gruff with need.

"Definitely," she responded, shooting him a sweet smile filled with what he wanted to believe was promise.

He had committed to taking things slow.

It wasn't going to be easy, but she was worth the wait. And with Diego's wedding later this week, Eduardo prayed that love and blissful futures were in the air.

# Chapter Five

Lourdes raced home early Wednesday evening, thankful her six PM shampoo, cut, and style had called needing to change her appointment. Usually late cancellations sucked. They meant less money. Not to mention Lourdes was still building her client list, and who knew if this new one would stick.

But today, she didn't care. There was some place else she'd rather be.

Nervous anticipation hurried her steps up the front walk to her building. Before leaving her apartment yesterday evening, Eduardo had asked if she planned on going to Diego's recreation league softball game tonight. Eduardo hadn't come right out and said it, but she knew he played on the team, too.

Various Chicago PD precincts fielded a team, with a competitive rivalry amongst them all. Later this summer, at Humboldt Park's Little Cub Field down the street at Humboldt Park, there'd be a friendly softball game between cops from different precincts and local at-risk youth. It was part of the Build organization's annual Peace League summer finale event. Last summer Diego had volunteered alongside the husband of one of Lilí's cousins, an ex-major league pitcher, to help out with a youth team. Sitting and cheering from the stands alongside Lilí had reminded Lourdes of Diego's T-ball years. Those hot and humid afternoons when she and Mami would watch together.

Only one year into her sobriety last summer, controlling that gut-twisting roller coaster of emotions and memories hadn't been easy. Lilí had held her hand, grounding her in the present. Reminding Lourdes that she had *familia* who believed in her.

This season she hadn't made many of her brother's games.

Usually, she pleaded the long work hours on her feet, volunteer commitments at the women's shelter and youth center or going to her own meetings. Mostly, though, it'd been to avoid running into Eduardo.

Last night, after their conversation and his gentle understanding of her fears, it was foolish of her to keep pretending she didn't want to be around him.

Once inside her apartment, she tossed her purse and keys on the worn sofa and went straight to her room. The clock was ticking, and she wanted to touch up her makeup. Swap her comfy work dress and wedge heels for something a little sporty. *Bueno,* as sporty as she could get seeing as how she'd never played on an organized team and her idea of exercise was dancing around the house when she cleaned. She was a better cheerleader—okay, more like heckler—than a participant.

For this game, she wanted to look her best. Only, not like she was trying too hard.

Fifteen minutes later, the bright summer sun still hung above the businesses and townhouses lining Division Street when she trotted down the cement steps on her building's front stoop. A quick glance at her cell confirmed she had just over thirty minutes 'til their seven PM game time. If she speed-walked, she could be there in fifteen and maybe get a chance to wish Eduardo good luck before they started.

Making a left on the cracked sidewalk, she headed west on Division. Señor Vega waved at her with one hand while shooing away some kids from in front of his *mercado* with the other. Lourdes laughed and returned his greeting. As far back as she could remember, there'd always been a group of teens hanging out by the Vega's corner store. They were usually harmless. But that *usually* could make a difference. And when they blocked traffic into his business, Señor Vega tended to get grouchy.

As she neared the intersection at California Ave, her gaze was drawn to the huge Puerto Rican flag replica spanning from one side of Division to the other. The red and blue steel art work proudly waving above the street traffic signaled the entrance to what many knew as *Paseo Boricua,* an area with a large Latino population. To her, it signaled home. A place she'd once thought lost to her. Not anymore though.

Her footsteps felt light in her Converse sneakers. A sense of pride and conviction filled her, hurrying her steps to the softball field a few blocks ahead. Earlier today she'd touched base with Rita. Her sponsor, like her therapist, had known about Eduardo's offer to tackle the hunt for family pics last night. More importantly, they knew her history with him.

Both women had cautioned her to take it slow. Be honest with Eduardo, and herself. Be mindful of any triggers.

Both had praised her progress, while also reminding her that, if needed, they were a quick phone call away.

Knowing she had those lifelines helped, though she was pleased that in almost a year she hadn't felt the need to call either one with an SOS.

Now, with the waning sun's rays smearing across the sky and clouds in dark orange and red streaks, a light humid breeze cooling the heated air, and the knowledge that Eduardo was aware of her past but still looked at her with caring and respect in his honey-colored eyes...Lourdes allowed herself to give in to the buoyant positivity humming through her.

She picked up her pace and soon found herself approaching the softball field on the south side of the park. From the looks of it, this was the place to be on a summer evening.

A group of kids tossed a baseball back and forth in a grassy field nearby. Picnic blankets and lawn chairs dotted the area on either side of the fence lining the field. The crack of the bat rang in the air as a team warmed up, a mix of players standing in their positions while a tall guy with a beer belly and a mop of gray hair hit ground balls from the batter's box. Over on the first base side, she spotted Eduardo's team in their navy T-shirts and white lettering gathered near the dugout. She veered her steps in that direction.

"*Oye*, look who finally decided to show up!"

Lourdes grinned at the greeting from one of the older guys on Diego's team. "Hola, Victor, looking good."

Sweat glistening on his round face, the chubby cop grinned back and patted his well-fed belly poking over the elastic waist band on his grey sweat pants. "Ha! Between the bakery's empanadas and pan dulce and my vieja's cooking, I'm losing the battle of the bulge here."

He stepped closer to wrap her in a big bear hug, and she chuckled along with him. If she remembered his *old lady's* contributions to church potlucks from years ago, Lourdes didn't see him winning that battle easily.

She high-fived hello with several other players, then exchanged cheek kisses with one of the girlfriends she knew from the neighborhood.

The sound of a cooler lid dropping closed had her peering through the crowd to see behind them. Eduardo and Diego stood beside a white and blue cooler talking.

They glanced in her direction, catching sight of her at the same time. Diego's shout of surprise was a welcome sound. But the pleased smile that curved Eduardo's lips and crinkled the corners of his eyes had butterflies fluttering in her chest. *Ay,* some things never changed. A simple look from this man had her knees wobbly.

Two water bottles clutched in his hands, Diego strode toward her. He held one out to her as he leaned in to brush a kiss on her temple. "Why didn't you tell me you were coming? Lilí's gonna be upset that she missed you. She's still at the clinic."

"I wasn't sure if I'd make it," Lourdes answered. "Turns out I had a late appointment cancel."

Eduardo hung back, twisting the lid off his water bottle. With his softball glove tucked under his left arm, a navy ball cap emblazoned with the Chicago PD logo shielding his eyes from the setting sun, muscular legs and arms on display thanks to his grey basketball shorts and snug-fitting team shirt, he looked ready to take the field. Frankly, he could take her anywhere and she'd —.

Lourdes immediately squashed that thought. Slow train, she reminded herself.

A lot remained unsaid between them. He may have dug into her past, but there were plenty of holes she needed to fill in about his. Questions that had plagued her over the years. Taunting her when she was low.

Like, did he ever get married? Have kids? Why had he stayed away?

In her darkest moments, she'd always found herself wondering if he'd forgotten about her. If he'd easily moved on with his life. Knowing now that he hadn't was like sprinkling water on the seeds of hope she'd believed had dried up and blown away in the harsh winds of time.

"Hey, Diego, what do you think about this line up?" A tall, slender cop Lourdes didn't recognize waved a piece of paper at Diego.

"Give me a sec, okay?" he told her, touching her elbow to excuse himself so he could check the team's batting order.

"Sure, I'm good."

As soon as Diego walked away, she slid her gaze back to Eduardo over by the cooler.

He flashed that sexy smile of his, then tilted his head with a little jerk to motion her over.

Lourdes bit the inside of her lip to keep her mouth from curving in a goofy grin. Anticipation pounded in her chest. Still, she took her time sauntering over, adding a touch of hip action for good measure.

Reaching his side, she turned to stand shoulder to shoulder with him. She stared at the baseball field, as if the other players warming up warranted her attention. The truth was, she and Eduardo hadn't socialized since his return. Not in public anyway. No sense doing anything that might get the gossipers flapping their lips. You know, like throwing her arms around him so she could give him the kind of hello kiss she'd dreamt about last night.

Only, in her dreams they hadn't stopped at kissing.

"Nice night for a softball game," she said in greeting.

A young woman playing in right field botched a practice fly ball, barely missing a beaning to the forehead. Lourdes watched the girl chase after the ball, waiting for Eduardo's response.

"So, this is how we're gonna play it?" he finally said.

"I'm not sure what you mean." *Mentirosa.*

"Liar."

Lourdes blinked in surprise when he voiced the name she'd

called herself in her head. "Hey, I walked all the way over here to watch my baby brother play. Running into you is—"

"Icing on the cake?"

She barked out a laugh and several heads turned their way. His snappy comeback had her imagining what it'd be like to lick frosting off of him. A delicious shiver trembled through her, and she shook her head, trying to dispel that image.

Eduardo chuckled beside her. Out of the corner of her eye she caught him take a swig of water. His big hand wrapped around the flimsy plastic bottle, his throat worked as he swallowed. The impulse to press her nose against his neck, inhale the scent of his musky, summer-heated skin, swelled inside her.

*Dios mío,* spending time with him the past few days had blown the lid off of the box where she'd stuffed all thoughts of romance and intimacy. Around him, her body came alive. And it had no interest in moving at the slow pace they'd discussed last night.

Pull it together, *nena*. The words whispered in her head. A warning.

This was not only the wrong place, but also the absolute wrong time in this new...whatever the *carajo* they had between them...for her to act on any carnal cravings.

"I'm, uh, going to head over to the concession stand. Support the youth league and buy a hot dog," she said. Food was the last thing on her mind. Getting away from Eduardo to regain perspective, however, might be a smart move.

"I'll come with you. I got off shift late and didn't have time to grab a bite on my way here."

Great. Suppressing a sign of frustration, Lourdes turned away from the field.

Eduardo fell into step beside her.

Diego looked their way, and Lourdes motioned toward the makeshift food stand Little League teams often set up as fundraisers. He frowned, his gaze going from her to Eduardo and back again. Her brother was probably wondering about her one-eighty. For months she'd been keeping a mile-wide distance from her ex. Now they were grabbing a bite together?

Only ball park food. Not a date and definitely not a move that should cause *bochinche* amongst any gossipers from their neighborhood. Still...

She hitched a shoulder, hoping Diego would take it for the *no big deal* she meant.

Ha!

If it was no big deal, then why was she feeling like they'd time-warped back to high school? When Diego played Little League and Eduardo would join Lourdes and her mami for a game. Back then they would have strolled hand in hand to grab snacks. Today...today they had miles of broken road behind them.

And while certain parts of her body might be screaming for his...

Her heart remained leery.

Her mind told her she needed answers.

She simply had to stop being a wuss and ask the questions. Starting right now.

# Chapter Six

The lights dotting the baseball field flickered on in the waning sun as Eduardo headed to the concession stand with Lourdes.

It'd been a crap day at work. He never enjoyed hauling in a kid for possession. Especially one barely in his teens who Eduardo had tried talking some sense into before. He'd even connected the kid with David, one of the managers at the Humboldt Park Youth Center. Sometimes, the pull of the neighborhood streets was too strong.

Maybe... hopefully...getting arrested for a minor offense would scare enough sense into the young teen. Before he graduated to major felonies.

Experienced enough to know that might be a big if, Eduardo had left the precinct feeling out of sorts. Disappointed. In the kid for not listening *and* himself for not getting through to the kid. Sure, Eduardo knew it wasn't up to him whether or not the boy made smart choices. Knowing that hadn't alleviated his guilt. Or lightened his mood.

If the team hadn't been two men down already, Eduardo would have gone straight home. His papi had texted to say he'd leave a plate with Eduardo's dinner in the microwave, *arroz con pollo* with *amarillos* and green beans on the side. His mouth had watered at the thought of chicken and rice with a side of the sweet plantains that'd always been his favorite. After his day, he'd been tempted to bag the softball game and head straight home for a tasty home-cooked meal paired with a cold beer.

Lopez razzing him about being a punk for not coming to play ball had made Eduardo head to the park.

Now, with Lourdes sauntering besides him in her figure-hugging red leggings and black tee, the words "Phenomenally Latina" in bold white letters across her chest making his pulse rev, Eduardo figured he owed Lopez.

A grilled ballpark hot dog and sports drink shared with Lourdes beat any meal, hands down. Apologies to his papi.

"Good evening, what can I get for you?" the middle-aged woman behind the long folding table serving as a makeshift counter asked in greeting.

Eduardo angled his body to face Lourdes, gesturing with an open palm for her to order first.

Lourdes glanced at the boxes of snack-size chip bags, candy bars, and sweets that filled one end of the table. Behind the woman stood a gentleman in a matching red polo embroidered with a white paw print under the word "Bears" manned a portable grill. Steam floated up engulfing him in a cloud pungent with the scent of meat cooking and drippings falling onto the hot coals below.

"I'll take a hot dog and Diet Coke," she said.

"What? No Peanut M&Ms?"

Her lips curved and he sure as hell hoped that, like him, she was thinking about the number of times they'd shared a bag of the candy while watching Diego playing ball.

"I'm an adult now," she told him, "So, I've gotta practice some restraint."

His answering smile faltered. Her life post-rehab was all about self-control. Avoiding temptation, making the right choices. The last thing he wanted to do was remind her of that.

"But don't worry, I'll be back in the fifth inning. A *chica* can only hold out so long when it comes to chocolate and peanuts, *verdad?*"

"Definitely right," the woman taking their order agreed. "I swear, every time we work this stand helping raise money for my son's team, I eat a week's worth of junk food."

"A moment on the lips, *siempre* on the hips!" The two women finished the Spanglish version of the saying in unison.

Lourdes's rich throaty laughter and the sparkle in her dark eyes as the other woman joined her were like a boxer's one-two punch to Eduardo's gut. He sucked in a quick breath, keenly aware of his body's response to being near her again. Damn if he didn't want to whisk her away to a private area where they could keep working on clearing away the past and all the sticky cobwebs impeding their ability to move forward. Preferably together.

Reining in his lust, Eduardo dug his wallet out of his shorts pocket.

"I got you covered," he said. "Two hot dogs, a Diet Coke and a Gatorade. And two bags of Peanut M&Ms."

He winked at Lourdes's huff.

"That way you won't risk missing me hitting a home run 'cuz you're over here grabbing dessert."

"*Egoista*," she mumbled, but the ghost of a smile softened the word.

The mom made quick work gathering their order and taking Eduardo's cash. He and Lourdes dressed their dogs with mustard, with her adding enough relish for both of them, then they headed back toward the team.

Eduardo angled his steps toward a cement picnic table under a shade tree off to the right. Lourdes followed. She stepped over the same bench he did, her shoulder bumping against his when she leaned left to swing her purse on the tabletop.

"Sorry," she garbled around a bite of her food.

Without thinking, he reached up to swipe a drop of mustard from the edge of her mouth. Lourdes stopped chewing. Her eyes widened with surprise. Desire flashed in their depths, and he swore time stopped.

The sounds of the birds in the trees and the teams gathered on the field behind them quieted. The kids bouncing a basketball on the hardcourt nearby melded with the green grass and shade trees into a blurry haze. His entire world zoomed in on her, this moment. A juxtaposition of what had been and what he craved now.

The tip of Lourdes's tongue swooped over the same corner of her mouth seconds before she reached up to wipe the moisture away with the back of her hand. She swallowed and leaned the tiniest bit away from him. Enough to let him know he'd overstepped. Her gaze dropped to the handful of napkins he'd grabbed from the condiment stand. Silently, she tugged one out of his grasp before slowly sinking onto the cement bench.

Eduardo joined her, making sure to leave several inches of space between them.

"You can't do things like that," she said, her tone flat.

"I wasn't—"

"It's not fair."

He started, nearly dropping his Gatorade. *"Not fair?"*

"Uh-huh." She took another bite of her food. Chewed slowly. Swallowed.

Meanwhile he couldn't have taken a bite of his even if a perp held a damn gun to his head and ordered him to do it.

"Lourdes…"

Her name hung in the stilted air between them. Wanting answers. Hating feeling like he stood in a field of landmines with her on the other side. One wrong move and…*BOOM!*…any shot of making his way back to her would be blown to smithereens.

She popped the top on her can of Diet Coke, the hiss of carbonation releasing mimicking the hiss of frustration he fought to hold inside.

"Look," Lourdes finally said. Head bent, she traced a finger around the circle of the aluminum can's top edge. "I don't like being at a disadvantage. And I'm at one here. You left over fifteen years ago, and my life, well…*se fue pa' el carajo.*"

"And you don't think my life went to hell, too?"

Lourdes jerked around to face him so fast, soda spilled out of the can, plopping onto the cement table in a dark splotch.

"Did it? I have no idea. That's the problem. You've played detective, using your cop contacts to dig into my life. Finding out about crap even the *bochincheras* in our neighborhood don't know."

Shame stamped her round face. Two deep grooves carved a path in between her brows.

"But me? I'm in the dark when it comes to you. Did you go to college like you talked about? Did you wind up marrying someone else? Did you…" She rubbed at the space between her brows, as if she was trying to erase the deep lines from her frown. "Do you have kids?"

Each question she threw out hit him right in the chest with a dart champion's accuracy.

"All I know is that you stayed away. You never came back. How come?" Her voice cracked on the last question. Bullseye. The pain and devastation in her words pierced the center of his heart.

"Hey, Santana, are you playing ball or stuffing your face?" Lopez yelled from the dugout.

Lourdes flinched at the interruption.

"You know what? This was a mistake." In one swift move she closed the foil wrapper over her half-eaten hot dog and balled-up napkin, then reached for her soda can. "I shouldn't have come."

"No! Wait!" Eduardo grasped her forearm, suddenly afraid if she walked away now, they'd go back to her shutting him out again.

One knee raised, ready to swing her leg over the bench and flee, Lourdes paused. With her chin tucked, her shoulders rose and fell on a heavy sigh. She looked up at him, tossing her dark waves out of her face when the humid summer breeze blew over them.

"Look, it was dumb of me to think I could show up here. Hang out and pretend like you were a normal guy and I was just a normal girl feeling our way around whatever I thought this might be."

"I don't want a normal girl."

Her face scrunched in a grimace she probably didn't intend to be adorable. But it was.

"I mean, I'm not interested in just any normal girl."

"That's not much better," she grumbled with a roll of her eyes.

"*Dame un chance, por favor,*" he pleaded, praying she'd agree. If she gave him a chance, gave them a chance, he'd get it right this time. He swore he would.

Her gaze slid past him toward the ball field behind him. She gave a quick shake of her head, and Eduardo turned to glance over his shoulder. Diego stood in the dugout's opening, glove clenched in both hands, his expression a thunderous mix of worried and pissed off.

*Coño.* One guess as to whose neck her brother felt like wringing. A string of words much stronger than *damn* slid to the tip of his tongue.

Diego had warned him about not hurting Lourdes, or Eduardo would answer to him.

Yeah, well, get in line, buddy. Because if he wound up hurting Lourdes again, Eduardo would never forgive himself.

"Stick around, please. Let's talk after the game, okay?"

Head tilted, she narrowed her dark eyes at him. The wind teased her hair, tugging apart several curls to dance across her cheek. Lourdes set down her drink, then tucked the hair behind her ear. Still, she remained silent.

"Eduardo! Right field!" Diego's call was more command than question.

"Go." Lourdes waved Eduardo off.

"Will you—"

"I'll think about it."

Not the answer he wanted. But better than flat-out no.

Grabbing his cold, untouched food, Eduardo tossed it in the trash as jogged to the dugout. Win or lose, he didn't care. This game couldn't get over fast enough.

# Chapter Seven

*Dios mío,* could she have screwed that up any worse?

Blurting out her questions. Interrogating the guy like he was on the witness stand. Only, they were in the freaking park. With a team of cops, including her overprotective brother, less than fifty feet away.

*¡Que estúpida!*

Lourdes gave herself a mental swat upside the head.

Things had been going good. Casual conversation. Him remembering her favorite candy. And then...poof! Old insecurities reared their evil heads, like ghosts slinking in to rattle her chains and leave her trembling on shaky emotional ground.

Making her run off at the mouth instead of ease into their muddy past.

Annoyed with her own impatience, Lourdes watched Eduardo slow his jog as he neared the dugout. Diego said something to him, but she couldn't read her brother's lips. Whatever it was, it drew Eduardo to a stop. He gave a brisk nod, then stepped inside the dugout without a backward glance at her.

*Ay,* Lourdes huffed out a breath in frustration. That was her baby brother for you. Always wanting to ride in and save the day.

Sure enough, Diego's gaze cut over to her again. She knew that expression well. It said, "You want me to take care of this?"

Like he could.

Still, this was a positive change for Diego. That expression used to mean more like, "I'm going to take care of this." As in, whether you want me to or not. Lourdes liked to think maturity and her making the decision to check herself into rehab had mellowed that machismo streak of his. But she knew it was really Lilí's doing.

The girl had Diego wrapped around her pinky. In the best of ways.

Saturday's wedding would be a happy celebration of their love. Lourdes refused to be the cause of any cloud of negativity over the fiesta.

So, despite the emotional tornado swirling inside her chest with gale force winds, Lourdes threw Diego what she hoped passed for an *it's all good* smile. Picking up her soda, she saluted him as she yelled, "Go use those big muscles of yours to hit me a home run, *hermanito!*"

He shook his head, one side of his mouth quirked in that self-deprecating grin he flashed every time she called him "little brother." The answering laugh that burst from her at his reaction smoothed the edges of her jangled nerves.

Pushing herself up from the cement picnic bench, Lourdes trudged over to the bleachers on the third-base side of the field. Sure, this was the opponent's territory and she probably could have bummed an extra folding picnic chair from another family member cheering for their team but sitting on the uncomfortable metal bleachers gave her some distance from Eduardo. Distance to gather her runaway mouth and thoughts.

The guys huddled up, hands sandwiched one on top of the other in the center. A deep voice counted, "One, two, three!" and together they all yelled, "Let's do this!" before racing to their positions.

She couldn't stop herself from tracking Eduardo's progress. Arms swinging at his sides with his elbows bent, glove already on his left hand, his long strides ate up the distance to right field. Once there, he bent at the waist to stretch his legs, then straightened and swiveled his upper body from side to side as if loosening his back. A ball cap shielded his eyes from the sun, leaving his handsome face in shadow. While their pitcher continued warming up, Eduardo sidestepped in the outfield, moving almost to center field. Lourdes frowned. She'd never played softball but had cheered for enough of Diego's games to know Eduardo was no longer standing in the right place.

When he took a few steps forward, craning his neck, she realized he was trying to get a glimpse around the dugout at the picnic table where they'd been sitting.

She knew the moment he spotted it, empty, because he straightened abruptly. His head moved slowly from the group of people gathered along their first-base side to the smattering of fans sitting in chairs behind home plate to the group gathered on and around the bleachers.

It didn't matter that he was too far away for her to see his eyes. The way her skin tingled, a delicious shiver chasing across her shoulder blades, told her who he sought in the crowd. Eduardo tipped his cap to her. His gaze glued in her direction, he moved back into position and punched his right fist into his mitt, ready to play.

Lourdes's gut clenched. Suddenly, she didn't want to know the answers to all those burning questions she'd thrown at him. What if he *had* married and divorced? Or worse, been widowed? She didn't want to think about him falling in love with another woman. *Making love* to another woman.

Jealousy tasted bitter on her tongue.

It was silly. Infantile, really, for her to think he'd never been with someone else in all these years. Then again, love made a girl think foolish thoughts. Do foolish things. She had the track record as proof.

Her multicolored hobo purse vibrated against her hip, the sound reverberating on the metal bench. Lourdes ducked her head and dug in her bag for her cell. A huff of relieved breath pushed through her lips when she saw her sponsor's name flashing on the tiny screen.

"*Hola,* Rita, how's it goin'?" Lourdes answered.

"Just dropped my daughter at rehearsal, figured I'd touch base. How's the ball game?"

Translation: How was Lourdes coping spending time with Eduardo.

A car honked on Rita's end of the line and she muttered a curse at some "idiot." She might as well have been talking to Lourdes over here making idiot moves herself.

"I'm hanging in there," Lourdes answered. "Almost bailed before the game even started, but currently enjoying the cozy sensation of metal bleachers cushioning my butt."

"Bailed? Why?"

Lourdes rolled her eyes at the question she should have expected.

Rita was like one of those gifs repeatedly flashing the same word. *Why? Why? Why?* The woman was always saying, "Figure out the emotion, the reasoning, behind your actions. Get to the root of the problem. If not, it'll keep popping up like damn weeds choking the garden you're trying to grow."

Lowering her voice to deter eavesdroppers, Lourdes filled Rita in on her impressive witness-questioning skills. The annoying "why" poking eventually got Lourdes to admit her insecurities had mushroomed in the aftermath of the desire that had whooshed like a wildfire scorching her entire body when Eduardo's thumb had brushed the corner of her mouth.

There was no holding back when it came to talking with her sponsor or her therapist. No matter how embarrassing or humbling. Not if Lourdes truly wanted to keep going in the right direction.

"You sticking around to wait or what?" Rita finally asked.

By now, Eduardo's team had trotted back to the dugout after getting the first three outs. He stood outside the cement structure, watching a teammate taking practice swings in the batter's warm-up circle. Leaning against the fence, hands raised head level and fingers crooked over the thin metal that made up the tiny squares of the chain-link fence, he struck a casual pose. Part of her longed to join him. Talk about their day, the weekend events ahead. The regular chit-chat people usually filled conversation with.

Only, they weren't usual people. If she wanted them to be, they had to clear the air.

"Yeah, I think so," Lourdes told Rita.

"Good for you. No need for me to reiterate the obvious, right?"

"Yeah, you're on my favorites call list if needed. *Gracias.*"

"Anytime." Rita ended the call mid-curse at another driver.

Lourdes dropped her phone back into her purse with a grin. Finger-combing her hair out of her face, she looked back over where Eduardo…had been standing.

Instead, he'd backed away from the fence and held his arms

open wide as a younger woman with long brown hair and a killer highlight job, wearing a burgundy sheath dress that hit her slim figure mid-thigh launched herself at him. Eduardo spun the woman in a circle. Her high-pitched laughter danced on the breeze at the same time her kicked-up heels stomped on Lourdes' heart.

¿*Qué carajo*?

Heat burned Lourdes's face as she watched Eduardo set the woman down, then bend to press a kiss on her cheek. The same *what the hell* question wailed an alarm in her head. The couple squeezed each other in a tight hug. Their joy at being in each other's arms was a glaring reminder that Lourdes had no clue about his private life. She'd purposely avoided any knowledge of it, afraid of how much the info would hurt.

Dumb move on her part.

Now she knew the truth. And it hurt worse than she'd expected.

She had absolutely no interest in meeting Eduardo's girlfriend. Nuh-uh. Not tonight. Probably never.

Sliding along the aluminum seat, Lourdes hopped off the end, then made a beeline for the shade trees over by the hardcourt. She'd text Diego later, give some excuse like a call from a friend in her group. Keep Eduardo out of it. If she mentioned him, her brother might be inclined to butt in, which could only lead to hard feelings stinking up the wedding's atmosphere on Saturday.

*Coño*, the wedding! Lourdes picked up her pace, anger fueling her steps. Damn indeed. Eduardo was sure to be there with this chick.

For a millisecond the idea of skipping the entire event flashed in Lourdes' brain. She quickly snuffed it out. No way she would do that to her brother.

Whatever. It didn't matter who Eduardo brought. The church and reception hall would be packed with *familia* and friends. Loads of people to help keep her from having to socialize with him. A crowd of revelers packing the dance floor, so she wouldn't have to watch him with another woman cradled in his arms.

*Ay*, despair burned her chest. Lourdes doggedly ignored it. Saturday wouldn't be easy, but she could do it. She'd focus on her brother and the new *familia* he assured her the two of them would be joining.

It was time she forget about the past and focus on her new future.

A sliver of sorrow pierced Lourdes's soul. One foot in front of the other, she forced herself to ignore the pain. It would eventually fade.

Wednesday, 9:27 PM

**Eduardo:** Hi, you didn't stick around for the game. Wanted to make sure you were okay.

**Lourdes:**


Thursday, 10:14 AM

**Eduardo:** Hola, I never heard back from you last night. Any chance you're free? Café con leche at the corner bodega?

**Lourdes:**


Thursday, 2:42 PM

**Eduardo:** Message received. You don't want to talk right now. I don't like it but will respect your desire.


Lourdes squeezed her cell phone in her hand, her right pointer finger poised to tap the screen and bring up the tiny keyboard. Her finger hovered in the air, the devil on one shoulder telling her to keep ghosting Eduardo. He deserved it. The angel on her other shoulder urged her to be a bigger person and acknowledge his attempts to reach her.

Ultimately, the need to look herself in the mirror at the end of the day, confident she had tried to do the right thing in any given situation, had her tapping out a response.

**Lourdes:** *I'm good. Busy. Appreciate you giving me the space I need. Cuídate.*

There. Hopefully he'd see her "take care" as a hint that the space she wanted from him had returned to the mile-wide kind. As in, infinite. As in, they weren't meant to be together.

So what if her entire body tensed with longing when she thought about him late at night, alone in her bed. Or that whenever she reached for a bag of Peanut M&Ms at the bodega, her heart ached when she remembered him teasing her at the park. She had shoved the candy back on the shelf.

Eduardo had moved on. Maybe he sought her friendship. And maybe one day she'd be strong enough to meet him halfway.

Today was not that day. This weekend was not the right time.

Friday and Saturday were all about Lilí and Diego's wedding. Lourdes would plaster on a happy face with her makeup and play the role of happy, devoted big sister. She had the devoted down, no problem. The happy? *Bueno,* she might have to work on that.

## Chapter Eight

Eduardo's gut clenched as Lourdes stepped through the archway connecting the church vestibule to the sanctuary. A dress the color of sand that'd been kissed by the ocean's waves clung to her amazing curves, pooling around her strappy heels and pink painted toes. Head held high, shoulders straight, she oozed confidence.

The late afternoon sun shot its rays through the church's stained glass windows, bathing Lourdes in a dusty glow. Like an angel once tempted by a darker side, but strong enough to conquer it, she stood at the end of the aisle. Proud and beautiful.

His desire for her, always on simmer, threatened to boil over.

Several people gathered around, and she dipped her head or brushed her cheek against another's in hello. At first glance, her sleeveless dress appeared modestly cut. High in front, the top edge hit above her collar bones, encircling her elegant neck and draping over her torso before cinching at her waist, then falling loosely to the floor. But when she turned to greet a dark-haired, athletic-looking guy in a navy suit, her bare back, smooth and tan, played peek-a-boo beneath her long, dark curls. The guy's thick arms snaked around her for a hug. His large hand like a paw splayed against the center of her back.

Eduardo's jaw tightened. He swallowed a curse, reminding himself he had no claim on her. Jealousy was an unwelcome guest here.

He'd been keeping an eye on the exact spot where Lourdes stood since he and his sister had gotten settled in their pew on the right side of the aisle, along with the rest of the groom's *familia* and friends.

In the ten minutes or so it had taken him and Frankie to sign some fancy book near the main door, greet a few neighbors, and exchange pats on the shoulders with a few cops from the precinct, he'd been busy scanning the premises. Peeking at a group gathered near the Blessed Virgin Mary statue by the choral risers to the right of the altar. Eyeballing another group huddled on the far left near the door leading to a smaller adoration chapel at the back of the main church. Desperate to catch a glimpse of the woman who'd been dodging his steps the past few days, while invading his dreams all night.

Now that she had arrived, the need to speak with her had his feet shuffling. Itching to go to her. Instead, he gripped the curved wooden backrest of the pew in front of him.

"Isn't that...?" Frankie elbowed him in the ribs as her whisper trailed off.

"Lourdes, yes," he answered.

Hand still plastered on her back, the handsy guy escorted Lourdes toward the front. She leaned into him, head thrown back in laughter at whatever he was telling her.

She looked relaxed. Happy. Completely different from the anguished, uncertainty she'd clearly felt around Eduardo at the ballpark.

Maybe it was selfish of him to want to make amends. Try to start over. Maybe what he wanted didn't, shouldn't matter and he needed to let her go, start fresh. Without him.

Pain seared his chest at the scramble of thoughts, robbing him of breath.

Halfway down the aisle, she reached them, her step faltering as their gazes met. She looked from him to his sister. A flash of remorse—no, determination—sparked in her dark eyes in the millisecond before she wrapped her right arm around her escort's waist and continued moving to her reserved spot in the first pew.

"Wow! She looks amazing." Frankie leaned to her left, watching Lourdes until she took her seat.

Amazing. Gorgeous. Hot.

Uninterested in giving him the time of day.

Eduardo's fingers curled in a fist on the pew backrest.

Frankie covered his hand with hers. The gentle pressure of her cool palm as she gave him a firm squeeze soothed his frustration.

"You gave up a lot to stay in Puerto Rico helping raise me. Taking care of Mami when Abuela physically couldn't anymore. You're a good man, *hermano*. She will see that. If not, Lourdes doesn't deserve you. *Me oyes?*"

"Yes, I hear you," he muttered.

A good man who'd made big mistakes. His only hope was that he hadn't waited too long to return home and win her back.

Eyes closed, he sent a desperate prayer to the heavens.

---

"So, you gonna tell me why I'm playing your buffer to the cop who's been glaring at me since you and I walked out of the church together?"

Lourdes sipped her Diet Coke with lime, eyeing Alfredo Fernández over the rim of her clear plastic cup. She'd met Lilí's cousin, a baseball coach in Puerto Rico, at last night's rehearsal dinner. Friendly guy, definitely easy on the eyes, with zero interest in scoring a wedding hook-up. That made him the perfect candidate to enlist in her plot to get through today's festivities with a smile on her face. No matter how fake it might be.

"Old boyfriend. A first love kinda thing." She figured she owed Freddie the truth, seeing as how he was her co-conspirator for the day. "He moved back to the neighborhood about two years ago after living on the Island for a while."

"Get out! What part?"

"Hey, you're not supposed to get chummy with him." She wagged a finger in the air. "Don't fail me now, Freddie. We have a mutual agreement to help each other combat the 'when are you getting married' harassment from the older generation at this fiesta."

Freddie grinned. The laugh lines around his dark eyes and generous mouth deepened in his tanned face. With his trim beard and curly black hair left long enough to brush the top of his suit jacket collar, he possessed a roguish sex appeal that turned the heads of every single woman lining up to catch Lilí's bouquet. You'd think the man's ego and machismo would blow the roof off the parish reception hall. And yet, he'd been nothing but polite and friendly since they'd wound up sitting next to each other at the Italian restaurant. They'd bonded over shared tiramisu.

From the reception line, through the buffet, and all the first dance hoopla they'd stuck together. Marveling at the absolute joy oozing off Diego and Lilí, while professing their non-interest in joining the married club.

Watching her brother and his new wife mingling with their guests, arms wrapped around each other's waists like they couldn't stand to be apart, a pang of envy knifed through Lourdes's heart. She had wanted that, once, with Eduardo. But it wasn't meant to be.

Disheartened, she stopped herself from sneaking a peek around the room. A glutton for punishment, desperate for a glimpse of Eduardo looking like some sexy GQ guy, all mind-blowingly hot in his suit. But if she looked, she'd also find his young, nubile date. No need for the visual reminder that Lourdes has misread his signals, projected her desire for more than friendship onto his actions.

"I got your back, girl," Freddie said. "Just wanting to know who might be trying to stab mine in the process." His playful wink took the edge off his observation.

Lourdes chuckled, thankful for the distraction Freddie provided.

Relief washed over her, diluting the anxiety she'd been fighting the past few days. When she wasn't stressing about Eduardo, she'd struggled with a crippling fear over how all these new people instantly part of her and Diego's once small *familia* circle would judge her and her past. Diego had promised she had no need to worry.

*Gracias a Dios* her brother had been right. Lilí's cousins—like Freddie and his two brothers—all the *tías, tíos,* and other extended *familia* from Puerto Rico and their Chicago suburb of Oakton had welcomed Lourdes with open arms. No questions. No side-eyed glances.

"You don't have to worry," she assured Freddie, stirring the thin black straw in her mock-tail. "Eduardo's actually one of the good guys. Though I can't speak for his new girlfriend. I don't recognize her from the neighborhood."

"Hmm." Freddie took a hurried sip of his beer bottle. "Looks like we might find out. He's bulldozing his way over as we speak."

Lourdes sucked in a shocked breath. Unfortunately, that made her swallow the small chunk of ice she'd been chewing, and she wound up in a freaking coughing fit. She smacked her chest with her palm as she plunked her drink on the round table.

"Come on," she wheezed. "Let's dance!"

She reached for Freddie's hand at the same time another one came into view. *¡Ay Dios mío!* Busted!

Slowly, her gaze trailed past long, tapered fingers to the strip of white dress shirt peeking out from under a coat's hem encircling a tanned wrist. Like a bystander gawking at an accident in motion, she couldn't stop herself from taking in the broad shoulders and muscular arms stretching the seams of Eduardo's cappuccino-colored suit jacket. His light brown eyes piercing with intensity, chiseled jaw tight, he stood beside her, arm held out to shake Freddie's hand.

"I don't believe we met. Eduardo Santana. And you are?" Despite the flash of his smile, tension vibrated off of Eduardo's tall frame like the DJ's speakers throbbing with a deep Reggaeton bass.

The same younger woman from the softball game hovered to his right. She smiled stiffly and stepped in to fill the gap between the two men. The peachy material of her halter-style cocktail dress complemented her ponytail, its highlighted dark and honey brown tresses draping down her collar bone and ending in a curl just below her chest. Gold hoops dangled from her ears, matching the gold strappy stiletto sandals she wore.

Damn, Lourdes bit back a grimace. She wanted to hate the chick, not admire her style.

"Actually, Freddie and I were about to dance," she lied, desperate to avoid a scene. "If you and your girlfriend will excuse us."

"My what?"

"Waaaiit a minute!"

Eduardo and his date spoke at the same time. She punctuated

her exclamation by bringing up her hand to shove a stop sign in the middle of their cozy little circle.

Lourdes had already grabbed Freddie's elbow, ready to drag him toward the dance floor. But her buffer didn't budge.

Instead, Freddie stared back and forth between Eduardo and the younger woman. A deep frown marred Freddie's previously friendly expression. He shook Eduardo's proffered hand, exchanging one assessing glance with another. "Alfredo Fernández. I'm thinking my cousin and her new husband knew what they were doing when they sent out their invites. So, we're not going to have any problems here, are we?"

"Uh, no! We are *not!*" The other woman stuck out her dainty hand, a clear indication that the men should release their death grips on each other. "I'm Franchesca Santana, Eduardo's—"

"Franche—Frankie?!?" Lourdes lurched forward in surprise. Unfortunately, her heel caught on her dress and she nearly tripped, bumping up against Freddie.

He clasped her forearm to steady her at the same time Eduardo's left arm reached around her waist, searing her lower back. His palm splayed along her hip like a brand scorching her soul.

"You okay?" Freddie asked.

Lourdes nodded dumbly, shocked that this…this woman was actually Eduardo's quiet, mousy little sister. The same one who'd devoured books and played with Barbie dolls back when she was eight or nine years old and they babysat her.

"You two know each other?" Freddie released her forearm as soon as Lourdes regained her footing.

"Yes, uh…" Lourdes nudged Eduardo's hand off of her hip with her elbow. *Por favor,* she had enough trouble thinking straight right now. Let's not add lustful urges exacerbated by his touch. "Frankie's, um, Eduardo's little sister."

"His *younger* sister," Frankie cut in. "Now in the process of studying for the bar."

"*¿No me digas?*" Lourdes gasped.

"Yes, I do say!" Frankie teased, her hazel eyes sparkling as Lourdes gaped at her. "Not so little anymore, right?"

Overjoyed at finally seeing her again after all these years, Lourdes wrapped Frankie in a big hug. "*Ay Dios mío,* girl, you are all grown up."

"That I am."

They rocked side to side for several heartfelt moments before Lourdes eventually stepped back, still thrown by this jaw-dropping revelation.

Frankie and Freddie introduced themselves while Lourdes scanned the reception hall, pretending an interest in the remnants of the wedding cake and buffet line along the right wall. Her gaze lingered on the white lilies wrapped with red ribbon adorning the tables along with the few remaining tulle memento pouches filled with five Jordan almonds, each symbolizing health, wealth, happiness, children, and long life for the new couple.

Basically, she was trying to avoid having to make eye contact with Eduardo. Talk about feeling foolish for the leap she'd made at the softball game. A leap that had her landing flat on her ass because of how wrong she'd been.

"So, about that dance you mentioned earlier..." Freddie crooked his elbow at Lourdes.

Eduardo edged closer, his jaw muscles tightening.

Undeterred, Freddie tilted his head toward the DJ in the far corner. "A quick spin around the dance floor before I wind up having to partner with all the *tías.*"

The same aunts scheming for him to end his bachelor ways. She and Freddie had agreed to be a lifeline for the other in the sea of matchmakers high on happy wedding vibes. And besides, she owed him. The guy had been ready to go toe to machismo toe with Eduardo if need be.

"Come on, I seem to recall someone else promising me at least one dance on the drive over." Threading her arm through her brother's, Frankie tugged Eduardo toward the area clear of round tables and chairs in one corner of the parish hall.

Lourdes watched them weave through the crowd, Eduardo tossing an annoyed glance over his shoulder back at her.

Freddie guided her in the same direction, pausing for the occasional kiss on the cheek or thump on the back from another wedding guest. As they stepped onto the dance floor the song changed to a sultry *bachata*. The updated, Spanish-English version of "Stand by Me" by Prince Royce was one of Lourdes's favorites.

Nearby, Rosa and her husband Jeremy were wrapped in a loving embrace, slowly swaying to the beat. Rosa gave her a loose-fingered wave. Lourdes returned it, fondly recalling the woman's warm thank you for the pictures Lourdes had shared, along with Rosa's heartfelt, "I'm excited to have another sister."

Lourdes stepped into Freddie's waiting arms, quelling her spurt of disappointment that he wasn't the person she really wanted to be with. Maybe not, but he was the right, the safest, partner for her.

"Here's the deal," Freddie said once they'd settled into the four-count *bachata* rhythm together. "Lilí's like my little sister. Now that you're *familia*, same goes for you."

Lourdes craned her neck to frown up at him. "Ooo-kay?"

"So, here's my brotherly advice."

"¡Ay no! Not you, too!"

A chuckle rumbled up from his chest.

She tucked her chin, shooting him a disbelieving glare.

Suddenly, Freddie's friendly smile melted away, leaving his mouth a grim, pinched line. Disconcerted by his unexpected mood change, Lourdes paused.

His feet and hips continued moving to the music, but a soulful sadness filled Freddie's dark brown eyes. That kindred sadness spoke to her.

"Fine. I'll give you one pass," she told him, falling back into step. "Lay these pearls of wisdom on me."

"Maybe I don't know your history, but the vibe I'm getting from your ex...it's one of a man who's desperate to fix whatever went wrong. A man who's seen the error of his ways."

Lourdes huffed out a breath. "You got all that from a handshake?"

Freddie stopped dancing. He gazed down at her, serious and intent. "I've known since I walked you down the aisle at the church and you nearly freeze-framed in front of him who you were avoiding. Believe me, I've kept my eye on him. Watching him watching you. I've seen that look before in my own mirror. I know how he feels. And, damn, if I had the chance to make things right with the love of my life, you better believe I'd do whatever it took."

Around them, couples of all ages moved to the love song's beat. In her periphery she caught Diego and Lilí, a blur of white and black from her mermaid wedding gown and his tux, foreheads pressed together as they danced.

An older woman smiled at Lourdes, motioning for her and Freddie to join in again. His stark, pain-filled eyes rooted Lourdes's feet to her spot.

"If you love this guy," Freddie continued. "If there's a chance you think he's the one, don't walk away. I promise, it'll be something you will always regret."

# Chapter Nine

The second Lourdes stopped dancing, Eduardo went on alert. He couldn't hear what Lili's cousin was saying, but Lourdes's eyes welled with tears. Her chin trembled. A little line marred the skin between her brows at her frown.

Freddie ducked his head closer as if emphasizing whatever point he made. Even though Lourdes nodded, her expression remained distraught. No way could Eduardo ignore his need to check on her.

"I'm sorry, Frankie. I've gotta go." He stepped away from his sister, shooting her an apologetic glance.

"Eduardo, what are you...?"

The rest of her question was swallowed up by the crush of guests crowding the floor as the music bled from the *bachata* into a popular hip-shaking salsa. By the time Eduardo reached Freddie, Lourdes was already gone.

A flash of dark sand material and her long, brown curls hugging the far wall near the buffet table drew his attention. He tracked her movements, figuring she was headed toward the patio door up head.

Determined to follow, he sidestepped Freddie, only to be stopped with a firm hand on his chest.

"What the hell, man?" Eduardo grumbled. He glared and knocked Freddie's hand away.

A group of young teens huddled together nearby turned at Eduardo's gruff complaint. Recognizing a few of them from the youth center in Humboldt Park, he tipped his head in greeting.

"Hey, if you go storming after her, machismo flag flying, you're not doing yourself any favors. Just sayin.'" Freddie's easy-going shrug, palms raised like a perp surrendering, made Eduardo pause.

Reining in his temper, he watched Lourdes slip through the door. The desperation he'd barely held in check the past few days clawed its way up his throat.

"I'm not stopping you. But, *cuidado con ella*. Clear?" Eddie backpedaled off the dance floor, an eyebrow arched to punctuate his warning. *Be careful with her, or answer to him.*

Eduardo respected the guy for protecting Lourdes. It said a lot about Lilí's cousin.

Right now, though, he had absolutely zero interest in convincing Freddie of his intent. Finding Lourdes, offering her a shoulder to lean on—whatever she needed—that's all he wanted.

After a chin jut in response, Eduardo pushed past Freddie and strode toward the patio door.

The reception music swelled as the patio door opened, and Lourdes shrank behind the oak tree's large trunk. If luck was on her side, the party-goer only wanted to cool down with the evening breeze for a few seconds, then hurry back inside to rejoin the fun.

The rough bark poked at her back as she heaved a tired sigh. Luck and fun. Seems like she'd been missing out on both lately. If only—

"Lourdes?"

She started at Eduardo's voice.

The click of his dress shoes on the cement drew closer. Her breath caught in her chest, and she squeezed her eyes shut against a flood of emotions. Hope. Fear. Need. They all clashed like warriors, with her heart as their battling ground.

"Hey, *estás bien?*"

The gentle question, roughened by the husky timbre of his voice, had her peeking up to find him a few feet away. Hands in his pants pocket, he stood on the patio edge, his handsome face creased with worry.

"Yeah, I'm fine," she lied. "Just getting a little fresh air."

He nodded slowly, his mouth curving in a frown as he gazed

out at the empty school playground nearby.

"Care for some company?"

*Ay*, yes. And no.

Mostly yes.

His gaze cut back to her when she didn't answer. The heartfelt entreaty in his light brown eyes gutted her. No way she could give him the brush off. Not when she'd be denying herself as much as him. Freddie's advice about regret and love pushed her to not take the easy, and potentially wrong, way out.

"Sure," she murmured. "I don't mind."

Eduardo's broad shoulders visibly relaxed underneath his cappuccino-colored suit coat.

Soft music from the reception serenaded them, another sultry *bachata* meant for lovers. Overhead, the evening breeze rustled the old oak's leaves. Lourdes poked her toe at the grass and dirt broken up by the thick tree roots, uncertain and nervous.

After a while, Eduardo shuffled his feet, then took a step closer. He cleared his throat. "I'd like to, uh, tell you what I would have the other night after the game."

The night she'd peppered him with questions and then mistakenly assumed Frankie was his girlfriend. *¡Que idiota!*

"You don't owe me any explanations. Or answers."

"Yes, I do. You should know…" His words trailed off, then he nodded as if coming to a decision. "Look, I know we were still kids when I moved. But what we had didn't feel like kid stuff. Not to me. Not back then, or now. I swear, I planned on graduating and coming back to you. Only, every time I mentioned it, Abuela reminded me how much my parents relied on me at home. With Frankie, and my mom."

He speared a hand through his hair, then gripped the back of his neck. "Especially with Papi working two jobs to pay the medical bills. As Mami's ALS worsened, caring for her became too physically demanding for Abuela. That fell on me."

Lourdes's heart ached thinking of his mom, a quiet, devout woman who'd been so kind to her when she and Eduardo had dated. Watching her slowly getting worse had to have been so damn difficult for her *familia*.

"Breaking up so you could move on seemed like the fair decision. But you have to know... *Dios mío,* it practically killed me, Lourdes. I checked out after that. Kind of disconnected, emotionally, for a while. Going through the motions. School, babysitting, caring for my mom. By the time she was gone, and Frankie started high school, I tried to get in touch with you. But you weren't—"

"But I wasn't making it easy for most of the people I loved to find me," she finished. *Dios,* how their lives had twisted and turned based on their decisions and those of others. "I'm so sorry."

"You don't have anything to be sorry about. Not where I'm concerned. I'm the one who needs your forgiveness."

Anguish tightened his features and he reached out to her.

The need to soothe his worries overwhelmed her and she met him halfway, linking their fingers together. They stood like that for several heart-pounding seconds. Arms outstretched, far too much distance between them.

Lourdes held her breath, desperate for them to get this right. Afraid they may not be able to.

Finally, Eduardo stepped onto the grass, edging his way toward her. "Yes, I have dated. I was even engaged once."

Her fingers flexed instinctively around his. As if resisting the idea of someone else having the right to do so.

"But we never even set a date," he rushed on, moving close enough to cup her jaw with his left hand.

She closed her eyes, concentrating on the warmth of his palm, the soft brush of his thumb along her cheek. Not the sharp pain of regret at the thought of him marrying another woman.

"I couldn't do it," he admitted, his voice gruff. "Eventually, she realized the truth. I couldn't commit. Not in the way she deserved. Someone else already owned my heart."

Her heart skipped. Hopeful. Scared she might be wrong.

"*You* have always owned my, Lourdes," Eduardo murmured. "You always will."

Relief filled her at his words, seeping into the darkest corners of her soul, and Lourdes rose on her toes to press her lips against his. Her arms wrapped around his waist as she pressed herself against him. Eduardo's tongue brushed against her lips, teasing them open. She obliged, moaning with pleasure.

Their kiss deepened. He tasted like coffee and chocolate and forever all rolled into one delicious dessert. Years of unmet need and desire clamored to the surface. She wanted more. Craved more.

As if he sensed the desire threatening to blaze out of control inside her, Eduardo broke their kiss. He cradled her face with both hands, dropping delicious little kisses on the corner of her mouth. Her cheek. Her temple. Her forehead. Then he slid his arms around her shoulders, engulfing her in his embrace.

She squeezed her arms around his waist, anchoring herself to him. Breathed in the woodsy, spicy scent that was his and his alone. The smell of home. Of love.

"I know you're working hard to make a good life for yourself. And you're doing incredible, *querida*."

Her heart swelled with love at his endearment. *Beloved*. Such an old-fashioned word. She adored him for it.

Lourdes arched back in his arms to smile up at him. "I am."

He chuckled. "Such humility."

"*Bueno*, you said it. I'm simply agreeing with you."

His arms tightened around her, and he ducked down to steal a quick kiss that ended far too soon.

"You know what's good about starting over?" she asked. "Anyone can do it. And even when it's hard, if you have the right people around you. With you. Loving you. It's so much better."

Eduardo pressed his forehead to hers. He gazed into her eyes, his expression serious. "I'm not going anywhere. Not again. Not without you. I'm yours, *siempre*."

"Always. I like the way that sounds."

She smiled, her eyes drifting closed as Eduardo sealed their promise with another heart-stopping kiss.

# About Priscilla Oliveras

Priscilla Oliveras is a USA Today bestselling author and 2018 RWA® RITA® double finalist who writes contemporary romance with a Latinx flavor. Her novels have earned praise in the *Washington Post, New York Times, Entertainment Weekly, Redbook,* and *Publishers Weekly,* amongst others.

A devotee of the romance genre, she's also a sports fan, beach lover, Zumba aficionado, and hammock nap connoisseur. Follow her antics and learn more about her books at https://prisoliveras.com/books/.

# Home Sweet Home

## by Hope Ramsay

# Chapter One

Isa Alvarez pushed through Atwood Construction's glass doors, her high heels hammering on the tile floor. Papi had asked her to come here today.

To forgive.

She wasn't sure she could fulfill that promise. What she really wanted was to spit in Patrick Atwood's eye. So she'd dressed to the nines for this meeting in her charcoal-gray Lafayette 148 New York spandex dress—the one that showed off her full figure. She'd paired the dress with the gently used Christian Louboutin shoes she'd found online.

She felt like a million bucks. Which was the point. She needed the expensive clothes like she needed armor. So when Patrick Atwood looked at her, he wouldn't see the same little Latina girl he'd bullied all those years ago. Instead, he'd recognize that she had become powerful and rich in her own right.

And if she signed the contract for the Food Network show, she'd most certainly exceed Mr. Atwood's wealth. And that made her feel good in a very bad way. And not at all in the spirit of forgiveness.

She stopped at the receptionist desk, which was manned by a twentysomething woman with a fresh face and blond hair.

"Can I help you?" the young woman asked.

"I'm here to see Mr. Atwood," Isa said.

"Did you have an appointment?"

"No." Isa knew better than to ask for an appointment. The old man would have said no. This was, strictly speaking, a forgiveness ambush. One she might have happily forgone except for the deathbed promise she'd made to her father, who'd died a week ago. Papi wanted her to "find closure" on the worst part of her personal history.

"Well, I'm sorry, but you really need—"

"Just tell him that Isabella Alvarez is here to see him," Isa interrupted.

The woman blinked a few times. "Oh my God, you're the cocktail lady, aren't you? I saw something on CNBC about your business. I'm a business major at Virginia Tech, and I'm always so impressed when I hear about local women launching successful enterprises. I'm just interning here for the summer." The young woman made it sound like interning at Atwood Construction was a huge disappointment.

Isa gave the woman a big smile. "I guess we have that in common, because I'm a Hokie too."

The woman made the ridiculous gobble sound that all Virginia Tech students learned on day one at the institution. It always struck Isa as idiotic that a university with the reputation of Virginia Tech would choose a turkey as its mascot.

"So," Isa said, "as one Hokie to another, can you please let Mr. Atwood know that I'm here and would like to speak with him?"

"Well, I guess so. But I'm not supposed to—"

"I know him. I grew up here in Sweet Home. My father was his construction foreman for many years. Unfortunately, Papi recently passed away."

"Oh. I'm so sorry for your loss." The young woman picked up the phone and hesitated for a moment before she buzzed the inner office. "Mr. Atwood, Isabella Alvarez is out here. She'd like to have a word with—"

The receptionist pulled the handset away from her ear as Mr. Atwood's voice sounded through the small speaker. "I guess he really does know you, huh?" the young woman said as she put the handset back to her ear.

Just then the door to the inner office opened, and Collin Atwood stepped out into the reception area.

Collin, not Patrick.

Isa's stomach dropped down to her knees, and goose bumps raced over her skin. Was she hot or cold? Damn. Collin hadn't changed much since that day eighteen years ago when they'd run off to the Richmond Courthouse together. Oh, he'd aged, of course, but the years had been kind to him. He seemed taller and more masculine than he'd been before.

She lost her breath, and her usually reliable confidence eroded. What would he think about the extra padding around her hips and waist? She might be wearing thousands of dollars in designer clothes, but she suddenly felt fat and frumpy. Like an impostor.

"Isa," he said on a long exhalation, his hazel-eyed stare running up from her shoes to her face and back down, stopping for a long moment on her chest. Well, that hadn't changed, had it? Collin had always loved her breasts.

And there was so much more of them to love these days.

"I, uh, was looking for your father."

He blinked a moment. "He's not here."

"Oh. Well, I'll come back again some—"

"He no longer runs the business," Collin said. "He's living at the Shady Brook home these days."

"Oh... Really?" Wow!

Isa was having a hard time wrapping her brain around the idea that Mr. Atwood had grown old enough to live in one of those assisted-living places. Also, the idea of Collin running the family business was equally absurd. Back when they'd been teenagers, Collin had never wanted any part of his father's life. He'd been adamant about that. And besides, he'd been on track to play professional baseball.

The last time she'd seen him had been the day the San Francisco Giants had taken him in the first round of the Major League Baseball draft. He'd been nationally touted as a top pitching prospect, but he'd never made it to the majors. What had happened to derail his dreams? She didn't know. She'd walked away and kept her promise to his father.

"Why are you here?" he asked.

Well damn. She couldn't exactly tell him that she wanted to forgive his father for what he'd done all those years ago. He had no knowledge of what his father had done to her. And she had every reason to keep that a secret even though Papi had died.

And besides, she didn't want to reconnect with Collin... much.

"I wanted to speak with your father," she said, sticking with the truth but not providing any motive.

"What? So you could thank him for handing you a bribe all those years ago?"

A bribe? Had it been a bribe? Well, maybe from Collin's perspective. Maybe she'd allowed Collin to believe that. But she sure didn't like that word, and she sure didn't like the way the receptionist was watching this conversation like an avid tennis fan, glancing back and forth as each of them spoke.

"I'm sorry," she said and turned her back on him. It was easier to breathe when she didn't have to look at his handsome face.

"Yeah, well, I didn't accept your apology back then, and I still don't," he said to her back.

She stopped and looked over her shoulder. "I guess I don't blame you," she said in a low voice, which trembled despite her efforts to keep her emotions in check. Funny how she could understand his bitterness now but had been blind to it all those years ago. Back then so much had been on the line. Back then she'd been powerless.

But now...

Things had changed, but they'd also stayed the same. There was still someone depending on her secrecy, and Collin still believed the lie she'd told all those years ago.

There was no reason to tell the truth now. Water under the bridge and all that. So she strode out of the office on her expensive shoes and didn't look back.

Isabella Alvarez—Isa—was as beautiful as she'd ever been. Maybe more so now that she was older and rounder. One look at those dark Spanish eyes and that olive-colored skin and it was like taking a punch to the diaphragm. Collin momentarily lost the ability to breathe, while a sudden acute pain radiated from the center of his chest.

But he'd shown nothing. He'd stood his ground. He'd told her to leave. And she'd gone, her backside swaying as she strutted through the door on those high heels. He didn't know much about women's apparel, but those shoes had red soles, and he remembered Jessica telling him that red-soled shoes could cost six or seven hundred dollars a pair. Who spent that much money on shoes?

Isa apparently. She'd come a long way from the girl he'd once known. The one who'd been afraid to dream big.

But maybe she'd fooled him all those years ago. Because she'd taken Daddy's bribe and walked away from Collin. And he hated her for it. Her success had been built on the rubble of his shattered heart.

He turned his gaze on Madison Thatcher, the summer intern from Tech. She sat wide-eyed at the desk she'd been using while she reviewed the company's profit-loss statements for the past several years.

"What are you staring at?" he asked, aware even in the moment that he was channeling his father's anger. He hated that, but it was too late. The words had been spoken and the young woman had jumped in her seat.

"Nothing," Madison said and turned back to the work he'd given her this morning.

He turned on his heel and stalked back into the office that had once been his father's domain. A big pile of paperwork sat on the desk — details of his father's business for the past five years — years during which Daddy's mind had been slowly deteriorating. Just looking at the mess made Collin feel guilty. If he'd been present in Daddy's life, things would not have slipped so badly.

In fact, up until a year ago, Daddy's construction foreman, Isabella's father, Julio, had been effectively running the business. But when Julio got sick and retired, everything fell to crap. Daddy hired out subcontractors who bled him blind and did shoddy work.

And no one had clued Collin in because he'd been too deep in his own funk, working his way through Jessica's untimely and unexpected death. Even so, Collin had been across the country, living in California. How much could he have done to stop the slide?

Cousin Alice's call six months ago had changed all that. A

county sheriff's deputy had found Daddy sitting in his car by the side of the road, confused about how to get home. According to passersby, Daddy had been sitting there for more than half a day. And he'd only been a mile and a half from home.

Collin had come when Alice called, and he'd discovered his father losing his mind and the once-successful Atwood Construction tottering on the brink. In an effort to start his life over by going back to the beginning, Collin had decided not to haul Daddy back to San Francisco. Instead, he'd put Daddy in a memory-care facility right here in the county and he'd come home for good.

In truth there hadn't been much holding him in California. Just a lot of bittersweet memories of a life that hadn't gone the way he'd planned.

So he'd sold his small construction company and the house Jessica had chosen just six months before she'd been diagnosed with stage-four ovarian cancer. He'd packed his SUV with the essentials and sold the rest. He and Liam had driven across the country, stopping at a few landmarks on the way. They'd settled down in Momma and Daddy's house in Sweet Home, Virginia. And now his eight-year-old son was a rising third-grader at the same school Collin had gone to as a boy.

Come to think of it, Isa had gone to that school too. And she'd been in his third-grade class.

He stared vacantly at the big pile of invoices he'd been going through this morning. His heart wasn't in the work. His heart wasn't in much these days. Jessica had passed away three years ago, and he still loved her and missed her. She'd been his confidant, his cheerleader, and the mother of his son.

So feeling desire for anyone but Jessica was a betrayal. And yet, inside the hard shell of his hurt, a small seed of love still existed for the Isa of his faulty memories. Even after all these years and a successful-but-short-lived marriage, he'd been unable to pulverize his memories of Isabella Alvarez into oblivion.

But he needed to pulverize something. So he turned and put his fist through the Sheetrock wall in his father's office. It didn't make him feel any better.

In fact, he bruised his knuckles.

## Chapter Two

The parking lot at Shady Brook Assisted Living Center had not one iota of shade. In fact, the grounds of the brand-new facility didn't have a single mature tree and looked to Isa as if it had been built in the past two or three years on land that had once been a farm.

Its whitewashed walls and Greek Revival colonnade hearkened back to Virginia's past. The main section of the building bore a striking resemblance to Mount Vernon, George Washington's home, which stood an hour north of Sweet Home on the banks of the Potomac.

A trickle of sweat dripped down Isa's back as she strode up the serpentine footpath to the facility's front door. It was one of those hot, humid July days, and her dress-for-success outfit wasn't exactly breathable. So much for her plans to face her nemesis looking like she owned the world. She'd be a melted mess by the time she came face to face with Mr. Atwood.

She pushed through the door, a rush of arctic air turning her sweat-damp dress cold and clammy. Boy, they had turned up the AC, hadn't they? Sudden gooseflesh rippled over her skin.

She squared her shoulders and marched to the high reception desk where a woman in her late fifties sat reading a paperback. The gatekeeper looked up from the page, and her eyes went wide with *the look*. That look of recognition still surprised Isa. Her path to success had been riddled with potholes and wrong turns. But when someone recognized her it was an affirmation that hard work and focus paid off, even if it was also vaguely discomforting.

She didn't like being recognized. And her small bit of fame had already caused her a lot of problems with Jason, her ex-boyfriend.

Who had not been good for her ego. And probably still wasn't.

"Oh, my God," the woman said. "You're the cocktail woman. The one on the early evening news every week."

Isa forced a smile. "I am," she said.

"Oh, my word. My husband and I are huge fans of the cucumber martini garnished with raspberries. It's our favorite summertime cocktail. We have your book."

"Thanks for buying it. And the cucumber martini is one of my favorites too."

"What are you doing here?"

"Well, actually, I was wondering if I could see Mr. Patrick Atwood."

"Do you know him?"

"I do. I grew up here in Sweet Home."

"Really? I'll have to tell my husband. Imagine that."

Isa smiled. "As a matter of fact, my father used to work for Mr. Atwood. Unfortunately, Papi passed away a few days ago, but he asked me to visit Mr. Atwood. It was something of a deathbed request."

"Oh well, of course." The woman turned toward her computer. "He's in room 38B. You need to take the elevator to the third floor. He'll probably be out in the lounge watching television."

"Thank you."

"You're welcome. Honestly, I can't believe it. Someone famous grew up in Sweet Home. It's kind of hard to process, you know? Nothing ever happens in this little town."

Isa walked to the elevator and pressed the button, all the while thinking about the woman's comment. The receptionist was wrong. Eighteen years ago, the regional newspapers — including the *Washington Post* — had been all over the news that Collin Atwood had been drafted by the San Francisco Giants.

Back then, Isa had been a nobody living on the wrong side of town. Collin had been a star.

The elevator took her to the third floor and opened its doors onto the television lounge — a large area with tables and chairs and a collection of ancient people, some of them in wheelchairs and some of them so far gone that they'd been wheeled out of their room in their beds.

Damn. This wasn't an assisted-living place. This was a nursing home. A memory-care place where they looked after Alzheimer's patients.

She stood there for the longest moment, her gaze shifting from one resident to the next until she saw Mr. Atwood. He wasn't in a wheelchair or a bed, thank goodness. He sat on a couch in front of the large flat-screen television, which was tuned to CNN.

He'd aged. A lot. He was almost bald, and the years had diminished him. He didn't look formidable sitting there in a blue-and-white golf shirt, baggy khakis, and a pair of plain white Nikes.

Half a lifetime ago, this man had terrified her. He'd held Papi's future in his hands. And he'd been prepared to crush her family to get what he wanted.

She had hated him for a long, long time. But when she'd confessed her big secret, when she'd told Papi what Mr. Atwood had done to her all those years ago, her father had made it his last, dying wish that she seek the man out and forgive him.

Until this moment, forgiving Mr. Atwood had seemed like an impossible task. Had Papi known Mr. Atwood was losing his mind? Had Papi realized that the only emotion she'd feel upon seeing him was sadness?

Maybe so.

She hauled in a gigantic breath and blew it out before she crossed the room to stand in front of him, blocking his view of the television. He didn't complain. He might be staring in the direction of the TV, but he sure hadn't been watching. His gaze was vacant and unfocused.

"Mr. Atwood," she said.

He blinked a moment and looked up at her. "Emily?" he asked, his sparse white eyebrows arching and a spark coming to his eyes.

Emily? Wasn't that Collin's mother's name? Damn.

"No, I'm not Emily," she said. "It's Isabella Alvarez. You remember me, don't you?"

He blinked a few more times. "Alvarez. Julio Alvarez's girl?" He frowned.

"Yes. I'm Julio's daughter. And I came here to tell you—"

He pointed his finger at her. "You're the one. You're the one," he said, standing up. He still towered over her even with his crooked stance and her three-inch heels. For a moment, she reconnected with the terror this man had once engendered in her.

She waited for him to say something crude or racist or ugly. But he just stood there pointing his finger, his hand trembling slightly.

She drew in a deep breath. "I came to tell you that I forgive—"

"You're the one who ruined him," Mr. Atwood interrupted, taking a menacing step forward. "He would have made it to the majors except he was brokenhearted about you."

What? She'd walked away from Collin because Mr. Atwood had threatened her family. Because Mr. Atwood had been convinced that she was the distraction that would cost his son a place in the major leagues. And now he was blaming her for doing what he'd forced her to do?

All her plans to grant Papi's dying wish disappeared. How could she forgive this man, even if his actions had put her on a trajectory for success? And more important, how could she forgive him for the way he'd exploited her father over the years? Without Papi, Mr. Atwood would never have been the success he'd become.

She didn't have to stand there and take the blame for something that wasn't her fault.

"I didn't ruin Collin," she said, forcing herself not to step back. "I did exactly what you told me to do. I walked away so he could focus on his career. If he was ruined, you're the one responsible. And for the record—"

"What the hell are you doing here?" The voice came from the general direction of the elevator, and Isa recognized it. She looked away from Mr. Atwood to find Collin standing there with his hands on his hips and an expression on his face that mirrored his father's. Behind him, a large male nurse in green scrubs was advancing on her. She was about to be tossed out on her butt.

Mr. Atwood turned around. "Collin? Is that you? Have you come to visit all the way from San Francisco? Emily will be so happy to see you."

Collin's expression sagged, and the momentary resemblance

between father and son disappeared. There was so much pain in Collin's eyes.

There would be no closure. No forgiveness. What had happened in the past had happened, and there was nothing she could do about it. She only had the future to work with.

"I'm sorry," she said, meeting Collin's gaze.

"Why are you here?"

She didn't answer him. She merely shook her head, turned on her stiletto heel, and walked to the elevator with as much dignity and grace as she could muster.

---

Isa peeled out of Shady Brook Assisted Living's parking lot and headed down Route 3 to the northeast side of town, a slow trickle of tears streaming down her cheeks.

Dammit all. She pounded on the steering wheel in a vain attempt to rid herself of her frustration. Why was she crying? Why was she so angry?

Why should she be so surprised that she couldn't accomplish what Papi had asked? It had been a ridiculous thing for her father to ask in the first place.

Which kind of begged the question why he'd asked her to do it. If anyone had known Patrick Atwood, Papi had.

"Well, whatever you had up your sleeve, it didn't work, Papi," she said to no one at all—or maybe the ghost of the father who might be riding shotgun right now. She glanced at the empty passenger's seat. She didn't believe in ghosts. Much.

Her tears redoubled. She would miss Papi with the same intensity as she'd missed Mami all these years. And she'd missed Mami with all her being. Not a day went by that she didn't think of her mother. And when she cooked, it was almost as if Mami was there beside her.

Like Papi now. Riding in the car like he used to do in the last year of his life, when he'd been battling bladder cancer and she'd driven him to radiation treatments.

"I should go home and make some empanadas," she said out loud. She'd make the traditional kind with ground pork and potatoes.

She managed a smile through her tears. Papi used to shake his head when she started experimenting with empanada fillings. He would taste test her inventions with broccoli and goat cheese, shake his head, and say, "*No tan buenas como las empanadas que tu abuela solía hacer.*"

And maybe he'd been right. Her grandmother's traditional empanadas were the best. She remembered sitting in Abuelita's kitchen in Bogota, helping Mami and her sisters fill the savory pastries. Mami and Isa went to Bogota every summer so Isa could improve her Spanish. Papi stayed in the US because he had to work and also because he didn't have his papers. Mami's family had benefited from the Reagan Administration amnesty program, which had allowed Mami to become a naturalized US citizen. Isa had been born in the United States.

But not Papi.

She drew in a deep breath remembering the family around Abuelita's kitchen table. It was a fact. Empanadas made together as a family with the traditional ingredients were comfort food in so many ways. She needed comfort right now.

So she took a detour right into the grocery store—the same one Mami had shopped at for years and years. She bought everything she would need to do some serious cooking. Not just for empanadas but other dishes as well. She suddenly wanted to make a whole dinner of traditional Colombian food. If only that could bring her parents back.

How could a grown woman feel like an orphan? But she did, even though she still had family nearby. It wasn't quite the same with her parents gone.

By the time she pulled to the curb beside the house where she'd grown up, her tears had dried and her mind had focused on the cooking to come. The house stood on Laurel Street beside dozens of similar houses—one-story structures with front porches. Mami used to sit on her porch and visit with the neighbors. But that had been long ago.

The porch had been abandoned when Mami died. And now it had become a rickety thing, lopsided and sagging, a star jasmine vine that had gone untended for too many years crawling over a trellis and up over the eaves. The vine's scent was heavenly, but the plant needed to be removed or significantly pruned. The disrepair and neglect were a testament to Papi's lack of interest after Mami died and his failing health over the past few years.

She stood in the weedy yard, staring at the dingy white paint, the old windows that leaked cold air in the winter, the window air-conditioning unit in Mami and Papi's bedroom. This house, which her parents had worked so hard to buy, was hers now.

And they would have told her it was their legacy to their only child. But they had given her much more than this. The house was just a thing. She would cherish her memories of the parents who put family above everything else.

And hadn't she done the same thing?

"Isa, why are you standing in the front yard?" Aunt Gabriela opened the front door and put her fists on her hips. Gabriela Rojas, Papi's younger sister, had gray hair, cut short, and sharp brown eyes behind her bifocals. She wore a pair of mom jeans and a sleeveless cotton T-shirt in a bright floral print. Gabriela always wore colors. She was like a rainbow when she walked into any room.

"I was looking at the house," Isa said. Something would have to be done about it. Gabriela had been living there for almost fifteen years, looking after Papi. A new widow fifteen years ago, Gabriela had moved in shortly after Mami died. Her devotion to her brother had freed Isa to pursue her dreams.

Gabriela deserved a better place to live. Maybe now, Isa could get the renovations done and give her aunt the nice home she richly deserved. Isa had been trying to fix up the house since her book on mixology made the *New York Times* bestseller list. That was five years ago. But Papi was a proud man.

"What about the house?" Gabriela asked.

"It needs a renovation," Isa said, continuing her journey from the curb to the front door, lugging several plastic grocery bags in each fist.

"You didn't have to go food shopping. I have plenty to—"

"I didn't shop for you. I went to the grocery store for me," Isa said with a smile. "I have everything we need to make empanadas the way Papi liked them. And *sancocho de carne*," she added, using the Spanish name for the Colombian beef stew that had always been Papi's favorite.

"I should have known," Gabriela said, stepping aside as Isa sailed through the front door and into the kitchen where Mami had taught her how to cook. This kitchen wasn't at all like the one in her condo in Baltimore, which was ginormous and carefully laid out for efficiency. This kitchen was tiny, with limited counter space, and about as inefficient as a kitchen could be. But it had been Mami's, and cooking here still brought unbridled joy to Isa's heart.

She'd learned everything about the power of food in this kitchen and the *cocina* of her Abuelita in Bogota.

"When the going gets tough you head for the kitchen," Gabriela said, taking one of the bags from Isa's hands and starting to unpack ingredients. "Based on the quantity of food you have just purchased, your meeting with Mr. Atwood did not go so well."

Isa dropped her own bags onto the small, Formica-topped kitchen table. "My meeting with Mr. Patrick Atwood went nowhere at all. I saw him, but I didn't really converse with him. He's at Shady Brook Assistant Living Center in the memory-care unit. He didn't recognize me at first. If only I could say the same thing about his son." She started hauling groceries out of the bags.

"Collin is here? In Sweet Home? Why did I not know this?"

Something in Gabriela's denial triggered Isa's internal BS detector. She hesitated, a plastic bag of masarepa in her hand, and gave her aunt a raised eyebrow. Gabriela shrugged, her round grandmotherly cheeks growing a little red.

"What are you up to?" Isa asked.

"So you saw him? Collin?" Gabriela asked, turning an avid gaze on Isa.

"I did see him. At Atwood Construction and then later at the nursing home. He was not happy to see me either time. And you know what? I can't even blame him for that."

"Yes, you can."

Isa slammed the bag of corn meal down on the table. "No, I can't." She didn't explain. Gabriela had no idea what had happened eighteen years ago. She didn't know that Isa and Collin had gotten married in Richmond. And she didn't know anything about what Mr. Atwood did in response to that monumental act of disobedience.

Isa wasn't going to tell her aunt because Gabriela was in the same situation as Papi had been. She didn't have papers.

"*Chica,* everyone knows that boy missed out on a good thing when he went off to California without a backward glance."

"He went because I told him to go, Gabriela."

"You did not."

"I did."

Gabriela cocked her head. "That is not what your mother told me. She said the boy left you."

"Well, he left, and I went to college and that's the end of that. And I think it was Mami who used to say that we should leave the past in the past. And look to the future."

"Yes, she used to say that."

"So, speaking of the future, I want you to know that you don't have to worry about anything anymore. I'm going to take care of you the way you took care of Papi. First, I'm going to feed you. And then, tomorrow, I'm going to find a contractor, and we're going to fix up this house for you. And I'm going to stay here for a while, you know. So you won't be alone. I'll stay at least until Carolina's wedding. And if you need to, you can come live with me in Baltimore or LA while the house is renovated."

Gabriela came into Isa's arms. "You are a good girl."

After a long warm hug, Gabriela pushed away, giving Isa a watery smile. "You know you have to hire Atwood Construction for this renovation."

"Gabriela, what are you up to? Atwood Construction is the last company I would use after—"

"I'm not up to a thing," Gabriela said. "I'm just pointing out that your father all but ran that company for many years, and many of his friends work there. He hired a lot of the people down there, you know. And from what I hear, the company isn't doing so well as it used to when Julio was in charge. If you're going to pay for someone to fix up this house, then you need to use your father's friends. To be honest, they could use the work."

Isa squinted at her aunt. Clearly Gabriela knew a lot more about what was happening at Atwood Construction than she'd let on earlier. She knew Collin was back in town and running his father's company. Did she think love could blossom between them again? Well, she didn't have all the facts, and she hadn't seen the angry look on Collin's face this afternoon.

Isa crossed her arms over her breasts. "So you knew Mr. Atwood was in the nursing home?"

Gabriela shrugged and gave her a sly smile. "I'm sorry, *chica*. I've been told that Collin came home several months ago to save the company. And he decided to stay here because, well, he was married, but his wife died."

"He was married?" Why did that hurt so much? He'd married Isa once. But the marriage had been wiped off the books. Like it had never existed. He probably told people he'd only been married once.

Just like she told people she'd never been married.

"Yes. His wife died of ovarian cancer."

"Oh, my God."

"He has a son. I don't know how old. School age. And you know what?" Gabriela said. "I hope he succeeds in building Atwood Construction back to what it once was. Our friends need those jobs. But mostly because I always liked that boy."

Isa had to stop from saying that she'd liked him too, once upon a time.

# Chapter Three

Collin refused to spend Saturdays in the office. Jessica had insisted that weekends were family time. And seeing that they'd only had a few years together, Collin was glad she'd established that rule. He'd kept it up after she'd died. Because life was short. And Liam was growing like a weed.

He stood just inside the open door of Daddy's three-car garage, staring at the tarp-shrouded vehicle.

"That's it?" Liam asked.

The little boy had heard a lot of stories about Collin's 1991 Ford F-150. The truck had been ten years old back in 2001 when Daddy had bought it for Collin. It had needed work then, and Collin had made some big plans to take the rusty paint down to steel and restore the thing.

But like many teens, he'd never started the project.

"Yep," he said glancing down at his eight-year-old son. Liam was probably too young to help with a project like this, but for some crazy-ass reason, this morning Collin had the urge to come out here and pull the tarp off, see what damage the decades had done, and maybe get his son interested in tinkering around with cars.

The way Collin had tinkered around as a boy.

Of course, he was telling himself a big lie. It wasn't a crazy-ass notion that had brought him out here to the garage. Yesterday, Isa Alvarez had walked back into his life on a pair of sexy, red-soled shoes. The truth was, he couldn't think about Isa without thinking about the truck, and vice versa.

The image of her, pissed off and stalking out of the nursing home with her backside swaying, had burned itself into his retinas. And his libido. He'd had some wild-ass dreams last night.

He stepped up to the truck and pulled the dirty blue plastic away. A cloud of dust lifted into the air, the morning sunshine highlighting the motes. Man. The years hadn't done the vehicle any good. Dry rot had attacked the tires, and Collin had no doubt that the engine probably wouldn't turn over. Everything would need to be rebuilt.

But the project enthused him in a way it had never done when he'd been eighteen. It almost seemed as if the truck had been waiting here for the past eighteen years — half his lifetime. As if it wanted him to come home and finish the job.

"It's kind of a mess, isn't it, Dad?" Liam asked.

He turned and squatted down to be on his son's level. Liam had the same middling shade of brown hair as Collin, but his eyes were a sharp blue, like his mother's. Sometimes it made his heart ache when he gazed into his son's face.

"Yeah," he said. "It is kind of a mess. But we're going to fix it up. And then it can be yours."

"I'm too little to drive."

"Yes, but it's going to take me a long time to get it ready for you. You're going to love this old truck. I have a lot of great memories of it."

He glanced up at the faded blue paint, memories of a rainy day eighteen years ago playing through his head.

"So what do we do first?" Liam asked.

Good question. He probably needed to see if the old truck would turn over. He stood up and was just peeking through the driver's side window to see if the key was in the ignition when a bright yellow Mini Cooper pulled up the drive.

"Who's that?" Liam asked.

"I have no idea," Collin said as he turned away from the truck and strolled out of the garage. He'd just reached the drive as Isabella Alvarez opened the driver's side door and got out. Dammit. What was she doing here? And why the hell did she leave him breathless?

She was wearing skintight jeans, high-heel sandals, and a bright pink top with a frilly edge that hugged her curves and showed a ton of cleavage. She was carrying an aluminum pan covered in tin foil. His body reacted, in spite of himself.

"Hi," she said, tossing her head just enough to make her high ponytail sway. "I, um, brought you some food, you know, as a peace offering. Empanadas. The traditional kind, no goat cheese." Her smile seemed nervous and her gaze flashed away, taking in the old truck and then Liam standing there with his head cocked like a curious puppy.

She blinked a few times. "And who's this?" she asked.

"Liam," Collin said, his voice coming out flat and angry. But the anger was mostly self-directed. What kind of idiot was he, anyway, getting hot and bothered by a woman he could never trust? A woman he didn't want his son to meet or ever know.

"Hello Liam," she said, cocking her own head in a mirror image of the boy. "I'm Isa. I used to know your papi when we were young."

"That was a long time ago. Why are you here?" Collin put his hands on his hips.

She glanced at the truck for a moment, her face going a little pale, before she turned her gaze on him. That wasn't an improvement. Isa had deep brown eyes that showed every emotion. And right now, she wasn't showing anything close to anger.

Why had he trusted those eyes? Why had he trusted anything about her?

"I came for two reasons," she said, a smile hovering at the corners of her sensuous mouth. "First, because I made more empanadas than Gabriela and I can possibly eat and I remembered how much you liked them. And second, the truth is, I was wondering if I could hire Atwood Construction to renovate Papi's house."

"What?"

She shrugged. "I promised Gabriela that she could stay in the house for as long as she wanted. But it needs major repairs. I was wondering if someone could come out and give me an estimate."

"No."

"No?" She blinked. "Why not?"

His mouth thinned. "I don't need a reason," he said. "Now please leave. And take the empanadas with you."

A slow rage filled Isabella as she stood in the blistering hot driveway and stared at Collin for a solid minute. How dare he?

He stood there tall and stiff, his own anger radiating from him in righteous waves. Yes, she had walked away from him, but she'd been given no choice. The money his father had waved in her face hadn't been a bribe, it had been a fig leaf that she'd used to avoid exposing Papi to deportation.

Papi never knew anything about what Mr. Atwood had threatened to do until she'd told him all about it a few days before he'd died. The money had protected her father from the knowledge of what kind of man his employer had been. And it had absolved him from carrying the burden of her bad choices.

She should have known not to fall in love with the boss's son.

Besides, taking a small amount of money from Mr. Atwood had been a great way of keeping the truth from Collin. It had allowed him to go off to California and live his major-league dream without having to carry any kind of guilt about anything. She'd let him off the hook. She'd let him think that she'd dumped him for money.

So maybe he had good reason to be angry.

She put the pan of empanadas down on the roof of her little car and took a step forward. "I didn't take a bribe, Collin," she said.

"No? Weren't you just playing me along until you could hit my father up?"

She shook her head. "If you remember, I told you to leave me alone. Dozens of times before I finally agreed to take that first ride with you out to Old Man Canaday's pond."

"Yeah, so. You were playing hard to get."

She shook her head. "No. I was playing by the rules — staying away from the boss's son."

"But—"

"No buts." She took another step forward and looked up into his beautiful hazel eyes. "I took a small amount of money from your father. That is true. But it wasn't a bribe. It was part of a deal.

He gave me money and refrained from calling the INS on my father, and I let you go to California without me."

She looked away, remembering that summer of innocence. It had been 2001, just a few weeks before the September 11 attacks. Before the Immigration and Naturalization Service became ICE. It was, in so many ways, the summer of her innocence.

"He what?"

"Papi didn't have papers. He came on a student visa back in the 1990s and overstayed. Your father told me he would turn Papi in to the INS if I didn't walk away from you."

"Why would he do that? Julio was Daddy's most trusted employee. Without Julio he would have been—"

"I know, Collin. But here's the hard truth. Your father exploited my father. And when I had the audacity to marry you, he threatened to destroy my family, and he had the power to do it."

Collin blinked, almost as if he'd been slapped in the face by her words. Good.

"Julio was undocumented?"

"He had documents. They were fakes. And your father knew it."

"You never told me—"

"Of course not."

"Why?"

She rolled her eyes. "What did you expect me to say to you? *My father works for your father, and by the way, he used fake documents to get the job?* That made both our fathers guilty of breaking the law. The only problem is that the penalty for your father would have been a small fine, and for my father it would have been deportation."

"But you took money. He told me you took—"

"He offered to pay for my college tuition. As it turned out, he paid for the first year and that was it. After you were safely out of town, he reneged on the deal."

"Oh my God, I didn't—"

"No. You didn't know. I kept it all from you so that you could go and have your dream."

"And yesterday? You wanted to what? Rub his nose in his

failure?"

"No. I wanted to forgive him."

"Why?" Surprise laced Collin's tone.

*Good question.* She pulled in a breath. "Truth is, I didn't want to forgive him. But I promised Papi I would. And you know what, I've been thinking about it for the last day, and I realize that I probably never would have gone to college if things had turned out differently. Remember how you were trying to convince me not to go to school but to follow you out to California? Remember how you were going to make millions and we were going to live in a fabulous house where I could make empanadas for you?"

He blinked in the sunlight. "Is that really what I thought? Boy did I have the wrong idea about Major League Baseball… and women's rights."

"You were always a dreamer. I loved your dreams back then. I didn't really have that many of my own. College was something I was going to do because Papi wanted me to do it, even though we were going to have to go deep into debt for it to happen."

"And did you? Go deep into debt?"

She shrugged. "Your father stopped paying after freshman year, so yeah. But by then I had changed my dream. I've been lucky. I paid off my college loans."

"Yeah, well. I'm not such a big dreamer now. I'm a realist."

"Okay. So as one realist to another, I hear that your father's business has fallen on some hard times. I'm ready to hire you. Are you still going to refuse?"

He jammed his hands into the pockets of his khaki golf shorts and looked down at his beat-up sneakers. "I guess that would be stupid, huh?" he asked, not meeting her gaze.

"It would. I'm just asking you to come out to Papi's house and give me an estimate on what it will cost and how long it will take. How about Monday afternoon?"

He looked up, meeting her gaze. Wow. Something seductive and powerful still sparked deep in those eyes of his. He might be here without his big dream, but he was still Collin. The boy she'd once loved.

The boy she'd never stopped loving.

Collin nodded soberly. "Monday after five," he said.

"Okay. I'll see you then," she said, turning away before she gave her emotions away. She picked up the pan of empanadas and took them to the little boy, who was not at all like his father. He was smaller than Collin had been, and his eyes were the color of a bright spring sky. He must favor his mother. He was a very handsome child.

It was odd and unsettling to think about Collin with anyone else. But clearly it was time to leave the past where it belonged. She'd have him fix up the house. And she would go to LA, where she would expand her business from cocktails to Latino foods. The contract with the Food Network was the first step in a dream that was much bigger than any Collin had ever dreamed for her on those nights when they drove down that old dirt road.

She squatted down to be on Liam's level. "Hello, Liam. I made these delicious empanadas. They have meat and potatoes in them. And your father used to love them. So I'm leaving these with you so you can try them. And remember, you should never say no to food you are unfamiliar with. If you don't taste something when it's offered, you will never know what wonderful thing you have missed. And life is too short to miss wonderful things."

The boy took the pan and gave her a little smile. And there, suddenly, she saw Collin in his face.

It was almost five o'clock on Monday afternoon when Collin finally got to the house on Laurel Street. He pulled his Atwood Construction pickup to the curb and got out. But even though he'd been running late all day, he found it impossible to rush up the sidewalk to the front door.

Instead, he stood in the yard staring at the house, his own memories rooting him to the spot. He'd forgotten about the jasmine.

The vine climbed up the eaves of the house Isa had once lived in and looked as if it wanted to pull the porch from its moorings.

He took a big breath. The air was humid and heavy with the smell of it. Sweet. Heavenly. That scent would forever remind him of Isa and those balmy summer nights when he had to wait for

Mrs. Alvarez to leave the porch. When he had to stoke his patience some more until the light in her parents' bedroom had gone dark.

Only then could he sneak around to the back and tap on Isa's bedroom window like some crazy Romeo. It was a one-story house, so at least he hadn't had to risk his life climbing to a balcony. But he would have climbed if necessary because he'd been just as crazy for his Isa as Romeo had been for his Juliet.

His parents and her parents hadn't feuded like the fabled lovers. Still, until Saturday, he'd never fully appreciated the fact that Momma and Daddy had never approved of Isa.

His outrage upon learning this truth was long overdue. He'd had no idea that Daddy was taking advantage of Julio Alvarez. Julio's steady leadership, insistence on quality workmanship, and professionalism had been one of the main reasons Atwood Construction had become so successful. When Julio had retired, things had taken a decided turn for the worse.

But back then, on those crazy summer nights, Collin had been a clueless teenager. Worse, really. He'd been privileged and blinded by that fact. He'd been the hero of the baseball team and from the "right" side of the tracks, and he'd never once considered how difficult his pursuit of Isa might have been for her. He'd loved her. He'd loved the scent of jasmine that followed her wherever she went. He'd loved the round curves of her body. He'd loved her brown skin and her dark eyes and her black-as-night hair curling in the summer heat.

And when she'd betrayed him, he'd lost a piece of himself.

"You gonna stand out there forever or come in and talk to me?"

He shifted his gaze from the overgrown vine to Isa standing on the porch, wearing a pair of faded jeans and an oversized top that fell off one of her shoulders. She stood there with one hand on her slightly jutted hip. Her hair hung down beyond her shoulders, and the summer humidity had done its job raising little curls around her forehead.

Man. He'd seen her strike that pose a million times, the light sparkling in her dark eyes. Sass in her posture. She'd never let him get away with any BS. She'd never let him get too high up on his horse. She'd always kept him grounded, even when the major league scouts had been coming to every American Legion ballgame he'd pitched.

What might have happened if she'd been there when he'd injured himself? Would she have pushed him harder? Would she have stopped him from feeling sorry for himself?

Most probably.

He shook off his regrets and put one boot in front of the other. "Hey," he said as he stepped carefully up the porch. "The jasmine has kind of taken over, hasn't it?"

The corner of her sensuous mouth twitched a little. "I'm afraid it's going to have to come out. It's sent down roots everywhere. But the smell is heavenly, isn't it? Mami loved it so much." She turned, her hair swinging behind her. "Come on in. I've been sorting through Papi's things and doing some cooking. Gabriela is over at Aunt Luisa's house, so it's just us."

He stepped across the threshold into the small sitting room at the front of the house. Her parents' bedroom door was to the right, and the small kitchen and dining room were straight ahead. Isa's room was off the kitchen in the back of the house.

"The layout has to be changed," Isa said. "It's always been stupid. I'm thinking we want to move the kitchen into where the master is now and open everything up. I loved cooking in Mami's kitchen but mostly because of Mami, not the kitchen." Words continued to tumble out of her mouth, and it occurred to Collin that Isa was nervous or maybe uncomfortable in his presence.

That made two of them.

But then he'd never been comfortable standing in this living room, facing her father. Julio could be intimidating at times. Collin had only been truly comfortable when the two of them had been cruising around Sweet Home in that old truck of his. And even then he'd been in the grip of teenage hormones most of the time.

He followed her into the kitchen, where another heavenly and exotic aroma grabbed him. "What are you cooking?" he asked, interrupting her monologue about kitchen design and open-concept floor plans.

She stopped talking turned toward him with a smile that reminded him of that night when they'd been lying in the bed of his pickup and got caught in the rainstorm. The rain had chased them into the cab of the truck. His heart thumped against his rib cage. The storm had raged all around them that night, and she'd never stopped smiling.

"It's *sancocho de carne*. Colombian beef stew," she said, pulling him away from his memories. "You want some? It's been cooking all morning, and it's just about ready."

His stomach chose that moment to rumble. He'd been operating all day on a couple of donuts and a not-very-satisfying egg salad sandwich. "Uh, yeah, sure."

She gestured toward the small dining room. "Sit. And I just want to say that we have to rearrange things so that Gabriela can have the whole family over. This dining room has never been big enough."

He sat, and she returned to the kitchen. A moment later she brought out two bowls filled with big chunks of meat and potatoes and corn on the cob and other things he didn't quite recognize. The bowls had been placed on big plates with a helping of rice, sliced avocado, and a small dab of some kind of salsa. He stared down at it.

"That's called *hogao*," Isa said, pointing at the salsa. "It's a mix of fried green onions and tomato. It's delish. You put some in your stew."

"And what's that?" he asked, pointing to the unknown vegetables in his bowl.

She leaned forward, close enough for him to feel the heat coming off her body. "That looks like plantain, and the other stuff is yucca root. And the green on top is cilantro."

"Yucca? Really? Is it spicy?"

She shook her head. "No. Colombian food isn't usually all that spicy. Try it, Collin."

He looked up at her, memories tumbling through his mind. "You used to say that all the time."

"And good thing too. Because you would never have discovered empanadas if I hadn't." She sat down in the chair next to him.

"And you told Liam the same thing on Saturday."

She cocked her head, her gaze so solemn and so deep. "He's a very handsome boy. I hope he tried some."

"Yeah, he did. And he told me you could make them for him anytime."

She shrugged. "Like father, like son."

For an instant it felt almost as if they'd rediscovered themselves, but then she looked away, her face a portrait of sorrow.

"I'm sorry about your father," Collin said. "He was a good man. He made a real contribution to Atwood Construction. I mean it. When he retired…"

She nodded, her mouth going thin. "He was a good man." She looked as if she intended to say something else. She certainly deserved to say something else. But she swallowed back whatever words had almost broken free. Instead, she looked back, her eyes liquid. "Eat. In honor of Papi. This was his favorite thing. That's why I made it today."

# Chapter Four

Collin brushed Isa's wrist with velvet-warm fingertips. He massaged her skin with a gentle touch, setting off an odd, almost electric, hum up her arm. He had always known exactly how to touch her, and that was the problem.

She knew he'd intended this contact to soothe and console, but his caress was anything but comforting. It sent gooseflesh up her arm and distracted her. She edged her hand away as she turned back to meet his gaze. He withdrew his hand like a guilty child and looked down at his *sancocho de carne*.

"Eat," she said again. And turned her attention to the food. The food comforted in a way his touch never could.

"It's really good," he said a moment later, in that surprised tone he'd used the day she'd fed him his first empanada. The truth was, Collin Atwood had lived a very sheltered life. Maybe that's why he'd once been a dreamer.

But he was a sadder and wiser man now. The shuffle of life, broken baseball dreams, and the loss of a wife had changed him. Oddly, it had made him more mature.

She swallowed her food and cocked her head, studying him. He was so handsome, with that square jaw and those forthright dark green eyes that changed colors with his mood. His eyes were dark now, as if he also felt the chemistry.

"So what's your dream now?" she asked. A provocative question for sure, but she suddenly needed to know, especially if she let herself fall under his spell for the second time in her life.

"I want to save Atwood Construction."

A surprise.

Once, a long time ago, she might have laughed at that. She

might have told him he was thinking small. She might have wondered why he wanted to be like his father. But that was before she'd started her own business. She had more than twenty employees up in Baltimore producing the flavored liqueurs she'd promoted in her book on mixology.

It was a small business, but it was growing, mostly because of the book's surprising success. Cocktails were a trend, and she'd managed to catch it at exactly the right time.

"It's a good dream, Collin. I love being in business for myself."

"So you have a business?"

Obviously he didn't watch the local weekend news program where her cocktail recipes were featured. It was okay. He'd just moved back here. And besides, this was Sweet Home, where people favored long-necked Buds, not trendy cocktails.

She told him all about her business. About how she'd graduated from Virginia Tech's Pamplin College of Business with a BS degree in hospitality and tourism. How she'd managed a couple of high-end hotels in DC where she'd dated a bartender. How she'd experimented with infusions just for the hell of it.

And how all of that turned into a business and a best-selling book on mixology. She didn't say one word about the offer from the Food Network. That would have been like bragging. Besides, she wasn't sure she wanted to leave the mid-Atlantic to live in LA. She wasn't sure she needed that kind of fame.

What she wanted was to write another cookbook—on Colombian cuisine. But that was unlikely to be a bestseller.

"You know, for the girl who didn't much like to drink, I find it amusing that you're in the business of selling alcohol," Collin said.

She shrugged. "It's not really about the alcohol, you know. It's about the taste."

He nodded, scooping up the last drop of his *sancocho de carne*. "Uh-huh. I totally get that." He eyed his empty bowl.

"I have more in the kitchen."

He pushed his bowl in her direction, and she jumped up to refill it. She loved nothing more than cooking for people. She'd gotten that from Mami. Food equaled love in this house.

That thought brought her up short.

She did not love Collin Atwood. At least not anymore.

But she still felt a certain joy as she refilled his bowl. And the awkwardness they'd felt earlier disappeared as they sat together at Mami's tiny dining table, talking about Gabriela's house while he made notes on a legal pad between bites of stew.

When the food and conversation ended, she got busy washing dishes while he poked around the house, making measurements, and peeking up into the attic space to figure out which walls were load bearing and in which direction the joists ran. It was well after seven o'clock by the time he finished. Isa had just dried the last dish when he returned to the kitchen.

"I'll write this up and send you an estimate. It's not going to be cheap to get what you want," he said. "I'll give you a few options, okay?"

"Okay, but Gabriela deserves the best."

He nodded and stood there for a moment as if reluctant to leave. Her heart rate kicked up a bit because she didn't want him to leave. Maybe she should offer to make him a cocktail. Or not.

"I'm sorry. I've kept you so late," she said. "I'm sure you need to go relieve the babysitter."

He shook his head. "Liam's with his grandparents. They've taken him off to Williamsburg and Busch Gardens for a few days. They don't get to see him very often now that we've moved east. They live in San Francisco."

"Oh. Well, I'm sure Liam is having a great time being spoiled."

"I'm sure he is." Collin smiled, and Isa's heart rate climbed a little higher.

"I gotta go," he said before she could offer the mixed drink.

She walked him to the door and followed him out onto the porch. And then she stood there watching him walk back to his truck. He had an athletic stride, as if he was always walking on the balls of his feet. She remembered people saying that for a pitcher he was fast on the bases.

And he'd always looked like poetry in motion fielding his position. Even Papi said so. Sometimes she and Papi would go to his American Legion ballgames together. Papi had expected him to become a major leaguer too.

Everyone had.

He reached his truck, and deep in her heart she willed him to stop and look back. She held her breath, and then...

He did. He got as far as the drivers' side, and then he studied her across the bed of the truck. "So, uh, are you doing anything tonight? Maybe we could..." He shrugged again.

"Go for a ride?" she asked, her heart almost bursting in her chest.

"Yeah."

"Let me lock the door."

Harry Canaday owned a farm with a pond on it. The spot was posted NO TRESPASSING, but that had never stopped Collin as a boy. The property line ran adjacent to Daddy's land, and Harry and Daddy had a silent agreement. No one complained when Collin biked down to the pond to go fishing. Or when he drove his old Ford truck down the dirt road when he'd been a teen.

The road was paved now, and Harry Canaday had long since passed away. His heirs, a son in Chicago and a daughter in Seattle, had sold the land in parcels. Some of it—the area near the pond—was still a farm, but instead of cows, the new owners kept horses and they frowned on trespassers.

The rest had gone to developers. Which had been good news for Atwood Construction—for a time, anyway. There was still business to be done in this county if he could hire back some of the good workers who'd left after Julio had retired. Unfortunately, Northern Virginia Contracting had hired a lot of those workers over the past couple of years. Getting them back wouldn't be easy.

"Nothing's the same," Collin said as he turned the company's pickup onto the road.

"I don't know," Isa said in that deep, lilting voice of hers. "The more things change the more they stay the same."

"You think?" he asked, nodding toward the stone gates on the left side of the road. The exclusive homes—mini mansions on tiny plots of land—had been built over the past five years. Sweet Home was turning into a bedroom suburb for Washington, DC and Richmond.

"Well," Isa said, turning so her hip rested against the seat back, "look on the bright side; the Atwoods aren't the only ones in town with a pretentious house anymore."

"Duly noted," he said, giving her a glance. She'd never let him get away with much. And he'd loved that about her. He'd loved the way she'd always seen the silver linings.

He'd never had to do that as a kid. There hadn't been any rain clouds in his life. Hell, from a certain perspective, the rain had brought only good things his way.

The memory tumbled through his mind, and he couldn't help but smile.

"What are you thinking?" she asked, her voice husky.

He pulled the truck off the road and over a berm into a pasture that had been sodded over with Bermuda grass and millet. The field where they'd gone years ago hadn't been so well kept. It had been overgrown with crown vetch and crabgrass and all sorts of weeds that were probably bad for horses.

This was the spot, right here. He stopped the truck and set the brake. "I was thinking about senior prom night," he said, turning toward her.

Her lips were parted, and he had no doubt she was thinking about that night too. The night they'd come out here, alone, dressed in their finery. It had been a warm, humid night in late May. The smell of the wildflowers had permeated the air. They'd spread a couple of old plaid blankets in the truck's bed and shucked off their shoes and then most of their clothes.

And they'd rested in each other's arms, looking up at the moon as clouds scudded by. He'd wanted her for so long. He'd pursued her. He'd wooed her. He'd been patient.

And it had paid off that night. Even when the thunderstorm had come rolling in, soaking their clothes because they'd left them out in the bed of the truck when they climbed inside the cabin to finish what they'd started.

He chuckled.

"What?" she asked a little too sharply.

"I was just thinking about the look Momma gave me when I came home that night in a tuxedo that was soaked right through.

I remember her looking at me and asking me if I didn't have enough sense to come in out of the rain. Little did she know."

Isa's beautiful lips quirked at the corner. "Mami was so angry with me. About the dress. Aunt Luisa had spent many nights making it for me, and it was ruined. I think she knew what I'd done though." She let out a big sigh. "She told me that I should be careful about you. She was very smart, my Mami."

"I never meant you harm. I fell in love with you that night."

"I know. I felt the same. I didn't want to, but I did."

They stared at each other. The years falling away just as a distant rumble of thunder reached them.

She was the first to laugh. "Oh no, not again."

Her words pierced his heart even though he didn't want anything to happen between them again. Much.

How could that be? He'd spent half a lifetime being angry with her. Unfairly, as it turned out.

A distant flash of lightning lit up the sky, reminding him that it was different now. On prom night, they'd come here after midnight. The moon had been high in the black sky before the storm clouds raced in. But it would be hours until the moon rose this evening.

He sat there for a long moment listening to the wind as it picked up and whispered, reminding him of the way this place used to look, reminding him of the promises they'd made to each other.

Not just on prom night, but six weeks later, on her eighteenth birthday, when they'd run off to Richmond and gotten married at the courthouse there. Had those beautiful promises meant nothing?

Maybe they hadn't had a beautiful wedding with a minister or a priest. But he'd still made a promise that day. And the words had meant everything to him. Back then, he'd been so sure of a lot of things: He'd expected to go high in the major league draft a few days later. He'd expected Isa to go with him wherever he landed.

He'd been a such a boy. Blind to the world. Blind to the fact that when the heavens had opened that night, there might never be a way to close them back up again.

"I would have fought for you," he said after a long moment. "If you'd let me."

"Oh, Collin."

He turned toward her, a big lump in his throat. "It wouldn't have mattered to me that your father didn't have papers. I would have stopped Daddy from bullying you. I would have."

"You would have tried," she said. "But I didn't believe that you would succeed. I was so afraid that Papi would be sent back to Colombia, and Mami would have to go with him or be alone. And I couldn't be the cause of that."

"That wounds my pride, you know."

She nodded. "I know."

"It would have been so much better to have been able to fight for you instead of thinking that you didn't care."

"It was a long time ago, Collin. And you have loved since."

"And lost." He swallowed hard. This wasn't about Jessica. But it was in some weird way. Loving was a hard thing. It always ended in heartbreak.

And even now sometimes, when he saw a woman with blond hair and just the right kind of build, his heart would soar and he'd think, for just a moment, Jessica is still here. And then reality would come crashing down, and he'd have to endure another wave of grief as the truth of her loss settled more deeply into his bones.

And hadn't he been the same way about Isa for all those years before Jess had come into his life? Hadn't he always seen her in a crowd? Hadn't he always hoped to see her when he'd come home to visit? Hadn't he never stopped looking for her? Never really stopped loving her even though he'd been so angry and so hurt?

And now here she sat in the cab of his truck. It was a different truck at a different time of day and a different season. The road was different. The land was different. But Isa was the same as she'd always been.

A man would have to be crazy to let this chance slip through his hands even though heartbreak might be awaiting. She was here. He had a second chance that he'd never have with Jess.

He reached out to caress her cheek, and damned if she didn't lean into his touch.

He pulled her up into a kiss that was like coming home. Her mouth was warm and sensuous and tasted faintly of the cilantro she'd used in the delicious stew she'd fed him. But more than that, this kiss held a promise of something strong and powerful and utterly alive.

The skies opened as her lips parted, and the heavens rained down, pounding against the metal roof above them like the thundering of his heart.

## Chapter Five

One night. Isa had given Collin one night in the cab of a truck, and another in a cheap motel on Route 1 not far from the theme park King's Dominion. Her wedding night.

And eighteen years later, she'd done it again. Given him a night in a truck. And even though they were adults, and he could have taken her home to his Daddy's big pretentious house. He'd driven her back to the house on Laurel afterward.

And by then, Aunt Gabriela was home, the light shining from the living room windows. So she'd kissed him one last time and left him, knowing as she walked up the path to the sagging porch that it was impossible to go back to the beginning.

She had the distinct feeling that Collin hadn't been with a woman since he'd lost his wife. And right there was a problem. Because she sensed that he still loved Jessica. That was her name.

And, of course, time flows in only one direction. Can't swim upstream or go back.

So she squared her shoulders and walked through the front door determined not ever to do that again. He was, officially, out of her system.

Except he wasn't. Even though the next few days were busy ones, filled with conference calls, decisions about her business, and the looming deadline for the Food Network contract, her mind kept turning back to the past, and the not-too-distant present.

She'd fallen for him again. Foolish woman. This time he was in love with someone else. But Isa had years of practice shoving Collin's memory aside, so for the next few days, she dived into work while simultaneously helping Cousin Carolina prepare for her wedding coming up on Saturday.

On Tuesday, she and Gabriela went to Aunt Luisa's house to help with the final alterations of the bridesmaids' gowns. Aunt Luisa was quite a seamstress, so the bridesmaid dresses had been handmade with a little help from Gabriela. Isa, who was all thumbs when it came to sewing, kept the kitchen going with good food and munchies for the many additional aunts and cousins from Mami's side of the family who'd arrived for the festivities.

On Wednesday, Isa drove up to Baltimore to deal with a few business issues and to tape her local TV segment.

And on Thursday, she met early in the day with Carolina and her fiancé, Scott Royce, to make the final choices for the signature cocktails that would be served at the wedding. The couple taste tested several recipes and settled on two drinks, one for the ladies and one for the gentlemen.

The ladies' cocktail was called the "Rosy glow," which was made with Reposado Milagro Tequila, a few teaspoons of fresh orange juice, and a couple of ounces of the rose-flavored liqueur made by Isa's company. It was served in a lowball glass with a squeezed orange garnish.

Carolina and Scott chose the birch and bourbon for the gentlemen's cocktail. This one was simpler, just an ounce of her company's birch-flavored liqueur and two ounces of bourbon. For the wedding she would garnish the drink with birch swizzle sticks, also sold by her company.

Finally, Isa had recommended a signature nonalcoholic drink for the children and others who wanted something festive but without the booze. The couple chose a vanilla soda concoction made with vanilla extract, some chamomile syrup flavoring that her company was experimenting with, and sparkling water.

The day Scott and Carolina came by for a cocktail consultation was also the day Isa learned that Collin Atwood was Scott's best man. "You mean you and Collin stayed in touch all these years?" she asked the groom as they were leaving Gabriela's house.

He shrugged. "Yeah. We did. Even though I went off to play baseball for the University of Michigan and he went to the minor leagues. We kept in touch. I got a job at Boeing, after college, and moved to Seattle, and Collin was in San Francisco. We got together for ski trips every winter." He paused a moment. "I'm the one who introduced him to Jess."

"His wife?"

Scott, a tall thin guy with a military-short haircut, nodded. "Yeah, she was a dancer who interned for a while at Boeing. But she got a chance to dance with a company in San Francisco, so I gave her Collin's email address. Shortly after she arrived in San Francisco she tore her ACL, and that ended her dancing career. But she met Collin and the rest is history. I was the best man at their wedding."

"Oh."

"We just wanted to make sure you knew," Carolina said. Carolina had been twelve the year Isa had run off with Collin to get married. Of course she didn't know one thing about the marriage. No one had been told in the family.

But everyone knew she and Collin had been going steady in high school. And Carolina had completely romanticized the relationship. She might have been a little girl back then, but she'd had an enormous crush on Collin's best friend. Who would have thought that she'd be marrying Scott all these years later?

"It's fine. I've seen him recently. I've hired Atwood Construction to update Gabriela's house."

"Oh good," Carolina said on a long breath. "I've been so worried. I should have told you sooner but—"

"It's not a problem."

"And don't worry. He's going to be seated at the main table, so if you don't want to talk to him, you don't—"

"I've already talked to him, Carolina. It's fine. You have plenty of other things to worry about."

Carolina gave Isa a big warm hug. "I do. And I'm a little crazy. So thank you so much for all your help. I think everyone is going to love the Rosy glow." She giggled. "I just love the name of that one."

And with that she glided out the door on the arm of her love, glowing just the way a bride should.

Isa stood on the porch and heaved a giant sigh. How many wedding cocktails had she created? Hundreds over the past decade. Would she ever create one for her own wedding?

Probably not.

Collin rolled his neck, a bone-deep ache running down his shoulders and back. He'd been overdoing it in the garage the past few days. With Liam off in Williamsburg and his confusion over what had happened on Monday, it had seemed like a good idea to pull the tarp all the way off the old Ford truck and get to work restoring it.

He'd gotten out his power sander and attacked the rusty spots, grinding the paint down to clean, shiny steel. And there was something to be said for sanding through those layers of time. As if the work was saying that it might be possible to go back and start again.

Scary thought. He'd spent so much time being angry with Isa. Where had the anger gone? And could he start over? Could he go back? And what would that mean to the love he still felt for Jess?

These questions turned in his mind as the sander whirled.

They were still in his mind today as he stood on a curving walkway at Columbine Plantation, an eighteenth-century house located on the road between Fredericksburg and Williamsburg. According to the historic literature in the front hallway of the small bed-and-breakfast, George Washington had surveyed the land where the house stood. And rumor had it that Washington might have slept there once. The map of northern Virginia was dotted with homes like that. Washington really must have gotten around.

Scott's wedding wouldn't be in the house though. It was planned for the lawn out back where a pergola of obviously twentieth-century vintage had been built for the express purpose of providing a classic backdrop for weddings. This particular pergola had a verdant wisteria growing over the trellis.

It was probably nice in the spring, but if Collin was going to choose a runaway vine, he'd go for the jasmine every time.

He turned toward Liam, dressed in an adorable gray suit with a bright purple clip-on bow tie. He hunkered down to be at eye level. "So you're going to behave, right? You'll be sitting with

Uncle Scott's mother and father."

"I'm good," he said running a finger with a torn nail under his collar. Collin had told the boy he could ditch the tie, but Liam had insisted that he wanted to look his best for this occasion.

Collin hadn't fully understood why until Isabella Alvarez arrived and his young son's eyes lit up. He pulled away from Collin with a big smile on his face.

"Hi, Isa," he said in a voice much too loud right before he gave her a big hug.

Collin stood and turned. Isa looked... stunning dressed in a bright red-orange strapless dress that exposed the gloriously brown skin over her shoulders and down her back. She'd left her hair down, and it fell to her shoulders in beautiful glossy waves. She wore a pair of ridiculous high heels that made her legs look delectable. And as always, her voluptuous, hourglass figure made him yearn to touch her everywhere.

Their gazes met across the space. He felt the heat and saw it mirrored in her eyes.

"I'm glad you're here," Liam said, breaking away from his hug and looking up at Isa with adoring eyes. "I really liked the empanadas."

"So I heard. And you were gone for a while. You went to Williamsburg."

He shrugged. "Yeah. The houses were kind of boring, but the cannons were fun. I mean it. I really, really liked the empanadas."

She laughed. "Your father told me."

The boy smiled and turned to look at Collin. "He did?"

"Yes. While you were gone, he came by to look at my aunt's house. He's going to fix it up." She shifted her gaze. "If he ever gets an estimate to me for the work."

Collin shrugged, trying to dispel the attraction. His estimate was finished, but he'd been putting off the phone call. The evening spent in his truck had confused the hell out of him. He wasn't sure he trusted himself around Isa. Plus he'd been worried about Liam and whether his son would be okay if he dated someone.

Obviously, that wasn't going to be a problem. Isa seemed to have a natural way of talking to Liam. Right down to complimenting him on his purple bow tie, which made the little boy smile.

Damn. Was Liam falling in love with Isa too?

"Hey, dude, get to work. The guests are arriving." Scott came down the walk, looking like the typical stressed-out bridegroom. Why on earth did people do this to themselves?

Collin and Jess had opted for a small wedding in a park with just friends and family. No giant extravaganza at an eighteenth-century plantation house for him.

No sir.

And then the memory of the first time followed. Well, getting married at a courthouse classified as the understated wedding of the century.

Collin's gaze landed on Isa. "Bride or groom?" He asked the traditional groomsman's question even though he knew the answer.

"Bride," she answered.

An instant later, he found himself with Isa's hand tucked into the corner of his arm as he walked her down the path to the area behind the inn where the folding chairs had been set up.

Isa had been his wife for a couple of days. But this was the very first time he'd ever walked her down the aisle. Of course, he was walking her in the wrong direction. Still, his heart kicked against his rib cage, leaving him a little breathless. Awareness coiled deep in his belly.

"You know," she said in a low voice that thrummed through him. "The bride traditionally takes this walk with her father."

It was only then that he saw the tears pooling in her eyes. He was a jerk. Here he was thinking about the past and the future and last Monday in the truck. And she was thinking about Julio. He stopped at the reserved section for the bride's family and looked deep into her dark eyes. "I'm sorry for your loss," he said, the words feeling strained and trite on his tongue.

She gave him a small, trembling sigh as she slipped her hand from his elbow. And he turned quickly and scooted back up the aisle before she could say anything else.

## Chapter Six

Isa shouldn't have said one word about Papi. Maybe if she'd kept her mouth shut, that moment of walking down the aisle with her hand tucked into Collin's arm would have lasted a little longer.

Or maybe she could have found a way to properly say what she'd felt in that moment, instead of bringing Papi into it.

Except that it was a reality that Papi would never walk her down the aisle. Not that she had an itch to settle down or get married.

The truth was she wasn't unhappy about the way her life had turned out. She had a strong and growing business in a niche of the food-and-beverage industry that was on the rise. She had made a local name for herself. She'd written a book that had made her wealthy. And she was probably going to move to California and become a nationally recognized expert on cocktails.

So why was she thinking about things that could never be? Or things that once had been but hadn't worked out?

There wasn't one reason to stray from her chosen path. She'd forged it with her decisions. She'd made a success of herself. And she couldn't go back.

Could she?

Did she even want to?

Yes.

When Collin left her and retreated as if he wanted nothing to do with her, she wanted desperately to turn back time.

"I see you're picking up where you left off," Cousin Vivian said the moment Isa sat down in the folding chair. Of course she'd ended up here, sitting next to Vivi, her least favorite cousin.

"What's that supposed to mean?" Isa asked.

Vivi turned and gave her a dark-eyed stare. "Really, Isa. Everyone knows about what you and Collin did all those years ago."

Did they? Did they know how Mr. Atwood had threatened her? Did they think she'd taken a bribe? Did they know she and Collin had gotten married?

No. The family knew nothing about her short-lived marriage to Collin Atwood. All they knew is that she and Collin had broken up right after he'd been drafted by the Giants organization.

She wasn't going to let Vivi's jealousy ruin her day. Her cousin, who lived in Florida, had always been jealous because Isa had been Abuelita's favorite. But that had only been because her grandmother loved to cook. And Vivi hated every moment she was forced to be in the kitchen.

But the jealousy remained, even now, years after Abuelita's death. Isa had done well. Vivi hadn't finished college, and her first and second marriages had failed.

So Isa settled down in her seat and tried very hard not to listen to Vivi's complaints and commentaries on everything and everyone. She was the most dissatisfied person Isa had ever met.

In her own opinion, Scott and Carolina's ceremony, although very traditional, was also super emotional. The couple looked so happy together. And that warmed Isa's heart. Scott was a good man. He'd made Carolina happy.

After the ceremony, Isa escaped her cousin by allowing herself to be pulled away from the festivities to supervise the cocktail hour. The caterers had some questions on how to properly mix the Rosy glow, and she was happy to provide instructions and pitch in to help mix drinks.

Besides, she felt more comfortable behind the bar. It gave her something to do instead of watching every move Collin made as the photographer lined up the wedding party for photographs.

He looked incredibly handsome and grown-up in that summer-weight suit. And the yearning she'd felt earlier returned threefold. Did she want to chuck the opportunity in LA for a chance with him?

And his adorable little boy?

Her heart yearned to say yes, especially when Liam escaped from Scott's parents to come sit on a stool by the bar, sipping his vanilla soda mocktail while he raved about how yummy it was.

The way to this child's heart was clearly through his taste buds. In fact, the little boy bent her ear for half an hour about his father's less-than-stellar cooking. The kid was looking for a cook, for sure. But maybe not a new mother.

Scott's mother found Liam after a while and pulled him away with a big apology. Isa told her that no apology was needed, but Scott's mom clearly thought it was inappropriate for an eight-year-old to hang out at the bar.

Aunt Gabriela showed up a few minutes later and physically pulled Isa away from the cocktails. "This is a family celebration," she scolded. "Not a catering job."

Gabriela forced a Rosy glow into her hand and dragged her off to visit with her aunts and uncles from Mami's side of the family, but after a short time, cocktail hour ended, and it was time to be seated for dinner under a big circus tent.

Where, of course, someone had thought it appropriate to seat all the unmarried people at one table. So Isa found herself once again having to endure Cousin Vivi, who was seated across the table next to a couple of Scott's unmarried cousins—all of them much younger than Vivi or Isa.

That didn't stop Vivi from going into all-out flirt mode though. Isa tried not to be embarrassed for her cousin while she concentrated on her not-very-interesting salad and the unspectacular chicken dinner. She occupied herself by sneaking peeks at Collin, seated at the head table.

Damn. Every time she looked at him, he seemed to be looking right back at her. And every time she shifted her gaze, Vivi noticed.

She was grateful when the time came for Collin to give the best man's toast. She could look at him without trying to hide it. He was so handsome. And his speech about Scott had half the room weeping when he mentioned how his best friend had introduced him to Jessica.

She got that message loud and clear. Now, if she could only

escape without half the family noticing her early departure. She planned to wait for the DJ to get rolling with the first dances. But just as the music started, Liam Atwood appeared at her table wearing his suit jacket and his slightly crooked purple tie.

"May I have this dance?" he asked with a determined look on his young face.

She fought against the urge to glance at Collin. Had he set her up? Had he sent this cherub her way in order to melt her heart?

Absolutely not. Collin's speech had been crystal clear. His lack of even a telephone call after their brief encounter in his truck had been message enough.

But still; who could refuse such a beautiful little boy?

So she sucked it up and nodded her head. "I would be delighted," she said, putting her hand in his much smaller one and letting him pull her onto the dance floor.

The DJ had just started playing "Lucky" by Jason Mraz and Colbie Caillat—not quite a slow dance, but not a foot-stomping number either. Just the same, Liam wasn't about to let go of her hand. He held on tight and started stepping in an impressive manner, suggesting that at some point in his young life the little dude had taken dancing lessons. He even knew how to twirl her around.

At the age of eight? Wow.

Collin, who had never danced with Isa ever, hadn't taught his son this trick. Collin would have signed the boy up for T-ball, not ballroom dancing. This was Jessica's doing.

Damn.

How could Isa possibly compete with a mother like that?

The best man's toast was dispensed with, thank God. Collin had never been much for public speaking, and he'd struggled over the speech until his mother-in-law had suggested that he just speak his heart.

After all, Scott was his best friend. Scott had introduced him to Jess. And Scott had been the guy—all those years ago—who'd told him not to listen to the bigoted people in high school. Scott had told him that if he had a thing for Isabella Alvarez, then he ought to go do something about it.

And now Scott was a member of Isa's family, and Collin was here, living in Sweet Home. A lonely widower.

He turned away from the bar, with his cocktail in hand. He took a sip just as that Jason Mraz song came on — the one Jess had loved so much.

But instead of driving him from the room with sad memories of Jess and Liam dancing around the living room, the song made him smile.

Liam had no interest in sports, but the boy loved to dance. And his mother had put him in dance classes from the time he was a toddler. He was usually the only boy in the class, but that never fazed him.

Recently he'd told Collin that dancing classes allowed him to make friends will all the cute girls. Maybe the kid had something going there. Because right this minute Liam was out on the dance floor with the most beautiful girl in the room. And he was making her smile.

Time stopped for a long moment, and a promise hung in the air. Collin could look at this situation one of two ways. It could leave him sad and missing Jess, or he could accept it as a sign.

Maybe, up there in heaven, Jess was telling him it was time to move on. He would never forget her or stop loving her or loving the son they'd made together. Hell, how could you not love Liam when he looked like her?

But Liam was moving on. And clearly, the kid had put on that jacket and bow tie for the woman whose empanadas had worked their way into his heart. Just like they'd worked their way into Collin's heart years and years ago.

Maybe it was possible to go back. Not to re-create the way it had been when they were kids. But to go back in order to move forward. To forgive her for something she never should have been blamed for in the first place.

So he put his birch and bourbon down on one of the tables and strode across the dance floor just as the song ended. He tapped his son's shoulder. "Can I cut in?"

Liam looked up at him with Jessica's eyes. "Sure, Dad. She's a good dancer. You should probably let her lead."

He gave Liam his best imitation of Jess's evil eye, but the kid just laughed. Collin turned to face the woman he'd once loved with all of his being.

And just then, the DJ came over the sound system. "This next song is by special request of the bride and groom." The opening chords of the classic wedding song, "When I Said I Do" by Clint Black, drifted from the sound system.

"It's a waltz, Dad," Liam said. "Remember? One-two-three, one-two-three."

"Get out of here," he said to his child.

The kid turned with a grin as wide as Texas and scampered over to visit with the bridegroom, who gave Collin a grin and a thumbs-up.

What the hell? Had he just been set up?

Maybe. But perhaps he'd needed that push. He took Isa's right hand in his left and placed his left on her waist. The feel of her body under his palm was almost enough to make him forget all those dance lessons Jess had dragged him to.

She'd been determined to teach him how to waltz. She'd joked that it was so that they could dance at Liam's wedding one day. But he wondered now if she'd known her time here on earth would be short. Maybe she'd been preparing Collin for this moment.

He led off and Isa followed, her brown eyes wide with surprise. "She taught you this," she said. Not as a question but as a statement.

He nodded. "She was a dancer. She had dreams that didn't come true." He looked deep into those Spanish eyes of hers. "Let's not talk about her," he said.

She gave him the smallest of nods and then relaxed into his arms. Damn. All the years he'd danced with Jess she'd always been trying to teach him to take charge of the dance, at the same time she'd be leading him.

But Isa put herself into his arms and moved wherever he led. They had never danced like this. Ever. Not in public or in private. Collin had been all left feet. And even at school dances, where he could make up the steps to the grunge music they listened to half the time, he'd never danced with her.

Because dancing had embarrassed him.

But now it occurred to him that she might have seen it another way. He'd loved her, but he'd done a lot of things to keep that love secret. And when he'd married her, it had been a quickie thing, an attempt to force his parents' hand.

He hadn't been like the man in the song they were dancing to. That man was singing about true love. The kind of love that overcomes the ups and downs. The kind of love that's shouted out loud. The kind of love that sees through the BS.

He should have loved her better all those years ago. He should have known what his father was up to. He should have been there for her.

"I'm sorry," he whispered, breaking all the rules Jess had taught him about maintaining a "frame" for the dance. He pulled her deeper into his arms and stopped worrying about where he put his feet. Instead he put his lips against her temple and felt her snuggle deeper into the embrace.

His heart pounded, aware that most of the room was watching them. And he didn't care. Having Isa in his arms after all this time seemed right. When the song came to its close, he took a small step back, cupped her face in his hands and kissed her.

Hard.

In front of everyone under the wedding tent.

Collin Atwood was delicious and more intoxicating than any cocktail Isa had ever mixed. He tasted of sweet bourbon and earthy birch spiced by a carnal bouquet of sex and passion. Maybe she should call this flavor "love." If she could bottle it, she'd make a fortune.

He released her, and Isa stepped back, dazed. What had just happened? Collin had danced with her. Really danced with her. He'd waltzed her around as if he'd known what he was doing. He'd held her close, and it was as if his body and the music merged.

When she'd said *I do* all those years ago, had she really made a promise of forever? Obviously not. She'd been so young. She hadn't understood anything. But maybe she was ready for a second chance to get it right.

They faced each other. His eyes dark, his ears a little red, his mouth kiss swollen.

"I'm sorry," she said.

"There's nothing to forgive," he murmured into that silence between songs on a dance floor.

She waited for the music to start again. She needed the music. She needed to *move*.

But instead, the DJ came over the sound system. "It's time for the bouquet toss." And the next thing she knew, Cousin Juanita grabbed her by the arm and dragged her away from Collin.

"You have to catch the bouquet," her teenage cousin said. "Especially now." The girl giggled, and Isa looked over her shoulder toward Collin, who stood in the middle of the dance floor with his head cocked slightly to one side as if he, too, didn't quite know what had just happened.

A moment later, Isa found herself in a group of unmarried women, most of them younger than she was. There were many cousins and a few of Carolina's college friends that Isa didn't know well.

Carolina looked right at Isa and shouted, "*Esto es para ti.*" She turned and made an overly dramatic windup motion.

In that split second, before Carolina let the bouquet fly, Isa came to a surprising decision. She wasn't going to sign the Food Network contract. She didn't want to move to LA away from her family.

Away from Gabriela, who was getting up in years and probably needed some help. Away from Luisa whom she loved with all her heart. Away from Carolina who was settling here with her new husband.

Away from the promise in Collin's kiss.

She wanted a home in Sweet Home.

And maybe, for the first time in her life, she wanted to position herself to snag that bouquet that her cousin had just said was coming in her direction. Which she did, inadvertently elbowing

Cousin Natalia in the process.

Collin found his birch and bourbon where he'd left it and took a bracing drink as he watched the bouquet toss. Of course Isa caught the damn thing. It was like fate, or maybe everyone was pushing them together.

Which was okay. Really okay. Kind of stunning, actually, given what his father had done to some of the members of this family.

He had so much to atone for, but maybe there was forgiveness at the end of this road. Maybe he could find his way back to the man he used to be. The man who believed in miracles.

But instead of a great big, major-league miracle, maybe he just wanted a small one. The miracle of forgiveness. The miracle of finding a love he'd thought he'd lost.

"Well, the fix is in."

He turned, finding one of Carolina and Isa's many cousins. He couldn't remember this one's name. Isa's family was enormous on her mother's side. There were cousins from New York, Florida, and Colombia here for this wedding. Scott had told him last night that even he had trouble remembering the names of all the cousins and who belonged to whom.

"What do you mean?" he asked. The woman was about Isa's age, he'd guess.

"The family is trying to keep her from moving to LA."

"What?" He turned to face the woman.

"Didn't she tell you?"

"Tell me what?"

"She's got a deal with the Food Network for a show on mixology. And she's in negotiations with her publisher for a cookbook on Latino cuisine. Her cocktail book was a bestseller, you know. I personally think the family is crazy if they think she has any intention of staying in this little town." She leaned in. "Carlos said her net worth is probably more than a million dollars by now. Imagine a millionaire living here in the middle of nowhere."

"A millionaire?"

"She's done well for herself. Although if you ask me, she

walked all over that boyfriend she had in her twenties. He was a bartender at the hotel where she worked. Taught her everything she knows about cocktails. But when she wrote her book, he didn't even get a mention in the acknowledgments."

She lifted her glass. She was drinking a Rosy glow. "Here's to the bride and groom."

He lifted his own glass mechanically as the woman turned and walked away.

What the hell? Isa was a millionaire? She was leaving? She'd built her fortune on a lie?

He knocked back the drink.

He should have known better. You can't go back in time. And miracles, even small ones, were a myth. They never happened.

Ever.

The bouquet was a fragrant collection of sweet roses and peppery lilies that tickled Isa's nose as she turned to look at Collin.

She had hoped to see a smile on his face. She had expected to see the same dark longing in his eyes that she'd seen just moments ago.

But something had changed. She remembered that look from the other day, when she'd walked through Atwood Construction's front doors intent on proving something to herself.

She hadn't really gone there to seek forgiveness. Not then, anyway, even though it was all she wanted now.

The music blared from the sound system, and the guests had finally reached the perfect level of inebriation. Suddenly everyone wanted to dance, and the DJ had moved from sentimental songs to loud ones.

She felt like a salmon swimming upstream as she fought the crowd. And when she reached Collin, she knew immediately that something had happened.

"What?" she asked.

"You didn't tell me about the Food Network."

"Oh, for goodness' sake. I haven't signed that deal yet and—"

"And what about the bartender?"

"What bartender?"

"The guy you screwed over."

"What?"

"Your cousin just told me there was a guy in your life."

"Well, there was a woman in yours, Collin. I haven't been celibate over the past eighteen years. Yes, I had a relationship with a man who was a bartender."

"And you stole his ideas?"

She sagged. Jason Clawson was a gifted mixologist and a total screwup as a human being. She'd met him as a twentysomething and had been totally swept away by his grace and beauty behind the bar. He'd been pretty good in bed too.

But he had no ambition. And he drank… a lot. And he was abusive when he got drunk.

She got out of the relationship after just a year and a half. But he'd spent the past few years, since her book was published, telling anyone who would listen that she'd stolen his ideas.

She hadn't stolen anything. She'd learned a lot from him about cocktails and life. He had always complained about the limited choice of cocktail flavorings, but he'd never done one thing about it.

When she'd left him, she'd been sad and sorry, but she'd learned early that food and drink would lift her up. So she'd eaten too much, put on weight she'd never lost, and she'd started experimenting. She'd created the cranberry liqueur first, and she'd used it to make a signature drink for the hotel bar where she'd been employed.

That drink had been a hit. And the rest was history.

Jason Clawson had been a memory until her book hit the *New York Times* bestsellers list.

"I didn't steal anything," she said.

"No? Not even to get ahead? Clearly you've got a dream to follow, and you'll do just about anything to chase it. I know exactly how that feels."

He turned on the balls of his feet, always graceful, and walked away.

# Chapter Seven

Isa's head hurt on Sunday morning when she cracked open her eyes. After Collin had left the wedding, she'd made herself one too many Rosy glows. They hadn't left her feeling very rosy.

Thank God it wasn't a sunny day. The rain beat hard against the roof, and the light around the window shade was a dreary gray.

So began the first day of the rest of her life. Yesterday she'd momentarily made a bunch of plans that were based on thin air. Today she'd fallen back to the ground.

No matter what she did, Collin would never trust her again. She'd destroyed his trust the moment she'd let his father bully her into walking away. She'd been so young and foolish. She'd lost a true love without even realizing how precious it was. She'd broken his heart.

And even if she'd had perfectly good reasons for doing what she'd done, damage like that could never be repaired.

She'd substituted a career that gave her plenty of freedom and money and even a little fame. It was the consolation prize for the mistake she'd made all those years ago.

Not a bad one as it turned out. She didn't hate her life. She just wanted more from it. She didn't want to give up her career, she just wanted to shape it so she could spend more time with family.

But staying here in Sweet Home wasn't possible. Not if Collin was going to be here rubbing her nose in the mistake. She needed to get away, regroup, move on.

So maybe she would sign that Food Network contract. Or maybe she'd go back to Baltimore and lick her wounds. She'd give Gabriela all the money she needed to fix the house, but she didn't want one thing to do with it anymore.

She didn't want to see Collin's face or hear his name or remember the past that she'd screwed up so badly.

So she got up and padded into the bathroom, drank a gallon of water from her cupped hands and took a shower.

Gabriela was waiting for her at the small kitchen table. "You're going, aren't you?"

"I am."

Gabriela gave a small nod. "It was a foolish hope we had." She blew out a sigh. "Which your cousin Vivi had to destroy because you know that girl. She destroys everything she envies."

"Vivi?"

"You didn't know? She's the one who filled Collin's head with poison."

Isa sat down and accepted a cup of coffee from her aunt. Could she undo the damage? She thought about it for a long time and jettisoned the idea.

"You can't make a man trust you after you've broken his heart," she finally said. "It wasn't Vivi who destroyed my second chance. I destroyed all my chances eighteen years ago. When I said *I do*, I should have meant what I said. It took me exactly two days to break that promise."

Gabriela frowned. "What promise?"

Isa pressed her fingers against the headache that had formed right in the middle of her forehead. "You didn't know? Papi never told you after all these years?"

"I didn't know what?"

"Collin and I ran away and got married at the courthouse in Richmond. We came home and told Mami and Papi. He told his parents. And let's just say that when Mr. Atwood found out, he made a big deal about Papi's forged papers."

"Oh no."

She nodded. "We didn't just break up, Gabriela. I dumped him. I broke his heart and I never told him why. And even though I recently told him the truth, the damage has been done. Plus, you know, he lost a wife. It's hard for a man like that to trust. And I'm the last person on the face of the planet that he can trust."

"I'm so sorry."

She shrugged. "I need time to think about what comes next. For a moment, I was thinking about coming home to Sweet Home. But maybe it's not a good idea."

"And not going to LA?"

She shook her head. "I'm not sure I want to be that famous, you know? I'd lose my privacy. Look at all the crap I had to endure from Jason after the book came out."

"Jason is a *caremonda*."

Wow! Gabriela was not one to swear, but she'd just basically called Jason a dick, although the literal translation was face of a penis. And really, the description fit.

"I'm going home to Baltimore," Isa said.

Gabriela did nothing to stop her, even though Isa halfway hoped she might try. But really, even Gabriela understood the difficulty now.

An hour later, she pulled her Mini onto the main road out of town with the windshield wipers flapping in the downpour. She got as far as the turn off toward Mr. Canaday's pond.

She slowed for a moment, and then her hands moved on the steering wheel almost of their own accord. She wanted one last look at the place where, once upon a time, she'd fallen in love.

Her little car would never be able to jump the berm up to the sodden pasture, but she pulled to the side of the road, turned off the engine, and listened to the rain beating on the metal roof of her car, just as it had done all those years ago, when the thunderstorm soaked them to the skin.

Collin got up early on Sunday morning and let Liam sleep. He went out to the garage, fired up the sander and went back to work on the truck.

He hadn't slept all night.

Funny. After Jess died, he'd gone through a long period where sleep had eluded him. The experts on grief had told him that this was perfectly normal. Sleeplessness was part of the shock of losing a loved one.

The experts had been right. Eventually he'd learned how to

sleep again, just like he'd learned to ignore the hole in his heart. He'd learned how to laugh again. And he'd gone on with his life. A lonely life.

Until Isa Alvarez walked into the office last Friday a week ago. He'd lost a lot of sleep since then. Mostly yearning for her. And last night, he'd paced the floors grieving again.

Not for Jess, but for Isa.

He fired up the sander and started grinding the paint. He worked for a long time until someone tugged on his jeans. He turned off the power tool and looked down at his son.

Damn. He'd forgotten about getting him some breakfast. "You must be hungry," he said.

The kid rolled his eyes and folded his arms over his thin chest. "Like I'm not able to pour some cereal into a bowl," he said.

"Good to know. Guess I can give up making you waffles on Sunday."

"I don't want waffles," he said, jutting his stubborn little chin. He looked exactly like Jess when he assumed that position.

"No?"

The kid shook his head. "No. I want to know why we left the wedding early last night. I wanted to dance more."

Collin turned his back. "Because."

"Because why?"

"Just because."

"Because you had a fight with Miss Isa?"

Collin shrugged.

"You did have a fight with her. I saw it. Why?"

"You're too young to understand."

"Dad!" Liam drew out this word in a truly irritating fashion.

"What?" Collin turned around and glared at his son.

"You like her," the kid said. "I like her. I like her cooking too."

"I'm not getting involved with a woman just because of her cooking."

The kid rolled his eyes. "Uncle Scott said she was your girlfriend when you were a kid."

"Yeah, so?"

"He said you used to take her out on dates in that truck."

"I did."

"And you still like her, right?"

Did he still like Isa Alvarez? Hell yes. He still liked her. A lot. But could he trust her?

"I think you should go over to her house and talk things over."

It was a bit chastening to hear his own words echoed back to him. Last month Liam had gotten into a fight with his bestie, Leo, over something stupid. A Lego structure they were trying to build together. And Liam had moped around the house for two days until Collin had dragged him over to Leo's house and made the boys talk to each other.

He leaned on the truck's fender for a long moment. Maybe he should go talk things over. Maybe he had jumped to a stupid conclusion. After all, why the hell would her cousin make such a point of dishing dirt on her?

"So you gonna do it?" Liam asked.

"You want to come with me?" Collin turned around and faced his son.

"Nah. I think you should be alone. But I called Leo, and you can drop me at his house on the way."

※

Isa wept. Sitting in her tiny yellow car, the tears fell like the rain beating on her roof. She cried for Mami. She cried for Papi. And she cried for the love she'd lost forever.

She felt so alone in those moments. What good was a dream if the people you loved, the ones you'd sacrificed for, were gone? She hadn't been selfish that day she'd decided to let Collin go. She'd done it to protect her family. And maybe, in the back of her mind, she'd bought into Mr. Atwood's arguments that Collin needed to focus on his career.

So in a weird, twisted way, she'd done it for Collin too. But she'd been so wrong about that.

And then she remembered something Mami had told her that night when she lay in her bed crying her eyes out, mourning the dreams she and Collin had planned all those nights when they'd sneaked out here to this pasture.

"He'll find you," Mami had said. "If his love is true, he'll find you."

But he never had found her. He'd never come back. And she'd never explained. She'd never even tried. This time, though, he hadn't even wanted to listen to her explanations.

But maybe he would now. Maybe she should try again. Maybe Mami was wrong, and she shouldn't be waiting for him to come find her. Maybe she needed to go find him.

To try one more time.

She wiped the tears from her eyes. "This is probably going to shatter my heart," she said to no one in particular, except maybe the ghosts in her head.

She fired up the Mini and turned around, heading down the old road that was paved over now. She reached the intersection and was about to turn left to go back into town, when an Atwood Construction Truck pulled up to the corner and turned.

The truck stopped and the driver's side window came down, the rain pouring down between them. Had Collin come to find her? Oh God, maybe he had.

She put down her own window. "I was just coming to find you," she said.

"Gabriela said you were going back to Baltimore."

"I was. But I couldn't drive past the turnout. Collin, I am so sorry that I broke your trust. But you need to hear me. I didn't steal anyone's ideas. My old boyfriend was abusive and controlling, and he's unhappy about my success. And I haven't signed any contracts with the Food Network. I've been carrying around the papers for a few weeks, trying to decide. And that should tell you something right there. If I had to think about it that hard, maybe it was because I knew that going to LA wasn't for me. I don't want that kind of fame or fortune."

"No?"

She shook her head. "And you shouldn't listen to every word that comes out of Vivian's mouth. She can be spiteful at times."

His mouth twitched seductively. "I figured that out. Come on, follow me," he said, rolling up his window.

He headed back down the road, and Isa made a U-turn and

followed him until he pulled off by the pasture. She stopped her car behind his truck and waited for a moment. Did he want her to brave the downpour?

No. A moment later, Collin emerged from his truck and sprinted through the rain to her passenger's side door. He climbed in, bringing the scent of the rain and himself with him.

His plaid work shirt was halfway drenched, and his hair dripped down his forehead, reminding her of prom night all those years ago when she'd licked the rainwater off his neck.

"I don't want you to go," he said. "I don't know what happened yesterday. I just got…"

"Scared?" she said, a lump in her throat. "You had a good reason to be. I broke my promise, and I'm so sorry for that."

"You were forced to break that promise."

She nodded. "I guess I was. I was so young. I was so stupid."

"I forgive you. And I hope you forgive me for being an idiot yesterday."

"There's nothing to forgive." She inched closer, the damn console in the way. Her Mini was not nearly big enough for any kind of serious fooling around.

He touched her face. "You've been crying."

She nodded. "I don't want to go. I want to make a home here in Sweet Home. I want another chance to get it right. I never stopped loving you Collin. All these years. I love you still."

"And I love you too." He pulled her forward, and the gearshift poked her in the ribs.

"Ow," she said. "Damn. Can we go someplace else? I mean, we're adults now. Do we have to always make out in a car or a truck?"

He laughed then. "There's a bunch of travel motels down the road."

"Good idea," she said starting the engine. "We'll leave your truck here, and I'll drive for once."

Fifteen minutes later they checked into a Holiday Inn that was ten times nicer than the place where they'd spent their wedding night.

He pulled her close into the shelter of his arms, and she tucked her head under his chin. "I promise to be faithful and true," she said, bending her neck to look up at him. "For the rest of my life. And this time, I really mean it."

And then he kissed her.

# Acknowledgments

I'd like to thank Nancy Vargas and Diana Vargas Lanier for their help in directing me to sources on Colombian cooking, and for introducing me to empanadas a number of years ago. If you've never had one, you're missing out.

I'd also like to give a shout out to Lelaneia Dubay, co-owner of the Hartford Flavor Company, maker of Wild Moon Liqueurs, for her help in the cocktails selected for the wedding in this short story. Check out their website to learn more about the kind of naturally-flavored liqueurs that the heroine of this story was making and for recipes for all the cocktails mentioned in this story. I am personally a huge fan of the Wild Moon Cucumber Liqueur. A cucumber gin martini garnished with a raspberry is a luxurious, sophisticated, and yummy summer time drink.

As always, I'd like to thank the writers in the weekday morning chat room, for just being there. Dana, Debbie, Marin, Lenee, AJ, Cynthia, and our latest addition to the crew, Elizabeth.

Finally, many thanks to the other writers at Fiction from the Heart for inviting me to be one of their sisterhood. Over the last difficult year, they have carried my water more times than I can count.

# About Hope Ramsay

**Hope Ramsay** is a *USA Today* bestselling author of heartwarming contemporary romances, set below the Mason-Dixon Line. Her children are grown, but she has fur-babies galore. A senior cat named Simba who was born in Uganda, a kitten named Pete, who was found wandering her neighborhood at the ripe age of eight weeks, and a precious Cockapoo named Daisy, who thinks Pete is her best buddy. Hope lives in the medium-sized town of Fredericksburg, Virginia and when she's not writing, she spends her time knitting, playing in the garden, and noodling around on her collection of guitars. You can learn more about Hope and her books at www.hoperamsay.com, or connect with Hope on Facebook.

# Inseparable

by Barbara Samuel

# Chapter One

In the softening light of approaching sunset, Nina Callahan drove between the shoulders of two peaks and into the small mountain town of Peach Ridge, where her son would finally be getting married.

It had been a long drive over mountain passes and across the high plains of the Colorado Rockies from her home in Colorado Springs. She didn't love navigating the narrow roads on her own, and once upon a time, her husband Jason would have taken the wheel. They would have played an audio book to pass the time, or sung along with a playlist he'd created from his vast collection of music.

She especially wished Jason could be there to see their son marry at last. Nathan had been a headstrong and heedless teen, giving his parents no end of worry, but once he'd discovered screenwriting in college, he'd settled into himself, growing into a man with strong convictions and a heart as big as the world. Jason would be proud.

And Nina was proud of herself. The drive had been over four hours, but now the GPS prompted her to turn onto a picturesque street lined with trees and Victorian-era buildings. Two blocks down, nestled against a stream, was the B&B her son had booked, The Larkspur Inn. She pulled into a small graveled lot and got out, stretching her back.

As if the world had been waiting for her to get ready, the sun dropped behind the towering, craggy peaks that surrounded the little town, making a perfect bowl. The sky blazed a bright, pure gold, lining the edge of the ragged mountains and then softening into lavender. Nina practically held her breath, wishing to take out her sketchbook and capture it, but that would waste the best of the show. Instead, she stood there with her hands on her hips, taking it in. Pink and lilac scarves of clouds fluttered across the darkening blue above the forests of aspen and pine, and were reflected back by a lake in the distance. The air was so still it was like a song.

A red-tailed hawk sailed overhead, an extravagance that made Nina laugh aloud. "Thank you," she whispered, feeling a sweetness settle through her, an expectation of happiness that had been lost for a long time.

As the shadows rose in the wake of sunset, a chill came along. Even in late June, the mountain nights could be cold, and she headed for the trunk to get her sweater and her bag to check in. Find some dinner, maybe. Her son wouldn't be arriving until tomorrow afternoon, but Nina had wanted a day to wander the town, sketch and shoot photos. She pulled the sweater out first and stuck her arms in. As she reached for the bag, a low warm voice said, "Let me get that for you."

"Oh, really, I'm—" she began, and halted in stunned surprise.

Because the man standing before her was not a stranger. Despite the thirty years that had passed, despite the way he cut his hair practically to nothing against his perfectly shaped skull, despite the laugh lines etched deeply around his eyes, and the goatee he'd been too young to grow back then, she knew him instantly. "Marcus!" she cried, "What are you doing here?"

"I could ask you the same question."

Oh, lord, that voice! She'd forgotten how smooth and rich his voice was, like a cello, like caramel, like—

They moved at the same instant, murmuring the same words, *oh my god,* as they came together in a massive hug. His arms wrapped around her, pulled her hard against his lean body, and at the smell of his skin—spice and warmth and summer nights—she felt a latent, nearly forgotten electricity bolt through her body. With her face buried in his shoulder, she remembered a million moments of longing and satisfaction, laughter and tears. Her veins buzzed, bringing life and awareness to every single inch of her skin.

They didn't speak. His big hand was at the back of her head, and her arms were so tightly wrapped around his waist that she could feel a button on his jacket biting into her neck. Twice she thought it had gone on too long, and twice she felt him gather her closer.

It made her dizzy.

Finally, after long minutes or maybe hours, she couldn't say, they released each other simultaneously. She looked up, up — he was always so tall, even in high school — and was glad of the cover of evening to hide her blush. "What are you doing here?" she asked softly.

"My daughter is getting married."

"Not Giselle?"

"Yes. Do you know her?"

Nina laughed, touching his arm. "Yes, I do. She's marrying my son Nathan."

"No!" He laughed, too, and the sound normalized the strange, shimmery tension surrounding them. Reaching for her suitcase, he swung it easily and slammed the trunk closed. "I suppose they'd rather not know our history."

"I'm quite sure they would not."

They walked across the parking lot in the quiet, their feet crunching gravel. "Is your husband with you?" he asked, much too politely.

"No. I'm a widow."

"I'm sorry. I hadn't heard. He was a doctor, wasn't he?"

"Yes. He set up clinics in rural places. He was drowned when a river flooded in a monsoon." With a small smile, she looked up. "It was six years ago, and Nathan and I have always said it was the way he would have wanted to go — on a mission."

"There's something to be said for living fully."

She forced herself to ask the question, "And your wife?"

"She's gone. Breast cancer, seven years ago."

"Oh, no. That's terrible."

"It wasn't an easy death," he agreed. He held open the door to the B&B. A shadow in Marcus's eyes in his eyes told her it hadn't been easy for him either.

The door opened into small room with a coat tree and tile floors — no doubt a practicality in such a sloppy place in the winter time—and a carved wooden bannister along a staircase that led upward to a large stained glass window that had lost most of its color in the darkening evening.

A woman bustled in, athletic-looking with a wild mass of curly red hair. "Hello! I'm Clara, the owner. I assume you have a reservation?"

"Yes. Nina Callahan."

Clare looked up. "Not the *artist* Nina Callahan?"

It was so very, very rare that this happened, and Nina beamed. "Yes!"

The woman settled her palm over her throat. "Oh, my goodness. I am such a fan! One of your collages is hanging in the breakfast room. A print," she hurried to add. "No offense but I couldn't afford the real thing."

"No offense taken." Nina laughed, and reached for the woman's hand, closing it between her own. "I'm honored, thank you."

"Let's get you settled. I'm moving you to the best bedroom. It has great views and a spectacular bathroom."

"Oh, you don't have to do that!"

"Please, it would be my honor."

Nina glanced up at Marcus, who had watched the exchange with a smile playing on the edges of his wide mouth. For a second she snagged on his lips, and suddenly remembered kissing them, full and soft and generous, and another wild ripple traveled through her body, shimmered over her skin.

Swallowing, she turned back to Clare. "Thank you. That would be very nice."

They finished the check in, and Nina took her key. Marcus hefted the small carryon she'd brought with her, and she protested. "I can do it, I swear. You don't have to lug it."

"I don't mind," he said in his quiet, sure way.

Clare led. As they climbed the stairs, Marcus behind her, Nina was acutely aware of her legs beneath the summer skirt she wore, and her rear end, and the set of her shoulders. In the narrow stairwell, she smelled his skin and heard him humming very softly beneath his breath. She remembered another stairway, the back stairs to the isolated art classrooms where they'd met, once upon a time, a thousand million years ago.

She felt that young ghost of herself stirring, wanting to look over her shoulder.

They climbed to the third floor, where a door opened into a charming room tucked between a trio of dormers. The color scheme gave it a sense of spring, with pale green walls and curtains and a white bedspread with green vines. Pillows in dark green and violet accented the bed and the sofa.

"It's lovely," Nina said.

Clare pointed out the coffee maker and mini bar and a basket of snacks, and last, the lingering light over the mountains. A whisper of a breeze blew in through a window, carrying the sound of the stream far below. A bird whistled goodnight in the trees.

"If there's anything you need, let me know," Clare said.

"I will."

Marcus settled her suitcase on the stand, and turned toward the door, too. She watched him move, his long legs, his athletic frame, and wondered what to say, how to keep him here.

Both of them spoke at once. "I can't believe—" Nina said

"I don't want to—" Marcus said.

They faced each other. His unfathomably dark eyes fixed on her face. "You first."

She found her hands clasped together. "I can't believe that you're here. After all this time."

"I don't want to stop talking to you. It's been so long." He searched her face. "Giselle won't be here until tomorrow."

"Nathan either."

"Let's find some dinner and catch up. What do you say?"

She nodded too vigorously, relieved. "Yes, I'd like that."

"Good." He stood there, as if he, too, was shaken and lost inside this odd reunion. "I'll give you some time to get unpacked. Meet you downstairs in twenty?"

"That's perfect."

He lingered one long moment more, as if he would say something else, then abruptly turned, ducked beneath the doorjamb and closed the door behind him.

Nina sank down onto the bed, putting her hands to her cheeks, which felt as hot at the rest of her. Her hands were a little shaky, as if she was fifteen again, and painfully in love.

She and Marcus met on the first day of ninth grade, at the brand new high school in a still treeless, raw subdivision that had sprouted up on the east side of Colorado Springs. No one knew anyone else, and all the seating was assigned by last name, so she found herself sitting next to him in two classes. The first time, in English second period, she noticed him, a tall black youth with hands too big for his wrists and a haircut so short that she figured he was from a military family, since every other black kid at school was wearing an Afro. He gave her a nod as he sat down, but nothing more.

The second class was biology, where they formed a group of four with two other kids, one a total stoner by the look of his red eyes, and one a shy nerd with glasses. Marcus gave her a smile this time, and she smiled back.

The third class was art, where there was no assigned seating, only wide, open tables. He sat down beside her. "I figured we might as well sit together here, too," he said. His eyes danced. "I'm Marcus."

"I know."

"What kind of art do you do?"

"All kinds, really, but I like painting. You?"

"I like everything, too, but my dad hates art, so I haven't had many chances to explore. I want to sculpt something, maybe."

"Why does your dad hate art?"

He shrugged, his face going blank. "It's sissy. Not for real guys."

Nina eyed his broad shoulders, his beautiful hands lying on the table in front of him. "You look like a real guy to me." It was the boldest thing she'd ever said to any boy ever.

He smiled.

From that day until the middle of their senior year, when everything had come to a brutal crashing end, they'd been inseparable, a couple people knew by one name, NinaMarcus or MarcusNina.

Every day. Four years.

Now he was here, right in front of her, the father of her son's bride.

And again family dynamics would make it impossible for them to pursue anything real.

But Nina was a grown woman now, sophisticated from her travels, grounded in reality as she never had been back in those starry-eyed days. She stood up to apply fresh lipstick and brush her very short-cropped hair.

It was only dinner. It would be fine.

## Chapter Two

As they walked toward the center of the tiny village, a deeply awkward silence fell between Nina and Marcus. The night was cool but pleasant, and Nina was glad of her sweater to wrap around herself, maybe in protection. Marcus had changed into jeans and a long-sleeved shirt topped with a bomber jacket aged to perfection.

The awkwardness was partly the roaring attraction she felt—completely inappropriate, considering everything—but partly, where to begin? How did you "catch up" after so much time had passed?

He seemed equally ill at ease. Hands in his jacket pockets, hands clasped behind him, hands swinging. For a while, he spun a key ring with a single key around his finger.

Finally, Nina said, "This is weird. I don't know where to start."

He gave a short laugh. "Me, either."

She took a breath. "How about this, then? How are you, Marcus? You look well. You look hot actually and I mean that in the best possible way."

"I'll take it that way. Thanks. So do you. I love your hair short like that."

"Do you?" She smoothed a hand over her bare neck. "I chopped it off seven or eight years ago. Jason hated it, but I love how easy it is."

"Not as easy as mine," he joked, running a hand over the barely-there shadow with a rueful smile.

"You've always had a great-looking head." She felt her shoulders ease slightly. "Where's home these days?"

"LA. I've been a lawyer out there since law school."

## Inseparable

"Lawyer, huh? I bet your dad loves that."

The awkwardness rose instantly, a prickly dinosaur standing between them. "Sorry," Nina said, shaking her head. "I don't know why I said that."

"I do." In the pause, Nina remembered her terror of the Colonel. "But yes, he does love it. He brags about me every chance he gets."

"That's nice. He must be...what? In his eighties by now?"

"Yes. Eighty-three, as a matter of fact. Still lives in the Springs."

"Huh. So do I."

"I did know that."

She looked up at him in surprise. "You did?"

He paused, lips turning down. "I've followed your career now and again."

"Really. You could have emailed or something."

They stopped in front of the restaurant, a fussy place with white table cloths. "I'm not feeling this," he said. "How about you?"

"No way." She looked up and down the street, and spied a sign that said Flanigans. "Pub?"

"Much better."

They made their way across the street, still accompanied by the prickly dinosaur of awkwardness. Maybe it had been a mistake to come out with him. Maybe there was too much time and history between them.

But she was there now. May as well get through it. She had to eat anyway. They settled in a high-backed booth. Celtic music played in the background, and a girl with blond hair shimmering down her back nearly to her rear-end came over to plop down two laminated menus. "How are you two tonight?" she asked, and her consonants were precise. A summer job, Nina thought, for a graduate student.

"Doing well, thanks," Marcus said, and she liked him for being a human being with the girl. "Will you bring me whatever brown ale you have on tap?"

"Of course. And you, miss?"

Nina smiled at the *miss*. "I'll have the same."

She buried herself in the menu, feeling the depth of her

famished emptiness. The listings were hefty, full of sandwiches designed to refuel skiers and mountain bikers, and she settled on a Rueben.

When she looked up, Marcus was studying her with a gentle expression. "What?" she asked.

He shook his head. "Just looking at you."

"Noticing all my wrinkles?"

"Not at all. I would have known you anywhere."

She studied his face in return. She'd always loved painting him — the contrasting angles, the warm burnt sienna of his skin, the thick eyebrows that had always driven him crazy but gave his adult face a power that probably served him well in his profession. His eyes were large and luminous, the singular thing about him that people always said, even then. *Marcus has the prettiest eyes.* She loved the addition of the goatee, a tidy salt and pepper mix that added a dash of sexiness.

"Also, I bet I know what you're going to order," he added.

"Doubtful."

He took a pen from inside his bomber jacket and wrote on the napkin, hiding it from her. His eyes sparkled as he finished. "We'll see."

The server returned with two pints of red-brown ale. "What would you like to eat?"

Marcus gestured toward Nina. "No, you first," she said, suddenly wondering if she should change her order.

"I'll have the cheeseburger," he said.

"No pickles," Nina inserted, "or ketchup or mayo or condiments of any kind." She met his eyes. "Right?"

He smiled, dipping his head in acknowledgement. "Correct."

"And I'd like the Rueben," Nina said. "No thousand island dressing."

"Got it." The woman grabbed the menus and hustled away.

Marcus held up the napkin on which he'd written REUBEN in blocky letters.

Nina laughed. Marcus's face eased, breaking into a smile that showed his laugh lines and good teeth tended by military dentists, while she'd been at the mercy of her single mother's meager resources and still had a crooked eye tooth. She touched it with her tongue, thinking how self-conscious she'd been about it. Now she'd grown to love it. It was a part of her.

He lifted his beer. "To old friends."

She clinked glasses. "Old friends."

"Tell me about your life, Nina," he said. "Do you have a studio where you work? Did you go to New York?"

She smiled softly, hearing the echo of the dreams they'd had — to grow up and go to New York for art school, paint and find fame together. "I did go to New York for grad school, which is where I met Nestor Young, the writer whose stories I first illustrated. And I do have a studio in my house. It's a converted shed in my backyard. The light is just amazing. Jason had it built for my fortieth birthday."

"That's great. You've done what we said we would. I admire that."

She looked down. Turned her pint glass in a circle on the napkin, then met his eyes. "And you? Do you have studio space?" She knew the answer. "Did you go to New York?"

He didn't flinch. "No on both counts, as you know. But I was never the artist you were, Nina. We both know that."

"That's your father talking," she said with an edge, but forced herself to take a breath, lighten up. All water under the bridge. "I can imagine you're a great lawyer, too. What kind of law?"

"Entertainment. Mostly film."

"That must be pretty interesting."

He shrugged. "Day to day, it's a lot of contracts, negotiations, a lot of business. But sometimes, it can be glamourous. I've been to some film premieres, worked with some people you'd know." He took a sip of beer. "Mainly, I love it because I'm helping people like you — an artist — avoid getting ripped off out of passion for a project."

"I thought that was an agent's job."

"Sometimes, but there's a lot of crossover."

"Have you ever worked with anyone famous?"

"Many times." He winked. "But I'm no name dropper."

She laughed. "Of course you aren't. You were always the best secret keeper." She remembered a conversation with Giselle about her father. "Giselle told me that she became interested in the business because of your work."

"I thought for a while she might become an actor, which is what everybody wants, but she was always focused on the behind-the-scenes world—how did they decide what to wear? How do you design scenery? How did you figure out who would play a role? She's remarkably good at casting."

"What did her mom do?" Nina sipped her beer. "And what was her name, your wife?"

"Beverly. She was...a mom. A wife. She kept things moving in our lives, organized the entertaining, all that." He sounded slightly defensive.

"I'm not judging her," Nina said. "Or you. I was just curious about what influenced Giselle to that kind of creative background work."

"Ah. Well, Beverly loved interior design, and helped all of her friends do their houses. She loved her garden, too, and it was one of the most beautiful in the neighborhood." He shook his head. "I hired a gardener after she died, and he's maintained it, but the heart is gone."

"She sounds like a wonderful person."

He took a breath. Nodded. "She was." Clearing his throat, he said, "Tell me about your husband."

Nina shook her head. "Another time. You can keep talking about Beverly. Tell me all about her and how you met and where you got married. All those things."

"Not now," he said, his voice rich and warm. "Another time. I'd rather hear about you."

She smiled. "And I want to know about *you*. It seems the woman you loved would be a big part of that."

For a moment he paused, looking down, his hands busy rearranging the salt and pepper shakers, the parmesan cheese in a round glass container. "I miss her today," he said at last. "She would be in such a happy tizzy over Giselle's wedding." He swallowed. "Giselle had to pick her wedding dress with friends instead of her mother."

Impulsively, she reached across the table and settled her hand on his. "I was thinking almost the same thing on the way over the pass. Jason would be so proud of the man Nathan has become."

"Yes." He shook his head. "I can't believe I didn't know Nathan was your son. He's a great guy. You've done an amazing job."

"Thanks. He was a crazy teen, but we got through it."

"Giselle was the opposite. She was so focused and made so many plans that I worried she wouldn't be able to manage failure." He took a breath. "And then her mom died and she showed me just how great she'd be."

"Our kids are getting married, Marcus!" She laughed. "How crazy is that?"

The server brought their food. Nina's sandwich was exactly perfect—grilled pumpernickel and sauerkraut with cheese oozing out. She bent in to smell it.

Marcus laughed. "You still love your food."

"I do." She gestured ruefully to her ample hips. "And it shows."

"I always knew you'd be a little plump."

"Oh, thank you very much!" She picked up a French fry and ate it defiantly. "Unlike some people here. How do you stay so slim?"

"I got fat for a while, but doc ordered me to find something aerobic to do or have a heart attack, so I picked up a walking habit."

"That's all, just walking?"

"Four miles a day, six days a week."

"Men!" Nina rolled her eyes. "I've been doing that for years. Doesn't help."

He chuckled. The sound was intimately familiar, deeper now, but still the same rhythm, the *heh, heh, heh*. The sound swirled around her body, found its way into her ribs, her belly, so her cells were primed to notice when he licked a smear of cheese from his thumb. Time slowed and she was transfixed, watching his lips purse and the way he gave a little suck, and she flashed suddenly on the way they had discovered each other's bodies, long, long ago.

Desire, unfamiliar and unsettling, pooled in her belly over the memories—Marcus bent over her, her throat, her chest, her abdomen—

He noticed her staring. His hand fell to the table, but their gaze tangled and held. "Your eyes," he said quietly. His nostrils flared ever so slightly, and some part of her that recognized his signals flushed hard, a warmth rushing down her neck, over her shoulders, as if she'd added a cloak of awareness. In a low voice, he said, "Your eyes always said so much."

Someone laughed too loudly at a table nearby. Nina jerked back to the here-and-now, not a lifetime ago when they were young and hungry and horny as cats twenty-four hours a day. As teenagers were programed to be, she told herself. They'd been young and biologically prompted to mate.

She looked at her sandwich, tried to remember what she was doing. Desire still washed over her, embarrassingly intense, as if she were sixteen again and new to it all.

"Hey." He took her hand. "I didn't mean to embarrass you."

The weight and heat of his palm connected to all the sensors in her body, sending another wave of hot blue light over every inch of her body. It was almost impossible to even breathe around it, and in self-defense, she pulled away. "You didn't." She dropped her hand to her lap. "It's all just so strange, you know, seeing you again. There's so much—"

"I know. Me, too."

This time, she let her defenses down, took in a calming breath and let it go, allowing him to see it. "It's strange, Marcus, but I'm glad." She picked up her beer. "Let's eat."

<hr>

A little wall came down then, and they talked about little things, about preferences that had stayed the same and things that had changed—he no longer ate candy all day long, popping peanut M&Ms in his mouth from a seemingly endless supply in his pocket; she no longer hated all vegetables. They talked about their friends from school and what had happened to them. Mostly, they didn't know. It was a military town, and a lot of them had simply moved on with their family's next duty station.

"Have you been to any of the reunions?" he asked.

"All of them," she admitted. "I'm still friends with Nancy Smits, remember her? She does all the organizing, and I'd never live it down if I didn't show up. The thirtieth was fairly thinned out." She wiped her greasy fingers. "You should come to the next one."

He shook his head. "You're the star, I bet."

"Kind of," she admitted with smile. "Alexander High is a musician but I think I might be the more famous of the two of us."

He laughed. "Good."

Their plates and glasses were empty. "Let's walk back."

Outside, Nina shivered a little at the layer of cold that crept along the sidewalk out of the mountains. "I have to remember to wear jeans at night," she said. "It's cold up here!"

In a flash, he took off his coat and flung it around her shoulders. "No, Marcus, you don't have to do that! I was just commenting on the weather."

He lifted his hand. "Let me be a gentleman."

The weight was delicious — and yes, warm. She tucked her arms into the sleeves smiling up at him as she unconsciously tugged the collar up to smell it.

The scent of him, all those summer notes of pine and night and a morning wind, had soaked into the fabric and the leather like a heady perfume. "I forgot how good you smell," she said without thinking.

He swallowed, touched her shoulders lightly and they kept walking. It seemed strange to not take his hand, as she might have done once upon a time. She forced herself to talk about something else.

"Remember the project in tenth grade when we had to do a series of birds in any medium we wanted?"

"I do. You did peacocks with collage."

"And you did birds of prey in graphite and watercolor."

"Red tailed hawk," he said, his voice rich with happiness. "My favorite."

"The whole series was amazing. Do you still have those paintings?"

"No, I don't have any of that stuff. When we moved to Alaska, we had to pare down hard."

Alaska was where he'd gone in the middle of senior year. A

shattering loss—for both of them. But to think he hadn't saved any of his work gave her an entirely different kind of pain. "You're kidding, Marcus! You didn't save *any* of the work you did? You were so good!"

He let go of a soft laugh. "*You* were good, Nina. I was only competent."

"That's not true. What about the abstracts?"

"Only competent."

She halted. "No," she said firmly. "They were extraordinary."

"You were just looking at them with eyes of love."

"One of them won an award!"

He glanced over her shoulder, seeing something in the past that she couldn't decipher.

"You never believed enough in your voice and vision," she said. "Your dad wouldn't let you."

Overhead, the sky was thick with stars. Crickets whirred in the grass. Far in the distance, a single car made its way down an unseen street. And standing in front of her was a man she'd dreamed about at least once every six months for her whole life, dreaming they'd met again, or fought, or had sad conversations about what had gone wrong.

*Soul mate.*

Against the stars, his profile was beloved and familiar, the brow, his nose, his strongly carved chin, all memorized a thousand years ago. Once they had believed they were soul mates, destined by forces much larger than themselves to go through life together, and then it had all come crashing down.

Impulsively, she said, "Let's go hiking tomorrow and sketch."

"I don't have anything with me."

She made a dismissive noise. "I have at least five hundred and ninety-two sketchbooks in the trunk of my car alone. A bag full of materials."

He hesitated. "I haven't done anything in a long time."

"Doesn't matter. We'll just have fun. That's all."

They had reached the B&B and Marcus paused beneath a gently rattling aspen tree. Behind it, the stream chuckled quietly. "And if we go, hiking and drawing, what will we do about this?"

"About what?" She whispered, but her body was already swaying toward him, and when his hands cupped her face, she heard herself take a breath, sharp and quick, in anticipation. Her hands lit on his chest, fingers spreading wide to gauge his ribs. He tilted up her chin, and for a moment stolen from one of her dreams, he looked at her, his gaze touching her brows, her nose and cheeks, and finally her mouth. "I've thought of you so many times," he said. "So many times."

"Me, too," she whispered, and then he bent and kissed her, and all there was in the world was his mouth, his lips, so soft, so very very soft, and yet commanding, and delicious. The smell of him enveloped her, and his hands slid down around her neck, to her shoulders, pulling her closer. Her arms slipped around his waist, and their bodies pressed together — chest to chest, belly to belly, as Nina tilted her head back and opened to taste him more fully, and they pressed tighter, heads tilting, tongues meeting and dancing, and she fell far away into the world that had always belonged to the two of them alone, their secret, sacred place. Her blood sang.

He raised his head ever so slightly, and Nina made a sound of loss that embarrassed her and she nearly pulled away completely, but he only hauled her closer, his arm hard around her back beneath the jacket, and bent his head again.

They kissed and kissed and kissed, as if kissing was the cure for all disease, as if they could mend the history of the world with just that act. Nina dissolved into him, whirling around the center that was Marcus.

They might have kissed for a hundred years, but a car swung by, flashing them with headlights, and they broke apart. Marcus didn't let her fly away into the stars, but caught her hand to pin her to the earth.

The car drove on, and Nina came back into her body bit by bit, dizziness slowing. His hand anchored her, so much bigger than her own, so comforting. She touched her mouth and looked up at him. "Wow."

He squeezed her hand. "Me, too."

"The kids can't know."

"Oh, no." He laughed.

Nina laughed, too. "Nathan would die of embarrassment."

"Giselle is pretty down to earth, but she...I don't know."

The thought of the bride and groom sobered Nina. "It will be our secret."

He gave her a sad smile. "I guess we had plenty of practice with that."

Nina felt a familiar sense of mingled anxiety and loss. The Colonel had despised Nina practically on sight—the working-class daughter of a divorced mother who waited tables. He tolerated her until Marcus had become serious about art, and then Nina became Public Enemy Number One.

She let go of his hand and shook off his jacket, handing it back as they headed for the B&B. "Sometimes, I can still get pretty angry about that."

"You have every right. I didn't know how to stand up to him."

"I know." She shook her head. "It's all right. We were so young."

Before they reached the door, he caught her hand again. "I'll go hiking tomorrow."

Nina smiled up at him. "Good."

"I'll walk you up."

"No, thank you." She didn't trust herself, and if he came to her door and kissed her again, she would not have the will to send him away. She needed to keep him at arm's length, at least a little bit. There were too many factors, too many possibilities of disaster, too much of a chance that she'd be shattered if she didn't keep her head.

He nodded, as if she'd spoken all of it aloud. "I'll see you at breakfast."

"Good night."

In her room, Nina shed her clothes and stepped immediately into what turned out to be the shower of the century, a big stone-tiled space with multiple heads and an overhead rain shower. There was even—if she so desired—a steam option. She laughed, playing with the controls for a while, then stood under the rain head for a long time, luxuriously washing her hair. Maybe, she thought, she should book a massage while she was here.

Or maybe she should just let Marcus massage her. As she wrapped herself up in fluffy towels, she admitted to herself that was what she wanted, Marcus's hands on her body, his weight pinning her down, his mouth on hers.

The thought sent a shudder down her spine, and she shook her head wiping a circle clean on the steamed-up mirror. What would it be like, all these years later? She'd had other lovers since then, and learned her body in ways no teenager could ever hope to know. The two of them had fumbled and experimented and figured out the whole business of making love, but that was teenage hormones and lush young bodies. It couldn't help but be the most amazing sex in the world.

Maybe it wouldn't be like that at all now.

The face that looked back at her from the mirror was not dewy or young. Wrinkles had creased her skin here and there, but it was more that she'd lost color. Lost the peachy cheeks, the rosy lips, the bright shimmer of youth. Her skin was a bland beige now, verging on sallow even when she'd had plenty of sleep. The face that looked back at her was in late middle age, no question.

And her body, too, was aged. Breasts soft and not so pert. Hips too wide, butt too big, thighs…oh, thighs. She sighed. As much as she might want to, how could she take off her clothes in front of Marcus?

Who had aged, but not the way she had. Men never did. He still looked fit, and he'd probably still—

"Oh, stop it." She flung the towel aside and faced herself in the mirror. "This body has supported us through everything. Don't you dare start making judgments."

She gave herself a rueful smile, and let go of all that. She brushed her teeth, donned her decidedly ordinary pajamas that were soft and silky and just right for her, and climbed into the ridiculously comfortable bed.

What a day, she thought, listening to the sound of the stream far below her window. What a lovely, lovely day.

## Chapter Three

When Beverly fell ill, Marcus had taken up meditation to cope with his emotions. His partner at the firm, a long-time Buddhist and yogi, had suggested it, and Marcus found the simple practice to be helpful beyond all reasonable expectation. Day by day, ten minutes at a time, he settled himself enough that he could be the support his wife needed to navigate the hard road she had to travel.

This morning in Peach Ridge, he sat down to meditate in his quaint—he would maybe even call it cloying—room. His windows faced west, so he had a view of the mountains bathed in delicate early sunlight. Getting comfortable on the couch, he affixed his headphones to his phone, and played a simple musical arrangement he'd been using for years. He closed his eyes.

His thoughts were all over the place, as he'd already known, bouncing between the present and Giselle and her wedding, to the past and Nina, to Beverly and her laughing on their wedding day, to his unexpected, powerful attraction to the woman he had not seen since they'd parted almost forty years ago.

*Ping, ping, ping.*

Breathe. Center. Breathe.

He had barely dated anyone in the years since Beverly passed. He'd felt no need, really. His life was full with work and travel and all the comforts his career had brought into his life—a beautiful home, and the ease of doing most of what he wanted, and being able to jovially help his daughter, still building her career in a very expensive city. Friends had set him up a couple of times, and he'd been asked out at least a dozen more.

He'd ventured into the waters a few times, but he'd never felt a single spark.

When Nina turned around and he saw her face, so much emotion had poured through him it was as if a long-forgotten jar in his heart had been kicked over. Standing next to her, he'd felt himself trembling slightly. Over dinner, he'd want to catalogue every millimeter of her face, her throat, her hands.

And kissing her, kissing her—

He had not felt those things in a very long time. Felt so much. Felt so deeply.

*Ping ping ping.*

He let the thoughts sail away, brought himself back to his breathing.

Time, wedding, Beverly, cancer, Nina, high school, his father, art.

*Ping ping ping.*

Guilt.

He felt exhilarated and guilty in equal portions. What if Beverly had not died? Would he have felt these same emotions toward a girl he'd left behind?

Breathe. He exhaled and let it all go. The only thing that existed was the present moment. The eternal now. A splash of sunlight came around the edge of a window and touched his cheekbone, his neck.

A promise.

Whistling under his breath, he stood to get dressed for a day of hiking and art.

Art. He laughed. He'd left his art behind with youth and never thought about it at all. Or at least not much. Despite Nina's comments, he'd never been particularly talented, not like she was.

But—what the hell. Maybe it would be fun.

He didn't see Nina right away when he came into the dining room. Instead, he was snared by a giant print of one of her garden collages hanging on the wall, a vivid field of poppies and little yellow flowers, all shards of color pieced together like a very intricate quilt, giving it a sense of depth, a feeling that you could walk into it, wander around. He would have known it was one of her pieces anywhere.

"Good morning," she said.

He turned. She sat by the window, dressed in hiking pants and a simple turquoise t-shirt. His lungs expanded, filling with joy and a sense of possibility. "Good morning," he said, and as if she were someone he saw every day, a good friend or maybe his wife, he bent and kissed her cheek, smelling soap and the cinnamon undertone she carried, something so particular he could have smelled it on the wind any moment of his life and known she was close by.

His kiss flustered her. She wasn't the type to blush, but she ducked her head and rearranged her silverware and then dropped her hands in her lap and looked up.

He felt like an idiot. "Sorry. I don't know why I did that."

"I didn't mind," she said. The t-shirt made her eyes look even brighter blue. She didn't wear any makeup, and he somehow liked that, that he could see her naked skin, the slight circles under her eyes, the laugh lines. "Why don't you sit down?"

He did, scooting his chair a little too loudly. It was a fussy kind of room, all wicker and flowery fabrics, and he felt like a clumsy bear, all shoulders and too-big paws. He narrowed his eyes. "Why are these places always made for women?"

Nina grinned. "Because we like them and we make the reservations."

A woman in jeans and a bibbed apron came over. "Coffee, sir?"

"Please," he said. As she poured, she rattled off the menu for the morning, offering egg casserole, danish, or porridge.

"Casserole," he said, "and danish. And grapefruit juice, please."

Nina had seemed uncomfortable the night before, but now she ate her breakfast calmly, and commented, "I slept like a teenager."

"Me, too. Must be the mountain air."

Diffuse light fell on her face, across the upper slope of her breasts. The material of her shirt rested softly against the swell of flesh, which was much fuller than the skinny Nina of old had boasted. He'd loved her breasts in those days, small and pale—

"Eyes up, soldier."

He jerked his gaze upward and felt as idiotic as a twelve-year-old. "Sorry."

She lifted her tea cup, eyes glittering. "Pregnancy gave me quite the bosom," she said. "It happens to all the women in my family."

He shook his head, laughing. "I'm really sorry. This is just so completely unexpected. I'm not a cretin, I swear."

"I know that. You could never be a cretin."

To shift the conversation, he gestured toward the print. "I would have known that was your work. You have always had such a strong point of view, even when we were kids."

"I like it there. It brings a lot of light into a dim area."

"I feel like I could just walk into it, smell the flowers."

"Really? Thank you."

"Have you been able to make a living with art?"

"Yes." She shrugged. "Not always a big living, you know, but enough. Some years are better than others."

Something about that satisfied an ache in his gut. Had he ever wanted to live with that insecurity? Maybe not. "Even now?"

"Now I'm okay," she said with a smile.

"A rich and famous artist."

"Don't forget beautiful." She seemed utterly calm, but there was a tease in the words, in the slight lift of her brow. A woman's tease, not a girl's, a woman utterly sure of herself and her place in the world.

It was sexy as hell.

"Beautiful," he said, "is not really enough of a word for you."

She blinked. "No?"

The woman brought his food and he leaned back to let her place it while he kept his gaze on Nina's face and considered what word he would use. Her features were rather plain, all told—a straight, ordinary nose, eyes that were only notable because the color was so bright, a nice enough mouth that was thinner than it had been. It wasn't the face itself, but the energy behind it, the glow of her confidence, the sweetness of her smile, and that earthy, earthy way she had of holding his gaze, the way she was doing right now, that made him think of sinking into her, kissing her, bodies naked...

"No," he said. "You are pulchritudinous."

Nina laughed outright, the sound a roaring delight. He'd always loved this about her, the way she laughed so unselfconsciously, mouth open, entire body engaged. It was not delicate or light; she would never cover her mouth to hide it. "Mrs. Wilber's spelling lists! Oh, my God, I forgot those." She raised a hand. "Well done."

He slapped her palm in the air.

"Now, let's eat and get out of here before it gets hot," Nina said. "I already loaded up my pack with stuff. You have to carry the water."

The whole day stretched ahead with her, he thought in wonder. The mountains, the sky, a trail and some art supplies. "Just like old times."

"Yep. Better eat up. You're going to need your strength."

He raised his brows.

"For hiking, Marcus. For hiking." But she did that thing with her mouth, sucking her lower lip under her teeth, and she swept a glance at his mouth, and he knew that she'd been thinking just as much as he had about certain things.

He dug into his breakfast and ate every last crumb.

# Chapter Four

Nina loved hiking. Growing up in Colorado Springs, the options had been endless and free, and she and her mother often spent weekends hiking one trail or another, picnicking by streams before coming back down to wallow in the pure sleep granted by fresh air and vigorous exercise.

She'd researched various trails around Peach Ridge and had chosen one that was supposed to be especially picturesque and relatively mild in terms of altitude gains. They made their way along the creek, which led to a trail that followed a shallow river into a break between high ridges. Aspen groves rattled their welcomes and insects whirred in the grass. A bright blue mountain bluebird dashed between pine trees, and a woodpecker was invisibly busy somewhere in the trees. The trail was not terribly busy, but they saw other hikers, a lot of mountain bikers, and the odd runner, most of them coming back after an early venture.

Marcus and Nina walked in companionable silence, taking in the fresh, clean air, the views, the sound of the river. He walked easily beside her, keeping pace even though she knew they must be well above 9000 feet here. "You must hike in California."

He nodded. "We have a hiking group at my office. Go out a couple of weekends a month, and people join in when they can."

"That's great. How often do you go?"

"Most of the time. It's one of my hobbies." He looked down at her. "How about you. Does your mom hike with you still?"

"No." She gave him a sad smile. "She's been gone a long time. Almost fifteen years. Lung cancer. Shocking, I know." Nina's mom had been a devoted smoker.

"I bet you miss her. She was good people."

"She loved you to pieces."

"It was mutual." He paused. "Those meatballs she made, oh my god. Best in the world."

"She was a really good cook," Nina agreed. Her skin sweated lightly and her legs warmed up. "I wonder sometimes now how she made it work. It wasn't easy being a single mom in those days, and she didn't have any help from anybody. She worked forty- and fifty-hour weeks for a creep of a boss, but still managed to give me home-cooked meals every day."

"All hamburger, all the time."

"Right? It was really cheap in those days."

The trail shifted upward and they focused on climbing for a bit. At the top of the bluff, Marcus stopped to drink water, and gave Nina her bottle. They looked out across the valley, green with all the recent rain. "I miss Colorado," Marcus said. "It was my favorite of all the places we lived."

It made her feel like Colorado Springs had been just a stop along the way, one of many great experiences he'd had. Which, she realized with the rational part of her brain, it actually was. With his father in the Air Force, he'd lived in a lot of great places.

But his time in Colorado had been very powerful for *her*. She managed to keep her voice light. "It's here anytime."

He inclined his head in agreement. "True. But my work is in LA, and so is Giselle."

"So is Nathan," she said.

"Have you given any thought to moving?" He screwed the lid back on the metal water bottle. "They'll have children eventually."

"Not really. I love my home, my town. All my friends are there."

He nodded. "I can understand that. Flights are what? A couple of hours?"

"Two from Denver."

"Huh," he said in a non-committal way.

"What?" Nina asked.

"Nothing, just absorbing what you said. How far do you want to hike?"

"I have a spot in mind. It shouldn't be that much farther."

As they walked on, they talked about the birds, naming them as they once had. Nina named plants, too, and trees. They'd often taken sketchbooks and tins of watercolor out into nature, into a mountain park where there was a stream, or a long park in the middle of town, to sketch leaves and plants, little animals. "Remember the chipmunk village?" Marcus asked.

They liked picnicking at a stream in Cheyenne Canyon, where a group lived in a big red cliff. "They were so cute," Nina said. "I still love their little faces. Bandit babies."

"Mice with better coloring."

"More or less, but what's wrong with mice?"

He grinned and just like that, she was staggered again. Everything about him had always pleased all of her senses—his height and loping easy grace, his big hands and silky skin, and always that big, big laugh. Her stomach flip-flopped, and she forgot to look where she was going, and she tripped, hard, on a branch growing across the path.

It happened too fast to catch herself, and she went down hard, slamming palms and her right knee into the earth, but before she even registered the ground, he scooped her up in one arm. "Whoa, there."

She looked at her palms, scraped but not severely, and then examined her knee. It stung worse that her palms, but the hiking pants were not torn. She was aware of his hand on her ribs, beneath her left breast, and the heat of his thigh along her hip. "I'm all right," she said, moving out of his grip. "Thanks for the save."

"Anytime."

Resolutely, she started up the trail again, hearing Marcus behind her whistling softly. Her knee stung, but didn't ache—just a scrape. She didn't turn around, but she knew he'd be looking around at the world, cataloguing the shape of Ponderosa pines and blue spruce, the white and black bark of aspens, the tufts of pale green grass. She started doing the same thing, forcing herself to forget Marcus and pay attention to the world around her, and gradually she came back to herself, to the spicy scent of sun-heated pine needles and dust, to the deliriously happy feeling of being on a trail. This was why she'd come early, to hike and then find some agreeable place to sketch.

When they came to the lake, a solid few miles from the start, Nina paused in deep satisfaction, her hands on her waist as she admired the view. "Now that was worth it, wasn't it?"

The lake was not large, but it was perfectly positioned to reflect the peaks surrounding it, peaks that were still covered in snow, even in June. Purple summits gave way to thick glaciers, and the sky above them was the deep blue of high altitude, the atmosphere so thin that space shone through.

"It was," he agreed, and pointed. "Let's walk over there. Might be a great view back down the valley, too."

"Sure." Nina followed as he led her around a grassy clearing and into a stand of pines surrounding a circle of pale green grass. Gratefully, she dropped her pack and stretched her arms over her head.

They spread a picnic cloth over the ground and sat down. Nina pulled out her square sketch book and a bag of watercolor pencils and set them to her right. "What are you in the mood for?" she asked, rummaging around in the pack, pulling out a small blue book, a classic notebook with hard sides, and a heavy-weight watercolor book. He chose the latter, and Nina smiled. "So, paint, then?"

"If you have it."

"Yes." She produced a battered metal tin, a handful of brushes rubber-banded together, and a plastic container full of water. "And these, if you want to try them." She added a pair of water brushes, their clear plastic bases filled with water.

To give him a chance to settle in and explore his materials, she flipped open her sketchbook and used a blue watercolor pencil to capture basic shapes—the irregular oblong of the lake, the rounds of the granite boulders littering the scene, triangles and lollipop shapes of trees sticking up like sentinels all the way around it. Sun heated her back and the top of her head, and she tugged a floppy hat out of the pack, too.

Marcus only sat beside her, looking at the view, making no move to do anything. She took a pencil from the pack and said, "Draw. Don't think, just do."

"I don't know where to start."

She looked out over the scene. "Draw that hill with the boulders."

He dutifully opened the watercolor book on his knees, and spread his hands over the pages, making them flat. It brought back a memory she hadn't visited in long time, the way he always smoothed his work area with his palms, wiping away anything that might get in the way, make a mark on his work.

Now, he still just sat there.

Nina had taught many, many workshops with beginners and she recognized a person frozen with terror. "Marcus," she said gently. "It's just a drawing. Not the cure for cancer."

He let go of a little sound, nodding.

"How long has it been since you've drawn or painted anything?" she asked gently.

His jaw corded. "Since the last time I saw you."

"Oh, Marcus!" Impulsively, she reached over and touched his arm, silky hot. "What a terrible day."

He raised his head, met her gaze. Nodded.

The last day they'd seen each other was three days after Christmas Day their senior year. His family was moving to Alaska, but the plan had been for Marcus to stay behind with friends to finish his senior year, then join them in June. Marcus and Nina had been heartbroken to learn of the transfer, but they had hatched a plan to apply to art school together, then at the very worst, they'd only be parted for the summer.

But Marcus had shown up at her door that morning, distraught. She opened the door, and he flung his arms around her, pulling her into a hug silently and fiercely. By then he'd grown into his full height. His shoulders were as broad as a man's, but his body was still thin. She felt his ribs under her arms. "What is it?" she breathed, rubbing her hands on his back. He wasn't weeping, but everything felt lost.

"My dad found the art school acceptance. He's making me move with the family. Now."

She pulled back, staring up at him to see if it was some terrible joke. "What? You can't! You've spent your entire high school years at this school! You have to graduate with us."

"He doesn't care." He shook his head. "He's so mad."

"Let's sit down." She led him to the couch.

Marcus dropped his head in his hands and repeated, "He's so mad. My mom's been trying to talk to him, but he just keeps going on and on about how hard he's worked to give me a better life than he had."

Nina was terrified of the Colonel, of his autocratic bearing, his hard eyes. He'd spent his childhood in some place he didn't like to talk about, and joined the Air Force at seventeen, and distinguished himself, working up the ranks through wartime service and posts no one else wanted. He didn't like Nina because her mother was a single working mom, because she was working class, but most of all, because she was an artist and distracted Marcus from the goals the Colonel wanted him to have.

Despite his harshness and hard standards, Marcus loved him. He was an only child, and Nina understood the requirements that fell on the child of a parent who loved you. Nina's mom was delighted with her artistic abilities, proud as a strutting peacock when she placed in school shows, and even regional student shows. Marcus placed in those shows, too, but only his mother ever came. It crushed Marcus every time.

"Maybe he'll calm down in a few days," Nina said, hopefully.

Marcus shook his head. Misery pulled down his features. "He already called the art school and cancelled my enrollment."

"That's not fair!" Nina cried. "He doesn't get to rule your whole life! He can't tell you who to be!"

"But I can't do it without him."

"Why? You mean to pay for it? We'll work all summer and apply for all the scholarships and grants. We'll make it work."

He took her hands. "Nina. I can't."

"Can't or won't?"

He took a breath, tightening his grip on her hands. "Can't *and* won't. I love my parents. I don't want to disappoint them."

"But you've been disappointing your dad the entire time we've been together! He's always wanted you to be with those girls from the officer's club. And you didn't care then!"

"Because I love you. Because I know he's wrong about you."

"But if you love me—" Nina felt tears, burning hot, rushing upward from her throat, a tsunami filling her eyes and nose and mouth as she realized what he was saying. "We'll never be together again if you go."

"Yes, we will." He pulled her onto his lap, holding her close. "Yes, I promise we will. We'll write letters. Oh, please, Nina, don't cry."

But then he was crying, too. They bent their heads together, hands tight, and cried because they both knew he couldn't stay. Nina was flooded with loss and anger and a sense of…shame. That she wasn't good enough, that she was not worth fighting for. Very quietly, she asked, "What about disappointing *me?*"

He raised his head, stricken. "You know I don't want to. But we're still kids."

"No," she said. "We're nearly adults. We've made plans for our adult lives, together."

For a long moment, he didn't say anything. Then he lifted a hand and brushed a lock of her hair, stuck to her wet cheek, away from her face and tucked it behind her ear. "I love you. But I can't be at war with my dad. It will break my mom's heart."

"Your mom knows who you are. She's seen your work. She knows what you can do! She'll stand up for you."

He shook his head. "I'm not the artist you are, Nina. You have a great future ahead of you in art, but I'll probably always just be a broke wanna-be." He lifted his mouth on one side. "I can't be that guy. I need to be somebody. And not for my dad. For me."

A sense of betrayal rocked her and she pulled back. "How long have you been feeling this way?"

He lifted a shoulder. "Not long. Maybe since the acceptances came in."

"Acceptances? Plural?"

"Yeah." He took a breath. "I got into Northwestern, too."

"What will you study there?"

"I don't know. Maybe poly sci. Maybe psychology. I really liked psych this year."

Airlessness squeezed her lungs. With effort, she stood up, backing away, and forced herself to take a breath. One of her collages, a cat made from diamond shapes of tissue paper and bits she cut out of a magazine, hung framed on the wall. Her mother didn't really have money to frame things in a shop, but she'd found a dime store frame that fit and hung it proudly in the living room.

Because her mom believed in her, she could believe in herself. She turned, arms crossed. "You've never really believed you could be an artist, but you can. If you want it, you can have that life."

"I don't know if I do."

"You're just afraid!" she cried. "You can't live a creative life looking for guarantees! You have to just dive in and see what happens. The good thing is, if you live the life you were meant to live, you're happy no matter what else happens."

"No," he said, standing up. "You're wrong about that. My dad never had that luxury. He was so poor he didn't have any shoes as a child, and everything he's done, every move he's made, was to give me a life of financial security, to position me to have more than he did." His voice softened. "I can't let him down."

Abruptly, Nina sank to the floor. "When will you move?"

"The end of the week." He sat down beside her. "We'll write letters, every day. I'll get a job and pay for long distance and we can talk all the time."

She shook her head.

"If we're meant to be, we'll make it through a separation."

"No," she said clearly. "I'm not going to live like that, pining for somebody far away. We're supposed to be inseparable, soul mates, but all this time, you haven't told me the truth."

"I'm telling you now."

She looked up at him, heart shattering. "You need to just go."

"But—"

"You've made your choice."

After a long, long time he finally stood and left her. Nina bowed her head and sobbed. How would she get through without him?

# Chapter Five

In a high mountain meadow, nearly forty years later, Marcus took her hand. Her long fingers were delicate against his, so graceful. "We were so young."

"You lost so much that day. I hate it that you also lost your art."

"I didn't lose it," he said, feeling oddly embarrassed, "I left it behind. With you."

She gave him a small smile. "My heart was so broken."

"I know. Mine, too." He wove his fingers through hers. Sunlight warmed his shoulders and back. "I wrote to you."

"I still have them."

"You do?" He laughed, and the sound came from somewhere deep, filling his chest. He saw himself at seventeen, pouring out his heart in the dark of morning in Alaska, pining so much for Nina that he felt like he had a sickness. "Those must be really something."

"They're beautiful."

"Why didn't you ever write back?"

"I did. Dozens of times. But you never got them, and eventually, I gave up."

A thud of loss dropped into his belly. He stared at her, trying to take the information in. "What do you mean?"

She ran her free hand through her cropped hair, smoothed it down, shrugged. Her mouth was so sad he felt his heart cracking all over again. "I wrote back, Marcus," she said, meeting his eyes. "But someone must have intercepted my letters."

"I couldn't believe that you'd just give up on us like that," he said.

"Like you did?"

"I didn't give up on you. I gave up on the idea of an art career."

She pulled her hand from his. "That was your dad speaking through you."

"No. It was my choice. I wanted more stability." He sighed. "I loved art, loved painting, but I didn't burn with it the way you did. And I did feel that I owed my father to reach for the highest rungs on the ladder that I could, to make him proud of me."

Her eyes shone suspiciously bright. "Why didn't you just tell me that?"

He saw the girl she'd been in the set of her shoulders, the press of her palms to her thighs, the way she looked away to hide her emotions.

Such strong emotions.

"I didn't know how, Nina. You'd spun this beautiful world for us, and I wanted to live there with you, but I also wanted it to have a really nice car in the garage."

She swung around to look at him—and burst out laughing. "You always were so much more mature than I was."

"You were a dreamer. I loved that about you. I guess I imagined that I could be the sensible one and you could paint the world with stars and moons."

"Or cut stars and moons out of magazines and glue them to the world."

It was his turn to laugh.

"Truce?" she asked, holding out her hand.

"Truce," he agreed, and they shook.

All the way up the trail, he'd been feeling a loose, distant sense of well-being, a pleasure in her company, in the curve of her jaw and her rear end, the easy way she moved. Now, looking into her bright eyes, he fell over into molten desire, everything in his body dissolving in an urgent need to kiss her. He tugged her closer and reached for her, and the awkward shape of their position tumbled them sideways, so she was lying on the blanket, looking up at him, so much older and still herself, and he felt the same roaring sense of rightness, the same need to merge with her that he always had.

"Marcus, maybe this—"

He bent over her body, so much smaller than his own, and kissed her. No, more than kissed her. Captured her mouth, coaxed her lips open and dove in, inviting her back. Her arms circled his neck and she made a sweet sound of yearning, pulling him closer, closer, closer. Their bodies twined, his arms around her waist, their legs scissoring. Sunlight covered them, and they kissed intricately, reassembling the world they once made together, their own, unique, intimate place.

He felt his emotion rising in his throat, a sense of pure wonder, that it was really *Nina* in his arms. He raised his head and she gazed back up at him, touched his cheek, his jaw, his nose. Her eyes shone with tears. "Kiss me some more," she said.

"Gladly."

It was so oddly complete, just to kiss. He fell to his side and brought her with him, the pair lying face to face, legs tangling, hands respectful but questing. He gauged the shape of her shoulders and waist. She traced his goatee and pressed her palms to his chest.

"Do you remember our first kiss?" she asked.

"Of course. We were walking around the park and you stubbed your toe, and it started bleeding like you'd cut if off." He ran a finger over the center of her throat, pressed his fingertip to the artery pulsing life to her brain. "I took off my shirt and wrapped it around your foot, holding on to stop the bleeding."

She grinned. "What I remember is looking at your back and your belly, and your skin was so smooth and perfect that I just wanted to rub my hands all over it."

"And you did."

"Yes, I did."

"I still have a belly if you want to try it again."

She swallowed, running a hand downward over his shirt. Her hand opened over his middle. "This feels volatile, like I won't be able to control anything about it."

He nodded.

"Maybe I'm too old for that."

Urgently, he moved, wrapping her close, pressing as much of himself to her as he could. "No, you aren't," he said, and this time he kissed her with all his hunger, his need to feel her skin next to his. She responded with a hot gasp, and he cupped her bottom in one hand, and slid the other beneath the back of her shirt. Her skin burned his palm and he sucked her lower lip, feeling her arch against him, making a low noise. He moved to her face, her jaw, that place on her neck that he suddenly remembered made her wiggle and shiver, and ran his tongue in circles around it, taking his time. She wiggled, closer, pressing her thigh against him.

She pushed him slightly away and tumbled him backward, then tugged up his shirt to run her palms over his stomach, which wasn't the hard, sleek surface it once had been, and he suddenly felt old and embarrassed. He grabbed her hand. "I'm not seventeen anymore."

"Pssh. Me either." She tried to take her hand back but he held her wrist, and she suddenly gave in, letting him hold the wrist while she bent and pressed her mouth to his skin, his belly. She didn't go lightly, either. She nibbled. Bit lightly, and he forgot he was holding her hand until she took it away and climbed up on top of him, straddling him. "Take off your shirt," she said.

"Only if you do," he countered.

She didn't even hesitate, simply pulled the shirt off over her head, revealing a yoga bra that wasn't much of anything, just a scrap of pale dark blue stretch that barely contained the flesh within.

He swallowed. "Wow."

"I'm not seventeen either," she said, and pushed up her breasts with her hands, not an action she ever would have taken at that age. The flesh swelled up over the top.

He was electrified. "No," he said in a raw voice, and reached for her.

She slapped his hands. "Shirt."

He sat up, stripping the t-shirt off over his head. She straddled his lap, and he wrapped his arms around her, feeling skin against skin, belly against belly. She cupped his face and kissed him slowly, thoroughly, moving against him, sliding her inner arms down the outside of his, pressing her breasts into his naked chest.

Marcus gathered her tighter, aching, everything ached. Heart, head, body, and parts that just needed to plunge—

A crack of a branch, then another, shook them awake. Marcus held her, protectively shielding her as he looked for an intruder—

Nina tightened her grip, whispered almost inaudibly right next to his ear. "By the lake."

He turned his head slowly. A black bear ambled through the trees a few yards away, headed for the shoreline, stopping to pause at a tree to rub her back along the rough bark of a pine. She didn't appear to notice them.

All at once, two cubs tumbled into view, galloping for the water.

He'd lived in the depths of Alaska, where the bears were not the relatively friendly black and browns you saw in the mountains of Colorado, but grizzlies, who were much larger and more aggressive. He'd taken in everything he was taught about dealing with bears, and one thing that was true about all bears was that mothers protecting cubs were extremely dangerous. It was too late to make noise and too late to stay away from the cubs. All they could do for the moment was to stay where they were, and hope the wind didn't shift.

# Chapter Six

Nina's heart pounded as they watched the mama bear and her two cubs frolic in the water's edge. The cubs chased each other while mama drank water placidly.

Marcus held her calmly, one hand on her shoulder, the other on her waist. She rested her hands on his shoulders and left them there. They kept their eyes on the bears, but Nina could feel sweat building between them, against their bellies, against her breasts. His breath was slow and steady, moving sometimes against her shoulder.

At first, adrenaline diverted all blood and emotion into the energy needed to flee if they had to, but as the minutes stretched, as they stayed where they were while the bears puttered at the water's edge, the adrenaline turned to hunger.

His skin beneath her fingers was smooth and even without moving an inch, she could sense the muscles beneath, the blood coursing through him. Her breast just touched his chest, and she ached to move back and forth. She could hear his breath moving in and out of his lungs, which seemed deeply intimate.

It was one of the strangest, most erotic moments of her life. No dream could possibly have been weirder or more charged—that she should be straddling Marcus du Bois, both of them semi-naked, while bears frolicked nearby.

They were in no hurry, the bears. She and Marcus simply had to wait them out. Every one of her senses was exaggerated. She smelled grass and water, fresh clean air, a hint of Marcus's sweat and his skin, growing more heady with every passing second. She had not been touched this way in a long, long time. Nerves she'd forgotten hummed with the feel of his body under her, around her, against her, and she couldn't help rocking ever so slightly against him even as she kept her eyes on the bears, who splashed each other and dashed into the water and then out again, while Marcus moved his hands very slowly, down her arms, down her back.

His mouth brushed her jaw, and she jumped a little at the zigzagging electric thrill of it. "Easy," he whispered, his hands holding her steady, and then he kissed her neck in a trail, very very slowly—one, two, three—ending at the junction of her shoulder, a place that had always been a secret erogenous zone.

Which he seemed to remember. He swept his lips back and forth, very lightly, then opened his mouth and pressed the heat and wet against her skin and began to suck and kiss, play and press. Nina tensed against him, arousal flooding her body, her fingers gripping his shoulders. Beneath her, he, too, was aroused, and it raised her awareness a hundred-fold. Memories of their explorations tumbled through her imagination—the rocking joinings in her basement while her mother was at work; the time they rented a motel and had sex on a waterbed; the way he would sometimes tease her with a slow burn for days, making the eventual sex incandescent, atomic. She didn't know in those days that it was so rare, that men would not usually spend so much thought on her pleasure.

He had not lost that gift. Instead of kneading her breasts, or peeling away the thin fabric of the yoga bra—which she would have welcomed—his hands moved on her arms, and he stayed with the spot that made her crazy, sucking just enough to arouse her without leaving a mark. He licked her throat, and kissed the hollow.

Oh, lord.

"Marcus!" she protested softly, but didn't pull away. She found herself moving against him, as if they were making out in a car long ago. His hand on her back slid to her buttocks and gripped her, and as if he couldn't stop himself, he bit her a little, sending a hard, sharp jolt through her body, between her legs.

The bears started to walk along the lake toward the opposite side, and Nina bent her head, using her hands to drag Marcus's face up to where she could kiss him, and they fell into that, rocking and kissing, deep and hard. Her brain was gone. She could only feel, arousal so intense she thought she might have an orgasm right there, with their clothes still on.

Swallowing, she raised her head. His eyes were glazed and his breath was unsteady, and he pulled her into him, as if they could join right through their clothes; bit her shoulder, sucked on that erogenous spot. "This is still the place, isn't it?" His voice rumbled so deep she could feel it against her breasts, which desperately wanted his hands, his mouth.

"The bears are gone," she managed. "We need to get out of here."

"Hmm." He stopped and raised his head, a sultry depth to his eyes that made her bones weak. "Do we?" His hands skimmed over her back, up over her shoulders, and down her torso, skimming over her breasts, her belly. "I don't know if I can walk in this condition."

"Me, either," she said, and realized that she was older and wiser, that she didn't have to be at the mercy of his delicious games, but could employ one of her own. "But we have to. Everyone is arriving for the rehearsal dinner tonight. Nathan is supposed to be here by three."

Willing herself to move, she pushed off his shoulders, standing up, adjusting her bra straps and jeans. He watched for a moment, then gave a nod and stood nonchalantly, picking up his discarded t-shirt. In that way men do, he adjusted himself beneath his jeans, his eyes on her face. "I'm a little uncomfortable, but I guess you are, too."

"I'm fine."

"Are you?" He closed the space between them until their skin was only millimeters apart. Without touching her, he bent and said over her lips, "Later."

"Our kids will be here! We won't have a chance."

"We'll find a way." He caught her lower lip between his teeth, then smoothed it with his tongue, and she wanted to start all over again, knock him to the ground and mount him and have raw, mindless sex.

No. She pushed him away. "We have to go." She picked up her

shirt and tossed it over her shoulder as she began to collect the art supplies scattered over the blanket. Gathering them one by one, she tucked them back into the little bag she carried.

"Nina," he said, and there was something in his voice that made her turn. "Will you let me draw you?"

"Now?"

His face held something that she hadn't seen in a long time. Something raw and lost and revealing. "Yes."

Suddenly, she was afraid of everything that was happening here. "Maybe we should get back down the hill."

He took the t-shirt off her shoulder, brushed fingers down her arm. "Please."

He wanted to draw. Nina found herself sitting back down, letting him get comfortable. "How do you want me?" she asked.

"However you're comfortable."

He sketched and sketched, asking her to take various poses. She stared into the distance, and leaned on one arm, and just sat cross legged. His hand moved feverishly, but she didn't ask to see, just let him do what he was doing.

It gave her a chance to study him, too. He was the same and not—that same glitter of humor, the twist of his smile, his low, full laugh, but he was also more sophisticated, more measured, not so impulsive. She loved the way time had whittled his features into their essence.

She wanted him. Badly. Wanted a night of hot sex and reminiscing and all that. She couldn't even remember the last time she'd had sex.

Years. It had been years.

Impulsively, she straightened and peeled the yoga bra off over her head, leaving her torso bare. "There, Jack," she said, quoting a movie they'd seen together. "Do you want to draw me like this?"

He only looked for a long moment, then nodded, sketching with verve and energy, his hand moving, his arm, looking at the page, then her, then turning the page and drawing again. "Damn, I wish I had a charcoal."

"Not something I carry," she said.

"Lean back on your hands."

She did.

It felt like heaven to have sunshine on her bare breasts, to have his gaze on her. She wasn't seventeen and she wished things were less—squishy—but she didn't think he minded.

At all.

His eyes felt like a caress, traveling over her shoulders, her belly. She thought she knew when he was drawing her nipples by the tingling of his gaze touching her, circling, over and over.

She wanted him.

And yet.

What if they did have sex? What then? How could she walk away now that she knew he was in the world again; now that he'd walked back in, how could she let him walk back out?

There was also the problem that he wouldn't just be a roll in the hay. She would know him now, know that he was the father of her daughter-in-law. Know that they'd shared this...whatever this was turning out to be.

"People coming," Marcus said, tossing her the t-shirt, which she tugged over her body as fast as she could. The yoga bra she crammed in her pocket. They busied themselves picking everything up while the people hiked on by. "Nice day!" one called.

"Gorgeous," Marcus called back with a wave.

When the hikers had gone, Marcus gave her a little smile. "Shirt's inside out."

She started laughing, giddy with sunshine and hunger and the very real fact of Marcus du Bois standing right in front of her. He laughed, too, and it broke the tension.

"We do have to get back," she said.

He nodded.

"Are you going to show me what you drew?"

"No." He held the sketchbook close to his body.

"Okay." She made a turning gesture. "Turn around so I can get this bra on."

"Turn around? I've been sketching you for a half hour."

"This is different." She kept her hands in her pockets, standing there in an inside out t-shirt.

"That shirt is scandalous."

"Is it?" Following some impulse she would never have indulged as a green teenager, she looked down and ran her hands over the outline of her breasts. "Huh. I guess it is. Turn around."

"I'd really rather just watch."

Nina suddenly remembered what they'd called "the naked game," which involved each of them being naked, or semi-naked, sitting at some distance from each other. One would tell the other something to do to his or her own body and they watched until they couldn't bear it.

"I just remembered the naked game," she said, swallowing.

"Me, too."

"Jeez, we were sophisticated for teenagers."

"We had a lot of time on our hands," he said. "And good imaginations."

Her heart was pounding, and a buzz in her limbs made her shiver. "We don't have time now."

"No."

"Turn around."

"No."

"Fine. I will." Nina yanked off the t-shirt, and then struggled into the stupid yoga bra with a lot of stupid manipulations, including squishing her breasts flat and having to move everything around to get it right, and pulled the t-shirt back on. "There. Let's go."

He was grinning, that big, generous expression that always disarmed her. Nina's heart sank. She'd already let her guard down. It was too late to get it back up.

"Come on," he said, hiking the pack on his shoulder and holding out a hand.

She didn't take it. "We have to be careful tonight at the rehearsal dinner," she said. "They'll be so embarrassed if they know we—"

"I think it's safe to say we knew each other back in the day," he said, as they started walking back down. "We know each other too well to have met just today."

"Yeah, that's true. We knew each other in high school. That's good." She frowned. "Is your dad coming?"

"No, he hasn't been well. My mom passed a couple of years ago and he just hasn't been the same."

Sympathy welled in her. "I'm sorry. I didn't even ask about your mom. She was always so supportive."

He nodded. "We all miss her."

The rest of the way down, they were quiet, commenting on birds or rocks or the way the river looked, but nothing personal. The closer they got to the hotel, the more Nina realized she'd been foolish. High in the mountains, with sun and the intoxicating thin air, making out with Marcus had seemed normal. Now it seemed foolish, something a teenager would do, not a grown woman whose son was getting married in less than twenty-four hours.

She stopped in the shade of an old cottonwood, its roots stuck deep in the stream behind the B&B. Hiking her pack a little, she said, "Marcus, we can't—do this."

He paused, looking down at her with his starry eyes. "Do what?"

"All of this. Make out and—act like teenagers."

"Okay," he said easily, and glanced over his shoulder before he stepped close. "Let's just be adults and go have wild sex."

She closed her eyes. "I just don't think I can stay...aloof."

A faint smile played at the edges of his mouth. "You always did think too much."

"But this is—crazy! Our kids are getting married. *To each other.* They will die of embarrassment if they find out their parents are hooking up."

"What they don't know won't hurt them."

So reasonable. And damn him, just standing there, he looked like a magazine cover for the sexiest man of the year. Her skin whispered, her molecules all leapt toward him, and she—

"Hey, you two!" called a male voice. "I've been waiting for you!"

Nina gave Marcus a look that said, *see? Close call.* "Nathan!" she cried, and ducked around Marcus to dash across the parking lot and give her son a hug.

"I'm so glad to see you!" He was every inch his father's child, tall and lean, with thick gold hair that caught fire in the sunshine.

With a happy roar, he swept her up in a giant hug.

"Me too," she said into his neck. "This is the best weekend of all time."

He set her back down on her feet, and his face glowed with anticipation. "It totally is. I really can't wait." He reached out to shake hands with Marcus. "How are you, Marcus? Good to see you."

"You, too, son. You look good." Marcus gave a nod. "Is Giselle here yet?"

"She's already gone up to the hotel to get ready for the rehearsal dinner."

"I'll see her there, then. I'm going to have a shower and some food before the festivities. We just hiked the Columbine Trail to the lake."

"No kidding. How was it?"

Nina didn't look at Marcus. "We saw a bear mother and her two cubs."

"What?" Nathan looked from one to the other. "That must have been kind of terrifying."

"Nah, it was fine," Marcus said, and it wasn't her imagination that his voice had dropped a notch.

"Marcus was Grizzly Adams back in the day," Nina said.

Nathan frowned. "Who?"

Marcus laughed. "I'll leave you two to it. See you in a bit." He touched Nina's shoulder, raised a hand to Nathan. As he headed for the door, she heard him whistling. She knew that whistle. It meant he was up to something. As he reached the door, he turned back and gave her a grin. She shook her head.

"You two seem cozy." Nathan cocked his head. "You just met at the hotel and went hiking?"

"Oh." Nina stuck her hands in her back pockets. "Uh, no. Believe it or not, we went to high school together."

"That's crazy!"

"I know." She tried to keep her face in a normal arrangement, but what did a normal arrangement feel like?

"So you were friends or something?"

"Yes. We met the first day of ninth grade."

"Huh." He studied her with a strange expression on his face, and Nina wondered if she was giving away the entire day, if the imprint of Marcus's hands and mouth were stamped all over her body.

"Why does that seem so weird?"

"I don't know," he said. "You're such an artist and he's…a lawyer."

She smiled. That. "Well, once upon a time, he was an artist, too. We were really good friends, and it was great to go hiking today and catch up. Do you want to have a beer or something?" The words tumbled out too fast. She forced herself to slow down. "I'm parched but I've got to get myself in the shower pretty soon."

He glanced at his watch. "Nah. I've got to get over to the hotel myself. The guys are waiting for me."

"You're not doing a bachelor party the night before, are you?"

"No way. We already did that." He lifted a shoulder. "I'm ready to end that part of my life and start this family."

"I'm so proud of you." She hugged him. "I wish your dad was here to see this."

"Me, too."

# Chapter Seven

Nina found herself taking extra care with her preparation for the rehearsal dinner. She had been obsessed with shopping for the wedding for months—the mother of the groom dress and the dress for this evening. She and her friend Valerie had been on mission after mission, trying things on, and in the end, Nina settled on a floaty silk dress with a pinched waist and a forgiving skirt that skimmed her more generous thighs and butt. The color was the selling point, a print in vivid pinks and muted greens that no one else in her world would have chosen, but it made her think of one of her own paintings. As she stood in her room, examining her reflection, all she thought about was what Marcus would think.

Which was silly. Her only son was getting married, and all of this was for him.

And his bride, Giselle, who met her at the converted silver mansion before the dinner. "Hey, my nearly mom!" she said warmly.

"Hey!" Nina cried as she came in. "You look stunning."

"Thank you!" Giselle turned in a little circle, making the hem of her mid-century halter dress spin out in a bell. The cut showed off her lean arms and shoulders, and the cool green color gave her skin a rose gold sheen. She wore a diamond bracelet on her arm. "Did you have a great day? Nathan said you and my dad went hiking."

"It was a beautiful day," Nina said, and wondered how she'd never guessed that Marcus was the father of this beautiful young woman. She had his eyes and his broad, inclusive smile. "You really look a lot like him."

"I do." Giselle looked away.

Nina took both of her hands. "Missing your mother?"

She ducked her head, touching one finger to her eye. "I thought I had it together, but it just doesn't seem fair that she's not here."

"It is *not* fair." Guilt rushed through her as she imagined how angry and hurt Giselle would be if she knew that Nina had spent the past twenty-four hours lusting after her widowed father. "I'm so sorry."

Giselle took a breath and straightened to her full height—nearly five ten without heels. Her hair fell to her shoulders in a cloud of curls she'd studded with sparkling pins and braids woven away from her face. "It's one of the things that brought Nathan and me together, losing a parent. She would have loved him just as much as I do."

"And Jason would be so proud to call you his daughter."

"Thank you." She bent to hug Nina. "I'm so lucky."

"We're the lucky ones." Emotion welled up—guilt that she hadn't thought more about Jason, excitement over the impending nuptials, happiness that her son had found such a good wife. "Now, let's get this party started, shall we?"

The dinner seating had already been arranged, and much to her relief, Nina and Marcus were on opposite ends of the table. Unless she leaned forward, she couldn't even see him, which made it much easier to relax and enjoy the feast. The minister gave last-minute reminders, and friends made funny speeches. Nina gave a simple toast to the couple, welcoming Giselle into the family. Marcus, too, gave a toast, but Nina didn't hear a word of it. He'd always liked dressing well for special occasions, but they'd grown up in the casual 70s, when lipstick was "plastic" and jeans and bare feet ruled the world of their high school.

In the intervening years, he'd gained an air of sophistication and elegance that outshone everyone in the room. He wore an exquisitely cut black linen and silk jacket over a pale green shirt that matched his daughter's dress, which she found unbearably touching. As he gave a tender speech that included Giselle's mother, a tear welled in the bride's eye, and in Nina's. She discreetly wiped it away, clapping and toasting with everyone else.

The small party moved into a larger room, where a small bar was set up in the corner, and a DJ played music for the rest of the guests who'd driven or flown to the location. The room was long and bright, with a series of french doors thrown open to the golden light pouring over the mountains from the west.

Her part done, Nina mingled, greeting people she knew, introducing herself to those she didn't. Nathan found her after a while and gave her a hug. "This is beautiful, Mom. Thanks." He looked as if he might float away.

"You are so handsome," she said, touching his cheek.

"Just like Chris," he said with a grin. With his sharp cheekbones and bright blue eyes, he looked like Chris Hemsworth. It was a joke between them, but in LA, sometimes people actually thought he was the actor. "I brought you a beer."

"Thanks." They watched the people for a few minutes. "Did you finish the script?" He'd been anxious to get a rough draft off his desk before the wedding.

"Yep." He offered a hand for a fist bump.

She obliged. "Now you're free to enjoy your travels." They were booked on a month-long European tour, ambling back roads and exploring thing off the beaten path. "Here's to no Tahiti."

He clinked her glass. "It was weird how many of our friends wanted us to do some tropical beach resort. Neither one of us is a resort kind of person."

"No. This will be better."

"You really never had a honeymoon with dad?"

"No, he didn't want to travel, which you can understand. He traveled for work all the time."

"Yeah, I guess. You should do more travel now, though."

"I've traveled!" she cried in her own defense.

"Not that much, Mom. And you'd better hurry up because we're going to have children as fast as possible and we'll need you to babysit."

"You'll have more than me, you know." Across the room, Marcus listened intently to a young guy talking with big gestures.

"Marcus can do it, too."

"It's hard to see him with a baby."

"You think?" She could see it easily, a little girl cooing up at him as he—

*They would have grandchildren together.*

Her grandchild and his would be the *same child.* The knowledge squeezed her heart so hard that he must have felt it himself across the room because he suddenly looked up, right at her. For the space of a few seconds, only the two of them existed.

Nina looked away, up at her tall son. He didn't seem to notice anything strange, and to distract herself, she said, "One thing those children are going to be is very tall."

"Right?" Nathan sipped his beer. "The Colonel is a solid six four, even now."

"It's too bad he can't come."

"I know. Giselle was really sad about it. He's one of her favorite people in the world."

Nina frowned. "Really? He was a pretty hard man when I knew him."

"You've met him?" Nathan looked at her. "You must have been really *good* friends with Marcus."

Nina glanced over at him, and now a woman of about their age was standing close, her hand on his arm. Flirting.

Of course she was. It probably happened all the time. She imagined an LA party, filled with glittering, well-tended, slim women who would all find him as tasty as catnip.

He was so out of her league. He always had been.

"Mom? How did you know the Colonel?"

"Just here and there. School things, you know. He picked us up from games or skating or whatever."

"Skating?" Nathan echoed. "Like, ice skating?"

"No," Nina said. "Like roller skating. Skate City."

"Wow." He snorted. "Okay."

Marcus had patted the hand of the woman talking to him and now ambled in their direction. He moved with the same grace he'd always carried, long-limbed and supple, and in those fine fabrics, so exquisitely cut, he looked like a model for an expensive car.

When he joined them, he gave Nina a smile. "Nice toast."

"You, too." She sipped the beer in her hand for something to do, and said, "Tell my son that roller skating was hip when we did it."

"It was the thing, man," Marcus said with a grin. "You could get close to the girls like that." He playfully slid an arm around her waist, miming the skate they'd done a million times. She looked up at him and he met her eyes, and his fingers stroked her side where no one could see. "Everybody wanted to skate with your mom. She was the hottest girl in school."

Nina rolled her eyes. "The weirdest girl, you mean."

He let her go. "That, too."

Nathan said, "I'm being paged. You too have fun reminiscing about the good old days."

They said nothing as he left, but Nina could feel every inch of his body alongside hers.

"Do you want to step outside for some air?" Marcus asked.

"Absolutely." She set her glass on the table behind them and followed him out into the mild evening. They sat on a bench a little way from the main action and looked at the view.

"Imagine this was your life," Marcus said. "You came out from the east, where you were a nobody who lived in some shack in a city, so you made your way west to find a better life. You did some mining, and struck a vein of silver that made you richer than a thousand families back home. So you married the prettiest girl you could find, and built her a big house and at night, you would look at this."

It touched her, this flight of historical imagining. He thought of the world in deeper, wider terms than anyone she'd ever met. "Good to know you're still a geek," she said lightly, and nearly reached out to touch his hand.

He laughed. "Takes one to know one."

The evening light richened suddenly, turning a particularly gilded shade that caught on hillocks of grass and limned the branches of trees. The mountains washed out to an uneven curtain drawn across the sky, and pines stood sentinel in sharp, narrow triangles. She slid her phone from a pocket hidden in her dress and shot a photo.

"A future work?"

"I don't know, maybe."

The sun gilded him, too, edging his brow and nose and shoulder. His hands rested easily on his thighs and the light cast a reddish glow over his fingers, his oval nails. She shot a dozen or more photos of his face, and his hands, and then the horizon again as the light changed, maybe keeping the camera up as armor. When he looked at her soberly, she shot his eyes, too, so deep and dark, and yet always so full of light.

"What do you see?" he asked.

"A man..." she took a breath, easing the pinch in her heart, the one that reminded her that this weekend was temporary, that they would both go back to their worlds and carry on. "...who is even more of what I thought he'd be when we were kids."

He took the phone without a word, and shot photos of her. She tried to endure the scrutiny as he had, trying not to squirm or look away. It had been so much easier this afternoon when he drew her.

When he drew her. She saw herself ripping off the yoga bra and wanted to crawl into a hole somewhere. How could she have imagined her body would be anything he'd want to draw?

Except that he had.

"What do you see?" she asked.

"Your eyes are the color of morning," he said. "And your lipstick is gone, so you don't have any color on your face at all."

She laughed. "Thank you?"

"I'd still rather look at you than anyone in the world right now." He lowered the camera, looked at her as he handed it over. "Text me those shots."

"I will."

"Now. Before you forget."

"I won't forget, Marcus."

"Now, please."

She nodded, opened up the messenger screen. "What's the number?" She typed it in, then went to the photos. Her face looked back at her, but not the face she ever saw in the mirror. With his talent for composition, he'd shot only portions of her face—her right eye, glowing with the light from sundown, a shimmer of gold over her nose and (colorless) mouth. That same mouth and her throat, with a tiny diamond winking in the hollow between her collarbones.

And one of her entire face, her eyes full of emotion—yearning and hope—

Humiliated, she kept her head down as she sent him the photos. "What's wrong?"

"Nothing." She lifted her head and smiled. "I sent them."

"I saw."

All around them, guests came in and out. He moved his foot until his ankle touched hers. "How did I hurt your feelings, Nina? Because I said you were colorless?"

"No." She shook her head, smiling, and took a lipstick out of her pocket, opened it, and smeared it on. "Better?"

"It was fine before, but that looks good."

"It's one of those weird things about you that you always said things straight out. So, it makes it easier to trust you."

"You don't trust me now."

"It's not you. It's the situation. It's risky and weird and nerve-wracking."

From inside came a crash of music. They both looked at the doors. "Is that...."

"It can't be..."

But it was. *Take a Chance on Me*, which had played on every speaker in the known universe the year they were juniors. Nina couldn't help it, she started laughing and crossed her hands on her chest as if to protect her heart.

Marcus stood, holding out his hand. "Come on. You know they didn't play this song for the young ones."

"You hate ABBA." She cocked her head teasing as she accepted his hand. "'Whitest band in the world.'"

He lifted a shoulder, still holding out his hand. "You love them."

"I do." And she couldn't help it—the music soaked into her bones, and she dance-stepped into the ballroom, where virtually everyone else was dancing, too, including Giselle and Nathan, who waved them over. Nina danced over, swinging her head as if she had hair. She and Marcus danced easily together, playacting, mugging for the kids. "I can feel my Farrah Fawcett bangs," she said to Marcus, leaning in so that he could hear her.

"So much hairspray!"

Nina laughed. She danced toward Giselle, and then Nathan, who laughed and said, "Did you guys skate to this?"

"Probably," Nina said, turning back to dance with Marcus, who, it had to be said, looked hot in his grown-up clothes with his grown-up body, so easy in his skin, so much himself. Her belly flipped, and he gave her the very smallest of winks.

Giselle and Nathan hammed their way around them. Marcus and Nina answered, all four of them shaking and sliding, and it was pure fun. All of Nina's anxious imaginings, projections for the future, sadness about the past, just fell away. Dancing with Marcus felt like exactly the thing she should be doing right that minute, celebrating the wedding of their children.

The next song was another from the same era, *We Will Rock You*, and Nina laughed again. Nathan and Giselle ambled away. Nina might have followed, but Marcus caught her hand. "We may as well give the young ones something to laugh at."

"At least it's not *Fat Bottom Girls*," she quipped, and he laughed, too.

"I think somebody's been to the movies lately," he said.

They just…played, forgetting everybody and everything, and at the same moment, when the beat got tangled in the melody, making it hard to dance, they both dropped their arms and flopped around, and Nina was so delighted that they both remembered at the same moment that she laughed aloud, throwing her head back to fully express it. It was loud, even against the music, but she didn't care.

She did not care.

The music shifted, down down down, but it was still a seventies song, "Let's Get it On" by Marvin Gaye.

Nina tilted her head. "Really?"

He laughed.

"It's almost like this DJ knows exactly what all our favorite songs were."

## Inseparable

He wiggled one eyebrow and held out his hands. "Couldn't all be your favorites, could they?"

Right then, in that second, she fell all over again. Her heart was sucked right out of her. "Marcus," she said, recalling too many memories, anticipating too much.

"One more," he said in that smooth voice, and there really was no choice. As if he was a magnet, she was pulled into the circle of his arms, and against his body. They began to sway together, just the way they had a thousand times at school dances, at parties. He was wearing cologne, lightly spicy, and the fabric of his coat was silky and nubby at once, and every place their bodies touched — palms, fingers, chests — her body pulsed with recognition. "You're such an adult," she said.

"Happens, doesn't it?" Their legs weaved together, and they shuffled around in a circle. "I can't stop thinking about what might have happened if my dad hadn't intercepted your letters."

"No, don't go there," she said, shaking her head. "Our lives went the way they were supposed to."

"Did they?" He slowed ever so slightly, his hands hot on her back. "We were inseparable."

It was what the yearbook labeled them at the end of their freshman year. Young Marcus, skinny and serious, and a long-haired Nina were photographed with heads together over an English book. Some clever yearbook person had stamped *Inseparable* over the picture. In tenth grade, it was a shot of the pair of them just like this at the Christmas dance, heads close, looking intently into each other's faces. Again, *Inseparable*. Junior year, a picture of them sitting outside on the grass, eating lunch, Marcus stretched out long and lean, Nina in a peasant blouse that flowed around her. *Inseparable, still* the caption read.

The senior year photo had been taken just before Marcus moved, in December at the Christmas art show. Nina and Marcus stood arm in arm in front of their award-winning paintings, looking happy and ready to conquer the world.

"I guess we weren't," she said.

"I guess not." He sounded sad.

A vast yearning overtook her and for a moment she closed her eyes, wishing she could nestle her cheek into the hollow of his shoulder and listen to him hum along with the music. She swayed a little, and then caught herself and stepped away slightly, putting distance between their bodies. "We need to look like we were only friends," she said.

"Do we?" His hand moved on her back, eased her closer. "Maybe just find each other very hot, and it has nothing to do with the past."

"Still. Our kids are missing their lost parents. It would be such a slap in the face for us to—"

"Nina, Nina, Nina," he said, "You've gotta stop thinking so much."

She looked at his mouth, thought of the kissing this afternoon. His legs scissored between hers, trousers brushing the bare skin of her inner knee. She found herself staring at the salt-and-pepper hairs of his goatee, and couldn't help thinking about sinking into the perfect lips they framed.

Chemistry. It was all just chemistry.

The song ended and Nina stepped away, but he caught her hand.

"One more," he said, and now she could see the earnestness in his face, as if he were afraid she'd say no, and when the first thrums of the music came over the speakers, she hesitated.

It was *Reunited,* by Peaches and Herb. They had played it a million times, after they'd had a fight. A make-up song.

"The kids are going to catch on."

He glanced at them, lifted his chin in their direction. "No, they won't."

When Nina looked over her shoulder, she saw the couple dancing in a very small, tight circle, foreheads together. It made her smile. Turning back, she let Marcus swing her back into his arms, this time more loosely, more playfully. He exaggerated his movements, trying to make her laugh, and succeeded.

It wasn't until the song was over that she realized what they'd acted out—the actual reality of their lives, the one they were trying to hide. They were reunited and *it felt so good.* As she swung into his arms, close enough to kiss, close enough to feel his breath, she flashed on him naked, over her, in her, below her, and the image was so powerful she nearly stumbled.

He caught her. "Me, too," he said in a low voice.

"Me, too, what?" she asked, and her words were slightly breathless.

"I'm thinking about kissing you all over. And how dangerous that feels." He swung her around, subtly pulling her even tighter against him. His knee bent, brushed her knee. His hips swayed against hers. His hands moved on her back.

A thready pulse moved in her throat as she looked up at him, at his deep, liquid eyes, and the arch of his brows, and that mouth that had given her so many hours of pleasure. "When you left, I didn't know how to get up in the morning, Marcus."

"Me, either. I didn't sleep for months."

"I just don't think I can risk feeling that way again."

He gripped her hand tightly. "What I know is that if we leave here this weekend without making love, we will wonder all the rest of our lives about what might have been."

But Nina suddenly saw what it might be like after this weekend—pining again for what they'd had, pining for what they'd lost, having to start all over again with that emptiness at the center of everything. "You know, I didn't even go on a date for nearly four years." They were barely swaying, their heads close. "You didn't stand up for me, for us, and you should have."

He caught her waist in a strong grip. "I know that, Nina." His voice was fierce. "I didn't date anyone either, not till I got to law school. I missed you like a limb."

Her heart squeezed so hard that she couldn't speak, thinking of the two of them, each going through their college years alone when they could have—

She stepped away, forcing him to let her go or make a scene everyone would notice. "I can't do this," she said, and walked way.

On the way out, she paused to give Nathan and Giselle a hug, promising to see them in the morning.

Then she fled.

# Chapter Eight

A brisk wind was blowing as Nina made her way back to the hotel, and along the horizon, lightning needled through the clouds that had started moving in while they danced. The cool air helped blow away the heat and overwhelming emotions that had swamped her while she danced with Marcus.

But even so, she couldn't stop the tears. Tears as hot as the air was cool, tears that came no matter how hard she told herself to stop. Tears that dripped right off her jaw.

A swirl of images surfaced, one after the other—herself, sitting in her bedroom, writing one earnest letter after another to Marcus, then decorating the envelopes with colored pencil; late afternoon in the art room, finishing some project while Marcus painted nearby; the hours and hours and hours they'd spent in her bedroom while her mom was at work, exploring each other's bodies and tastes and delights; eating lunch with him in the school cafeteria; walking home with him. Watching movies, dancing, talking about everything.

No other guy measured up. They were too slow or too slippery or too boring. They came on too strong or they had a strange scent or—

Whatever. The only thing wrong with them, really, was that they were not Marcus.

Out in the dark beneath the cottonwood tree, she paused to try cleaning up her face before she went in. An old tissue had lodged in the corner of her purse and she used it to blot away the smears of make-up as best she could. Took a deep breath of the cool, dry air of the mountains, and looked up to the stars.

The clouds had not yet hidden the sky overhead, and in the

high mountains, she could see a million, billion stars. The Milky Way spread across the center of the view and she let herself imagine a million planets with billions of beings each.

It did the trick—as wonder over the spectacular universe filled her, it made her silly problem seem small and insignificant. Once, she'd loved Marcus du Bois, but it would cost too much to love him now.

A crunch on the gravel behind her let her know he'd followed her. She didn't even have to turn around. Hadn't she known he would, in some part of her?

He pointed to a fuzzy blur. "Do you see Andromeda?"

She nodded.

He only stood beside her, his hands in his pockets. "Do you still watch the stars?"

"Sometimes," she said. "I bought a new telescope a few years ago and it's pretty amazing. I've been shooting photos with a tripod, too."

"I have one, too, but I have to leave the city to shoot. Death Valley is decent." His voice was hushed with awe as he added, "It's not like this, though. This is amazing."

"Yeah."

And although it was a smaller wonder than the vast universe, it was amazing that he was here, too, that *they* were here, after so much time.

"It's easier when you're young, isn't it?" he said quietly.

"Easier how?"

"You just believe in things. You think if you work hard and do the right thing, that it will all turn out okay in the end."

She let go of a soft sound of recognition. "And then life happens."

"And then life happens." He took her hand. "But we're still standing here."

Another small wonder was his face and the way he looked at her and the possibilities contained in a single moment.

"Shall we take a chance?" he asked.

"Yes," she breathed, and her fingers tangled with his. She let herself be led into the hotel. No one was in the lobby, and he simply took her up the stairs to her room under the eaves. When he held out his hand, she dropped the key in it, and he unlocked the door, pulled her through, and locked it behind him.

Light shone through the windows into the dark room. Music came faintly from somewhere, and the rain-scented breeze blew the curtains up softly. Nina simply stood right where she was, safely on this side of the line from whatever was about to happen next. A fine tremor moved beneath her skin, and her stomach held a thousand butterflies, and she knew her heart must be racing, but she only stood there. Looking up at Marcus.

He tossed the keys on the bureau by the door, then took her hand again. "Let's sit down," he said gently.

"No," she said, suddenly sure. She lifted his hand and pressed his palm to her cheek, holding it there with one hand as she closed her eyes and brought herself into the moment, into what was happening here. His warm hand, his long fingers against her face. The scent of him filling her whole head, kindling the desire that had been on a low simmer for the past twenty-four hours.

"I want you," she said quietly, and met his eyes. "So much."

"Good. Because I think I might spontaneously combust if I can't get my hands on you very soon."

She laughed softly, and pushed him into the room, walking him backward into a patch of light coming in from below. He started to take off his jacket, and she shook her head, stopping his hands. "Let me."

He dropped his hands. Nina ran her hands up his chest, feeling the shape of his ribs, his shoulders, and then the labels of the silky coat. "This is very nice fabric," she said.

"Thank you."

She tossed it on the sofa, then stood before him, looking up first as she unfastened the first button of his shirt. "It was so touching that you wore the same color as Giselle. Did she ask you to?"

"No. I helped her choose the dress and surprised her with the match tonight."

"Mmm. That's very sweet."

She unbuttoned the rest of the shirt, all the way down, remembering in time to unfasten the cuffs of his sleeves, too, and skimmed it off, leaving his torso bare. Light edged his shoulders, and she touched those rounds of muscle, his shoulders, his chest with its sparse scattering of hair, and his sides, leaning in with a dizzy sensation to kiss his skin, here and there, and here again, her hands as light as the breeze.

"My turn," he said. "Turn around."

Nina obliged, and he unzipped the dress she wore, pushing it from her body, his hands following the path of the fabric as it fell to the floor, revealing a slip that had cost nearly as much as the dress, the color just the shade of the clouds first thing in the morning. Nina stepped out of her dress and turned as he laid it carefully on the sofa next to his coat and shirt. She kicked off her shoes and immediately was three inches shorter, reminding her of high school, when they'd started at a fairly close height, and then he grew and grew and grew until he towered over her.

"I like this," he said, running his palms over the slip.

"Thank you," she said, shivering a little.

"I think I should get it out of the way, before things get rough."

She shivered at the visual that flashed over her mind. Sometimes, they'd had such wild sex that they'd fallen right off the bed. His fingers stroked her breasts as he eased the silk slip from her body, tugging it over her head.

And now she stood only in her panties and bra, her soft belly revealed and her big, not-so-smooth thighs — but when he touched her, lightly skimming the top swell of her breasts and then her waist, and bending to kiss her, she forgot that her body was not what it had been. At the searing press of his naked torso against hers, she gasped, and he bent to capture the sound with his mouth, his hands on her bottom to pull her hard into him. His tongue plunged into her mouth, and Nina made a noise that was so unlike her it —

But he matched it, a groan that came from deep inside his chest, and he kissed her so hard that she felt her tooth nick his lip, tasted salt and blood, and as if that was the match to gasoline, he hauled her up, lifting her off the floor and walking toward the bed, where he fell with her into the mattress.

She cried out as his weight pinned her, her legs circling his waist, thighs rubbing against the fabric of his slacks, his chest hard against her breasts. His mouth devouring her, her mouth, her neck, her shoulders. He hauled down the straps of her bra and kissed her breasts, covering them over with kisses until Nina was out of her mind with pleasure, with need.

"Take off your clothes," she panted.

He stood up and shed his trousers, his socks, his boxers. Nina watched, half-mad with a dizzy, consuming hunger she had never felt, never, and at the sight of his entirely naked form, the long legs and flat belly and everything in between, she unhooked her bra and scrambled out of her panties and said softly, "Come. Here."

"Gladly." He dove toward her and they tangled, arms and legs and mouths and bodies, kissing and rolling, touching and exploring, but mainly, driving toward the singular, searing moment when they joined, both crying out. Nina gripped him with her entire being, and he paused there for the longest time, deep within. They kissed and moved and then it was too intense for anything except the pure, powerful, hungry movements of lovers too long apart.

They cried out together, gripping each other as if they could entirely merge, bones and blood and skin and hearts.

As if they could make it possible to never part again.

Marcus came back to himself a tiny bit at a time. His feet and head, his belly against hers, their hands gripped together. Slowly, slowly, he raised his head and kissed her, gently this time, and eased his weight off of her, rolling them to their sides. He felt shaken and shaky, dizzy with the intensity of their joining.

He rested his hand on her tummy, kissed her shoulder. "You all right?"

She laughed. "All right is a bit of an understatement." Taking a breath, then letting it go, she covered his hand with hers. "You?"

"Yeah. Better than that." He leaned in, admired the way light fell across the lower swell of one breast, the side of her arm, her jaw. Words seemed far away, but he remembered that she liked them, especially at this point, right after they'd had intense sex, as if words somehow grounded her again after they'd dissolved into each other. He moved his hand lightly, tried to think of what to say, and ended up with, "I think I lost my mind in all of that. Might have to give me a minute."

"That's all right." She let one hand fall against his arm. "Me, too."

What he was thinking, really, was that it felt like his soul was communing with hers as they lay there, bodies revealed and spent. He kissed her shoulder, skimmed upward and cupped her breast. Her fingers moved along his thigh, up and down.

"I always thought I must be exaggerating how it was with us," she said softly. "I wasn't."

"No," he whispered, pulling her closer, into his arms, feeling her skin against his, her hair against his nose. He wanted to pour out a thousand emotions, *I missed you so much and you smell like everything good in the world and I love your soft skin and I love you as much as I ever did.*

He didn't say any of them. Just held her and held her, and in a while, she turned to him and lifted up on one elbow and kissed him, slowly, slowly, slowly, so thoroughly, skimming her hand down to rouse him. And to his delight, he was just as ready as the first time, as if he were still young, and when she mounted him, he took the pleasure she offered, and lost more of his soul to her body, and it didn't matter. As they moved together, he felt the world righting itself, as if things had been out of order.

Nina, Nina, Nina. Whatever had brought him here was worth it.

# Chapter Nine

After a time, Nina felt her stomach growling. It must have been past midnight, because the lights had blinked out along the street, one by one, and the only sounds were the stream and —

"Do you hear that?" Marcus said quietly. She heard him through her right ear, which was open to the world, and through her left ear, which was pressed against his chest.

She listened and a sound wafted through the room, "Hoo hoo hooooo." And again, "Hoo hoo hoo hoooo." Rising on one elbow, she cocked her head. "Is that an owl?"

"A great horned owl," he said.

"How lucky."

"Why?"

"Because you always loved them, so he came to tell you all is well."

Marcus laughed softly, moving his hand along her spine. "You know I don't believe in all that."

"I do." She shrugged. "The day I arrived, a red-tailed hawk was circling when you showed up."

"Seriously?"

"Yes." She flung off the covers. "Do you want something to eat? I'm absolutely starving."

"Yes. Do you have anything?"

"Of course." She picked up his shirt from the couch. "Do you mind?"

"Not at all." He shifted to lean against the headboard. "What did you do with the art supplies? Are they in here or your car?"

Nina pointed in the corner, where she'd dropped her backpack on a chair in the rush to get ready for the rehearsal dinner, then busied herself pulling things out of the mini bar and the box of dry goods on top.

"Nice," she said, admiring a bottle of grapefruit San Pellegrino. She grabbed two and carried over some peanut M&Ms, a plastic box of pistachios, and a tube of Pringles, which she dumped on the bed, then rearranged the pillows and tucked her feet under the covers. "I could eat a whole herd of cows," she said, popping open the chips.

He'd slid back into his boxers and padded over to the backpack. The way he bent and straightened was not the move of a young man; it was stiffer and more considered, though in no way old, but it pierced her to the quick. They had been apart such a long time!

Then he turned, a fistful of watercolor pencils and a notebook in hand, and there was Marcus again in the pleasure he carried with him, in the way he leapt on the bed and plopped down beside her, grabbing a chip out of her hand with his mouth.

She laughed. "Get your own, greedy."

"I will." He turned on the lamp beside the bed and sat cross-legged, picking up the soda and drinking deeply, then popping open the M&Ms. "Mini bars have come a long way," he commented.

"I don't have that much experience." She plucked a blue M&M out of the bag. "Have you traveled a lot?"

He nodded. "Mostly work, but we went somewhere every year on vacation."

A ripple of yearning moved through her. "Where did you go?"

"All over. Europe—Spain and Portugal one year, Germany and Italy another." He pursed his lips, sipped the soda, continued, "Hawaii, of course."

"Of course," she said wryly.

"Didn't you take vacations?"

She looked down, embarrassed a little. "Jason traveled constantly for his job, so when he was home, he just wanted to be home. And I got it, but sometimes it would have been nice to see more of the world with him. He'd been everywhere."

"Why not go now? Or why haven't you gone since he died? It's been awhile now."

Nathan had pushed her to do the same thing. "I don't know," but she actually did. "I guess I've been afraid to go alone. My friends are mostly all still married, and I am not experienced enough to know where and how I should go."

For a moment, he was silent, his eyes on her face. "I hate that, Nina." He almost looked as if he would weep. "You were the one who wanted to get out and see the world."

She deflected. "That was just the townie talking. All the military kids got to see everything, and I never even went to Denver much."

"Still." He touched her knee. "You need to do it. Before you can't."

She met his eyes, confessed. "I'm scared."

With an urgent gesture, he leaned in and took her face in his hands, kissed her hard, then leaned back. "I'll make you a deal."

"I'm listening."

"I'll take an art class if you plan a trip."

"How will I know you did it? How will you know I did?" The words came out before she realized how pathetic they sounded. "I don't mean—"

He raised a hand. Shook his head. "You'll tell me. And I'll tell you. We'll make a promise, okay?"

She bit her bottom lip, thinking. "I want to see the work you did this afternoon."

He was still for a moment. "Why?"

"Just because it will help you get ready to take that class."

"Okay, I'll show you, but first, where would you like to go?"

"So many places," she sighed.

"The number-one place, highest on your list."

"Morocco," she blurted out.

He smiled, very slowly, something new in his face. "Not Paris or Hawaii or Ireland?"

"No. Morocco. All those colors, the buildings, the desert."

"Beautiful." He unfolded, stood, and plucked his phone out of his coat pocket, carrying it back to the bed. "The pictures."

The file showed a series of about ten sketches, all angles contrasting softness—the curve of her head and the angle of her chin pinned by the softness of mouth; the sharp angle of elbow and soft shoulder with the arch of breast. Strong lines, but not strong enough for his tastes; she saw where he'd broken the tip of a pencil with his force. "You really wanted some charcoal, didn't you?"

"Yeah." He very meticulously broke apart a pistachio shell and took the nut out, crunched it between his teeth. The gesture contained the past and the present, and she felt Marcus-the-youth and Marcus-the-man mingling, going in and out of focus. "It's hard to get the shadow right without that weight."

The sketches were strong. A little clumsy, but not as much as she might have expected after so many years. "You really haven't done any art at all?"

"No time." He took apart another pistachio. "I shoot a lot of photos, but then everybody does these days, right? It used to be something, but it's not so much now, just a good eye."

"No," she said seriously, "I don't think that's true at all. You've always been brilliant with composition. I thought that again at the rehearsal dinner, when you took the photos of my face. And you did the same thing here." As matter-of-factly as she possibly could, she pointed out the strength of the sketches. "Perfect balance, those spare lines, the soft and hard."

"Thanks," he said.

"You don't believe me."

"I do."

She grinned. "You think I'm just telling you nice things so I can get in your pants."

"You already did that, I think."

Sitting there, half-dressed, eating junk food and talking about art, Nina felt as comfortable as she had in years. "Do you date much?" she asked suddenly.

"No." He made a noise. "It's painful."

"Right?" she cried. "Everybody is so set in their ways. They all make these pronouncements, like they expect you to fall in line."

"Oh, yeah. And the rules. So many rules, unspoken and spoken."

"When I go to somebody's house, I'm always thinking, 'this

doesn't feel right. How could I live here?'"

"I never even get that far," he confessed, his mouth twisting into a rueful smile. "Dinner takes too long and I get bored and want to get back to my workshop and my study."

She laughed. "We're set in our ways, too, I guess. What kind of projects?"

"All kinds of things. Shelves and tables, a few chairs."

"Wait. You build furniture?"

"It's just simple stuff, really."

"Marcus! That's art. Don't you realize that?"

"It's not art the way you do art."

"And I don't do art via furniture." She pushed the food and paper out of the way, and climbed in his lap. It was only as she dropped her arm around his shoulders that she realized how unselfconscious she was, which was so unlike her usual encounters that it sent a little ripple of warning through her.

*What would happen after this?*

His hands molded the small of her back and a slight smile curved his mouth, a mouth she bent and kissed. "You need to promise me that you'll stop making apologies for your art."

"I'll try." He slipped his hands under the shirt, stoking her bare bottom with his palms. "And you need to stop being afraid of the world."

"I'll try." She brushed his nose. "What are we going to do, Marcus? The kids will be so embarrassed and upset if they know their parents have hooked up."

"Why, though? Maybe you're ascribing something to them that's just not true."

"Oh, no," she said, waggling a finger. "One thing I know is that kids hate, hate, hate, hate, hate to imagine their parents having sex, much less with the parent of their significant other." She wiggled a little, enjoying the slow stoke of his hand up her back and back down, feeling an impossible surge of new desire. He would think she was a nympho freak. "Just imagine your dad having sex with my mom."

He squeezed his eyes tight. "Ugh. No. Now I need to shower my imagination. Your poor mom."

"See what I mean?"

"Yeah." His hands slid over her thighs, and back up. "Your skin is so soft. I love feeling it."

"Thank you," she whispered, and kissed his nose, his eyelids.

"Maybe," he said in a voice growing a little rougher, "we don't have to figure it all out right this minute."

"No?" His hand slid between her thigh and she gave a little squeak. "Marcus! Are you sure?"

"Why don't you see for yourself?"

She reached between them, and kissed him, and then there was no more talking.

An urgent knocking on the door woke Nina the next morning. She bolted awake to bright, blazing sunlight on her face. "Mom!" Nathan cried. "I need to talk to you. Are you up?"

She was naked. So was Marcus. She slammed her feet to the floor in a panic. "Just a minute!"

Marcus was already on his feet, running across the room to grab his clothes and dive into the bathroom. He poked his head back out and threw her the bathrobe from the back of the door. She scrambled into it, gathering the empty bottles and M&Ms and pistachios, tucking them all in a drawer. She felt slightly sore, and her mouth was tender, as if she'd kissed for about a million years—she had! The imprint of the carnal, thoroughly delicious night was stamped all over her, body, and a thready panic made her pause before the mirror to make sure…what? That no words were written on her forehead to announce that she'd had sex with Marcus?—and flung open the door. "Hey," she said, feigning a yawn. "What's up?"

"You're not up yet?" he cried. "The wedding is in three hours!"

She recognized the mood he was in. High drama. He'd worked himself into some kind of a scenario he couldn't live up to, and now he needed to come to grips with real life. "That's three hours, sweetheart. I don't need that much time to do my face, I promise." She took him by the arm. "Come sit down. What's going on?"

He plopped down on the sofa and slammed his head into his hands. "What if I'm the worst husband who ever lived?" he cried.

"What if I can't live up to all the things I want to do? What if we don't take good care of each other, or I get caught up in my work and don't pay enough attention to her and she falls in love with somebody else?"

Ah, Nina thought, suppressing a smile. This. "Those are good questions, son. I can answer the first one—you won't be the worst husband who ever lived. I think that's reserved for Henry the Eighth ."

He didn't smile. "You know what I mean. I haven't always been the best person."

"Oh, honey!" She brushed hair from his forehead, rubbed his shoulder. "You've always been a good person. Just because you were a crazy teenager doesn't mean you're going to be crazy as an adult. Being a teenager is about learning how to cope, learning all those skills. You did that."

"Did I?"

"Yes." Out of the corner of her eye, she spied a shoe, lying right in plain sight in front of the chair. She could also see a scatter of pencils and the sketchbook on the bed, face down, thank God, because she'd done a series of sketches of naked Marcus when their bodies would no longer cooperate with making love again. He drew her and she drew him and it was only as birds started to twitter in the trees that they had let go of the night to fall asleep.

She forced her attention back to Nathan, and the fact that she needed to made her feel like the worst mother in the world. What kind of mother indulged her own longings at her son's wedding?

Her, evidently.

But she knew what she needed to do. She took Nathan's hand. "Listen. Marriage is not always easy. You won't always take care of each other the way you should. You'll have times you don't like each other. You'll get on each other's nerves. But if you remember to be kind, and take the time to have your own—"

"Please don't say sex."

She chuckled. "That's also important, but I won't say it." She smiled at him. "I was going to say 'space.'"

"Oh."

"The truth is, you two know each other. You're very well suited and your families are happy you're getting together, so you have tons of love and support. You're just getting cold feet."

"No, it's not cold feet. Not at all! I am so in love with her that I would walk on hot coals for the rest of my natural life if that's what it took."

"You must be a writer or something," she teased, and was rewarded with a smile.

"I just don't want to let her down."

"You will," she said, "and she'll let you down, too. But it'll be okay. I promise."

"Promise?"

She nodded. "Now, get out of here so I can get myself together."

He hugged her, hard. "Thanks, Mom."

"It's going to be great, sweetheart. Trust me."

She hustled him to the door and out, waiting until she could see him walking through the parking lot before she knocked on the bathroom door. Marcus was dressed, except for his shoes. "All clear?"

"Yes. Did you hear him?"

"I tried not to invade his privacy too much. But you were great."

"Thanks. Now you really do have to get out of here because we did oversleep."

He reached for her, bending in for a kiss. "Later, alligator."

"Take care, teddy bear," she said against his mouth.

"Bye-bye, butterfly." He straightened. "I'd better get out of here before anyone comes to my room."

Her stomach growled. "I'm going to miss breakfast."

"I'll pop in there and grab some muffins, bring you some."

"Would you? That would be great. I'll leave the door open while I shower."

His eyes darkened. "Don't tempt me."

"Don't even think about it." She shoved his chest. "Coffee, too?"

He winked. "Done. See you later."

# Chapter Ten

The day was exquisitely perfect for a wedding—skies so blue you could swim in them, scudded with perfectly drawn white clouds for decoration. The mountains stood shoulder to shoulder over the scene, revealing peeks of pale green meadows and cropping of red rock. The air was neither hot nor cold, the sun bright and clear. Nina wore a pair of low clogs as she walked the four blocks to the church from the hotel. Her good shoes were in her bag.

A fairly large number of people had already gathered—despite her protests to the contrary, it had taken nearly the whole three hours to get ready, partly because she kept falling adrift in her memories of the long, delicious night and partly because that long night really did show on her face.

Ah, youth. She had joked to a friend once that she now spent hours trying to look the way she once had looked when she first woke up.

Beneath a towering pine a half a block from the church, she paused to change shoes. Into the bag went her clogs, for later dancing, and onto her feet went the highly impractical, wonderfully sexy four-inch heels with a thousand straps. She smoothed down her dress, which had taken months to find, a froth in turquoise tissue with a white underlay. It was simple, a scoop neck front and back, and a fitted waist with a swirly skirt that fell in a handkerchief hem. She wore her grandmother's sapphire necklace, the only jewelry of any note that her mother had owned. Touching it, she said, "Wish you were here, Mom. I miss you."

Smoothing her skirt one last time, she walked the rest of the way to the church. Quite a few people were there already, standing on the steps or the sidewalk, talking. Giselle and Nathan

## Inseparable

had wanted to keep the gathering small, and they worked hard to do it. Each of them had only a single attendant, and because of the distance and trouble, they would have a reception in LA when they got back from their honeymoon.

Still, it was a surprisingly robust crowd, mostly thirty-somethings who'd made the trip because they loved the couple, but also because it was such a great location. Nina greeted several people, most of whom she'd met the night before.

From inside the church came a soft playlist of popular love songs and classical music, and for a moment, she felt unbearably lonely. She was supposed to celebrate this day with Jason. None of her family had made the trip, not that there were many of them to do so.

And Marcus was off on his own, doing whatever he was doing.

Was she going to spend the whole rest of her life like this? Enjoying an evening of pleasure that dried up in the morning, leaving her alone again?

*Ugh. Don't start,* she told herself.

Instead, she went to check on Nathan, who was getting ready with several of his friends in tiny room off the altar. "Mom!" he cried when he saw her. "You look amazing!"

"Thanks, son. How are you doing?"

"Fine, now. Thanks. I talked to Marcus for a minute, too."

She squeezed his arm, trying to think of something to say that wouldn't feel wrong. "I'm glad," she said.

She greeted Giselle, too, still cloaked in a peach dressing gown, and simply gave her a card and a small gift to remember the day, a necklace with a small sapphire to connect to the one Nina wore herself. She hugged Giselle. "I can't wait to call you daughter," she said, and Giselle hugged her hard.

Back out on the sidewalk, she had to admit to herself that she was looking for Marcus. If Nathan had spoken to him, he had to be close by, but she ambled around the church twice and he was nowhere to be found. She was starting to feel silly standing outside when so many were seated in the church.

A black Lincoln pulled up and Marcus leapt out of the driver's seat, coming around to the passenger side to open the door. He looked exquisitely well-pressed in a medium blue suit, double-breasted, with tiny pinstripes. Natty, she thought, and felt a funny thrill that they were matched, even without discussing it.

He opened the door, and a man unfolded. He was very thin, and pushed a cane out in front of him, but as he straightened, Nina felt her heart drop.

The Colonel.

He had not lost a bit of his hair, and it was a white cloud over his heavily wrinkled face. He had always been clean-shaven but now sported a white mustache. His posture was as straight and perfect as ever, the military bearing giving him dignity. Although he carried the cane, he didn't seem to need it.

How had she never realized how much Marcus looked like him?

Before she could turn and dash up the steps, the Colonel caught sight of her, and Nina froze, unsure whether she should run away or simply greet him politely. He was only six feet away when he said in a booming voice, "Well, well, well, if it isn't little Nina Callahan, all grown up."

She looked at Marcus. He gave the slightest possible shrug, like *I don't know, either.*

Nina shook herself. She was a grown woman who'd raised a son, buried a husband, and created a shining career doing what she loved. Whatever her teenage self had feared from this man, those reasons were long gone. With a smile, she held out her hand, and took his bony fingers into both of her own. "It's good to see you, Colonel," she said, and instantly wondered if the title was still appropriate if he was retired.

But he beamed. It was startling, actually. He'd only ever been severe back in those days—when, she realized, he'd been younger than she was now by a decade or more—and his smile transformed his face. "You, too, child. My wife was so proud of you. I know she'd want me to tell you that."

A tear sparked in Nina's eye. "Thank you, sir. I appreciate that."

Marcus said, "We probably need to get inside."

"Walk with us," the Colonel said, offering his elbow. "Tell me what brings you to the wedding. Do you know my granddaughter?"

"I do know her, but it's a very funny coincidence—I'm Nathan's mother."

"What?" The old man paused and looked from Marcus to Nina, scowling. "You're kidding me."

"Nope," Marcus said. "My daughter is marrying Nina's son."

The Colonel stood there for a long minute, his rheumy eyes resting on Nina's face. "Well, isn't that something."

Music poured down the steps of the church, and without another word, the trio headed inside. "I'll see you at the reception," Nina said, lifting a hand to Marcus. He didn't smile as he gave her a nod, and she wondered what he was thinking.

But it didn't matter. Not now. Not today. The usher escorted her to the place of honor on the groom's side, and she gave her son a giant smile. He looked calm and radiant, light coming off him in waves.

Marcus and his father were seated just opposite, on the bride's side. She glanced over, and Marcus was still standing, tenderly waiting for his father to make his way into a sitting position, then giving him his cane. He sat down on the aisle, as Nina was, and her heart squeezed hard. He looked so handsome and dignified in the blue suit, his beard trimmed neatly, his hands in his lap. As if he felt her gaze, he looked over, his eyes sparkling, and raised his eyebrows.

She shook her head ever so faintly, widening her eyes.

Then the bridal march swelled through the room and they all stood, waiting for Giselle to appear.

When she did, a soft collective gasp came from the gathered number, because there could never have been a more beautiful bride in all the history of the world. She stood nearly six feet tall in her heels, and her hair had been swept into an elaborate series of princess braids laced with tiny roses and daisies and greenery. Her dress was mostly white, with a simple bodice that showed her toned shoulders and an antique garnet necklace Nina knew had belonged to her maternal great-grandmother, made of silver filigree in the shape of delicate roses. The skirt was fine net over a white underskirt, the hem and each panel embroidered with roses and leaves along the hem. The bouquet echoed the theme of a roses and vines with an elegant simple posy.

She beamed as she walked up the aisle, alone, because she had refused to have anyone "give her away," saying she belonged to herself.

Nina glanced at Marcus. He wore an expression of transcendent pride, and there were unmistakable tears in his eyes, which gave her tears in her eyes, and when Giselle caught sight of him, there were tears in her eyes, too. As she passed, she stopped to kiss him on the cheek.

Nina took the handkerchief out of her pocket.

She needed it. Giselle and Nathan were radiantly happy, extraordinarily beautiful, and she wept for their happiness and their commitment. As they said their vows, she felt the future that waited for them, all the good and all the trials. She thought of Jason, and how happy she'd been to say her vows to him, and how proud he would be today, and shed a few tears for him, too.

Mostly, they were tears of joy. The future spun out in hazy happiness—Thanksgiving meals, Christmases or Fourths of July, with children playing, pets.

Children. Her grandchildren.

And Marcus's. She glanced at his profile, and imagined a boy with his face, Nathan's infectious giggle, Giselle's kind eyes. Maybe even the Colonel's posture and bearing.

They would be connected for life, now. And once a child was born, it would be eternal. She didn't know why that made her tears flow all the more.

The reception was held in a converted barn around the corner from the church, and they all trooped over in their finery, not an unusual sight in the town since they'd set it up for destination weddings like this. Nina had been enveloped by well-wishers who accompanied her into the barn, but then she found herself alone again, looking for her next step. Tables were set up around the perimeter of a dance floor, all decorated with roses and vines. Strings of lights hung overhead for later.

*Inseparable*

Nathan called her. "Mom! You're here."

She joined him at the round head table, where Marcus and the Colonel were already seated. She had already kissed and hugged the bride and groom, who were alight with the day, so she looked at the available seats. The best man and matron of honor sat next to Nathan and Giselle, and there were several open seats, then Marcus and the Colonel. Would it look strange if she sat next to them?

Marcus gave her a wry smile and pulled out the chair next to him. "I won't bite."

With relief, she sat down, and nearly swooned at the smell of his cologne. "Congratulations, Dad. The bride is stunning."

"Congratulations, Mom," he said and kissed her on the cheek, as he'd done at breakfast yesterday. So casual, so touching.

Brunch was served, with mimosas and Bloody Marys and buckets of coffee, quiche and potatoes and baskets of pastries, steaming fried apples and biscuits and orange juice. "This is amazing!" Nina said. "Good job, Dad."

"I didn't plan it," he said.

"Just paid for it."

He acknowledged that truth with a dip of his head.

Under the table, their politeness was belied. Marcus moved his leg to touch hers, hip to knee, and he'd taken her hand, which he held until they needed to eat. The Colonel was hard of hearing, so she was spared the need to lean over and engage him in conversation. Marcus took care of that, while Nina talked with one of Giselle's aunts, a spare woman in a no-nonsense suit who revealed herself to be the Colonel's sister.

Of course.

It felt like disaster might be averted, that the tinderbox of the Colonel's knowledge of their long-ago romance would go unlit, until the speeches were finished and the dances were underway.

"Shall we?" Marcus asked quietly.

Nina met his eyes, conveying with a look what she could not speak. "Sure," she said, and hoped it was casual. She glanced across the table, but no one seemed to notice. The aunt had gone to powder her nose, while Giselle and Nathan were already out there dancing.

The song was part of a playlist that the couple had put together very thoughtfully, full of love songs both fast and slow, from across the decades. She'd heard some music from the 50s and some from the aughts, and this was something she knew vaguely from the radio.

But it didn't matter. The second Marcus took her in his arms, everything else dropped way.

"I missed you," he said quietly.

"Me, too."

"I wish we could have sat together at the wedding."

Nina nodded. Under her hands, she could feel the muscles of his shoulders, and it was the same and different from before. Just like now was the same and different. "I almost fainted when I saw your dad."

"Tell me about it." He glanced over her shoulder at the old man. "He paid a taxi to drive him up here. Must have cost a fortune, but he won't hear of me paying."

Nina chuckled.

"Is he going to blow it for us?"

"I don't know. It's out of our hands."

They danced silently for a while. Marcus asked, "When do you go back?"

"Tomorrow morning." She looked at him, feeling a sense of grief that sometime tomorrow afternoon, she wouldn't be looking at him anymore. "How about you?"

"Same." He swallowed. "Can you stay?"

She shook her head. "I have a meeting on Monday morning with my gallery. Can you come to me?"

"I have to get back by Tuesday for a court date."

Her stomach ached. She wanted to touch his goatee, his mouth, his ears and neck. "It's crazy, but I'm going to miss you."

"Not crazy." He took a breath. "I wish I could kiss you right now."

"What do you think would happen?"

"I don't know."

"We have to let the kids have their day."

"Only the day?"

"I don't know," she said. "I guess we can play it by ear."

"Are we going forward then? Me and you?"

"Do you want to?"

He gripped her waist. "Are there stars in the sky?"

She smiled. "Me, too."

The song ended and they reluctantly broke apart, just in time to see the Colonel pick up the mic from the table. "Can you hold off on the music for a minute? I want to say something."

Nina and Marcus froze. "Oh, no," she breathed.

"I'm sure it's nothing," Marcus said.

"For all of you who don't know me, I'm Colonel du Bois, Giselle's granddaddy. I think you all agree with me that she is the prettiest bride that ever was."

Whoops and clapping.

"What you don't know is that her groom is the son of a woman I was pretty hard on, once upon a time."

Nina shook her head, starting to step forward and stop him, but Marcus stopped her by grabbing her hand. He stood protectively close. "Here we go."

"You see, Marcus, my son over there, the good looking one wearing the fancy suit—"

Laughter.

"Used to be head over heels in love with that girl and I didn't like it, not one bit."

Stillness rippled through the room. Nina glanced at Giselle and Nathan, but their faces didn't show any expression whatsoever. Her heart was pounding.

"Not because she was white, now. I've never cared about that. No," he looked at her. "She was an artist. An artsy-fartsy, unrealistic, hippie dreamer. It was her fault that Marcus started studying art, started getting off track."

Marcus stroked her hand with his thumb.

The Colonel shook his head. "Back in those days, I was a pretty hard man. And I have to tell you that I made a big mistake."

"Grandpa." Giselle stood up. "Wait one second."

"Hold on. I have something to say."

Giselle rounded the table in her fluffy skirt and took the mic out of his hand. "So do I." She kissed his cheek. She took the mic and looked at Marcus and Nina. Nathan joined her, and they were both smiling.

"So, this was supposed to go down a little differently, but we'll just go with it. Weddings are never perfect." She inclined her head. "A couple of years ago, Nathan and I helped my granddaddy move out of the house he'd been in for twenty years to a new one that was a little easier to manage, and while we were there, we found some letters that were written by a girl with the same name as Nathan's mom."

Nina swallowed.

"They were from Nina to my dad, back when they were teenagers, and while I didn't read them all, I read enough to know that they were only one side of the story."

The Colonel leaned over Giselle. "I hid them."

Giselle laughed. "Yes. That's what I figured out." She shifted her skirt a little. "I did some digging to see what I could find out, see who this girl was. I looked up the yearbooks online, and that's when I found out that Marcus, my dad, and Nina, were madly in love in high school. The yearbooks called them inseparable." She smiled. "Until they were separated because of a move. My dad wrote to Nina, and Nina wrote back, but this guy," She put her arm around the Colonel, "intercepted Nina's—for reasons that were all about love. He wanted his son to have a good life."

The Colonel nodded.

"Eventually, my dad gave up."

A soft sound of sadness rounded the room.

"So Nathan and I talked about it. Both of them were widowed, right? We cooked up this plan. To see if we could get them in the same space again, see what happened."

Marcus laughed. It was his big, booming laugh, so big and wide it seemed to hold the heavens themselves.

"If any of you saw them dancing last night, I think you know what happened."

Nina looked at Nathan, who was grinning at her, and gave her a thumbs-up.

*Inseparable*

"And you see them standing there, holding hands right now, don't you?" The room clapped, and Nina looked up at Marcus. Quietly, she asked, "Are you okay with all of this?"

In answer, he bent down and kissed her, hard. "Yes."

Another round of whoops and hollers went out, and although Nina was only looking at Marcus and he was only looking at her, they both heard Giselle say, "This song is for them."

The first, familiar threads of Ella Fitzgerald's *At Last* floated out into the room. Nina laughed, and so did Marcus, and when he opened his arms, she went gladly, tears streaming down her face. He held her hand close to his chest, and kissed it. "Do you want to do this?"

"Yes." There was no question in her mind whatsoever. Whatever, wherever, whenever. If the team was Marcus and Nina, everything would be fine.

He kissed her, and others milled around the dance floor, but they didn't matter at all. "See," he said, raising his head, "we really are inseparable."

She laughed.

"I love you, Nina," he said. "I don't think that ever went away."

She raised her hands to his face. "I know I never stopped loving you."

Giselle and Nathan came over. "Too much, you guys?" Giselle asked.

Marcus kissed his daughter's head and Nina let Nathan hug her. She said, "We were so afraid you'd be freaked out."

"It was a little weird to see Marcus's shoe on the floor this morning, but that's when I knew it worked." Nathan squeezed her hand. "And this way you can be in LA when the baby is born."

"Baby?" Nina said, whipping around to look at Giselle.

She nodded, discreetly resting her hand on her belly. Nina realized she'd not had a drink at all. "Okay."

The four circled in a swaying celebration.

At last.

# Epilogue

The light was a dusty gold, the buildings turquoise and pink and yellow, with courtyards filled with plants and jars; the markets crammed with beautiful things. Nina's sketchbook was crammed with images she'd captured during a two-week tour. She'd arranged it herself, nervous, but thrilled, and joined a tour group. This morning, they'd parted and Nina waited at a luxurious hotel for the second part of the trip.

She sat at a table on the veranda of the hotel, drinking freshly squeezed orange juice and sketching the scene before her.

A man walked in the bright sunshine, wearing tropical khakis and a hat to cover his head. He was perfectly at ease in his body, moving as loosely as a lion. His goatee had gained more white. He climbed the stairs and stood for one moment looking at her. "You're a sight for sore eyes."

"You, too." She reached out a hand, mindful that they should not kiss in public, and patted the rattan seat beside her. "Come sit down. Show me your sketchbook."

He'd taken a life drawing course intensive while she toured Morocco, the bargain they'd made a year ago. In between had been a big move—two actually, because they'd found a house near the beach to start their lives fresh—and a grandson, and a quiet wedding. On the second part of their trip, they would ride camels into the desert and explore Egypt and then fly to Venice, just because Nina wanted to paint there.

Quietly, they sat together viewing the scene, holding hands beneath the table.

"Did you ever think we'd be here like this?" Nina asked.

"As a matter of fact, I did." He flashed her a smile. "And here we are."

She grinned back. "Here we are."

**The End**

# Acknowledgments

All my thanks go to my Fiction from the Heart sisters. It's been a true blessing in my life to get to know you, ladies. I look forward to many more hours of discussion, help, celebration, commiseration and projects. Special thanks to Priscilla, Jamie, and Liz, who did a lot of cat-herding.

# About Barbara Samuel

Barbara Samuel sold her first romance when she was still in her twenties and has since written more than 75 books. She loves to head out for far away places, splash around with watercolor, and walk miles and miles. She lives with her partner, an English endurance athlete, and their three cats and two dogs. She has won seven RITA awards from the Romance Writers of America and was inducted into the Hall of Fame in 2012. Read more about all of her books at www.barbarasamuel.com./

# A Morning Glory Wedding

by Liz Talley

# Chapter One

Brandy Robbins's mother had named her after a popular song of the 1970s, thus ensuring that Brandy would forever be the girl in the port that no sailor would ever commit to. Oh, sure, Brandy was a fine girl and what a good wife she could probably be... but catching a guy who wanted to put a ring on her finger was as likely as the ancient Greek Tantalus getting that cool drink of water.

*Stay thirsty, girlfriend.*

Of course, Brandy might have had better luck had she not been an absolute idiot, falling for the wrong guy her first year back in Morning Glory. She'd single-handedly destroyed the marriage of *the* power couple of the small Mississippi town... which was why she couldn't believe she was sitting in her grandmother's floral shop across from the emissary of the betrayed Jess Culpepper, talking about a bridal bouquet for the upcoming Reyes-Culpepper wedding.

"Do you think orchids will look good?" Rosemary asked, running her hand over the rounded bump of her stomach for the *thirteenth* time. Pretty Rosemary was five months along and glowing.

"Well, you said she liked orchids," Brandy said, drawing a loop-the-loop on the top of her order pad to quell her nerves.

"Yeah, but there was no plan to use orchids in the original bouquet. Angie had special ordered peonies and protea in shades of lavender and blush, but, well, that's..." Rosemary shrugged and petted her stomach. *Fourteen* tummy rubs. "We'll just have to do the best we can do."

Jess Culpepper would never darken the doorstep of Flowers for

You herself—she hated Brandy—so the fact Brandy was working with Rosemary Genovese wasn't the surprise. It was the fact that the wronged Jess would consider using Brandy as her florist in the first place. Brandy had figured that when word reached Jess that Posy Mart, her floral shop of choice for her wedding in six days, had burned to the ground, the panicked bride would go with someone out of nearby Jackson. But then Rosemary had called to schedule an appointment with Brandy, guaranteeing an exorbitant rush fee for a last-minute wedding order. Brandy had pinched herself three times in a row and said yes to doing the wedding that would take place that upcoming weekend.

In January, Brandy had made a new business plan for her grandmother's floral shop, Flowers for You, but she could have never imagined that her last flippant line to "burn down the competition" would be a literal, actionable item. Of course, it was faulty wiring that had burned Posy Mart down. But Brandy hadn't felt as bad as she would have had the owner not been one of the horde of women who'd stopped talking to Brandy after she'd been branded the "other woman" after the breakup of Jess and her ex-husband.

Brandy couldn't blame the woman. Or maybe she could. Because no one in Morning Glory had bothered to point a finger at Benton Mason, Jess's ex. No, they assumed Brandy had chased the handsome, charming former quarterback like a crazed rabbit-boiling stalker set on tearing apart the vows of every meant-to-be couple in town.

Thus, the scarlet *A* was still firmly affixed on Brandy's enhanced chest.

Brandy re-centered her focus on Rosemary, who seemed overly contemplative about those peonies. "How about something more Jess-like than ruffled peonies and exotic sugar-bush? When I think of Jess, I think of wildflowers. They're tough and beautiful. Resilient but still spectacular. They say Southern and simple."

Rosemary narrowed her eyes. "You don't really know Jess."

Her words were true. Brandy *didn't* really know Jess. Oh, they'd gone to high school together, but Brandy hadn't come close to hanging out with the Fab Four—Rosemary, Jess, Lacy, and Eden. No, Brandy was the girl everyone forgot they knew. She'd see people she'd known for years in the grocery store and say hello, and they would return a "who are you again?" stare that told her they didn't remember the girl who'd sat next to them in American history. In high school Brandy was wholly unmemorable—a mousy brunette with wide gray eyes, pale skin, and toothpick legs that should have earned her nicknames like Praying Mantis or Stick Girl. But, alas, she was too inconsequential to qualify for such a moniker. *Forgettable* was the best word for the girl Brandy had been.

"True." Brandy didn't say more. Instead, she waited. She'd learned that when it came to dealing with brides—or emissaries of brides—it was best to listen and allow them to talk it out. But Rosemary stared at her and didn't follow up with anything more. Her stare wasn't hostile. Rosemary was way too polite to show any residual anger at Brandy, but the woman didn't seem interested in making Brandy comfortable either.

After a few seconds, Brandy finally sighed. "Why don't you follow me to the back, and I'll show you what I have available? I can also show you some bouquets I've done in the past. If I can't get my hands on particular flowers in those examples, I'll find a serviceable replacement."

Brandy rose and walked toward the back, expecting Rosemary to follow.

When she realized the woman wasn't behind her, she turned around. Rosemary stood, looking at the photos strewn across the counter. As part of her New Year's resolution, Brandy had decided to clean out the junk drawers beneath the counter. Old receipts, funny clippings, and former bulletin board photos she'd crammed in the recesses fanned across the Formica. One in particular, the only image Brandy had of her and Benton, sat on the top.

Damn it. She should have thrown that out before Rosemary showed up, but she'd gotten busy with a shipment and forgot about the mess she'd left.

Rosemary picked up the black-and-white photo-booth strip, her pretty face a mirror for her emotions. She stared at the images of Brandy and Benton Mason clowning around and then looked up at Brandy. "We told Jess not to use you—that she didn't need a reminder of her past on her wedding day—but Jess wants fresh flowers. She said you're the best florist in town." Rosemary tossed the strip onto the counter like it was something covered with dog poop.

Brandy looked down at the pictures scattered across the counter. Then she walked over, picked up the trashcan, and scraped everything into its depths. She set the metal can down with a clatter and looked Rosemary in the eye. "I'm the *only* florist in town."

The woman wearing the pink sweater set stroked her stomach. *Fifteen.* "Why did you sleep with him, Brandy? How could you do that to Jess?"

Brandy blinked once. Then she swallowed hard. "You know, you're the first person with enough guts to come out and ask me that question."

Rosemary didn't reply. She watched Brandy, a sad expression on her face. Brandy wasn't sure if it was for her best friend Jess, whose first marriage had ended, or if it was for Brandy, who had reached for something she ought not have. Perhaps both.

Brandy had thought about how she would answer that question if someone ever asked her why she had done what she'd done. She could have told them how her therapist back in Dallas diagnosed her with borderline histrionic personality disorder. After her freshman year of college, a miserable year where she'd existed as a ghost on TCU's campus, Brandy went to a party, drank some tequila, and broke out of the cocoon in which she'd been moldering for years. The freshman fifteen had given her a few curves, and by the end of her sophomore year, Brandy had dyed her hair platinum, gotten breast enhancements, and was using sex as a way to be loved. Her endless cycle of "am I good enough?" had caused her heartbreak and led to depression that she had finally gotten a handle on in her late twenties. What would perfect Rosemary say to something like that? Could she even understand being a nobody in a world where everyone was somebody?

Or maybe Brandy could tell her about how she'd moved back to Morning Glory because her grammy, the only person who'd ever loved her, could no longer remember how to count back change or where her house was located? Could Rosemary understand living in a small town with people who didn't remember attending grade school with her... having her heart broken by a grandmother who'd also forgotten her?

Brandy really wanted to tell her about Benton and how he'd come by almost every day for a month to flirt with her. How he'd once ordered a bouquet of flowers for a "pretty girl," walked out the door, and then come right back and handed them to her. He'd said, "I bet you never get flowers," and she'd fallen half in love with the guy who wouldn't have given her a second look when they were in high school. Or perhaps she could tell Rosemary how Benton had lied to her when he said that he and Jess were over, that the two of them had agreed to split but were waiting until they were both on their feet financially before moving out and filing for separation. How Benton had sworn that he and Jess were living in separate rooms and that Jess was corresponding with a new romantic interest online. He'd said that Jess had told him he was free to move on and be happy. Would Rosemary understand how much Brandy had wanted to be loved by a man like Benton?

Would Rosemary believe that Brandy had been the stupidest, most pathetic woman this side of the Mississippi River when she'd tried for something she'd always wanted and never had — a chance at a happily-ever-after?

Should she show Rosemary all the returned letters she'd written to Jess, begging her forgiveness? Or the pathetic ones she'd never mailed to Benton after he'd left her for Deidre Pierpont... one month after he'd vowed he was in love with Brandy and wanted to marry her?

Yeah, there were so many things she wanted to say about being the woman who busted up Jess and Benton's marriage, but those words wouldn't come. Because Rosemary wouldn't believe them anyway.

So instead she said the one thing she knew about herself. "Because I'm a horrible person."

## Chapter Two

Geoffrey Harper opened the door to Arbor Assisted Living and grinned at the woman standing behind the receptionist desk. The retirement community was divided into two distinct sections. One contained small cottages for independent living, a pool, and a walking trail, and the other was for those who needed more care and could no longer live on their own. This particular side was housed in a structure designed to look like an old antebellum house with floor-to-ceiling window covers with plantation shutters and rocking chairs across the front porch. Welcoming everyone was a large woman with a gap-toothed smile, big hoop earrings, and a wig that was shockingly red. Effie Jefferson ran this department of the Arbor with compassion, humor, and efficiency. Her only problem was she liked the wrong football team.

"Told you the Saints were going to win the division," he said with perhaps a bit too much gloating.

"Ha." Effie rolled her eyes. "You know my Cowboys were down a few good linemen and that's the only reason they didn't take care of those ugly ol' Saints in the playoffs. You mark my words—if dem boys would have been healthy, they'd be wearing those rings."

"Pay up," Geoff said, extending his hand over the shiny wood of the reception desk.

Effie made a face but pulled her famous sour cream pound cake from the depths of a bag at her feet. "I'd hope you choke on it, but you're a preacher and all, and I don't want to go to hell."

He laughed and tucked the foil-wrapped package under his arm. "I know you love me."

Effie grinned as big as Dallas... the city from which she hailed.

"That's what you tell yourself anyway. Oh and look, here comes my girl. Brandy, tell this man the Cowboys would have whooped the Saints—again, I might add—if we would have played them in the playoffs. You're from Texas. Back me up."

Geoff turned to see Brandy Robbins, the quiet beauty he saw almost every time he visited his parishioners at the Arbor.

"What playoffs?" Brandy asked, pushing her grandmother down the hall toward what he assumed were the winter-weary gardens. The day was unseasonably warm, but the landscape outside the large picture window was decidedly gray. "Are you talking about basketball or football?"

Effie rolled her brown eyes. "Lord Jesus, I will be praying for this one. How do you grow up in the South and not know anything about sports?"

Brandy smiled, and Geoff felt a flutter of something he'd been trying to ignore brush against his ribs. "Miss Effie, have you seen me dribble a basketball or throw a football? You would know why I know next to nothing about sports. Besides, I'm not truly from Texas. I was raised here."

"All I'm saying is you don't have to know how to play a sport to appreciate all those good-looking men in those tight, shiny pants," Effie said.

Brandy rolled her eyes and then looked at him. "Good afternoon, Father Geoff. Sorry you have to put up with this kind of harassment." She tossed a good-natured look at Effie, who had already sat down and pulled out her crossword puzzle. The older woman was now officially ignoring them.

Effie made a choking noise, or maybe it was a harrumph. Okay, not totally ignoring them.

"Comes with the territory, Brandy. And how's your grandmother today?" he asked, looking at the older woman who slumped in the wheelchair. The woman wore a velour jogging suit, slippers, and her hair stuck up at odd angles. Pearl Havers was essentially comatose with occasional fits of anger, sadness, or odd laughter. Still, Brandy came four or five times a week, bringing cheerful flowers from the flower shop to brighten her grandmother's room. She also made bouquets for some of the other residents. He'd often seen her playing a game of dominos with some of the elderly gentlemen or conversing with some of the ladies in the cafeteria, and her kindness never failed to touch him.

"The same," Brandy said, bending over and smoothing the cowlicks that stood at attention on the older woman's head. "But she's still here, so that's something. We're taking a stroll. Maybe we'll see if the roses are starting to wake up. What do you think, Grammy?"

The older woman didn't respond. Brandy looked up and smiled softly. "I think that means yes."

"Can I join you?"

Something cautious flashed in her eyes before she nodded. "Sure."

"Bye, Effie. Thanks for the victory cake. I will think of the Cowboys with every bite."

Effie huffed. "Oh, if you weren't a man of God…"

Brandy laughed, and the sound was unexpected. For such a serious woman, she had a lovely laugh. The lightness in it matched her sun-streaked hair and clear gray eyes.

"She really loves me." He grinned, falling in step with her.

"Effie loves everyone. It's just hard to see it sometimes." She rolled her grandmother down the hallway past landscapes painted by many of the former residents and into the area that was a bank of windows. A small alcove containing comfortable chairs overlooked a lush garden that Effie assured him was normally full of roses, daylilies, and other plants native to Mississippi. But at the beginning of February, the garden sat awaiting new growth, its only cheerful offering several bird feeders from which hungry blue jays and cardinals fed.

"Sometimes you wear your, uh, uniform, but other times you don't," Brandy said, nodding at his black clerical shirt with its white collar. He wore a black jacket over it along with a pair of slim black pants. His black chucks peeked out from the hem.

"Most of my congregation here at the Arbor are traditionalists, so I try to look somewhat pastorly, but I'm not required to wear the trappings of my profession all the time."

She smashed her foot onto the wheelchair brake and rubbed her grandmother's shoulder. "My grandmother took me to the Baptist church. I don't know much about priests."

He didn't want to talk about his faith, which was contrary to his calling. He should want to talk of Christ and salvation, but at that moment he wanted Brandy to see him as a man. Not a man of the cloth. "Technically I'm a pastor like any other man of God. But we're just regular people. How are things at the shop? You mentioned last time I saw you that you were worried about staying open."

Brandy froze for a moment, glancing down at her grandmother as if she were afraid the woman might hear. "I forgot I told you that. You must really be good at your job. I mean, people bare their souls to you and all."

He smiled. "I'm not Catholic and don't hear confessions. Still, I'm always willing to lend an ear to those who need it."

For a moment she didn't say anything. "I actually have a bit of good news. I got the Reyes-Culpepper job next week."

"That's right. The other floral shop will be out of commission. Such a loss, but it delivers a nice silver lining for you. Jess's parents are members of Saint Paul's congregation. The wedding is at the church."

"Guess you'll be seeing me over the next few days. I mean, I see you most weeks, but you know, at your place." She stepped around her grandmother and rubbed at a smudge on the window. Outside in the garden, tiny wrens scattered, and a pretty goldfinch flew onto a branch of the redbud tree that was covered in tight purple buds.

"At my place," he repeated with a smile in his voice. "I'm not sure I've heard anyone call the church my place. The chapel is lovely. Have you been there?"

She nodded. "Always reminded me of something in England. Not that I've actually been to England." A flicker at her mouth made him want to ask her what the joke was.

"I know you'll do a good job for Ryan and Jess. Everyone seems to be anticipating this Valentine's wedding. Perfect time to declare one's love."

At that she snorted.

"What?" he asked, noticing how pretty she was in the thin winter light. Her cheekbones looked sculpted by a master, those unwavering eyes wide and fringed with thick lashes. Her mouth was almost a slash in her porcelain face, softened only by a full lower lip. Her nose tipped up just so. The tangle of honey-streaked brown hair reminded him of Farrah Fawcett in her heyday. His dad had had an old picture of the '70s pinup star in his garage, and Geoff used to think she was the prettiest woman he'd ever seen.

"Nothing."

"You don't believe in love?"

Brandy lifted one shoulder. "Maybe. I always wanted to believe that true love existed, but to be honest, Father, I haven't seen it too often in action. Seems everyone has a hustle, something that they want to get from someone else, and they use words like *love* to get what they want."

He wasn't certain he'd ever heard someone be as cynical about such a pure thing as love. "So your mother didn't love you? She hustled you?"

Brandy turned to him. "My mother had me when she was eighteen. She dropped me on my grandmother's doorstep when I was nine months old and ran off to Alaska with some guy who was working the pipeline. She never called, wrote, or sent me one nickel or thought. I don't even know if she's still alive, but what I do know is that she never loved me."

He stilled at the thought of a mother abandoning her child in such a manner. His own mother had smothered him with love, affection, and expectations—things he'd fought like a prisoner struggling against steel handcuffs. He'd given his parents much cause for tears as he rebelled against their rules, but eventually, after almost a decade of bad choices, he'd come back to the light… And now he helped to spread that brightness to others. His journey to his current profession had not been easy or without sacrifice, but he loved pursuing good. "I'm sorry to hear that, but your grandmother surely showed you love."

Brandy glanced down at the older woman. "That's true

enough. Maybe I'm talking about romantic love. You know, tingles, roses, and poetry."

"This from a florist who capitalizes on people wanting to express such sentiments."

Brandy put her finger to her lips. "Shh!"

He chuckled. "Okay, it will be our secret."

"Right. You can't tell because you're a priest, um, pastor. That's like the law or something." Her smile made him feel warm all over. It had been quite a while since he'd felt interested in a woman in a romantic sense, but something about Brandy drew him. Obviously, she was attractive—curvy in the right places and pretty enough to turn heads—but there was something more. She was kind to people when no one was looking, when there was no gain in doing so. And perhaps there was the sense that she had been wounded and needed someone like him to lean upon.

"Since you'll be providing the flowers and be there for the wedding, why don't you be my date for the reception?"

Her eyes widened. "Um, aren't you not supposed to, uh, be with a woman?"

"Are you talking about celibacy? That's true in the Catholic faith, but Episcopalian priests are allowed date and marry. Of course, I'm not asking you to marry me. Just be my plus-one for the reception. I can promise you cake."

She bloomed an adorable shade of pink. "Uh, well, I would love to... I mean, it's not you, it's just that I'm pretty sure Jess isn't going to want me there."

Geoff hadn't expected her refusal to ding his ego the way it did. After all, he'd been the recipient of a lot of casseroles and pound cakes the week he'd been appointed to Saint Paul's and moved to the rectory. Thanks to the single ladies of Morning Glory (and their mothers), he hadn't had to cook for a good three weeks. "Okay. I'm not sure why Jess wouldn't want the person providing her floral arrangements to have a slice of cake, but I can take a hint."

Brandy bit her lower lip. "Well, it's not that I don't find you attractive. I do. I mean, uh, that's sort of embarrassing because... but it's more about... you know."

He shook his head. "What?"

"Oh," she said, her face growing serious. "Maybe you don't know."

"Know what?" He'd only been in Morning Glory for a few short months. Obviously, something had occurred between Brandy and Jess Culpepper.

Brandy turned back toward the plate glass window. "I'm the 'other woman'—the one who broke up Jess's first marriage."

## Chapter Three

Brandy set her purse on the kitchen counter and pressed the button on the answering machine. Yes, her grandmother still had an old-fashioned answering machine, and for some strange reason, Brandy had been unwilling to retire it. Probably because every time she checked the machine for messages, she heard her grandmother's cheerful voice asking the person to "leave a message, and I'll get right back to you, darlin.'"

Her grandmother had been so funny, so lively. Having her relegated to a shell taking up space was like swallowing a knot of tacks every time Brandy visited her. Very, very hard to get past. Or was that passed? Either way, it hurt.

Chess leaped onto the counter, and Brandy stroked his soft, shaggy fur. "Hiya, Chess. How was your day? See any mice?"

Chess purred and paced back and forth under her hand. When she'd first arrived at her grandmother's house several years ago, she'd nearly fallen over in disbelief. The pier-and-beam farmhouse, once freshly painted and sporting window boxes even florists in Charleston couldn't touch, had fallen into serious disrepair and housed several mouse families. Brandy had hired Clem Aikens to repair the sagging porch, paint, and replace the damaged shutters. Then she'd gone out to Crazy Ted's and brought home a mouser to cull the mice the exterminator hadn't managed to relocate. She'd laughed when she'd seen the cat the next morning with a victim limp in its mouth and said, "Checkmate, mousies."

And that's how Chess got his name.

Brandy had kept her grandmother with her as long as she could. Pearl deserved to stay in the home and community she loved, but after she'd become combative and then escaped to roam the streets in her bathrobe, Brandy knew she could no longer manage her grandmother. The Arbor was the best alternative, and she knew they took good care of her grandmother, especially after the stroke that left her nearly comatose. Still, it was lonely to come home to an empty house every day. Thank goodness for Chess.

She set the mail on the counter next to the toaster and grabbed the coffeepot. Nothing like a cup of coffee to help her open all the bills she could no longer pay. Her savings were depleted, her grandmother's checking account empty, and the note on the refinance of the floral shop past due. Opening the mail was awfully fun these days.

As she cleaned the coffeepot, her mind went back to the handsome priest.

A date.

The man had asked her on a date.

"Poor Father Geoff," she said to Chess, who had walked along the counter to the sink and now watched Brandy fill the carafe. "He's too green to know that I'm the absolute wrong woman for him to go on a date with. At least not in this town."

The cat meowed.

"That's what I said, but he's all forgiving and stuff." Brandy gave a chuffing laugh. "Guess that's what real Christians are. Not that I've experienced much of that around here."

As soon as she said it, she knew that wasn't necessarily true. Sure, many in Morning Glory were still stuck in medieval times with their fiery torches and pitch forks of morality, but Brandy wasn't relegated to living on the outskirts or wearing a scarlet letter on her chest. She had friends. Like Lucy, her next-door neighbor, who should be arriving—

"Yoo-hoo," a thin voice called out. "Brandy?"

"Come on in, Lucy. I just started a pot of coffee. Oh, and Father Harper gave me some of Effie's pound cake. We'll eat like queens."

Lucy poked her head around the corner. "There you are. What's this I hear about cake?"

"Effie Jefferson made it. I talked the good Father Harper into parting with a few pieces."

"Oh, that yummy Father Harper. Almost makes me wish I wasn't Jewish. Oh, the things I could confess," Lucy said with a titter, her rheumy brown eyes sparkling in her lined face. Blue hair carefully coiffed sat pinned atop her crown, and she wore a pair of jeans with rhinestones on the pockets and a turtleneck to cover what she called her turkey neck.

"He doesn't do confession. He's Episcopalian."

"Well, darn. I wanted to shock him with my exploits. I wasn't always old and fat."

"You're not fat," Brandy said right as she realized she'd walked into that one.

"But I'm old, right?"

Brandy smiled. "Well, you're no spring chicken, Lucy."

The older woman cackled and rubbed her hands together. "Damned right. I have no use for spring chickens, especially of the male variety. After Percy died, I decided I wasn't picking up any man undies anymore. Percy's were bad enough. Plus, at this point, all those men just want my money." She glanced over at the stack of mail, a red PAST DUE stamped on at least two of the envelopes.

Brandy's gaze followed Lucy's, and her stomach clutched at the sight of the unpaid bills.

"Why don't you let me help you, sugar?" Lucy said.

"You can't. It's not your burden."

Lucy frowned. "It's not a burden. I got all this money and I'm too old to spend it. It would make me so happy to help you."

Brandy shook her head. She knew Lucy had inherited a lot of money from her East Coast family and had plenty to spare. Still, Brandy didn't want to be bailed out. She'd made her own bed and now she had to sleep in it. "I know it would, but don't worry. I just got the Reyes-Culpepper wedding, and with Valentine's Day the weekend after, I'm pretty much the only game in town. Of course, I feel bad that someone else's misfortune may pull me out of bankruptcy, but I believe in silver linings."

Lucy smiled. "Nothing wrong with silver linings. And Jess Culpepper, huh? Who would have thunk it?"

"I know. She hates my guts… and every other part of my body.

I thought for sure she'd go without flowers before she hired me for her wedding." Brandy ground the beans and scooped the fragrant coffee into the filter. She poured the water into the coffee maker and sliced the pound cake she'd talked Father Geoff into giving her. When it came to his time, smiles, or pound cake, the good father seemed more than willing to part with a share.

"Jess wasn't born yesterday. She knows what role Benton played in all that nonsense."

"Lucy, I slept with him. I knew he was married, and I still did it."

"But he told you he was separated. He baited that hook and dangled it right in front of your nose. Any other time in your life, you would have swum on past, but he knew what he had to do to get your knickers off, and he did it." Lucy took her cup and plopped down at the old scarred table with the vintage napkin dispenser and Conway Twitty salt and pepper shakers. Her grandmother had had a thing for the country music singer, so the man's image was peppered (no pun intended) throughout the house.

Her neighbor's words weren't incorrect, but that didn't make them right either. It was true Benton had sniffed her out the way a shark scents a wounded seal from miles away. She'd not been in town but six months when her grandmother had the stroke. For several weeks, she wasn't sure if her grandmother would even make it. The day Benton Mason waltzed into the floral shop, Brandy had just found the DNR papers along with her grandmother's will and had been crying in the bathroom for a good part of the morning. She felt like tissue paper dropping into a pitcher of water, unable to stop her world from disappearing.

Benton Mason had appeared at her counter, as handsome as ever. Time had filled out his face, emphasizing his five-o'clock shadow and bright eyes with crinkles that made him look like a weathered, sexy ski bum instead of a small-town businessman.

Benton hadn't remembered Brandy—no surprise there—and had introduced himself with a charming smile and a flicker in his eyes that he'd never, ever used on her in high school. After he'd been suitably sad for her about her grandmother, Benton's eyes dropped from her face to skim her body. She didn't have to be a rocket scientist to see he liked what he saw. She also knew he was married to the pretty Jess Culpepper Mason and had no business checking her out the way he was. But she couldn't help feeling something at his flirty words and interest. It was way better than "the disease is progressing" and "she needs care you can't give her."

He'd ordered flowers for a funeral and promised to visit again soon.

And he had.

His office was only a few blocks away, so every time he went past the floral shop, he popped in. Sometimes he brought her a coffee from the Lazy Frog. Other times he dropped the *New York Times* crossword puzzle on the counter because she'd confessed to loving the challenge. She began to look forward to his visits too much, telling herself that a man like Benton could be her friend as much as Lucy could. A few weeks after he began their friendship, he told her he and Jess had been having marital problems for almost a year. Their marriage was pretty much over, and he'd moved into the guest bedroom. They'd married too young, without having dated other people, and both agreed they shouldn't have married their high school sweetheart. Once they were both on their feet financially, they'd file for separation and put the house on the market. Benton was practically a free man.

God help Brandy, but she'd believed him.

Because she'd needed someone like Benton to say those things to her. She was lonely, hurt, and without any friends outside of Lucy. Yeah, yeah, there was no excuse for what she'd done. She should have known he'd lied to her. How many other times had she believed men only to find out that she was the stupidest cow this side of Texas? Let's just say if she had a quarter for all the times she'd believed that love could find her, she'd be able to pay those damn bills sitting on the kitchen counter.

"Brandy?" Lucy's question jarred her from her memory of her biggest mistake.

"I let him convince me. I wanted him to want me."

"You're human, honey," the older woman said.

"No, I should have known better than to trust Benton. Losers like him always stick to me like a three-day funk. I don't know why I always fall for assholes, Lucy."

As soon as she said those words, Father Geoff Harper's image appeared in her mind.

A priest—a veritable superhero of morality and goodness—had asked her out. Well, not out out. More like a *you'll be there, I'll be there, let's sit together* sort of date. But it was a date nevertheless. Of course, it wasn't a date if she didn't take him up on it. She'd told him she would let him know and then wheeled her grandmother as fast as she could toward the front of the building.

"Then you need to find you a non-asshole." Lucy popped a piece of cake in her mouth.

"Or swear off men forever," Brandy said, grabbing her mug of fragrant wonderfulness and joining Lucy at the table. "I might just eat cake, get fat, and stay single forever."

"Hey, that's my plan, and it's working for me," her neighbor said.

## Chapter Four

Geoff set the notes for his sermon Sunday on the desk and pushed back his chair. He'd been doing a series on positive living and was on the last sermon, which would center around how to stay the course and keep joy present in one's life. He'd pored through tomes and scoured liturgical practices that would complement his message for his congregation, but now his eyes felt like they'd crossed.

He needed a break... and it had nothing to do with the fact that Brandy Robbins was in the sanctuary getting some measurements.

Eh, maybe it did.

He rose and smoothed his hair, smiling at himself for his vanity.

*I'm the other woman.*

The way she'd said those words to him days ago had made his heart fissure. She'd sounded so broken... so hopeless. Brandy Robbins had let her past mistakes define her, of that he was certain. When he thought about someone making that sort of mistake... and then looked out the window at the town in which it had been made, he felt even more sorrow for her.

Morning Glory was as pretty as its moniker, a startlingly cheerful bit of Mississippi that gave a passerby a little lift in his step. Quaint and quintessentially Southern, the small town slightly southeast of Jackson was full of delightful characters, wide front porches, and good places to catch a catfish or two, but it was also a typical small town that housed some matching small minds. He knew firsthand because there had been many opposed to his appointment. Perhaps it was his stint in rehab or the fact he had been a social justice worker before he was called to ministry that set some against him. Or perhaps it was his shaggy hair, preference for running in actual running shorts and a tank top, or his high-top Vans that had gotten him more than one double take... and suggestions for a good barber. His secretary had bought him a pair of penny loafers "on sale" so he could look "appropriate." Oh, the townspeople meant well, but they had notions, and those notions were the kind that often gave Christians a bad rap.

So he couldn't imagine being the woman Benton Mason had cheated on Jess Culpepper with.

Still, that didn't mean Brandy had to be the Hester Prynne of Morning Glory. She was deserving of forgiveness just like every person in the town. And she was worthy of a second chance at—

He stopped.

What was he thinking?

He had to be honest with himself. When she'd said those words, he'd been disappointed. Mostly because he was interested in her. But Brandy being someone who'd contributed to the breaking of a sacred vow made him hesitate. After all, he was the new leader of Saint Paul's Episcopal, and there *had* been a good bit of opposition to his appointment.

Brandy had baggage... a nice, big luggage cart tipping with baggage. Perhaps he didn't need to be the one to help her pull that weight. Sometimes his heart was bigger than his common sense. Still, he couldn't stop thinking that Brandy needed him, and perhaps he needed someone like her to complete a missing piece of his own puzzle. Truth be told, he was lonely, and no other female in town had piqued his interest... until he'd seen Brandy laughing with the old guys at the Arbor after beating them soundly in dominos. The way she'd grinned and teased them, the way the light had fallen on her hair, the way her pretty lips had curved. He'd been sucker punched by that image.

"Miss Elaine, I'm stepping out for a minute," he said, not bothering to wait for her questions.

His administrative assistant always had questions. He closed the door on her "what about..."

He entered the sanctuary, admiring for the umpteenth time the way the light fell into colorful patterns on the gleaming pulpit and prayer rail. The high ceilings with the wooden joists and gleaming chandeliers lent a solemnity to the holy chapel, which smelled of beeswax and old hymnals. The place never failed to bring him peace and contentment.

Standing on the steps leading up to the pulpit were Brandy and a plump woman with frizzy red hair.

"Father Geoff." The tape measure snapped into place as Brandy turned. "I didn't realize you were here."

"Didn't mean to scare you, and please just call me Geoff," he said, smiling and jogging up the steps to where she stood. Her hair was gathered into a low ponytail, and she wore stretch pants and a long shirt with a ruffle around the hem. Soft pink ballet slippers completed the outfit, making her look so far away from a predatory woman that it was laughable.

"All right then, Just Geoff, this is Shelia. She's going to be helping me with the flowers for the wedding. We were measuring to make sure the vases I have will fit and not crowd the wedding party."

"If you need some different-sized vases or urns, I'm almost certain there are some in the sacristy closet. You're welcome to borrow them," he said, looking over at the woman standing beside Brandy and eying Geoff with reservation. "Nice to meet you, Shelia."

"I go to the Baptist church," the woman said by way of greeting.

He smiled because people always followed their initial greeting with where they were churched as if to fend him off. Always made him feel like a traveling salesman peddling wares. *Sorry, sir. We already have a good vacuum cleaner.*

"Pastor Sandlin?" he asked with a smile.

She nodded. "Been my preacher since I was knee-high to a grasshopper."

"He's a good man. We serve on the First Friends Advisory Council together."

Brandy had turned toward the windows. "Do you know what the light will be like at five o'clock? Those stained-glass windows throwing color on the flowers could mess up my palette."

"I can check for you this afternoon," he said, eying the glass.

"Hey, have you two had lunch yet? The Ladies Auxiliary set out some sandwiches for the clergy and there's plenty left over."

"What kind of sandwiches?" Shelia asked.

"Chicken salad. Mrs. March made them. Supposedly hers are the best in town." Geoff gestured toward the door where he'd entered. "It's right down the hall. Turn left just past my office."

Shelia must have known where to go because she disappeared faster than a goose on Christmas Eve.

Brandy turned and watched the door close behind Shelia. "Guess she's hungry."

"Or can take a hint," Geoff said.

Brandy flushed, and something about that innocent response endeared her even more to him. He'd not been able to say much to her after she'd confessed she'd been the woman who'd broken up Jess Culpepper's first marriage because as soon as the words were out of her mouth, Brandy had turned her grandmother's wheelchair back toward her room. He'd offered her some of Essie's pound cake and she'd taken it, but he could tell that she needed some breathing room. The last thing he'd said to her was "Hey, Brandy, we all have things in our past we aren't proud of. One mistake doesn't define you."

She'd looked back, one hand on her grandmother's shoulder, the other gripping the handle of the wheelchair. "Yeah? Well, someone should tell all the people in this town."

And then she'd walked away.

"Maybe we should tell them together," he'd called back to her.

She'd turned around then, her pretty face so sad, and had given him a small smile. She waved at him and then disappeared around the corner. At that moment he felt the weight of injustice, the same siren call that had driven him to lead marches and deliver fiery speeches about human rights and corporate greed. He'd long learned that time, compassion, and compromise did more good than screaming at people, but right then he wanted to march against the narrow-minded bigots who'd pigeonholed this woman and kept their foot on her throat for too long. For many, forgiveness was an abstract concept.

Yes, what Brandy had done had been wrong. Very wrong. But

after knowing her for only a few brief weeks, he realized she was complicated, sincere, and devastated by her participation in the destruction of a marriage.

Now looking at her, he felt those same stirrings, but there was something more beneath his spirit of generosity. Something like the fact he was a man. And she a woman. And even standing in this most holy of places, a pulpit where he shared about God's grace and goodness, he wanted to kiss the ever-loving hell out of her.

"You look pretty today," he said instead.

"Oh, well, I'm not wearing any makeup or anything, so thanks." She touched her hair self-consciously.

"You don't need it."

She rolled her pretty gray eyes. "Men always say that, but put them in the club and they go for the ones all dolled up every time."

"We're not in a nightclub," he said with a teasing grin.

"Far from it," she said, looking around. "I always liked this church. It's very beautiful."

"It is." He joined her in her perusal of the sanctuary. "Have you given any more thought to being my date for the wedding?"

She looked at him then, her gray eyes the exact color of a thunderstorm cloud. "I'm not sure I should. Um, for Jess's sake. It's her day, and I don't want to ruin it. I hope you understand that it's not about you. I would love to have... I mean, if it wasn't *this* wedding, I would love to be your plus-one."

He'd opened his mouth to argue, but at that moment the doors to the sanctuary flew open and four chattering women tumbled in, a gust of wind following them, ripping at the wreaths on the doors.

"Holy hell, that's some wind," Jess Culpepper said, pushing back hair that had stuck to her face.

"Shut the door quick." Rosemary shook out her own normally perfect coiffeur.

Geoff looked down at his Apple Watch and realized he'd forgotten the appointment to finalize the Reyes-Culpepper ceremony. Looked like Jess had brought consultants to make sure everything was just right.

Once the doors were secured, all four women fell silent, their eyes affixed to where he stood with Brandy.

Uncomfortable silence ensued.

The bride-to-be, Jess Culpepper, was a long-legged beauty with curly brown hair and the prowess of an athlete. Beside her was the pregnant Rosemary Genovese, who always reminded him of an auburn-headed Grace Kelly with her pearls and classic features. Then there was Eden Voorhees, small, dark and the quiet one of the bunch even though her startling blue eyes hinted at a bit of fire. She stood beside her sister, Sunny David, who was likely the prettiest of all the women with her lush figure and blond hair. The first three women had been friends forever, or so everyone said. They'd tragically lost the other member of their squad years before to cancer.

Yeah, this town talked, and these three women along with Sunny had been the topic of conversation quite often even though Jess and Eden no longer lived in their hometown. He didn't know them well, but the times he'd met them, he'd thought them all warm and welcoming.

"Hello, ladies," he said, donning a smile. Beside him, Brandy stood, frozen in place like a doe awaiting the crack of a rifle.

"Father Geoff." Jess darted a glance to Brandy and then looked back at her friends. They all wore wary expressions. "I hope we're not too early. The weather's getting bad out there. A storm on the horizon."

Geoff walked down the steps toward the group of women, thinking about those words. *Storm on the horizon.* "No, it's fine. I was just helping your florist with some measurements."

Jess looked again at Brandy, who had by this time occupied herself with snapping photos with her phone and writing something on the small pad she'd been carrying. "Good."

He shook their hands. "Nice to see you all again. Why don't you ladies go on to my office and I'll be right there? If you're hungry, there are some sandwiches in the parlor along with bottled water and tea. I'll join you all shortly."

"Thank you, but we just ate. Sal made lasagna for the special today. I brought you a piece." Rosemary pulled a foam container from her large bag and handed it to him.

"So thoughtful. Thank you, Rosemary."

"You're welcome. We have to keep you fed," she said with a smile. Then she turned to her friends. "Look at me. I'm turning into an Italian mother already."

"You're not Italian, Rosemary," Eden muttered, rolling her eyes. "You're about as Irish as they come. Between you and Sal, this kid will be plump and guilty all the time."

"That's *Catholic* guilt, Eden. Oh no, wait. Sal's that too." Rosemary made a face.

Sunny laughed at her sister and Rosemary. "Come on. I heard Joann March made chicken salad sandwiches. Bet those are the ones in the parlor."

"You just ate," Eden said as the women moved past him and made their way out of the chapel.

Jess lagged behind, eyeing Brandy. "You girls go on. I need to talk to Brandy for a minute."

Her friends stopped and turned to look at her, casting glances at Brandy, who had frozen at Jess's words.

"Go," Jess said, giving them a smile. "I'll be there in a sec."

The three women exchanged curious glances. Eden shrugged and opened the heavy door. They exited, leaving Geoff with Jess and Brandy.

He wanted to protect Brandy, but that was ludicrous. Jess Culpepper was a perfectly nice woman. He'd counseled her and Ryan Reyes a few times in preparation for the ceremony and knew her to be even-keeled, generous, and wholly in love with her fiancé. Still, bad blood sat between these two women, and it felt wrong to abandon Brandy.

"Do you want me to stay?" he asked Brandy.

"I want to *talk* to her, Father Geoff. That's it." Jess's expression was bemused, and for a moment he felt silly for acting as if something bad was going to play out in the chapel of his church.

Brandy looked over at him and nodded. "It's fine, Geoff."

His name on her lips was soft and somehow meaningful. A shift into trusting him, into a friendship. The thought warmed him. He looked at Jess. "I'll be waiting in my office. Don't leave me too long or Rosemary will have new slipcovers ordered for the parlor and custom curtains for my office. She's a force, that woman."

Jess laughed. "Well, that's the risk you take when Rosemary's around, but don't worry, she's too busy working on her new line of quilts and managing my wedding to fit you in. You're safe until at least April."

Geoff cast another look at Brandy as he walked to the chapel door. She seemed resigned and perhaps a tad bit relieved. He sensed the two women had not said much between them. Perhaps now was as good a time as any to say what needed to be said.

As he slipped from the chapel, he heard Brandy say, "How can I help you, Jess?"

# Chapter Five

Brandy didn't want to be left alone with Jess, not because she was afraid of the woman but because she wasn't sure she could find the words that needed to be said after all this time. Of course, she'd rehearsed a million times what she would say if ever she had the opportunity to do so. She had three letters in her bedroom drawer that she'd penned. Of course they'd been returned unopened. She'd seen Jess around town a few times, but the woman had either shot her a hurt look or one of anger before turning her back to Brandy. Brandy had choked down the apology that hovered on her lips like a wasp over a flower, tentative, fleeting, liable to leave a sting.

"Thank you for agreeing to do the flowers for the wedding on short notice," Jess said, moving toward her, trailing a hand over the carved edges of the pews as she walked toward the front of the church. Jess wore a blue dress that stopped just above her knees and a pair of black suede booties that made her somehow taller. Her curly hair framed an oval face, pouty lips, and wide leonine eyes. Jess was everything a woman could ever want to be… and soon to have a new husband who looked like a cover model. She'd rebounded from her hurt well.

"Of course. Why wouldn't I?" Brandy asked, standing perfectly still though she clutched the pen as if it were a knife. Okay, she was being a bit dramatic, but her nerves demanded it.

"Because of what happened between us," Jess said, looking up at the cross that hung above the organ pipes.

"You did nothing to cause what happened. It wasn't between us, not really." Brandy looked down at her feet. "I, uh, I've needed to apologize to you for a long time, Jess. I could say I put it off because you moved and don't live in Morning Glory any longer, but… it's mostly because I've been so ashamed. You were kind to me, and I— "

" —believed my stupid ex-husband when he lied to you?"

Brandy snapped her head up, her gaze finding Jess's. "What?"

"Benton came to Florida a few weeks ago, and he confessed to his crimes. Seems he has a new girlfriend who's a therapist and is requiring him to jump through some hoops. Anyway, he's making positive changes in his life, and one of the steps is being honest with himself about his own flaws and giving restitution to the people he wronged with his actions. In fact, you might be getting a call soon."

"That's what that was about?" Benton had left a message on her grandmother's machine not too long ago, asking her to meet him for coffee. She'd erased it without a second thought.

Jess sank onto the first pew. She glanced at the other end and nodded, so Brandy obliged her. Her thighs had started trembling with emotion, and her throat felt oddly scratchy, so sitting sounded like a great idea.

"Benton admitted to telling blatant lies in order to get you into bed. He said he told you our marriage was over and we'd agreed to divorce. He said he intentionally manipulated you into thinking he loved you. He took advantage of you."

"But I let him," Brandy said, twisting her fingers into a knot. "He didn't have to push too hard, Jess. I was lonely and vulnerable, but that wasn't an excuse. I knew I should have waited for you to split, but I didn't."

Jess nodded. "That may be true, but I know Benton. I know how he operates. Once he has something on his mind or in his sights, he doesn't rest. He wanted out of our marriage, and he used you to do it. You were a tool, and he bent you to his will. You may have bent easily, but I don't think you set after Benton or hooked your claws into him. He admitted as much. He lied to you. He deceived you. And he hurt us both… maybe even you more than me."

Brandy swallowed hard. "Doesn't change the fact that I did what I did."

Jess lifted a shoulder. "Maybe not. But I know you've been

punished enough. I can see past my grief and pain now. I'm happier than I've ever been because I'm loved like I've never been loved. I just wanted you to know that I forgive you, and I'm very sorry that this town has treated you so poorly."

Brandy felt something break loose inside her at Jess's words. *I forgive you.* "I don't know if I can ever forgive myself." She looked up at Jess, not bothering to wipe the tears coursing down her face.

Jess moved closer, reaching into her purse and withdrawing a tissue. She held it out, a white bit of fluff that seemed somehow more than what it was. A peace offering. A surrender. A kind gesture. Brandy took the tissue and swiped at her face.

"I hope you will forgive yourself, because we all make stupid mistakes. You wanted to believe in love. There's nothing wrong with that."

Brandy shook her head. "It is when he's married."

Jess's mouth quirked. "Well, yeah, there's that, but even so, I have the complete picture now, and while I suppose we'll never be friends, I wish you happiness. Life's too short to hold on to the things that hurt us, Brandy. Don't let Benton and what you did keep you from happiness."

Brandy nodded because she wanted to believe Jess's words were true. She wanted happiness and still nurtured hope for a future with someone who loved her. Still, the past few years, the out-and-out crumbling of her life, had beaten her down. "Thank you."

Jess smiled. "You're welcome."

Brandy stood and shoved the tissue into her pocket. "I wanted to make sure you like the flowers I'm using. Did Rosemary consult you?"

"Rosemary hasn't consulted me on much, and that's cool. Because I really don't care. But don't tell her that. She loves this sort of stuff. It's odd because when I married Benton, I wanted everything perfect. But now I see that life isn't perfect and that's okay. I stopped planning so much and embraced what life has given me, and that life is good."

Brandy felt a bit like the Tin Man when she smiled at Jess—a bit rusty and creaky. "I'm very glad for you, Jess, and I'll make sure the flowers show that."

"I suppose I better get in there before Rosemary changes the whole ceremony. She's all big on using sand since we live on the beach. Something about mingling the sands..." Jess gave a big sigh and walked toward the double doors. "I'm glad things are cleared between us. I feel better about getting married this weekend, knowing that everything in the past is in the past."

Brandy nodded and as the door clicked shut, she sank again onto the pew, her emotions whirling, tears still leaking from her eyes.

Jess had forgiven her.

She lifted her eyes to the cross, a singular simple brass cross sitting high as a focus for the congregation. *There is power in forgiveness.* Was that a hymn? A verse from the Bible she'd shelved long ago? She wasn't certain, but she knew there was truth in that phrase. A huge burden had been lifted from her soul when Jess had uttered those words, and though she was not a religious woman, she whispered, "Thank you, God."

There was no answer from on high, but a heavy peace descended upon her. For the past few years, she'd borne the censure of Morning Glory. The dirty looks, the loss of customers, the once-welcoming town giving her the silent treatment, and she'd allowed it because she believed she deserved it. Not only was she a cheater, but she was a stupid one because she'd thought Benton really loved her. So she'd taken her lumps and expected nothing good from her life.

But that was no way to live.

Maybe she was plumb tired of being a tragic figure, beleaguered by her one big mistake.

Perhaps Jess was right — it was time to forgive herself and stop hiding from her past.

Brandy rose and set her pad on the pew and walked over to the rail surrounding the pulpit. Colorful embroidered cushions invited the weary to sink onto their knees in prayer. Brandy hadn't prayed in so long she wasn't sure she remembered how, but she sank to her knees all the same. Folding her hands together, she looked up at the cross. "Dear God, it's me, Brandy. I don't know if you can even hear me. I'm not good at this stuff. But if you're real and you have power and all, could you maybe forgive me for what I did with Benton? It was wrong. And if you do that, will you help me to forgive myself... and maybe help me find some happiness? 'Cause that would be good. Really good."

She stopped and bit her lip, trying to remember if there was something else she was supposed to do. Was there, like, a special ending other than amen?

"Thank you. And amen."

Brandy rose and felt a little silly, but she also felt pretty good. Like she'd been baptized by Jess's forgiveness and her life could be new. Or as new as she could make it. She had a lot stacked against her—a sick grandmother, a lonely house, a failing business, and very few friends—but she still felt better than she had in a long time. The money she'd receive for doing this wedding paired with the Valentine's orders that had already poured in would help her pay the overdue bills. Not to mention she had an offer for a date for the Reyes-Culpepper wedding.

A devilishly good-looking date... who was also a priest.

She liked that oxymoron.

The door swung open and Shelia entered, carrying a plate. "Hey, I brought you a sandwich and a cookie. They're danged good."

"That was nice of you," Brandy said.

"I can be nice. Sometimes," Shelia said with a saucy smile. "Now let's get moving on this. Ginger called from the shop and said she's got fifteen orders for Valentine's bouquets. We're going to be busy for the next few weeks. Things are looking up."

Brandy nodded. "That's what I've been thinking."

# Chapter Six

He never should have mentioned to his assistant that Brandy Robbins was his date for the wedding. Elaine Jansen was as bad a gossip as any woman in Morning Glory, and by the time he was ready to conclude the afternoon and head home, he'd fielded two phone calls and a drop-in from one of his parishioners who had plopped a photo montage of her two daughters onto his desk. Her words were "These are my girls. They're single and ready to mingle... at weddings, barbeques, where ever you might need a pretty, wholesome, Christian lady on your arm."

It was as if by asking someone to sit with him at a wedding, he'd unleashed the kraken of potential mothers-in-law. Ones who wanted to save him from tainted women who might lead him astray. Though he was fairly certain debating the choice of buttercream over Italian crème cake with a woman who'd sinned wasn't going to send him to a life of eternal damnation. Because everyone sinned. It was the human condition.

"I'm heading out, Miss Elaine. Have a good evening," he said, walking through the outer office.

His administrative assistant looked up and smoothed her teased bonnet of silver hair. "I hope you have a good evening too, Father Geoff. And that you find a suitable plus-one for the Culpepper girl's wedding. There are plenty of *nice* girls here in Morning Glory."

He left his hand on the office door and turned. "Are you saying my choice is not nice?"

She lifted her brows. "Oh, heavens no. I don't presume to judge. I meant I'm so happy to see you finally thinking about companionship. I guess I don't have to tell you that there are a lot of women curling their hair about now."

His mind went to an image of women squirting on perfume, sharpening their claws, and stretching their hamstrings, all in an effort to catch the Episcopalian priest new to the singles scene. "Uh, I'm not sure that's what I'm doing. It's just sort of a date."

"Sort of?" Elaine arched an eyebrow.

"Brandy and I are friends. We often visit with one another at the Arbor. She's already going to be at the wedding because she's doing the flowers... so it's a plus-one sort of thing." But he wanted it to be a real date... even more than he had before. For one, he didn't like being told he couldn't do something because uptight people thought they knew what was best for him. And for another, he really liked Brandy. But no need to fuel the gossip monster in town by telling everyone it was a date.

Earlier, when he returned to the chapel after Jess and her friends had left, he'd been surprised to still find Brandy there. She and Shelia had parked themselves on a pew and were going over all the needs for the wedding party.

"Still here?" he asked, smiling at them as they sat with their heads together.

"Oh, I'm sorry, Father." Brandy rose and handed her notepad to Shelia. "It was so quiet in here that we took the opportunity to get our details completed. Once we go back to the shop, we'll be swamped with Valentine's orders. I'm not complaining, mind you, but it will be hectic."

"And we're done now," Shelia said, tucking everything into a bag she slung over her shoulder. "I'm heading back to the shop and calling the supplier. I want to make sure we can keep the hydrangea for the reception arrangements fresh."

Brandy nodded. "I'll be there shortly. I have to drop the deposit by the bank before it closes."

Shelia huffed and puffed out the chapel door.

Brandy turned to him. "I'll get out of your hair now."

"You understand that I'm not running you off. I've always thought the quietness of the chapel a nice reprieve from the world. I'm glad you were able to focus here."

Brandy glanced around. "I haven't been in a church in forever.

Oh, I mean, I do weddings and stuff but rarely feel like I'm in a place that's holy. I'm sure that's horrible to admit."

"Not at all," he said, moving toward her. "Many people feel uncomfortable in structured religious settings. When I first started going to church, I went to a cowboy church in Alabama."

Brandy made a confused face. "A cowboy church?"

"The Lord said, 'Where two or more are gathered in my name' as a definition for a church. It's not always as grand as all this. Sometimes people meet in barns… or in their homes. I once went to a church in a barber shop."

He didn't want to talk about church even though he was standing in the one he pastored, wearing his collar and tunic, looking very much the priest and not the man he was beneath his profession. And he was a man… a man who wanted Brandy to see him as such. But then again, he'd just quoted scripture, so there was that.

"I suppose that's true." She picked up her purse and hooked it on her arm.

"Was everything okay with Jess?" As soon as he asked the question, he knew it was nosy. And it had put him in a fatherly advisor-like role. A "come talk to me, child" invitation.

"Oh, yeah. It's all good." She bit her lower lip. "You remember that I told you about my role in the breakup of her first marriage? Well, I hadn't actually spoken to Jess since then. I had some things I needed to say… and I guess she did too."

He wanted to ask her what that was, but he had no reason to need to know. That was Brandy's business.

"She forgave me," Brandy said, her voice soft and filled with what sounded like gratitude.

"That's wonderful. After seeing how you felt about your past and how that's affected your present here in Morning Glory, I'm sure it feels like a burden has been lifted."

She nodded. "And since Jess has let our past go, I think it's okay if I go with you. I mean, if you still want me to go to the reception with you."

"Of course I do. I asked, didn't I?" He grinned, his heart feeling much lighter now. There was such discord in life that it was nice to see two people untangle a hardness between them. True forgiveness seemed seldom sought.

"So I suppose I'll see you this Saturday. We'll be here around noon to start setting up. Will there be someone here to let us inside?"

"How about I give you my personal number and you can call me? The church should be open. Our custodian usually gets here early on days that there are special events, but this way you can reach me if there's an issue. Or even if there's not." Did that sound sketchy? Smarmy? A total pickup line?

"And I'll give you mine. Never know when there might be a flower emergency," she said with a grin.

Her smile was so pretty he felt it deep within his soul. Again, he had the inclination to take her into his arms and hold her against him. It had been so long since he'd filled his arms with a woman, drawing in the soft scent, feeling his heart beat next to another. Brandy drew him like a flickering lone candle drew a moth, and he seemed helpless to stop himself from wanting to spend more time with her. The anomaly of Brandy Robbins intrigued him.

He pulled his phone from his jean pocket and handed it to her.

"No security code?"

He shrugged. "My life is an open book."

She tapped on hers until it brought forth the home screen. "And mine has been closed for so long I don't remember how to open it."

# Chapter Seven

Brandy twisted the wire on the bouquet and set it in the box designed to hold them. She'd been unable to locate some of the flowers she and Rosemary had decided upon, but the delphiniums, scabiosas, and tiny daisies with cascading greenery gave the perfect boho-chic vibe she'd been going for. Not that Jess was boho-chic. More simple and natural, but somehow the bouquets worked with the livelier colors in the big urns sitting on either side of the altar. Geoff had found a gorgeous antique arch in the back of church storage, and Brandy had wound flowering vines and cheerful greenery around it to create a magical bowery. A beautiful display with the bride's family Bible and a unity candle sat beneath. The effect was simple, heartfelt, and a bit of spring delivered to the winter-weary township.

"Wow," Rosemary said, bustling in, wearing the soft lavender gown that hid her baby bump perfectly. The high-waist bridesmaid dress wrapped and tied beneath her breasts. Strappy sandals peeked out beneath the ankle-length hem. "Those look terrific. I was worried when you said there were no peonies or dahlia. But that's really nice, Brandy."

Brandy stood back and looked at the altar, nodding. "Thank you."

Rosemary walked toward her, and her eyes looked a bit misty. "I can't believe Jess is getting married again. She wanted to do a justice of the peace, but I talked her into a church wedding. After all, it's Ryan's first wedding."

Brandy swallowed. "And it's her forever wedding. The first one…" She was going to say "didn't count." But it had. Jess had married Benton and lived with him for many years before Benton had cheated on her... with Brandy. Those years could not be discounted because Brandy wished them to have never existed.

Rosemary slid her a glance. "It's okay. I know what you mean. Jess is getting a do-over with someone who loves her so much he'd walk barefoot across a briar patch while his clothes were on fire to get to her."

"It must be nice to be loved like that."

"It is," Rosemary said with a soft smile. Then her face grew serious. "I wanted to say I'm sorry for being such a... well, not a bitch, really, because I didn't talk to you or anything. But that was sort of... Well, Jess was so hurt. I really hated you for a long time."

Brandy felt the knife in her heart twist. For the past few days, she'd been trying to forget her past transgression and claim some happiness. But Rosemary's words dragged her right back. A small noise escaped her before she could find her old emotional armor and don it.

Rosemary caught her arm. "We all talked about what happened last night after the rehearsal dinner. I don't mean to hurt you now. I just wanted to say, uh... I don't know what I'm trying to say. I guess I feel really bad that I was so angry at you, and I don't want to be that way anymore."

Brandy sucked in a deep breath and blew it out. "I'm thrilled for Jess today. She deserves to be happy."

"Last night I had this dream. I mean, the dreams you have when you're pregnant are crazy cakes, but anyway, you were standing in the woods all alone. Just wandering around from tree to tree, peeking out at all the rest of us. We were eating fried chicken and riding in paddleboats. I know. Weird. But anyway, you were crying the whole time. I wanted to have fun with everyone, but I knew you were there and you were sad. I tried to go in the woods to find you, but you turned into a deer and ran from me. I couldn't find you to bring you back to eat chicken."

Brandy didn't know what to say to Rosemary and her dream revelation. The whole thing had come out of nowhere. Paddleboats and fried chicken?

Rosemary didn't seem to be put off by Brandy's silence. "Well, that's when I realized that all this time you've been hiding from life, and we're the ones who put you out in the woods because we loved Jess so much and because you were part of what hurt her. But this morning I realized that you need to come on out and have some fried chicken. I know this is really strange, but my dreams always have meaning. It's a gift really." Rosemary looked at her with utter conviction.

"Well, it's very kind of you to, uh, share that. But I'm done with hiding. Jess forgave me, and I'm working on forgiving myself." Brandy wanted to believe that was absolutely true. She *was* done with hiding. Accepting Geoff's offer was the first step. She deserved to have a second chance at a life in Morning Glory, and she deserved to have a guy as good as Geoff.

"Oh." Rosemary pulled her into a hard hug. "I'm so glad. That makes today an even happier day. Both of you are getting a do-over."

The door to the church opened and Shelia came in, carrying the rest of the bouquets. Jess had only three bridesmaids, and Shelia had done the smaller, matching bouquets for them. "I'm here. I brought the tape you forgot and the boutonnieres."

"That's my cue. I'm off," Rosemary said, delivering a genuine smile that made her light up. Her auburn hair had been teased into a semibouffant that should have looked ridiculous but on Rosemary was perfect. Total throwback. "Send me the bill for the flowers."

Brandy nodded and turned back to Shelia. "Thanks for getting those. I need to run out to the country club to check all the flowers for the reception and then change really quick."

"Tom took the van. I thought you were wearing that."

Brandy looked down at the faded navy pants and cream sweater with the small moth hole in the right sleeve and frowned. "I probably need something nicer to wear to the reception."

"I can take you," someone said from the doorway.

Geoff stood there in all his priestly splendor.

"Oh, well, don't you have to be *here*?" Brandy asked suddenly nervous. She'd spent the past few days playing off the excitement she had at sitting next to Geoff and being his date. Everyone in town seemed to know that he'd asked her, and she had been

## A Morning Glory Wedding

telling herself it was no big deal. Still, she was anxious about what people would think... and she was nervous about living up to the expectation that Geoff seemed to have for her. She liked him and wanted to know what it was like to be loved by a good man. To feel his arms around her. To take her breath away.

God, she hoped he would take her breath away.

"Still an hour and a half until the music for seating even starts. All I have to do is be here for the vows," he said with a wink. The man was darned handsome and so nice. She should be on cloud nine and not worrying about disappointing him. Still, a small voice said *"He's too good for someone like you."*

That inner voice made her doubt so much about herself. She'd spent the past few years drawing as little attention to herself as possible after being the talk of the town for a good two months. Now she was about to be out in the spotlight again, people's eyes on her, everyone wondering how she'd seduced their new boy wonder out from under the noses of their eligible and way more pure daughters. She'd already broken up a marriage. Would she now drag a man of God into her pit of sin?

Okay, maybe she was being a bit melodramatic, but she'd lived long enough in Morning Glory to know that it was a town that loved its own, and she'd ceased to be one of them the day she'd allowed Benton Mason to unhook her bra in the back of the florist shop.

But if she was going to face her critics, she might as well do it in something other than old clothes and no makeup.

"Okay, let's be quick," she said.

# Chapter Eight

The trouble with keeping a low profile around town meant having very little to wear that was suitable for an evening wedding.

"Hmm," Brandy muttered, stooping to pet a purring Chess while she contemplated her lack of fabulousness in the closet. She still had some sexy dresses she'd brought back from Dallas, but those were more club vibe than tasteful wedding. She had one nice black dress perfect for a funeral, but it might look too severe for a wedding. Earlier she'd settled on a pair of slacks, white ruffled blouse, and a pair of serviceable shoes that would allow her to be on her feet as needed, but now that outfit hanging on the bathroom door seemed so... office-like and frumpy.

Why hadn't she bought something new?

Because she hadn't wanted to get her hopes up about Geoff. That's why.

"Yoo-hoo," Lucy called from the hallway. "It's Lucy."

Brandy smiled. "I know who it is."

"That handsome priest let me in. Goodness, he looks so good in that vestment thing or whatever they call it that I'm now wondering how he might look underneath it," Lucy called from the other side of her bedroom door, loudly enough for Geoff to hear her comment.

Brandy hurried over to the door and jerked it open, hiding behind it because she wore only a lacy bra and pair of undies. "Stop saying such things."

"Don't worry. I like them," Geoff called, his voice laced with amusement.

Lucy's eyes danced. "I really like this guy."

"Get in here," Brandy said, tugging the older woman's arm

firmly enough to show she meant business.

Lucy slipped in. She wore a silk pantsuit and Chinese-patterned shoes that curled at the toe. She also wore her "good" wig, which was a platinum-blond pageboy. Big diamonds winked on hands that carried a black garment bag. "I brought you something to wear."

"What do you mean, something to wear?"

"A dress, Cinderella."

Brandy narrowed her eyes. "What dress? You don't know my size."

Lucy laid the bag on the bed and unzipped it, revealing a soft cream-and-black taffeta dress. "It's vintage, but vintage is all the rage. This one was my sister's, and I kept it because it was Dior. I longed to have big enough ta-tas to fill it. But alas, still flat-chested. I thought it would look perfect on you. You're about Stella's size. Well, her size back then." She pulled it out, and with a soft swoosh there emerged one of the most beautiful dresses Brandy had ever seen.

"I can't wear that," she whispered.

"Why not?"

"Everyone will look at me."

Lucy grinned. "Exactly. It's a 1952 design. Perfectly tasteful with this little bolero-style matching jacket. You don't need fancy shoes. Those black stilettos right there will do fine." She pointed to the three-inch heels in the closet.

Brandy ran a hand over the material. It wasn't a party dress, though the skirt was rather full. It would be perfect for a wedding. Perfect.

"Here are some pearls," Lucy said, dropping a small velvet ditty bag atop the bodice. "Now hurry up. That good-looking priest said he'd give me a lift to the wedding. Don't worry, Janice Brown said she'd bring me home after the bride cuts the cake."

Her fairy godmother disappeared before Brandy could argue with her.

Brandy snapped her mouth closed and looked at what her neighbor had brought her.

Cinderella.

Without much more thought, Brandy traded her bra for a strapless one and unzipped the haute couture dress that looked like it had slipped from the pages of *Vogue* magazine. She stepped into the full black skirt and pulled it over her hips. The zipper hung only once, and though it was a bit snug, the dress fit her like it had been made for her. She slipped the shoes on, fastened the glowing white pearls around her neck, and went to her bathroom. Quick as she could manage, she twisted and pinned her hair into a classic chignon before doing her makeup, emphasizing her eyes with her best mascara and carefully painting her lips a shade of vermillion. When she stepped back and caught herself in the full-length mirror in her room, she gasped.

She looked like... sin.

"Oh, God," she whispered to herself, spinning around, letting the skirt swoosh around her. "I look like a bad, bad girl."

She couldn't do it. The dress made her look like what she was— a scarlet woman. She should scrub off the lipstick and wear flats. Then she glanced at her alarm clock. Out of time.

"Brandy, I hate to bother, but your priest has a wedding to get to," Lucy called out.

"Crap." Brandy looked at herself, shrugged, and grabbed the bolero jacket, praying it covered enough to make her presentable. Then she walked out to the living room.

※

Geoff nearly swallowed his tongue when Brandy emerged from her bedroom. She looked like a 1950s pinup girl. Rita Hayworth had nothing on Miss Brandy Robbins.

"Wow," he said, mesmerized by her even though Brandy seemed hesitant. "I mean wow."

"I knew it. You make that dress look like a million dollars, girl. Total babe. Marilyn Monroe just called and wants her status as 1950s bombshell back. I wish I still had the gloves my sister wore with it." Lucy prattled, but her eyes showed triumph.

Brandy had almost turned the color of the lipstick she was wearing. "Is it too much?"

"You look gorgeous," he said, letting his eyes travel up the length of her body from the lean legs to the nipped-in waist to the plump breasts barely concealed beneath the jacket to the lush caramel hair pinned back to show the delicate beauty of her face. "I don't know if I've ever seen a woman as beautiful as you."

"Let's get going. You both have things to do, and I'm going to sit in the back of the church and visit with Jess's grandmother Josephine. I ain't seen her in a coon's age." Lucy grabbed her mink coat and shrugged it on.

Geoff glanced at his watch. "We really do need to go."

Brandy bit her lip and glanced down at the dress again. At that moment, he understood. She felt exposed in what she wore.

He winked at her. "You're stunning. I promise."

She gave him a smile then, and he felt his heart skip.

"Okay, let's do this," she said.

Geoff extended his arm. "Shall we?"

Brandy curled her arm into his and he gave her another flirty wink, making her blush again. He'd never been so amused, turned on, and protective of a woman before. He said a silent thank-you to God for giving him the opportunity to have this night with Brandy, because God willing, he was going to convince her they deserved a second date. And a third. And fifty.

Geoff walked over to the colorful, funny older woman with the odd outfit and obvious wig. "And you too, madam?"

"Now this is a man, Brandy. Don't let him get away."

"Lucy," Brandy said, a warning in her words. She rolled her eyes when he glanced at her.

"Get away?" Geoff laughed at the older woman. "I'm tempted to flop on the floor and refuse to ever leave."

Brandy's eyes widened, but she managed to laugh before saying, "It would be hard to vacuum around you."

And that might be the moment he started falling in love with her.

# Chapter Nine

Geoff watched as the bride, grinning from ear to ear, met Ryan Reyes halfway for the kiss that united them as man and wife. The handsome groom tipped Jess back, making her squeak before bestowing a second kiss on his new wife.

"Family and friends, may I introduce for the first time... Ryan and Jess Reyes," he said, smiling as the two joined hands and Jess retrieved her bouquet from Rosemary and turned to the congregation. Everyone was crying, smiling, and clapping as Jess lifted her bouquet in triumph. Geoff's gaze found Brandy's. She'd been sitting near the back, but her eyes weren't on the bride and groom hurrying down the aisle. Her gaze was on him.

And it felt prophetic.

The wedding party paired up and trounced down the steps toward the back of the church, and the congregation followed. He watched as many of the townspeople glanced in surprise at Brandy sitting on the end of the second to last pew. She seemed aware of their curiosity, but she remained serene, and her smile seemed genuine as the happy couple disappeared through the carved oak doors.

Brandy looked beautiful... and perhaps a bit sinful in the back of the Episcopalian Church.

Geoff sort of dug that about her.

Ten minutes later, he opened the car door for her and started the engine of his red Mustang. Yeah, it wasn't a priestmobile like his mentor Father Paul drove, but he couldn't seem to let his old girl go. He'd had her repainted last year before accepting the job in Morning Glory. He knew some disapproved of their pastor driving a "hot rod" as he believed Elaine called it, but he didn't really give a rat's patoot. He liked driving it.

"Nice car," Brandy said, buckling the new seat belts he'd had installed.

"Thanks." He looked over at her. A few tendrils of hair had escaped to frame her face. "You look perfect sitting in it, wearing that dress."

"This is a 1952 Christian Dior. Mustangs didn't roll out until 1964."

He clutched his chest. "A woman who knows cars? I'm done."

She giggled, and he decided it was the best sound he'd heard in forever.

When they pulled up in front of the country club, he found that Rosemary had reserved parking for the bridal party and clergy. That made him grin because the woman had thought of everything for the wedding and had only lost out on the mingling of the sands. Jess had put her foot down on that bit of hokey symbolism.

"I heard Jess's mom ordered the cake from New Orleans. It's supposed to be some fancy place with the best buttercream frosting in America." Brandy unbuckled, then reached for the door handle. She'd grown quiet on the way to the country club, and he wanted her to laugh again. To smile at him. To make his heart skip a beat.

"Nope, don't. Let me," he said, hopping out and pocketing the keys. He ran around and opened her door. "This is a date, remember?"

"Elaine Jansen told Maryanne Williams that you said you only asked me to come because we were friends and both going to be here anyway," Brandy said, accepting his hand as she stood.

He shut the door and turned to her. "Who told you that?"

"No one told me. They just said it loud enough so I could hear it from the back of the church," she said, her voice a bit cautious. "It's okay, Geoff. I know that's mostly true. You're a nice man who felt bad for me."

Around them, people swarmed, carrying wedding gifts, shifting looks their way. He could feel the question in their eyes, hear the slight whispers. He could tell that Brandy felt them too.

At that moment, he felt angry on her behalf. Angry on his too. People needed to mind their own damn business.

"It's very much a date, and it has nothing to do with feeling sorry for you."

She licked her lips and then glanced around. The light was fading from the day and the entrance to the country club was particularly festive with white twinkle lights arching above the stone path. Pretty paper lanterns hung from the oak trees and the overall effect was magical. "It's okay if it is though."

"Brandy, look at me."

She turned those pretty, vulnerable gray eyes to meet his, and in their depths he could see a million things. Okay, not a million. But he could see hope, fear, embarrassment, anxiety, and the plea for someone to love her the way Ryan loved Jess. The way a man loved a woman. The way Geoff hoped he could love her one day. If she would let him.

Geoff cupped her cheek and then lowered his lips to hers.

He felt her surprise as he kissed her. She tasted of the Juicy Fruit gum she'd popped into her mouth earlier and something sweeter than he'd ever imagined.

Brandy Robbins, the woman a town had painted as a scarlet woman, tasted like his future.

It was a simple, sweet kiss, and the good Lord knew he wanted more. But he lifted his head and looked into her eyes. "It's a *date*, Brandy."

She swallowed hard and then nodded. "Okay."

Then she grinned.

Then she chuckled at what he assumed was the kiss they'd shared in front of half the town.

She took his hand and turned toward all the people watching them with their mouths slightly open. "I can't wait to dance with you, Geoff."

He lifted her hand, brushing her knuckles against his lips. "Hate to tell you this, but I'm terrible at dancing."

"But not at kissing."

"Eh, I'm decent at that." He winked at Elaine as he passed her and her husband George. Then he waved to several of his congregation who were watching him. Some had amusement in their eyes, some seemed more interested in getting in line for the buffet, and some looked a little taken aback. But he didn't care.

He was a priest who loved God, but he was also a man who might have found what he'd been looking for. He smiled down at Brandy as they walked beneath the twinkle lights. "So, you have plans for Valentine's Day?"

"I'll be exhausted on Valentine's Day. We have so many orders."

"How about I bring you dinner and we practice dancing?"

Her eyes were shiny with unshed tears when she looked up at him. "As long as you don't bring me flowers."

"I wouldn't dream of it. I'll bring fried chicken."

Brandy stopped and her eyes got big. "Fried chicken?"

"I'm good at frying chicken. My grandmother taught me."

The woman threw back her head and laughed. "Well, I'll be damned. Fried chicken. You know, someone recently told me I should eat some fried chicken."

He smiled, not quite understanding but not really caring. "Well, I think I'm your guy."

Brandy shook her head as if in wonder. "I do believe you are."

# About Liz Talley

Liz Talley is the author of twenty-five heartwarming stories. A finalist in both RWA's Golden Heart and Rita Awards, Liz makes her home in Louisiana where she likes to read, volunteer and avoid housework. Her newest release *Come Home to Me* is an emotional southern story about the power of forgiveness. You can sign up for her newsletter at www.liztalleybooks.com or find other Liz Talley books at http://bit.ly/LizTalleyAmazon

Made in the USA
Middletown, DE
04 June 2019